READER'S
DIGEST
CONDENSED
BOOKS

The Reader's Digest Association Limited
11 Westferry Circus, Canary Wharf, London E14 4HE

The Reader's Digest Association South Africa (Pty) Ltd
Reader's Digest House, 130 Strand Street, Cape Town

For information as to ownership of copyright in the
material of this book, and acknowledgments, see last page.

Printed in France

READER'S

DIGEST

CONDENSED

BOOKS

The Reader's Digest Association Limited
LONDON • NEW YORK • CAPE TOWN

FIVE PAST MIDNIGHT

James Thayer

In 1945, holed up in his hidden bunker in Berlin, Hitler is proclaiming that he will fight 'until five minutes past midnight'; in other words, to the bitter end. It leaves the Allies no choice but to send in fearless commando Jack Cray to track the dictator to his lair. A fast-paced, action-packed thriller that tells how the war *might* have been won.

PUBLISHED BY
MACMILLAN AT £16.99

ONLY LOVE

Erich Segal

There are some passions that time can never dim. This is the story of just such a love, between Matthew Hillier and Silvia Dalessandro. It begins in the seventies, when both are training as doctors. Through war, injury and long separation, the flame of their love burns on. Twenty years later, it is put to the toughest test. . . A deeply moving romantic novel by the author of *Love Story*.

PUBLISHED BY
PIATKUS AT £17.99

KILLING FLOOR

Lee Child

Jack Reacher, recently laid off from the
military and content with life on the road,
decides, on a whim, to stop off in Margrave,
a small sleepy town in mid-Georgia. Without
warning, he is arrested and accused of murder.
As he strives to clear his name, he is drawn
into a hunt for the real killer—and a police
crackdown on an extraordinary fraud.

PUBLISHED BY
BANTAM PRESS AT £9.99

THE SHADOWY HORSES

Susanna Kearsley

Verity Grey is working on an archaeological
dig in Scotland, trying to find out what
happened to a Roman legion that
disappeared without trace in the early 2nd
century AD. But as bizarre events occur,
Verity finds herself distracted—by a
Scotsman who steals her heart, and by a
tantalising presence from the past.

PUBLISHED BY
GOLLANCZ AT £15.99

JAMES THAYER

FIVE PAST

MIDNIGHT

Could one man put an end to the Second World War by killing Adolf Hitler? That is the question President Roosevelt is asking.

For Jack Cray—an American commando with nothing left to lose—the answer is an unconditional yes.

Until he discovers that the Third Reich has set its most determined police detective on his tail. And until he meets beautiful German war widow, Katrin von Tornitz . . .

Victory is a thing of the will.

—FERDINAND FOCH

 # PROLOGUE

The White House, April 4, 1945

onovan never recorded the meeting in his journal, but he would remember it in fine detail to the end of his days. It began when the usher tapped lightly on the massive oak door, then pressed a small button hidden in the wainscoting to notify the Secret Service watch officer that the spymaster was about to enter the office.

'He's expecting you, General,' the usher said in a low voice. When he pushed open the door the spymaster stepped through.

Franklin D. Roosevelt was sitting behind his desk, his face green in the light of a banker's lamp. The chandelier had been doused and the blackout curtains were drawn across the windows, so the walls of the Oval Office were a periphery of darkness. The President waved the general into the room.

General William Donovan, Director of the Office of Strategic Services, placed an envelope on the desk, pushing it across to the blotter so the President would not have to use the tongs he kept in a drawer. White House carpenters had raised the desk six inches to accommodate FDR's wheelchair, and when Donovan sat in the low leather chair the desk top came almost to his shoulders.

Roosevelt made a production of weighing the envelope. 'You are a lawyer by profession, Bill,' he said in his silky, compelling voice. 'You write briefs. But you never write anything brief.'

Donovan should have chuckled dutifully. Not this night. The

9

contents of the envelope precluded levity.

Roosevelt pulled a Camel from its pack and stabbed it at a Bakelite holder that had white teeth marks on the stem. His hands trembled, and only after three attempts did he succeed in planting the cigarette. When he leaned forward for his Ronson, the President's face came into the lamplight. Donovan's breath caught.

Twenty-three of Roosevelt's sixty-two years had been spent in a wheelchair. Yet he had been the most vibrant man Donovan had ever met, exuding health and virility and energy. In the three weeks since their last meeting, though, Roosevelt's skin had taken on a ghastly pallor and the bags under his eyes had darkened.

Roosevelt inhaled the smoke deeply, then let it trail out of his nostrils. 'Can you spare me all the reading, Bill? It's late.'

'Mr President, I can summarise in three sentences.'

Roosevelt grinned appreciatively.

'First, each and every day the war continues in Europe, twenty-eight thousand men, women and children die.'

The President's smile vanished.

'Second, a group of German officers is ready to assume leadership of the Third Reich if an opportunity arises, and will instantly surrender. Finally, we have confirmed General Eisenhower's report that the SS is preparing a national redoubt in the Bavarian Alps, where Hitler may be able to carry on for two more years.'

President Roosevelt started to speak but his throat rattled and he bent low over the blotter, caught in a coughing fit. He was finally able to rasp, 'The bastard is going to outlive me, isn't he?'

Donovan avoided the question. 'Hitler has recently pledged that he will fight "until five minutes past midnight".'

The President blinked several times, and his mouth moved silently. He seemed awash in melancholy. He gripped the wheelchair rims and backed away from the desk, then he rolled to a window overlooking the lawn and pushed aside the blackout curtain, a small act that seemed to consume the last of his strength. It was ten o'clock in the evening. Streetlights and the Washington Monument were dark for the duration, so there was nothing to be seen.

Yet he peered into the blackness for a full minute. Then, without turning away from the window, he said softly, as if in the presence of the dead, 'You take care of it, Bill.'

That was enough. General Donovan rose from the chair, retrieved the envelope and fairly sprinted out of the office.

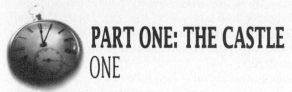

PART ONE: THE CASTLE
ONE

Berlin, April 7, 1945

O tto Dietrich was curled on the metal cot under a tattered blanket that smelt of urine and old blood. The blanket was alive with vermin, yet he lay motionless, too uncaring to scratch. They always came at noon. A few more minutes. They had left him his watch so he would know when his moment arrived. His belt, shoelaces, badge and wallet had been taken. And his bridgework—lest he slash his wrists with his false teeth, he supposed. With an effort that made him moan, he struggled to a sitting position. He would meet his fate with dignity and would stand when they came for him. He doubled over with a grinding cough. Pneumonia, he suspected. His lungs rattled with each breath.

Dietrich levered himself from the cot. He placed a hand on the oozing wall to steady himself. He spat into a palm and pawed his face with it, trying to wipe away the filth. They had reduced him to an animal's existence, but every day he cleaned himself as best he could. He straightened his foul clothing and turned to the door.

Dietrich's cell was in Wing B of Berlin's Lehrterstrasse Prison. The prison had been a busy place since July 20, 1944.

On that day, at Hitler's headquarters at Rastenburg in East Prussia, Colonel Count von Stauffenberg's briefcase bomb had only slightly wounded Hitler, because the attaché case had been shunted aside by another officer and Hitler had been shielded by the conference table's heavy leg. Colonel Stauffenberg, Generals Beck and Halder and several other plotters had already met their ends. Five thousand others—army officers, writers, doctors, clergymen, most with utterly no knowledge of the plot—had also been executed.

Before his arrest Otto Dietrich had been chief criminal inspector with the Berlin Kriminalpolizei, known as the Kripo. In 1928 he had solved the murder of the heiress Elisabeth Hoffer, whose headless corpse had been found in the Spree, put there, Dietrich learned, by her younger sister. Two years later he tracked down the two killers of Director Dräger of the Mercedes Palast cinema, murdered during a kidnap attempt gone awry. In 1938, when Karl Schwandheist reported that two brigands had carried off his wife, Dietrich found her alive and well in Geneva, spending with her husband the 400,000-mark insurance proceeds he had claimed. Otto Dietrich was a household name in Berlin.

From the door came the scrape of a key, followed by the shriek of metal on rusted hinges. The executioner stepped into the cell.

Sergeant Oscar Winge had a drinker's face, blotched and purple, with red capillaries showing on his nose.

He was followed by Gestapo case officer Rudolf Koder. The agent had a pinched face, with deep lines. He wore street clothes and the ubiquitous Gestapo black leather coat belted at the waist.

'Let's see what today brings, shall we, Inspector?' Koder said.

Winge secured Dietrich's arms behind his back with handcuffs. He prodded the prisoner through the door into the corridor. A line of dim overhead bulbs marked the way to the death chamber.

Otto Dietrich was an inmate in the prison to which he had sent so many convicted criminals. His crime was as insignificant as it was damning. His brother Joachim had stolen the 'L' relay and detonator used in Colonel Stauffenberg's briefcase bomb. The Gestapo had taken only three weeks to discover Joachim's complicity in the plot, and he had been executed within twelve hours of his arrest. Otto had known nothing of the plot, but his blood relationship to Joachim was an adequate indictment, and his anti-Party behaviour over the years sealed his conviction.

Rudolf Koder opened the chamber door.

It is little known that the guillotine is the German execution device. Dissimilarities in the German and French guillotines reflect their differences as people. The uprights on the French guillotine rise to the heavens; the German machine is short and thickset, its purpose more evident. In France, the severed head drops into a woven basket which compares favourably to the rough plank onto which the German head falls. The French trestle, where the condemned lies, is decorated with a carved fleur-de-lis to remind him of the state's authority by which he has found himself in this predicament. The Germans do not bother with such trifles.

Winge shoved Dietrich onto the trestle and wrapped leather straps round his chest and knees. The neck beam was lowered and secured with a metal clasp. Lying on his stomach, Dietrich could see the plank and surrounding stone floor, blackened by a century of blood. He fought for breath, trying not to sob.

The Gestapo agent moved round the guillotine so that Dietrich could see him out of the corner of an eye. 'Have you truly told us all you know about Joachim, Inspector?'

'I have,' he whimpered. 'I have nothing left to tell.'

It was the truth. The Gestapo agent had broken him. He was bitterly ashamed of his weakness, but he had been helpless against them.

'Well, it hasn't made any difference anyway, has it? Get on with it, Sergeant.' Dietrich closed his eyes, blocking out the light for the last time.

With a searing squeal, the blade dropped in the post grooves. It fell for an eternity, for the blink of an eye. And, with a ringing crack, the blade stopped one inch above Dietrich's neck.

'Not today, then, Inspector. Not today.'

The executioner released the neck brace and pulled Dietrich upright. He was propelled back along the corridor into his cell. He collapsed onto his cot.

Dietrich pulled the vile blanket over him and brought his legs up against his chest. His frame shook with relief. For twelve days he had been taken to the guillotine, then returned to his cell.

All he wanted was to get out of this cell. Or out of this life. He didn't care which.

Colditz Castle, Upper Saxony

THE AMERICAN was seated at a table in the casualty ward. He scraped at a rusty nail with a fingernail file. The filings dropped to form a red pile on a copy of the *Overseas Kid*, the German propaganda newspaper for POWs, used mainly for toilet paper. The American worked until the nail shone like new.

Next he began filing a piece of charcoal. A cone of shavings grew on the paper. Leaning against the grey stone wall was a baseball bat he had carved from a pole stolen from the castle workshop.

Built on a high promontory jutting out over the Mulde River, which flowed north to the Elbe, Colditz was perhaps the least attractive, least romantic castle in Germany. Two Moorish cupola towers were the structure's only ornament. The citadel consisted of a series of wings erected over the centuries, resulting in a figure-eight shape, with two baileys in the middle of the wings. And, with its current guests' propensities for escape in mind, the castle had recently been further modified. A machine-gun tower had been built in the north-west corner of the terrace outside the walls, and catwalks had been erected to eliminate guards' blind spots in the courtyard and on approaches to the gate. The castle's eighty-foot-high exterior walls were floodlit. Microphones and primitive seismographs had been planted in the walls to detect digging. Guards were on duty all night in the courtyard.

But, since D-Day, escape had lost much of its allure, and attempts had largely stopped at Colditz and other POW camps. General Eisenhower had recently ordered POWs to stay behind the wire. 'We'll get to you soon,' Colditz's senior POW officer had heard Ike say over the camp's hidden radio; the prisoners knew Ike would keep his word, and so did the guards. The POWs could now hear Allied guns night and day to the south.

Only the American had tried to escape since Eisenhower's order; he had made the attempt six times since his arrival, receiving twenty-one days in a solitary-confinement cell each time.

The other POWs knew the American as John, and they knew it was a pseudonym adopted to protect his life, for reasons they could only guess. The American had told only two men, the senior Allied and American officers, his true name.

The American rose from the table and lifted a pot from the stove near the door. The ersatz coffee smelt like a wet dog. He stirred in the nail rust and charcoal powder. Rust prevented anaemia and the charcoal helped control dysentery.

He carried a cup of coffee to a bunk where Captain Lewis Grimball of the Wiltshire Regiment was shivering under his blanket. The spring thaw had not reached the castle's interior. The American helped him to a sitting position. Grimball coughed raggedly. The American wiped spit from the corner of Grimball's mouth, then held the cup to his lips.

Grimball sipped, then wheezed, 'This tastes like dirt, John.'

The American also served coffee to Lieutenant Richard Cornwall of the Essex Scottish (Canada) Regiment, who was lying on his bunk near the stove. The bunks, table, a few chairs and the stove filled the small room. Nails had been hammered into the ends of the bunks to hang clothes. One shirt was hanging on a nail near a wash bucket filled with water and prunes, raisins and sugar from Red Cross parcels. Fermented a month, the concoction would have a horse's kick. When guards approached the ward, a POW would yell, 'Goons up!' and the hanging shirt would be tossed into the wash bucket. The guards assumed a POW was doing his laundry.

As the American returned to the table, the door opened and the senior Allied officer entered the ward, followed by the ranking American officer.

The American quickly rose to attention.

'At ease,' the SAO said. 'May we have a few words with you, John?' Group Captain Ian Hornsby had lost his Handley Page Halifax and three fingers of his left hand over occupied France.

'We thought perhaps you could tell us what's going on,' said Harry Bell, the senior American POW. Major Bell's bomber had been shot down during the Regensburg raid, August 17–18, 1943.

The SAO said, 'We've gone along with your determination to remain anonymous, believing that you faced a firing squad if the Jerries found out who you were. You told only me and Bell, and we've told no one. Except London, when you first arrived here.'

The American might have nodded. His angled face had lost its usual trace of merriment. The skin had sunk round his cheekbones and jaw. He asked, 'A message on your radio?'

The POWs knew a radio was in the camp somewhere, because BBC war news was known almost immediately after a broadcast. Only Hornsby and two others knew that the radio was hidden in a table leg. Half a year ago Hornsby had devised a wireless code, a multiple substitution with frequent changes. When a Geneva Red Cross official visited Colditz, Hornsby had asked him to take a message for his wife and cable it to her from Geneva. It had contained the code, which England accepted. Hornsby had been receiving coded instructions since then.

Frowning, Bell spoke, clipping his words for emphasis. 'Captain Cray, we've been ordered to get you out of here.'

The corners of the American's mouth lifted. He had not lost teeth like many of the POWs, and his were even and white. 'My friends call me Jack.'

'You've told us nothing about yourself,' Bell said angrily. 'All we know about you is that you are a crazy escaper.'

Cray smiled. 'There must've been more to the message.'

Hornsby looked at him closely as if trying to divine his thoughts. 'A Berlin address and a code word. Horseman. Does that mean anything to you?'

'Not a thing.'

'The message directs you to divert and distract on your way to Berlin,' Hornsby continued. 'That's the term it uses. Divert and distract. Why, do you think?'

Cray rubbed his chin. 'So the Germans will use up a lot of men and material searching for me, I suppose. Maybe my mission is just to be a feint.'

Hornsby stared pensively at the American. Finally he said, 'Well, we've got to get you out of this castle. I've got an idea, a good one. You willing to try it?'

Cray grinned widely. 'Can I go today?'

KATRIN VON TORNITZ walked carefully along Lasslerstrasse, stepping round a crater filled with murky water, then round an uprooted tree torn from its planter by a high-explosive blast. It was ten in the evening, and Berlin was black. The few cars in the street had tape over their headlights. She carried a heavy suitcase, a prewar Rugieri from Milan. On Katrin's lapel was an ornate lily brooch designed by the Berlin goldsmith Emil Lettine and given to her on her twentieth birthday. The case and the brooch were among the last bits of the life she had once known.

She ducked into a doorway to let a column of Home Guards march by, some with Panzerfausten—antitank rocket launchers— over their shoulders, most carrying only shovels. They were old men, bedraggled and ridiculous.

Across the street was a building that had been a bakery. Most of the roof had been blown away. On the door was a placard reading, ACHTUNG! MINEN! An unexploded bomb was inside.

The old men's footfalls faded. Katrin glanced nervously along the street. Most of the tenements on the road had been destroyed.

Katrin saw no one, so she briskly crossed the street. She had developed the *Berliner Blick* (the Berlin look), the habit of glancing over her shoulder for the Gestapo. She pushed against the bakery's shattered door and stepped inside. Glass shards snapped under her shoes. They were 'Goebbels shoes', flats with pressed-cardboard soles, now sodden with rainwater. She wore a gaberdine coat and green felt hat. She was met by the scent of decaying flesh. The rescue squad had missed a body somewhere under the rubble.

She climbed some stairs to the first floor, which was open to the sky. She placed her suitcase on a chair and flipped the clasps. Inside was her radio, a pack wireless with a powerful amplifier and frequency multiplier. She pulled a small compass from her pocket, squinted at its tiny needle, then squared herself to the northwest.

Unrolling one of the wire antennas, she picked her way across the room to the window. She retrieved a drawing pin from her coat pocket. The end of the antenna had a tiny loop. She pressed the pin through the wire circle and into the window's wood casing. She did the same with the second wire antenna.

The two wires made a broadside array antenna. She brought up her wristwatch. Five minutes to go. Through the gaping holes in the ceiling she could see the red night sky, coloured by the fires set by American bombs that day.

Katrin von Tornitz had not visited Berlin until her twenty-third birthday, seven years ago. In 1902 her grandmother, Countess Voss-Hillebrand, had been one of the Ladies of the Palace. When the Kaiser appointed new Ladies of the Palace ranking above her, the countess stormed out of the court and left Berlin for the family estate in the Mecklenburg area, swearing her family would never return to the city. Not once in her fifty-five years had the countess's daughter—Katrin's mother—visited Berlin. Only when her grandmother died—of an accumulation of bile, the family suspected—could Katrin venture to the great city.

During her first evening there, at the Hotel Esplanade, a gallant Wehrmacht officer, Captain Adam von Tornitz, had approached her as she was standing near a terrace fountain. He whispered into her ear that she was *das Ewig-weibliche*, the eternal feminine, a phrase from Goethe. They were married ten days later.

Katrin was convinced then—and still fervently believed—that their love was a unique creation, unattainable by other humans. She had found her fulfilment. Then, on July 28, 1944, Adam von Tornitz was arrested, tried for complicity in Colonel Stauffenberg's plot and taken to Plötznsee Prison. He was hanged by piano wire from a meat hook. Rumours circulated in Berlin that a motion-picture camera had been in the death chamber, and that Hitler watched the films at night. Katrin never learned what, if anything, her husband had done to assist Stauffenberg.

Her grief had made her a traitor to the Fatherland. At Adam's funeral, one of his friends, Colonel Wilhelm Becker, expressed his sympathy, then added cryptically, 'Katrin, if you would like to do something in memory of Adam more substantial than tossing flowers onto his coffin, let me know.'

She had been fired from her post as a radio operator for OKW (the high command of the Wehrmacht) the day Adam was arrested. Had she not been so disconsolate after Adam's death, she might have feared for herself, because the Gestapo often arrested the accused's family members. But she was numb to everything but grief. And then rage began to kindle.

So she had visited Colonel Becker at his home. Three days later she received the pack wireless and a one-time pad, a booklet with codes printed in red for enciphering and black for deciphering, and made of cellulose nitrate, which burns quickly and leaves no latent images. She was also given a route that took her south of the city centre then back to the Friedrichstrasse Station, during which she checked three drops. She was to transmit whatever message she found, but there had never been any.

Colonel Becker had also told Katrin of the Gestapo's new radio direction finder, a circular antenna mounted on a black Opel. She was not to broadcast twice from the same location, and she was never to send for more than thirty seconds. Buildings with ACHTUNG! MINEN! on them were free from squatters and looters. She knew the risk, but she no longer feared anything.

Berlin was a city of widows, and they had grown to look alike, with vacant eyes, compressed lips and the timid expressions of those fearful of more dreadful news. Katrin had fought this sameness. She wore lipstick and eyeliner, though not much because heavy use of make-up was unpatriotic. Her face was slightly overfeatured, with vast Prussian-blue eyes. Her eyes had once been able to switch from glacial to gay in an instant. Now they were only mournful. She could not remember the last time she smiled.

She waited until the dial on her watch clicked onto the hour, then removed her hat to place the headset over her hair. The set pinched her ears. She tapped her call sign and sent a series of Vs so London could precisely tune to her signal. Her next letters were NA, meaning she had no message to send that night.

From her headset came a series of Vs. England was acknowledging her signal. The Morse ended. She was about to remove her headset when the receiver stuttered into life again. An actual message. She fumbled for the pad. Unable to see the paper clearly in the dark, she jabbed her dots and dashes across it. Twenty seconds later it ended. She clattered an acknowledgment.

The message was brief, so she decoded it as she sat there, squinting hard, as if that might help her see better in the dim light. The message said only, 'Follow Horseman's instructions.'

She knew of no one named Horseman, and she was worried.

She would have been more worried had she known of the black Opel, only two blocks away, coming closer and closer to her. But when Katrin ended her broadcast the car slowed, then stopped, having failed again to find her in time.

LAGEROFFIZIER LIEUTENANT Gerd Heydekampf detested these marches, but the Geneva Convention allowed them, so he bit down and paced along the wall near the chapel, waiting for it to end. Every time news of an Allied victory reached Colditz Castle, the POWs would march in brisk formation to and fro in the tiny yard, flaunting the Allied achievement. Today they were marching to celebrate the United States Ninth Army's capture of Essen, an event that had happened just the day before, April 9.

The POWs were using an American marching chant: 'She left. She left. She left, right, she left. You had a good home. You had a good job. You had a good life, but she left, right, she left.' The interminable refrain crawled up Heydekampf's back. With the war going as it was, the POWs marched every day.

The chant abruptly stopped, and Heydekampf's head jerked up at a new sound. The wail of a cat whose tail was being pulled. Or the screech of fingernails dragged across a blackboard.

He blew his whistle and the parade halted. 'What is that noise?' he demanded in English.

Harold MacMillan, of the Argyll and Sutherland Highlanders, called out, 'Bagpipes, sir.'

Heydekampf charged across the yard. MacMillan, barely five foot one, held the bag under his arm. He said in a Scots brogue, 'The windbag has the Black Watch pattern. Lovely, isn't it?'

The German sputtered, 'Where did you get that, MacMillan?'

'Lieutenant, may I speak with you?'

Startled at the voice, Heydekampf turned to find the camp commandant, Colonel Janssen, standing at his shoulder.

'Of course, sir.'

The colonel led him to a spot near the delousing shed.

He said, 'I am allowing the prisoners to accompany their marches with that infernal instrument. I see no harm in it.'

The parade resumed to the bagpipes' caterwauling. Through

clenched teeth Heydekampf asked, 'Where'd it come from, sir?'

Colonel Janssen's face was carefully deadpan. 'I purchased it at a curiosity shop in Leipzig yesterday.'

Understanding creased Heydekampf's face. 'And you received a good-conduct testimonial in return—is that it, sir?'

The colonel drew himself up stiffly. 'You are being insubordinate.' Then he softened. 'I know you are dedicated to the service of this camp, Lieutenant, but your devotion to the Reich should not cloud your understanding of what is to come for us.'

Heydekampf asked with acid sweetness, 'You are saying that we must look out for ourselves—is that it, Colonel?'

'POW Captain MacMillan signed a paper saying that I treated him humanely during his two years at Colditz. This document may get me through difficult times in the weeks to come.'

Heydekampf chewed back his anger. Good-conduct testimonials had become a currency in the camp. Some of the guards gathered them as children collected stamps before the war, believing that if they could present twenty of the testimonials their blamelessness would be proven at any war-crimes trial.

Shouts came from the marching formation. Heydekampf and Janssen turned to the sound. A fight had erupted among the prisoners.

Heydekampf rushed towards the fray, then hesitated, swinging his gaze the length of the yard. Fist fights were classic POW ruses, designed to draw attention away from an escape. The lieutenant saw nothing unusual. He started for the two brawlers.

'Break it up,' he bellowed in English. He waded into the crowd.

Another shout, a desperate animal shriek of fear, instantly halted the fight. Heydekampf pivoted to the sound. He saw a body slam into the ground.

'No,' he gasped, then sprinted towards the body. The broken form had come to rest face down at the base of a five-storey wing of the castle. A brown cardboard suitcase made from a Red Cross bulk food box had hit the ground nearby.

Heydekampf rolled the body over.

'Damn it to hell,' he said softly. 'It's the crazy American.'

Blood was coming from the American's ears, which Heydekampf knew was evidence of a fractured skull. The blood was gathering at his neck and flowing onto the ground. One of his eyes was blackened and filling with blood. A ruptured eye socket. The POW's arm projected behind his shoulder at a twisted, unnatural angle.

Commandant Janssen and Group Captain Hornsby came to the front of the crowd.

Heydekampf reached for the POW's wrist. He waited a long moment with the American's wrist between his finger and thumb before he announced, 'No pulse. He's dead.'

'Of course he's dead,' Group Captain Hornsby said bitterly. 'He fell five bloody storeys and hit your stone courtyard.'

'*Scheisse*,' Heydekampf muttered.

Janssen ordered a guard to get a bag from the infirmary.

Heydekampf moved along the crowd of POWs to the senior Allied officer. 'Your fight and the noise of the bagpipes were a ruse, were they not, Captain Hornsby? A little choreography to distract my guards?'

Hornsby said nothing..

Anger clipped Heydekampf's words. 'You see what has resulted from your game? A good soldier is dead, thanks to your escape pranks. You live with that for a while.'

'We'll bury him today, Group Captain Hornsby,' said Commandant Janssen. 'I will issue some wood and white paint from the shop if you will have one of your men construct a cross.'

SS PRIVATE BRUNO PATZER knew the garden had once been a lovely atrium, with fountains, a tea pavilion and a greenhouse full of hyacinths and jasmine, the blossoms the Führer preferred on his table. The garden would have offered little solace on this bitter night, though, even if bombs had not destroyed it. The private shifted his hands, trying to keep his cold fingers away from the colder steel of his Mauser, gripping instead its wooden stock. His post was the camouflaged guard tower that had a view of the Reich Chancellery garden. His sentry box was unheated and the day had been unusually cold for April, with heavy rain.

Most of the private's view was ruin. The greenhouses had been shattered by a bomb blast, and glass splinters littered the garden. Uprooted trees and broken statuary seemed to have been tossed casually about. The largest structure in the garden was the blockhouse, a thirty-foot cube of concrete near the rear of the Old Chancellery. The blockhouse's steel door led to the Führer's bunker. The private had never been through that door.

SS Private Patzer was one of fifteen guards on duty in the garden, and he was proud of his service in the Liebstandarte-SS Adolf Hitler. On that day two years ago when Private Patzer had taken his personal oath of obedience to the Führer, Hitler had walked down the line of soldiers, shaking each hand and looking into each pair of eyes. When the Führer reached him, it was the greatest moment of Patzer's life. The Führer had not spoken to him that day or any day since, but Patzer was as close to the German saviour as he was to his mother. He loved the man.

A guard at the blockhouse blew a boatswain's whistle. Patzer quickly squared his helmet and his belt, and brought his Mauser in line in front of him.

The two guards stationed at the blockhouse door jerked themselves to a rigid attention. From the black doorway, emerging out of the darkness, walked the Führer. He was wearing a grey greatcoat, scarf, black gloves and a field-grey peaked cap. Beside him was Blondi, his white Alsatian. The dog leapt to the end of his leash, eager for the trees and bushes of the garden. Hitler moved slowly, cautiously, as if testing each step.

Patzer wanted to weep for the man. Hitler shuffled along the gravel path, wobbling like a drunken sailor. He used his right hand both to grip the dog's leash and to hold his dead left arm close to his body. In the darkness Patzer could not see Hitler's face, only a glint off the nickel-rimmed spectacles he always wore except when in front of cameras.

Patzer removed his gaze from the man to stare precisely ahead, as ordered, when the Führer passed. When Hitler's footsteps stopped Patzer braved a look down.

The Führer's head was tilted back, and he was peering straight up the tower at Patzer. Astounded, the private swayed on his feet.

'It's cold up there,' Hitler said. 'Much too cold for April.'

Patzer tried to bark out his response as he had been trained. Instead, his voice was tremulous. 'Yes, my Führer.'

'Your hands are wet and are going to get blue.'

'Yes, my Führer.'

'Here.' Hitler peeled off his gloves. 'Can you catch these?' Hitler tossed the calf gloves skywards. Patzer could catch only one of them. The other fluttered back down to the ground.

Hitler stepped off the path into the mud to retrieve the glove. 'We Germans don't play cricket like our enemies. So you can't blame me for a lame toss.'

'No, sir.'

Hitler reared back again and launched the glove. Patzer snatched it easily.

'Put them on your hands,' Hitler lectured lightly. 'Don't stick them into your pocket to keep them for a museum somewhere.'

'Thank you, my Führer.' Patzer shoved his fingers into the gloves. The rabbit-fur lining still radiated Hitler's warmth. Patzer was giddy with the intimacy. He had taken his SS oath in the presence of his leader. Now he took another one, in silence. He would stay with the Führer to the end, to the very end.

 # TWO

The farmhouse was fifty yards off the road, down a dirt drive. Cray walked towards the house, avoiding ruts and potholes. An apple orchard was to the north, the trees new in their spring leaves. To one side of the stone house stood a goat shed and an open machine shed in which there were a two-bladed plough and stacks of apple boxes. Wooden planks had fallen from the goat shed, shingles were missing from the farmhouse's roof, and ivy had grown up and over the porch. The farm was clearly in decline.

Cray neared the house. No vehicle in the driveway. No farm animals. The porch creaked when he stepped onto it. He leaned to his right to peer into a sitting room. Empty. He walked to the rear of the house, where a garden contained a row of bean stakes and a torn bird net which was hung over small pear trees. The back doorknob turned easily.

When Cray stepped into the kitchen, he was met by the smell of fresh baking, a fruit pastry of some sort. Tendrils of scent wrapped round him, making him feel light-headed. His stomach loudly rolled over at the prospect of being filled. A strudel and several old newspapers were on a sideboard near a wood stove.

Cray gazed at the pastry. A flaky crust round apple halves.

He stepped into the sitting room. An overstuffed chair, a wall clock. Then he walked across a hooked rug past a fireplace to the bedroom. A four-poster bed, a hat on a wooden rack, a dresser and a mirror. A farmer's spartan home. Cray was satisfied no one was at home. The house was cold. He could see his breath.

He rifled through the dresser and found a man's clothing. Cray peeled off his shirt and trousers. He put on a shirt with wooden buttons, too tight but wearable, a pair of trousers and a work coat.

He returned to the kitchen and opened a drawer for a fork. He lifted the strudel reverentially and sniffed the pastry. He lowered the plate to the table, sat on a sturdy chair, carefully cut off a small piece of pastry and lifted it to his mouth.

The muzzle of a shotgun bit into the back of Cray's neck. His fork froze.

'This is my house,' a voice behind Cray said. An old woman's voice. 'And that's my strudel.'

Cray sat utterly still. His knife was under his belt.

The shotgun barrels lifted from his neck. The woman came into his view. She was wearing a long green coat, a crocheted shawl and a frown. She sat on a chair, propping the bird gun on the table edge, its barrels pointed at Cray's throat.

'You are an escapee from that awful castle over in Colditz?'

He answered in German. 'Yes.'

'So you must be dangerous.' The woman wore her silver hair in a bun on top of her head. Her face had deep lines. She was thin, with her coat hanging loosely from narrow shoulders and with wrists the width of broom handles. Her dark eyes were far back in her head. They were alert. Cray suspected they missed nothing.

'You speak our language,' she said. 'I should shoot you now.'

'Will you wait until I eat this strudel before you shoot me?'

A corner of her mouth lifted slightly. 'If I wait until you eat the strudel, then I'll have a dead body in my kitchen and no strudel. But if I shoot you now, I'll have a dead body but I also have the strudel. So it would be smarter to shoot you now.'

Cray suggested, 'How about if I eat half, then you shoot me?'

'All right,' she said. 'Cut the strudel in half, then I'll choose which half you eat.'

Cray visually measured the pastry, then cut it precisely in half with his fork. The old lady nodded at the piece to Cray's left. He instantly dug into it with the fork. The strudel seemed to burst inside his mouth, filling him with flavour down to his feet.

'You are a good cook, ma'am.'

'I didn't have fresh fruit, so I used apples I bottled last autumn. And I had to stretch the flour by adding some sawdust.'

'I wondered about the piny taste.'

'How did you learn German?' the woman asked.

He hesitated. 'My parents came from Berlin.'

'I have an unerring ear for the truth,' she said. 'And I didn't hear it just then. Maybe I should shoot you now, just so I don't have to listen to lies.'

'How's this, then? After I received a degree in mechanical engineering in the United States, I did postgraduate work at Berlin Polytechnic, in 1936. I learned the language in Berlin.' He lifted more strudel on his fork. 'Why is it so cold in here?'

'I don't have any firewood.'

Cray said, 'But I saw a big stack of wood just outside.'

'I have bad arthritis in my fingers and hands and shoulders. I can't swing an axe at all. So I sit in here all day, cold. I made that strudel using only wood chips for heat. Those I can carry in.'

Cray scratched his nose. 'Why don't I cut some firewood for you? In exchange for the other half of the strudel.'

'Then when do I shoot you?'

'After I chop the wood and eat the last half of the strudel.'

'The axe is out by the woodpile.'

Cradling the shotgun in her arms, the old woman followed the American out of the kitchen door. A maul, a wedge and an axe were lined up against the house. She stayed by the door as he centred a log on a chopping block. He tapped the wedge into the centre of the log and then swung the maul in a large circle. It landed on the wedge with a crack. He swung again and the log split in half. He pushed the halves to one side and reached for another log.

Cray said, 'May I ask your name, ma'am?'

'Helga Engelman.'

'Are you running your farm alone, Frau Engelman?'

'Two summers ago during the harvest my husband lay down between two apple trees and never got up again. A heart attack. You look better in his clothes than he did.'

Cray split another log, then another.

'You are a commando,' Mrs Engelman said. 'Am I right?'

'Well, not really . . .'

'Remember.' The shotgun wiggled. 'I have an ear for a lie.'

'I'm a commando.' Cray lifted the axe.

'What's the worst thing you've ever done to my homeland?'

Cray turned to her, the axe hanging at his side. 'Why would I reveal that to a German woman pointing a shotgun at me?'

'Because I'm pointing a shotgun at you.'

He lifted another piece of wood. 'I sank a submarine once.'

'You sank a submarine? By yourself?'

Cray nodded. 'The submarine belonged to the Kriegsmarine's Tenth Flotilla, and was in a pen at Lorient, on France's west coast. I was parachuted into Brittany, and I got inside the base by burying myself in a locomotive's coal car. Then, with a satchel charge in a rubberised bag, I swam out to *U-495*. I dropped the satchel into the forward hatch. Then I slid back into the water. The blast tore the sub in two.'

Cray began again with the axe. The pile of split wood grew rapidly.

'I told you I have an ear for a lie.'

'Yes, ma'am.'

'That submarine isn't the worst thing you've done to my country, is it?'

Cray didn't stop his mechanical motion. 'No, ma'am.'

'I don't suppose I want to know the worst, do I?'

'No, ma'am.'

She leaned the shotgun against the wall. 'You could have flicked me aside like a bug, shotgun or no. Isn't that so?'

Cray replied, 'The thought never crossed my mind, ma'am.'

She smiled, revealing yellowed teeth. 'Will you help me put the firewood inside the house before you go?'

Cray carried a load of wood into the house and stacked it in the cradle near the stove. Then he made five more trips.

When the hopper was full, she said firmly, 'It will be my duty as a German patriot to report that you were here.'

'Can you wait three hours?'

'One hour.'

'Ninety minutes?'

'All right. Ninety minutes.'

She wrapped the rest of the strudel in a sheet of newspaper and passed it to the American. 'You'd best hurry.'

Cray tucked the pastry under his coat. 'Maybe I'll come back and visit you, Frau Engelman. After the war.'

'If you do, bring coffee. I won't have any, most likely.'

Cray smiled at Frau Engelman, then left her house. He heard her call after him. 'And cream, I take mine with cream.'

OTTO DIETRICH woke to the rasp of the key. The sound at his cell door was out of turn. He had been to the blade and back an hour before. Now they were coming for him again.

'This is against your rules,' he said meekly as the door opened. 'I've been to the guillotine once today.'

The executioner, Sergeant Winge, entered the cell carrying two buckets of water. A towel was draped over his shoulders. 'You have an appointment. You need to get ready.'

Agent Koder came next. He was holding a pair of trousers, a shirt and a leather bag. 'Take your clothes off,' he ordered.

Dietrich surprised himself by finding a reserve of dignity. 'I'm not going naked to the guillotine.'

Koder's voice was bitter. 'You are to go to the Prinz Albrecht Strasse headquarters as soon as possible. Here's a razor and soap and scissors. You'll find shoes to fit you in this bag, along with your wallet, police ID, and your false teeth.'

Dietrich tried to cut his beard with the scissors.

Sergeant Winge said, 'Your hands are shaking so badly you're going to stab yourself.' He took the scissors and quickly cut back the beard to stubble. Then he dabbed soap lather on Dietrich's face. 'My father was a barber,' the executioner said. 'I was going to enter the trade, but I found the army first. So, instead of cutting off hair, I cut off heads. Funny how life works.'

The sergeant rapidly shaved Dietrich, dipping the straight razor into the bucket several times. Then he wiped the detective's face with the towel. He stepped back to admire his work.

'Good as new,' Winge said proudly.

Dietrich inserted his teeth and snapped his jaw several times to test them. He was too weak to stand on one leg, so he leaned into the sergeant to pull the trousers on. Nothing quite fitted him. The sergeant pulled Dietrich's pistol—a Walther—from the bag and passed it to him. Dietrich shoved it into his belt.

Koder and the sergeant led him from the cell, along the dim corridor, then up the stairs to the main floor. When they stepped through the doors, Dietrich had to bring his hands to his eyes. He had not been above ground for three months. Daylight was blinding. The sergeant grabbed his elbow to lead him across the pavement to a waiting Mercedes with silver swastika medallions above its bumpers.

Sergeant Winge opened the door. Dietrich tried to lower himself to the seat, but his legs buckled. Winge caught him and gently placed him on the seat.

Dietrich had smelled nothing but mould and rot and his own fear for months, and the limousine's odour of leather and cigars was intoxicating. He turned to the window as the car pulled away. They were passing through a valley of rubble that rose steeply on both sides.

'With all the wreckage many streets are too narrow for cars and trucks. So we've brought narrow-gauge trains from the Ruhr mines, and laid the tracks for them.' The SS driver spoke in a rehearsed manner, as if he frequently gave tours.

The Mercedes veered round a crater, then came to a line of fallen telephone poles that blocked the road. The SS driver backed up, then turned onto another street, but here high-tension cables lying across the road were marked with a warning sign. Again he put the car into reverse, this time going two entire blocks backwards before finding a roadway that was clear, but which had not been swept. It was a river of glittering glass, crackling under the Mercedes's tyres. At the next crossroads they passed a field kitchen with a long line of haggard women and blank-faced children holding tin bowls.

The Mercedes turned onto Berlinerstrasse, then came to the Tiergarten. Dietrich's mouth turned down at his first view of the lawns. They were a moonscape of room-sized craters. Many of the chestnut and lilac trees had been blasted down or cut for firewood. The ponds, once blue gems, were now filled with rubble pushed there by bulldozers clearing nearby streets. The Victory Column was surrounded by ramshackle squatters' huts.

They drove along the once-elegant Kurfürstendamm, where the café society had reigned. The street was bombed out and boarded up, the restaurants' striped awnings lying along the gutters. At the top of the avenue they came to the Kaiser Wilhelm Church, where the tower clock had been frozen at seven thirty since the day in November 1943 when Allied bombers destroyed 1,000 acres of the city. Berlin had become a second Carthage.

'The city will never be rebuilt,' Dietrich said.

The car stopped in front of Gestapo headquarters on Prinz Albrecht Strasse. After an SS guard opened the Mercedes's door, a Gestapo agent showed the detective into the building. Dietrich was led to the third-floor office of Gestapo leader Heinrich Müller. Dietrich was astonished when the door was opened to reveal all the chiefs of the Reich's criminal and political police organisations sitting round Müller's conference table, silently waiting for him.

'Please sit down, Chief Inspector Dietrich,' Heinrich Himmler said.

Dietrich had never before met the man. Himmler was smaller than his photographs portrayed, and more kindly in appearance. His undersized chin, delicate moustache and watery eyes behind rimless spectacles gave him the look of a clerk. His hips were wider than his shoulders and he had gained a pot belly over the years sitting behind his desk. Himmler excelled at desk work.

Displaced from his chair at the head of the conference table by Himmler, Heinrich Müller sat stonily to the Reichsführer's left. He had been too long inside Gestapo headquarters, and his skin had faded to a leprous white and was marred by pockmarks. His nose was flat and his mirthless brown eyes were set deep in his skull. His dark hair was combed straight back and kept in place with gleaming pomade. Müller stared at Dietrich with undisguised hatred.

Gestapo Müller was Dietrich's great nemesis, the ever-present threat and the constant danger.

Ten years before, in 1935, Dietrich had arrested him for the murder of his mistress, a teenager from the Bavarian mountains. Müller had set her up in a flat just off the Kurfürstendamm. Dietrich had never determined what had driven Müller to his murderous fury, but the girl's body had been punctured with a knife eight times. On the basis of the report of a neighbour who had seen Müller leave the premises with a bloodstained overcoat, Dietrich arrested Müller, who spent two months in the Lehrterstrasse Prison before the Nazi Party could effect his freedom. Despite Dietrich's pressing the issue, Müller was never rearrested or tried. And Müller had been after Dietrich ever since, trying to catch him in a mistake. Finally, the Stauffenberg plot had been enough.

General Eugen Eberhardt, head of the Reich Security Service (RSD), was at the table. Dietrich knew him to be highly competent.

'I have flooded the Reich with copies of this photograph,' General Eberhardt said.

Dietrich's eyes followed Eberhardt's gaze to the white wall, where the image of a man's head was projected.

The photo had been taken on the prisoner's admission to Colditz. The POW's mouth was slightly arched, and his eyebrows were lifted as if he were amused. Dietrich could not tell the prisoner's eye colour, but the man had fair skin and short blond hair. His jaw was aggressive. A boxer's face.

'His name is Jack Cray,' Eberhardt said. 'He is the American who escaped from Oflag IV C at Colditz yesterday afternoon.'

General Eberhardt had spoken with the Colditz commandant, Janssen, by telephone. Janssen had not determined how it had occurred, but he had apparently buried a man alive in the castle cemetery. After the graveside service, the minister who had said words over the grave had begun searching for edible portions of apples on the ground in the orchard next to the cemetery. The minister saw the POW emerge from his grave, like a demon from the centre of the earth. According to Colonel Janssen, the minister was still trembling from the ordeal.

'The POW was spotted at Böhlen, a village ten kilometres north of Colditz,' Eberhardt added. 'An elderly woman found him in her house, eating pastry.'

Himmler had never heard of Böhlen. 'North of Colditz?'

'Yes, sir.'

Allied POWs usually headed east towards the Soviet lines. It was known among POWs that the Red Army would gladly assist them in getting home. Then why had this Colditz escapee journeyed north towards the heart of the Reich, not east?

'There's more,' Eberhardt continued. 'It seems the old lady and the POW had a talk. She said the POW claims to have sunk the submarine in the pen at Lorient. Remember that?'

Eberhardt's expression shifted as he glanced again at the POW's photograph. 'Moreover,' he said, 'there is no question that this same Cray was the guerrilla who entered the Vassy Chateau.' Eberhardt spoke slowly, letting his words take full effect.

All German police and military personnel knew of the Vassy Chateau disaster. On a moonless night last August, a Wehrmacht division was bivouacked in a chateau near St Lô. Sleeping soldiers were scattered about the main room, some on sofas, some on a Turkish rug. It was believed the enemy commando was in the room less than ten minutes. He knifed eight Germans, every other one he came to. Soldiers woke up sandwiched between two dead comrades. Eberhardt leaned slightly towards the projected photo and said, 'One of the sentries patrolling the chateau that night reports that the American sneaked up behind him and spun him round. The sentry believes the American deliberately let him see him.'

Dietrich now realised that he had been released from prison for his investigative skills. He was determined to prove himself to avoid a return to his cell.

'The American let the sentry live?' Dietrich asked. 'Why?'

'I don't know, Inspector. Perhaps he wanted his description to become known, as a terror tactic.'

Himmler nodded. 'That is an American trait, you know. I have studied our enemies. Soldiers reflect their homeland's national peculiarities. British soldiers are courteous even when killing you. French servicemen refuse to fight on empty stomachs. Wanting to become famous for his exploit is certainly American.'

Eberhardt glanced at his notes. 'We have another report about the American, this from Berlin Polytechnic. Jack Cray was a student there for two terms in 1936. He took the fluid dynamics course. According to information on his enrolment forms, he was born in the western United States, in a town called Wenatchee in the state of Washington. His father was an apple grower.'

Himmler interrupted, 'But what is important is that this Jack Cray is loose now and appears to be heading for Berlin.'

'Are we certain he is not still in Böhlen?' Müller asked.

'General Reinecke ordered a class-one house-to-house search,' Eberhardt explained. 'The village was circled by members of the Home Guard, Hitler Youth, the League of German Girls, the police and prison-service guards. The American is no longer there.'

Himmler said, 'Jack Cray is coming to Berlin to attempt to assassinate the Führer.'

'How do you know that?' Dietrich asked.

Himmler was so unaccustomed to questions that his mouth snapped shut.

General Eberhardt said, 'At this point in the war the enemy can accomplish virtually all of their military objectives by using their bombers. There is no need for the Americans to go to extreme lengths to free this commando unless they have some delicate but very important task in mind. We must assume the worst.'

'You have very little evidence,' Dietrich persisted.

Eberhardt replied, 'That's the difference between your job and mine, Inspector. As a policeman, you must find enough evidence for a jury to convict a criminal. But the duty of the RSD is to protect the Führer. Since the beginning of the war, we have thwarted eighteen assassination attempts. I must act on supposition, on the slightest of suspicions, on the hint of a rumour.'

'If the Reich is to survive, the Führer must survive; it is as simple as that,' Himmler said. 'I am told you are the best man-hunter in the Reich. You are to stop this American.'

He removed a pen from his breast pocket and opened a folder. As he wrote on a piece of stationery, he continued, 'Jodl and Goering agree with me regarding the urgency of your task, and they have pledged that whatever you need—manpower, communications, equipment—will be yours instantly.'

He passed the letter to Dietrich. At the top of the page was the emblem of the Reichsführer-SS. Dietrich read the scratchy handwriting: 'This is Chief Detective Inspector Otto Dietrich. You are to obey his orders as if they were my orders. Himmler.'

The Reichsführer said, 'This note will assist you, I trust.'

Otto Dietrich would go to his grave wondering where he found the courage to say, 'Where is my wife?'

Himmler's eyebrows rose. 'General Müller?'

'At a facility outside Munich,' Müller said. 'She is being detained pending investigation as your accomplice.'

'You release her from that place or I won't do a thing.'

Müller coloured and half rose from his chair. His mouth opened, but Himmler's cold glance cut him off.

The Reichsführer waved his hand airily. 'She will be released within one hour, and will be brought directly to Berlin.'

General Eberhardt handed the detective the RSD file about the American. Eberhardt said, 'This American, this Jack Cray. Put a bullet in him. From a great distance, if possible.'

'I understand, sir.' Dietrich started towards the door.

He was brought up by Müller's piercing voice. 'Your wife will be released, Inspector Dietrich. But the Gestapo is like the Lord. What it gives, it can take away. Remember that.'

Reichsführer Himmler clucked his tongue at Müller's boorish threat. But he added in a pleasant tone, 'Now, Inspector Dietrich, kindly begin your work, and do not fail us.'

THREE

Ulster Rifleman David Davis and Major Harry Bell held their breaths and stared at the senior Allied officer. Ian Hornsby rarely let indecision cross his face, but he was clearly agonising.

Otto Dietrich had spread out a selection of doughnuts on paper on a table in the prison ward. 'Go ahead,' he urged, 'they aren't poisoned. Offering pastries isn't some new German interrogation technique.'

Heydekampf translated the words into English.

When Hornsby slowly reached for one of the doughnuts, Bell and Davis leapt for them.

Davis crammed one into his mouth, then mumbled, 'You almost had a bloody mutiny on your hands, Captain.'

Bell chewed frantically. 'I would have joined Davis.'

The first thing Otto Dietrich had done after leaving the Gestapo headquarters was to re-enter the Mercedes. When the SS chauffeur baulked at driving the inspector without further instructions from the Gestapo, Dietrich produced Himmler's letter. With a laugh, the driver started the engine. On the inspector's orders, the driver took him to the Adler Bakery on Hermann Goering Strasse. The baker swore he had no pastries that day. Flashing Himmler's letter quickly resulted in four dozen doughnuts.

Then Dietrich had visited his district police station to requisition the talents of Peter Hilfinger, his assistant for the past six years. On first sight of Dietrich, Hilfinger had grabbed him in an unprofessional bear hug, and then had been quick to drop whatever he had been working on to join him.

They had stopped briefly at an orthopaedic surgeon's clinic on Krummestrasse, where Dietrich and Hilfinger conducted an interview while the driver waited at the kerb. Then they drove to a haberdashery. Gestapo Müller's Fieseler Storch aeroplane had then taken Dietrich and Hilfinger from Berlin to Colditz. Dietrich did not know whether his nausea during the ride was motion sickness or came from the rich pastries.

Dietrich walked round a bunk to a barred window, giving the POWs more time to sate their sweet tooths. To help support himself, he put his hand against the window frame. His legs were still weak from his time at Lehrterstrasse.

'Captain Hornsby,' he said, turning from the window, 'you are the senior Allied officer at Colditz. Major Bell is the senior American officer. Colonel Janssen believes that you, Captain Davis, are the Colditz escape committee chief. I trust his instincts.'

Dietrich paused, allowing Heydekampf to render his words into English. Then he said, 'I asked you to meet me because you three undoubtedly planned and assisted Jack Cray's escape.'

Hornsby furrowed his brow, then glanced at Bell, who shrugged. Captain Davis licked icing from his fingers. They had no idea where the detective inspector was leading.

Dietrich continued, 'It would be impossible for me to trick you into divulging information about the escape, but I don't need to. I am going to tell you how you and the American did it.'

Dietrich stepped round a support post in the centre of the ward. 'Your challenge was to make Jack Cray look dead,' he said. 'A fractured skull—one smashed against cobblestones from a great height—has a certain damaged appearance.'

Colonel Janssen protested, 'It looks just like Cray's did.'

Dietrich breathed on a hand. His cell in the Lehrterstrasse had been warmer than the Colditz ward. 'What Cray did was to pull down his lower eyelid and put a small slice on the inside of the eyelid with a knife. The tiny blood vessels there bleed profusely. He probably dabbed a little chimney soot on his cheekbone to make it look bruised. Altogether, it would have been a convincing replica of a ruptured eye socket.

'Bleeding ears are another classic sign of a fractured skull,' the inspector went on. 'And Jack Cray's ears had blood in them. But it wasn't Cray's blood, was it? One of you gentlemen cut yourself with a blade, on your arm or thigh or somewhere else, collected the blood in a cup, and at the right time poured it into Cray's ears. If I were to search you, I would find such a gash.'

Ian Hornsby wiped doughnut crumbs from the corners of his mouth. His face was a carefully composed mask.

The detective was wearing black trousers and a fur-lined waistcoat which he had procured from the haberdashery with Himmler's letter. Dietrich's shoes were also new, and squeaked when he walked. He said, 'Cray also appeared to have shattered his shoulders and arms when he hit the courtyard.'

Heydekampf nodded fervently as he translated.

'It must have been a difficult task, Group Captain Hornsby.' Dietrich touched the support post, of roughly milled timber. 'Cray stood with his back against this post. One of you pinned him in place so he wouldn't slip round the column. Then two more of you dislocated his shoulders.'

Colonel Janssen's mouth opened.

'The pain must have been excruciating, but I doubt Cray called out. Am I right?'

Harry Bell helped himself to a chair. He gave Hornsby the slightest of glances.

Dietrich had not expected an answer. He continued, 'The Reich's Office of Medical Information, which gathers statistics regarding accidents, reports that a person who falls three storeys has a fifty per cent chance of surviving. A person who falls four storeys has a fifteen per cent chance. And someone who falls five storeys, as Jack Cray ostensibly did, has virtually no chance.'

'I saw him fall, Inspector,' Heydekampf almost shouted.

'Lieutenant, you saw him land.' Dietrich moved to the iron-barred window for the second time. 'Cray landed in the yard below this very window.'

He gripped a bar and pulled. It easily came off in his hand. When he gripped a second rod and tugged, it also came away from the window. The inspector held up both metal shafts.

'The fist fight was a planned distraction,' he went on. 'The instant the brawl began, Cray leapt from this first-floor window. He fell three metres, not five floors.'

'But I saw him fall,' Heydekampf objected.

'You heard Cray scream, and turned in time to see him fall a few metres, Lieutenant. Your imagination filled in the rest.'

Heydekampf did not bother translating these last revelations.

Dietrich asked Janssen, 'Where do you suspect the POWs got the metal saw or file to cut the bars?'

The commandant lifted his palms. 'Stolen from a maintenance crew probably. Or perhaps they have picked the workshop lock. They can get into the workshop and infirmary and kitchen at will, it seems.'

Heydekampf began translating again when the inspector said, 'Jack Cray's will-power can be measured by his posture after he landed. A man who is in a great deal of pain will reflexively curl up into a ball, but a dead man has a sprawled, boneless look to him. That's how you found Jack Cray. His flaccid posture alone would have led you to think he was dead.'

'He wasn't breathing,' Heydekampf blurted in German.

'He was breathing, very shallowly and slowly under his loose coat, and in checking everything else you missed it.'

Dietrich placed the bars on the floor and turned to the table. Hornsby and Bell had finished their doughnuts, but David Davis still had one in each hand and was taking bites out of each alternately.

'But he had no pulse,' Heydekampf argued. 'I swear it.'

'You are correct. Cray had no pulse.' Dietrich brought out two lengths of rubber from his jacket pocket. 'This is surgical tubing. When a surgeon amputates an arm, he wraps this round the patient's upper arm, right under the shoulder. It prevents bleeding during the operation, and it blocks off all detectable pulse.'

Colonel Janssen's face whitened.

'Cray had tourniquets round both arms under his shirt and coat. Maybe not surgical tubing, maybe lengths of twine.'

As he interpreted, Heydekampf's voice lowered to a chagrined whisper. The POWs leaned towards him to hear the translation.

'The blood on Cray's neck was smeared there so you wouldn't check the carotid pulse in his neck. When it's easy to check his wrists, no sense bloodying your hands by checking the neck.'

Janssen said quietly, 'So that's how he did it. I've never heard of anything like it, not from Colditz or any other POW camp.'

'That's not all of it,' Dietrich said. 'Your report indicated that Major Bell and Captain Davis placed the American in the burial bag. To make him fit, they had to relocate his arms. Another excruciating ordeal for Cray. They also threw a knife into the bag so that Cray could cut himself out of it. And they may have removed the tourniquets, or Cray might have done it himself. The POWs who dug the grave made sure it was shallow.'

Janssen only nodded.

'And then there was the shortness of the ceremony at the grave,' Dietrich continued. 'None of the POWs offered to speak a few words over the body, knowing that Cray could last only a few minutes below ground. The minister who saw Cray rise from the earth estimates he was in the grave less than ten minutes.'

Hornsby's head came up. He had not known about the minister seeing Cray emerge from the ground. So that was how the Germans were alerted so quickly.

Otto Dietrich locked his gaze onto Hornsby's. After a moment the investigator buttoned his coat. 'Goodbye, gentlemen. You told me nothing, but I learned a lot.' He stepped to the door. Janssen and Heydekampf followed.

THE LINE OF REFUGEES at Sergeant Hans Richter's checkpoint was growing. He rose to his toes to glance back along the line. There must be three hundred people waiting to pass through, he guessed. They were hollow-eyed with fatigue. Some had blankets over their shoulders. They pulled carts and pushed wheelbarrows. Horses drew wagons piled with furniture.

He looked again at the photo of an American on his clipboard. At the briefing that morning Sergeant Richter's captain had warned that the fugitive was to be shot on sight.

A horn bleated, and a Horch limousine parted the refugees as it approached the checkpoint. The driver stopped the car at the barrier and rolled down his window.

Richter bent to the window. 'May I see your papers, please?'

From the back seat came a bark: 'I am Wehrmacht General Dräger. I am needed in Berlin. Let me through immediately.'

'I must see your identification, General. Those are my orders.'

The general leaned across the seat back to bellow, 'And I'm giving you new orders. Raise the barricade right now.'

Sergeant Richter put his hand round his Schmeisser submachine-gun grip. 'Sir, I have gone the whole war without shooting anybody, and I'd hate to begin with a Wehrmacht general.'

Accompanied by a spewing curse, the documents were passed through the window. Richter took his time with them, flipping through the pages with a studied insolence. He earned more profanity from the back of the Horch.

Richter handed the documents back through the window. 'Stay where you are while I search the boot,' he ordered. He lifted the boot lid. Nothing but changes of uniform. He closed the boot and walked slowly to the Horch's bonnet. He opened it to reveal the eight-cylinder engine.

'You idiot,' the general shouted from inside the car. 'Nobody could hide under the bonnet.'

Moving even more sluggishly, Richter latched the bonnet. He used a mirror mounted on a pole to look under the car, then walked to the barrier. 'Please proceed, General.'

The Horch shot forwards, trailing curses like exhaust. Richter laughed. He was able to pass several more refugees through, and then a cargo truck arrived, an Opel Blitz two-axle vehicle.

As he passed his papers through the window, the driver asked, 'You looking for anybody in particular?'

Richter returned the papers. 'Not you. Your ears stick out too much and you're about a foot too short.'

The driver smiled thinly. 'I guess a lad carrying a submachine gun is allowed to have a smart mouth.'

'Your cargo doors locked?'

The driver shook his head.

While one of his men searched the truck's underside with the mirror, Richter went to the back. He lifted the hasp and pulled open the doors. The cargo was beef carcasses, hung from rods in two rows. The carcasses were still swaying from the truck's stop. They dripped blood from their butchering, five tons of meat of a kind not seen by most Germans for two years.

Gasps came from the refugees. 'My God, look at all the beef. Enough to feed a village.'

'A load for Wilhelmstrasse?' came from a refugee. Wilhelmstrasse was Berlin's diplomatic and government quarter.

A woman dropped her cloth bag to shake a fist. She raged, 'My boy starved to death in the east. And look at all that meat.'

The crowd had transformed into a mob. Sergeant Richter raised his Schmeisser until the stubby barrel was pointed at the sky. He squeezed the trigger. The submachine gun bucked and brayed. Spent shells fell to the roadway.

The mob instantly halted.

'I'm not going to have to use this damn gun in earnest, am I?'

The refugees stared at him with fear and hatred and hunger, but slowly the crowd ebbed from the meat truck. Sergeant Richter stepped onto the Opel Blitz's bumper, then into the cargo bay.

Richter searched the length of the truck, looking behind each swinging bovine cadaver, making sure no one was hiding behind the suspended carcasses. Blood stained his uniform.

He peeked back out of the truck, then stepped behind a side of beef, drew his service knife and cut a dozen jagged sirloins from the hanging carcass. He was no butcher, and he struggled with the beef cuts, taking several minutes. He tucked them into his coat under an arm. For a month his men had been eating nothing but *Eintopfgericht*, a wartime stew consisting of butcher's-shop sweepings, the men suspected. Tonight would be different. Holding the sides of his coat so that he wouldn't drop his prizes, he jumped down to the road, closed the truck's cargo doors and waved the driver through the checkpoint. When the woman who had shouted that her son had starved in the east passed for inspection, he slipped her one of the sirloins. Her startled and grateful expression almost made the war worth while for the sergeant.

When the meat truck was two kilometres west of the checkpoint, Jack Cray's knife emerged from between the breastbones of a bull carcass. The blade slashed through the twine he had used to tie the ribs together after he had entered the organ cavity. He slithered out of the bull, dropping like a newborn calf. His hair was matted with sinew and blood, his clothes sodden.

He pushed open the cargo door, waited until the truck slowed for a corner, then leapt into the undergrowth at the side of the road. He rolled twice before finding his feet. He put his knife into his waistband, then pulled a compass from his pocket.

The compass had been made by the Colditz escape committee out of a moulded phonograph record, a sewing needle and a magnetised strip of razor blade. Cray sprinted across the road, climbed over a pole fence and entered a glade of trees.

The compass needle pointed north, and Cray headed in that direction. North, towards Berlin.

 # PART TWO: THE ARMOURY
FOUR

Otto Dietrich stared between the strips of blast tape crisscrossing the bedroom window out onto Kammlestrasse. Charred pieces of his neighbours' homes had been pushed into piles at even intervals along the pavement. Across the street, old Frau Fodor tended an iron pot hung over a fire, stirring it with a wooden spoon. Passers-by stopped to stare into the pot and nod, enjoying the steam that wafted across their faces. Frau Fodor's home resembled a pile of kindling, and she was living in her toolshed.

The detective moved from the window and slumped down on a three-legged stool next to his wife's bed. He could hardly bear looking at Maria, her sunken face, her convict's haircut. Her face was rose-red and splotchy with the same rash that covered most of her body. She had moaned much of the morning, but now she was quiet, and Dietrich knew the end was near.

He had been told by the doctor that it was her time in detention and not the typhoid fever that had wasted her away.

Dietrich had been waiting at the same window when the Gestapo vehicle brought Maria home. The detective's voice had risen suddenly. 'There's my wife.'

Dietrich yanked open the front door and hurried down the four steps to the black Horch. The driver and front-seat passenger made no move to get out of the vehicle.

Dietrich pulled open the rear door. 'Maria, I'm here, and—' Emotions chopped off his words.

She sagged out of the door and he had to catch her. He was startled at how little she weighed.

'Maria,' he blurted. 'It's me. It's Otto.'

She was unconscious, her eyes closed, her body limp.

'Let's get her inside.' The doctor had followed Dietrich.

Dietrich was unable to move. The doctor put his arms round Maria's still form and carried her from the car.

His physician, Kurt Scheller, waited with him. Scheller had given Maria a few days, and he had been generous. Now her time was up. Dietrich sat squeezing her hand, wondering how he would continue after today. Long ago he had determined that only two things were certain in his life: the love between Maria and him, and his investigating skills. Now one of those constants was leaving him.

He turned towards a photograph of them on their wedding day, rather than look at her. She was her old self in the photo. A flash of teeth, merrily angled eyes, mischief right there for all to see. Time and time again when he was in the Lehrterstrasse Prison, Dietrich would reconstruct that day. The bouquets, the champagne, his father-in-law's lederhosen, the cream and strawberries, every imitation pearl on Maria's dress. Next to the photo were his service pistol and a manila envelope containing the photograph of the escaped POW.

Feeling he was being unkind—looking at her in the old photograph rather than as she was now, drawn and skeletal—he turned back to the bed. Her chest rose and fell, just a suggestion of movement. He wiped a bit of spittle from the corner of her mouth, then caressed her forehead. Her eyes were closed as they had been since the Gestapo had delivered her.

Maria suddenly shuddered and gasped. Her body straightened as if pulled from both ends. She inhaled loudly and let the breath out. Then her head moved on the pillow and her eyes opened. She looked at her husband for a few seconds and whispered his name, 'Otto.'

Then she was still. The life went out of her, with her eyes still open. He knew she was dead: he had seen enough dead people to know.

Otto Dietrich stared at his wife for five more minutes, or it might have been thirty. Then he closed her eyes with his fingers and bent to kiss her forehead.

He stepped across the room to the dresser. She was gone, and now if there was anything left of him it was his ability as a policeman. He pulled Jack Cray's photograph from the envelope, staring at it with the same intensity with which he had gazed upon his wife. He put the envelope in his pocket, then lifted his pistol. He went downstairs and out of the house to his car.

TWILIGHT LINGERED in Leipzig. The sky was washed in reds and purples. Dust and ash from the day's bombing runs had not yet settled. They never settled; persistent Allied airmen saw to that. The particles softened the city by obscuring the distance, letting citizens occasionally forget that the skyline of their ancient city—the spires and towers—was now a series of rounded mounds.

The man who shuffled into an alley between two destroyed warehouses was apparently a refugee. He walked into the wind, arms across his chest, the tails of his thin coat flapping behind, his feet crunching the rubble. A scarf covered his hair and ears.

Jack Cray stepped out of the alley and continued down the road, the third time he had walked this circuit. His gait was a perfect imitation of a refugee's—a dispirited, halting walk that broadcast hunger and despair. Cray had found the neighbourhood by walking in the direction from which came loaded military cargo trucks. He had found an armoury on the bank of the Parthe River.

Cray had only been able to get within a block of the building. The armoury was surrounded by concertina wire, and soldiers patrolled the exterior of the building. Many important buildings in the Reich were now patrolled by the old and infirm, but this Leipzig armoury still commanded regular troops, and they were well armed. Cray had found no way to penetrate the wire and the patrols. He hobbled along the street.

When a troop truck passed, its wheels throwing mud, he felt the eyes of the driver on him. Cray reached down to the cobblestones for a discarded tin can, running his fingers inside the container, searching for anything edible. He licked his fingers. The truck's driver did not look a second time at Cray.

Three blocks from the armoury Cray turned towards the Parthe River. He passed a coal yard and a row of five gutted trucks, reduced to blackened hulks in a bomb raid. Then came a machine shop and a glassworks, both intact and operating. Workers' shadows were visible on blackout paper on the windows. The sweet scent of brewery malt turned Cray's nose. Their city was devastated, yet Leipzigers could still run a brewery. He grinned at the thought of a beer, his teeth flashing like a half-hidden knife.

On the riverbank were the remnants of a warehouse, hit long ago, only a concrete foundation, burnt and fractured timbers and scattered brick and glass shards remaining. Glass crunched under Cray's feet as he moved across the warehouse floor. He walked carefully in the grainy purple light, leaving the warehouse by wooden steps that went down to the river. Passing through damp grass, he neared the water. He stabbed his shoes into the mud for traction as the river bank steepened.

Defenders usually overestimate the value of water. Cray was guessing that he would be able to approach the armoury from the river side. He removed the scarf and his coat, and lowered a leg into the water. The Parthe was shockingly cold. Yet Cray let himself sink into the river, then shoved himself away from the bank. He idly kicked his feet, doing most of the work with his arms, a silent breast stroke with the current. In the failing light the surface of the water shone like oil. Cray bumped into something floating in the water. A dog's body, its belly and eyes eaten out by rats. He ignored it and pulled himself along.

A barbed-wire fence ran along the edge of the armoury property and into the water. Cray kicked round the fence posts and drifted towards the shore. When his feet found the soft bottom, he started up the bank, mud sucking at his boots. Then he heard a laugh. Two cigarettes glowed near an armoury door. A guard shouted and was answered by laughs from more soldiers further along the brick wall. The water side of the armoury was well guarded.

Cray slipped back into the river. An icy hand seemed to be squeezing his chest. The water had begun its work of killing him. He closed his eyes. His face hardened, resolution rekindling.

He drifted along the bank. The south end of the armoury had been destroyed by a bomb, and only the north portion was in operation. But all of it was guarded. Cray glided through the water. A new scent caught him. Sewage. In the dim light he saw an effluent pipe that jutted from the bank, most of it underwater. He paddled up to the pipe, which was about one and a half metres in diameter. Cray gripped the edges and held himself against the outflow. The human waste was warm, surging round him. He began to feel his chest and shoulders and arms again.

The pipe seemed to head underground in the direction of the armoury. Cray was comfortable hanging in front of the sewage pipe, and was tempted to stay for a while. But a splinter of wood drifted into him from the pipe, then more small pieces of wood, and then bits of floating plaster not yet fully soaked.

Detritus was falling into the sewage not far up the line. Cray lifted himself on the pipe to peer into the armoury's yard. Two men in overalls were negotiating a path through bomb rubble. One of them must have kicked debris into the open sewage pipe.

Cray smiled thinly. He had found the breach. He lowered himself again to peer into the pipe. He might have seen a slight suggestion of indigo down the pipe—a reflection of the dying day's light—but he could not be sure. He breathed deeply, lifted his legs until his feet found the concrete lip and crawled inside.

Sewage filled the pipe except for the top seven inches. Cray twisted his neck so that his mouth and nose remained above the surface. The air was putrid, but Cray knew it wasn't the scent but rather the methane and the absence of oxygen which would kill him if he was too long in the pipe. He scrambled along, his feet slipping on slime that coated the pipe walls under the surface. He held his breath as long as possible, then let it slowly out. When at last he had to inhale, neon spots began appearing before his eyes. He dug his feet into the walls and pushed off again and again.

That distant purple spot seemed no nearer. He could see nothing except more neon colours. He lost his bearings and drifted sideways, his shoulder bumping the pipe wall. He kicked and kicked against the walls, vaguely hoping he was still going towards that patch of purple.

Abruptly he rose in the waste. He had found the cleft in the pipe caused by the bomb blast. Cray gulped air.

He was in a conical bomb crater, with a short horizon of dirt all round, as if he were standing at the bottom of a funnel. He stood slowly so that the muck dripping off him would be soundless. He placed a foot on the dirt to test his weight. When several pebbles fell into the sewage, Cray froze to listen for the guards. He heard only good-natured chatter from a patrol near the river. With small and careful steps, he rose to the crest of the crater.

Debris hid Cray from the guards. He crawled towards the armoury, moving one limb at a time. When he heard new voices, he paused to cup both ears with his hands, then rotated one cup downwards, a hunter's trick which allowed him better to gauge the direction of the conversation. Sentries were to both his left and his right. Again Cray crawled forwards.

In lieu of a fallen wall, tarpaulins had been hung from beams. Cray moved the last few yards to a tarp. He slowly lifted a corner.

Sounds of machinery and men came from the far end of the building. Down an aisle of wooden boxes, workers were pushing containers into two trucks that had backed into loading bays. He slipped under the tarp and moved to a stack of crates.

They were stamped with STIELHANDGRANATE, FLAMMENWERFER and MP/2. Stick grenades, flamethrowers, submachine guns. He would turn to the weapons after he had obtained a change of clothes. He moved to a container painted in camouflage brown. He opened it and pulled out green fabric—trousers and shirts, windproof anoraks, boots, greatcoats and caps with short cloth peaks.

Then he lifted out a canvas bag and dug inside to find shoulder patches showing rank. He brought out a patch with two pips, for a captain. He stared at it, then whispered, 'I deserve a promotion.'

He brought out two braided major's patches.

'That's better.' He added the patches to his cache.

THE SS GUARDS eyed Sergeant Ulrich Kahr as he approached the cement blockhouse just as they did every day, looking at him as if he were some species of vermin. He detested the haughty SS.

The sergeant slowed, not wanting to enter the bunker one moment earlier than he had to. At the blockhouse door Kahr lifted his stiff grey linen identification card from a pocket and gave it to a guard. The SS guard studied Kahr's face, comparing it with the photograph on the pass. Sergeant Kahr's mouth was crooked, lower on one side, giving him a carping look, even though he seldom carped. His eyes were dark and faded, with only a suggestion of life left in them.

Finally the guard nodded. When the other guard opened the heavy steel door, Sergeant Kahr entered the blockhouse. The door clanked shut behind him with the deep finality of the last sound on earth.

Kahr descended the stairs to one landing, then another, circling anticlockwise. The fetid smell reached for him, dank and sour. The bunker was surrounded by ground water, and with every heavy rain the sewers backed up. Then he heard the whine, his whine. Sergeant Kahr may have been the only person assigned to the bunker whom the ventilator system's drone did not bother. Most compared the sound to a dentist's drill. He was one of the bunker's ventilation technicians, whose duty was to maintain the equipment that sucked in new air and blew out old air. He took pride in his task and appreciated the whine because it reminded bunker denizens of his importance.

At the bottom of the stairs was a foyer, lit so brightly by overhead bulbs that Kahr had to squint up into the faces of the two tall SS guards posted there. One guard examined his pass, then checked the duty rota on his clipboard. The other searched Kahr, running his hands up the sergeant's uniform to his armpits, along his lower back, then down and up his trousers.

'All right, Sergeant. You can go in,' the clipboard guard said.

'*Bleib übrig*,' Kahr said pointedly. Survive. Lately, Berliners had been using the phrase instead of 'goodbye'. Kahr knew it irritated the SS guards, who viewed the new saying as defeatist. So he said it again. '*Bleib übrig*.'

'I'll survive, old man.' The guard laughed meanly. 'From the looks of you, you may not.'

Kahr could only nod agreement. The war had beaten up Ulrich Kahr, had ravaged his face and his body, and he knew it. He hadn't seen front-line duty because he was fifty-five years old, born the same year as the Führer. But the war had etched deep lines into Kahr's face, and he walked now with a stoop like an old man.

Kahr had been a widower for fifteen years, and had raised his sons on his own. Last summer his oldest boy, Eswald, a Wehrmacht infantryman, had been killed on the Normandy coast. Then, just this past Christmas, Kahr had learned that his second son, Theodor, an armoured car driver, had been killed during the Ardennes campaign when his vehicle rolled over a mine.

Now all that was left of Ulrich Kahr's family was his youngest son, Max, who was on the eastern front. Every time Kahr saw the regimental chaplain he held his breath, hoping the chaplain wasn't bringing bad news, as he had already done twice. Kahr knew he could never again be whole, but he had one slender hope. The chance that he might see his son Max again, home and alive, was a fragile prospect, too perilous to nudge by dwelling on it, but it was all that was left for Kahr.

He stepped into a long central corridor just as Field-Marshal Keitel emerged from the conference room. Kahr heard the golden voice that had once lifted Germany: 'And, Keitel, you tell him it must be done. There can be no other course of action.'

The general turned and answered, 'Of course, my Führer.'

Kahr gave the conference room the swiftest of glances. The leader was bent over a map table. He was wearing the pearl-grey tunic with the olive shirt and black trousers that he always wore in the bunker. On his left breast were his golden Party badge and the Iron Cross won in the Great War. Then General Jodl stepped round the table and Sergeant Kahr's view was blocked.

He walked straight ahead. Lockers were to one side, where Foreign Minister Ribbentrop was conferring with an SS general. Ribbentrop fidgeted with a tunic pocket that contained a packet of cigarettes and politely herded the general towards the door, apparently anxious to get outside for a cigarette. Smoking was forbidden in the bunker. Even matches were prohibited, some said for security purposes, but most believed their banning was an extension of the Führer's loathing of cigarette smoke.

Kahr glanced at his watch, wondering if he had time to visit the galley. One of the cooks was sweet on him and would slip him pastry or a plate of veal. She would make a production of looking over her shoulders to ensure no one was looking as she passed the food to him, but in truth no one cared. The SS guard at the door would glance at the food and say nothing. Kahr's wristwatch indicated he had better forgo visiting the cook this day.

The sergeant had noticed a stratification in the bunker's society. Those who spent most of their time below ground—the Führer's cooks and secretaries and waiter, his personal aide and bodyguard SS Colonel Günsche, his valet Heinz Linge, Party Chancellor Martin Bormann, the blonde woman with the chirpy Bavarian accent Kahr had heard called Eva, the SS guards at the bunker's entrances and a few others, including Kahr and the other technicians—were treated as family. The Führer listened to their problems and gave them advice. When one of his secretaries, Trudi Reymann, weepingly reported that her fiancé had jilted her, Hitler sat beside her for half an hour, patting her hand and cooing softly.

On the second level of bunker society were men whose duty often brought them underground and the sycophants who had somehow gained both the Führer's favour and valid passes. They included Keitel and Jodl and Ministers Goebbels and Speer. These visitors were handled with less patience and less solicitude.

Battlefield commanders arrived at irregular intervals, mud on their boots, faces haggard, anxious to report and get away. As often as not, they would be summarily promoted or transferred or dismissed, and they rarely knew their fate when they arrived. In their demeanour and haste, these generals brought shocking reality into the bunker, where eight-foot-thick concrete walls muffled both bombs and unpleasant reality. The contempt felt for those safely ensconced below ground was visible on every battlefield commander's face, and those in Führerbunker society were just as relieved to see them go as the commanders were to do so. These front-liners were certainly not members of the underground family.

Kahr rang the buzzer of the second door on the left with that day's signal: two rings, then one, then one more. Hans Fischer, a Wehrmacht sergeant, pulled open the door, and Kahr entered his domain, a cubicle filled with machinery. At the far end were two diesel generators, quiet for the moment because electricity had been patched through to the bunker. Many times a day the bunker would be plunged into darkness. The beating heart of the Reich would be still until Ulrich Kahr came to its rescue. With the help of a torch, Kahr would pull the cord on a petrol starter motor and then engage the diesel generators. It was a nervous business, because the most important people in the Reich were just a few metres away.

'Anything new?' Kahr asked the sergeant.

'There is still a small oil leak at the base of starter one,' said Fischer. 'No better, no worse. I telephoned a mechanic and he said he was on his way, but he must have been detained.'

Fischer signed out on the rota, nodded goodbye and left the room, still stretching the aches out of his limbs. The job mostly involved sitting on a hard chair staring at dials.

The generators and starter engines and the fan boxes occupied much of the room, and an instrument panel took up much of the remainder. The panel—gauges and toggles and warning lights—monitored the generators and the ventilating system, some of which Kahr had designed. There was also a cage with yellow canaries in it.

Kahr looked at the oil- and water-pressure gauges, making notes in the machinery logbooks. He lifted a rag from the wall hook behind his chair and checked six dipsticks, two for each of the diesel engines and one each for the starter motors. Then he took a pinch of birdseed from a cloth bag and dropped it into the wood cup at the side of the canary cage. The birds were an alarm, as they would die from gas poisoning before humans, thereby allowing people in the bunker time to find their gas masks.

On the wall above the panel was a diagram of the ventilation system, showing the routes of the piping and the locations of the fans, filters, outlets and inlets, even the locations of the canaries. Switches on the panel activated dampers and gates, allowing Kahr to direct the flow of air. In the event of a gas attack he had been trained to shut off the fresh-air intakes and allow only captured air to circulate. The pipes were purposely made too narrow to allow even the smallest of men to crawl through them.

Kahr lowered himself to the chair. With the dipsticks checked and the canaries fed, he had completed his work for the shift, until the lights went out and he had to bring the generators to life. And, with nothing to do, his thoughts invariably returned to his boy Max. Perhaps, if he loaded God with prayers, God would allow a small mercy. Kahr closed his eyes and whispered a new prayer, so softly it was hardly audible above the ventilator fans' whine.

The signal came from the buzzer above his desk. Two rings, then one, then another. Kahr was puzzled. Few people visited the generator room. He threw the bolt and opened the heavy door.

'Sergeant Kahr,' the visitor said.

The voice, the golden voice. Kahr stepped away from the door so quickly that his chair spilled backwards and the startled canaries chirruped and frantically flitted round their cage.

Kahr straightened his backbone, slapped his arms against his sides, thrust his chin up and sucked his belly in.

'Sergeant Kahr, we are a family here below ground,' Adolf Hitler said, entering the room slowly, with more a shuffle than a walk.

'Yes, my leader.' Kahr fought for breath.

'I have tried to take some of the burdens off my family, especially now that we must live down in this terrible place.'

'Yes, my leader.'

Even though Kahr worked within two dozen metres of the Führer almost every day, he seldom more than glimpsed the man, so his image of Hitler had remained fixed: the glowing giant on the posters. Now Kahr was startled at Hitler's rapid decline. The Führer's pale blue eyes—his one distinctive feature—were bloodshot, the pupils filmy. Hitler's face was bloated and the skin was chalky and yellow. His hair had turned grey within the past two months, not a dignified silver but a drab mouse grey. Hitler's left arm was palsied and useless, and he gripped it with his right hand to prevent it from shaking.

But, still, the voice. 'I cannot let my intimates suffer alone.'

On his nose were the nickel-rimmed spectacles that most Germans knew nothing about. He brought a sheet of paper up to his eyes, and then Ulrich Kahr knew the reason for the visit.

Hitler said in a tender voice, 'Your son, Max, has been lost near Stettin, on the Oder.'

'Lost?' Kahr said in a fogged voice.

'His commanding officer writes that Max did not come back from patrol. He is presumed dead. The Bolsheviks are not taking prisoners. I thought it better that I inform you myself.'

Kahr reached blindly for his desk. His legs were suddenly unable to support him. Hitler stepped into the small room and put his good hand on Kahr's shoulder. 'I am very sorry,' he said, bending forwards so as to gaze into the sergeant's watering eyes. 'But at least you know that his loss was for the Fatherland.' Hitler left the room.

Kahr turned back to his control panel. The dials and gauges were scrambled by his tears. Max. His last son. He could not see beyond that minute, that hour, that day. His business with this world was done. Ulrich Kahr's last hope was gone for ever.

 FIVE

S ergeant Georg Keppler stepped on the starter, but the truck's battery was dead and the engine wouldn't turn over. He had been travelling south on a road parallel to the railway line. When he had stopped the truck at a level crossing, it had stalled.

'Get out and check the generator belt,' he ordered. 'Maybe it's gone.'

Private Werner Enge opened the Krupp's door and slid off the seat to the ground. He struggled with the latch before he could push up the bonnet.

'Gone,' he called. 'We've been running off the battery.'

Sergeant Keppler slapped the steering wheel. 'The lieutenant is going to hang us from a power pole, Werner.' He climbed down from the truck.

The private nodded. 'I suppose he will.'

Private Werner Enge was sixteen years old. His green eyes were still lively with innocence, and his mouth seemed permanently set in a smile of wonder. His uniform hung loosely on him.

'The lieutenant does not listen to excuses,' Sergeant Keppler said darkly. Keppler was a veteran of the eastern front, and wore fresh maps of scars on his legs from a mortar shell that had found him in the Ukraine. 'He might just hang us.'

Keppler turned at the sound of an approaching train. 'Damn it, we should be back at that field by now, picking up our unit.'

Keppler and Enge had dropped off their squadron, then travelled south to Linthe to look for fuel, and had been returning for their soldiers when the Krupp broke down.

'It could be worse,' Enge laughed, eager to please the sergeant. 'Our truck could have stalled right on the tracks.'

'Here they come.' Keppler leaned against the truck's bumper. 'Blown up, shot, burnt and broken, the lot of them.'

Private Enge watched the train. Six carriages passed, each with a red cross on a white banner below the windows. Window glare hid most of the passengers, but Enge could see a few bandaged heads as they sped by. The last two wagons were converted cattle trucks used for the wounded on litters. The wagons' slats had been covered with tarpaulins and the red cross.

'Let's walk.' Keppler pulled Enge's rifle from the Krupp's floor and passed it to him, then reached for his own Mauser.

As the last cattle truck pulled away from them, a mound on the track caught Enge's eye. The train had left something behind. A lump between the two tracks. The lump rose from the sleepers and gravel and transformed itself into a man. Someone had been run over by the train, maybe. The man rose, turning towards them.

Enge was relieved. The man couldn't be hurt too badly. He was a Wehrmacht major. Enge and Keppler hurried towards him.

The major staggered and fell. Then, as the soldiers neared him, the man rose again with something in his hand. He moved with startling speed towards them, bringing his hand round in a vicious arc. Enge saw only a crease in the day, a horizontal blemish against the background, and then heard a solid thump. Keppler collapsed to the ground, a stone the size of a fist hitting the ground next to him. The man had thrown a rock at the sergeant.

Enge's rifle strap snagged for an instant on a shoulder button. He yanked it free and brought the barrel up, wildly searching with his finger for the trigger, but too late. The man in the Wehrmacht major's uniform grew in front of Enge, a wall rushing at him.

The day blinked out. Nothing but blackness.

The private woke a moment later, his nose in the mud, the side of his head a mass of pain. He pushed himself up with one hand. Sergeant Keppler was still on the ground, his forehead bleeding. Many Sergeant Kepplers, swimming in front of Enge, whose eyes refused to focus.

'Is this all you have to eat?' the voice above him asked in German with a flat accent.

Enge rolled over and shaded his eyes with a hand. The man was backlit by the dull sun, a dark mountain hovering over Enge. He was rustling round in Enge's pack. His blond hair was short and spiky, and his nose was blunt. He was thin, and his skin was stretched tautly across his face.

'You're the American, the one who was at the Vassy Chateau.' Private Enge's voice wavered. He pulled a flier from his coat pocket. Jack Cray's face was printed on it.

Cray studied the flier. Below his face were the words NATIONAL ALERT, and then in slightly smaller type, VASSY CHATEAU KILLER ESCAPES POW CAMP. On the bottom of the flier was Cray's name, and under that SPEAKS GERMAN FLUENTLY. 'That's me, all right. Where'd you get this?'

'Everybody has one. They're posted all over Germany.'

Groaning, Sergeant Keppler rolled onto his belly.

Cray returned the flier. 'Let's go.' He lifted Enge's rifle.

Enge was startled. 'Go? Go where?'

'North.'

'If you wanted to go further north, why didn't you stay on the train?'

'I held on as long as I could,' Cray replied. 'Let's go.'

The private shook his head solemnly. 'I'm not going without my sergeant.' He pointed at Keppler, who was now sitting with his legs splayed out in front of him, a hand touching his head.

'You don't have a lot of say in it,' Cray said. 'Get in your truck and let's go.'

Enge said with satisfaction, 'The truck doesn't work.'

Cray stared at Private Enge's face, an open face incapable of a lie. 'Then let's walk.'

The private shook his head. 'Not without Sergeant Keppler.'

'You read that flier.' Cray smiled. 'You are talking to a dangerous fellow here. You should do what I say, and quickly.'

Another adamant shake of the private's head. His lip was out.

Cray shrugged. 'All right. Let's get him to his feet.'

One on each side of him, they pulled Keppler up. He swayed, but could move his legs. They began walking north. The sergeant's rifle was left behind. Cray carried the other Mauser in his free hand.

After a while Sergeant Keppler shook off their help and walked unassisted. He said nothing. Red welts were forming on his forehead where the stone had hit him. Cray dropped a pace behind so that he could watch both of them. The country lane ran alongside the railway tracks, and the three of them passed several farmhouses.

'Where did you get that Wehrmacht major's uniform?' Enge asked. 'Did you kill some poor guy to get it?'

'From a box in a warehouse.'

'I'll bet you took it off a dead body,' Enge insisted.

Sergeant Keppler scowled at Enge.

'I promise I didn't.' Cray moved his hand across his uniform. 'Cross my heart.'

That satisfied the private.

Keppler said his first words to the American, 'Where are you taking us?'

'As far north as I can get.'

'Why don't you kill us now and save us the walk?' Keppler asked.

Enge's eyes widened. 'Is he going to kill us, Sergeant?'

'Enge, you read about him. Why would it be any different for you and me than for those poor bastards at the chateau?'

'But he seems friendly,' Enge argued.

Cray smiled to prove it. 'Americans are friendly people.'

'Enge, you are stupid even for the Wehrmacht,' Keppler said. 'You and I are dead. This man just needs to decide when.'

'What town is that?' Cray nodded north.

'The outskirts of Potsdam,' Enge answered. 'Berlin is a few kilometres beyond.' Enge paused and squinted down the road. 'Something is coming.' He pointed. 'A motorcycle and sidecar.'

Cray reached into his boot and brought out a two-edged knife. He removed the clip from the Mauser and put it in his pocket, ejected the shell from the chamber, then handed the rifle to a startled Enge. He abruptly caught Sergeant Keppler round the neck, the knife at Keppler's throat but the blade hidden in Cray's hand.

'Tell them I'm your major, and that I've been injured.' He pressed the blade into the skin of Keppler's neck.

'What if they don't believe me?'

'The minute I sense they are doubting you,' Cray said, 'I'm going to cut your throat from ear to ear. So you'd better put your heart into your acting.' He dragged his left foot as if it had been injured, and sagged so that Keppler and Enge had to lean into him to support his weight. They each held one of his arms.

The BMW and sidecar stopped in front of the three walkers. The passenger was holding a Schmeisser, its barrel pointed at the ground. Both riders wore motorcycle coats and shiny metal ornaments that read FELDGENDARMERIE, military police.

'Get off the motorcycle. I'm commandeering it,' Keppler yelled at them. 'I've got to get to the aid station.'

A bit defensively, the sidecar passenger said, 'We've been ordered to look for the American commando. He's been—'

Keppler growled, 'Do the three of us look like an American commando? Now get out of my way or you'll be responsible for my major's death.'

The driver shook his head. 'This belongs to my unit.'

'I'm giving you an order,' Keppler barked.

'Damn know-it-all sergeants.' The driver turned to his sidekick. 'Hang on.' The driver accelerated the engine, kicked the motorcycle into gear and sped away to the south. Cray brought his hand away from the sergeant's neck. He pulled the Mauser away from Enge and inserted the clip.

'You weren't really going to kill Sergeant Keppler, were you?' Enge's eyes were wide. 'With that knife of yours?'

'Nah. I was pretending.' Cray's knife had disappeared.

Keppler said, 'Enge, you are dumber than a stone.'

'I'm going on alone,' the American said. 'You two walk back in the other direction.'

'Really?' Enge blurted. 'We can go free?'

Cray nodded. 'Walk back the way you came.'

He started north, his boots splashing in puddles of rainwater. He rested the rifle on his shoulder.

Enge followed him. 'Our lieutenant is going to murder us for being absent without leave.'

'That really isn't my concern.' Cray increased his pace.

Enge matched the American step for step. 'The SS is shooting soldiers for running away. You'd have that on your conscience.'

Cray sighed. 'What do you want me to do?'

Enge pulled out his flier. 'You can write a note to my lieutenant.'

'Write him a note?'

Enge nodded. He pulled a pencil from a front pocket and pushed it and the flier into Cray's hand. 'Write: "I am the American terrorist whose photo is on this poster. I kidnapped Sergeant Keppler and Private Enge so they were late to return to duty."'

Cray transcribed the dictation. 'Anything else?'

Enge thought for a moment. '"They acted honourably and bravely, especially Private Enge."'

Cray added the sentence. 'Anything else?'

Enge pursed his lips. 'How is the lieutenant going to know it was really you who signed this?'

Cray offered, 'I'll add something about the Vassy Chateau that very few people know.' He scratched his chin. 'The third soldier I killed had a white patch over one eye. How's that?'

'Perfect.'

Cray finished the note, then passed the flier back to Enge. 'The Russians will overrun this place soon. Don't let them kill you.'

Enge cackled victoriously as he rejoined his sergeant. 'If you couldn't kill me, neither can the Russians.'

Cray resumed his walk north. 'No, probably not.'

 SIX

The sound of car tyres came from behind her. Katrin looked over her shoulder. A black saloon was slowly following her, running without headlight slits. Then she saw a circular antenna on the car's roof. This was the Opel that Colonel Becker had warned her about. The agents inside the car must have been able to fix on her broadcast, and had been following her since she left the abandoned house. A window rolled down on the car's passenger side, and a hand holding a pistol emerged.

Desperation and fear abruptly wrapped round her like a coat. She walked faster, approaching her brick front path. Then she broke into a run, slipping on the brick but catching herself.

The Opel accelerated to her front path, then slowed. Two men in dark coats leapt out before it was fully stopped. The driver stayed in the car. Katrin climbed the eight steps to the porch, uselessly fumbling for her keys.

The Gestapo agents scrambled up the front steps and into the porch behind her. The taller agent clubbed her with the butt of his handgun. Katrin sagged against the door, then slid to the mat. The second agent caught her suitcase as it fell. He was a plug of a man, with his weight in his chest. He slipped his pistol into his belt and opened the suitcase. The plug grinned. 'A pack radio.'

The agents lifted Katrin by her elbows, then carried her down the stairs and along the path towards the car.

The taller agent opened the back passenger door. Darkness hid the driver. Gestapo cars have the inside lights disconnected to hide comings and goings. The tall agent bent to enter the car first.

The plug waited behind Katrin. He said tonelessly, 'You can tell us about your radio broadcasts on the way to Prinz Albrecht Strasse. It'll save us time once we get there.'

The plug put a hand on her head and pushed her down towards the door. He shoved her onto the back seat.

Everything inside the car was entirely wrong. Instead of the tall Gestapo agent, a blond, square-jawed man sat in the middle of the leather seat, a knife in his hand. Blood dripped from the knife onto his trousers. The body of the tall Gestapo agent was pushed against the far door, crumpled and slack, blood gushing from a wound in his throat. In the front seat, the Gestapo driver was bent over his steering wheel, his hands loose at his sides.

The blond man held a finger to his lips. He was smiling narrowly behind his hand. He wore a Wehrmacht major's uniform.

When the plug bent to enter the car, the blond man reached across Katrin, gripped the agent by a coat lapel and jerked him inside. The blond man brought the agent's head down over the knife, and the blade worked swiftly. The momentum of the plug's body carried him across Katrin, and he came to rest on the first agent. In one smooth motion, the agents had entered one door alive and ended up against the other door dead.

The blond man wore stubble across his chin. His face was full of harsh angles. The knife disappeared somewhere.

With a broad accent, the blond man asked, 'Do you have anything to eat?'

KATRIN SAT ON THE ONLY piece of furniture left in her bedroom, a Gothic armchair of carved and gilded wood with velvet upholstery. The one-time pad was on one knee and her pages of dots and dashes on the other. The room was meagrely lit by an oil lamp resting on a windowsill at her shoulder. On a bitterly cold night three months ago, Katrin had ripped apart her bed and used the frame for firewood. Then onto the fire grate went the antique desk on which she once wrote letters to Adam. She had watched the flames eat away the old wood, so happy to be warm she hadn't given the heirloom another thought.

She decoded the last line and stared at the page. She had come to call the faceless sender of messages the Hand. This message made little sense to her, and it was not meant to. It was addressed to the Horseman. She scratched a match head, then put the flame to the pages she had torn off the one-time pad.

Katrin's head snapped up at the scent of meat. She had not had any kind of meat for six weeks, maybe longer. The odour seemed to lift her from the chair and pull her from the room. She carried the message with her as she descended the stairs.

The American was in the kitchen, shuffling the meat in the frying pan. She held out the message. 'It's for you.'

He must have been more interested in the meal, because he put the message on the worktop without looking at it. 'I had no idea . . .' Her voice faded.

'You had no idea the Horseman would be the man on the posters all over the city, the Vassy Chateau soldier?'

She shook her head.

He smiled. 'I had no idea I was the Horseman either, until a few days ago. Somebody gave me the name. I'd like that job. Sitting in a room dreaming up code names.'

He took a pinch of salt from a bowl and sprinkled it over the steak. Also on the stove were potatoes and carrots in boiling water. On the worktop and table was a vast treasure of food: jars of jam, cheeses, sausages, tins of butter, three chickens, bread, bottles of wine. And pastries. French éclairs, an apple tart and a blackberry strudel.

Her finger dipped into the icing on an éclair and she brought it to her mouth. The sweetness made her giddy.

'Don't spoil your dinner,' the American said lightly. His German was gnarled by an accent, but fast and understandable.

Katrin picked up a cloth bag from the worktop and held it to her nose. She closed her eyes. 'Coffee. Real coffee.' She glanced at him. 'Is the Gauleiter still alive?'

He looked up, wearing a startled expression, perhaps for her benefit. 'Of course he's still alive.'

'Then how did you get all this food?'

In the Opel, after the American had told her he was the
Horseman, he had asked where the nearest food was, and she had
pointed at Gauleiter Eckardt's house. The Gauleiter always had an
inexhaustible amount of food because he controlled the city's warehouses. The American had told her to go into her house, and that he
would be along in a few minutes. He had returned while she was
upstairs decoding the message.

The American said, 'The Gauleiter was upstairs with a lady. I
heard them giggling and singing. I went in by the unlocked back
door into the kitchen. They didn't hear a thing, and so much food
was in his larder he won't miss the little I took.'

'Where did you put the car, the car with the bodies?'

'I left it in a park a kilometre from here.'

She nodded at the stove. 'And the wood?'

He grinned again. 'It's coal, not wood.'

'I've been out of coal for months.'

'I found a few chunks that had fallen into the ash bin below the
furnace.'

She had heard a few things about America and Americans. They
were naive and full of energy, children really. American women
shaved their armpits, and New York City lay in ruins after Luftwaffe
bombings. That was all she knew about them. She had never before
met one. In fact, she thought, this one looked German. Stout and
blond and agate-eyed.

'Is your heritage German?' she asked abruptly. 'You look German.'

He pulled at an ear lobe. 'I had an uncle who was German. He
came to America to work in a pram factory.'

'Yes?'

Cray said, 'He was fired after two weeks.'

'Why?'

'Because every time he tried to build a pram, it turned out to be a
machine gun.'

It took her a moment. Then she said, 'You are a child.'

'Looks like the steaks are done.'

He slid them onto two plates, then fished out the carrots and potatoes. He broke the potatoes open and spread butter on them, then
tore off large chunks of bread and scraped the meat pan, letting the

grease soak into the bread. He handed her a plate, a knife and a fork. She followed him into the adjacent room, where a fire was in the grate. The fire was the only light in the room. He lifted two cushions from a sofa and tossed them in front of the fireplace. He lowered himself to a cushion, his feet out to the flames. She followed him down to the other.

The house had been in Adam's family for eighty years, and this room still looked as it had since the turn of the century, everything in its place. In the middle of the room was a carpet, and centred on that carpet was a table; in the middle of the table was a crocheted mat, and in the centre of the mat was a flower vase. Round the table were six chairs with plaited cane seats and red plush backs. Dark curtains hung over the windows.

'Aren't you going to read the message?' she asked.

'Until I eat this steak, I don't care what's in that message.' He cut off a large portion of meat and shoved it into his mouth.

She bit into the grease-soaked bread, then said round the wad in her mouth, 'I've never tasted anything better than this.' They ate in silence, the only sound the rush and pop of the fire. She could not take her eyes off him. He cleaned his plate with the bread, and only when the last of it was gone did he go to the kitchen for the message. When he returned, he was also carrying an open bottle of wine and two glasses. He sat next to the fire and used its light to read. Then he read the message again.

He asked, 'Do you know what this asks me to do?'

She shook her head. 'It's in English. I transposed the letters without understanding it.'

The American poured wine into the glasses and passed one to her. 'What's your name?'

'Katrin von Tornitz.'

'Why was I sent here to you? Because you have the radio?'

'That's the only reason I can think of.'

'Your hand is shaking.' His mouth turned up. 'You're splashing wine out of the glass.'

She dabbed at the wine drops on the floor. 'I'm afraid of you.'

He seemed genuinely puzzled. 'Why?'

'I just saw you kill three men with a knife. Then you use your same knife to cut the steaks. Then you eat a huge meal as if nothing happened at all.'

He shrugged. 'I'm a soldier.'

'And you are frightening to look at.'

'We'll get along better if you don't try to flatter me.' He grinned. 'Besides, I'm not the tough one. You are.'

She looked away, into the fire. After a moment he said, 'I need to visit the Reich Chancellery.'

She turned to the fire and brought her knees up under her chin. 'The Hand has ordered you to kill the Führer, hasn't it? That's the only reason someone like you would be sent to Berlin.'

He drank from the glass. 'Are you going to help me?'

She was silent.

He said, 'The Hand must think it will help win the war.'

Her gaze swept back to him. 'Win the war? I'm not going to help you win the war.'

'Your radio transmissions are—'

She cut him off angrily. 'I'm going to help stop the war, not help you win it. You fat and happy Americans—up in your big, comfortable bombers—you don't know anything about anything.' She looked away, in time to hide her tears from him. After a moment she said, 'I just want it all stopped.'

He watched her for a while. 'Is your husband dead?'

'All our husbands are dead.'

'How did it happen?'

Her voice was bitter. 'He was a German and he believed Germany should have a future. That's how it happened.'

'I've lost my loved one, too,' Cray said, his voice a whisper.

'Please don't share anything with me,' she said. 'I already have enough of whatever you are going to tell me.'

He might not have heard her. 'Wenatchee is a little town on the Columbia River, in the state of Washington. Although I've not been to all the small towns in America, Wenatchee is probably the loveliest. We grow apples, and in May the valley is covered with apple blossoms. I was raised there, and so was my wife. My memory doesn't run back to a time when I didn't know her. My wife—her name was Merri Ann—once told me that she knew from first grade that we would be married someday.'

She didn't want to know any of this, but the American was now staring into the fire and speaking in a low voice, and she found she could not stop him. She took a sip of wine.

'Merri Ann was killed by a drunk driver.' He might have been talking to the fire. 'So I know something of what you are going through.

Some mornings I wake up and wonder whether it's worth getting out of bed.'

After a moment, she asked, 'Do you know why the Hand has chosen you?'

'The Vassy Chateau, I imagine. And that I speak German.'

'More than that.'

He finally looked away from the fire and at her.

'The Hand knows about your wife,' she explained. 'You don't have much to live for, so the Hand believes you will go places and do things that a person who wants to survive will not.'

He shrugged. 'I don't go through a door unless I know I can get back out.' Cray lifted the message and reread it.

She said quietly, 'And I'm telling you, the Hand is sending you on a suicide mission.'

A DEAD DOG in a wheelbarrow was Cray's ruse, and it was working. Stooped and limping, he walked from the park to Hermann Goering Strasse. The Reich Chancellery garages and guard quarters were on his left. SS guards stood at the doors to the barracks.

Cray joined a stream of refugees, shuffling ahead, slowed by despair and grief and hunger. Many glanced covetously at the dead dog, knowing its owner would eat well that night. One man wore rags wrapped round his legs. A woman with an empty sleeve pinned to her coat led a ten-year-old girl with a bandage over her eyes. Crutches and canes were common on this street, and Cray's was not the only wheelbarrow. One family nudged along a railway porter's cart loaded with possessions.

Up ahead a horn bleated, and the refugees were shunted towards the kerb as six Wehrmacht troop trucks rolled down the street, the last one pulling a fifteen-centimetre infantry-support gun. When the convoy had passed, the refugees refilled the street.

Cray was wearing two wool jackets, one over the other, a grease-stained felt hat and trousers so short they showed his ankles. His eyebrows and hair were blackened with fireplace soot, and a bandage was over his left cheek and ear. He shuffled along, bent and slow, indistinguishable from hundreds of others on the street.

He looked at his watch. Only he among the crowd knew that an American air strike was due in twelve minutes.

Cray was nearing Potsdamer Platz, still within sight of the Chancellery, when the air-raid sirens began their plaintive wail. The sirens usually gave Berliners ten minutes. Many refugees looked around wildly, searching for bomb shelters. Cray pushed the wheelbarrow to the kerb, then climbed the steps of an abandoned building. Perhaps because he walked as if he might know where he was going, he was followed by a dozen refugees and a serviceman. A woman behind him held an infant in her arms. He led them into an apartment, down some stairs and into a cellar.

Cray sat on the floor against a concrete wall. The woman with the baby and the others also lowered themselves to the floor. The serviceman, a Wehrmacht private, sat at the other end of the room. He was missing his cap and was not carrying a weapon.

A low sound came from the north, a persistent and growing rumble. Dust fell from the ceiling. The baby grinned at Cray.

Cray couldn't see the sky, but he knew it would be laden with bombers in perfect formations, as well as smaller American fighter escorts. The bombers had taken off from England, but the fighters had joined them from captured German airfields.

An SS officer scrambled down the stairs. He glanced at the Wehrmacht private, who ducked his head. Then he sat next to Cray. The collar tabs on his grey-green greatcoat collar identified him as an SS-Standartenführer, the equivalent of a colonel. A silver death's-head was on his grey peaked cap. The man was an SS bureaucrat, an author of orders and a keeper of files.

The first bombs tore into the suburbs. Debris flew skywards and had started its descent before the sounds reached Cray. The basement's walls trembled, then bucked. Cray's ears popped with the sudden changes in air pressure. Empty jam jars fell from a shelf and shattered on the floor. The baby wailed.

Cray's thoughts—those that could form between the pounding of the explosives—settled on Katrin and their conversation last night. She had thought his comments about Merri Ann to be manipulative, offered to show that Cray and Katrin were kin in suffering. But Cray's memory of his wife, and of her death, had come forth unbidden, as it did every hour of every day, and he had not told Katrin all of it. The horror of that day and of the subsequent weeks and months had remained locked within him. Katrin had been right. The Hand knew of his wife's death and of Cray's wild grief and guilt, and was using them. The Hand knew that Jack Cray gave most of his energy to accomplishing his assignments and little to getting back to safety. Cray had lied when he said he didn't go through a door unless he knew he could get back out. If he got out, fine. If not, well, he deserved to find the door closed.

If he could just have that night back. Just that one night.

Time in the cellar had an odd elasticity. Cray could not determine whether the raid—and his dreadful memories—lasted five minutes or an hour, but finally the last bomb detonated and the weight of the sound was lifted from the cellar's occupants. Cray rose, dusting off his shoulders.

'You.' The SS officer stabbed his hand towards the Wehrmacht private. 'Your ID and orders, quickly.'

The private, no more than seventeen years old, whitened and stammered, and it was instantly apparent he was a deserter. The civilians hurried up the stairs, anxious to get away. Except Cray.

The colonel reached inside his greatcoat for his service pistol. The young soldier backed into the wall, his hands out. 'You are a deserter,' the colonel exclaimed, levelling his Walther at the soldier. 'A disgrace to the Fatherland and the Führer.' The colonel held the pistol at full arm's length, then hesitated, maybe wondering whether to arrest the young soldier or to shoot him.

Cray saved him the trouble of making the decision. He quickly stepped to the colonel and put his arm round the man's waist. 'Let's give the lad a break. What do you say?' He held him tight, a friendly embrace except for the knife deep inside the colonel's chest cavity. Blood bubbled at the SS officer's lips.

'Beat it, Private,' Cray ordered. 'And find a helmet and a rifle. You look like just what you are.'

The private hesitated, nodded at Cray, then rushed away, climbing the stairs two at a time. Cray could hear his footfalls above his head. He let the SS officer sink to the floor.

Cray searched for the man's ID and found it in the inside breast pocket of his service tunic. The grey linen card identified him as Colonel Kurt Schwenninger, an SS liaison officer to the Chancellery.

Jack Cray had called in the bombing run so that he might study the government quarter, learn the emergency routines and observe evacuation plans, searching for a flaw in the Chancellery's defences. But when the SS colonel had to seek refuge in the cellar, Cray had been offered more than an opportunity to study.

He emerged from the cellar ten minutes later wearing the colonel's uniform and no longer shuffling like a refugee.

Potsdamer Platz was obscured by smoke and dust, so thick that a fierce fire across the square could be seen only as a golden glow. The all clear mixed with the thin wail of fire-truck sirens. In the gutter were two bodies, naked, their clothes blown off them. A grocery shop had been hit, and a stream of fluids—honey, condensed milk and marmalade—oozed out of the front door. Berliners rushed into the store to plunder it. A horse pulling a newspaper vendor's cart had been killed. Three women with carving knives whittled at the horse's shanks. More starving Berliners hurried to join them.

Cray quickly approached the city-block-long Reich Chancellery. It had been hit. Cray saw that, despite the smoke and confusion, the SS guards at the door were closely examining the faces and identification cards of those who entered the building.

Cray turned away from the guards, brought his knife up to his forehead and slashed the skin above his eyebrows, left to right, dragging the blade against bone. Blood instantly poured down his face. The knife disappeared and he turned back, pulling out the colonel's identification card. He held up the card and stepped forwards.

The guard looked at the card. A second guard patted Cray down, keeping his fingers away from the dripping blood. The first guard said, 'Dr Niedhardt is inside, Colonel. He'll fix you up.'

Cray nodded and stepped into a hallway with a green marble floor. Smoke filled the room. A woman stepped out of the haze, stared with wide eyes at Cray, then took him gently by the elbow. She said, 'The doctors are this way, Colonel.'

She led him into an anteroom, where a surgery had been set up. An examining table, three beds and an X-ray machine filled the room. Two of the beds were occupied by guards who had remained at their stations during the raid. A physician tended to a third guard, probing a wound on his arm.

The woman lowered Cray into a chair by a window and patted him on the arm, 'He'll be with you as soon as he can.' She continued to stand near him, waiting to catch the doctor's eye.

Prompted by the sudden good fortune of an SS uniform and ID, Cray's makeshift plan had been to see as much of the Chancellery as he could, open a few doors and walk into a few rooms, and if he found his target take advantage of the opportunity. At the very least, he would discover the layout of the seat of German government. At best, he would accomplish his mission.

The American wiped blood from his eyes, wondering when this good-hearted woman would leave him so that he could continue his reconnaissance. He turned in his seat to peer out of the window. Behind the Chancellery was a garden. The smoke was lifting, and Cray saw that it must have been an elegant park at one time, with pergolas and fountains. At the west end was a massive concrete block with a steel door in it. The block stood by itself, and its door surely led below ground to a bunker. Two SS guards stood at the door. And to one side of the block Field-Marshal Keitel and General Jodl were bent in conversation, smoking cigarettes.

Cray recognised both generals from photographs, and he knew that neither Keitel nor Jodl ever allowed himself to be far from Hitler. And when Keitel and Jodl threw aside their cigarette butts and re-entered the blockhouse, Cray knew that Hitler was no longer ruling the Reich from the Chancellery, but instead was in a fortified bunker below the Chancellery's garden.

Adolf Hitler had gone to ground.

When the helpful woman walked over to talk to the physician, Cray rose quickly and left the room, walking out by the same door through which he had entered the Chancellery.

 # SEVEN

Katrin spun round. She was lost, once again.

Like most Berliners, she frequently became lost, sometimes only blocks from home, what with rubble piles obscuring the horizon, landmarks torn down and the location of the sun hidden by smoke and ash. She could not get her bearings. And, because many buildings were crazily canted, the perpendicular was distorted. The war had taken away many things, none more surprising than the ability to tell which direction was straight up.

She tried to push her hands into her coat pockets, but they were stuffed with bread rolls. She had been without adequate food so long that she had been unable to leave home without filling her pockets. She needed to be near food, even if she had to wear it.

She passed an elm tree lying on the street, its roots exposed. Two oxen were pulling a Schutheiss Brewery dray over the crossroads ahead of her. Perhaps she was near the brewery. Down the block came refugees, twenty or so of them. Refugees always marched west—seeming instinctively to know the way—so Katrin took her bearings from them and started north towards the Tiergarten. She glanced at her watch. She had twenty-five minutes.

A child's cry brought her up. Huddled near an overturned truck was a boy, maybe four years old, wearing three gunny sacks for a shirt and a pair of rolled-up man's trousers. His face was screwed up with the realisation that he was lost, that his parents had moved on without him. In his hand was a toy truck.

Berlin was full of lost children. Katrin took three more steps before, with a huge sigh, she turned back towards the boy.

She towered over him. 'Where are your parents?' A little too gruff. Lord, she didn't want this little boy's problems.

He peeked up at her but said nothing.

'Is your *Mutti* alive? Your father?'

'*Mutti*. But she's not here.' The boy's words ended in a wail.

Katrin asked, 'How long have you been lost?'

His chin trembled. 'Ten hundred hours and minutes.' He tentatively moved towards her, two half-steps, and with that little movement gave himself over to the kind lady. He was now hers.

Katrin understood. She rubbed her hand alongside an eye, trying to think. Then it came to her. She looked at her watch. Twenty minutes. She had to hurry. 'What's your name?'

'Artur.'

She reached for his hand, pulling him along. 'Come with me, Artur.'

A few moments later they were on the Kurfürstendamm, near the blackened skeleton of the Kaiser Wilhelm Church. At this crossroads were public notice boards, dozens of them, installed for government announcements—Jack Cray's face stared out from each panel—but lately plastered with private messages.

This was the place in Berlin where the lost might be found. A hundred or more people clutched their coats, went up onto their toes and called out, hoping against hope that the war would for once relent and allow their loved ones to appear at this spot. Occasionally a crushing embrace was seen, but most often people drifted away, hoarse and heartbroken.

Even Berliners who had misplaced one another while shopping knew to meet at these notice boards. And Artur's mother had worked out that her son might end up here. She leapt from the crowd and grabbed him, her face broadly creased by a smile.

The woman was dressed in a filthy Wehrmacht coat that hung to her ankles. She scolded him softly, but hugged and hugged her boy. Katrin looked at her watch. She had ten minutes. Finally, Artur's mother turned to Katrin, gripped both of her hands and whispered a thankyou.

Katrin pulled two cheese rolls out of her pocket and passed them to the woman, who might not have seen that much food in weeks. She grabbed them, then remembered to smile another thanks. Katrin dug further and pulled out three Kaiser rolls. The woman also took these, then turned to join her son. She shepherded him away. West, of course. An instant later they had disappeared.

Katrin almost ran past the ruined church towards Budapester Strasse. She reined herself in. To run in Berlin was to invite being stopped by the Gestapo. Wilhelm Becker had told her weeks ago that in an emergency she could always find him walking along the park side of Tiergartenstrasse at four in the afternoon.

She spotted him, emerging from the army headquarters building's double doors. She was startled by his appearance. His shoulders were hunched protectively. His eyes were shadowed and remote, and, it seemed to Katrin, fearful, darting left and right. His face was clouded. Becker had the look of one expecting a blow.

Katrin stepped up to him. 'Colonel Becker?'

He gasped when he recognised her. 'Why are you here?'

'I need to talk to you.' She gripped his elbow fiercely and turned him round. 'Walk with me to the park.'

When he baulked, she pulled him along as she had done to Artur. His arm trembled under the pressure of her hand.

'What has happened to you?' she demanded.

Becker was silent, glancing over his shoulder every few steps. He ducked his head as army officers passed. Katrin led him into the park. She conducted him towards a bench that had been blown backwards. He stood mutely while she righted it, then swept dampness from the seat with her hand before sitting down. After a moment Becker joined her on the bench.

'You ignored the message I left in the milk box,' she said. 'You recruited me, and now you've cut me off?'

'You have no idea what has happened.' Becker refused to look at her, staring at a bank of lilacs. 'My superior, General Etzdorf, has been arrested, and so have two others in my office.'

'Etzdorf is a member of your group?'

'There is no group,' he snapped. 'The general and I have . . . have

worked together on certain matters, and if he starts to talk . . .'
Becker stopped in mid-sentence. He turned on the bench and finally
looked at her. 'Why have you come to me?'

'I need your help, Colonel.'

He shook his head sorrowfully. 'That is impossible, Mrs von Tornitz.
I am under suspicion. I no longer . . . no longer have the courage or
strength to do . . . those things.'

'Colonel, you work in the office of army administration. You can
easily get what I want. I need the rota for the soldiers and SS troopers
assigned to the Chancellery.'

Becker's eyes widened and his breath rattled in his throat. Then he
tried to rise, but she dug her fingernails into his arm and pulled him
back down.

'Colonel Becker, you don't understand how important this is.'

He shook his head. 'It doesn't matter. I'm through with all that.'

With histrionic embellishment, Katrin reached to scratch the top
of her head. So apparent a signal was this that Becker leapt from the
bench and started towards the street.

He made only three steps. As if by sleight of hand, Jack Cray
appeared in front of Becker, perhaps from the lilacs, and gently
pushed him back to the bench.

The colonel's face blanched. Cray was wearing a Wehrmacht captain's uniform taken from Katrin's closet. A row of stitches covered
the new gash on his forehead.

He sat on the other side of Becker. The colonel's gaze pivoted back
and forth between Cray and Katrin.

She said, 'Colonel, I don't have time to fool with you. You are
going to obtain the Chancellery rota and bring it to me.'

He moved his head slightly, a negative.

'Colonel, look at this man,' she said. 'This is the man on the
posters all over the city. This is the Vassy Chateau killer.'

Becker's face whitened even more. His mouth pulled back in a
grimace of fear.

Katrin's voice was iron. 'He is going to slit your throat right now if
you don't agree to bring me that rota.'

Cray's face opened in astonishment. He blurted, 'No, I'm not.'

She persisted. 'Colonel, this American is a ruthless killer. Are you
going to do what I say, or are you living your last seconds?'

Becker closed his eyes in surrender. His voice could just be heard.
'I might be able to get a copy of the rota.'

Katrin stood. 'Place it in the drop by tomorrow evening.' She stared at him levelly. 'If it is not there, I will anonymously telephone the Gestapo about your activities against the state. They will come for you, irrespective of what General Etzdorf tells them.' She started back towards the street.

Cray said to Becker, 'She's been through a lot.'

'If you are planning to suborn someone on the Chancellery rota, hoping to get into the Führer's headquarters, you are too late,' Becker said. 'The Führer is leaving Berlin tonight.'

The American demanded, 'How do you know that?'

'When the leader leaves the city, hundreds of orders are issued. One of them is that the Chancellery guard is drastically reduced. I know because the orders are distributed through my office.'

'How will he leave Berlin?'

'Most rail bridges have been knocked out, so probably by plane. The Führer uses an airstrip in the Tiergarten.'

'Nothing's ever easy, is it?' Cray smiled at Becker. 'Don't forget the rota. Put it in the drop.' He ran after Katrin. At her elbow he asked, 'Will you kindly not do that again?'

'What?' she asked, all innocence.

'Use my face to frighten someone.'

As she neared the street, she turned to him. 'Don't you do whatever works? Isn't that what you commandos are trained to do?'

'Well . . .'

'That's just what I did.' She turned west, walking briskly.

He followed her. 'Well, you could hurt my feelings, doing that.'

She stopped dead. 'I cannot possibly have heard you correctly. Hurt your feelings?' She laughed brightly, so foreign and forgotten a sound that it startled her.

Cray kept pace with her. 'I didn't tell you all of it last night.'

'All of what?'

'About my wife, and what happened.'

'Maybe I didn't want to hear it.' She increased her pace.

'I've never told anybody else about it.' His voice was suddenly devoid of his American boldness, and there was a touch of pleading to it. She slowed.

Cray said softly, 'I was the drunk.'

She stopped. 'What?'

'It was a one-car accident. I was driving.' Only by force of will could he keep his eyes on Katrin. His voice was broken. 'We'd been at a restaurant, celebrating our second wedding anniversary. This was in the summer of 1941, almost four years ago. We held hands all night. I don't think my gaze left her once during the entire dinner. Our marriage was so . . .'

He stopped and turned away. Her hand came up, hesitated, then touched his arm.

His voice was rough. 'I loved my wife.'

'I know.'

'That night, I never laughed so hard or talked so much. And I never drank so much in my life. I drank too much.'

'What happened?'

'I drove us towards home, still laughing, her sitting so close to me that I could hardly shift the gears. I was going too fast. I missed a turn. Our car skidded off the road, then rolled down a ravine. It turned over and over.' Black grief was written on Cray's face. 'I was pinned behind the steering wheel, both my legs broken. Our car wasn't found for eighteen hours. I stared at my dead wife for those eighteen hours.'

'Were you prosecuted?'

Cray shook his head. 'The sheriff had been a friend of my father's. He didn't enquire into it.'

'So you ran away into the army?'

'After my legs healed.'

'You've been angry at yourself ever since. Your plan is to have a German soldier end it for you, rather than do it yourself.'

'I don't know if I had thought it through that far.' Cray ran a hand along his temple. 'But I sure didn't expect to last this long in the war.' He tried a laugh, but it was feeble.

Katrin took him by the arm and continued walking. 'Don't make me think about you, alive or dead. All right? Is that too much for me to ask?'

'I don't know. You might end up thinking about me a lot. When I put my mind to it, I'm quite likable.'

'No, you aren't.' But she squeezed his arm as they made their way towards the Zoo Station. 'Not in the least.'

HEINZ BURMASTER tramped along, close on the heels of the Home Guardsman in front of him. Burmaster's antitank weapon, a Panzerfaust, bounced on his shoulder with each step. He had found a woman's scarf—hand-knitted blue wool with a cat in the centre—

and had placed it on his shoulder as a pad, so now at least the Panzerfaust's metal stock was not banging against his collarbone. Burmaster turned his head left. 'Getting older with each day is the natural order of the universe, wouldn't you say, Rolf?'

Rolf Quast walked beside Burmaster. He had become accustomed to Burmaster's jovial prattle, and only occasionally encouraged him with a grunt; this he did now.

'Well, then, I have reversed the natural order, because I appear to be getting younger with each day.' Burmaster held up a hand to prevent Quast from interrupting, as if there were a chance of that. 'You ask, "How can that be, Heinz?"'

Rolf Quast cleared his throat, which Burmaster took as an invitation to continue. 'I was too old for the Great War, Rolf. I tried to enlist, but the army wouldn't take me. This was thirty years ago. But, as you can plainly see, I am not too old for this war. Hence, I must be getting younger.'

Quast asked, 'How old are you, Heinz?'

'Sixty-six.'

'Two years older than me. We are both too old to be lugging anti-tank rockets round the city. You ever fired one before?'

Burmaster followed the column to one side of the street to avoid a crater. 'We didn't have enough of them to waste them on training. So our instructor made us point them at a wooden mock-up of a British Matilda and pretend to pull the trigger and yell out "Shoosh" to imitate the sound of the launch. Then the instructor would call out "Boom" to show I'd hit the tank. I'm a good shot, apparently.' He tapped the Panzerfaust affectionately.

The column of old men wound its way along Plegerstrasse, dodging mounds of rubble, having to climb over others, as it had been doing for ten nights. It was a crisscrossing of Berlin which to Burmaster and Quast and the others seemed chaotic, but which was in response to the Berlin commandant's best estimate as to where the city's defences needed shoring up, an estimate that changed with each new bombing run.

The Panzerfaust was getting heavier with each step, and when the sergeant blew the whistle to fall out for a break, Burmaster slid the damned thing off his shoulder and laid it against the trunk of a tree. Quast placed his Panzerfaust next to Burmaster's, then levered himself down to the cobblestones and leaned back against the tree.

A few moments passed before Burmaster said, in a low voice, 'I'm never going to fire that thing. My Panzerfaust.'

'What do you mean?'

'I'm going to wait for the first chance I get, then throw up my arms in surrender and pray the Russians don't shoot me.'

'Maybe the Americans will get to Berlin first,' Quast said. 'I've heard they're nice people, once they calm down.'

'That's the first line of my evening prayer every night. "Please, God," I pray, "don't let George Patton's tanks run out of fuel."'

The whistle blew, and the guardsmen struggled to their feet. Heinz Burmaster grimaced as he turned for his Panzerfaust.

It was gone. And so was Quast's.

Quast drew air through his teeth. 'You don't have to worry about the Russians now, because the captain is going to shoot you and me, if he sees us without our weapons.'

Burmaster picked up a board from the kerb. He placed it over his shoulder as if it were his Panzerfaust, then he stepped into line. 'The captain has other things to worry about,' he said. 'He's never going to notice that our weapons are missing.'

Quast picked up a board, shouldered it and walked beside him. He asked nervously, 'You think so, Heinz?'

Burmaster half closed his eyes, then intoned in a low voice and in cadence with his steps: 'Please, God, don't let George Patton's tanks run out of fuel. Please, God, don't let George Patton's tanks run out of fuel. Please, God . . .'

ONLY FOR BRIEF SECONDS when the moon shed itself of clouds could Cray see the entire length of the landing strip. He could not locate a hangar, and he could not see a plane— not yet, anyway. But there was no doubt this was the emergency strip Colonel Becker had spoken of. Fourteen hundred metres long, ninety across, no trees, no debris. Cray lay on his belly on a sloping crater bank, the two Panzerfausts next to him. An aeroplane taking off would have to pass within forty metres of his position.

A grey movement at the eastern end of the airstrip caught Cray's attention. A soldier wearing a coal-scuttle helmet and a rifle over his shoulder had planted a flare in the ground. A second flare came to life, carried by another soldier. Quickly more were lit until they framed the landing field.

Cray looked at his wristwatch. Midnight. A low drone could be heard, and then a plane slid out of the night at the west end of the airstrip. It was a wing-over, single-engine Fieseler Storch. The model had proved itself scouting for Rommel in Africa. This plane had been reserved for Hitler. The engine gained power to turn the plane round, then it taxied along the airstrip, passing Cray.

The sound of other engines came from the southwest, from behind Cray and off to his left: the strident howling of motorcycles. Behind them was a car, a Grosser Mercedes, with windows thirty millimetres thick and doors reinforced with steel plate. The tyres had extremely low air pressure so that vibration would not upset Hitler's sensitive stomach.

Two other car followed the Mercedes, both black Horches. When the Führer's limousine stopped near the aeroplane, bodyguards emerged from both trailing cars to surround the Mercedes. They huddled round the car, forming a human shield, and began moving at a slow pace towards the plane. One of them gripped a wing strut and stepped onto the landing gear. He opened the plane's passenger door, still forming a shield.

A man rose from the group of guards, many hands assisting him into the plane. If Colonel Becker's news was accurate, Cray's target was fleeing Berlin, and in a few minutes he would have failed entirely.

The Storch's engine began winding up as soon as the guard on the strut jumped down. He and the others quickly retreated to their cars, holding on to their hats. The small plane lurched forwards, then gained speed, bouncing on the rough runway.

Jack Cray rose from his position, brought up a Panzerfaust and placed it over his shoulder. His hand found the trigger and he centred the approaching plane above the aiming stick. The plane gained speed on the runway. Cray's trigger finger came back.

Then the Storch's engine failed. At least, so it seemed to Cray. The plane slowed and finally stopped, still 100 yards short of Cray's position. For a moment Cray expected the doors to be thrown open, the pilot calling out his trouble to some mechanic.

And then Cray knew that he had been set up. The information that the German leader was leaving Berlin from this landing strip was the bait, and Cray had gone for it.

Cray slipped down into the crater, putting the Panzerfaust aside. He peered over the rim. To the north a picket fence of men, surely soldiers, walked slowly in Cray's direction. He looked west towards the cars. The bodyguards had taken up positions at the end of the airstrip. He glanced over his shoulder. Another phalanx of soldiers was closing in on him from the south. At the east end of the airfield a tank crawled out of the darkness.

Cray closed his eyes and said under his breath, 'Nuts.'

He pulled the pistol from his belt and scrambled up the crater's crumbling wall, leaving the Panzerfausts behind. He ran east in an infantryman's crouch. To his right came the sounds of soldiers closing in, heavy boots on loose soil.

A German voice called, 'Did you see someone?' Others barked replies, lost to Cray in the sound of his breath.

The most formidable weapon may also be the weakest. Cray was forty yards from the tank at the south end of the airstrip when the night was split by a dagger of harsh yellow light. Then another and another. Flares descended from the sky on parachutes. In a few seconds the airstrip and all that surrounded it would be brightly lit.

His legs churning, Cray glanced to the south. Soldiers seeped out between the trees. They had been told this trap had been set for the Vassy Chateau killer, and they moved warily. They squinted against the sudden light. A few saw movement and brought up weapons. A smattering of shots.

Dirt and stones splashed up at the American's feet. The tank's commander was standing in the cupola, the upper half of his body protruding from the turret. His eyes found Jack Cray just as Cray reached for a handhold on the spare track links on the tank's nose. He reached down into the cupola, shouting for his pistol.

The tank's loader also saw the American through a vision block, and he reached for the grip of his MG-34 just as Cray launched himself at the tank commander. Cray smashed the handle of his pistol into the German's temple. The commander began to sag back down through the hatch. Cray straddled the cupola and dragged him out of the turret, his hands under the German's arms.

Running towards the tank, soldiers hesitated because Cray used the commander as a shield, but a few bullets clipped the air, and a few more clattered uselessly against the tank.

A second bank of flares lit the night. More shouts and curses and orders.

Cray threw the unconscious commander off the turret and jumped down through the hatch. His feet landed on the commander's empty seat. Cray gripped the hatch rim, and let his knees buckle. He dropped fully inside the tank's fighting compartment.

The loader was aiming a pistol. Cray lashed out at him with a boot, thrusting his head back against the steel of the turret wall. The loader slumped.

At the same instant Cray's pistol turned towards the gunner. He was unarmed. He spread his hands, his eyes locked on Cray's pistol. Cray barked, 'Tell the driver to back up the tank.'

The gunner shook his head and said, 'The driver—'

He didn't get out another word. Cray shot him through his right biceps. 'My next bullet goes through your head.' Cray brought the pistol to the gunner's nose. 'Do as I tell you.'

The gunner blanched but pushed his mouth into the speaker tube and weakly called the order. Then Cray swung the hatch above his head closed and secured it with a lever. He was surrounded by steel thirty-four millimetres thick. He felt better.

The hatch to the driving compartment began to open beneath Cray's feet.

'Walter?' the radio operator called.

When the metal door opened further, Cray yanked it out of the radio man's hands and aimed his pistol down into the compartment at the driver. 'Get me out of the Tiergarten or none of you will ever leave this tank. Do you understand me? Back your tank up.'

'I can't see behind me.' The driver had a soft Bavarian accent. He looked up at the American.

'Do you think I give a damn about what's behind you?' Cray prodded the man's forehead with the pistol barrel. 'The question is, have you just taken your last breath?'

The driver wound up the Maybach engine, gripped the steering levers and released the clutch. The tank lurched backwards. It rose as it climbed a tree, then levelled off as the tree toppled under the tank's weight.

Orders had apparently been given to sacrifice the tank's crewmen, because a shell—perhaps from an armoured car—banged against the turret, but it had hit it at an angle and bounced off. The sound was like being inside a bell when it is rung.

Cray gripped the handle of the MG-34 and loosed a long string of bullets, warnings not to get close to the tank.

Cray's ears rang. He yelled down at the driver, 'Turn us round and head south across Tiergartenstrasse.'

The tank stopped, then wheeled about and took off again.

Cray shouted down into the driver's compartment, 'I've got a problem, driver. When I climb out of this tank, you are going to try to run me over or shoot me. So I've got a problem letting you live.'

'Sounds more like my problem, frankly,' the driver replied.

Cray shoved aside the injured gunner to peer through his sighting telescope. 'Where are we, driver?'

'Crossing Tiergartenstrasse. Buildings straight ahead.' His voice rose. 'If you're the new commander, give me directions.'

Cray wet his lips. He knew soldiers would be following the runaway tank. He also knew that a man is never more vulnerable than when trying to climb out of a tank turret.

'Straight ahead,' he ordered. 'Ram one of the buildings.'

'What?'

'Put your tank through one of those shattered buildings.'

The tank ground forwards, up the kerb, then up two steps of an apartment, knocking aside two cement planters. The building had been partly destroyed in a bombing run. The upper storey had tumbled out over the street, leaving bricks and masonry about.

The tank charged through a wall and into a living room, crushing a sofa and table, then to the back of the room, where the treads gripped the wall and rose. Cray could hear wrenched timbers falling against the turret. The wall buckled, and the tank climbed higher, its blunt nose almost at the ceiling. Then the treads spun without gaining more purchase.

'That's as far as we go.' The driver disengaged the gear. 'Now what?'

Cray rose to stand on the commander's chair to push open the hatch. Plaster fell away from the cupola. He pushed away debris, then grabbed the rim to lift his legs out. Here, inside the fractured building, he was protected from gunfire as he left the tank.

A family portrait was still on one wall, but darkness hid the rest of the room. Shots came from outside, from across the street.

He bent back through the hatch. 'Don't try to follow me.'

The driver shook his head. 'The notion hadn't occurred to me.'

Cray slipped off the turret to the wing, then down to the room's floor. The tank's weight had bent the room's back wall, revealing beams and sky above. The treads and wheels had sunk into the floor as if it were water. Exhaust from the tank's engine filled the room. Carrying his pistol, Cray stepped over a lampshade and through a door to a kitchen, where utensils were scattered over the floor, then out of a back door. He sprinted along the alley, then onto a side street, where the night took him in.

PART THREE: THE RANGE
EIGHT

Otto Dietrich's desk was cluttered with tokens of appreciation. The largest was a brass fire nozzle. Etched into the brass was TO DETECTIVE INSPECTOR DIETRICH WITH GRATITUDE FROM THE FIREMEN OF CHARLOTTENBURG STATION NO. 2. Dietrich had caught the gem-setter who, in a fit of pique resulting from a denial of a pay rise, had burned down his employer's jewellery store. Three firemen had died when a floor collapsed.

Dietrich seldom sat at his desk, but he did now, still weak from his time in the prison. He asked mildly, 'How many Jack Crays are out there now?'

Detective Peter Hilfinger stepped to the window overlooking Alexanderplatz. The day was fading, with red in the sky, some from the sunset, some from that day's bombing-raid fires. 'Nine, looks like. With his face covering almost every vertical surface in Berlin, we are getting an average of fifteen sightings and three arrests an hour.'

'Perhaps we should have anticipated it. Berliners will not tolerate a knife-wielding killer walking their streets.'

'No.' Hilfinger turned from the window. His face was inappropriate for a policeman. His eyes were set merrily, and the corners of his mouth were permanently turned up.

'That's why we've had this flood of reports.' Dietrich thought his own words lame. The truth wa80
s that his manhunt had failed.

Dietrich gripped the fire nozzle and slammed the desk with it, so uncharacteristic a gesture that Hilfinger flinched.

Dietrich exclaimed, 'I thought we had that bastard trapped last night at the Tiergarten airstrip. Damn the Americans anyway.'

After a moment he released the nozzle. He looked sheepishly at his subordinate, clucking his tongue by way of apology.

'There's something I can't figure out,' Hilfinger said after a moment, pushing aside a telephone so he could sit on the front of his desk facing Dietrich.

'Only one thing?'

'Why didn't he hide his progress towards Berlin?' Hilfinger asked.

'I mean, he had that conversation with that old lady, and he let those two Wehrmacht soldiers live. The American must have known they'd report to the authorities.'

'I think it's Jack Cray's way of boasting. He is telling us we can't catch him even if he gives us glimpses of himself.' Dietrich scratched his chin. 'Or maybe he doesn't care if we catch him.'

'Do you think Jack Cray is a feint? That the enemy has another plan under way and Cray's purpose is only to distract us?'

'I don't know, but, feint or not, I'm in charge of finding him.' Dietrich toyed with the fire nozzle. 'One of the few things I'm certain of is that Jack Cray is almost certainly still disguising himself in a German uniform. Not in a refugee's clothes, or some other civilian's clothes.'

'What makes you think so?' Hilfinger asked.

'Jack Cray is most comfortable in a uniform. Soldiers the world over think and act alike. Cray knows the soldier's walk and mannerisms. Because he doesn't have to be an actor when he's in a uniform, his job is easier.'

'What else do you know, Inspector?' The new voice at the doorway was dreadfully recognisable.

Dietrich spun in his chair to see Rudolf Koder. Dietrich tightened, as if expecting a blow.

The Gestapo agent smiled, perhaps in recognition of his effect.

'This is my office,' Dietrich managed, trying to make himself sound angry rather than afraid. 'Get out.'

'I'm your case officer,' Koder said in a tone of finality. 'We in the Staatspolizei close a file only upon the death of the subject. As long as you live, I am your case officer, and now General Müller has ordered me to assist you.'

'To watch me,' Dietrich corrected.

Koder pursed his lips. 'Your organisation and mine have different methods, to be sure. But I can be of help in your search.' He added pleasantly, 'While I watch you.'

Koder lowered himself to a chair below a bulletin board. To his right was a floor-to-ceiling map of Berlin, with coloured pins stuck here and there.

'I'll ask again, Inspector,' he said. 'What else do you know?'

Peter Hilfinger's face had gained the pink hue of anger. He had learned his craft from Dietrich and revered the man. Hilfinger knew the circumstances of Dietrich's disappearance into the Gestapo dungeon. And here was one of the devils, in their own midst, bullying the great man.

'I've learned nothing else,' Dietrich answered.

'Is that why, even though a killer is roaming the city, you and your boys are here rather than out on the streets looking for him?'

Reassured that Koder had not arrived to escort him back to prison, Dietrich regained a modicum of courage. 'How many people do you have reporting to you on, say, the Schiffbauerdamm?'

Koder studied Dietrich, perhaps wondering how he was being asked to incriminate himself. 'Three or four.'

'Three or four in the entire neighbourhood.' Dietrich glanced at Hilfinger. This lesson was for him. Rudolf Koder was beyond lessons. 'In the summer of 1941, I arrested a house painter who had murdered three young women in the street. He was convicted and executed. The neighbourhood was relieved and grateful, and now I have two hundred people on the Schiffbauerdamm who report to this office the slightest of peculiar circumstances. You rely on fear. I rely on respect.'

'Jack Cray is still out there,' Koder said flatly.

'But he can't evade me long. Not in Berlin. I have thousands and thousands of pairs of eyes looking for him.'

When the telephone sounded, Dietrich lifted the handset to his ear. 'This is Dietrich . . . Yes, I remember you, Captain.'

The detective grabbed for a pencil and rose as he dashed off notes on the back of an envelope. 'Von Tornitz? I don't know that name . . . His widow? And the American? Are you sure?' Dietrich cupped his hand over the phone. He ordered Hilfinger, 'Adam von Tornitz. A Wehrmacht captain. Get his address.'

He turned his attention to the telephone again. 'Thank you, Captain.' Dietrich lowered the telephone. He grinned meanly at the Gestapo agent. 'One of my pairs of eyes saw the widow of Adam von Tornitz walking with the American near the Tiergarten.'

Hilfinger ran his finger down a page of the city directory.

'Von Tornitz?' Koder asked. 'He was involved in a plot against the Führer. He was hanged, as I recall.'

Hilfinger wrote down an address. 'It's in the Nikolassee.' He handed the address to Dietrich.

Dietrich dialled, then barked orders into the telephone. Still grinning, waving the address like a prize, he sped past Koder on his way out of the office.

'HAVE YOU SEEN HIM, Nolte?' Dietrich whispered, even though the house was sixty metres away. He had just got out of his car. Night was almost complete, with only a faint purple left of the day in the western sky.

Nolte, the plain-clothes policeman, shook his head. 'I've been here ten minutes. A shadow crossing a window is all I saw. My men have the house surrounded, so if he's in there he can't get out.'

Dietrich carried binoculars in one hand and a pack radio in the other. He watched three cars pull up a block west of the von Tornitz house. Peter Hilfinger and Detective Egon Haushofer climbed out of the first car. More cars were arriving to the north, policemen spilling out.

'Sir,' Nolte blurted, 'he's coming out. In the front porch.'

Dietrich lifted the binoculars to his eyes and saw Jack Cray stepping down the stairs to the front path.

Dietrich breathed, 'It's him all right.'

Jack Cray must have had superb hearing, because just then his head jerked up. He cocked an ear. Dietrich heard nothing for a moment. Then from the south came the low growl of engines. Dietrich turned to see two armoured cars and three troop trucks roaring down the street.

'Damn that idiot.' Dietrich spun towards the house, in time to see Jack Cray rush back inside and close the door.

A black Horch rolled up next to Dietrich. Rudolf Koder and two other agents emerged from the car.

'That the von Tornitz house?' Koder yelled over the grind of the car engines. 'Have you seen the American?'

Dietrich was silent, furious that the Gestapo agent had muscled in on his police work.

Nolte replied, 'He's in that house. Just went back through the front door.'

At a signal from Koder, SS storm troopers emerged from the trucks and spread out round the house, joining the policemen. They carried Schmeissers and rifles, and moved with confidence.

Anger clipped Otto Dietrich's words. 'Who gave you authority to use the SS on this operation, Koder? This is *my* job.'

'The American is in the house, and the house is surrounded. Your job looks at an end, doesn't it?' Koder smiled. 'So who knows what you might be doing tomorrow or where you'll be.'

Dietrich had not been promised a pardon were he to capture the

American. Still, perhaps if he brought Jack Cray in himself, rather than allowing the Blackshirts and the Gestapo to do his job, some fate other than a return to the cell might await him.

'I'm going in after the American,' Dietrich said.

'You are a policeman, not a soldier,' Koder said. 'You don't have any idea what's waiting for you in that house.'

Dietrich walked towards the front porch. 'Better Jack Cray than you and your guillotine.' He motioned for Hilfinger to join him.

'At least let me help you with the door.' Koder gave an order to the armoured car's spotter.

The spotter yelled down into his hatch. A gun roared, yellow flashes dancing at the tip of the barrel. The door of the house blew inwards, leaving a ragged, smoking hole at the top of the steps.

Dietrich and Hilfinger paused at the front door. Pistols in hand, they stepped slowly through the door, ducking under shattered boards. There was a bitter smell of spent explosives. The armoured car's shell had done its work on the hallway, which was tossed and shattered and filled with rubble. They stepped round an overturned Chinese chest and a gilt-framed mirror which had been blown off the wall. Shards of mirror lay all along the hall. The chest was too small for a man, but Dietrich looked into it anyway. It was filled with china dishes, now mostly fragments. Rudolf Koder and six storm troopers followed them.

Dietrich led them into the sitting room, then into the kitchen. They pulled open cabinets. When a trooper came to the closed pantry door, he yanked back the bolt on his Schmeisser and loosed half a clip through the door, stitching the wood up one side and down the other. Then he kicked in the door, to find nothing but a few empty jars and bins.

'Learn that technique in Warsaw, did you?' Dietrich asked.

He led Hilfinger and the troopers up the stairs. The detectives peered into the bathroom. A trooper stepped past Dietrich, opened a cabinet and jabbed a bayonet into piles of stacked towels.

Hilfinger and the other troopers searched the three back bedrooms while Dietrich climbed to the servants' quarters in the garret. They opened closets and dressers. Armoires were pierced through with bayonets. Koder watched from the top of the stairs.

The basement was next. It was filled with boxes and bins, two bicycles, a pedal sewing machine and a laundry hopper. Hilfinger and Koder had obtained torches, and the thin, moving beams threw exaggerated shadows against the boxes and the walls.

Dietrich stuck his torch and gun into the furnace room at the same time, sweeping the light to the left into the coal bin.

'Nothing, not even coal,' he whispered to himself.

He brought the beam of light down to the ash bin below the furnace's iron lip. A trooper squeezed past Dietrich and thrust his bayonet twice down into the ash box, the weapon sinking each time until the front sight was below the ash.

Dietrich lowered himself to his knees to peer into the combustion chamber. He couldn't see up into the furnace, but nothing was on its floor. And he couldn't think of a way a man could get into it.

The bass cracking of a Schmeisser filled the basement. Dietrich turned to see the water heater leaking from eight holes.

'Don't fire that again unless I order you to,' he said wearily. 'I want to talk to this American first.'

'I take my orders from Kriminalrat Koder, sir,' the trooper replied.

'This is my investigation. I run it my way.'

Koder stared at him.

Dietrich detested the weakness in him that compelled him to explain further, 'And we don't know how involved this woman von Tornitz is.'

'She is the wife of an executed traitor,' Koder said.

'But that doesn't mean she herself is a traitor. So we shouldn't be in such a hurry to destroy her home.'

Koder smiled. Then he snapped a finger at the troopers.

Three of them turned their submachine guns on the cartons. The roar pushed Dietrich back against a wall. Wood splinters leapt into the air. Masonry chips shot out from the walls. Boxes shattered inwards, revealing old clothes and bric-a-brac. A glass-fronted bookcase ruptured. Spent shells skittered across the floor.

Then the troopers picked through the debris, pulled aside the bullet-riddled clothes and kicked in the boxes.

One of them said unnecessarily, 'The American isn't here.'

Dietrich's ears were ringing. He crossed the basement and climbed the stairs. Peter Hilfinger joined him at the door and followed him from the house and down the front steps. They walked between the two armoured cars.

'So where is Jack Cray?' Hilfinger asked.

Dietrich turned abruptly so that he could look again at the von Tornitz house. 'Peter, I saw him come out and go back into that house. He is still inside, damn it. But I don't know where.'

Rudolf Koder emerged from the house. His mouth was a grim line. He marched to the second armoured car and yelled an order. The troopers and agents backed away from the house, giving the armoured car a clear field of fire.

Dietrich rushed up to Koder. 'What in hell are you doing?'

'The American is in that house.' Koder did not bother looking at Dietrich. 'He leaves me no alternative.'

The sudden blare was like that of a bellows, a loud, windy howl. The night lit up, painting Dietrich and Hilfinger and all the others in orange light. A stream of fire gushed from a blunt nozzle on the front of the armoured car. Liquid flame surged across the lawn and coursed up the steps and into the house. Within seconds, nothing of the front façade could be seen. Fire rose three storeys and beyond. Everything—the dormers and parapets, the flues and chimneys—was lost behind the boiling curtain.

The von Tornitz house was still surrounded by Blackshirts and Gestapo agents and policemen, but they had to withdraw away from the heat. Dietrich and Hilfinger retreated to the far kerb. For half an hour they watched the conflagration. The blazing house fell in on itself and continued to burn angrily, the red core getting smaller and smaller. Clouds of smoke lifted skywards. The fire hissed.

Then the troopers returned to their trucks. The armoured cars, fire engines and other equipment receded, all loudly.

Koder crossed the street to join Dietrich and Hilfinger. 'Where's the American?' he said. 'He should have made a run for safety.'

Patiently, Dietrich said, 'He was in the house, and the house burned down.'

Koder's eyes dug into Dietrich, who would not look down, in contrast to all the times in the prison. Finally the Gestapo agent turned towards his car and walked away.

Dietrich stared at the remains of the house. 'Damn it, Peter, Jack Cray is in that house.'

'There is no house any more. Tomorrow they'll find his body in the ashes.' Hilfinger turned towards a car where other plain-clothes policemen waited for a ride back to the station. Dietrich nodded. He walked towards his car along the wooded lane.

Otto Dietrich would go to his grave wondering how he heard utterly nothing and saw utterly nothing. He was alone on the pavement, surely. But he wasn't.

An arm wrapped itself round Dietrich's neck. He felt cold metal press into the soft spot next to his Adam's apple.

The accent was strong. 'What did you want to talk about?'

Dietrich blinked. He was about to die and all he could think of was that Jack Cray's German was fairly good.

'What did you want to say to me?' The voice again.

Dietrich stammered, 'I . . . I wanted to ask if you . . . How did you escape the fire?'

'In the furnace ash pit.'

'The ash pit was stabbed with a bayonet a couple of times.'

'I was stabbed with a bayonet a couple of times.' Cray held his left arm over Dietrich's shoulder so that the detective could see it. The uniform sleeve was matted with ash. 'Clean through my arm. It hurts. I've got another long cut along my backbone.'

'How did you survive the heat?'

'I opened the coal gate. Cool air came in, sucked in by the flames. All the fire was above me. I dug down into the pit, and it was fairly comfortable. Except for being stabbed.'

Was the commando mocking him? It didn't seem professional. On the verge of death, Dietrich was indignant.

'I could hear you in the basement,' Jack Cray said. 'You sounded like a policeman. Not a soldier.'

'I'm a detective. A murder detective.'

'Would killing you be legal, then? A lawful wartime action?'

'No, surely not.' The American was having a fine old time at Dietrich's expense.

'How'd you set me up last night in the Tiergarten?'

Dietrich hesitated, but when the knife scraped his neck as if it were shaving him, the German said, 'We had the Chancellery issue orders as if the Führer were leaving Berlin. It is a complicated process, with hundreds of people involved. We figured there'd be a leak and you'd find it. We were right.'

'That was good,' Cray said. 'I like that.'

'Thank you.'

'Now what do I do with you?'

'You're going to let me live because you want someone to be able to tell people how clever you were escaping the fire.'

'I'm going to let you live because you argued against destroying her house.' The pressure at Dietrich's neck lessened slightly. 'Stay away from me. You'll get hurt if you get close again.'

The knife was removed. Dietrich could sense the American receding into the night. He waited a few heartbeats to be sure, then he turned round.

He saw nothing, nothing but night and the dark shadows of trees and a few sparkling embers, all that remained of the house.

Dietrich's hands were shaking and he had trouble drawing a breath. 'Bastard American show-off,' he said finally.

 # NINE

'Skin is just like cloth, isn't it?' the countess asked. 'Just poke and pull.'

'Take it easy, will you?' Cray spoke through clenched teeth. 'This isn't as much fun as it looks.'

'Do you want me to sew you up?' The old lady was cheery. 'Or are you going to walk round with holes in your arm?' She pricked his skin again, then pulled the needle through, the thread trailing behind it.

Cray grimaced. He was sitting at the woman's feet, leaning back against her overstuffed chair. She was bent over him, legs to one side, the needle gleaming in her hand.

'Are you going to tell me how you got these holes in your arm?' She tugged at the thread, closing the wound.

'A bayonet.'

'Didn't your mother tell you not to play with bayonets?'

Cray glanced over his shoulder at her. She smiled. The skin of her face was sallow and wrinkled like an elephant's leg. Her hair was too black—badly dyed—but her eyes were daylight blue and bright with humour. She was enjoying her work.

The American said, 'You're pretty good with a needle.'

'I don't want you to think I was always a seamstress, young man.' She slid the needle into his skin again. 'I was once a friend of the Casardis and the Fürstenbergs.'

'Never heard of them.' Cray winced. 'Take it easy, will you? You're killing me here.'

'But, when the bombs came, my friends all boarded up their windows and left the city. Some to Rome, some to country villas. Our family has been a bit embarrassed for a generation, if I may say, and I don't own a country retreat. So now I take in alterations and repairs.' She yanked the thread through Cray's skin.

Cray yelped. 'Kindly don't take it out on me, ma'am.'

'I'm properly called "Countess". Countess Gabriella Hohenberg. Before my society disintegrated, I was known for my table and my wit. Now I'm known for my sewing.' She stabbed him again.

Cray sucked wind through his teeth. 'I've heard other things about you countesses,' he said.

She giggled. 'I've heard things about you young Americans.'

'They are all true.'

'Oh, you.' She slapped his shoulder.

The small room was cluttered with mementos from her prior station and evidence of her new one. In one corner was a Louis Quinze armchair. Four Dresden china parrots lined the top of a bookshelf, and on a pedestal table were two Augsburg silver candle holders and a candle snuffer. These suggestions of the *belle époque* were surrounded by the more common paraphernalia of the seamstress. Cloth scraps were scattered about the floor near a treadle sewing machine. A pincushion was on the armchair.

Cray looked at a pole suspended horizontally from two wires. Wehrmacht and SS uniforms hung from the bar on hangers.

She followed his gaze. 'Senior officers come to me to tailor their uniforms. Sometimes they never come back to collect them. Killed in action, I suppose. You are welcome to them.'

'I might take you up on that. Nothing less than a captain, though. I have certain standards.'

She laughed, pushing her needle through his skin again. 'Just a couple more stitches.'

'Countess, how is it you know Katrin?'

'Her mother and I were friends since childhood, but she died several years ago.'

Cray said, 'Katrin calls you "Auntie".'

'Just a nickname. It's unlikely anyone would make the connection between her and me, if that's what you are wondering.'

A key sounded in the lock, then Katrin entered the apartment. She was carrying a burlap bag and breathing quickly from hauling it up the stairs. She had received a coded message on her pack radio, an address on Kordtstrasse, where she was to find an envelope in a milk box and a burlap sack near the box.

From the bag Cray pulled out three Tellermines, German antitank mines, each containing five kilograms of explosives.

'Just what I ordered,' he said.

Cray then used the countess's pinking shears to slit open the envelope. He pulled out its contents: three typed pages and several photographs. 'It's coded. More work for you.' He passed the typed pages back to Katrin, retaining the photographs.

One was an aerial shot of Berlin, taken from perhaps 900 metres. The second photo, taken at a much lower altitude, was of the Reich Chancellery—some of it open to the sky—and the garden behind it. A square blockhouse with two guards standing at each side of its entrance was clearly visible. The remaining photographs were of three POWs, each standing next to a camp guard. The prisoners wore Wehrmacht uniforms stripped of insignia. Judging from the guards' uniforms, two of the photos were taken in an American POW camp, while the third one was from a Soviet camp.

Katrin pulled off her coat. 'Auntie, may I heat some water? I found a little tea at the market. I think it's real.' She stepped round a basket of yarn and entered the small kitchen.

The events of the last days had complicated Katrin von Tornitz's assessment of Jack Cray.

On the day of the fire, she had been out making a radio broadcast. When she returned, her home was surrounded by policemen and troopers, and ablaze from front to rear. She had watched and watched from down the road. Over the winter she had burned her furniture for heat, and now this fire was taking away all the rest, everything she owned, every memento of Adam.

Only after a moment had she remembered that the American was in her house. There could be nothing left of him. She had never met anyone who had been on first sight more suggestive of trouble. His crazed grin, his animation, his stupid cheerfulness. Yet, watching the embers die, she had been sorrowful that he was gone.

She had surprised herself with that emotion.

Then, when everyone else had retreated from the destroyed house, and when she had turned to wondering where she would spend the cold night, she saw Jack Cray rise from the ashes—a ghoul emerging from the earth—and make his way towards the last remaining policeman, who was standing by his car.

She had been transfixed by his movement, utterly silent yet almost as fast as a sprinter and somehow eerily merging with the shadows, darkness on darkness. She understood why the Hand had called on him. His exuberance and affability were doubtless feigned. Jack Cray was nothing more than a proficient killer, and he was about to kill again.

But the crazy American said a few words into the policeman's ear and then let the man go. Just turned him loose. Yes, Jack Cray was continually complicating her assessment of him.

Katrin came in from the kitchen with three cups of tea on a tray. The pages were under her arm. She handed a cup to the countess and one to Cray, then pushed a hassock into the circle of light near the old lady and began the transcription.

'I visited Philadelphia once, over in America,' the countess said. 'This was in 1912. I had fewer wrinkles.'

'I haven't seen a single wrinkle.'

She tapped his arm playfully. 'You do have a way with the ladies, just as I suspected.' She reached for her scissors to remove the collar patches from his captain's tunic. 'Your country does not have nobility, and so I was entirely uncomfortable there. No one understood titles. I don't think I was called "Countess" once.'

'How dreary.' Cray smiled again.

'That's why I loathe that little man with his tidy little moustache who has taken over the Reich Chancellery. He is not sensible to Germany's thousand-year heritage. He doesn't understand the courtesy due to his betters.'

'Some people think he's done worse things.'

'I met him once. It was back in 1934, at a garden reception for Princess Maria Metternich-Wittenburg.'

Cray's eyes were now on the countess. 'What's he like?'

She put the patches into a basket. 'Nice voice. He could have been a singer if he hadn't become a dictator.'

Katrin passed Cray her completed transcription.

Cray read to himself for a moment. Then he summarised the message aloud. 'The Hand has found a second bunker on Hermann Goering Strasse, at right angles to the Chancellery.' He looked at the photograph. 'It's here, several hundred metres from the main bunker. The Hand thinks Hitler would probably retreat to this bunker were the main one knocked out.'

'How did it discover the second bunker?'

'POW interrogation, I suppose. Probably a German officer who has been inside the bunker earlier in the war.'

The countess lifted herself from her chair with a grunt, then crossed the room to the hangers. She pulled out a uniform tunic. 'Here's a colonel's. Why don't you just be a colonel?'

'I don't want a lot of people saluting me, noticing me.'

'I'll put your old patches on it, then.' She returned to her chair and began plucking at the stitching on one of the colonel's collar patches. 'You are going after Hitler, aren't you?'

Cray stared at her. 'I never said anything like that.'

'You didn't need to say anything, but I know.'

'Well . . .'

'And I remember one more thing about Hitler from that day in the garden. He is shorter than photos of him lead you to believe.'

'Yes?'

She added, 'So be careful not to aim too high.'

'YOU ARE ON THE LIST, Inspector,' the SS guard said, pointing at a line on a clipboard. 'This man is not.'

'Wait here, Peter.' Dietrich handed his Walther to Hilfinger, then spread his hands and feet for a search. The moon was hidden by high clouds. British bombers had not made their appearance yet that night. Any moment now.

Hilfinger stepped back to look again at the mammoth concrete block in the garden. 'I think I'd rather stay out here, anyway.'

Dietrich followed an SS guard past a telephone box and through the doors into the block. As he descended into the bunker, Dietrich felt his faith in his ability as a detective was being shaken. He had prided himself on his knowledge of Berlin. More than anything else, knowing the city's streets gave the detective an advantage over law-breakers. Yet here was an enormous structure, which Dietrich had heard rumours about without ever being able to confirm them, right in the centre of Berlin. It made Dietrich wonder what else he had missed.

The SS guard led him to the bottom of the stairs, where two more guards started to search Dietrich.

'How long has this bunker been here?' Dietrich asked.

'State secret.' The guard grinned. 'That and everything else about the place. You may go in.'

Dietrich stepped through a door that must have weighed more than a Panzer, must have been ten centimetres thick, solid steel. He stared down the corridor, recognising people he had seen only in newsreels, on posters and in newspapers. Dr Goebbels was speaking with Field-Marshal Keitel. When Goebbels turned towards the corridor's rear door, Dietrich noticed that the man walked with a limp. The Minister of Propaganda—the most visible man in the Reich now that the Führer had largely disappeared from public view—had a club foot, and Dietrich had never heard of it. Again Dietrich was disturbed. What else had he missed?

Also in the corridor were Minister Ribbentrop, Ernst Kaltenbrunner, head of the Reich Main Security Office, and a dozen senior SS officers. All appeared to be waiting. A high-pitched whine seemed to come from all directions. The air was dank.

An orderly at Dietrich's elbow pointed at a door and said, 'Go in, please.'

Kaltenbrunner's eyebrows rose, and others in the corridor turned to examine Dietrich, a man in plain clothes who apparently had precedence over all the rank in the corridor. Dietrich walked into a small study filled by a table covered with maps. He was alone with Adolf Hitler.

The Führer was wearing reading glasses, which Dietrich had never seen in posters or photographs. The detective knew Hitler was fifty-five, but he looked two decades older, shrunken, the skin on his face mottled. Hair hung down across his forehead, and it appeared greasy, needing to be washed. The moustache was uneven, bitten and dull, with speckles of grey.

The Führer looked up. 'Detective Inspector Dietrich.'

'Yes, sir.'

'Would you like some refreshment?' Hitler removed the spectacles and put them into his uniform pocket.

'Yes, sir.'

'Come with me.'

Hitler led the detective into a sitting room. The Führer motioned to a blue horsehair sofa set against a wall under a portrait of Frederick the Great. Below a grating was an oxygen bottle on wheels. A small marble bust of Frederick rested on a burnished wooden stand near the door. Dietrich lowered himself onto the sofa, while Hitler poured tea into a tiny engraved silver cup, then passed it to him.

Dietrich sipped it. 'What is this?'

Hitler smiled. Never had Dietrich seen a photograph of Hitler smiling. The man had bad teeth, yellow and small.

'It is just as well you did not join the Party, Inspector. Asking what refreshment is being served is not the proper protocol.'

Was Hitler making a joke? Humour was a characteristic Dietrich had never before associated with the Reich's leader.

Hitler returned the teapot to a stand, then with a groan sat in a leather chair behind a cluttered desk. His eyes found Dietrich. Found him with the force of a blow. Despite Hitler's appearance of age and infirmity, the eyes were blue, a milky blue, penetrating yet at the same time warm and guileless. So powerful was the gaze that it was a presence entirely apart from the decrepit, ailing man sitting across from Dietrich. The detective felt pushed back into the chair by the eyes, and laid bare.

'You never joined the Party, Inspector, but you would have done better in the Berlin police had you been one of us.'

'Yes, sir.' Was that all Dietrich could say?

'You have been assigned to search for the American killer.' Hitler spoke with his Lower Bavaria accent. His tone was charming.

'Yes, sir.'

'You missed him earlier.'

'I didn't miss him. That was the Gestapo. And, if I may say, they are interfering.'

'It's apple-peel tea, by the way,' Hitler said. 'You should never drink real tea or coffee. They'll kill you.'

'I'll keep that in mind.' Dietrich cleared his throat. 'May I ask why I was summoned here, sir?'

Hitler sipped his tea. 'Do you believe in fate, Inspector?'

'I've not given it much thought, sir.'

'One day during the Great War, when I was eating dinner with some comrades in a trench, I heard a voice in my ear. It said, "Go over there, quickly." I obeyed, moving twenty yards down the trench. And just then a shell burst over my comrades. All of them were killed. Fate spoke to me that day. Fate spared me.'

'Yes, sir.'

'I believe in fate, and my fate is tied to my city, Inspector. I will never leave Berlin.' Hitler lightly rubbed the side of his chin. 'And there's another reason.'

Dietrich said nothing.

'Our enemies believe we have a fortress in the Alps, where I will flee once the enemy appears at the city's gates.' Hitler paused. 'There is no such place. I have nowhere to go.'

'Yes, sir.'

'So, you see, I cannot meet my end at the hands of an assassin.'

'Yes, sir.'

'I asked you here to thank you for what you are doing. And to encourage you to work a little harder.'

'I will, sir. Work harder.'

Hitler opened a side drawer of the desk he sat at, to pull out a gilt picture frame. He held it out to Dietrich. In the frame was a photograph of Hitler. Dietrich gingerly accepted it.

Hitler rose from the chair and escorted Dietrich back into the conference room. 'Goodbye, then. And send Keitel in.'

Goebbels blocked the door into the hallway. He gripped a piece of paper in both hands. A smile so wide it seemed to hang from his ears was wrapped round his bony face. He fairly danced on his one good leg. 'My Führer, Roosevelt is dead.'

Hitler's eyes widened. He inhaled quickly. 'Dead?'

'Dead.' Goebbels was trembling with the news, the dispatch shaking in his hand.

'By God, we are saved, Goebbels.' Hitler's voice rose like a storm. 'The Reich is saved.' He breathed heavily. The news straightened his backbone and put colour into his face. He slapped a fist into a hand, then again and again.

'It was foretold to me, Goebbels. I have long known I would be taken up from these ashes. And now it has happened.'

Hitler turned away, back to his study. Goebbels followed him.

Dietrich had been instantly forgotten. He stepped into the long corridor. Keitel's face darkened when Dietrich indicated he should enter Hitler's rooms. Dietrich was oddly satisfied by the field-marshal's reaction. The orderly escorted Dietrich back up the stairs and out of the blockhouse door. Dietrich stepped between the SS guards into the garden.

Hilfinger was waiting for him. 'You returned. I had my doubts.'

'So did I.' Dietrich filled his lungs with the outdoor air. 'President Roosevelt is dead.'

Hilfinger chewed on the news for a moment. 'It won't make any difference.'

Dietrich nodded. 'Not to you. Not to me. Not to anybody below ground in that bunker. Not to Germany.'

As they walked away from the concrete structure, Hilfinger asked eagerly, 'What's he like? The Führer?'

Dietrich stared at the framed photograph. 'He almost convinced me, almost had me. I almost fell for him, like some schoolgirl.' Dietrich glowered, then tossed the framed photograph onto a pile of gravel. The glass shattered, a tiny sound by Berlin standards. 'Like some damn swooning schoolgirl.'

DIETRICH SLID HANGERS along the pole in the cupboard. 'Cray would take a military uniform, if there was one. Anything on that? A husband or son in the military?'

Hilfinger looked at his notes. 'She was a widow. Husband dead fifteen years. So, even if she didn't throw his clothes away, there probably wasn't a modern uniform here.'

'There's some man's trousers in here. Civilian. So maybe he's dressed again as a civilian.'

Dietrich and Hilfinger and Egon Haushofer occupied most of the small bedroom as they picked through the widow's belongings, looking for evidence of Jack Cray. During the night Dietrich's detectives had searched city records for Katrin von Tornitz's relations, and had found that she had a great-aunt who lived in Dahlem, or had lived there before the war.

The widow's home was a brick structure from the last century, covered with vines. It was dark—all Berlin houses were dark—but not shuttered. After spending almost an hour observing the house, the detectives had entered and found it empty.

Hilfinger rifled through a basket, then the drawers of a desk. 'Here's an address book.' He dropped it into a canvas satchel he had brought with him. 'And Christmas cards. A lot of return addresses on them. Maybe Katrin von Tornitz and her great-aunt have mutual friends, another place Cray might hide.'

'You don't follow orders, do you, Inspector?' A new voice, abrupt and coarse.

Dietrich turned to find Heinrich Müller at the bedroom door, with agent Rudolf Koder at his elbow.

The Gestapo chief stepped into the room. 'How long have you known about this address?'

Dietrich feared this man, but he would not let Hilfinger and Haushofer see it. In a level voice, he replied, 'About an hour.'

Müller rose on his toes, a bucking motion, his hands behind his back. 'I specifically ordered you to report all your leads to me.'

Dietrich sucked on a tooth before answering. 'With Himmler's letter, I unordered myself.'

Hilfinger smiled at his boss's dangerous impudence.

So did Heinrich Müller, but meanly. 'It is a lack of respect, isn't it, Inspector? You simply do not respect my organisation.'

Dietrich idly rubbed his jaw.

Müller bit down with such pressure that his lips paled. A signal must have passed, but Dietrich did not see it. Nor did he see the pistol in Koder's hand.

Koder took one step towards Peter Hilfinger, placed the muzzle of the pistol against Hilfinger's temple and pulled the trigger.

Hilfinger collapsed to the floor. Blood and bits of his brain dribbled down the wall. Koder swung the pistol towards Haushofer, freezing the detective's hand as it reached under his coat for his weapon. Hilfinger's bemused grin was still on his dead face.

'Perhaps you won't forget to report next time, Inspector,' Müller said pleasantly. He walked out of the widow's bedroom.

Koder shrugged and put his palms up, perhaps in a gesture seeking understanding, the pistol still in one hand, then backed out of the room, following Müller.

 # TEN

C ray lay on the earth, the scent of German loess rich and close. He was at the edge of a wood, and was concealed by juniper bushes. Ahead was a clearing, then a chain-link fence topped by strands of concertina wire. A pathway of beaten-down grass, made by patrols, paralleled the fence. The night was still dense, but the first grainy light of dawn was colouring the sky. Cray could hear Red Army guns in the east. To the south the clouds were a soft orange, reflecting the fires from that night's bombing raid on Berlin. He had left the countess's apartment at midnight and had pedalled a bicycle north for four hours.

Cray rose from the brush and sprinted across the clearing. The chain links were too small for footholds, so he gripped the fence and pulled himself up, hand over hand. Cray had experience with razor wire, and he had not come unprepared. The countess had sewn heavy oilcloth onto the palms of a pair of black gloves. Cray was wearing a black pea jacket and black dungarees.

He reached the top of the fence and gripped the wire. It was in loose coils, offering no support, so he spilled onto it, toppling forwards then cartwheeling over and down to the ground.

Cray sat a moment, taking stock. The wire had raked him. His dungarees were absorbing blood from slashes on his thighs. Both ankles were bleeding. He'd been hurt worse.

He rose and hurried on, bent low like an infantryman. When he had crossed almost thirty metres of soft earth, he encountered a second fence, this one with no razor wire atop it.

Parallel fences at a military base often meant a dog run.

The sound came at him from the north, a huffing and hissing, a rushing rumble, closer and yet closer. Cray leapt wildly, his fingers snaring the links. He was too late.

A Doberman sank its fangs into his ankle and held on. Another leapt, its teeth slashing at Cray's calves, snagging the trouser leg and his muscle, but then twisted and fell back to the ground. Cray climbed hand over hand, the first dog attached to his foot like a bear trap. His hands found the fence's top bar. With his free foot he kicked at the dog, first in the head, to no visible effect, then at its lungs. He kicked again, viciously, using the heel of his boot. The dog loosened its grip, and Cray lashed into it again. The animal slipped off, crashing to the ground. Instantly both dogs lunged upwards, snapping their jaws, Cray's blood dripping down on them.

Pulling himself up, Cray lifted a leg over the bar, then slid down the inside of the fence. Shuddering, he glared at the dogs. 'You two need a little work on your manners.'

Cray suspected the dogs had not been on guards' leads, and that no sentries were approaching. But he waited, his pistol in front of him. For a few minutes the dogs barked and paced, then they drifted away, back the way they had come.

Cray rose from the ground and limped north, travelling between fir and oak trees and over damp ground made soft by moss and decomposing leaves. He crossed a graveyard. Carefully arranged wooden crosses and stone markers gave way to rows of unpainted crosses with crude lettering. These were the more recently dead.

For a hundred metres he followed a gravel road past what had once been a petrol and diesel dump but was now a hole in the earth. Blasts of exploding fuel had pushed trees back as if with a giant hand. Dawn filled the woods with fragile blue light.

Through the trees came a sharp yell, then another, followed by a volley of curses and then a shouted order. Cray recognised the voice. They were the same the world over. A drill instructor. He skirted the parade ground, staying in the forested area, then stopped to study the map Colonel Becker had drawn for him. The base, just north of Berlin, was the home of the Wehrmacht's Third Army. Through the brush Cray could see the camp hospital.

The forest opened into a long rectangle of pasture, about a kilo-metre long and 350 metres wide. Cray stayed inside the cover of the trees, but edged close to the field. Bombers had mistaken it for an airfield, and it was cratered from one end to the other.

Cray settled onto his haunches behind an oak. And then he began to disappear.

Jack Cray did not believe in the mystical, so he could not explain how he could almost vanish. But he was so silent and still that the damp ground seemed to soak him up. He became part of his sur-roundings, invisible to anyone more than a metre away.

A low drone soared overhead, so swift that it was gone almost before it registered. Then a dull report, a flat, muted clap that echoed in the trees before fading away.

The sounds told Cray he had found the right place on the army base. He waited, invisible in the bush.

CORPORAL EWALD HEGEL lay on his belly, his chin against the rifle's check-patterned stock, his eye at the telescopic lens.

'Can you feel the pulse in your finger, Corporal?' The instructor stood above the shooter, his hands round a pair of binoculars.

'I think so, Sergeant.'

'Wait until you do. Pull the trigger between pulses. Otherwise the pumping of your heart will draw you off the target.'

The corporal squinted into the scope. 'Yes, Sergeant.'

The targets were above a butt 600 metres downrange. A cratered wasteland separated the shooters from the bull's-eyes. Corporal Hegel's weapon was a Mauser, but resembled the standard-issue Wehrmacht rifle in name only. The barrel was made of Norwegian steel—the entire steel plant had been barged across the North Sea to Germany—and was wider than a regulation barrel. The wooden stock and grip were also heavier than those on the standard Mauser. The weight added stability.

'Hegel, you've got a crosswind.'

'The rifle is clicked left two points, Sergeant.' Hegel waited, trying to sense the pulse in his arms. He thought he had it. He counted along with his heart, then brought back his finger.

The Mauser barked and kicked up. Downrange, a black circle on a pole rose from the butt, covering the new hole in the target.

The sergeant peered through the binoculars. 'Second ring, six o'clock. You've got a way to go, Hegel.'

'Yes, sir.'

'Let's rotate the pit.' He brought out a red flag and waved it above his head. When, 600 metres away, a red flag answered by crossing back and forth in front of the target, he announced, 'The range is now closed.'

'Hegel, you and Pohl are due at the target butt.'

As the instructor turned to his other sniper students, Corporals Hegel and Pohl rose from their firing positions, slung their Mausers over their shoulders and started for the target.

Hegel was eighteen, and graveyard thin. He trotted along, the stock of the Mauser bouncing against his hip. 'Do you think they'll finish with us in time?' he asked.

'In time for what?' Roland Pohl followed in Hegel's footsteps towards the target butt. The path was at the edge of the range, wedged between the trees and the bomb craters.

'In time for the war.'

Pohl laughed. 'We'll probably finish our sniper training just as the Red Army gets to the camp. That way our unit won't have to be shipped anywhere. We can put our education to use here.'

'If that's our duty, we'll do it.' Hegel held his arm out for balance as the path narrowed and he had to negotiate round the crumbling side of a bomb crater. 'We'll do what we are told.'

Ewald Hegel would never be able to recall what happened to him at that instant, would have no memory of it whatsoever. One moment he was chatting with Roland, and the next he was kneeling at the bottom of a bomb crater, gasping for breath. Roland Pohl was next to him, on his back. Hegel groaned and brought his legs up to try to stand. He wobbled, then collapsed into the mud.

Finally Hegel asked, 'What . . . what happened?'

Pohl looked as if he had been rolled in mud. 'The edge of the crater must have collapsed.'

'Then why does my head hurt so much?' Hegel pressed his temple. 'My head was hit by something.'

Corporal Pohl pulled his weapon out of the mud. 'Ewald, look at my Mauser. I'll bet the scope is ruined.'

Hegel pushed his hands through the mud, first in front of him then to both sides. 'Where's my rifle?'

'Under the water, probably.'

'And my grenades? Where are they?'

They searched for several minutes through the mud. Then they climbed out of the crater shivering, their uniforms dripping.

After looking through the brush and round the trees, Hegel said, 'My rifle is gone. Someone knocked me on the head and took my rifle and grenades. The sergeant is going to kill me.'

'Well,' Pohl replied, 'it'll save the Russians the chore.'

SERGEANT ULRICH KAHR dropped a handful of potato peelings into the meat grinder bolted to the workbench. He grunted as he cranked the handle round and round. Pulpy mashed potato skins oozed out of the spout and dropped into a wooden bucket.

It wasn't hunger that prompted Kahr to bring home potato skins and orange rinds and bread crusts from the Chancellery kitchen. It was thirst. The sergeant could make alcohol out of almost anything. His still was in the goat shed behind his farmhouse, just east of the Havel River. The duty rota allowed him three days at home after seven in the Chancellery barracks.

Kahr sat on an upturned nail barrel near his boiler. With the tip of his boot, he pushed a few embers back into the fire. It was a small fire, just enough to warm the shed and bring the mash to the boil, and it demanded just enough attention to dull his misery. With his family gone—all his sons—he spent more time in the shed than in his house. Every corner of the house brought back memories. He tossed a handful of straw onto the blaze.

His head came up. He'd heard a noise. He pivoted to face the door. Had it been the hinges? No, something else, a wood sound. Someone stepping on wood. Maybe out at the stack of firewood.

Kahr rose from the barrel and lifted the pitchfork from its wooden pegs. The fork had three prongs, each half a man long. He edged towards the door, bringing up the pitchfork.

'Sergeant Kahr?' A woman's voice. Somewhere out in the night. 'May I speak to you?'

Kahr was silent. He didn't know any women. And the voice outside the goat shed was young. And cultured.

Katrin von Tornitz stepped into the circle of frail light coming from the shed. She smiled at him. 'I rode a bicycle all the way from Berlin. Can I come in? It's important, Sergeant Kahr.'

Kahr lowered the pitchfork and said, 'Sure, come in.'

He led Katrin into the shed. He turned over another barrel, then dragged it towards the fire. 'Have a seat. Do you want something to drink?' He waved towards the bottles.

She shook her head at the offer, then said, 'Sergeant, I don't want you to be frightened.'

His chin came up. 'I'm not frightened.'

'Well, you are going to be when you see him.'

'Who? Who are you talking about?'

From the shed door came a new voice. 'Will you just make the introductions, for God's sake?'

Katrin repeated, 'I just don't want you to be afraid, Sergeant.'

Sergeant Kahr had seen the posters in Berlin, and now he saw the man standing at the door. At first he could do nothing but stare at Jack Cray, but then he scooped up the pitchfork and held it with the points at the level of Cray's neck.

'What do you have in those bottles?' Cray nodded towards the workbench.

'Schnapps, vodka. I don't know what to call some of it.'

'May I have a drink?'

The pitchfork was lowered slightly. 'That all you want?'

'I want to talk.'

Kahr peered at the American. 'What kind of talk?'

'About family.' Cray pushed the tines aside and stepped to the workbench. 'And what it's like to lose a son.'

Katrin said, 'We know your son is gone.'

'What's this?' Cray held up a jar of clear fluid.

'Made of apples. Peels and cores, actually.'

Cray sipped from the bottle, then sharply drew in air through his teeth. 'Could use another ten or fifteen minutes of ageing.'

'I tried to make it taste like schnapps.' Kahr returned to his upturned barrel. 'I add spices, when I can find them.'

With the bottle still in one hand, Cray dragged a sawhorse to the circle of warmth round the boiler. 'My father once made a barrel of this stuff. Where I'm from we call it applejack.' He passed the bottle to Kahr. 'Tasted about like yours.'

'Yeah?' Kahr sipped from the bottle, then passed it back to the American.

Cray leaned back, bringing his feet to the fire to warm them. He took another pull from the bottle. 'He'd use Red Delicious apples from our farm, in a place called Wenatchee. The best apples in the world, some of them almost the size of my head.'

'I used to grow those big red ones myself. Right out there.' Kahr waved at a wall. 'Sixty-four trees in perfect rows.'

Katrin interrupted. 'Two men sitting round a fire drinking, having a fine time. That's not why we came out here.'

Sergeant Kahr stared morosely at her.

So did Cray. He said to the sergeant, 'She's been a lot of fun, you can tell.' He passed the spirits back to Kahr.

'To business,' Katrin insisted.

Cray rubbed the side of his nose with a finger. 'You've lost three sons, Sergeant.' Colonel Becker had reported Kahr's missing sons to Cray. 'I'll give you one of them back.'

The sergeant's brow furled. 'That's a poor joke, friend.'

The American pulled an envelope from his jacket pocket. From it he withdrew a photograph. He held it up to the sergeant and said, 'Wehrmacht Corporal Max Kahr is a Russian POW.'

Ulrich Kahr stared at the photo. 'That can't be him.'

'Look closely.' Cray smiled. 'This photograph was taken within the past week.'

For a long moment the sergeant looked at the photograph. Then his voice was the ghost of a whisper. 'I was told my boy was dead.' Kahr blinked repeatedly, but he could not stop the tears.

Katrin said, 'We can get him released.'

'And returned to you,' Cray added. 'In a matter of days.'

Kahr was breathing quickly, joy flooding him. 'You have no idea what my boys mean to me . . . My last boy . . .'

'Well, there *is* one small catch,' Cray said. 'It's nothing, really.'

'Nothing?' Kahr repeated.

Cray smiled again, reaching for the bottle. 'A small thing.'

HALF AN HOUR LATER they left Sergeant Kahr to his distilling and walked round his farmhouse, then out onto the track. The moon's shadow was dappled by the boughs of elms that lined the driveway. Cray and Katrin approached their bicycles, which were leaning against the wall near Kahr's letterbox by the main road.

Cray pointed. 'What direction is that?'

'West.'

'How can you tell?'

'See the orange clouds that way?' She pointed, too, but at a ninety-degree angle to Cray's direction. 'Berlin burning, a reflection of the fires. Orange clouds are our unfailing compass.'

Cray glanced at her, an impish cast to his eyes. 'Thanks for the date tonight. I had a good time.'

'Date? What date?'

'You and me, sitting in front of the fire having drinks.'

'That wasn't a date. That was a . . . a business meeting.'

'We were sitting in front of a cosy fire,' he said. 'And the scent of spring was in the air.'

She glanced at him. 'It was the smell of old goats.'

'So it sounds like a date to me. You and me. A romantic evening in the Prussian countryside.'

'And we weren't even alone,' she protested. 'The sergeant was there, and once we made our deal he did most of the talking. No, it wasn't a date. Nothing of the sort.'

'Sure it was.'

'Not at all.' She laughed.

'There. You laughed.'

'I did not laugh. I'm a war widow. We never laugh.'

She laughed again.

ELEVEN

'They match?' Eugen Eberhardt bent over the table.

With a trembling pencil, Dietrich pointed at a portion of the photograph. 'Right at the back of the heel imprint. It's the trace of a nailhead.'

'And you see it on this photo, too?' Eberhardt adjusted the gooseneck lamp, centring it over the second photograph. 'Now I see it, the same nail print. Just as you say.'

'The first photograph was taken at von Tornitz's home, near the spot where Cray had his little chat with me. The second was taken at the rifle range, where those two snipers were attacked.'

'And you're sure that the rifle is missing?' Eberhardt lowered himself to a folding chair. The truck was cramped, and his knees were pressed against a metal cabinet.

Eberhardt and Dietrich were inside a Funkwagen, a mobile command post built for the military services by Volkswagen. The vehicle was almost four metres long and squat, with two rod antennas and a bedstead aerial attached to its roof. An RSD radio operator was also in the cargo bay, hovering over an array of dials and switches. Behind the operator was a bulletproof window through which the driver's head could be seen. Eberhardt's office on Potsdamer Platz had been destroyed the night before, and he had been promised a new one—somewhere—by noon. Until then the head of the RSD would conduct his business at a metal table in the Funkwagen.

'Military police turned the camp upside-down. That boy's rifle is gone. And so are his three grenades. Two were TNT, and one was a smoke grenade.' Dietrich grabbed the table edge with both hands. Since witnessing Peter Hilfinger's murder, he had been unable to keep his hands from shaking. Fear—his constant companion in prison—had returned with such force that it overwhelmed the grief he should have felt. He was ashamed of his weakness.

'There was a time when hardly a bullet could disappear in Germany without my learning of it,' Eberhardt said. 'The war has changed that. Rifles disappear all the time. So do machine guns.'

'Here's more bad news.' Dietrich unbuttoned a rifle case lying next to him to bring out a rifle with a scope on it. 'The base commander loaned me this Mauser. It's identical to the one Cray took off the young sniper.' He passed the rifle to Eberhardt. 'With this weapon Cray's range would be seven or eight hundred metres.'

Eberhardt's expression suggested that perhaps his boots were too tight. 'Do you realise how vastly more complicated my job has become, with Cray having a sniper's rifle—?' The general was interrupted by the sudden blare of an air-raid siren.

He muttered, 'Damn, I get sick of this, every day and every night, never failing. Let's go.' He signalled to the driver to follow them, then opened the Funkwagen's door.

The vehicle was parked near the Stadtmitte U-Bahn station. Dietrich and Eberhardt and the RSD driver and radio operator joined the flow of Berliners heading for the underground entrance. They descended the stairs and entered the long concrete cavern.

Dietrich found a place on a bench, then ceded it to an elderly woman wearing a scarf round her head. She smiled at him with grey teeth. A Kriegsmarine captain in a blue reefer jacket with four gold stripes on each sleeve walked along the platform.

'There aren't any boats left in the navy,' Eberhardt said under his breath. 'I wonder what that captain does to earn his pay.'

Dietrich chuckled, liking the RSD general.

Eberhardt said, 'In a way I owe you for my son's life.'

'How do you work that out?'

'My boy—his name is Ritter—used to follow your exploits in the newspapers with some relish. He'd read about some ghastly crime and how Otto Dietrich captured the perpetrator, and he became a policeman. So he has been spared the front lines.'

'I'll accept your thanks, however faulty your logic.' Dietrich hesitated, then added, 'And in return I'll ask a favour. Can you get Müller off my back?'

Eberhardt took a long breath. 'Otto, I've got my own problems with Müller. I don't think there's much I can do.'

Dietrich rubbed his hands together. The station was colder than the Berlin streets. He said softly, 'I'm afraid of Müller.'

'So am I,' Eberhardt admitted after a moment. 'But you met the Führer personally. Doesn't that make Müller hesitate?'

'Not that I've seen. Hitler thanked me, but maybe he also wants me still to be terrified of the Gestapo.'

The walls abruptly shifted, then shivered. Bombs were falling. Berlin was built on alluvial sand, so bombs had a rippling side effect through the earth. The platform bucked. Dust fell from ceiling cracks, and in a few places water seeped down the walls.

Finally the quivering stopped, and a few minutes later the all clear sounded. Dietrich again followed General Eberhardt, swept along by people desperate to leave the tomb of the underground and return to whatever was left above ground.

They stepped through the doors into a cloud of smoke and ash that hid buildings fifty metres away. The sharp scents of high explosives and ruptured sewage lines carried in the breeze.

From the haze came the sound of a vehicle's worn brakes, metal on metal, or so it sounded to Dietrich. Then it came again, an agonised wail, so out of place among the ruins that the detective could not identify it. A vast patch of the haze shifted and then was pushed aside by a mammoth presence. A trunk and tusks formed out of the smoke, then the rest of the elephant, moving fast, throwing one enormous foot out in front of the other.

'It's Fritzi, from the Tiergarten Zoo,' Dietrich said. 'He's got out of his pen.'

'He's been hurt.' Eberhardt stepped towards the elephant, as if he could help him. A gash the size of a door was open in his side. White ribs were visible, and torn muscles, and blood was gushing from the creature. Fritzi bleated again and again.

'My children and I used to feed him peanuts,' Eberhardt said.

The elephant had been running in fright and pain for blocks, but was now at his end. He lurched against a car, righted himself, then raised his trunk to cry out. He sank ponderously on his front legs, shuddered, then toppled onto his side. His huge chest rose and fell once, and then the animal was still.

Berliners gathered round the animal. Fritzi had been the star attraction of the Berlin zoo for twenty years. Now the terror fliers had killed him. Men and women began to weep openly, and gently touched the giant animal, trying to comfort him in death.

Eberhardt stared sadly at the elephant. 'This'll all be over soon. All of this destruction.'

The detective glanced at Eberhardt. 'Are you and I lengthening the war or shortening it, General? By trying to catch Jack Cray?'

'That's not for us to worry about, Otto. We've been told to catch Cray, and that's what we'll do.'

'YOU DON'T LOOK any better with brown hair,' Katrin said, her arm in Cray's, leaning into him as if guiding him along the pavement. A scarf hid her hair and much of her face.

'I used up all the countess's dye on my hair and eyebrows.' Cray adjusted the bandage that hid the right side of his face.

He was wearing a Wehrmacht officer's uniform borrowed from the countess, and he limped, using a black walking stock and favouring his right leg. Smoke rose from the block ahead of them, and in the east was a wide smoke column.

Katrin and Cray had not been near a shelter when the air-raid siren sounded, so they had climbed into the basement of a ruined building and huddled in a corner under a table, mouths open and fingers in their ears. When they heard the all clear, they emerged to find Berlin swallowed in smoke and drifting ash, the sun hidden in the haze. Their *ad hoc* shelter had been at the edge of the target area, and the new fires and craters and shattered buildings were to the south, the direction in which they needed to travel.

They picked their way along the street. A few Berliners crept out of cellars onto the pavements to squint against the gauze of smoke, craning their necks, trying to determine what was left of their neighbourhood. No one paid attention to the wounded Wehrmacht major. Berlin was brimming with injured servicemen.

'Do you smell perfume? Lilac?' Katrin asked. 'I can also smell fresh bread and mothballs, and a whiff of floor cleaner. It's always like this after a bombing. The air smells of better days.'

'I can't smell any of that.'

'Take a big breath, and tell me the scents you detect.'

Cray sniffed, pondered, then announced, 'Cordite and gelignite and high-explosive residue.'

She looked at him. 'Have you *ever* had a romantic thought?'

Katrin had been contacting the Hand twice a day since Cray had appeared. The Hand had given her no information during her last three broadcasts. The American had speculated that either the Hand was learning nothing to pass on, or perhaps it was saying nothing because Cray's mission was only a cover for some other operation, so it had other concerns.

'I'm hungry,' Cray announced. 'You'd think if the Hand is putting us to all this trouble it'd send us something to eat.'

Katrin asked abruptly, 'Have you ever read Kant?'

He shook his head. 'Did you say you smelled bread?'

'Or Leibniz or Hegel?'

'Not enough pictures in those books.'

She slowed their pace. 'What do you read?'

'*Popular Mechanics.*'

She hesitated. 'What's that?'

'A magazine about how to make crystal radios using junk,' he said. 'I made dozens of them when I was a kid.'

Her tone was patient. 'You don't know our literature or philosophy. Do you know anything about us Germans?'

'I aim and fire at them. What's there to know?'

After a moment she said, 'Is it just that your German is rough, or is it possible I'm speaking to a moron?'

'Now I'm smelling the bread, too. It's making me salivate.'

'Adam and I had wonderful conversations,' Katrin said.

'Is that what this is about? Trying to have a conversation with me to replace the ones you once had with your husband?'

'It was an absurd idea, come to think of it.'

'What's so absurd about it?' Cray helped Katrin step over a wad of singed blankets. 'I can have a meaningful discussion, but I can't talk about Hegel, if that's what you want.'

'How about your childhood—or did you spring from the ground, fully formed, carrying a knife and a grenade and a pistol?'

His look was of crushed dignity.

'I'm teasing.' Her voice was light and warm. 'Go on.'

Cray thought for a moment. 'I knew I was going to be an engineer when I was very young. Maybe ten or eleven years old.'

She nodded, encouraging him. 'What made you think so?'

'There wasn't a wire or a tube in a radio I didn't know. I rigged an antenna on our barn. I could hear stations as far away as San Francisco. Then I made a transmitter. There was a while when San Francisco might've been able to hear me.'

She laughed.

'It amused my mom and dad, having all those tubes and condensers and dials and switches all round. Until one bad day. A very bad day.' He paused. 'I made a radio detonator.'

She stiffened. 'Oh, don't go ruining this little talk.'

'And discovered—purely by accident, I told my dad—that match heads inside a length of pipe could be detonated at a distance, and would indeed destroy a toolshed.'

'Weapons. Is that all you ever think about?'

'Shovels, hoes, plant pots, rakes, shingles, bits of windowpanes, the works, all blown into the air. Some landed on our lawn; some I don't think ever came down.'

Katrin sighed heavily.

'Well.' He brushed his hands together. 'I do enjoy a nice chat.'

She asked abruptly, 'Have you ever examined your life?'

'A person shouldn't look too closely at himself.'

'You are a better person than you think, Jack,' she said. 'But that doesn't mean you aren't a moron.'

Her hand was on his arm as they walked, and now Cray put a hand over hers. He said in a diminished tone, 'I can get you out of here when this is over, Katrin. Out of Germany.'

Her eyes shone with emotions he could not read.

He said gravely, 'Even if the Gestapo doesn't find you, the Red Army will be here soon. The horrors have just begun for Berlin.'

Her mouth moved, trying to find the right words.

'I can get you out,' he repeated.

'You won't be able to get yourself out, much less me.' She smiled to take the edge off her words.

An arm—as thick as a hawser—went across her back as they walked round a scattering of bricks. 'I can get us out, both of us.'

She shook her head. 'I'm not leaving Germany. I know a few places I can hide.'

'We can talk about it later.'

'There's no need to. I'm not leaving.'

DIETRICH AND EBERHARDT stood in front of the barber's chair, which was brought into the room once a day for these few minutes. Hitler was getting a shave under the smiling and careful attention of an SS barber. A bib was across his chest, and Dietrich thought it peculiar that the bib was camouflage brown and green. Under the bib, Hitler was wearing a black satin morning robe over white pyjamas with blue piping. On his feet were black patent-leather slippers. Hitler's left arm trembled underneath the bib.

This was Hitler's bedroom, one room further into the catacombs than the map room. A Dresden vase and Carlyle's biography of Frederick the Great were on a night table near a low bed. Across from the bed was the blue horsehair sofa.

'You again, Inspector,' Hitler said, white foam parting at his mouth.

'Yes, sir. And General Eberhardt.'

'General Eberhardt has been working for me for thirteen years, Inspector, and not once has he brought me welcome news,' the Führer said. 'What is it this time, General?'

'I must be blunt, my leader,' Eberhardt said. 'We believe the American—Jack Cray—has obtained a sniper rifle.'

While General Eberhardt informed the Führer how such an event had come to pass and how it had been discovered, Dietrich sensed movement to his right and glanced round the room.

A woman with hair the colour of straw was rearranging tubes of lipstick and vials of perfume on the dresser, taking too long, perhaps with nothing else to do. She had a shade too much rouge on her cheeks, and her eyebrows were pencilled darker than her hair. She wore a snug-fitting blue dress with white ruffles at the neckline.

And when Dietrich—feeling like a thief for having glimpsed this woman—quickly turned back to the barber's chair, Hitler startled the detective by raising an eyebrow, just fractionally, but plainly and purposefully nonetheless. It was the silent and common question one bachelor asks of another: she's something, isn't she? Dietrich stood to attention, as straight as a shinbone, while Eberhardt continued with his briefing.

'So he will try to flush me out of the bunker.' Hitler was again all business.

'There is no other reason to obtain a sniper's rifle.' The RSD general spoke succinctly, a professional briefer.

'How will he do it, Inspector?'

The barber waited until Hitler had finished the question before scraping the blade across his chin. Strip by strip, the Führer's face was emerging from the foam.

'Perhaps a massive bombing raid. The Allies have a new bomb that penetrates several feet of concrete before exploding. It has been used with success on airfield runways.'

'This roof is considerably thicker than a runway, and on top of all the concrete is another ten metres of earth,' Hitler said, as the barber wiped away the last specks of lather.

Eberhardt said, 'Perhaps the bombers' goal will be not to destroy this facility entirely, but to chase you from it, to make it uninhabitable, so you will be forced to emerge.'

'Where Jack Cray will be waiting,' Dietrich concluded, 'with the sniper's rifle.'

Hitler rose unsteadily from the barber's chair. His face was pink and shiny. He pushed aside his forelock using his entire hand, the outsized gesture of a boy. 'My engineers tell me this bunker cannot be pierced by a bomb, any bomb. So I will stay in this place. For ever.'

'You are never leaving?' Dietrich asked.

'Last time you were here, I told you I would never leave Berlin. Now I am telling you I am never leaving this bunker. This American . . . what is his name again?' Hitler asked.

'Jack Cray,' the detective replied.

'Jack Cray won't have a target.' The Führer's blue eyes were as flat as paint. 'He'll be out there, waiting and waiting, but he'll never have anything to shoot at. And so all you need do, Inspector, is catch him. You don't need to concern yourself about me.'

The barber crisply bowed to Hitler and left the room. Thinking himself dismissed, Dietrich moved to follow him.

Hitler's hand on his arm brought him up. 'Tell me, Inspector. Are the Bolsheviks within mortar distance of Berlin?'

Dietrich was startled. How could the Führer not know this? 'Soviet shells are landing on the city day and night.' Again, Dietrich found reserves of courage he did not know he possessed. 'Don't your generals tell you?'

'Some do and some don't,' the Führer replied tonelessly. 'Some of the traitors have never told me the truth. They lie to me. It's a matter of who to believe. That's how I've come this far, Inspector. Knowing who to believe.'

Dietrich sensed he was witnessing the tide turn, the waning of reason and the waxing of something more dangerous. He had heard rumours of these sea changes. He hastily turned to go, Eberhardt at his heels.

'And amid all the traitors, I can trust you, Inspector.' Hitler's voice gained half an octave, and inklings of hysteria were at the edges of his words. A flood was coming. 'They have never told me the truth. They lie to me. And, worse, they conspire with each other to lie to me.' Hitler's face was turning red. Spittle formed at the corner of his mouth. His voice rose like a stormy wind. 'That's all I hear down here. Lies and more lies.'

The Führer caught himself. He shuddered with the effort to control his passion. He breathed quickly, air rattling in his throat. He turned to the blue sofa like a jerking marionette, his ruined body not cooperating in even this small motion.

He said over his shoulder, 'Send another one of them in as you leave, Inspector Dietrich. Any one of them, outside the door there, waiting for an audience, snivelling in fear, hoping I haven't discovered their treachery. But of course I have.'

OTTO DIETRICH held two corners of the map laid over the car's bonnet, while Eugen Eberhardt pinned down the other two corners. They were near the Food and Agriculture Ministry's building on Wilhelmstrasse. A company of Eberhardt's RSD troops were cordoning off the crossroads and 200 metres of Behrenstrasse, setting up wooden traffic barricades. Camouflage nets hung from lampposts made Wilhelmstrasse seem like a tunnel.

'It's all a matter of angles, really.' General Eberhardt stared down Behrenstrasse towards the church. 'We'll give Jack Cray a few, and we'll take away a few.'

'And you're sure the Führer would exit the bunker only by these routes?' Dietrich was bent over the bonnet, studying the map of the district that was the Reich's administrative heart.

'Otto, I have overseen his departure from the Chancellery hundreds of times. These would be his routes were he to leave. He usually gets into the limousine in the Honour Courtyard, and the limousine exits through the vehicle gate onto Wilhelmstrasse. Occasionally the limousine pulls up in front of the building, and he leaves from the Great Marble Gallery, nearer his office.'

'And are you certain you know all the places the Führer would go if the Chancellery bunker were uninhabitable?'

Eberhardt stiffened, lifting his hands from the map so that it flapped in the breeze. 'It's my duty to know these things. The SS bunker across the Chancellery garden would be the first refuge. The Wehrmacht command bunker in Zossen would be the second.'

'How would the Führer travel to them? Could he walk to the SS bunker?'

'Of course. It's just across the garden.'

Dietrich continued, 'And to get to the Zossen bunker he would have to drive, of course. It's quite a distance. So, if Jack Cray can force the Führer out of the bunker, the only place Cray can count on the Führer being in the open will be as he walks across the garden towards the SS bunker, or when he is at the vehicle gate or the Marble Gallery entrance. Is that right?'

'Yes, but you are supposing Jack Cray knows these things.'

Dietrich said, 'We must presume that the Americans and English have put a vast intelligence machine at Cray's disposal. And so we must assume Cray knows the Führer's escape routes.'

The RSD general nodded. Every part of this conversation had been spoken before by these two men over the last two days, and more than once. They acted as each other's cross-examiner, searching for Cray through the power of their intellects, sifting through the meagre clues he had left behind.

Dietrich began folding the map. 'But, Eugen, there's a chance the sniper rifle is only a ruse. Maybe Jack Cray stole it as a smoke screen. And his plan is something else entirely.'

The general pursed his lips. 'Otto, Cray went to a lot of trouble to get that rifle. I don't think it's a ruse.'

An RSD man blew his whistle twice, then yelled a final warning through a loudhailer. Other whistles sounded, indicating nearby buildings and roads were clear of people. 'Ready when you are, General Eberhardt,' he called.

Dietrich followed the general towards a low wall of sandbags. An RSD man waited there, one hand on the plunger of a detonator and the other round a pair of binoculars.

As he walked, Dietrich said in a low voice, 'You saw him down there, the Führer.'

'I see the Führer rather frequently,' Eberhardt replied, a touch of the bureaucrat in his voice. 'What's your point?'

'It's insane down in that bunker.'

'You shouldn't speculate . . .'

'For God's sake, you heard him down there. Talking of traitors, talking of his loyal soldiers like that, soldiers who've given their lives and families and homes to Germany. And their leader is raving and rolling his eyes, spit flying from his mouth.'

'Otto, these are dangerous things you are saying.'

'He's a certifiable lunatic.' Dietrich found his voice rising, just as Hitler's had. 'You saw it yourself. I never knew it until now.'

The RSD general gripped Dietrich's arm with force. 'Otto, if the wrong ears hear you, you'll be back in that dungeon.'

Dietrich was having trouble breathing. 'Yes.' He wiped his mouth with the back of a hand. 'Yes, of course.'

They stepped behind the sandbag wall. Eberhardt peered through field glasses to the century-old church with its high steeple, high enough that a man could stand on the bell platform and see over the Old Chancellery into the garden, to the blockhouse entrance to the bunker. The church had so far escaped explosives. Not this day.

Eberhardt nodded at the RSD man, who pushed the plunger handle. The grind of the small generator inside the box was immediately followed by the roar of dynamite from the church's roof. Smoke and splinters erupted from the base of the bell tower, and the tower sank, then toppled forwards. It had become a trifling scrap of rubble in a city that was little else.

Dietrich and Eberhardt rose from behind the sandbags. Eberhardt said, 'I wish we could just have posted a squadron at that church, and so spared the bell tower.'

The detective replied, 'Cray might have got past them.'

'We can't cover every single firing site Cray might use.'

'Of course not.' A gleam entered Dietrich's faded blue eyes. 'But we can cover two or three. Then maybe—just once—Jack Cray will appear where we want him and when we want him.'

 TWELVE

'You ever heard of her, Egon?' Dietrich asked, his hand on the dashboard, bracing himself. 'A Countess Hohenberg?'

'Not that I recall,' Detective Haushofer replied. 'She's not related to Katrin von Tornitz, then?'

'Not that we can find. I suspect the countess was a friend of Katrin von Tornitz's mother, but that's a guess.'

The Mercedes lurched and sank, then bounced up as it rolled between inclines of rubble on Heuwingstrasse, all that remained of the three- and four-storey apartment buildings that had lined the street. Dietrich commented, 'We got a break on this.'

Haushofer nodded. 'We needed a break.'

A woman who lived on the floor below the countess had been peeking out of her door when Katrin von Tornitz was walking up the stairs. She had recognised Katrin from the posters in the street.

Haushofer pulled on the steering wheel, and the Mercedes wound round a filing cabinet and a sofa in the road. A drumroll of rain sounded on the Mercedes's roof.

'Are Cray and Katrin von Tornitz still there, do you think?' Haushofer asked.

The canyon ended at a crossroads, and the car drove between low apartment buildings. This portion of Heuwingstrasse had been spared.

'The snoop said she hadn't seen them today, so probably not. But I want to talk to the countess.' Dietrich squinted through the rain. 'There's her building. Pull over.'

The clouds suddenly parted, revealing the sun. The road began to steam. Dietrich left the car and ran to the door to check for her name on the letterbox. HOHENBERG. He pushed open the door and began ascending the stairs. He drew his pistol.

The countess's door was open. Dietrich could see the old woman in a chair against the window. Knitting needles were on her lap, and a ball of yarn and a sewing basket at her feet. She was staring through the door at Dietrich, and her mouth was pulled back in a curl of fear.

Dietrich thought she must be afraid of his pistol, so he moved it behind his leg. He stepped to the door's threshold.

'Countess Hohenberg?'

She croaked piteously, 'Please don't hit me.'

Dietrich allowed himself a smile, a friendly one, he hoped. 'I wouldn't think of it. I'm Detective Inspector Dietrich. I just want a few words with you. May I come in?'

Her eyes were old and leaking, and mirrored a wild fear.

Dietrich stepped inside the apartment. 'Countess, I'm just a police officer. There's no reason to be afraid of me.'

Rudolf Koder stepped in from the kitchen. 'But she has good reason to be afraid of me.'

Dietrich's pistol involuntarily swept to Koder.

The Gestapo agent grinned at the weapon. 'We are on the same side, remember?'

Dietrich shoved the Walther into his trousers, and only then did he notice Koder was carrying a meat cleaver.

'Don't hit me again,' the countess intoned. 'Please.'

Dietrich could see Koder's knuckle imprints on the countess's cheek. Colour rose in his face. 'How did you find out about this lady?'

A vulpine smile. 'We listen to your telephone,' the Gestapo agent said. 'I know full well Jack Cray slept here last night. He left a pair of socks in a corner of the kitchen, in a bag. One of the socks has blood on it. But the so-called countess here won't tell me where he and Katrin von Tornitz are.'

'Maybe I can talk to her.' Dietrich sensed movement behind him. He turned to see another Gestapo agent. This one's pistol was out, its snout pointed at Dietrich.

'She won't say anything. I've already tried to persuade her, but it wasn't enough.' Koder brought up the cleaver. 'Never let it be said that distaste for a task dissuaded me from my duty.'

With a speed that belied his banker's manner, he snatched the countess's hand, slapped it against the table next to her and held it there as he viciously brought down the cleaver. The blade clapped loudly against the table top, and two of the countess's fingers fell to the floor, where they curled like grubs.

'I must apologise,' Koder said to her, still holding her hand. 'No doubt that smarts. But maybe it will freshen your memory.'

The countess moved her jaw, but no sound came. Blood dripped from her hand across the table, then fell into her sewing basket.

Dietrich rushed forwards. 'There's no reason to do that . . .' He brought up his pistol, unsure what he would do with it.

Koder swung the cleaver in a tight arc, catching Dietrich's jaw with the flat of the blade. The detective staggered, then collapsed to his knees. Koder dipped his chin at the agent in the doorway, who slammed the butt of his pistol into the detective's head. Dietrich pitched into a black void.

An age passed, or perhaps only a minute. The veil of darkness lifted in fits and starts, allowing Dietrich vague and puzzling glimpses of the countess's apartment as seen from the rug. He groaned and tried to push himself up from the carpet, but nausea surged from his belly into his throat, and he sank back to the floor. His head pumped agony down his neck and into his shoulders. The countess—several countesses—drifted in front of him.

The countess's fingers lay across the floor like spilt cartridges. Dietrich's vision was still not good enough to count them, but he trusted the Gestapo to finish a job, and there would be ten of them lying there. The countess was still sitting in her sewing chair. Her hands hung down on each side of the armrests, the frayed stumps of her fingers dripping blood like rows of little spigots.

A hand found Dietrich's shoulder. Egon Haushofer asked fearfully, 'Inspector, can you stand?' Haushofer pulled on Dietrich's arm, wrestling him to his feet. 'Are you all right?'

'No, hell, no, I'm not all right.' The floor seemed to be rolling like the deck of a ship. Dietrich palpated his head and brought away blood. His eyes found the countess's seamed face. She stared at Dietrich with the sightless reproach of death. A clean, perfectly symmetrical bullet hole was centred in her forehead.

Haushofer's words tumbled out. 'I was parking the car down the street when I saw those two Gestapo bastards leave.'

'Egon,' Dietrich said softly, 'look what they did to this poor woman.'

'Your pupils are dilated. I think you've got concussion.' Haushofer gently turned Dietrich to the door. 'Come on, Inspector. We'll get you patched up, then we'll go after Jack Cray.'

Dietrich touched away dampness from his eyes. 'Yes, Jack Cray.'

Haushofer tried to lead Dietrich from the apartment, but Dietrich said, 'Let's look round. If he's been here, he's surely left things, left part of himself, things the Gestapo would miss.'

SERGEANT KAHR had rehearsed this entry into the bunker a hundred times in his mind. He thought he'd be able to walk calmly up to the SS guards at the blockhouse entrance, receive the usual insults as they patted him down and go into the blockhouse. But, as he stepped up to the guard, the small box of matches taped on his right thigh seemed to expand in size and weight, forcing him to walk peculiarly.

The sergeant held his breath while he was patted down. The guard's hand came close, but he was searching for pistols or grenades, and he searched some five hundred people a day, so he missed the matches, just as Kahr had prayed he would.

'Go ahead, Sergeant.'

Kahr entered the blockhouse and started down the dimly lit stairs. Berlin had fallen into such dark chaos that the bunker no longer seemed so gloomy by comparison. At least here he could escape the ash and the hollow rattle of Bolshevik shells. The SS guard at the antechamber door frisked him but didn't find the matches either. To hide his nervousness while the guard studied his ID card, Kahr swatted ash from his shoulders.

'Enter,' the guard ordered, passing back the card.

Kahr stepped through the door, breathing for the first time in an hour. The bunker was so crowded he could not see the door at the far end of the corridor. And he gasped at the disarray. Three SS officers were in a corner, sharing a bottle of schnapps. General Gotthard Heinrici was raging at Foreign Minister Ribbentrop, his hand pumping like a locomotive's main rod. A card table had been set up outside the Führer's door, and two generals were hunched over it. On another table was a gramophone, playing Brahms. A cake with green icing was next to the record player. An SS adjutant was wiping away icing and letting the Führer's dog Blondi lick it off his finger.

Kahr pushed his way into the corridor, stepping round General Steiner, who was speaking to another general whom Kahr did not recognise. He walked past the Führer's open door. The nasal, rasping screech coming from the room could scarcely be identified as Hitler's voice, but of course it was. Kahr glanced around. Nobody else in the corridor seemed perturbed by the Führer's ranting. He passed the door to his generator ventilator room, climbed the circular stairs and entered the kitchen wing. The central passage here was used as a dining room. Kahr recognised Erich Kempka, Hitler's chauffeur, and Hans Baur, Hitler's pilot, sitting at a table and dining on soup. He walked to the end of the dining hall, then turned into the kitchen.

'So you are back again, Ulrich?' An agreeably flabby cook smiled over her rolling pin. A circle of dough lay on the table in front of her.

'I'm on business today, Helena.'

'You are never on business when you come into my kitchen.' She put the rolling pin to one side and wiped her hands on her apron. Baking trays were stacked on a shelf. She plucked a chocolate éclair from a tray and put it into Sergeant Kahr's hand.

'This is why you visit me,' she said with mock petulance. 'My food. Just my food.' Her smile was flirtatious.

Kahr normally appreciated Helena's modest attempts at being a coquette and would linger awhile, but today he had work to do. He ate the éclair in two bites and mumbled round the pastry in his mouth, 'You are stockpiling flour, sounds like.'

'All the time. And sausages, cabbage, vension, everything.'

Kahr licked chocolate from his thumb and index finger, hoping this little concern with cleanliness would disguise his agitation. 'I've been ordered to take as much flour off your hands as I can cram into my room. You'll get another load tomorrow.'

She clapped her hands together, raising a cloud of flour. 'So now we are hoarding? Are the Russians that close?'

Kahr swallowed. His fear had given the éclair—the Führer's favourite dessert—a rancid aftertaste. 'The end has been near since 1942, but don't tell anybody I told you so, lest I'm dragged before a court-martial. Let me into the pantry, Helena.'

She untied her apron and hung it on a towel bar. Kahr followed her through the supply-room door. Barrels and crates filled the room. Rounds of cheese, racks of wine, casks of olive oil, kegs of beer, shelves of spices, baskets of oranges and combs of honey.

'The flour sacks are there.' Helena pointed.

Kahr stepped round stacked boxes of carrots. He grunted as he lifted a bag up to his left shoulder. He guessed it weighed thirty kilograms. 'I'll be back for more.'

The crowd in the dining hall was growing. Kahr did not draw a glance. He carried the sack into the main hall, as crowded as ever. The pretty blonde woman—whom Kahr had once heard called *die Blöde Kuh*, the stupid cow, was sitting in a chair, teaching the eldest Goebbels daughter how to apply mascara. Kahr pressed the generator room's buzzer with that day's code, three rings then two.

After a moment—always just long enough to irritate Kahr—Sergeant Fischer threw the bolts and opened the door.

Kahr shouted above the whirr of the fans, 'We've got to keep company with the dry goods.' He lowered the sack to the floor.

Fischer said sullenly, 'First it's canaries, now it's the stores.'

The sergeant made five more trips to the pantry. At the end of his labours, he had moved 180 kilograms of flour into the generator room. His exertions with the bags—throwing them off his shoulder onto the concrete floor—resulted in a fine veil of flour on the big Benz generators. He pulled out a rag and began wiping down his machinery. He knew it was to be the last time he would ever do so.

RSD GENERAL EUGEN EBERHARDT stepped down from the Funkwagen, the cordoning-off order in his hand. He had overseen security for all the Führer's public appearances for thirteen years, and the guiding principle had always been the same: erect a wall of guards between the Führer and potential trouble. The SS, the RSD, the League of German Girls, the Hitler Youth, even the Female Police Auxiliary Helpers were used. Eberhardt understood these massive shows of force. But today's cordoning-off order was new entirely. It was a knotty scheme, and Eberhardt didn't like it.

Otto Dietrich was waiting for him on the street. The detective's driver, Egon Haushofer, was leaning against his car's bumpers, a dandelion cigarette in his hand burnt down almost to his knuckles.

Eberhardt waved the four-page order at Dietrich. 'Otto, there was a time when I thought all I had to do to protect the Führer was stop a bullet or defuse a bomb. Now this damn mess of an order.'

Dietrich said, 'Preventing Jack Cray from attempting to assassinate the Führer won't be enough, because Cray will try and try again. He must be caught.'

'He must be killed.' The new voice belonged to Gestapo Müller, who moved into their circle. 'I agree with the inspector. If we cordon off the Chancellery with fifty thousand men, the American will simply come back another day. We must let him think today is like every other day regarding the Führer's security. Let him think he is getting his chance with his rifle.'

Dietrich added, 'And we'll be there when he tries. We've left him five firing sites.' He and Eberhardt had overseen the destruction of fifteen structures that overlooked the Chancellery.

'Those sites will be like flytraps,' Müller said. 'Cray will find them easy to enter, but impossible to escape. We have ten men at each of them. Well armed, well trained and hidden.'

'And you are sure he is going to try for the Führer today?' Eberhardt knew Dietrich's theory, but he wanted to be convinced.

'The old countess told us so,' Müller said, rocking on his heels. 'Jack Cray said goodbye to her this morning. He wouldn't have told her he wasn't returning if he were staying in the city any longer. He's going into action today.'

General Eberhardt said, 'Your man Koder had no call to murder that woman, that countess, Müller.'

'Would you rather have sacrificed the Führer's life? That was our choice. Either she talked, or you wouldn't have a clue when Cray was going to make his move. Now you do, thanks to Koder over there.' Koder was leaning against the front bumper of a Gestapo car.

Dietrich wished he could fault Müller's reasoning.

'And we think Cray's plan will begin with a bombing raid. The

American planes always come between nine and noon. They will try to chase the Führer from the bunker.' Müller started towards Koder's car without saying anything more.

Dietrich glanced at Rudolf Koder. His anger bubbled up. 'I'm going to kill that son of a bitch Koder when I get the chance.'

Eberhardt gave him a corrosive look. 'The Russians will be here any day, and they'll surely do that for you. So don't do anything to get yourself hung, Otto.'

 # THIRTEEN

Ulrich Kahr knew the air raid had begun when his desk started to shiver. Only a little at first, but then the old Wehrmacht-surplus oak desk began to dance towards the generators, and the sergeant had to grab it and drag it back. When he rose from his chair, the room went black, a disorientating, impenetrable black.

Kahr moved unsteadily towards the door, to the torch that hung on the wall near the door frame. He moved the beam of light to the fan box and tripped switches so that when the bunker again had electric power the fans would remain still.

Then the light beam found the starter engine. Kahr planted his feet squarely—the floor vibrating under him—and yanked the cord. The little engine popped several times, then blared like a trumpet. The sergeant let it warm before pulling the clutch lever which engaged the first diesel engine.

Kahr withdrew a service knife from the desk drawer, then pulled a mattress from a cot onto the floor. He stabbed into the mattress and tugged out the stuffing until the cover was limp.

He put most of the wadding to one side, but retained a handful. He lifted his helmet from his desk and held it upside-down under a drain valve, then turned the tap. A thin stream of diesel oil fell into the helmet. Kahr dropped the stuffing into it. When it was saturated, he put it on the floor and dipped another tuft into the diesel. After a few moments all the fabric lay on the floor, oozing fuel.

The light bulbs abruptly regained their full brightness, and the control panel indicated that power had been restored. Normally, Sergeant Kahr would now shut down the generator. This time he left the big brass machine droning along.

He looked at his watch. Then he threw five switches on the control panel. After a few seconds, signal lights on the panel indicated that five gates in the ventilation system had closed. Instead of bringing in fresh air, the system was now recycling old air through its pipes. He opened a service gate on one of the pipes, then pushed wads of the damp mattress stuffing into the pipe. He compressed the wet wads, making sure they were not entirely blocking the pipe. Then he opened another gate and stuffed a wad of diesel-impregnated fabric into it. He repeated the procedure nine more times, until each pipe contained his preparations.

He unbuttoned his trousers and yanked on the matchbox. He grimaced as hairs came away with the tape. He opened the box to fish out a match. Again he checked his wristwatch. The time had come. He struck the match against the box, and it flared into life. He pushed the small flame into the opening of a pipe until it was against the fuel-soaked wad. The material caught fire. He quickly closed the gate, trapping the fire inside the pipe. In a few minutes he had set all the wadding on fire.

Next, Kahr engaged the fans at low speed, not so fast as to extinguish the pipe fires, but enough to move the black diesel smoke from his fabric fires through the system and into the bunker. He pulled his gas mask from its box and put it over his head.

And now he waited. The entrance buzzer sounded, and he heard a muffled, 'Sergeant Kahr. Open the door.'

Black haze began pouring into his room through the gratings. Five minutes more and he would turn his attention to the flour. The pounding at the door became louder. 'Sergeant Kahr.' One voice, then three voices, all yelling his name. The buzzer sounded again and again. He waited.

THE BOMBING RUN was unusual for the Americans in the spring of 1945. They came in low—at 2,000 feet, unheard-of for B-24s—and they came with only twenty planes. These twenty roared over the Reichstag and right between Wilhelmstrasse and Mauerstrasse, precisely on target, bomb bays open and sticks falling.

A swath of destruction chased the planes' shadows. Upper Wilhelmstrasse buckled and then turned over, as if raked by a giant plough. The Science and Education Ministry disappeared in a cloud of dust and fragments. On Mauerstrasse the Paris Restaurant ceased to exist in a white flash, nothing larger than twisted forks remaining.

Superheated air swept along the streets, yanking off awnings and signs, sucking out windows and carrying deadly debris. Power lines collapsed and lay across the street, sparking and hissing. Ribbentrop's Foreign Office—just next to the Reich Chancellery—was torn in two.

Then the planes were gone and the bombs had spent their fury. An eerie quiet settled over the area, broken only by the crackle of fire and the sound of the occasional beam or post giving way.

Berliners hiding below ground could not have known then of the careful placing of the bombs. Ruin had been vast, but not one bomb had sailed into the Reich Chancellery or its garden.

They were left alone. They were left for Jack Cray.

GENERAL EBERHARDT ran up the steps from the bomb cellar below the Air Ministry, four RSD men behind him. They sprinted east along Leipzigerstrasse, dodging new debris and craters. The all clear had not yet sounded, and no one else was on the street. Eberhardt knew another team would be closing in from the other direction, further east on Leipzigerstrasse.

Eberhardt could cover only one of the five potential firing sites, but he prayed Jack Cray would choose this one, the six-storey office building with a view of the Chancellery's vehicle entrance. It was the most likely of the five sites, the one Eberhardt would have chosen. With a combat team, Otto Dietrich was covering another site, hoping that his spot would be the one.

The other team was already at the office building's front door. Eberhardt nodded, and the troops rushed into the building and ran up the stairs, their weapons in front of them. The rear of the building—which shared a wall with the neighbouring restaurant—had been exposed by the bomb that ruined the restaurant, explaining the scent of horse stew in the building's lobby.

Eberhardt was breathing through his open mouth when he reached the sixth floor. His men—younger and fitter—were already inside the room that overlooked the Chancellery's vehicle entrance. The general swore to himself when he saw they were milling about, their weapons at ease. Cray had chosen another site.

He put the handset to his mouth, dispensing with radio protocol. 'This is Eberhardt. Anything at number two?'

A crackling voice. 'No, sir. Nobody.'

Eberhardt demanded, 'Number three?'

A different voice, made weak by the reception. 'Nothing, sir.'

Eberhardt's scowl deepened as each team in turn reported seeing nothing.

Then one of his soldiers entered the room, holding a scoped sniper's rifle. 'I found the rifle two rooms down, sir. This was with it.' The soldier handed Eberhardt a piece of paper.

The general read aloud, '"You can have this rifle back. I won't be needing it."'

And then—his face crimsoning—General Eberhardt understood that he and Dietrich had been wrong—perfectly and wildly wrong—about Cray's plan.

FOURTEEN

The intercom on Sergeant's Kahr's desk was buzzing, the telephone there was ringing and it sounded as if SS guards were working on the steel door with a crowbar. Kahr had helped design the door, and he knew it would hold for the few more minutes he needed. Black smoke was coming through the ventilator grates, the same smoke that was pouring into all the rooms of the bunker, and it was getting thicker. Kahr coughed into his mask.

He twisted the valves on the water pipes, closing down the bunker's sprinkler system. Then he opened a grating over the uppermost ventilation pipe on the wall. Air flowed through the pipe in a steady stream, but it too was smoky because the system was drawing air from the bunker and returning it to the same place. Kahr ripped open a flour sack, glanced at his wristwatch and then started pouring flour into the pipe. After only a few seconds his first bag was empty. He lifted the second bag, balanced it on his knee to yank out the thread and spilled its contents into the pipe. And then the third bag. Finally, he emptied the last bag. Flour began to drift through the air ducts.

Kahr brought out the box of matches and scratched a match against the score.

FOREIGN MINISTER RIBBENTROP struggled with his gas mask. A strap was caught on his ear. He wrestled with it, swearing and coughing. The bombing raid had just ended and the bunker had stopped its trembling. But it was filling with acrid black smoke which obscured the walls and ceiling.

Martin Bormann emerged from the conference room and held a handkerchief to his mouth. An SS orderly rushed up to give him a mask. The smoke was thickest near the ceiling. The throng appeared headless to Minister Goebbels, who was shorter than everyone else in the hall. Goebbels found someone to yell at—a hapless Propaganda Ministry aide. The Führer's dog, Blondi, howled.

Alfred Jodl stepped into the hall, breathing stertorously, tears running down his cheeks. He called, 'We must evacuate. Give the order.'

'No, sir,' replied a guard captain. 'Our orders are to remain below ground if at all possible, and it is still possible.'

The crew at the ventilator-room door jammed a crowbar's blade into the space between the steel door and the steel frame. Two guards yanked on the bar, but it lost its purchase and the guards had to prevent themselves spilling backwards. The captain plunged the crowbar again into the crack.

As smoke, now darker and denser flowed from half the grates, Field-Marshal Keitel marched over to the guard captain. 'I order you to evacuate the Führerbunker, Captain.'

He let up on the crowbar. 'Sir, there is no fire below ground.'

Keitel's chin went up. 'I will not stand for impudence from—'

'If there's no fire, we stay here.' A new voice.

The captain was relieved to see RSD General Eberhardt, who had just entered the bunker. Eberhardt's countenance was grim.

'Eberhardt,' Keitel said, 'it is time to leave the bunker.'

Not wanting a trace of self-pity to colour his words, Eberhardt spoke carefully. 'I have failed to stop the American commando. He is still out there, and I have no doubt he is near by.'

Keitel's black scowl dissolved as he coughed, a rattling hack that ended in a whistling wheeze. He managed, 'Look around, Eberhardt. We can't stay down here. We'll suffocate.'

General Eberhardt's voice was weary. 'Your mask is secure against the smoke, sir.'

Staring at the ventilation grates, Albert Speer said, rather idly, 'What's that new material coming from the vents? Chalk dust?'

Speer did not have long to wonder. At that instant, in the locked ventilator room, Sergeant Kahr dropped the match into the pipe and slammed shut the cover.

The flour and air mixture in the pipe ignited. Fire roared through the system. The guard captain heard the muffled explosion and turned from the ventilator-room door to see fire pour out of the gratings that lined both long walls of the hall of the bunker. He opened the sprinkler valves at his station in the corridor, twisting both valves to their fully open position. A few drops of water came from the overhead sprinklers, but nothing more. 'Extinguishers,' he yelled.

OTTO DIETRICH PICKED UP the telephone, rubbed the handset nervously for a moment, then returned it to the cradle behind the SS guard's booth. The detective had heard a muffled explosion, which had been followed by thicker smoke pouring from the door. General Eberhardt—eighteen metres under Dietrich's feet in the bunker—would call if there was anything Dietrich needed to know.

The massive blockhouse was in front of Dietrich, with its steel door open. Smoke continued to drift up the stairs and out through the door, joining the haze that filled the garden from the bombing run and obscuring the walls of the Chancellery. Six SS guards stood near the door and two more by the booth. They looked at the plain-clothes man with suspicion. Dietrich paced, ignoring the guards. Rudolf Koder no longer bothered to hide while he was trailing Dietrich. He waited near the blockhouse, watching the detective.

The telephone sounded. An SS lieutenant lifted the handset, said, 'Yes, sir,' and replaced it on the cradle. He told Dietrich, 'The rescue squad has been summoned.'

'Has an evacuation been ordered?'

'Not yet. They can hold out a while longer, General Eberhardt thinks.'

Dietrich nodded. He suspected Eberhardt would rather allow everyone to be parboiled than expose the Führer to Jack Cray out in the open.

And Jack Cray was out in the open. Cray was within a hundred metres of him, Dietrich was certain. Somewhere in the Reich Chancellery, in the ruined wing, maybe even in the garden, hidden somewhere, waiting for Hitler to emerge. Cray's sniper rifle had been found, along with the note, and so Dietrich's deductions regarding Cray's plans had been entirely wrong. Now Dietrich simply had no notion how and where Cray would strike. Dietrich had failed.

Guards at the vehicle entrance pulled open the iron gates. Men from the rescue squad ran through the gate, followed by a fire engine. A generator truck followed. An officer jumped from the running board, held his identification card up to the guard at the door and said, 'Captain Dreesen.'

The SS guard studied Dreesen's face, comparing it with the photo on the ID.

Finally Dreesen barked, 'Get out of my way, idiot.'

The SS guard waved Dreesen and his men through. A cable from the generator truck was clamped to an electrical box. If necessary, the truck would provide electricity for emergency lights. More rescue squad members trailed in. Several wore fire-resistant canvas vests with 'TeNo' (Technische Nothilfe) stamped on them in white. Some carried coiled ropes, others hauled oxygen bottles, crowbars and sledgehammers. They passed through the door into the blockhouse.

And then it came to Otto Dietrich, came with a force like a blow to his chest, crushing the wind out of him.

The SS guards had checked the TeNo captain's ID, but were allowing his men into the bunker without being screened. They had come into the garden as a group and were entering the bunker as a group, all in their white herringbone uniforms, wearing gas masks. No one was examining each TeNo face.

'Arrest them,' Dietrich yelled, waving his hand wildly. 'All of them. All the TeNo men.' He dug into his coat for his pistol.

The guards quickly surrounded the rescue squad members still above ground. Dietrich tore off the nearest man's gas mask. A dark-haired man with black stubble across his cheeks and chin. Looked nothing like Jack Cray. Dietrich ran to the telephone at the blockhouse door. He lifted the handset and pressed the button. He yelled into the phone at the guard captain, 'The American is in the bunker. Jack Cray is in a TeNo uniform.'

The detective grabbed a gas mask and ran into the blockhouse. He descended blindly, unable to see through the rising smoke, roughly pushing aside TeNo men slowed by their equipment. Dietrich knew any one of them might be Cray working his way into the bunker, but he suspected the American would have been one of the first men down the stairs. Cray was already in the bunker, he was certain. Koder followed Dietrich.

From below came cries of alarm, shouted orders, a dog's barking and the crackling of fire. Heat rose in the stairwell. Dietrich's mask leaked, and smoke stung his eyes. He reached the antechamber, where two SS guards held their weapons on some TeNo men, keeping them from entering the bunker.

'Arrest the TeNo men,' yelled a captain. 'Block them from entering the Führer's quarters. The American commando is one of them.'

A shot came from somewhere in the bunker corridor, a sharp slap which echoed back and forth in the underground compound. Screams, then a curse and orders for calm.

Dietrich stepped from the antechamber into the central corridor, Koder behind him. Fire worked along the floor. The carpet burned, sending runners of smoke into the already thick air. Dietrich could see little beyond his hand. He bumped into Gestapo Müller. His foot caught on a leg. The body of a TeNo man. An SS guard with a pistol blocked the door to the Führer's study and bedroom. He had just shot the rescue squad member.

'What are you doing, damn it?' Dietrich yelled at the guard. 'Don't shoot the TeNo. Arrest them. Round them up . . .'

Something clinked near his feet. He glanced down. A stick grenade flashed by. Then a second grenade.

'Down, down!' from somewhere near the door to the antechamber.

The detective lunged away from the SS guard towards the opposite doorway, which was to a dressing room. The smoke opened for an instant, and Dietrich glimpsed a TeNo man in a gas mask holding an SS guard in front of him as a shield. Jack Cray must be in that TeNo uniform.

Dietrich tripped on a chair and fell into the dressing room.

The first explosion was muffled, but the corridor filled with spewing, acrid, grey-green smoke.

The second grenade detonated.

The first had been a smoke grenade. The second contained TNT and shrapnel. The corridor filled with a brilliant white flash. The sound was that of a sledgehammer hitting an anvil, a metallic peal so loud it seemed to stab Dietrich's head. His pistol was still in his hand. He rose unsteadily and returned to the hall.

Two seconds of silence. Then moans and screams. Shrapnel had swept the room like a scythe. The SS guard used as a shield was sprawled face up on the floor, blood oozing from his chest. Near him on the floor, blood pumped from punctures in the SS guard who had stood at Hitler's study door.

The smoke thinned for an instant. The TeNo man stood there. Jack Cray. Face hidden by a gas mask, but surely it was him. Pistol in one hand, knife in another. Just standing there, next to the door into Hitler's quarters.

But just for that second. Then the smoke throbbed and the air clapped and Dietrich felt metal cut into his thigh and leg. Cray had thrown another grenade. And now the American spun from his place against the wall and charged into Hitler's study. Dietrich high-stepped over fragmented furniture, his leg in agony. The American commando's back was dead ahead, framed in the doorway to Hitler's bedroom. Cray was raising his pistol.

Cray twisted violently, ducking, just as a shot sounded from the bedroom. The American's knife arm slashed forwards. He stepped ahead into the bedroom again. The next sound was that of a melon dropped onto the floor. Then another. The commando pitched forwards into the bedroom, his gun and knife hitting the rug just as he himself did. Dietrich moved through the smoke towards the bedroom.

The commando was sprawled face down on the rug.

General Eberhardt stood near the pedestal, the bust of Frederick the Great in his hand. His right forearm was slashed.

Eberhardt smiled grimly. 'I hit him with Frederick.'

Dietrich grimaced with pain as he bent to the downed man. He rolled the commando over and pulled off the gas mask. 'It's him,' he breathed. 'Jack Cray. I'll be damned. You got him.'

'We got him,' Eberhardt corrected kindly.

Hitler appeared in the smoke. He asked drily, 'That was a little close, don't you think, General Eberhardt?'

Gestapo Müller rushed into the room. His uniform was dappled with blood. Shrapnel had creased his neck, and blood oozed over his shirt. He demanded, 'Is he alive?'

As if in answer, Cray moaned. His arm moved a fraction.

Müller said, 'I'm going to take care of this bastard right now.'

'I want to talk to him,' General Eberhardt said. 'See how—'

'Your job is over, Eberhardt,' Müller cut in. He yelled over his shoulder, 'Koder, get in here.'

The RSD general returned the bust of Frederick to the pedestal. 'My Führer, an interrogation—'

'I'm not interested in what the American has to say, General. The commando is now Müller's.' Hitler turned his back on them. He said over his shoulder, 'Now that you've got the American, tell the TeNo to put out the fires. It's a little warm in here.'

Koder rushed into the room and bent to grab Jack Cray's legs to pull him away. Dietrich put his pistol into his belt. When Cray's eyes fluttered open, Müller viciously kicked him in the head. An SS guard stepped into the bedroom to take Cray's other leg. He and Koder dragged the American into the corridor.

Gestapo Müller followed. In the antechamber he ordered Koder, 'Do it near the south end of the Chancellery. A bullet in his head. Take the body to a pit in the Tiergarten.' He turned back into the bunker's central corridor and was quickly lost in the smoke.

Agent Koder and the guard pulled Cray feet first up the stairs, the American's head bouncing on each step. Limping from the shrapnel wound, Otto Dietrich followed them up.

TeNo men and SS guards rushed about in the haze. General Eberhardt gulped air through his gas mask. He had done his job. Had caught the American commando. It had been close, sure. But the Führer was alive. Eberhardt was giddy with relief.

Cray had turned into the Führer's room, was bringing his pistol round and hadn't seen Eberhardt standing near the pedestal bust to his right. Eberhardt had fired his pistol, but the general had never been much of a shot. He missed. But then damned if he hadn't simply snatched the bust and lashed out at the commando. Smashed it twice into Cray's head. And down went the American.

THE LAST RESCUE SQUAD member to enter the bunker could see no better than any of the others, with the smoke acting as a film across his eyes, so he turned right and took six steps to the wall, then followed it past the cloakroom door and the conference-room door to the third door.

Like other TeNo troops, he wore a herringbone white uniform. The gas mask hid his face. He walked into the room. No one else was in the study. He stepped over ruined furniture and blackened pieces of maps and reports and walked into Hitler's bedroom.

The Führer was sitting on the blue sofa, a small mask covering his face, with a tube to an oxygen bottle on a stand near his feet. He was wearing the field-grey jacket that symbolised his role as supreme commander of the German armed forces. Hitler flicked his hand to dismiss the rescue squad member, silently indicating he did not need help. He turned back to the document in his hand.

Then Jack Cray removed his gas mask. He brought out a pistol from the folds of the rescue squad uniform.

Hitler looked up again. He pulled off the mask and put it aside. His face was blank. With difficulty, he stood.

'You are back. The Vassy Chateau killer,' the Führer said, his voice echoing in the concrete room. The Iron Cross on his chest, won during the Great War, testified to his bravery. He showed it now. 'You got past them all again. How did you do it?'

Jack Cray smiled. He fired the pistol. The sound was a flat clap. A hole opened between Hitler's eyes, and his brains dappled the portrait of Frederick the Great. Hitler collapsed to the blue sofa, his arm hanging to the floor, blood streaking the fabric.

Cray spun to a movement at the corner of his eye, bringing the pistol round. A soft cry came from a woman in a blue print dress who had appeared from the adjacent dressing room. She flew across the room to the body, ignoring the killer.

Cray returned the gas mask to his head, then backed out of the room and sidestepped the table in the study.

An SS guard rushed into the room. 'What's happened?' he demanded.

'The Führer,' Cray yelled. He re-entered the central corridor and was instantly lost in the smoke. A scream came from down the hall, then an answering scream and a shout for order.

Cray pushed across the hall—he had been told the route with precision—to the opposite wall, where he turned right. The SS crew had failed to prise open the steel door and were looking about for further instructions, one holding the crowbar. A guard held a submachine gun pointed at the door in front of him.

'New code,' Cray said. He pressed the buzzer. Five short, two long.

Instantly bolts scraped and the door opened. Wearing a mask, Ulrich Kahr stepped into the hall. He cried, 'The ventilators have failed. Where's the mechanic?'

Gestapo Müller rushed past the SS guard. He stabbed a pistol at Kahr. 'You. I'm taking you upstairs.'

Cray shot the Gestapo chief in the stomach. Müller folded and sank to the floor. The guard saw Cray's gun hand come round and ducked back into the smoke. Cray yanked Sergeant Kahr towards the exit. From somewhere in the smoke, a submachine gun fired. Bullets pocked the wall where Cray had been an instant before. Shrieks and shouts came from all directions.

Cray was four steps from the stairwell door, Kahr on his heels, when a hand found Cray's shoulder.

'You,' Eberhardt demanded. 'Where did you come from?'

Cray stepped up to the general so that their noses almost touched and stabbed the pistol barrel at Eberhardt's solar plexus.

'Say another word and I'll kill you,' Cray spat. 'Go out of the door and up the stairs.'

Eberhardt turned for the door, Cray and Kahr right behind. Cray's pistol disappeared into his uniform. They walked through the haze into the stairwell, past the SS guards, who did not give them a look because they were peering through the smoke into the corridor trying to discover the source of the resurgent furore.

At ground level in the blockhouse, the pistol was in Cray's hand again. 'Go back down the stairs, General.'

Eberhardt did not look relieved at the dismissal. 'I have failed to protect the Führer, haven't I? I have failed in my duty.'

The American grinned. 'And will you count to a hundred before you alert anybody?'

The general started down the stairs, but turned back to Cray. 'What did you do to Inspector Dietrich?'

Another smile from Cray. 'Go back down the stairs, General.'

Cray and Kahr waited thirty seconds before stepping through the blockhouse door into the smoke-blanketed garden. The guards, nervously pacing at their posts, speculating about the grey-green smoke rising from the bunker, were indifferent to the rescue squad man and the Wehrmacht sergeant who walked past them and then across the garden towards the vehicle entrance.

 # FIFTEEN

Cray stepped into a foyer in the ruined west end of the Chancellery. He held up a hand, indicating that Sergeant Kahr should wait for him there. Then he opened a door and walked into an office, pushing aside rubble hanging from the splintered first floor.

Otto Dietrich was holding his pistol on Rudolf Koder and the SS guard who had helped Koder drag Cray up to the garden. Koder and the guard were sitting on the edges of chairs. Koder was wearing his own handcuffs behind his back, and the guard was wearing Dietrich's. Koder glared malignantly at Dietrich.

'So you got back into the bunker?' Dietrich asked.

'In and out like grain through a goose.'

Koder's voice was tight with hatred and fury. 'You are a traitor, Dietrich. A traitor to the Fatherland.'

Cray lifted a finger towards Koder. 'Know this fellow, Inspector?'
Dietrich nodded. 'His name is Rudolf Koder, a Gestapo agent.
He is my case officer. He had my wife arrested and sent to a camp,
where she came down with typhoid fever and died. He almost killed
me, reduced me to nothing, nothing human. I'd like to shoot the
bastard.' The detective spoke slowly. 'But I've spent too much of my
life hunting down murderers to kill somebody in cold blood. It
would haunt me for the rest of my life.'

'It's not going to bother me at all.' Out came Cray's pistol. He
pulled the trigger, and Koder bucked back in the chair, then spilled
sideways. Blood pumped from the hole in his chest.

'What about the other one?' Cray asked. 'The SS trooper?'

'I don't know him,' Dietrich said. 'Never seen him before.'

Cray wagged his pistol at the trooper. 'Lucky for you, eh?'

The American used a key to unlock the trooper's handcuffs from
one hand. He attached one cuff to an exposed pipe.

The American picked up a large pack and slipped it onto his
shoulders, then led Otto Dietrich through the wing's maze of ruin.

As they reached Sergeant Kahr in the lobby, the all clear sounded,
and Cray looked at his wristwatch. 'There'll be another air raid in
thirty minutes. We'd better be there.'

He didn't say where, and Dietrich and Kahr had to satisfy
themselves with following him. They turned south to Leipzigerstrasse,
past the Hotel Esplanade, heading for the Tiergarten.

They were walking through a sea of rubble. On both sides of them
fire-blackened building façades stood like tombstones.

Dietrich stepped round a pile of books. 'Agent Koder was right.
I'm a traitor to the Fatherland.'

'Maybe so.' Cray led them round a truck lying on its side.

Dietrich raised his voice in exasperation. 'Isn't it incumbent on
you to argue that I'm a patriot and not a traitor?'

'It's incumbent on me to see that we don't die in the next few
minutes. I'll worry about your feelings later.'

They crossed Tiergartenstrasse and entered the park.

'Slow down,' Dietrich said, panting. 'My leg is killing me.' He
grabbed Cray's arm. 'I want you to listen to me for a minute, without
any of your ghastly American optimism or stupid jokes.' The air-raid
sirens began again, drifting over the Tiergarten. 'The Reich killed my
wife. She died in front of my eyes. It didn't break my loyalty to the
Fatherland. Not then. I pushed it aside, chasing you, doing my job.'

Cray was looking round, searching for the SS or the Gestapo.

'Listen to me, damn it.' Dietrich wet his lips. 'But my rage worked like a worm inside me. When I saw Koder was about to shoot you, I broke. And I knew how to strike back. Through you. So I drew my pistol on Koder and the guard, and let you go back down into the bunker with Koder's pistol.'

'I'm touched, really. Now let's get to the airstrip.'

Cray led them to an area west of Bellevue Allee, a road that cut diagonally across the Tiergarten. A short landing strip was wedged between craters. The strip had been cut into the park at the beginning of the war, and bulldozers immediately repaired the runway each time it was bombed. Cray, Dietrich and Kahr approached a copse of shattered trees, their trunks broken and split.

Katrin stepped from the trees. She was not carrying anything. Cray knew then that he had failed to convince her to leave Berlin.

Cray said, 'I'm glad you've come.'

'To say goodbye.' She paused, then added, 'And I didn't have anything else to do.'

Cray slipped the pack off his shoulders and unbuttoned it. 'Put on these shirts.' He handed the Germans large white dress shirts and began putting on one himself.

Kahr looked nervously across the park to the ruined buildings on Tiergartenstrasse. 'These white shirts will make us conspicuous.'

'Anyone not wearing a white shirt, or any vehicle that approaches our plane, is going to have trouble.' Cray's shirt—from the countess's rack of unclaimed tailoring—was much brighter than his rescue squad uniform. The tails hung out. Katrin declined to put on a shirt.

She shook her head. Dietrich held out the white shirt. 'I'm not going, either.'

'The Gestapo is going to hunt you down if you remain here.' Cray buttoned his shirt. 'And then there'll be the Russians after the Gestapo is gone.'

'I'm not going to England or the United States. I'm a German.'

'You'll be a dead German if you don't come along.'

'I have a few places I can hide.'

Cray argued, 'You can't hide from the Gestapo. There's no point martyring yourself when the end of the war is so near.'

Dietrich shook his head. 'I'm not going.'

Cray said only, 'Suit yourself.'

'There they are.' Ulrich Kahr pointed north.

The wind had torn great windows in the smoke. A bomber wing was approaching from the north. The B-17s were escorted by a dozen or more fighters, P-51 Mustangs. The roar of their Rolls-Royce Merlin engines raced out ahead of them.

Dietrich looked back at Tiergartenstrasse. 'Cray, they've found us.' Two black cars were winding round the rubble.

'A bulletin must have gone out from the bunker.' Dietrich pulled out his pistol. It looked tiny and useless in his hand.

'Where's our plane?' Kahr demanded.

The cars had jumped a kerb and were crossing the park. A side window came down in the leading car, a Horch, and out came a hand holding a pistol.

'Where's our plane, damn it?' Ulrich Kahr yelled. 'Where's the plane you said would be here?'

It dropped out of the sky from a parting bank of smoke, smaller and nimbler than the usual hardware over Berlin. It fluttered down, resembling a leaf in autumn. A twin-engined transport made by Douglas and called the Skytrain.

Kahr's head jerked left and right, searching for an avenue of escape. 'They're a hundred metres away. Eighty metres.'

'Don't worry about those Gestapo agents.'

'What?' Kahr exclaimed furiously. 'Do something.'

Cray smiled. 'They aren't wearing white shirts.'

The first Horch was fifty metres from Cray when the ground near it began to bubble. Clots of dirt burst into the air. Then the projectiles found the car and cut it in half from side to side, ripping through metal and glass and upholstery and flesh. The Mustang pilot lingered with the car in his sights, letting .50-calibre bullets reduce the vehicle to scraps. Then the fighter soared overhead.

Gestapo agents bailed out of the second car, but they were too late. The second Mustang in the strafing formation loosed long bursts at the car and all round it. Limbs and heads and trunks were pierced through and flicked into the air; then the car was shredded. The petrol tank burst and doused the remains in fire.

The Skytrain miraculously pulled out of its dive and plopped down on the runway.

Cray held out his arms and Katrin stepped into them. She tucked her chin into his neck and held him round his shoulders. 'Goodbye, Jack,' she whispered. Her tears were on his neck.

Cray's arm jerked. Katrin's head bounced forwards, and she

slumped into Cray's arms. In his hand was his pistol. He had just sent the butt into her temple.

'Help me,' he ordered.

When Cray started dragging her, Kahr lifted her legs. They carried her to the Skytrain, then handed her up to two crewmen.

Cray returned to Dietrich. The detective said, 'You're doing her a favour, taking her out of here.'

Cray said quietly, so that Dietrich had to lean forwards to hear, 'I'm not doing it for her. I'm doing it for me.' He scratched his chin. 'You know, I don't have a lot of friends.'

'That's entirely understandable,' Dietrich replied, a bit stiffly.

'I'd hate to lose one.' The pistol appeared in Cray's hand again, and he lashed out with it, slamming the butt against Dietrich's temple. Cray caught the detective as he fell and they retraced their route towards the Skytrain.

Ulrich Kahr climbed through the Skytrain's hatch, then turned to pull up Dietrich. Cray shoved and prodded, and between the two of them Dietrich was put quickly into a flight seat.

The pilot turned to look at them as they strapped themselves in. 'Who is that? I wasn't told about a third man.'

'He's a friend of mine,' Cray announced.

The pilot wound up the engine, and the Skytrain started down the runway. It bounced once, then again, and lifted into the air.

Cray looked at Dietrich. The side of the detective's head round his ear was purpling. 'Though he might not know it yet.'

AS THE SKYTRAIN sank towards the airstrip at Wittenberg—field headquarters of the US Ninth Army—Sergeant Kahr began rocking back and forth in his seat, as if that might hurry the plane. His forehead was pressed against the side window.

Cray opened and closed his jaw against the increasing air pressure. Otto Dietrich was slumped in his seat, rubbing his temple. Katrin was pressing a towel to her head and glaring at Cray. When she had come round, he had told her—with a grin that gave the lie to his words—that a Russian mortar round had blacked her out. He could hardly just leave her lying there on the runway.

The Skytrain touched down, then taxied towards the north end of the field, where three soldiers stood, two with M-1s and the third in a tattered Wehrmacht uniform.

'That's him,' Kahr shouted. 'That's Max. My God, look how thin he is.' Kahr turned in his seat to look at Cray. 'You did it, by God. You sprang him from the Bolshevik camp.' Kahr might have been about to add his thanks, but his eyes were abruptly damp and he could say no more. He shouldered open the door and leaned out of the plane until the Skytrain had stopped. Then he leapt to the ground and sprinted towards his son.

The pilot braked the plane into a half-circle, then shoved the accelerator knob forwards. The Skytrain bumped down the runway until its wheels lost contact with the ground once again.

Cray looked down as the plane banked north. Kahr and his son were still standing next to the airstrip in each other's arms.

THE SKYTRAIN WAS HEADING for the airfield near Eastwell Manor in Kent. Cray could see the rose garden, the topiary bushes and the fountains. The pilot said something into his radio.

'They'll never let it out,' Dietrich said abruptly.

'What?' Cray asked.

'That the Führer was assassinated. It doesn't fit into the legend. They'll say he committed suicide.' Dietrich thought again about the pretty blonde woman. She knew Hitler had died at the hands of an assassin rather than by noble suicide. Dietrich suspected she would never leave the bunker alive.

Cray shrugged. 'What're your plans, Inspector? Where are you going to go?'

'You mean I'm not a prisoner of war?'

'Why would you be a POW? You're a policeman, not a soldier.'

Dietrich said, just above the sound of the Skytrain's engines, 'Then I'll be a policeman. That's all I know how to do. I'll go back after things settle down. Maybe work for the occupation forces. They'll need homicide detectives in Berlin after the war.'

Cray said, 'The war won't have made much difference to murderers, I suppose.'

'And you won't be in Berlin, so it'll be safer.'

'I'm going back to Wenatchee, Washington. I inherited an apple orchard there,' Cray said. 'Katrin is coming with me. To help me out in the orchard. Eat some of my cooking. See what happens.'

'What?' from the back seat.

'You're coming with me to Wenatchee.'

'Wenatchee? I can't even pronounce the name.'

'It's a good idea, it seems to me.'

'A stupid idea,' she said, but without heat. 'Me, helping you grow apples in rural America?' She laughed. 'A crazy notion. Besides, I can just barely tolerate you.'

'I grow on people.' Cray grinned. 'I can be a pretty good convincer. All we need is a little time together.'

'I've already spent a little time with you. It seemed like half a century.' But her eyes were pensive. He looked back at her. That optimistic and brash American face. That battered face. Someone who cared for her, even if he was crazy. And an American.

She exhaled suddenly, loudly, her mind running away from her, running into absurd territory. Those wild thoughts, and what they revealed to her about her heart, had a force which pushed her back into her chair, as if the plane were taking off rather than landing.

The plane touched down on the ploughed field, and the ruts grabbed the wheels and guided the Skytrain along to the three men waiting. The pilot shut down the engine.

The pilot was first out of the plane, followed by Dietrich.

Cray had a foot on the ladder, ready to climb down, when Katrin touched his shoulder. 'What kind of apples, did you say?'

While the plot of *Five Past Midnight*, with its highly imaginative variation on the closing events of the Second World War, is pure fiction, the final scenes are rooted in fact—inspired by the actual structure of Hitler's last refuge, as Seattle-based author James Thayer explains.

'I visited West Berlin and climbed onto a platform that looked over the Wall into the wasteland beyond. All you can see now of the bunker is a grass-covered mound. The authorities weren't able to rip out the building, so they filled it in and grassed it over. But plans of the layout are easy to get hold of—they're in lots of books.

'There was a ventilation system in the bunker just like the one I describe in *Five Past Midnight*. But I got the idea for the fire from something I learned during my student days. I was working in a grain elevator—that's a huge, tall installation where the harvest is stored. As grain passes through the machinery, it creates a lot of very fine, flour-like dust. And if parts of it aren't cleaned adequately, a single spark can ignite the dust and cause an explosion and fire—just as it does in my novel.'

James Thayer's aim in his portrayal of Adolf Hitler was to make him more than just a two-dimensional stereotype of evil. 'We have to come to terms,' he explains, 'with the fact that such terrible villainy can be the work of a human being. That's why, in one scene, I have the Führer wink at our German hero. It's a ghastly notion that he's capable of such a whimsical gesture, given everything he's done. In another he takes off his gloves and, in a gesture of kindness, gives them to a soldier in the garden.'

The author, whose previous novel, *White Star*, was a huge success in Condensed Books, is now at work a new book involving an air crash caused by a bomb.

Only Love
Erich Segal

In Paris, in 1978, Dr Matthew Hillier met the woman of his dreams. Together they served as doctors in Ethiopia, providing voluntary medical care.

Now, eighteen years later, Matt is at the top of his profession—and alone. Unable to come to terms with Silvia's sudden, unexplained disappearance from his life, he has buried himself in his work.

Then, out of the blue, Silvia returns.

PROLOGUE

I have a terrible confession to make.

When I learned Silvia was dying I was not completely unhappy.

I know this may seem inhuman—especially from a doctor. But then I can't think of her as just another patient. In fact when I first heard she was coming to see me after all this time, I almost imagined it was a gesture of reconciliation.

I wonder what's going on in her mind. Does she regard our impending reunion merely as a last desperate attempt to save her life? Or perhaps, before the darkness falls, does she long to see me again as much as I long to see her?

And what about her husband? Even in the unlikely event that she hasn't told him about our relationship years ago, she would certainly have to *now*.

Whatever his feelings, he would be unable to prevent us from meeting. After all, he was a man accustomed to having the best in the world, and I guess in this field I am number one.

She is two years younger than I, a mere forty-three years old. And, judging even from the most recent newspaper articles, still very beautiful. She looks too radiant, too *alive* to be seriously ill. To me, she has always been the quintessence of the life force.

In our first telephone conversation, Rinaldi is polite and formal. Though speaking of his wife there is no trace of emotion in his voice. He takes for granted that I will be instantly at his disposal.

'Mrs Rinaldi has a brain tumour—can you see her right away?'

For all his arrogance I can sense an implicit acknowledgment that I have a power he does not possess. Consummate businessman that he is, he still cannot outbargain the Angel of Death. And that is a source of satisfaction.

Suddenly, almost as an afterthought and with a barely perceptible break in his voice, he adds, 'Please.'

I had to help. Both of them.

THE NOTES AND X-RAYS reached my office within the hour. As soon as I was alone, I tore open the envelope thinking, irrationally, that there might be something recognisably Silvia inside.

But of course these were only various high-tech images of her brain. And then the physician in me grew angry. Even the earliest scans showed evidence of neoplasm. What kind of people had she consulted? I leafed quickly through the notes but it was the usual antiseptic medical jargon. The patient, a forty-one-year-old married white female, first came to one Professor Luca Vingiano complaining of severe headaches. He attributed the cause to emotional stress and prescribed tranquillisers.

But then he had let slip a bit of personal detail. Evidently there was some unspecified tension in Silvia's life. Perhaps self-servingly, I immediately assumed that it involved her marriage.

For though she appeared with her husband in photos as a kind of marital ornament, she always seemed deliberately to exist on the margin of his life. Nico, by contrast, was a far more public person. His multinational colossus, FAMA, in addition to being Italy's largest car manufacturer, included construction, steelworks, insurance and publishing.

At various times there had been rumours in the press linking him with one or another talented younger woman. But the photographs were all shot at charity occasions, so this may have been mere scabrous speculation. Eminence always attracts gossip. I myself had achieved enough success in my field to know that.

Whatever the reality, the suggestion was like a lit match for the dry tinderwood of my emotions and I chose to ascribe the anxiety noted by the professor to Silvia's husband's alienated affections.

I forced myself to read on.

She had languished for an unconscionably long time before Vingiano took her seriously and sent her to a London neurologist with a 'Sir' before his name and an international reputation behind it. He found the tumour all right but adjudged it to be inoperable. Indeed, there was no way that the most skilled pair of hands could manoeuvre the tiniest microsurgical instrument and not cause serious damage. Or, more likely, kill her.

This made me the last resort. And it was an uncomfortable feeling. True, the genetic technique I pioneered had several times succeeded in reversing tumour growth by replicating the DNA with the fault corrected. Yet, now, for the first time, I fully understood why doctors are not meant to treat people close to them. I suddenly lost faith in my abilities, painfully aware of my own fallibility. I did not want Silvia as a patient.

Scarcely fifteen minutes after the envelope had reached me, the phone rang. 'Well, Dr Hiller, what do you think?'

'I'm sorry, I haven't had time to review the whole history.'

'Wouldn't a quick glance at her latest scans tell you everything you need to know?'

Obviously he was right. 'Mr Rinaldi, I'm afraid I agree with your doctor in London. This kind of growth is incurable.'

'Except by you,' he countered insistently. I guess I was waiting for him to say it. 'Can you see her today?'

Reflexively, I glanced in my diary. Why even look when I knew I would accede to his demands? 'How about two?' I proposed.

I should have guessed Nico would try for a better deal. 'Our apartment is only minutes away. We can be there immediately.'

'All right.' I surrendered with a sigh. Let's get it over with.

Five minutes later my secretary buzzed to announce the arrival of Mr and Mrs Rinaldi. My heart began to race. Within seconds my office doors would open—and with them a torrent of memories.

I saw him first: tall, imposing and intense. Receding hairline. He acknowledged me with a saturnine nod and presented his wife as if introducing her for the first time.

I stared at Silvia's face. At first it seemed unchanged by time. Her eyes were the same black flames, though they were deliberately avoiding mine. I could not decipher her emotions, but I gradually became aware that something was different.

Perhaps it was my imagination, but there seemed to be a weariness and nonspecific sadness that was not related to her illness.

I moved forward awkwardly (or so it seemed) and heard her murmur, 'It's good to see you again.'

Paris, spring 1978. Those of us who survived the initial third degree, and the rigorous training that followed, would be rewarded by being sent to Africa to risk our lives and save others. It was my first trip outside America.

Our flight arrived just as day was breaking. Ten thousand feet below, the city was stirring, like a sensuous woman shaking off the languor of sleep in the early-morning light.

Two hours later, I bounded up the steps from the Métro into the very centre of St-Germain-des-Prés, which pulsated with the *musique concrète* of the rush-hour traffic. I glanced nervously at my watch—only fifteen minutes to go. I checked my street map for the final time and then sprinted like mad all the way to the headquarters of Médecine Internationale, an architectural antique on the rue des Sts-Pères.

I arrived sweaty but just in time.

'Sit down, Dr Hiller.' François Pelletier, the irascible grand inquisitor, was a dead ringer for Don Quixote, including the wispy beard. The only difference was his shirt, open nearly to the navel. And the cigarette dangling from his bony fingers.

Appropriately enough, he was flanked by a balding Sancho Panza type—who scribbled compulsively on a pad, and was later introduced to me as Maurice Hermans—and a well-upholstered Dutchwoman in her early thirties.

From the moment the interview began, it was obvious that François had a chip on his shoulder about Americans, holding them collectively responsible for all the ills of mankind from nuclear waste to high cholesterol. He bombarded me with hostile questions about every microscopic aspect of my life. At first I responded politely but, when it became clear there was no end in sight, I began to retort sarcastically. For example, why did I not burn my draft card during the Vietnam War? I answered by asking if he had burned *his* when the French were fighting there before us.

He quickly changed the subject and we continued volleying unpleasantries.

'Tell me, Dr Hiller, do you know where Ethiopia is?'

'Don't insult my intelligence, François.'

'What if I told you that three other Americans I interviewed thought it was in South America.'

'Then you shouldn't bother with them.'

'You're right there.' He now jumped to his feet and began to pace. Then suddenly stopped and fired, 'Imagine you are in a run-down field hospital, in the wilds of Africa, miles from everything you ever knew as civilisation. How would you keep your sanity?'

'Bach,' I answered, unblinking.

'What?'

'Johann Sebastian—or any of his relatives for that matter.'

'Ah yes. From your c.v. I gather you're quite a musician. Unfortunately, our clinics don't include pianos.'

'That's OK. I can play in my head and get the same buzz. I've got a practice keyboard I can take. It doesn't make any noise. It'll keep my fingers nimble while the music keeps my soul in shape.'

For the first time that morning I seemed to have short-circuited the electric current of antagonism.

'Well,' he mused, 'you haven't cracked up yet.'

'You sound disappointed.'

François fixed me with his gaze then queried, 'How about filth? Starvation? Appalling diseases? How would they affect you?'

'I've done my year in the pits. I think I can take every conceivable medical horror show.'

'Leprosy? Smallpox?'

'I admit I've never seen either. Are you trying to turn me off?'

'In a way,' he conceded, leaning conspiratorially closer. 'Because if you're going to freak out, it's a lot better to do it here than in the middle of Africa.'

The Dutchwoman suddenly decided to put her two cents in.

'Tell me, why would you want to go to the Third World when you could be making house calls on Park Avenue?'

'How does wanting to help people grab you?'

'Fairly predictable,' Sancho commented as he took it down. 'Can't you come up with anything more original?'

I was rapidly losing my patience—and my temper.

'Frankly, you guys disappoint me. I thought Médecine Internationale was full of altruistic doctors. Not cynics.'

The three interrogators looked at one another, and then François turned to me and asked bluntly, 'Now, what about sex?'

'Not here, François. Not in front of everybody,' I retorted. By this time I didn't give a damn.

His minions broke into laughter and he did too. 'That also answers my most important question, Matthew. You have a sense of humour.' He reached out his hand. 'Welcome aboard.'

The three-week orientation course began two days later. Meanwhile, I would see the glories of Paris.

I checked into the Left Bank dump they had reserved for the candidates and decided it had atmosphere. It was one of those fleapits in which every room, I'm sure, was a garret and every bedspring creaked. Maybe François had chosen it to toughen us for the trip.

My brother Chaz had told me that it was impossible to get a bad meal in Paris. And he was absolutely right. I ate in a place called Le Petit Zinc, where you picked your meal from all sorts of exotic crustaceans displayed downstairs, which they then served on the upper floors.

The next two days were a shock to my system. Trying to see the artistic treasures of Paris in so short a time is like trying to swallow an elephant in one gulp. But I gave it my best. From dawn till well after dusk, I absorbed the city through every pore.

OF COURSE I REMEMBER the exact date: Monday, April 3, 1978. Yet it started like any other morning: I shaved and showered, selected my coolest shirt (blue button-down, short-sleeved) and then headed for the rue des Sts-Pères and Operation Ethiopia, Day One. By now I had recovered my confidence and sharpened my ideals and was ready for anything.

Except the emotional ambush awaiting me.

Most of the others were already there, chattering over paper cups of coffee. Between puffs on his cigarette, François introduced me to four French candidates—one a fairly attractive female—and two Dutchmen, one wearing a ten-gallon hat.

And Silvia.

I stopped breathing. She was a poem without words. Exquisite.

She wore jeans, a sweatshirt and no make-up. Her long black hair was pulled back in a ponytail. But this attempt at plainness didn't fool anyone.

'Don't hold Silvia's looks against her, Matthew. She's such an astute diagnostician that I picked her even though her grandfather was a Nazi and her father causes lung cancer,' François said.

'Hi,' I managed, though in oxygen debt. 'I can understand the sins of the grandfather, but what would make her dad carcinogenic?'

'Simple,' François grinned. 'His last name is Dalessandro.'

'You mean head of FAMA—the Italian car makers?'

'The very same. Arch-polluters of the highways and byways. Not to mention the chemical waste they produce.'

I looked at her and asked, 'Is he pulling my leg again?'

'No—guilty as charged,' she allowed. 'But notice that the latter-day St Luke forgot to mention that my ecologically delinquent father fought with the *American* army during the war. Where are you from, Matthew?'

'By coincidence another automotive capital: Dearborn, Michigan. Only my name's not Ford.'

'Lucky you. Coming from a well-known—or in my case notorious—family can sometimes be a drag.'

Pointing to me, François confided mischievously to her, 'By the way, Silvia, watch out for this character. He tries to come across as a simple clodhopper from the cornfields. But he's a serious pianist, and speaks Italian.'

'Really?' She looked at me, sort of impressed.

'It's nowhere near as fluent as your English. But I really needed the language to major in music.'

'Ah, *un amante dell'opera*,' she murmured appreciatively.

'You too?'

'Madly. But when you're born in Milan, you grow up crazy about two things: soccer and opera.'

At this moment François bellowed, 'Now everybody sit down and shut up.' Suddenly the banter ceased and we each grabbed a seat. François revved up: 'Let me make a prediction. Whoever doesn't already dislike me will absolutely hate my guts by the end of the first week in the field. It's going to be hot, stressful and dangerous. The conditions you'll encounter are like nothing you've ever known. Before this civil war, Ethiopia was already one of the

145

poorest countries in the world. The people live in a perpetual state of starvation, cxacerbated by endless years of drought. It's a fully fledged nightmare.' He took a breath and then said, 'Now, appropriately enough, we'll start with the plague.'

Project No. 62 of Médecine Internationale was under way.

SILVIA WAS NEVER ALONE. She was like the Pied Piper, moving with a swarm of admirers of both sexes wherever she went. Yet I soon realised how heavily escorted she was—in a rather sinister sense. On the first Friday I happened to arrive early. As I glanced casually out of the window, Silvia entered the building, and I noticed that in addition to her usual bevy of groupies there was a huge, barrel-chested, middle-aged guy trailing about a hundred yards behind her. I got the eerie sensation that he was stalking her.

During our half-hour lunch break, we all hung around eating filled baguettes. Silvia went down the block to buy a newspaper. And then, moments before we were about to resume, I saw her coming back. Further up the street, I recognised the same man watching her intently.

At the end of the afternoon session, when a bunch of us returned to the 'Termite Hilton', as we had dubbed it, I boldly asked Silvia if she would join me for a drink and a brief chat about a private matter. She agreed amicably enough and we repaired to a little *bistro à vin* two doors away.

'So,' she smiled, as I squeezed into our narrow booth carrying a white wine in each hand. 'What's happening?'

'Silvia, I don't want to upset you . . .' I hesitated. 'But I think someone's following you.'

'I know.' She was totally unfazed. 'There always is. My father's worried about something happening to me.'

'You mean the guy's your bodyguard?'

'Sort of. But I prefer to think of Nino as my fairy godfather. Anyway, Papa's not paranoid. I'm sorry to say there are genuine reasons . . .' Her voice trailed off.

I suddenly recalled reading about her mother's abduction and murder many years ago. It was worldwide news.

'Hey,' I mumbled apologetically, 'I'm sorry I asked. We can go back to the group now.'

'What's the rush? Let's finish our wine and gossip for a bit. Do you follow NBA basketball?'

'Not very closely. Why do you ask?'

'Well, FAMA has its own professional team in the European League. Every year we recruit players who get cut from the NBA. I was hoping that you'd noticed one of the Detroit Pistons who might still have a few minor-league seasons in him. That's one thing I'm going to miss in Africa. Whenever the boys played in England, my father flew over and took me to watch.'

'What did you do in England between games?'

'I studied there for nearly ten years after my mother died. I did my MD at Cambridge.'

'What are you specialising in?'

'I haven't made up my mind. But it'll probably be something like paediatric surgery. And you?'

'Well, at first I was attracted by the scalpel too. But I believe it will be obsolete in a few years and it'll all be done by genetic techniques. That's where I'd like to end up eventually. So, after Africa, I'll probably do a Ph.D. in something like microbiology. Anyway, I'm looking forward to this adventure, aren't you?'

'Well, just between the two of us, I sometimes wonder if I'll be able to cope.'

'Don't worry. François wouldn't have picked you if he didn't think you could handle the rough stuff.'

And, for the first time, I sensed that beneath that flawless exterior there were little fireflies of doubt. It was nice to know that she was human.

As we walked out of the door, I saw Nino leaning against a parking meter, 'reading a newspaper'.

'By the way, Silvia, is he coming to Ethiopia with us too?'

'No, thank heavens. Actually, being totally on my own will be a new experience for me.'

'Well, if it means anything, you can tell your father that I'll be there to protect you.'

She seemed to appreciate what I said. She smiled at me and, in so doing, destroyed all my autoimmune reactions to falling in love with her.

TOWARDS THE END of the second week of our course there was a once-in-a-lifetime event at the Opéra de Paris Garnier. A legendary soprano would be singing Violetta in *La Traviata* for the last time. I faked a couple of symptoms and left the seminar early to line up for standing-room tickets.

147

Needless to say, I was not the only person in Paris who wanted to see the performance. There seemed to be enough people ahead of me to fill every one of the two thousand-odd seats in the theatre. Around six thirty, when the queue had moved a mere twenty places and things were looking increasingly glum, I heard a female voice call out, 'Matthew, I thought you weren't feeling well?'

Caught in the act! I turned to see that it was none other than Signorina Perfect. She had loosened her austere workaday hairdo, letting the locks cascade onto her shoulders. She wore a simple black dress which revealed considerably more leg than her usual jeans. In short, she was stunning.

'I'm OK,' I explained, 'but I just had to see this opera. It doesn't look like I'm going to make it.'

'Well then, join me. My father's company has a box here.'

'I'd love to. But are you sure I'm not a little overdressed?' I indicated my frayed denim shirt and corduroy trousers.

'I'm the only one who'll see. Come on.' She took my hand and led me up the great marble staircase. As I feared, I was the only man not wearing a dinner jacket or tails. But then, I consoled myself, I was invisible. I mean, who could notice me when at my side I had the Venus de Milano?

A uniformed bellboy led us down a hushed corridor to a wooden door which opened into a crimson velvet box. We overlooked a high proscenium arch. In the centre of the vaulted auditorium was the opera house's fabled chandelier hanging from a gold-circled ceiling painted by Chagall.

I was in heaven as the orchestra tuned up. We sat in the two front seats, where a half-bottle of champagne awaited us. Calling upon years of experience as a waiter, I poured us each a glassful without losing a bubble.

'To my host,' I toasted. 'Fabbrica Milanese Automobili,' adding, 'and those nearest and dearest to the management.'

She laughed appreciatively.

As the lights began to dim, the bearlike Nino (also in a tux) entered and sat discreetly at the back.

'Do you know *La Traviata* well?' Silvia asked.

'*Mezzo, mezzo*,' I replied. 'I wrote a paper on it in college. And yesterday after class I spent about an hour playing through it.'

'Oh, where did you find a piano?'

'I just made like I was shopping in La Voix de Son Maître, took the score down from the shelf and started tinkling on one of their Steinways. Fortunately, they didn't throw me out.'

'I'd love to have been there.'

'We can go there tomorrow if you'd really like. The manager gave me an open invitation.'

'That's a promise, Matthew.' She raised her glass as if thanking me in advance. Her smile shone in the darkening theatre.

The opening chorus, *'Libiamo ne' lieti calici'* ('Let's drink up in happy goblets'), aptly reflected my state of mind. And even though I was intoxicated by the soprano's magical stage presence, I regularly stole glances at Silvia.

Half an hour later the heroine, Violetta, stood alone onstage and sang *'Ah fors' è lui'* ('Perhaps he is the one') recognising that, despite her many affairs, she was genuinely in love for the first time in her life, with Alfredo. As the Act I curtain descended to rapturous applause, another lackey appeared with canapés. Being a guest, I felt obliged to contribute something intellectual.

'Do you realise in that entire first act there wasn't even a single break in the music, no recitative, and not even a real aria till "*Ah fors' è lui*"?'

'I didn't even notice.'

'That's the whole trick. Verdi was diabolically clever.'

'So, apparently, is my companion this evening.'

The lights dimmed again and the tragedy began to unfold. There was a thunderous chord on the brass as Violetta realised she was doomed: 'O Lord! to die so young.' And finally the singer fainted, only to revive again long enough to sing an incredible high B flat— and immediately die from the effort.

The audience were so transported they were almost afraid to break the spell. Then, as the ripples of applause crescendoed into a tidal wave of adulation, I suddenly felt Silvia's hand in mine. I looked at her. She was in tears.

'I'm sorry, Matthew. I know I'm being silly.'

I placed my other hand on top of hers. She did not move, and we remained that way until the final curtain fell.

WHEN WE EMERGED from the theatre, Silvia linked her arm in mine and proposed, 'Shall we walk?'

She made a subtle gesture to her guardian, and we set off for a nocturnal promenade through the streets of Paris as Nino followed us discreetly. Passing the many brightly lit outdoor restaurants filled with theatregoers, we discussed the soprano's artistry.

'You know, it's not just her voice,' Silvia observed. 'It's the way she breathes believable life into the character.'

'Yes, even at her age she comes across as a frail young woman. Does *Traviata* always make you cry like that?'

She nodded. 'I guess Italians are sentimental.'

'So are Americans. But I've found that I relate the sadness I'm watching to events in my own life. It's a kind of socially respectable excuse to recall old griefs.'

Her eyes told me that she understood completely. 'You know about my mother?'

'Yes.'

'Tonight, on the stage, when the doctor announced that Violetta was dead, I couldn't help remembering the moment when my father said those same words to me. But then, I don't need an artistic pretext to mourn. I still miss her terribly.'

'How has your father coped all this time?'

'Not at all, really. I mean, it's been almost fifteen years and he's still like a man under water. Occasionally we have a conversation about it, but most of the time he's submerged in his work. He just stays locked in his office, away from people.'

'Including you?'

'I think especially me.'

I wondered whether the subject was getting too difficult for her. But then she talked on. 'I was only a little girl so I could barely appreciate the things she was—the first woman editor of *La Mattina*, committed to social reform, and very brave. That's a lot to live up to. But I like to think she'd be pleased with what I've become—or at least what I'm trying to become.'

I didn't know whether to answer with the usual pious platitudes, or say what I really believed, that dead parents survive only in their children's psyches.

She sighed and gazed out over the water as we crossed the Seine at the Pont au Change. Her unhappiness was palpable.

'Hey,' I said after a moment. 'I'm sorry. I probably never should have brought this up in the first place.'

'That's OK. There's a part of me that still needs to talk about her. And the occasion of a new friend provides an acceptable excuse.'

'I hope so,' I said softly. 'I mean I hope we'll be friends.'

She reacted shyly for a moment, then answered, 'We already are.'
Suddenly glancing at her watch, she said, 'Do you know what time it
is? And I've still got two more articles to read for tomorrow's class.'

Outside our hotel, at the virtual doorstep of day, she turned to me.
'I noticed how touched you were by the opera too. Would I be right
in thinking that—'

I interrupted her insight. 'Yes. It was my father. I'll tell you about it
some time.'

I then kissed her lightly on both cheeks and retired to the privacy
of my own dreams.

I LOVED MY FATHER, but I was ashamed of him. From as early as I
can remember, he lived on an emotional seesaw. He was either on top
of the world or overwhelmed by it.

In other words, either terribly drunk or painfully sober.

Yet unfortunately, in either state, he was equally inaccessible to his
children. I couldn't bear being in his company. There is nothing
scarier for a kid than to have a parent out of control. And Henry
Hiller was this in the extreme—skydiving from responsibility without a parachute.

He was an assistant professor of literature at Cutler Junior
College in Dearborn. I think his primary goal in life was self-
destruction, and he seemed very good at it. He was so skilful that he
even let his department find out about his drinking problem just a
few months before he was to receive tenure.

The way he and Mom explained this career change to my little
brother Chaz and myself was that Dad wanted to concentrate full-
time on his writing. As he put it, 'Lots of people just dream about
producing that big book that's in all of us. But it takes real courage
to take the plunge and do it without the safety net of a job.'

My mother, on the other hand, did not call a family conference to
announce that she would be taking over as both homemaker and
breadwinner. Since her husband was 'working' late into the night,
she would get up early, prepare our breakfast and packed lunch,
drive us to school, and then go to work at the hospital where she had
once been the head surgical nurse. Now, because of her need for flex-
ibility, she had demoted herself to being a roving understudy for
whatever department was short-handed.

I tried to grow up as fast as possible to assume my share of
the burden. When I was eleven I took over making dinner.

'Compliments to the chef,' Dad said cheerfully after my maiden effort. It gave me the creeps.

Whenever Dad was in a 'good mood' at dinnertime, he would interrogate Chaz and me at length about our school work. This would make us both squirm, so I got the idea of turning the tables and encouraging him to talk about what he had written that day. For even if it were not actually committed to paper yet, he would have pondered his topic—'The Concept of the Hero'—and come up with ideas worth hearing.

Indeed, years later in college, I got an A for a paper comparing Achilles and King Lear that was practically a carbon copy of one of his more stimulating evening lectures.

I'm glad I was able to catch a glimpse of how inspiring a teacher he once must have been, and after a while began to understand the tortuous retreat he had made from life. Yet being an expert on the classics, he was so daunted by their greatness that he ultimately gave up all hope of producing anything worthwhile.

In our house, dinner was usually brief—how long does it take to eat macaroni and cheese? Dad would dematerialise with the last spoonful, leaving Chaz and me to clear the dishes. Then we would sit down at the table and I would help him with his maths.

He was having problems at school, apparently being obstreperous and not paying attention. His teacher, Mr Porter, had already written one letter home, which my father had intercepted.

'What's all this about, Chaz?'

'Nothing, nothing. The guy just picks on me, that's all.'

'Ah,' Dad remarked. 'I thought so. Some arrogant philistine. Well, I'll have to go in and set him straight.'

I desperately tried to dissuade him. 'No, Dad, you can't.'

'I beg your pardon, Matthew?' He addressed me with eyebrow raised. 'I'm still the head of this family. As a matter of fact, I think I'll see this Mr Porter tomorrow.'

I was really worried and told Mom when she arrived home late from the hospital. 'Oh Lord,' she groaned, clearly at the end of her tether. 'We can't have him doing that.'

'How can you stop him?'

She didn't answer. But later that evening Chaz appeared in his pyjamas when I was in my room studying. He motioned to me to be quiet and come out on the landing.

We stood there in the darkness like two castaways on a raft as we listened to our parents bickering acrimoniously. In the loneliness that permeated every corner of our house, I could barely see the outline of my little brother's face as he looked up to me for reassurance. I could find nothing to say.

TWO

Silvia and I were both yawning the next day. I thought I caught her sneaking me a smile, but it might have been wishful thinking. I couldn't wait to speak to her.

Our guest lecturer on typhus, Professor Jean-Michel Gottlieb, of the famous La Salpêtrière hospital, specialised in 'ancient diseases'—the ones most people think have long been eliminated, like smallpox or plague. Or leprosy, which still claims millions of sufferers in Africa and India.

Any doubts I'd had about my decision to join Médecine Internationale were eloquently reaffirmed by Gottlieb. I thought I was a real doctor, but I had never in my life treated a case of smallpox. And I had seen only one case of infantile polio—the baby of a couple who had immigrated illegally from Guatemala. Even the most destitute welfare patients I had seen in America were vaccinated.

At precisely five o'clock, Professor Gottlieb concluded his presentation and wished us all good luck.

As I was putting some order into the chaos of the notes I had scribbled all day, Silvia came up, casually put her arm on my shoulder and asked, 'Will you play for me tonight? I promise we'll study afterwards.'

'On one condition,' I stipulated. 'That I take you to dinner.'

'That's not a condition, it's a pleasure. When should we meet?'

'The hotel lobby at seven o'clock.'

'Fine. How do I dress?'

'Very nicely,' I riposted. 'See you.'

She gave me a backward wave and plunged into her waiting cluster of admirers for the homeward parade.

When I caught sight of her that evening, I was not sure what she had changed in her outfit. Then, on closer inspection, I noticed that her jeans were black instead of blue, her sweatshirt did not have any company logo and seemed to fit a little more tightly. And she was, by her standards, bejewelled: a small pearl necklace.

My own appearance was enhanced by a light blue sweater I had bought that afternoon in Galeries Lafayette.

As we started out of the door, she remarked matter-of-factly, 'I've booked the Hôtel Lutétia.'

'Sorry,' I declared, asserting my independence. '*I've* reserved Le Petit Zinc. I told you this was my—'

'No conflict, Matthew. The hotel is just for your concert.'

What? The most elegant address in the whole arrondissement? I did not know whether to be flattered or annoyed. By the time we reached Boulevard Raspail and entered the sumptuous lobby, I was beginning to feel distinctly uncomfortable. And I was downright intimidated when I entered the enormous ballroom, with a grand piano standing propped open at the far end.

'Did you rent an audience too?' I said, only half joking.

'Don't be silly. And I didn't "rent" this place either. I simply phoned and asked the manager's permission. The moment he heard who you were, he agreed right away.'

'And who am I?'

'A passionate pianist from Médecine Internationale about to go abroad where he'll be thousands of miles from the nearest keyboard. He was very impressed by your dedication.'

My mood changed from minor to major. And I felt genuinely honoured. I was suddenly consumed with the desire to play that piano. On a nearby table stood two glasses of chilled champagne. 'You?' I asked her.

She shook her head and observed, 'There's a card.' I opened the envelope and read:

Dear Doctors,
   Enjoy your musical evening and know that people everywhere admire the 'harmony' you are bringing to the less fortunate of the world.
   Bon voyage à vous deux.

                                        Louis Bergeron, Manager

With my audience of one seated comfortably in a nearby chair, I began with Bach's Prelude No. 21 in B flat—a deceptively easy piece.

When I first placed my hands on the keys, I felt a kind of shiver. Except very briefly, I had not touched a piano in nearly three weeks, and there was an almost sensual yearning to reunite with the instrument. I had not realised how much it was a part of my very being.

I had not thought out a programme in advance. I just let my psyche lead my hands and at that moment they felt like exploring Mozart's Sonata in C minor. I launched into the octaves that crisply set out the tonality of the piece. I was so hypnotically involved I forgot Silvia was there.

After I don't know how much time, I became slowly aware of my surroundings once again. I played the last few notes with a controlled passion, then let my head drop, emotionally depleted.

Silvia did not say a word, but walked over, put a hand on either side of my face, and kissed my forehead.

A few minutes later, we were walking towards the restaurant to the sound of laughter filtering into the street from cafés and bistros. Silvia still had not offered the slightest comment.

At Le Petit Zinc we selected our meal from the array of sea creatures, then went upstairs, where the waiter opened a bottle of wine for us. Silvia picked up her glass but did not drink. She seemed lost in thought. At last she began awkwardly.

'Matthew, I don't know quite how to say this. But I come from a world where anything can be bought.' She paused and then, leaning over the table, said with fire, *'Except what you just did.'*

I did not know how to respond.

'You play like an angel. You could be a professional.'

I shrugged. 'Maybe, maybe not. But the point is, you can't play Bach to a child with TB until you make him well first. I mean, that's why we're going to Ethopia, isn't it?'

'Of course,' she said. 'It's just that I thought—I mean—you seem to have so much more going for you.'

I suddenly got the sense that she was ambivalent about taking this momentous step in her life. Perhaps understandably, for she would be going to one of the few places on earth where FAMA and its products were totally unknown.

It was eleven o'clock when we chose a table in the Café de Flore, ordered coffee and began working through the next day's diseases.

It took us nearly two hours to get through the complex material, which included a lot of statistics. Silvia finally declared us ready. 'Shall we have a nightcap?'

'Why not? Especially since it's your round.'

It had been a long evening, exhilarating but exhausting. We left the café and began to walk slowly back to the hotel.

'How did you get started in the first place?' she enquired. 'I mean with the piano.'

'Do you want the long version or the short version?'

'I'm in no rush.'

WHEN I WAS A KID, I had this fantasy that my dad would come to one of our school field-days and beat all the other fathers in the hundred-yard dash. Needless to say it never happened, because he was always 'under the weather' on the day of the competitions.

Sometimes he would lurch over and make an appearance, but then he'd sit on the side nipping secretly from his flask. So I never saw him physically active till that morning in the school yard when out of the corner of my eye I caught sight of him at the gate. He seemed to be heading for Mr Porter, my brother's maths teacher. I was trying to concentrate on playing half-court basketball when suddenly I heard Tommy Steadman shout, 'Wow, Hiller, your dad's fantastic!'

I felt a sudden irrational thrill. Unfortunately, my euphoria immediately evaporated. For what Tommy had so admired was the fact that my dad had thrown a punch at Mr Porter, catching him off-balance and knocking him to the ground.

By the time I ran over, the victim had regained his feet and was shaking a menacing finger at my father. 'You drunken fool,' he shouted as he retreated into the school building.

My father stood there out of breath, with one of his triumphant grins. He noticed me and called out, 'Hi, Matthew. Did you see me deck the wicked giant?' I was humiliated beyond belief.

'Dad, why did you do it? It'll only make things worse for Chaz.'

He bristled. 'I couldn't let that Neanderthal persecute your brother. I think you should be proud of me. Come on, I'll take you two out to lunch.'

'No, Dad,' I said quietly. 'We've still got four periods left. Why don't you go on home?'

I sensed he wouldn't leave unless I took the initiative, so I grabbed his arm and walked him towards the gate. When we reached the exit, I turned and saw my classmates watching, conspicuously silent.

I started back on the long, long road towards my peers, my gaze fixed firmly on the ground.

'Are you OK, Matthew?' I looked up and was startled to find it was Mr Porter. And he didn't seem to be angry with me.

'Yes, sir. I'm all right.'

'Is he like that very often?'

I didn't know how to answer. Should I increase my shame by admitting that he was a chronic drunk? Or should I try to save some molecules of dignity?

'Now and then,' I answered vaguely and walked slowly back to Tommy Steadman. 'Hey, are we going to play ball?'

'Yeah, sure, Hiller. Sure.'

And ironically, the thing that hurt the most about this hurtful incident was that my friends were so nice. So horribly, painfully, pityingly nice.

Fortunately my father made no more such quixotic sallies into the real world. He thereafter remained at home, 'working on his book' and railing against the injustice of the world.

At this point, I myself was not too thrilled about the hand that life had dealt me. My only release was in the evenings when Chaz was studying in his room and I was left alone to practise the piano, which I would do for hours on end, pouring out my anger and invoking all the discipline my father lacked.

By the time I was in high school, I was too busy to sit and listen to his rambling lectures and, besides, he finally pushed me too far.

I was sweating over Chopin's Fantaisie Impromptu late one evening when he appeared somewhat unsteadily in the doorway and snapped, 'I'm trying to work. Must you play so loud?'

I reflected for a moment, then locked into my father's gaze and, losing my temper, sternly answered, 'Yes.'

I turned back to the music and ignored him for ever.

I WAS QUIET for a moment and then I said tonelessly, 'A little while after that he killed himself.'

Silvia grasped my arm tightly.

'Although he never went anywhere, he kept a car in the garage and he would sometimes go out, sit there, and I guess fantasise that he was on the open road, heading for some destination. One day, in what I took to be the ultimate gesture of shutting out the world, he attached a hose to the exhaust pipe . . .'

I looked at her and she was at a loss for words.

'Anyway, I don't often bring this up in conversation.'

'No,' she agreed. 'You don't have to. It's just always there—behind a thin gauze curtain of memory—waiting to emerge when you least expect it.'

She understood, this girl. She *really* understood.

We walked the rest of the way in total silence. When we reached the hotel, she kissed me quietly, squeezed my arm again and then slipped off. It was the depth of night, a time I always hated. Yet at that moment I did not feel so utterly alone.

PARADOXICALLY, my father's death, though a difficult period for us, was a kind of liberation. It had been like watching a man teetering on a tightrope across Niagara Falls. Though it took a while until he actually let go, his fate was clearly sealed from the moment he began to waver. The fall itself was almost anticlimactic.

I had to respect the minister for not delivering a saccharine eulogy. There was no nonsense about a great man torn from us tragically in the prime of life. Rather, he spoke a few sentences about our common hope that Henry Hiller's troubled soul would find peace at last. And left it at that.

Not surprisingly, little changed. We were left as the family unit we had already become without him before he died. If anything, the pace of my life intensified. I was chosen to represent our school in the state keyboard competition and took second prize.

I wanted to go to med school and when, after a two-hour audition, the music department of the University of Michigan offered me a full scholarship, I sailed home from Ann Arbor on a cloud. But it really only sank in when I shared the news with my mother and brother. In the ensuing celebration, I told Mom to take the money she had been scrimping and saving for my education and get herself the new car she so badly needed. But she insisted that I spend it on something that would bring me pleasure. The choice was obvious: a secondhand piano.

My next four years resonated.

Though premed scientific courses were no doubt conceived to destroy the soul, majoring in music made mine indestructible. I explored beyond the keyboard into the riches of the orchestra and fell in love with opera.

The course of my life had changed dramatically. For as long as I could remember, I had been trudging through a dark labyrinth of work and worry. Now, at long last, I was on a sun-swept plain that stretched all the way to a blue and cloudless horizon. And I even discovered that these strange new feelings had a name: happiness.

My appearances as a soloist with various chamber groups made me something of a Big Man on Campus and added immeasurably to my confidence. Yet the most significant event of my entire freshman year was meeting Evie.

She was warm and pretty in a fresh-faced sort of way, with short brown hair, an infectious smile and wide hazel eyes that beamed with optimism. But most important, she was an extremely talented cellist. Ever since her childhood in Ames, Iowa, she had aspired to emulate her musical heroine Jacqueline du Pré. We would listen to every record we could get our hands on of Jackie on the cello communing eloquently with her pianist–husband Daniel Barenboim. We played them so often that we practically wore out the grooves in the LPs.

Although we spent almost every waking moment together, Evie was not a girlfriend in the romantic sense. We just found in each other the qualities we both were looking for in a best pal. She was already a sophomore when we met, and at first I suspected an ulterior motive in her friendliness towards a naive youngster like myself. I mean, cellists need accompanists and the one thing I can do with the best of them is sight-read.

I guess at the time we didn't fully appreciate the uniqueness of our relationship. We confided things to one another that we would never have revealed to anyone else. Not just about how we felt about whom we were dating, but, far more intimately, the fact that we had both wrestled with the problem of what to do with our lives. Mr and Mrs Webster were strongly against their daughter becoming a professional musician. They genuinely believed it was incompatible with marriage, which should be every girl's first career choice.

The most 'passionate' moments in those years were the times Evie and I spent practising together. We went through almost every major work for piano and cello. Sometimes more than an hour would pass without our exchanging a spoken word.

Of course we gave each other moral as well as musical support. One occasion was when I accompanied her in Fauré's *Sicilienne*, which she had chosen for her degree recital in the spring of her senior year. I knew my part well enough to be able to sneak glances at the professors' faces and could tell she was making a really good impression. As I predicted, she received a *summa cum laude*—and I received the longest, warmest embrace she had ever given me.

I have always been grateful that she was there to help me during my big identity crisis, for with each passing semester I was coming closer and closer to an unavoidable crossroads. Which path would I take? The faculty did not make it any easier. They seemed to be actively engaged in a tug of war, trying to pull me towards either music or medicine. I felt like I was being torn apart. Evie was the only person I could talk to about it.

'You can make it as a pro,' she asserted. 'I mean, you've got the divine spark that makes the difference between a keyboard technician and a virtuoso. You know that, Matt, don't you?'

I nodded. There was no question that I wanted to keep on playing music for the rest of my life. And yet a part of me could not imagine a life that did not somehow involve helping other people, giving something back—maybe a legacy from Mom.

The summer before my junior year was the crucible.

While Evie was off at the Aspen Festival taking a cello master class with Roger Josephson, I slaved as an orderly in the university hospital. I remember one night during my shift on the paediatric ward there was this comatose girl who seemed to be whimpering. I reported it to the nurses, who insisted she was drugged to the eyeballs and could not be feeling any pain.

Nonetheless, when I went off duty I went over, sat down and took the child's hand. She suddenly went quiet. I remained at her bedside till nearly daybreak. The girl must have been aware that I had been with her all the time, because when she awoke she gave me a little smile and said, 'Thank you, Doctor.'

I called Evie and told her I had made up my mind.

'I'm really glad, Matthew.'

'That I'm going into medicine?'

'No,' she said fondly. 'That you've finally decided.'

IN THE MIDDLE of her senior year, Evie received the good news that Josephson's intercession on her behalf had succeeded in winning her a scholarship to Juilliard.

She begged me to apply to med school in New York so that we could keep playing together. I thought about it. The idea was tempting—even though Chaz had been accepted by Michigan and would be arriving on campus the following fall. Anyway, I went to the medical adviser's office, got an armful of brochures for New York and began to study them.

At last the time came for Evie to leave. I guess most good friends would have gone out for a farewell meal or something, but we had other ideas. We went down to our favourite practice room at around 6.00pm and were still there at midnight. And so we concluded with César Franck's Sonata in A. The music was full of sadness and yearning, and we both attacked it with a depth of feeling that surpassed all other moments we had ever played together.

I took her to the airport the next morning. We hugged, then she was gone. I drove home in a very empty car.

THAT SEPTEMBER, Chaz arrived in Ann Arbor, all grown-up and ready to live. Of course, his idea of living was, no doubt, strongly conditioned by the psychic uncertainties of our childhood. He seemed in an enormous hurry to establish domestic stability. To prove this, before he even chose a major, he chose a steady girlfriend. In a matter of months he and Ellen Morris, a freckle-faced guitar-playing classmate, were living happily together on the top floor of a two-family house in Plainfield, a twenty-five-minute bus ride from the university.

Meanwhile, I was busy writing my senior thesis in music while suffering through organic chemistry. Several nights a week Evie and I would talk on the phone. It was not as satisfying as our 'live' conversations—and certainly not as good as making music together—but it was still nice to hear her views on everything from my dates to my dissertation on Verdi. She thought more of the latter than the former.

When Mom came to visit for Thanksgiving, she brought a surprise. His name was Malcolm Hearn, MD. My hunch that someone had recently come into her personal life turned out to be accurate. A divorced surgeon with grown children, Malcolm not only seemed like a warm, solid guy with a sense of humour (and a world view at the antipode of Dad's), but he was also something of a musician, a first tenor, to be exact. And a real one, who could hit high C without having to cheat and go falsetto. Mal was the star of the hospital barbershop quartet. Most important, he seemed really fond of Mom, who would now have a genuine second chance at happiness.

Evie was really pleased to hear about Malcolm. ('A surgeon, a nice guy *and* high C? That's too good to be true!') I told her she could make up her own mind when she met him at Christmas.

'Uh, I was working up the courage to tell you, Matthew. I'm afraid

I'm not going to be able to come out. Roger and I—'

'Roger?' I asked with an irrational pang of jealousy. 'Are you refer-ring to Maestro Josephson?'

'Uh, yes. Actually, he's the guy who just answered the phone.'

'Hey,' I said suddenly self-conscious. 'You should have told me I was disturbing you.'

'You never disturb me. Besides, I told him all about us. Listen, why don't you join us at Sugarbush for a week of skiing?'

'Gosh, I wish I could. But I'm snowed under with work. I'll barely make it home for one day. Anyway, Merry Christmas.'

I hung up feeling like a stupid ass. I had given Evie holiday greet-ings an entire month too early.

I STAYED in Ann Arbor for med school. That way I could see Chaz and Ellen regularly, even after they were married.

Marriage was epidemic that year. In August Evie and Roger also tied the knot at Tanglewood, where he was playing Dvořák under Zubin Mehta. Fortunately I went down two days early because while Roger was off at his bachelor party Evie had a fit of what I can only describe as cold feet. ('I mean, Matt, he's so famous and—so grown-up. Why does he want a kid like me?')

I managed to convince her that a guy like Roger was astute enough to appreciate what a special person she was. For that matter whoever married her would know he was the luckiest guy in the world. The crisis was forgotten by the time the corks and flashbulbs popped.

Afterwards, I went home and plunged into the world of doctoring.

THREE

Milan, September 1953. They stood in order of rank. God first. The Virgin Mary. And then the baby.

The more important guests who had gathered in Milan's cathedral were already on familiar terms with the first two. But the infant had just been born. She was the daughter of Gian Battista Dalessandro, the owner of FAMA, Italy's largest conglomerate. And this was her social debut.

As the Prime Minister held the child and the cardinal chanted the Latin words that baptised her Silvia Maria Dalessandro, her mother Catarina whispered to her husband, 'I wish I believed in God so I could thank Him.'

He smiled broadly and embraced his wife.

'He exists, *carina.* How else could we have found each other?'

Among the dignitaries who had flown in from distant corners of the world was Mario Rinaldi, Gian Battista's rival and best friend. He was chairman of Gruppo METRO, and the second-richest man in Italy.

Although the occasion belonged to Gian Battista, with industrial potentates orbiting him like deferential planets, Mario had one consolation: even after two marriages, and for all his money, Gian Battista had not been able to buy a son and heir. And that was something *he* had.

As the prelate sprinkled water on the infant's head, Mario whispered to the darkly handsome teenager at his side, 'She is going to be your wife.' Young Nico, all of sixteen, could not tell whether it was a command or a prediction.

THE HEIR to the METRO fortune reached his majority never having worked a single day in his life—and never intending to. To please his father, Nico had gone through the motions of a university education, subsidising a number of needy students who wrote his papers and even took his exams. He had better things to do. Since childhood he had been in love with speed: on the ground, in the air and in the water. This omnivorous passion afforded year-round opportunities for risking his life.

In the summer he moored his racing boat in Nice harbour and would expropriate the palatial guesthouse at his parents' estate with an ever-changing crowd of friends in tow.

Though her father had tried to develop in Silvia a wariness of strangers, he did not regard the son of his Riviera neighbour as an outsider. Nico was, among other things, Gian Battista's favourite tennis partner, and every year they battled each other in a marathon summer-long tournament. Neither liked to lose.

Silvia would always sit courtside and stand up periodically to announce the score in English, French and Italian.

Nico's latest *principessa*, the luxuriant Simona Gattopardo, was charmed. 'Your niece is very sweet,' she said.

'She's not my niece. She's my pal,' he offered, draping his arm round Simona as they walked off towards the terrace.

Silvia watched them go with a pang she did not yet realise was jealousy.

Naturally, Nico was too involved in his own pursuits to notice that the little girl adored him.

One winter her father and Mario took Silvia to see Nico race his bobsleigh in Cortina d'Ampezzo. Towards the end of the afternoon, his sledge hit a patch of water, spun out of control and crashed, rolling over several times. The brakeman fell free, unhurt.

Silvia burst into tears. Gian Battista picked her up to comfort her.

At the first-aid station the medics made an inventory of Nico's broken bones and prepared him for the helicopter ride to Milan.

'Will you be all right?' Silvia asked solicitously.

'Of course,' he replied with bravado. 'I'm indestructible.'

Gian Battista later visited the younger Rinaldi in his spacious top-floor hospital room and reported to his wife and daughter, 'I think he's going to be in there for quite a few months.'

'Maybe the doctors will transplant some sense into his head,' Catarina remarked with disapproval. 'Then maybe he'll find something worthwhile to do with himself.'

'I think he's already looking. His list of visitors looks like a *Who's Who* of the business world. I think that's where he'll compete for his gold medals from now on.'

'It's about time he settled down. What's he waiting for?'

Silvia, who had been playing quietly nearby, chirped up, 'Me.'

IN THE SPRING of 1965 Catarina Dalessandro was abducted by a revolutionary group and held for an obscenely large ransom.

In a swift and uncharacteristic burst of efficiency, the Italian police closed off all the Dalessandro bank accounts so they would be unable to surrender to the terrorists' demands.

At this point the Rinaldis, father and son, proved their friendship. To enable Gian Battista to meet the kidnappers' demands, Mario flew to London for dollars while Nico sped to Lugano to bring back Swiss francs.

Unfortunately the carabinieri, who had been tapping the phones, reached the terrorists before the money did. And in the exchange of fire that followed, Catarina was shot dead.

From the moment Gian Battista received the news, he closed

himself in his room, unable to face the world.

Although he knew his daughter needed him, he did not have the emotional strength to respond. It was like living behind a wall of glass. He could see but not touch other people.

The task of comforting Silvia fell to Nico.

The day before the funeral, while his father was with Gian Battista in his study, Rinaldi strolled up to the playroom. The place was empty, although toys were spilled everywhere. He then wandered downstairs and into the garden, past the silent swimming pool and the equally deserted tennis court.

At last he caught sight of Silvia seated on a bench, staring into space. Her governess was trying to distract her by reading aloud. The twelve-year-old child wore a look of utter desolation.

Nodding to her companion, Nico sat down next to the little girl and began to speak softly. 'Silvia, I can't tell you how sorry I am. I mean, for your mother . . . and for you.'

There was a moment of silence. Then she answered, her voice hollow. 'The world seems like such a horrible place.'

'I can see life must be unbearable right now. But you can't give up. You know what your mother would have wanted.'

'Nico, my father won't talk to me. Did I do something wrong?'

'Just give him a little time. He's coping the best way he can.' Nico looked out towards the horizon, then said as casually as possible, 'I don't know about you, but I'm cold. Let's all go inside and get something nice and warm to drink.' He extended his hand to her.

She slowly rose and the three of them walked back into the house.

The burial was private but a plague of paparazzi with telescopic lenses stood outside the cemetery, feeding like carrion on the victims' grief.

The mourners wound their way slowly behind the coffin. Nico held Silvia's hand as they walked a step behind Gian Battista and Mario Rinaldi. At the end of the service, as the dignitaries began to leave, Silvia remained beside the open grave and whispered, 'Goodbye, Mama.'

Then she turned, took Nico's hand again and walked away.

SUDDENLY THE ENTIRE population of Paris was reduced to only Silvia and me. We sat next to each other in class and in the evenings dined together in local bistros. Then, after ploughing through the assignments for the next day, we would close our books and just talk.

If there was a single quality that characterised Silvia it was passion. She embraced every aspect of life with enthusiasm. Somehow, neither the onus of excessive wealth nor her painful childhood appeared to have handicapped her in any way.

Or so it seemed at first.

It was interesting how often she mentioned her mother. 'When she married my father, Mamma was the editor of *La Mattina*, Italy's largest morning paper. After I was born, she converted a wing of the house into offices, and with motorcycle messengers, endless charm and a very loud voice, ran the whole show from home. And yet she wasn't like those women who are so wrapped up in their careers they have no room for their kids. She was always there when I needed her.'

From the vantage point of time and grief it was hard to tell whether this was a real memory or an idealisation.

'How did you manage afterwards?'

'Well, there was my father,' she said softly. Her tone revealed more familial loyalty than genuine conviction. She then confessed quietly, 'Although he needed my support even more than I needed his. Actually, Papa's never really recovered. He's still trying to work himself to death. I worry about him.'

'But who worried about you? Who played with you? Who took you to school?'

'Different people. I don't remember anyone in particular. It didn't seem like a big deal at the time, since all of them wore the same uniform. But Nico read to me.'

'Ah, Nico.'

'Yes. He also taught me how to play tennis. And chess. And he took me to the circus.'

'Then I guess you're going to marry him,' I stated, masking the sinking pessimism about my own chances.

'What makes you say that? That was ages ago. He's a hundred years old now.'

'To begin with, he's not. He's young enough for you to play with and old enough to look up to. Most of all, he always seems to have been there. And that's very important to you, isn't it?'

'You're right to a certain extent,' she conceded. 'He was really wonderful during the period I refer to as my "incarceration".'

'What do you mean by that?'

'Understandably, after what happened to Mamma my father was obsessed with protecting me. I mean, he pulled me out of school and had me tutored at home. And as far as my social life was concerned, I desperately missed other people.'

'How did you finally get away? Was that with Sir Nico's help, too?'

'Stop teasing,' she chided. 'But as a matter of fact he was always encouraging me to study abroad. Still, I couldn't really leave my father until he was on his feet again.'

How strange, the parental instinct coming from a child.

'And then I finally decided that if he was ever to rejoin the human race, I had to go. I thought that if I left him on his own he'd be forced to start looking for somebody else. Anyway, England was the only country whose security he approved of. Since the school had to be Catholic, this pretty much boiled down to St Bartholomew's in Wiltshire. I was happy there, although it took me a while to get used to all that religious stuff. The only thing I ever prayed for was that next visitors' day Papa would come with a nice new lady on his arm.' She then added wistfully, 'But he never did.

'I guess I've talked too much, huh?' she said apologetically. It was close to 1.00am, and we were standing in the empty lobby of the 'Termite Hilton'.

'Not at all,' I answered sincerely. 'How else can you get to know a person?'

'But knowing isn't synonymous with liking,' she ventured.

'Silvia, in your case it couldn't mean anything else.'

We exchanged good-night kisses on the cheek and went to our rooms. As I climbed the creaking stairway to mine, I thought— unless I was too drunk on hope— that there was meaning in her last remark. Nico had not won her yet. I still had a chance.

THE NEXT NIGHT in the Café de Flore, after we had covered the last item on our agenda—a thorough study of the onset, development and cure of schistosomiasis, a common blood infection caused by polluted water—we ordered a carafe of dry white wine and talked about the things that attracted us to medicine in the first place.

'To tell the truth,' Silvia said, 'I can't remember a time when, at some level, I didn't want to be a doctor. I guess it started as far back as Giorgio Rizutto.'

'Who was he?'

She hunched over the table as she always did when she was sharing her innermost thoughts with me. 'He was my first "boyfriend". We were both seven years old. He was skinny, with black saucer eyes, a lot smaller than the rest of us. During recess, while the other boys ran around, he would sit on the sidelines and I'd keep him company. But he could never come to our house and play. It turned out that every evening after school he had to go to the hospital for dialysis.'

She took a deep breath. 'Damn. Even after all this time, it's still tough to speak about it. Apparently he didn't have much longer to live. My father offered to pay for him to have one of those new kidney transplants in America. I was really proud. I thought Papa could never fail at anything.' She paused, then said, 'They operated on Giorgio in Boston General. He never woke up.' Silvia lowered her head. 'My father's been haunted by it ever since.'

I was silent for a few seconds and then said gently, 'So you decided to become a doctor.'

'Not consciously, but I must have carried those feelings with me. Anyway, I met a professor of medicine in Cambridge who directed a hospice for the terminally ill. One day he let me tag along while he made the morning rounds. He was wonderful. When he spent time with a patient, he made him feel like the most important person in the world. He listened to everyone's worries, and somehow found the right words to give each of them courage. I suddenly found myself wishing that Giorgio could have died in such a humane and caring place. That day was when I made up my mind.'

'I can imagine your father's reaction.'

'Actually, I don't think you can. Though obviously surprised, he seemed to accept my decision. It was only later that he started fighting it. Naturally, he began with guilt.'

'That's always a popular one with parents.'

'When that didn't work, he tried the rigours of a medical education.'

'Tell me about it, Doctor,' I smiled. 'Did he describe the three-day shifts without sleep?'

'In agonising detail. But I argued that if others had survived it I could too. Finally, after a summer of fruitless attempts at dissuasion, he surrendered. When he kissed me goodbye, he whispered that the most important thing in the world was that I do whatever made me happy.'

'Anyway,' I said testily, 'isn't it really a question of what you do until you marry Nico?'

'Oh Lord!' She looked at me with playful annoyance. 'You're worse than my father. What makes you so sure I'm in love with him? Did I ever mention that I was?'

'Well, it'd be a great stock merger anyway,' I said.

'I can't deny that much,' she conceded.

'Then have you set a date?' I was suddenly not sure I wanted to hear the answer to that.

'Actually,' she said with a mischievous smile, 'the fathers recently proposed the last weekend in August. Of course now they'll have to postpone it.'

At last I understood the extra dimension of her desire to join Médecine Internationale. Not only could she work with sick children, but she would be worlds away from Nico Rinaldi and all the familial pressures. 'Tell me, Silvia, did your decision to go to Africa by any chance involve not being able to attend your own wedding?'

She tried unsuccessfully to suppress a grin. 'As a matter of fact, I did explain that I needed time and space to think things over.'

'How did they take it?'

'They didn't have a choice. I'm my mother's daughter as well as my father's. She would have asserted all her independence. So now, Mr Enquiring Reporter, do you have all your answers?'

No, I said to myself, just a whole new set of questions.

FOUR

At five o'clock on the last day of our training, François made a few remarks. 'OK. We've finished the formal introduction which, as you'll see the moment you arrive, is no preparation at all. I'd just like to say to those of you I've picked on unfairly, I'm sorry. And, to those of you I haven't —don't worry, I'll get to you while we're there.'

There was a ripple of laughter.

We were scheduled to leave the next evening and so had three-quarters of a day in Paris to do what we wanted. Silvia and I went to the Rodin Museum in the morning, then showed up at Médecine Internationale for the last time. We had various documents to sign, including bank mandates, a health policy in case of medical catastrophe and life insurance for our next of kin. I designated Chaz and my mother each to become $5,000 richer in case of my demise. We then split up to do some shopping for our respective families.

That evening I paced nervously outside the bus. It was getting late and we would miss the plane if we didn't get going. I kept glancing at my watch, wondering what might have happened to her.

'Hey, Matthew,' François bellowed. 'Get on board. Don't worry, she can afford a limo if we leave without her.'

I found that neither reassuring nor funny, but I obeyed.

Just as I sat down, Silvia appeared on the top step of the hotel, followed by her usual shadow. She looked gorgeous in a blue sweater, tight jeans and black leather boots. Flopping down next to me, she patted my hand. 'I'm sorry. They just wouldn't get off the phone.'

I thought it best not to ask to whom she was referring.

The ever-faithful Nino had the back row all to himself. When I met his eye, I waved to him cordially to join us. But he stared right past me.

At Charles de Gaulle Airport, as we threw our luggage onto trolleys and began to push them towards the gate, her bodyguard still continued to keep watch over his charge from a discreet distance. At last, when we reached passport control, duties officially ended, he approached Silvia and me and said goodbye.

'I wish Signorina Dalessandro a good journey. I am sorry that I will not be there to look after her.'

'You're a sweetie,' she responded warmly. 'Thank you for everything. *Arrivederci.*'

He glanced at me out of the corner of his eye as if to say, I'm counting on you, mister. Don't screw up. Then he turned and walked slowly down the corridor.

'Are you going to miss him?' I murmured.

'No,' she answered categorically.

I took her hand and we hurried to join the others.

All eleven of us then hung around the departure gate, making small talk and trying not to appear as nervous as we all were. At last, Ethiopian Airlines called flight number 224 to Asmara, capital of the province of Eritrea. François stood at the door of the plane like a drill sergeant, making absolutely sure that every one of his carefully trained medical commandos had made it on board. He eyed the large rectangular package protruding from my knapsack. 'Pray tell, what's that, Dr Hiller?'

'It's my keyboard. I told you about it.'

'Yes,' he recalled. 'I look forward to not hearing it.'

As we fastened our safety belts, Silvia gave me a big smile. I reached into my pocket and gave her a gift-wrapped cassette I'd purchased that afternoon. 'For your new tape machine.'

'Thank you. Is it *Hiller's Greatest Hits*?'

'It's a hell of a lot better.'

By now she had opened the wrapping and seen that I had bought her selections from Gluck's *Orfeo ed Euridice.*

'I've never heard it,' she confessed.

'Well, it's got the most perfect expression of a lover's longing ever set to music.'

She handed me her cassette player. 'Find it for me.'

Putting on the headset I quickly fast-forwarded to the spot and then returned it to her. She closed her eyes and listened to '*Che farò senza, Euridice?*' ('What will I do without Eurydice?')

Half way through she grabbed me by the arm and said, 'Matthew, '*che farò senza te*?' What would I do without *you*?'

I leaned over and kissed her. Long. Slow. And sexy.

With a roar, the plane lifted off and soared into the evening sky.

WE REACHED Asmara at one o'clock in the morning. All of us were wide-awake with excitement.

I have vivid recollections of my first impressions of Darkest Africa. It was just that—dark. Once our plane landed, the runway lights were extinguished and it was eerie to see the blackness of the airport punctuated only by the glimmer of eyes and teeth.

Customs were perfunctory, and we all piled into the back of a van. Three other vintage trucks followed with our gear and a new infusion of pharmaceutical supplies we had brought with us. Silvia fell asleep on my shoulder as our caravan bounced along painfully through the darkness.

At last we reached Adi Shuma and the ramshackle compound of rectangular huts with corrugated-iron roofs that would be our home for the foreseeable future. I was billeted with Gilles Nagler, a stocky, earnest-looking Frenchman with wire-rimmed glasses. We unpacked by candlelight, since the primitive gasoline-driven electric generator served only the operating room and other medical areas.

Gilles noticed my huge package, which I had left wrapped. 'What's that?' he asked with undisguised concern.

'A piano,' I replied.

'No, really, be serious.'

'I am serious. It's a keyboard without the instrument itself.'

'Oh, so you mean it will not make any noise?'

'Noise? Perish the thought, Gilles. What it does make is music, but only in my head.'

'I must warn you,' he admonished as he withdrew five or six pairs of binoculars from his bag, 'I am compulsively neat. I hope you too will keep this place tidy.'

I couldn't help eyeing his collection of optical equipment.

'I am a birdwatcher,' he offered with some pride.

'Of that I have no doubt,' I commented and crawled into bed.

'If I'm very lucky, I will see the northern bald ibis.'

'Sounds wonderful. Good night.'

I don't know how long I actually slept, but I remember being up with the dawn. Our room was already humid and uncomfortable and getting worse by the minute. I went to the window to take my first look at Eritrea by daylight and was amazed by what I saw.

'My God,' I gasped.

My roommate suddenly woke, groped for his glasses, bounded out of bed and demanded, 'What? What's wrong?'

'Nothing,' I said. 'But I think there might be a big rock concert here tonight.'

'Are you insane?'

'Well,' I said, continuing to pull his leg, 'there seems to be quite a crowd of fans lined up. I can't imagine what else so many people could be waiting for.'

Gilles stared in amazement at the sight of a seemingly endless column of people—emaciated, dusty, obviously unwell—massing from the front door of the clinic to as far back as the eye could see.

'Don't they know we don't start till seven?' he gasped.

'Not all of them have their Rolexes, Gilles. Anyway, I'd say we've got a full day ahead of us.'

As we dressed and shaved quickly, Gilles chattered compulsively about birds. How, during our 'visit', he was hoping to catch a glimpse of such winged wonders as the wattled crane and—I kid you not—the brown booby. He chattered on as we headed for the refectory, a large barnlike structure clearly built in a hurry.

Most of the others were already seated at the long, sagging table, including Silvia, who waved that she was saving me a place. At the far wall was a kitchen of sorts, with a wood-burning stove.

Our breakfast was laid out on a counter: some papayas, bananas, and goat's cheese to be eaten with *injara*, a kind of rubbery bread roll made of *teff*, a local grain. The coffee urn had evidently had a previous life as a barrel of cooking oil. I sat next to Silvia.

'How do you feel, Silvia?'

'Scared to death. And you?'

'Well, I'd say my dominant mood is impatience. I want to get out there and get started.' As I wolfed down the food, I looked around at the other faces and sensed in them an urgent energy similar to my own. Only Silvia seemed subdued.

'Anything wrong?' I asked.

She shook her head. 'I've suddenly gone blank on the signs and symptoms for schistosomiasis.'

'Come on.' I put my arm round her shoulder. 'You knew it upside-down that night in the Café de Flore.'

She forced herself to smile and then remembered she had not introduced me to the young Tigrean sitting opposite her. 'This is Yohannes. I'm lucky. He's going to be my practical nurse, and he speaks the best English of anyone around.'

The young man beamed at this high praise. 'Surely the doctor is erroneous,' he stated. 'I am not so extremely linguistic.'

From what I'd heard so far, I agreed with him, and I hoped at least he could translate suitable medical questions to the patients—and, especially, transmit the answers.

I suddenly noticed François was missing. 'Hey, where's the great man? Don't tell me he's enjoying a little sleep-in?'

'Are you kidding?' interjected Denise Lagarde, an internist from Grenoble. 'François and Maurice have been in the OR since we got here last night. There were some badly shot-up guerrillas waiting when we arrived and they didn't want to risk putting them off till morning.'

As we were all about to disperse, Marta, François's Dutch assistant, called out, 'Remember, there's no lunch as such. The food is here, so just come and grab it when you can. Dinner's at seven thirty and we have a team meeting at nine. Believe me, it's a full day.'

'I believe her,' I muttered to Silvia as we walked out into the now-blistering morning sun towards the hovel known as the patient consultation building, to which she and Denise had been assigned.

As I kissed her on the forehead, she clutched my hand tightly for a second. 'Can I check with you if I need a second opinion?'

'Sure—but you won't.'

I puzzled over her uncharacteristic stage fright for roughly the next two minutes, approximately the time it took to get to my own examination room, throw on a white jacket, wash my hands and diagnose my first case of TB without even having to put on a stethoscope. This little girl was so patently infected I could hear the lesions on her lungs by the way she breathed.

From then on, I lost track of time.

In the next three hours I saw a more exotic spectrum of diseases than I had in my entire previous clinical experience. I think I encountered every one of the allegedly extinct afflictions that Jean-Michel Gottlieb had discussed, including leprosy.

My nurse was a seasoned veteran named Aida. She was tiny and tough, and I admit that at first I found her bedside manner a bit too aggressive. But I soon realised that she had evolved her technique from years of experience, for the many patients trying to push in front of one another obediently responded to her shouting and occasional shoving.

Also, she helped me begin my study of the Tigrean language, the first word I learned being the most gratifying for any doctor: *yekanyela*—'thank you'.

I was kept so constantly busy that it was only when I stopped to take the obligatory litre of water that I noticed how totally soaked in sweat I was.

While I savoured the moment of free time I had granted myself, I suddenly remembered Silvia. Leaving Aida to hold the fort, I took a quick break. The sun was now at its meridian, a fireball—the beginning of the three-hour period in which the staff had been forbidden to walk out for anything but the shortest distance.

Of course the patients had no alternative but to sit in the burning heat, protecting themselves as best they could with their tattered garments as they waited their turn to be examined by the white-coated medicine men and women from a different world.

Mothers sat nursing their whimpering infants as flies buzzed relentlessly about them. Old people, stick-thin, bent with the weight of years, stood mutely by. Many of them had walked over half a day to get here and were prepared to wait as long as necessary. That meant they would sleep where they stood and receive only water and a token bowl of porridge. I had only to look at their faces—which I tried not to do—and my heart ached.

When I arrived, Silvia's clinic was utter chaos—shouting, screaming and pushing. I instantly grasped that, for all his eloquence, Yohannes lacked Aida's ability to deal with the more assertive patients. My attention was immediately seized by the wails of a woman in great pain. Then I saw Denise suturing a jagged abdominal laceration as the patient was held down by volunteers.

'What the hell are you doing?' I asked her. 'Can't you give her some more lignocaine?'

'No,' she hissed between gritted teeth. 'I ran out a few minutes ago.'

'Well, I'll get you some,' I shouted.

She stared at me, her eyes burning with anger. 'There is none, you American fool. Now leave me alone. Do you think I am enjoying this?'

'Where's Silvia?' I asked in a chastened tone.

'I don't know. If you find her, tell her to get the hell back here and pull her weight.' Then her tone suddenly changed to a helpless appeal. '*Please*, Matt, I'm reaching my limit.'

I could tell she was on the verge of tears. Clearly, for some unfathomable reason, Silvia had deserted. I hurried to the refectory and, as I entered, nearly bumped into François. From the expression on his unshaven face, he was not in a jovial mood. He had obviously just come out of the OR.

'If you're looking for your girlfriend, she's taking the longest coffee break in history,' he said with disgust. 'I should have known better. But Dalessandro's bribe was too gross to ignore. I guess this is all too much for her pampered sensibilities.'

'What are you talking about?'

'She doesn't know, but when she applied, her father offered us a million bucks.'

'If you took her?'

'No, *if we turned her down*. That annoyed me so much that I accepted her. Now, if you don't mind, I've got work to do, and so have you.' He stormed out without another word.

I caught sight of Silvia seated at the far end of the table, head propped up on her hand, staring forlornly into a coffee cup. I tried to restrain my anger but I couldn't help feeling disappointed and, yes, embarrassed. For me as well as for her. But as I drew near I reminded myself that François had surely dressed her down already. She was clearly undergoing a crisis of confidence and needed some support.

'Hi, Silvia,' I said quietly. 'Wanna talk?'

She was silent for a moment, then: 'Matthew, I'm so ashamed of myself. All these months I'd been so confident about what I wanted to do. And yet the instant I saw those children my heart just broke and I fell apart.'

So that was it. She had lost her clinical distance.

'I should have been tougher,' she berated herself.

'If you were tougher, you wouldn't be you,' I said softly. 'François expected too much on the first day. By the way, have you been drinking water regularly?'

She avoided my gaze.

There was no point in castigating her further. I merely went over and brought her two litre bottles of water. 'Down one of these now and another during the rest of the day. And as far as everything else is concerned I have only two words.'

'Yes?' She looked at me anxiously.

'Grow up.'

For some reason that made her smile.

When we finally left the dining room ten minutes later, she was shored up to face the sternest medical challenges. Just outside the door she put her arms round me and said, 'Thanks, Matthew.' And then she kissed me with a passion that made our embrace on the plane seem like just a friendly peck.

IT WAS NOT an ordinary day.

Between dealing with the gunshot wounds of guerrilla fighters, I diagnosed and treated more patients than I could count. Many would have died had we not been there at this moment in their illness. Then there was the blindness our arrival prevented in at least a dozen kids with trachoma. This insidious eye infection, always at its worst where hygiene is at its least, would have cost them their sight. But timely dabs of the antibiotic doxycycline clears the condition entirely.

I will never forget the last trachoma case I saw that day. He was a bright little boy named Dawit who, in his many hours of waiting, had learned one or two words of English. He delighted in addressing me as 'Dokta' in various tones of voice, giggling after each one. A course of doxy would treat his condition, leaving no permanent damage.

But we had no more ointment on hand and I had Aida explain to Dawit's mother that she should bring him back the following morning. The next day mother and son were nowhere to be found.

During the rest of my time in Africa, I searched for this little boy to save him from a life of sightlessness. I never found him.

I think the best doctors are the ones who remember their failures as much as their successes. It gives them the necessary humility. That is why, when my thoughts turn to Eritrea, I think of those I didn't save. Of little Dawit.

And Silvia.

DINNER WAS AS SUBDUED as breakfast had been animated.

Sure, we had been warned a thousand times that this place was deprived. But none of us had ever seen human beings live in such utter squalor and neglect. I personally wondered how I ever could go out for a simple pizza again knowing how many children spend the nights groaning with hunger.

The day had been so hectic that it was difficult to remember back to when Silvia had been a problem. In the afternoon she had steeled herself. Her diagnoses were more assured, her manner reassuring. In fact she had one spectacular triumph.

Denise Lagarde was examining a child who had been given antibiotics for a chest infection a week earlier in her village by one of the roving UN medical teams. But now she had been rushed to our clinic, pale, sweaty, with a barely detectable, fast, thready pulse. When Denise had difficulty picking up heart sounds from the stethoscope, she called Silvia over to listen.

Silvia reacted instantly. 'Get the ultrasound machine in here right away.'

'What are you talking about, Dalessandro? This is a viral—'

Silvia cut her off and repeated to the nurse, 'Hurry, Yohannes.' He dashed off obediently and returned in a matter of minutes, wheeling the primitive apparatus we had brought with us. Silvia quickly switched it on and slapped the probe on the child's chest. Her suspicions were immediately confirmed.

'I knew it. She's got a pericardial effusion. Her heart's compressed. No wonder you couldn't hear anything. Are you sure we have no local anaesthetic at all?'

'Absolutely.'

'Damn it, I'll have to go in there cold.'

She commanded Denise to help Yohannes hold the young patient down, trying to bolster her own courage by saying, half aloud, 'Come on, Dalessandro. Just go in and do it fast.'

A moment later the child shrieked with pain as Silvia introduced a needle below the breastbone and quickly aspirated some cloudy fluid. In a matter of seconds the compression was relieved and the little girl began to breathe normally.

Silvia bent over, stroked the child's forehead and said gently, 'I'm sorry I had to do that. But there was no other way.'

By the time François called our flagging group to order that evening, everyone already knew about Silvia's inspired actions.

'I'll make this brief, guys,' he began, 'because I know you're all dying to sample the swinging local nightlife.' We were too bushed to grant him even a token laugh. 'The only thing we have to discuss tonight,' he continued, 'is how to make the best use of the few drugs the thieves have left us.'

'Did you say thieves?' Maurice Hermans asked with astonishment.

'Well, here they're called *shifta*. But by any name they're the same black marketeers who, wherever we go, somehow manage to rip off our medications.'

'With respect, François—' I began to protest.

'Cut the bull. You mean without respect—'

'Well, without respect, then. If you knew they would try to rob us, why didn't you post guards on the supply vehicle?'

'What the hell do you think I did, Hiller? Unfortunately, yesterday the "guards" themselves drove the whole damn truck away.'

Having made me feel like a squashed bug he now addressed the others. 'We've got to prioritise surgican procedures carefully.'

Murmurs of discontent grew louder as a handwritten list was circulated among us.

Maurice was livid. 'I don't believe this,' he stated, slapping the paper for emphasis. 'As I see it, we've no lignocaine, no erythromycin and only half the halothane we started with. What can we do, François? Some ingrown toenails?'

I particularly noted that in addition to these major drugs every tube of ophthalmic antibiotics had disappeared. For the foreseeable future, the dozens of children we would diagnose each day with trachoma would go untreated.

'When can we expect some refills?' I enquired.

'Not until our guys in Paris collect the insurance,' François answered. 'And don't start hassling me about red tape.'

At this moment Silvia raised her hand.

'Yes, Miss FAMA?' His irritation was undisguised.

'May I make a phone call?'

Without waiting for François to reply, the others shouted almost in unison, 'No!'

Denise even went as far as to sneer, 'Calling for the first flight out, Dalessandro?'

But Silvia was no longer the wilting lily they'd seen earlier.

'I know that I'm not very popular today, and I apologise to everyone—especially Denise—for screwing up this morning. However, my request was a legitimate attempt to help.'

'I'm listening,' François said, arms folded.

'I'd like to call my father.'

More groans and boos. Clearly the team had found a scapegoat.

Their smug self-righteousness really annoyed me. I rose and leaned on the table. 'All right, you guys, shut up. Let her talk.'

The derision subsided and Silvia spoke her piece. 'Being, as all of you know, a filthy capitalist swine, my father's got connections with others of his ilk in the pharmaceutical industry and might be able to expedite the shipment of the drugs we need.'

The first response was silence. All eyes fixed on our leader, whose reaction was surprisingly benign.

'Well, as the Ethiopian proverb might go, "It takes a *shifta* to catch a *shifta*." So why not give Big Daddy a try?'

He reached into his pocket, withdrew a key and handed it to her. 'While you're at it, ask him to send a few cases of Chianti Riserva.'

Silvia managed to walk straight-backed out of the room, knowing the mockery that would explode in her absence.

'Typical bourgeois,' Denise cracked. 'Running to Daddy.'

'Come on, give her a break,' I barked. 'Don't you think it took guts to volunteer her father's influence? I still think Silvia's really got the stuff.'

'Yes,' Marta concurred sarcastically 'It's called money.'

Moments later, their scornful laughter was interrupted by Silvia's reappearance. Everybody suddenly shut up.

'Thank you,' she said quietly to François, handing back the key. 'We can probably expect a stopgap shipment by the end of the week.'

'Bravo,' my roommate, Gilles, cheered. 'Well done, Silvia. By the way, that was a damn good diagnosis this afternoon.' His initiative was followed by some politely grudging applause. It was far from a love feast, but at least the Silvia-bashing was over.

'All right, boys and girls,' François proclaimed. 'The meeting's finished, everybody go and get some sleep now.'

In a matter of seconds Silvia and I were alone, each of us holding a candle. She smiled uneasily.

'Thanks for sticking up for me.'

'Thanks for doing what you did. It'll make a big difference.'

She looked beautiful in the flickering light.

'How are things in Milan?' I asked, trying to sound nonchalant.

'Fine . . . OK.'

'How's Nico?'

'I didn't ask.'

I suddenly wondered about the nature of the report Nino had inevitably given. And how much his employer already knew about me. I decided not to think about it any further. At least at that moment.

'Why are you looking at me like that?' she asked, as if she could feel my gaze on her cheek.

'Because I want to remember you exactly this way.'

Then, without another word, we each extinguished the tiny candle flames and stood close together in the darkness.

I put my arm round her and switched on my flashlight. We began to walk slowly back to her bungalow.

The compound was totally silent except for the distant cawing of night birds, whose exotic names were known only to the likes of Gilles. The huts and trees were mere shadows against the moon, and the temperature was verging on the tolerable.

'Do you know something?' she murmured. 'What started as the worst day of my life has ended as the best. And there's a single reason.' She squeezed my arm. 'How can I ever thank you?'

'It was nothing,' I replied.

We were now at her front door. She looked up at me.

'I don't want this day to end.'

A moment later we were inside, reaching out for one another by the light of a single candle.

Suddenly she stopped. 'I have something to tell you, Matthew,' she said. 'I'm scared. I've never been with a man before.'

I was genuinely surprised. I would never have imagined that of someone as sophisticated as Silvia. But from the expression on her face I could see it was true. Which left me to draw my own conclusions about what I meant to her.

And so we made love for the first time in a small room in a broken-down hut in a remote village in Ethiopia.

FIVE

It was not a dream.

I awoke in what seemed the middle of the night and found that I was still next to Silvia. That she was breathing peacefully in my arms. I could scarcely believe it. She looked more beautiful than ever. I wanted to kiss her and yet could not disturb her slumber.

I looked at my watch: it was after five. Through the makeshift shutter of her window, I could now see filaments of daylight beginning to radiate in the darkened sky. I had to get back.

Though I dressed as quietly as I could, she suddenly opened her eyes, raised up on her elbow and looked at me in the chiaroscuro of the new morning. At first she simply stared and then said, 'No.'

'No what?'

'You can't leave, Matthew.'

I leaned close. 'Do you want them to find out?'

'What does it matter? They'll see it on my face, anyway.'

'Yes,' I smiled. 'Can you see it on mine?'

She nodded. 'So you can stay.'

'No. I don't want to make Gilles jealous,' I joked.

As she laughed, I broke free of her spell and forced myself to do what I knew was the right thing.

Our charade continued for the better part of forty-eight hours. My teammates did not seem to notice any change in our behaviour, and we were happy for the privacy. And then on the third morning François dispatched the two of us to attend to an ailing chieftain.

When we returned, François was grinning broadly.

'Guys, I've had to relocate you. From now on you're both living in hut eleven. That's if you don't mind . . .'

Silvia and I exchanged glances.

'No,' I answered on our behalf. 'We'll force ourselves.'

Then I realised. 'Hey, there are only ten huts.'

'Well, some of our convalescing patients are terrific with their hands. They put up the compound's latest residential development in record time while you were away this morning.'

It certainly looked it. The structure was in its way an architectural classic, combining the rectangularity of a telephone booth and the gentle sloping of the Tower of Pisa. But it had the inestimable advantage of being on the far side of the storehouse, apart from the others. However humble, it was our first home. Silvia and I stood hand in hand looking at the freshly built abode.

'Happy?' I asked.

She smiled. 'I told you everyone would tell.'

'That's good. It saves us the trouble of telling everyone.'

Needless to say, our nights were memorable. And we were very happy together.

YET, IN THE MERCILESS HEAT of day, we could not be oblivious to our surroundings.

The earth was parched. Except for the defiantly bold violet flowers of the jacaranda trees, nothing seemed to blossom or grow. The landscape was oppressively monochrome—dull brown with a barely perceptible tinge of red. In moments of reflection I sometimes fantasised that this was the result of all the blood that killing ground had absorbed.

From our clinic, we could hear the occasional tattoo of gunfire. It was a troubling sound, not least because it signalled the imminent arrival of its victims for surgery.

Silvia's father knew how to make things happen. Before the first week ended, helicopters from an oil-exploration rig on the Dahlak Archipelago were ferrying new shipments of drugs from Asmara Airport safely to our back yard. The patients thronging nearby cheered and broke into a welcome dance for the magic-bearing whirlybirds. We, on the other hand, celebrated by performing surgery. And giving doxycycline to the sufferers of trachoma.

Except for when we were on duty, Silvia and I spent every waking moment together. For the others the exhausting sameness of each day inevitably wore them down. For us it was an endless repetition of pure happiness. Yet the unacceptable losses we sustained each day eventually took their toll.

I could exorcise my own pain by practising on the dummy piano. But Silvia had no such outlet and needed to talk about her feelings. She would come home, change into her bathrobe and hurry to the makeshift outdoor showers.

When she returned, she would sit on the bed close to me as I played feverishly, the instrument stretched out across my knees.

Without music there was no way she could tell what piece I was working on, so I explained, 'It's the second movement of Beethoven's so-called "Moonlight" Sonata. Whoever gave it that stupid title never heard this part.' Then with wild movement and crashing chords I pounded the keyboard for emphasis. Yet the only audible sound was of pads hitting wood.

'You played that very well,' she said, kissing the back of my neck. 'Such total involvement.' She smiled. 'I sometimes hear the music, too.'

Then I would stop and we would talk about our day. It was the only way we could preserve our sanity.

Since the refectory was the only 'recreational' building with electricity, we all hung around there after dinner, reading week-old newspapers, writing letters, talking shop or—yes—smoking. The stress was really brutal and one or two of us had relapsed into old habits. Often we would try to catch the news on the BBC World Service on the short-wave radio. We listened avidly, especially when they mentioned the Eritrean rebels' fight for independence from Ethiopia. They seemed to know more in London about what was happening on our doorstep than we did.

There was nothing else left to while away the hours till bed but gossip. Gradually we learned each other's life stories, and, as time passed, phrases like 'when I'm back in Paris' began to creep into everyday conversation. Now and then we all had to remind ourselves of the idealism that had brought us to this troubled place.

One night in early May we heard on the radio that Aldo Moro, the former prime minister of Italy, who had been kidnapped in March, had been murdered by left-wing terrorists. Silvia was shaken. Not only did it bring back shuddering memories of her own mother's fate, but Moro had been a personal friend of her father's.

I tried to comfort her, 'At least you're safe from that sort of thing here.' I made her promise not to listen to the news again. 'Might as well take advantage of being in the middle of nowhere. We have enough to worry about with our patients.'

She nodded and clasped my hand. 'You're right, we should treasure these moments.' For me these words had a penumbra of sadness. They served to remind me that the idyll could not last.

Once in a while I dared to ponder the future. But it seemed fraught with pain. There was no way I could envisage a life in the real world where we would be together. Would she come back to Dearborn with me and practise medicine? Not likely. Would I go to Italy? I couldn't see myself being welcomed into her Milanese social circle. I began to believe that we were the playthings of a cruel destiny. Inevitably I could not keep these thoughts from Silvia, who readily confessed that her own mind was besieged by the same spectre of separation.

'Look, we're so happy now,' I insisted. 'Why can't we just go on living like this for ever?'

'I agree.'

At first I could not believe I had heard her correctly.

'Everything's perfect now,' she reasoned. 'Why can't we stay here in Africa? There's a lifetime of work to do.'

'Are you serious, Silvia? You mean you'd actually give up all the other things in your world?'

'Love and work are all that matter, Matthew. My world begins and ends right here.'

'Well, I'd like to share my life with you, if you're sure that's what you really want.'

'That *is* what I really want.'

'Then will you marry me?'

'I have three words to say to that: *yes*, *yes* and *yes*.' Her dark eyes shining, she flung her arms round me. 'Why don't we go and see a priest? Perhaps in Asmara?'

'That's OK with me.' It didn't matter how we got married as long as we did. I volunteered to phone the Catholic cathedral in Asmara for an appointment. When did she want to go?

'The sooner the better,' she replied. 'Actually, now that we've decided, I'd be happier if we could present my father with a *fait accompli*. I can't explain it, it's just my instinct.'

I knew she was right. The longer we waited, the more likely it would be that somehow word would reach this very powerful man who could move heaven and earth—and certainly Eritrea—to pluck his daughter away from me.

Without saying why, we asked François for a long-overdue furlough so we could go to Asmara.

'Of course,' he agreed good-naturedly.

Two days later we started out at 7.00am and well before noon we were at the outskirts of the capital of Eritrea, a full mile higher in altitude. The change in weather was dramatic: we had left the inferno of summer and driven into spring. As we entered the city, we experienced a cultural shock. After so much time in the barren African wilderness, we suddenly came upon what looked like a suburb of Milan. And not without reason. The majority of the architecture dated back to the Italian conquest of the city in 1889, after which this became the seat of Italy's African empire.

Asmara, the 'Forest of Flowers', lived up to its name, with bougainvillea and jacaranda everywhere. The streets were immaculate, with outdoor cafés and real shops instead of market-day merchandise on blankets. Yet our beat-up half-track did not look out of place. Nearly half the traffic was horse-drawn.

We headed straight for the Catholic cathedral, a huge Italianate structure that dominated its surroundings. With a few minutes to kill, we strolled round the interior, and I was suddenly sidetracked by something wonderful. Without stopping to ask permission I found myself quickly pulling out the stops of the cathedral organ.

Naturally it would have to be Bach's great Fugue in G minor and the first measures were halfway to heaven when a loud voice shouted over the powerful music.

'May I ask who you are?' it demanded.

I was so elated to be playing again that my answer may have been slightly disrespectful. 'Right now I'm nothing but a humble servant of J. S. Bach. We've got an appointment with Monsignor General Yifter. Do you know where we find him?'

'You have,' the man replied, adding magniloquently, 'Welcome, my children. You have obviously flown here early on the wings of love. Will you both come this way?'

Like most of his countrymen Monsignor Yifter was compactly built. He was balding and slightly jowly, with wire glasses pressed tightly against his face, giving him a look of sharp intelligence. Coffee for three was waiting in his book-lined office. As we sat down I could not help but notice the proliferation of Latin texts.

'So, my children, you are very far from home. Did you meet here in Africa?'

'No, Monsignor. Three months ago in Paris while we were training for the trip.'

'Ah,' the cleric remarked, 'then you haven't known each other long?'

'I suppose in bare chronological terms it's a short time,' I answered. 'But we've been living together—by that I mean working night and day—ever since. In those circumstances you really get close to a person.'

'Ah, yes,' Monsignor Yifter allowed. 'News of your good work has reached us even here. You are to be congratulated. Now, where shall we begin?' He leaned back in his chair, pressing the fingers of both hands together, and looked at Silvia.

'Marriage is a very serious undertaking, Miss Dalessandro. And it is, of course, an eternal and unbreakable bond.'

Silvia glanced at me. My expression revealed growing impatience with his patronising manner.

She turned and said in a conciliatory tone, 'We understand that, Monsignor. That's why we've come to put ourselves in your hands.' Now she pressed him. 'Will you marry us?'

'Of course, of course, all in the fullness of time. But it is a practice of the Church to prepare couples for matrimony with a series of five or six visits. Are you prepared to meet on a monthly basis?'

I wasn't sure, but I thought he had just postponed our wedding by half a year. I was wrong.

'Of course in this case,' he appended, 'we have a non-Catholic partner.' He looked at me. 'You are willing to take instruction?'

'Yes. And do I understand that I don't have to convert formally if I decide not to?'

'Yes, as long as you agree to raise the children in the true faith.'

For a split second I did not react. I had already told Silvia that I was willing to have Catholic children, but I did not like this guy putting me under pressure. Still, I knew there was only one word that would get us out of there, so I said it: 'Yes.'

'Excellent. I'm sure for someone of your education that would not involve more than an additional three months.'

It was now a nine-month delay. I merely nodded.

'Splendid.' He rose to his feet. 'Then is this time of day convenient?'

'Yes, Monsignor,' Silvia said politely.

'Very well, shall we meet in . . .' He reached into the pocket of his robes and withdrew a leather diary. Leafing through the pages studiously he proposed, 'Shall we meet again on the 24th?'

That was three weeks away.

'Fine,' Silvia answered for both of us and with that grabbed me by the arm and pulled me out of the office. The moment we were beyond earshot she whispered, 'Deep breaths, Matthew, take deep breaths. Wait till we're in the street.'

To reach the car we had to return through the cathedral porch.

It was only then that the plaque on the back wall caught our eye. It was dated 1922 and commemorated the original benefactors of the church. They included none other than Vincenzo Dalessandro, founder of the FAMA corporation.

'Well, that explains a lot,' I remarked. 'Did you know this was a family chapel?'

'If I had, do you think I would have suggested it?'

She then looked at me with those beautiful eyes and asked tenderly, 'Do you still want to marry me?'

'Of course, Silvia. Anyplace but here.'

Our experiences at the Italian and American embassies were a complete contrast. The affable local functionaries promised to do everything they could to expedite their respective governmental permissions to marry abroad. They both assured us that we could schedule the event for two weeks' time.

We had a quick espresso before setting off home.

'What are you thinking about, Matthew?' Silvia asked.

'About how long it's going to take your father to bust us up.'

She grabbed my hand. 'Don't be silly. Nothing could separate us.'

'Don't be too sure.'

'Be realistic. We're over twenty-one. How could he stop us?'

'Silvia,' I said, 'with your father's connections he could send you on the first Italian space mission to Mars.'

'No, FRANÇOIS, you can't make me do this.'

If this had been the army I would have been court-martialled for disobedience. When I'd committed myself to this mission I thought that there was no task too odious or disturbing, but I was wrong. I discovered that I was incapable of aiming a weapon at another human being and pulling the trigger. Ironically, it was François of all people who was testing my pacifism.

'Look, Matthew, be realistic. There's a war going on barely a hundred metres outside these gates. You may find yourself having to protect your patients' safety.'

Yet body language betrayed his real feelings. I could tell from the gingerly manner in which he dangled the .38-calibre automatic pistol from his fingers that he too was repelled at holding an instrument of death in a hand trained to save life.

'I'll tell you what. To assuage your guilt, I propose a compromise. Learn to use this thing, and defer the decision about firing till the problem stares you in the face.' He stopped, took an exasperated breath and added, 'At least promise me that you'll acquire the option.'

I surrendered. At 6.30am for the next two weeks we all gathered in a remote corner of the compound while François showed us how to dispatch, with merciless accuracy, three cardboard 'people' with concentric circles pasted on their hearts.

We had arrived in 1978 just as the civil war had reached a new and dangerous phase. The Soviets had intruded upon the scene, massively rearming the Ethiopian regime. Their vastly increased firepower turned the tide against the Eritrean rebels and wrought bloody havoc everywhere.

These setbacks displaced masses of people, and UN relief workers were frantically setting up refugee camps. The latest one in our area, some forty miles east of Kamchiwa, merely had two nurses, first-aid equipment and some 'holding' staples like dioralyte for the inevitable dysenteries that took such a toll, especially on the children. Since we were the closest equivalent to a hospital, we regularly sent out pairs of doctors to treat the more urgent cases among these refugees.

Though it did not seem reckless at the time, Silvia and I looked forward to making these trips together. For us they combined the opportunity to display altruism and to enjoy each other's company for hours on the road. And yet we were aware that the journey was not without its perils. Ethiopian troops, rebels and just plain *shifta* fought regular and pointless battles for turf.

We were about to leave for our third trip to Kamchiwa. In the final moments of preparation, François helped us check the supplies we had loaded into the back of our well-worn half-track. Without comment François removed the pistol from the glove compartment and checked that it was loaded.

As one would expect from the heiress apparent of FAMA, Silvia drove with panache. If I had let her, she would have kept the wheel the entire way. The early-morning weather was temperate, and driving vaguely resembled a pleasure.

Silvia seemed pensive. 'D'you think we'll ever go back?' she asked.

'Where?'

'You know, where we came from.'

'Yeah, for our first grandchild's wedding.'

She smiled.

By the time we had driven for two hours, the air was already an oven. When we reached a cluster of eucalyptus trees I made Silvia pull over. We both drank tea with honey—part of Mother François's recipe for washing down salt tablets and keeping heat stroke away—

and then I took over the driving duties. A few minutes later the road opened out onto a broad expanse of high ground. We had been warned that this topography was the most dangerous, since potential aggressors could see us without being seen. But then we were young and in love and who the hell would want to hurt us anyway?

A moment later we found out. At first it sounded like a piece of gravel. In the middle of the African nowhere? Obviously I was unwilling to believe that what had pierced the right side of the bonnet was a bullet. But then, with a huge hiss, the steam from the punctured radiator began to spray out. It was all I could do to keep control of the vehicle and bring it to a halt.

'What is it?' Silvia asked, suddenly frightened.

'Not what,' I corrected her. '*Who.*'

I could feel the veins in my forehead pounding as I reached into the glove compartment, grabbed the pistol and clambered out to see what was going on. At that moment, I came face to face with our aggressors: two wiry mahogany-skinned fighters with bandoleers crisscrossed on their chests. They were full of menace, holding what even I recognised as Russian rifles.

I attempted to engage them in discourse. 'What do you guys want?' I growled in my best Tigrinya. My heart was pumping so loudly against my ribs that I was afraid I wouldn't hear their answer.

They were taken aback for a second by a gringo speaking their own language. The taller of the two eyed me fierily.

'You come with us,' he barked. There was no way on earth that I would let Silvia be taken by these characters. It would literally have to be over my dead body.

'Get out of our way!' I yelled back, adding some choice curse words I had learned from hearing our patients in great pain. The rich vernacular momentarily stymied them again. I called back to Silvia to get into the driver's seat quickly and let me know the instant she was ready to shift gears.

She was obviously in shock. 'No, Matthew, maybe we should do what they say.'

'Listen to me,' I snapped, trying to rouse her from paralysis. 'You don't want to be their prisoner. Now do what I told you!'

At this point one of the ambushers motioned me with his rifle to come towards him. I refused to move.

'Hurry, Silvia!' I shouted again. There was still no reaction from inside the half-track.

The man's eyes blazed with anger and his intentions were clearly homicidal. At that moment I became a creature of instinct—an animal who would protect his mate at any cost.

A bullet whizzed past my ear, cutting my final link with civilisation. In a furious rage I aimed my gun and fired straight at his chest. I came perilously close to hitting him as he dropped to his knees to avoid the shot.

Before he could scramble to his feet I had jumped onto the running board. Suddenly I spied a third gunman on the other side of the road. He was lifting his rifle to his shoulder, aiming straight at Silvia.

Instinctively, I fired.

He recoiled backwards. My God, I had just shot a man. It was the most horrifying moment of my life, and yet I had no time to think twice about it. I quickly reached over, shook Silvia and shouted her name at the top of my lungs. She suddenly came alive, shifted gears and we took off.

By now there was a hail of bullets coming from both sides. As we slowly gained momentum I emptied my pistol at the enemy.

In the next instant I felt something tear at my temple. The inside of my head was suddenly flashing like the Fourth of July.

Then everything went black.

PART II   SIX

Summer 1978. A gentle sunlight was streaming through the windows, caressing my face as I slowly regained consciousness. I gradually became aware that I was in a hospital bed. My skull ached, there was a drip in my arm. Standing above me, her face tired and careworn, was my mother. What was she doing here? Where was I?

Mom looked enormously relieved that I had opened my eyes. 'Matthew, can you understand me?' she asked apprehensively.

Though scarcely awake, my instant reaction was: '*Where's Silvia?*' I tried desperately to speak, gulping air but unable to create the sounds.

I felt a hand touch mine affectionately and heard the sound of my brother's voice. 'Take it easy, Matthew,' he said. 'You've been through a hell of a lot. You'll be able to boast to your grandchildren that you got shot in the head and lived to tell the tale.'

At last I managed to get the words out.

'Chaz, is she all right? Did she get away?'

He seemed not to understand my question and simply answered soothingly, 'Try to relax. The main thing is that you're OK.'

'No, it's not,' I protested, growing more and more agitated.

A stocky grey-haired man in a white coat came into my field of vision, interrupting the conversation. He spoke in strangely accented English. 'Dr Hiller, do you know where you are?'

At this point, I wasn't even sure *who* I was.

The gentleman politely explained, 'My name is Professor Tammuz. You are at the University Hospital, Zürich. Five days ago we admitted you with a bullet lodged in the spheroid bone, very close to the brain. The situation was quite serious. I operated immediately and I am pleased to see that you are back with us.'

My head was groggy but what I was hearing was doing nothing to make things any more coherent. 'How did I get here?'

'Apparently you were flown in a private air ambulance,' Chaz volunteered.

I looked desperately at the professor. 'Who else was with me?'

'A young neurologist and a nurse.'

'Wasn't there an Italian girl?' My eyes were imploring him. 'I mean, there had to be. Silvia was with me, I know she was. She's beautiful, dark-haired, about five foot ten '

'I'm afraid there was no one else on the plane,' Tammuz repeated with surgical finality.

I still did not even know if Silvia was alive. The very thought made my soul ache. 'Chaz'—I looked up at my brother—'how did you find out where I was?'

'We got a call from a doctor in Milan. He told us that you'd been injured and were being flown to Zürich to be operated on by the best neurosurgeon in the world. From what I've seen, everything he said was right.'

At this point the professor intervened again. 'Can you remember anything that happened before the bullet?'

I tried to think. Yet the mental effort to recollect the most recent events was indescribably difficult. Despite the discomfort, I tried to assail the fortress of my memory and breach its stone walls.

'There were these two guys—three. With rifles. They tried to take us prisoner. They opened fire. I shot back. I think I hit one of them.' Even at this moment I could not confront the possibility that I had actually killed another human being. Suddenly I shouted to no one in particular, 'Silvia Dalessandro was with me when we were attacked. Will someone please tell me what happened to her?'

My mother answered. 'Matthew, we don't know any more than the doctor's told you. Back home there was a small item on the news wires. It said that an American volunteer had been shot in Eritrea. There was no mention of any other victim.'

I was at my wits' end. 'This can't be possible,' I exploded. 'She can't have just disappeared.'

'Maybe Dr Pelletier knows something,' Chaz offered, trying to calm me down. 'He phoned yesterday and we promised to inform him the moment you woke up.'

'Good idea,' I agreed eagerly. 'Let's try him right away.'

It took nearly two hours to get through to Eritrea, but at last I heard François's voice speaking through a mattress of static. 'I'm glad that you're back with us again, Matthew. I admire your bravery, but whatever possessed you to indulge in such cheap heroism?'

'Cut it out, will you? Is Silvia alive or dead?'

He hesitated for a second and then said tonelessly, 'Alive, of course, thanks to you. She was the one who brought you back.'

'Then where is she?'

'I honestly don't know. And that's the truth, Matthew. I assumed she was with you in Zürich. The last thing I saw, she was holding your hand as they lifted you into the helicopter.'

'What helicopter?'

'One of those Italian choppers from the Red Sea oil rig that helped us move the drugs from the airport. Remember? It picked you up, and she went along. I mean, man, you saved her life!'

'François, do you have her phone number in Milan?'

'Yes. But I doubt it will do you much good.'

What did he know that he wasn't saying?

'Give it to me anyway.'

I handed the phone to Chaz, who jotted down the series of digits François gave him. I then said a quick goodbye and ordered my brother to get me the number right away.

A man with a deep voice answered. 'May I speak to Silvia Dalessandro?' I asked politely in Italian.

'I'm sorry, sir,' he replied laconically.

I couldn't even wring out of him whether Silvia was there or not. As a last resort, I decided to go for broke. 'May I speak to Mr Dalessandro, please?'

'*Prego?*'

'Look, don't play stupid. Put your boss on. This is about his daughter—the one whose life I saved.'

Somehow this made an impression. He put me on hold. A few moments later a gentleman who spoke English with the patina of a BBC announcer picked up the phone.

'Good evening, Dr Hiller. Dalessandro here. I can't thank you enough for what you did. And I'm delighted to hear you're better. I was most concerned until I heard the latest prognosis.'

Amazing. The guy was actually monitoring my condition and never thought to call me and thank me. Something told me my time would be very short, so I blasted to the point.

'Where's Silvia?'

His riposte was as smooth as silk. 'She was very upset, Matthew. I'm sure you can understand that.'

'Can I speak to her?'

'I don't think this is the moment.'

'Well, when do you think the moment will be?'

'I think it's best that we not continue this conversation,' he answered politely but firmly. 'Goodbye, Doctor.'

I had a strong premonition that this was to be my last communication with the Dalessandro family, so I was determined to hang on tenaciously and get everything in. 'Damn it, Mr Dalessandro, don't you realise I killed a man for her?'

Not even this wild outburst moved him. He replied with unruffled composure. 'Matthew, I'll always be grateful to you for saving my daughter's life.'

And then he hung up.

I fell back on my pillow in total agony.

And wished that the bullet that had pierced my skull had gone all the way.

IN ITALY, 'ROYAL MARRIAGE' UNITES TWO DYNASTIES

Milan, August 4, 1978

The closest thing to a royal wedding modern Italy will ever see took place in Milan today. It united that country's most eligible bachelor, Niccolo Rinaldi, 41, son and heir of the chairman of the multinational METRO corporation, and Dr Silvia Dalessandro, aged 25, daughter of the director of the still bigger conglomerate FAMA.

Observers predict that this will inevitably lead to the biggest corporate merger in the history of Italian industry.

The ceremony was private and attended only by the immediate families. The bride, a native of Milan, received her medical degree from the University of Cambridge. The couple will make their home in Milan.

Naively, Mom and Chaz first tried to keep the news from me.

They did not realise that the whole world loves this sort of fairytale event. It was broadcast on every one of the television channels in the hospital. So I watched it innumerable times.

During the next few weeks my emotions oscillated between incredulity and paranoia. At the height of my insanity I imagined that those thugs had been hired by Silvia's father to kill me and steal her back. But most of the time I was bewildered. I did not know what to believe about Silvia, about the world, about myself.

Late one afternoon, three days before I was discharged, I was sitting by the open door to the terrace, trying to read and get some air. The nurse suddenly entered to announce an unexpected visitor: a young woman who had identified herself merely as 'Sarah Conrad, a friend of a friend'.

She was undeniably pretty, with short, shiny chestnut hair, gentle eyes and a soft voice, with an educated English accent. I sensed why she might have come and asked to be left alone with her. She looked at me, a trifle uneasily I thought, and at last enquired, 'Are you all right?'

'That depends on who's asking,' I answered suspiciously. 'Did she send you?'

Sarah nodded.

'Were you at the wedding?'

'Yes.'

'Why did she do it?'

She shrugged. 'I don't know. I'm not sure she knows herself. I suppose marrying Nico was always on the cards.' She seemed to weigh every syllable she spoke with extreme care.

'But that was before Paris—before Africa.'

At first she didn't answer. She sat on the edge of her chair like a prim schoolgirl, holding her clenched fists tightly together. She could not look me in the eye, but at last produced an envelope. She got up, handed it to me and started to leave.

'No, wait,' I shouted. And then apologetically added, 'Please.'

She sat down again nervously as I tore it open.

My dearest friend,

I owe you my life and an explanation. I will be forever grateful that I spent even a small part of my life with someone as wonderful as you. I only wish the ending could have been otherwise. As it is, I can only say that I did what I thought was right. For both of us. Please forget me. I am sure you will find the happiness you deserve. I will treasure the joy of our encounter for the rest of my life.

Love, Silvia.

Up to this point, I now realised, I had not completely given up hope. But Silvia's own hand had destroyed the last refuge of my self-delusion.

'Tell me honestly, how did they make her marry him?'

'There was no gun at her head,' my visitor replied almost in a whisper, then reddened, obviously regretting her choice of metaphor. She stood up.

'It was nice meeting you,' she said awkwardly. 'I mean, I'm glad to know you're going to be all right.'

'Can't I give you some kind of answer to take back to her?'

She gestured helplessly.

'So this is it?' I demanded, as much to myself as to her. 'We meet, we fall in love and then she just disappears from the planet?'

'I'm sorry, Matthew,' Sarah murmured.

Then she was gone. And I was alone with Silvia's final words.

WHEN THEY FINALLY declared me well enough to leave the hospital, Professor Tammuz gave me strict orders to take things easy and avoid all stressful situations.

Chaz and I took Mom to the airport. She hugged me goodbye and with obvious misgivings boarded the plane back to Michigan. Two hours later my brother and I were on a train streaking across the Swiss countryside.

'Where is this place you're taking me?' I demanded irritably. Chaz was a saint to put up with this cantankerous behaviour, but somehow I couldn't help finding fault with everything. 'Switzerland has a surplus of two things—cuckoo clocks and mountains. So why do we have to go all this way just to see another overgrown hill?'

'First of all, the trip itself is beautiful,' he began patiently. 'Second, we're going practically to the roof of the world where you can see all the way to the Matterhorn. Third, there's absolutely nothing to do there but walk, relax and look at snow on the glacier. You might even find the person you're looking for.'

'Yeah? Who?'

'Yourself, you idiot.'

We got off the train at Sion and walked two blocks to the funicular railway, which went straight up and deposited us a mere twenty minutes later a mile higher in the town of Crans-Montana.

Whether by chance or design the Hôtel du Parc had in the early part of the century been a sanatorium for tuberculosis. An atmosphere of recuperation somehow permeated the corridors. It also commanded a reverential view of the Matterhorn. Even the most inveterate misanthrope would have his pessimism shaken at the sight of this huge snowcapped mountain reflecting the bright summer sun—the view from our terrace at breakfast. The bread had come from the baker across the street, the butter from a neighbouring cow and the cheese from the next village.

After a week of wandering through tranquil forests and unspoiled towns and villages, I began to regain some strength. One day we were walking through the town's main square, looking for a place to have lunch, when I caught sight of a poster outside the church announcing a forthcoming piano recital by the fabled Vladimir Horowitz. Crans, strategically located between Geneva and Milan, attracts an extremely cosmopolitan crowd.

That afternoon, in the middle of the stark, white-walled sanctuary, stood a platform graced by a magnificent ebony grand piano, polished to perfection. As the time of the concert approached I began to feel excited. At four o'clock the small church was packed. Horowitz walked on stage, bone-thin and stoop-shouldered. He appeared nervous. But the moment he sat down he emanated supreme confidence even before playing the first note.

It was an unforgettable experience. I have never heard anyone play so delicately and at the same time convey so much emotion. His last piece was both a surprise and a thrill for me. It was Horowitz's own arrangement of John Philip Sousa's *Stars and Stripes Forever* played with such velocity and panache that when he imitated the *piccolo obbligato* in the grand finale it sounded as though he had three hands. I was first on my feet, cheering both out of patriotism and sheer worship of the man's genius.

As I stood with many other admirers waiting to shake the maestro's hand after the concert, I glanced at the ivory keys of the magnificent Steinway with the lust of a man who has been on a desert island seeing a voluptuous woman for the first time.

Chaz could not help but notice my fixation and whispered, 'Stick around and play after he goes.'

Horowitz finally escaped his well-wishers and a few moments later the hall was empty.

'Go on,' Chaz said. 'Give yourself a treat. I've got to buy some postcards. I'll meet you back at the hotel.'

It looked so tempting. I sat on the bench for a long time, not daring to touch the keys. At first I wondered what I should play.

And then I wondered what I *could* play.

Slowly, with mounting horror, I realised the answer: nothing. Absolutely nothing.

It was then I knew that I could perhaps survive the loss of Silvia physically, but the music was irretrievably gone.

From my hands. From my head. From my heart.

I MADE UP MY MIND to tell no one about my inner muteness. I would burden no one else. Back at the hotel I did my best to make lively conversation during our meal, well aware that sooner or later Chaz would ask me the painful question. As we were sitting peacefully on the terrace later that evening, he enquired, 'How'd your reunion with the keyboard go?'

I moved my right hand from side to side to indicate 'So-so'.

He was unperturbed. 'Give yourself a chance. It'll come back.'

He didn't know. How could he?

After a few days of quiet brooding I came to a decision. I would stop mourning. I would not be a source of pain to my family. If they hadn't been around, I suppose I would have thrown myself off a picturesque cliff. But now Ellen was going to make me an uncle. And it was time to stop hiding in this fantasy world where the scenery was too beautiful to be real.

Later that day I began to act on my decision. My brother stood by in dismay as I threw my clothes into a suitcase.

'You're not serious, are you?' he demanded. 'You're not really going back to Africa?'

'It's called honouring your commitments, Chaz. I signed on for three years and they need me badly. I'm going back to where I can do some good.'

He could tell I was immovable and resigned himself to the task of helping me prepare for my return to the wilderness. We had plenty of spending money since all my medical bills had been covered by Médecine Internationale who had also continued to pay my salary while I was in the hospital. So I bought presents for everybody.

It was only when we were sitting in the departure lounge and we heard the last call for my flight that Chaz grew agitated. I patted him on the shoulder.

'Don't worry, Chaz. I'll come back in one piece, I promise.'

'You said that last time,' he smiled wryly.

'Give Ellen a special kiss from me.'

We embraced, and I did not look back as I boarded the plane.

AS HE HAD PROMISED on the phone when he jubilantly received the news that I had booked my flight back, François himself was waiting for me on the tarmac in Asmara. He threw his arms round me, and though I protested my health and strength he insisted upon carrying my bags to the car.

During the journey he filled me in on almost every event: the changes of personnel and even the most minor incidents that had occurred in my absence. It was something of a bravura performance that he never once mentioned Silvia's name. And as the rest of the evening proved, her vanishing act was complete, for she had been expunged from everyone else's vocabulary as well.

'We've missed you,' François stated in a tone surprisingly devoid of his usual sardonic humour. 'It was only in your absence that I realised how valuable you were. Anyway,' he slapped my thigh, 'with you we're back at full strength again. I managed to get this Australian fellow I had short-listed.'

'How is he?' I asked.

'As a doctor, first-rate. As a human being . . . Apparently humility doesn't flourish down under. And he's not as irresistible as he thinks.'

As usual, François's social observations were right on target.

Everyone was waiting up for my return and one by one they all came up and hugged me. All except a big muscular-looking guy who merely offered his simian hand and introduced himself in a broad Australian accent. 'Doug Maitland,' he announced. 'Too bad I wasn't there when you got winged, mate,' he added modestly. 'I could have sorted you out right on the spot.'

'Oh?' I enquired. 'Are you a brain surgeon?'

'No, orthopaedics. But I know my way around the skull and from what I hear you didn't get it too badly. Anyway, mate, it's good to have you on board.'

Wait a minute, I thought to myself. That's my line, or did he think he had been here first? François must have had to dig very deep to come up with this character.

It was good to see everyone. Marta, François's assistant, gave me a big kiss, as did Aida, who was especially touched by the perfume I had brought her.

I had managed to travel several thousands of miles from Zürich avoiding any thoughts about what really awaited me. François had not changed the sleeping arrangements while I was gone. I was given a flashlight and Gilles helped me carry my stuff to hut number eleven. He left me at the door and I entered alone. I flashed my light over to the bed. It was neatly made with a light blanket folded at the foot. Scarcely three months ago Silvia and I were here together making love, and now I was alone and it was as if she had never existed. How the hell would I sleep here tonight?

The answer was—with difficulty.

WHEN DOUG MAITLAND first arrived he had been billeted with poor Gilles. It was, to say the least, a clash of cultures. It seemed our Australian colleague had joined us with a sense of entitlement even larger than his boots. Within days of my return, François asked if I would allow Gilles to share hut eleven.

'Sure,' I replied.

It didn't take me long to get resynchronised with the routine. The patients had changed, their ailments hadn't. There was still so much needless suffering. We continued to lose sick people who under ordinary circumstances we would have treated on the spot and sent home to live long lives.

Before we sat down to dinner one evening, François cornered me and remarked, 'By the way, Matt, tomorrow's Tuesday.'

'I'm glad to hear that—especially since today's Monday.'

'Come on, Matthew. You know what Maurice and I do every Tuesday afternoon.'

It suddenly came back to me. 'It's cataract day, isn't it?'

'Yes, and I'd like you to scrub up with us.'

'Since when do you need help with a procedure you've done a thousand times?'

'Since this.' He held his hands in front of me and I clearly saw the swelling in the knuckles that was either recent or that I had failed to notice before. It looked ominous. 'Go ahead, Matthew. Make the diagnosis. It looks like rheumatoid arthritis, and it is.'

'Oh, I'm sorry.'

'I've had time to get used to it. Fortunately I enjoy teaching, and frankly I'm looking forward to the bright lights of Paris. Meanwhile, there's a ready solution to the problem out here.' He looked me in the eye and smiled. 'You, *mon cher*. As of tomorrow you begin training to succeed me as cataract surgeon.'

'Doug won't like that,' I remarked, knowing how this would confer special status on me as François's deputy.

'Well, I don't like Doug, so we're even. It's a straightforward operation and our organisation has always trained nonsurgeons to specialise in this one ophthalmic procedure.'

I didn't know how to react. Among other things, I knew this had to be very difficult for someone like François.

'Matthew, why do you look so miserable?' he chided.

'Well, this may come as a shock, but I actually like you.'

'Thanks, but for heaven's sake don't tell anybody. I don't want to lose my image.'

'However will we manage without you, François?' I said.

'Very well, I think. They'll be getting a first-rate leader in you.'

I returned to the hut that night with completely different thoughts in my head. The day before I had been feeling sorry for myself. Tonight I had something more meaningful to think about: feeling sorry for François.

I could not sleep and wandered over to the empty dining room, reheated a mug of last night's brackish coffee and began to read up on my impending surgical specialisation. 'Cataracts are probably the greatest cause of blindness in the world and the biggest workload . . . the high prevalence in the underdeveloped world is probably related to high sunlight levels.' In places like Eritrea the incidence of this disease is at least twenty times as great as in Europe and America.

The next day François was his usual acerbic self. I'm sure he was aware that I was observing him with new eyes, studying him not merely as a doctor but as a leader. It was only in trying to imagine what it would be like that I realised how incredibly difficult and complex his job really was.

The following Tuesday, with my own hands I restored the sight of five blind people. It was the most thrilling experience of my life. An old man saw his grandchildren for the first time. A woman saw her grown son whom she had last seen as a little boy.

The moment François officially turned over the operation to my absolute control, the rumours began to fly. And socially I was in limbo: no longer one of the peons, but not yet the commander.

The only person who seemed at ease with me was Gilles, who was happy as a lark (so to speak) about being my roommate again.

With my eminence imminent, I was now granted a paraffin lamp to allow me to work at night, which aroused no small amount of envy. Of course the illumination also enabled Gilles to keep up his ornithological reading.

One night, as I was going over some records, Gilles posed a question.

'Matthew, could I ask you something?'

'What's that?'

He set his book down and took off his glasses. 'It's about your little piano.'

It was bound to come up sooner or later. 'What about it?'

'I never see you play it any more. Have you given it up for some reason—if I'm not intruding?' he diffidently added.

'No, that's OK,' I lied. 'I just don't have the time.'

I could see I was not convincing him.

'People say you were very good. Very good indeed.'

'I guess I was—once.'

He sensed that I was unwilling to open the door to my psyche any wider. Yet as he turned over in bed, he could not suppress an involuntary, 'That's too bad.'

'What is?' I asked, now slightly uncomfortable.

He raised his head and looked at me, myopic without his glasses. 'I've been in a room while a great pianist was playing and never heard a note.'

EVER SINCE FRANÇOIS had told me that I would be running the whole show, I'd had occasional spasms of doubt as to whether I was up to it without him there as a living encyclopedia. Then, gradually, as the months went by, I found myself almost looking forward to his departure so that I could institute some of my own ideas, especially a public health programme I had long been pondering.

During the week before officially taking over, I made a point of having a heart-to-heart conversation with every one of the doctors. I assured them that nothing would change in their jobs unless they wanted it to. (As usual Doug Maitland was the exception. He demanded to do the cataracts and I refused him.) It was gratifying to learn that the team was pleased that I had been selected. Everyone promised to help me get through the early difficult days.

On the day he flew home, our boss wanted no fuss and insisted I keep the clinics open as usual. Only myself and a driver were excused to take him to the airport.

The next eighteen months were a time of building. In a way it turned out to be an advantage to have François as our man in Paris because he was close to the purse strings. His diplomacy got us grants. And he performed miracles with the financing of my grandiosely named Public Health Campaign. I was determined to leave something permanent for the greater health of these long-suffering people. According to my records, by the time I left we had immunised nearly forty thousand children against smallpox and polio. We also trained twenty-four nurses and set up two mobile clinics to teach basic hygiene.

Interestingly enough, in all this time we had only one defection in the ranks. Doug Maitland, the mighty Australian Tarzan, couldn't take it. No sooner was the ink dry on his c.v. than, strangely, the climate began to affect an old rugby injury of his. It soon became— like the man himself—intolerable. Though it would wreak havoc with our work schedules, I let him go with a mere fifteen days' notice.

ERITREA IS A COUNTRY where nothing seems to end. The drought had begun in 1968—more than ten years earlier—and seemed as if it would go on for ever. Famine remained an unaltering fact of life.

The civil war also raged on unabated, with no sign of either side losing the will to fight.

This endlessness took its inevitable toll on my staff, to whom the morning queues never seemed one patient shorter, and on the trauma team, who were still removing bullets from wounded fighters day and night. By the following Christmas I could see that everyone was dreaming of home. Even I was growing weary of trying to boost their morale while maintaining my own.

When their contracts neared expiry no one signed up for an extension.

From the time we had spent together in Switzerland, my brother had learned how to win arguments with me without seeming to be arguing. He recognised that my psychic pendulum was currently swinging towards altruism and never once invoked our family—not even my little niece Jessica—as a possible reason to lure me home. Instead he pointed out the subtle connection between the new genetic sciences and the preventive medicine project I had been running on the ground.

'Just imagine,' he wrote. 'Some day we won't have to worry about curing diseases like diabetes because they won't exist. Instead of manufacturing artificial insulin for those who lack it, it's possible now to use new techniques to repair the genes in the body that should be doing it naturally. Don't you want a piece of this action?'

I was hooked again.

And I guess Chaz knew it when I asked him to send more stuff.

During the last six months of my contract I applied to various universities to pursue a doctorate in microbiology. My rather special field experience obviously made a positive impression on the schools I applied to, because they all accepted me.

I decided to go to Harvard purely so I wouldn't have to spend the rest of my medical career explaining to people why I hadn't.

The night before I left, we had the traditional drunken party with mocking speeches and lugubrious farewells. I was already feeling nostalgic but tried not to show it.

With such an early flight I would have no time next morning to say a proper farewell to the most important people there: the patients. So after closing my luggage and tying up my books, I strolled over and visited the various campfires of those waiting to be seen the next day. By now I spoke fluent Tigrinya and could trade quips with them.

I recognised a pregnant woman I had treated whose first child had died from dysentery. I wished her all sorts of better luck with her new one. She thanked me for my kindness. I kissed her goodbye and walked back to the hut.

Gilles was waiting anxiously for my return.

'Hey, look, Matthew, you almost forgot this,' he said, holding up my silent keyboard.

'That's OK,' I said. 'I don't need it any more.'

'But it would be a shame to just throw it out.'

I agreed and suggested to him that he give it as a gift from me to the pregnant lady sitting at the nearby fire. I could tell he was baffled about what *she* would do with it. But then he looked on the bright side and said, 'Perhaps it will inspire her child to become a virtuoso.'

'You never know.' I smiled and walked inside.

I still miss the people, the patients, even the tortured countryside. And when I said goodbye to my Eritrean friends I felt sad at leaving them to go back to a place where I could put my feet up, open a beer and watch *Wide World of Sports*.

A little more than two months before my leave-taking, we had begun to build a twenty-four-bed hospital with a well-equipped OR. It may not seem like much, I know, but it was a start.

And if there is one thing that I brought back from my experience in Eritrea it was that *I made a difference*.

PART III ─── SEVEN ───

New York, 1991. When I started at Harvard, the field of genetic engineering was in its infancy. It had been less than thirty years since Crick and Watson discovered the structure of DNA, providing a key that would in time unlock every secret of the body's seventy-five trillion cells. Yet there were already visionaries who believed that all diseases would ultimately be cured by the infusion of a repaired version of whatever gene was defective.

I was one of those dedicated zealots.

I spent the first four years after my return from Africa rooted in front of my electron microscope, running trial after trial, searching for the precise molecular match that could be used to reverse a tumour. My obsessive search for a single gene reminded me of Gilles, scanning the horizon for a glimpse of an elusive bird. And my compulsion to vanquish disease kept me up all night. Can man survive on pizza alone? For years philosophers have debated the question. But as a graduate student I tested it empirically. When you're in hot pursuit of a specific strand of DNA, you don't waste time on dinner or whatever meal the hour warrants. Pizza is the be-all and end-all.

The project for my dissertation was, not surprisingly, in the realm of neurobiology. When you have been shot in the head it is no exaggeration to say that your brain is often on your mind. Thus I took to searching the cerebral hemispheres, exploring neural pathways, leaping across synapses to see what I could find in this still little-known domain.

After finishing my research in molecular biology in 1984, I stayed at Harvard as a postdoctoral fellow. I guess inertia had a lot to do with it. Labs look pretty much the same everywhere, and Boston seemed as good a place as any to eat pizza.

Besides, on the rare occasions we did eat out, I always conned my buddies into going to the North End, the old Italian section of town where you barely saw a sign or heard a word in English.

Every time I went there I imagined I saw Silvia. Sometimes I thought I heard her voice or glimpsed her walking just ahead of me.

Even at night I would dream that she had reappeared, only to wake and find myself alone. I guess it wasn't simply the pursuit of science that kept me locked up in the lab.

As I began to publish my research findings, I received various enquiries from institutions sounding out my willingness to move. One particularly attractive offer came from Cornell Medical School in Manhattan. By this time Chaz was near despair, certain that I was turning into a 'frumpy old bachelor'. He was anxious for me to move. He touted New York's infinite cultural opportunities—theatre, concerts, operas and the like. Not to mention that the eminence that would immediately surround me if I took the job would be a lodestone to the best and brightest women.

I decided to go. It was time for a change. I was especially lucky to find a really nice apartment for sale on East End Avenue with a view of the river that inspired me to begin jogging. (My waistline appeared to be advancing even faster than my career.)

And so I moved down from Boston in June, when the early evenings were still cool enough to tempt the novice jogger.

My contract provided two laboratory assistants who definitely speeded up the output of my work. I also spent three afternoons a week as a paediatric neurologist. Though in the main I was dealing with cases for whom, unfortunately, we could offer a diagnosis and nothing more, I enjoyed the interaction with my young patients. This also served to remind me why I was doing all my research.

By the late 1980s, genetic engineering was finally producing some concrete results. In my own case I had developed a technique that enhanced T-cell reaction and helped reverse certain tumour growths in mice. Not that it was all work and no play. I mean, at least once a year I found myself at conventions in exotic places like Acapulco, Honolulu and Tokyo. And I *had* to go because I was now chairman of the school.

We were all in such a hurry then. And I think French Anderson, one of the pioneers in our field, best expressed the urgency we all felt: 'Ask the cancer patient who has only a few months to live. Ask the AIDS patient whose body is shrivelling . . . The "rush" arises from our human compassion for our fellow man who needs help now.'

But if our branch of medicine was ever to take wing, the bureaucrats in Washington had to find the courage to allow us to try out our therapies on human beings.

All sorts of moral as well as medical issues were involved. The notion of tampering with God's work was one doctrinal objection. There was also the legitimate fear that since the body contained at least one hundred thousand genes we might activate the wrong one by error and create some neoplasmic nightmare.

And yet, until we could find someone from the Food and Drug Administration willing to take a leap of faith, our struggle would remain a drama with no final act. Someone had to force them to let us intervene while there was still a breath of time. It fell to my lot to do just that.

I met Josh Lipton, a charming, tousle-haired eleven-year-old, when he was on his deathbed. He had been transferred from

Houston where the medulloblastoma growing in his brain had already been unsuccessfully attacked with chemotherapy, radiology and surgery. He now had at most a few more weeks to live.

Both Josh and his parents were fighters. And, as he clung tenaciously to life, they continued to look for other methods. I decided to appeal to Washington to treat Josh on a compassionate dispensation. I got two world experts to submit affidavits stating that this little boy was beyond all known medical help. And they urged the governmental honchos to let us try my procedure which—at least in laboratory experiments—had succeeded in reducing tumour growth.

As the bureaucrats sanctimoniously debated and discussed, Josh's life was quickly ebbing away. I examined him late one afternoon and realised that the next document to this endless paper chase would be a death certificate.

Though I did not know the man personally, I called the chairman of the committee, Dr Stephen Grabiner, and laid it on the line. 'Do you want me to read the FDA approval at his funeral, damn it? Get serious, Doctor. Take a chance. It's my neck, not yours.' (Actually, it was Josh's neck, but in the heat of these battles patients sometimes find themselves pushed to the periphery.)

Something seemed to be happening at the other end of the wire. A heart had informed a mind which had awoken a will.

'Point taken, Dr Hiller. I'll see if I can convene the committee over the weekend.'

IT IS CURIOUS the trivial details you remember about momentous events. It was nearly 3.00am on Thursday, March 14, 1991. We were sitting in the lab about to sample a new culinary delicacy, a smoked salmon pizza that I had ordered specially from Le Mistral, when the phone rang. 'Hey, Matthew, it's Steve Grabiner. I'm sorry to call you so late, but I knew you wouldn't want me to wait until morning. I won't bore you with the details, but the bottom line is that we're granting permission to do it *once*. I'll fax confirmation in the morning.'

I was speechless. 'Dr Grabiner—Steve—what can I say?'

'Well,' he replied with a light-hearted weariness, 'you can tell me that you're absolutely sure there's no way this could turn into a horror show.'

'Well, I can't, you know that.'

'That's why I'm going to have a very large Scotch and go to sleep. Good night, old buddy.'

As I scribbled a list of staff members to wake up, the qualms began. I had taken on the responsibility of a human being's life on a voyage to the unknown. And though Josh's parents had sworn to me that they held out no false expectations, I could not bear the thought of what my failure would do to them.

Time was so precious that I phoned the on-duty nurse in Josh's ward to have his parents summoned immediately to sign the informed consent. She replied that Mr and Mrs Lipton were already in their son's room.

Obsessively aware of every particle of sand slipping through the hourglass, I sprinted across the courtyard, took the elevator to Josh's floor and dashed towards his room. Barbara and Greg Lipton were now waiting outside in the corridor. There was an air of festivity that seemed unsettlingly premature.

'Oh, Dr Hiller, this is such wonderful news,' Barbara said.

'Thanks, Doctor,' the father acknowledged with more sobriety. 'You got us another chance.'

The boy was already awake and we exchanged a few friendly words while Resa, my senior lab assistant, prepared the apparatus.

I asked my young patient if he knew what this was all about.

'My dad says it's another new drug or something.'

'Not exactly a drug,' I explained. 'It's just a way I've worked out to rearrange the cells in your blood so they'll go back inside you and gobble up that tumour once and for all.'

He nodded sleepily as I took the syringe from the tray. I reached for the boy's emaciated arm and tried to find a vein that had not been ravaged. I went in as gently as I could and drew blood. Resa then hurried back to the lab where two other assistants were waiting to begin the slow, tricky process of reprogramming his gene to attack the tumour *in vivo*.

By 6.00am, the apparatus in my lab was humming and the replication was under way. This would all take time, the one thing in short supply. With nothing to do, I walked up and down the lab. Resa was the only one who had the guts to upbraid me.

'For heaven's sake, Matt, can't you find somewhere else to pace? You're getting on everybody's nerves.'

Just then the phone rang. It was Warren Oliver, the hospital press officer. 'Hey, Hiller, what's happening?'

I was hardly in the mood to make my anxieties public so I tried to dodge him. But he persevered.

'What's this I hear about you getting the go-ahead from the boys in Washington, DC? That's news, man. That's great news.'

'Only if it works.'

'It will, won't it? Besides, even if it doesn't, we can get mileage just out of you being the first to be granted permission.'

I tried to keep my temper and reminded myself that he was in the business of getting column inches into newspapers, which was fast becoming a medical speciality.

'I'm sorry, Warren. I've really got my hands full right now.'

'Well, just don't forget I'm here, Matthew. And we're a team. You're the inside man and I'm the outside man.'

I hung up on his pep talk and vowed not to do unto my lab staff what Warren was doing unto me. I let it be known that I was going out of the hospital for breakfast and would not be back for several hours. They did not disguise their gratitude.

Three days later we completed the retroviral gene transfer, and the new cells were ready to be introduced into the sick boy's bloodstream. Though officially no one knew what was about to happen, there was a palpable tension even in the corridor outside his room. His parents stood on either side of his pillow holding their son's hands as I sat on the bed and infused a minute quantity of liquid—less than a teaspoon—into a vein.

'How do the cells know exactly where to go, Doctor?' Barbara asked me afterwards. 'Isn't there a chance that they might get lost in a different part of the body?'

That was the nightmare version. I tried to look confident. 'Well, each one has a specific DNA address. I'm hoping that my virus has the right zip code.'

In the days that followed, I almost never left the hospital except to jog and collect my mail. At the end of the fifth day we took Josh to radiology for his first postinfusion scan. We all crowded round Al Redding, the chief radiologist, as he strained to dictate his findings into a microcassette recorder.

'Tumour measures at one point five by two by two which, compared with previous reading on the fourteenth, indicates no net growth.'

Murmurs among the onlookers.

'Did I hear you right, Al?' I demanded. 'Are you suggesting that the tumour hasn't grown at all?'

'That's what I've just reported, Matthew,' Redding answered

deadpan as he moved aside so I could take a closer look.

At this moment I indulged in a wild burst of hope. Yet I did not have the courage to share it with anyone, not even Josh's parents, whose reaction was the polar opposite of our cautious radiologists.

Barbara began to sob quietly. 'You've done it, Doctor. It's not growing any more.'

'We can't say that for certain yet,' I warned. 'Besides, as long as there's a trace of tumour there's always the risk of haemorrhage. This could just be a temporary remission. Meanwhile, I'm going to infuse some more of the new cells we've made.'

The scan four days later showed a twenty per cent reduction in the size of the tumour. It was getting harder to hide my elation, especially when at the end of the second week Josh was able to sit up in bed and dangle his feet over the side.

The miracle occurred three nights later. I was finishing my rounds and decided to visit Josh. I turned a corner and could not believe my eyes. At the far end of the corridor I saw him walking with his parents. *Without holding on to either one.*

It was an unbelievable sight and I was overwhelmed. I rushed to him. 'How do you feel?' I asked breathlessly.

'OK, Doctor. Cool.'

'He's more than OK, he's terrific,' laughed Greg.

We didn't stand on ceremony and request an appointment. I simply told a nurse to inform radiology that we would be bringing the kid up for a scan immediately. They didn't keep us waiting.

The results were sensational. The tumour had shrunk to half its former size and was no longer pressing against the brain.

The phlegmatic Al Redding finally defrosted his emotions and shook my hand vigorously. '*Mazel tov*, Matt. You've done it.'

'No, Al. It's Josh who deserves the credit.'

Back in my office, I called the various people in my life. My mother and Malcolm, Chaz and Ellen were all thrilled beyond words. The instant I set the phone down it rang again loudly.

'Now what's the story, Matthew?' Warren Oliver asked impatiently. 'In case you've forgotten, our research programmmes cost money and reporters are conduits to our contributors. I especially owe a favour to the gal from *The New York Times*. Come on,' he urged. 'Play the game. Tell me, have you got anything significant to report?'

'Not yet. Anything I tell you might inspire false hopes.'

'Did you just say "inspire"? Come on, Matthew, *give*.'

I was defeated, and, against my better judgment, agreed to go down to Oliver's office to be interviewed for fifteen minutes and give a sound bite or two.

This publicity meant nothing to me. With one bizarre exception. I wondered if the story would be picked up by the Italian papers.

IT WAS CLEAR that I had no escape. The press seemed to have got hold of every number at which I could be reached. My only recourse was to turn off my pager, duck into a movie and hide.

Or a concert. As I leafed through the Sunday *New York Times*, I studied the multitude of musical treats on offer. Yet I knew immediately which one I would attend. That very afternoon at Carnegie Hall, Roger Josephson, my old pal Evie's cellist husband, was playing Mozart, Chopin and Franck. She would doubtless be in the audience and I could catch up on her news.

The place was almost sold out, but I managed to get a single at the far end of the first row. Josephson had put on some weight and his hair was streaked with grey. His more distinguished aspect matched the greater maturity of his musical technique. He seemed to be approaching real virtuosity.

As an erstwhile accompanist, I could not help but notice the skill of his pianist, an attractive Mexican woman named Carmen de la Rochas. The two had obviously played together a lot.

I looked for Evie during the intermission, but the hall was crowded.

Roger and his partner played an exciting last movement to the Chopin, amply earning the rapturous applause they received.

I don't usually have the guts to do this sort of thing, but in my euphoria I walked to the stage door, identified myself as a friend of the Josephson family and had no trouble getting admitted.

Naturally the cellist's dressing room was packed with toadies, well-wishers, managers, publicists and the like. I was a bit hesitant to dive into that mob and instead stood on tiptoe to see if I could spot Evie. At that moment the Mexican pianist approached me and asked with a very alluring smile, 'May I help you?'

'Thanks,' I replied. 'I'm an old friend of Mrs Josephson and—'

'*I'm* Mrs Josephson,' she reacted, with a spark of Latin possessiveness. It took me about a second to catch on.

'But . . . what happened to Evie?' I responded gauchely.

'I did,' she grinned, her dark eyes flashing. 'They've been divorced for several years now. Don't you read the papers?'

'Uh, actually, I've been out of the country,' I explained in an apologetic tone. 'In that case, I'd better be going.'

'Why not wait? She'll be here any minute to pick up the girls.'

It was both good news and bad. I was about to be united with a very dear friend. At the same time I'd learned that the intervening years had not been kind to her.

'No, I can't believe it.' The voice was mezzo-soprano, the tone joyous, the timbre like a bell. It was Evie, looking at first glance no different than she had all those years ago. Her brown hair was cut short and her large hazel eyes shone as brightly as ever.

Heedless of the onlookers we rushed to embrace one another. Her perfume was the scent of spring flowers.

'Where have you been all the past years?' she demanded, continuing to hug me unselfconsciously.

'It's a long story, Evie. And I take it there have been one or two changes in your life.'

'Yeah, you might say that,' she acknowledged good-humouredly. 'Come and meet the two most important ones.'

She approached a pair of young girls, each wearing blue sweaters over white blouses. They were chatting to a Hispanic woman who turned out to be a temporary nanny. They looked like miniatures of their mother. Lily, thirteen, and Debbie, eleven, reacted with enthusiasm when Evie introduced me.

'This is my old friend, that genius pianist I've told you about.'

'The one that became a doctor instead?' asked Lily.

'And went to the jungle and never came back?' said Debbie.

'Almost right,' their mother laughed.

'How did you hear I was in Africa?' I asked.

'I have a source,' Evie answered playfully. 'It's called the *Michigan Alumnus*. Your brother's been terrific about keeping the old grads up to date on your activities. Your family must be very proud.'

Only then did she take a careful look at the left side of my forehead. 'It's barely visible,' she said sympathetically. 'I guess you were a little lucky, huh?'

'You might say that,' I said, intending to sound ambiguous.

'What brings you to New York?'

I immediately realised that my fraternal chronicler had been a little less forthcoming about my more recent movements.

'Well, I suppose I'd have to say Cornell Medical School. I'm a professor there.'

'Really?' she asked delightedly. 'Has doctoring turned out to be everything you hoped for?'

'Do you want a simple yes or no answer—or can I take you and the girls for an early dinner somewhere?'

'Oh, yes,' her daughters cheered.

'Are you sure you haven't got anything more important planned?' Evie asked with a twinkle.

'Absolutely.' I then addressed the two girls. 'Do you like the Russian Tea Room?' They both nodded eagerly.

Evie somehow caught her former husband's attention. They exchanged waves that obviously signalled the transfer of authority for their children, and we walked out. Once we reached the street the girls instinctively walked ahead, allowing me to say what was uppermost in my mind to their mother.

'Hey, I'm sorry the marriage didn't work out.'

'I wouldn't quite put it that way, Matthew. We've got two wonderful girls and I wouldn't trade them for anything.'

'But still, bringing them up on your own—you are on your own, aren't you?'

'This is New York,' she answered. 'The ratio is hardly what you would call favourable to single women.'

The moment we reached the Russian Tea Room our attention shifted to blinis and sour cream and, of course, tea from the samovar.

It had been such a long time since we had seen each other that a great deal of basic information had to be exchanged. Not unexpectedly, she chose the girls as a high point and Roger's opting for the fiery Mexican as the low point. She spoke quite candidly in front of the kids, who had obviously lived through it blow by blow. My own source of pride was the clinic in Eritrea with the low point inevitably being the bullet. This left a whole further occasion to discuss Silvia.

Evie seemed as indomitable as ever, strong, resilient, optimistic, prepared to take the good with gratitude and the bad without self-pity.

After the divorce she had obviously modified her career plans but Roger had been generous enough to get her appointed at Juilliard where she tutored privately, taught master classes in cello and still performed with various chamber groups.

'How do you spend your summers?' I asked, trying to confine our first discussion to neutral topics.

'Well, the girls join Roger and'—you could see she still had trouble saying it—'Carmen for a month. Lately I've been going out to Aspen for the music festival. Now why don't you tell me what you've been hiding? What's her name, and how many kids do you have?'

'What are you talking about, Evie?'

'What do you think I'm talking about? Your wife.'

'What wife?'

'The wife every halfway decent guy in New York always seems to have.'

'I'm sorry to disappoint you, but I haven't got one.'

She stopped, obviously unsure of how to deal with what to her was a genuine anomaly. I knew what her next question would be. 'Oh, did it not work out?'

'Uh,' I replied evasively, 'I'll tell you about it another time.'

'If it's not too painful for you.'

'Oh, it isn't,' I said unconvincingly.

When dinner was over and the girls had polished off their charlottes russes, I hailed a cab and took them home. To my delight I discovered that they lived just down the block from me in the legendary Beauchamp Court.

'Your building is famous,' I told the girls. 'People have nicknamed it Carnegie Hall East. They say it's the only apartment house in New York where every flat comes with a fridge, freezer, stove and Steinway.' I looked at Evie and she smiled.

'That was one advantage of my getting sole custody. There was no pressure about who got the apartment. Now tell me what I've been dying to hear. What are you doing musically at the moment?'

I groped for a reply. 'At the moment I'm going through all the Mozart piano concertos.'

'That's terrific!' Evie exclaimed.

And then I added sheepishly, 'Only I'm letting Daniel Barenboim do the actual playing. I mean, I'm so busy in the lab that the best I can do is play the CDs. But anyway, that's a long story and we can talk about it next time—which I hope will be soon.'

In the elevator I could see Evie holding a wordless dialogue with her daughters and their signals of agreement.

'Uh, Matt, the girls and I would like to have you come over for dinner.'

'That would be lovely.'

We went through the complicated exercise of harmonising diaries. The first day we could clear was nearly a fortnight later, which I welcomed since I would need time to organise my thoughts.

Rediscovering Evie had opened up a vein of memories. Of missed opportunities, of chances lost. I should never have allowed us to drift apart. One thing was sure. Now that we had found each other once again, our friendship would begin precisely where we had left off. And this time there would be no intermission.

EIGHT

The trouble with being an eccentric is that everybody notices when you act the slightest bit normal.

Thus when, two weeks later, I left the lab at 6.00pm, letting it be known that I would not be returning till the next day, tongues began to wag. I had even kept the details from my secretary, Paula. I had her mark the evening merely as 'dinner 7.30'.

Carnegie Hall East lived up to its reputation. As I entered, I recognised a famous pianist and his wife obviously headed for a concert. And the Italian elevator man, Luigi, chatted about music nonstop as he brought his clientele up to their destinations.

When I arrived at Evie's floor, it was no surprise to hear Rachmaninov's Third Piano Concerto emanating live from her neighbour's apartment. But what struck me most at that moment was the pungent aroma of tomatoes and garlic wafting from underneath Evie's door. For some strange reason it made a deep impression on me. Of a real home dinner, not a restaurant or microwave. And waiting for me now to join them: a real family.

Debbie opened the front door, announcing that her mother had been held up at a faculty meeting, and had arrived home but minutes earlier. 'Can you come back a little later?' she suggested helpfully. 'We're not ready yet.'

'Debbie,' called Evie's disapproving voice, 'bring Matthew to the kitchen this minute.'

Evie smiled when I entered. 'Hello. As the head waitress just told you, I'm running slightly late. Would you open the Chianti?'

While Lily grated the Parmesan cheese into a bowl, Evie poured the pasta into a colander.

We kissed each other on the cheek.

During dinner I shared memories of Eritrea. Afterwards, the girls patently ignored Evie's unambiguous order to repair and do their homework. She eventually had to spell it out as a command and with that they both decamped. Though a reluctant Debbie stretched the time out by petitioning her mother to allow her to return and 'listen when you guys start playing'.

'No one said anything about playing,' Evie countered with a slight hint of embarrassment. 'Matthew's had a long day and may just want to sit back and relax.'

To emphasise the change of subject she then turned to me and asked, 'What time do you usually start at the hospital?'

'Actually, sometimes I spend whole nights at the lab.'

This personality defect in me mistakenly impressed the girls.

'You mean you don't go to bed at all?' Lily asked, wide-eyed.

'Oh, I always get a few winks curled up on my couch.'

'Is that why you're not married?' Debbie asked ingenuously.

Evie's face turned red as she pulled rank. 'That's quite enough, young lady. You are now officially dismissed.'

'OK. See you guys later, I hope.'

'Gosh, they're cute,' I laughed. 'How can Roger bear to be without them?'

'Oh, he manages,' she answered, her displeasure undisguised. 'I think he even schedules his tours to coincide with their vacations, so they couldn't possibly be with him.'

'I'm sorry, Evie,' I offered sympathetically. 'That's not really fair to you. I mean you should have a chance to tour as well.'

'Maybe when the girls are old enough. I'll just have to wait. Now you—we've heard about your medical exploits. Tell me what you're really doing musically.'

I had come without illusions, knowing that the topic would inevitably be broached. After all, it used to be our common bond. What could I offer as a rational explanation? The trauma of the gunshot? I had never revealed this to anyone. And only now, in opening my heart to Evie, did I begin to comprehend the full extent of the painful silence I had been living in all these years. I also realised as we talked that Evie was the only person in the world I could have shared this with. I started with that afternoon after the concert in Crans.

'My God, Matt.' Evie grabbed her forehead in disbelief. 'How can you stand it? It must have been devastating.' We exchanged no words for a few minutes. Then she looked at me earnestly and said, 'Tell me everything. Please, Matt, don't be afraid.'

We talked late into the night. Of Silvia. Of Paris. Of Africa and then Silvia's total disappearance.

Evie simply listened. At last, when I had finished, she looked at me for a moment and observed, 'You're still in love with her.'

'I don't know. I guess she's still a presence in my psyche.'

'All the time?'

'Of course not. Now and then. Hey, it's not a big deal any more.'

'That's not how it sounds to me,' she answered with concern. 'Damn it, Matthew, why are you still pining after all this time? I mean, do you believe she ever thinks of you?'

'I don't know,' I prevaricated. And then, 'Unlikely.' And finally, 'Of course not. Not at all.'

'You bet she doesn't,' Evie said with anger. 'For heaven's sake, Matt, music was the breath of life to you. How could you let her steal your very being?'

I had no answer for that.

'Come on, Matt. It's me, your old friend Evie. Look me in the eye and say that you can bear to live without your music.' She put her hand on mine and said this was the worst thing she could ever imagine happening to an artist.

I reminded her that I was a doctor.

'That doesn't make you any less an artist,' she replied. She thought a moment and then asked, 'Have you tried at all since then? Even playing something simple like the Minuet in G?'

'Evie, it's all gone. Every note. I've more or less grown used to it. I mean, as a doctor I've saved lives. That was a kind of privilege. Believe me, if I had to choose . . .'

'But why should you, Matthew? Why should you be punished like this?'

In a way I now regretted having told her. And yet in my heart I knew that had our paths not crossed again I couldn't have survived much longer.

I BLAMED MYSELF for staying much too late. Yet we'd been so caught up in talking we hadn't noticed the time.

When I got home I even had to fight off the ridiculous notion to call her as we used to in the old days, just to say thank you.

I was unwilling—or unable—to give in to sleep, so I sat down and tried to dream up a casual pretext for another such encounter. Perhaps I'd invite Evie and the girls to a concert or a matinée, a Sunday morning bike ride through the park, then brunch at Tavern-on-the-Green. As I mulled over the alternatives, I noticed that they all involved us as a pseudo-family. Why had I not thought about inviting Evie out to dinner on her own? Was I perhaps afraid of something like emotional involvement? *But then, you idiot, what would you call the heart-to-heart communication you had with her tonight? You couldn't be much more involved than that.*

I had an inner dialogue with Chaz, who asked sarcastically, 'What's the problem now, big brother—scared of being happy?'

Answer: yes.

I called the next morning and thanked Evie. She emphasised that the girls had really liked me and had begged her to ask me again soon. 'Incidentally,' she enquired, 'are you interested in coming to a Mozart party a week from Saturday? Every year a bunch of friends get together in his honour. Everyone who wants to gets a chance to perform.'

Sounded like a bit of pressure, but she quickly reassured me.

'Anyone who doesn't play an instrument can play the audience. So all you'd have to do is sit and listen and forgive the mistakes.'

'Mistakes?'

'Sure, they're a real mixed bag of musicians. My best pal, Georgie, teaches viola in our department at Juilliard. Her husband, Harvey, is an accountant and a real sweetie, but to put it mildly he's a keyboard klutz. We kind of close our ears because he's so enthusiastic. Would you like to come?'

'Sounds like fun. What time should I pick you up?'

'Is eight o'clock OK?'

'Great. I look forward to it.'

I WAS NEVER very good at parties, which is why I was always so grateful for the chance of making music. Mind you, this time I was not at a loss for conversation since the subject was familiar and I could hold my own discussing the new artists on the scene.

Good old Amadeus's repertoire got a workout, with much emphasis upon the strings. Then they reached the quintets. The E flat was the showpiece for our host, the philharmonious accountant. Evie told me that he'd been practising for this all year long.

While the other participants cheerfully took their places, tuning up and chatting, he stood anxiously and scanned the audience. For some unknown reason his glance fell on me.

'Uh, I've noticed you're not playing. Would you be able to turn pages for me?'

'I'd be happy to.'

We commenced, with Harvey labouring like Hercules just to keep up with the music. I felt like when I'd been an intern watching a particularly maladroit physician botching up a simple operation. Thankfully it ended. And then Evie and some faculty friends came up to play a string quintet. As she passed by she gave me a kiss and whispered, 'You did a terrific job, Matt.'

'Thanks,' I laughed and kissed her back.

Evie was careful not to allude to my past as a pianist. But it was quite evident she had confided in a friend or two about my future as a . . . partner? For almost everyone I spoke to gave an unsolicited endorsement of her as a person and as a musician. One man offered the opinion that her ex-husband Roger was a total creep to give up a gal like that. 'Sooner or later he'll come crawling back.'

Not if I had anything to do with it.

We stayed late. When we at last returned to Evie's apartment, Bob the night man waited patiently to see if he should take me down. I wasn't sure what Evie wanted, but thank heavens *she* was.

'We haven't had much chance to talk this evening. Why not come in for a while?'

'Fine,' I answered, and Bob disappeared.

'I'll make coffee, and we can have it in the studio,' she said, pointing towards the room to the right of the front door.

I walked into the studio and switched on the light. It was a musician's paradise. Whatever wall space wasn't lined with books was soundproofed in cork. Evie's library seemed to contain every work that had been written on the cello. Her music stand was set up by the window so she could gaze out at the river while she played. There was also a Steinway grand.

Evie entered with a tray of coffee just as I had taken one step closer to the instrument. She had the infinite delicacy to say nothing.

I took the tray, set it down on a table, and put my arms round her. We held each other tightly for a moment. Then we kissed, no longer merely friends, now on the verge of being lovers. It felt completely natural. I disengaged myself from her after a moment and gently closed the door.

I WAS BORN AGAIN that night. I knew that I would wake and Evie would be there. Not just tomorrow or the next day, but an infinity of future mornings. I would now open my eyes, reach over and touch her. For the first time I felt an intimation of eternity.

Hours later the rising sun seemed to welcome us as a part of nature's scheme of things.

I woke up in love.

And then we had to scramble. The girls were still asleep, so there was time for us to make a semblance of propriety. Evie hurried to her room while I dressed quickly and straightened up the studio to look as if I had decided to 'stay over' at the last minute.

In any case we all had breakfast as a family and, when they went back to their rooms to do whatever girls do on Sunday mornings, Evie and I sat smiling at each other.

'Well, that happened rather fast,' she laughed.

'I hardly think knowing each other for about twenty years would put us in the hasty category. Don't you agree?'

Her expression said it all without the need for words. The only question was: now what?

We sat drinking coffee and pretending to browse through sections of the Sunday papers when we both were bursting to discuss our common future.

'Are you going home?' she asked.

'Eventually. I mean, sooner or later I've got to at least change my shirt.'

'But after that?'

'I don't know. What do you have in mind?'

'Well, Matt, we started something—how do you propose we continue?'

'By doing precisely that, Evie, by continuing. The only problem is my apartment barely has enough room for your cello, much less your daughters.'

'So why don't I invite you to stay here for, let's say, a week?'

'What about the girls?'

'Well, I agree there might be a problem there,' she acknowledged, smiling. 'I don't think they'd ever let you leave again.'

And that's exactly what happened.

A week became a month, then two, then three. One evening Debbie, never one to mince her words, enquired without a blush, 'Matthew, can I call you Daddy?'

I looked at Evie as I replied, 'That depends on whether your mother will let me call her Mrs Hiller.'

I had decided long ago, and was merely waiting for the right time to ask her.

'Well, Mom, are you going to say yes?'

Evie was beaming. 'If you and your sister will be bridesmaids.'

'Does that mean we get to wear new dresses?' Lily suddenly popped out from wherever she was listening.

'Yes, my darling,' Evie answered. 'That will mean a whole new everything.'

A week later, Judge Sydney Brichto made a house call and united us as man and wife in the presence of Evie's daughters. Georgie, Evie's violist friend, was matron of honour and my assistant Dr Morty Shulman held the ring for me. As a special treat, Georgie's husband Harvey played what sounded like the wedding march.

I was alive for the first time. I only realised this after the first month of marriage. How could I have wasted so many years of utter incompleteness? Never really having lived with anyone, except in Africa, I had no idea what marriage was like on a day-to-day basis. I wondered if someone as obsessively involved with his work as I could cut the mustard as a husband. Yet by taking for granted that I could, Evie gave me the confidence to prove her right.

She also taught me how to be a parent. I was soon visiting the girls' school, talking over academic problems with their teachers just as if I had been doing so throughout their lives. (Roger's participation ended with his signature on each semester's cheque.) In a way, I had already learned so much in observing Evie that I had a head start on life's least user-friendly occupation.

Then came the watershed.

The following summer I was invited to address the annual meeting of the International Neurological Society, this year being held in Rome. I wavered. Evie guessed the reason instantly.

'What are you afraid of, Matthew? Is Silvia beginning to assume mythical proportions in your mind?'

'Evie, I'm not afraid of meeting her.'

'Then you're afraid of *not* meeting her.'

'I'm not afraid of anything. Just let me tell you what I'd like to do.'

'OK, I'm listening,' she said impatiently.

'Well, as I see it, Italy's not just a country. In the summer it's one great big music festival. There's a million different kinds of concerts:

opera in the Baths of Caracalla, the arena in Verona, you name it. Why should I deprive you guys, and me, of this incredible experience? Let's spend at least a whole month there.'

As she threw her arms round me, I let out a sudden groan.

'What's the matter now?' she asked.

'Now I have to come up with a speech.'

THE IDEAL TOPIC was obvious. For my keynote address I would present the most up-to-date results of the procedure that had worked so well on Josh Lipton and, since then, half a dozen others. Evie was terrific, helping me prepare. She even insisted that I do a complete dress rehearsal in our room before delivering it to the vast throng of international nit-pickers.

With their infinite gift for sensationalism, the Italian media picked up my research and I found myself being lionised by an excited swarm of reporters.

I confess that when the girls went out shopping on the Via Condotti, I went to the hotel operators' station and leafed through the Milan phone book.

Needless to say, Silvia's number was not listed.

I HAD PREPARED a special surprise for the girls. Evie's lifelong dream had been to visit Venice. So I arranged for us to spend the entire last week there before we flew home.

The legendary city with the liquid streets exceeded all our expectations. We heard choirs sing the sacred music of Giovanni Gabrieli in St Mark's Basilica, and the Albinoni horn concertos performed under the magnificent ceiling by Titian in the Church of Santa Maria della Salute. The next afternoon, crossing the great piazza in the pastel sunset, we cringed as geriatric orchestras in neighbouring cafés scratched out the corniest of pop tunes.

I suddenly realised that I was as happy as a man had any right to be. Impulsively, I kissed the girls and hugged my loving wife.

The following day we visited the Gran Teatro la Fenice. This classic red-velvet jewel box of an opera house had been the site of the first performance of *La Traviata*, the opera that had also been my 'first date' with Silvia. Now I stood for a long while behind the back row gazing at the empty stage. And somehow I felt the final curtain had at last descended. The heroine was no longer waiting in the wings, poised to appear when least expected in the theatre of my memory. I would no longer be time's hostage. *Finita la commedia.*

A seemingly mundane incident proved the turning point.

Evie was not a vain person. Yet when we were in the Hotel Danielli I was surprised when I came out of the shower to see her looking at herself in the full-length mirror, pinching herself at the waist.

I knew exactly what she was thinking.

'You're fine, Evie. You have a lovely figure.'

She blushed with embarrassment. 'You don't have to flatter me, Matthew. I know I've put on nearly five pounds.'

'I never noticed,' I said lovingly.

'Well, *I* have. And I've got to do something about it before it turns you off. I'm going to get up and jog tomorrow morning.'

'Where do you expect to jog in Venice?'

'I'm told that at dawn the Piazza San Marco is like Central Park. Will you come with me?'

At 6.00am I hauled myself out of bed, quickly downed some black coffee and shuffled out to the piazza, where we joined at least a dozen motley—no doubt all American—fitness freaks, in outlandish garb and expensive footwear.

As I plodded along, I watched the look of determination on Evie's sweating face. She really loves me, I thought to myself. She wants to stay attractive in my eyes. She doesn't want to age. I guess she doesn't realise that one of her most endearing qualities is the fact that her beauty transcends time.

From that moment on I looked forward to growing old with my wife. I mean, I had already learned the difference between a *coup de foudre* that strikes a twenty-year-old and the profound love that captures a mature adult by slow and powerful osmosis. This kind of emotion endures because it adapts to change. I could imagine Evie with grey hair, and I knew she would care for me when I had lost all of mine.

Mature passion is not immutability. It is growth.

Suddenly I realised that in my imagination Silvia had never altered from the last moment I had seen her. In my daydreams she had remained for ever young.

How could Evie's reality compete with Silvia's timeless perfection, unchanged and unchanging?

And then a thought occurred to me. What if I had walked by Silvia at some point during this last month. How would I have known? Perhaps her raven hair was now streaked with silver, her face slightly lined. Perhaps, like Evie, she had put on a pound here and there. The Silvia I was remembering no longer existed.

I grabbed Evie's hand. She slowed down and stopped running.

'Hey, tiger,' she smiled, herself slightly out of breath. 'You'd better get in shape.'

'You're right,' I grinned back. 'Especially with a young wife like you.'

Our arms round one another, we walked slowly back to the hotel as the Piazza San Marco filled with sunlight. And my heart with love.

NINE

The next years had the serenity of Beethoven's 'Pastoral' Symphony. We were very happy. For a long time anyway. Then out of the blue came that astounding phone call from Nico Rinaldi. Ironically, maddeningly, just when I thought I had finally exorcised her, Silvia reappeared in my life.

I should have said no right away. That would have been easier for all of us. It would have been over—quickly and painlessly.

Thank God for Evie. She had come along and rescued me from the emotional paralysis that gripped my life. And now she was the only person in the world that I could speak to. I checked her Juilliard schedule in my diary, called and got her out of class.

'Matt, is something wrong? Are you all right?'

And then I told her what had happened. Quickly and succinctly. Like a young clinician offering a case history to his professor.

'I'm sorry, Matt. Will you be able to help her?'

'Maybe, I don't know. I'm worried, Evie.'

'What about? She's just another patient now, isn't she?'

I didn't answer instantly.

'*Isn't* she, for heaven's sake?'

'I guess so.'

'Then what are you afraid of?' Only Evie could have asked that question so directly. 'Matthew, listen to me. You've got nothing to worry about. You don't love her any more.'

'What makes you so sure?'

'You love *me*, you idiot. It's OK. You'll cure her. And then you'll be cured of her. She'll finally be out of your system for good and we'll live happily ever after.'

'Yes, I suppose you're right.'

As I hung up I could not help thinking, I hope you are.

WHY DID I NOT SAY NO? What was there possibly to gain by seeing her? Apologies? Some sort of spiritual retribution?

All this time I'd known that Silvia was still alive because I'd read it in the papers. I'd come across the public messages announcing to the world that she was married, had two children. Did she ever once attempt to find out how I was?

The violence of my anger took me by surprise. I had never realised that I harboured such a resentment.

Just then the door to my office opened.

'Mr and Mrs Rinaldi,' my secretary announced.

Curiously, I looked at him first. I suppose I wanted to see what she preferred to me.

Tall, broad-shouldered, high forehead. We were both losing hair, but he more stylishly. Nico wielded his charisma deftly. Firm hand-shake, voice secure and modulated. Wholly in control.

'Dr Hiller,' looking me straight in the eye, 'thank you for seeing us so swiftly.'

'Please sit down.'

Did I betray the slightest hint of tremor in my voice?

At last I looked at her. By any standards she was beautiful. The brilliance of those eyes had not diminished. Nor the seductive power of her smile. Despite illness and the passage of time she'd lost none of her magic.

She avoided my gaze even when she murmured, 'It's good to see you again.'

And then it became clear: she's afraid of me now, I thought.

Nevertheless, in this woman—exquisite even in the shadow of death—I recognised the person I had loved so passionately.

And like a man standing on the edge of the seashore suddenly gripped by a powerful undertow, I felt myself losing balance.

They sat down side by side in front of my desk. Rinaldi held her hand. It was territorial, of course. He was reminding me that although they were petitioning for my help, she belonged to him.

For her part, she sat passively, saying nothing.

Nico took the initiative. 'Well, Dr Hiller? I assume you've had a chance to study my wife's notes?'

'Yes, Mr Rinaldi, I have.'

'And?'

'I'm sure I'm telling you nothing new when I say that the tumour is very advanced.'

He seemed to take this as implicit criticism and felt obliged to defend himself. 'I was being cautious, Doctor. I thought the surgeon's knife was too great a risk. She's had the chemotherapy and radiation. In most cases that would have been sufficient.'

Merely to demonstrate that I had studied the folder well, I made a few general comments to them. Then standard procedure required that I check the back of her eyes with an ophthalmoscope. I had performed this routine a million times before. Never before had I given any thought to the dimension of intimacy involved. But this was not an ordinary patient. This was Silvia.

I recognised her perfume. It added a certain reality to what seemed a dream. I then bent over to look into her pupils. They were the same eyes I had gazed into half a lifetime ago. Inevitably our foreheads brushed. She was silent. I wondered if the same sensual memories were leaping to the surface of her skin. And I was surprised that I could feel so strongly after all this time. My reverie was suddenly interrupted by the impatient voice of Rinaldi.

'What is your opinion, Doctor?' he asked curtly.

I didn't answer him directly, but merely suspended my examination, stood up and retreated behind the ramparts of my desk.

'Mr and Mrs Rinaldi, I've been giving this serious thought. I really think for everyone concerned it would be better if another doctor treated you.'

'But you're—' he started to object.

'I don't mean by another method, since I do think the genetic route is all that is open to you now. But there are other experts. My colleague Dr Chiu in San Diego—'

Silvia looked at Nico with helpless panic. She seemed about to say something to him but he silenced her with a wave of his hand.

'I'll take care of this,' he declared in Italian.

He stood up in what was perhaps unconsciously intended as intimidation. 'Now, Dr Hiller,' he began, 'without going into detail, I can understand your reluctance to take on this case. I respect your feelings in the matter. On the other hand, we all know that you pioneered this work. Your record is the best.'

He approached my desk, fixing my eyes with a saturnine gaze.

'Can you deny this to my wife?' His right fist hit my desk.

At this point Silvia said in a frightened voice, 'Nico, I think we'd better go.'

He ignored her and remained determined to persuade me. But his tone this time was unmistakably a supplication. I could hear his voice almost choke as he said, 'Please.'

Clearly he loved her.

For the next few moments we all remained silent, thinking our own thoughts and wondering what I would do. At last I heard myself say, 'OK . . . OK, Mrs Rinaldi.' I took a deep breath and began. 'I can't say I like what I see. There's considerable swelling of the optic nerve, indicating intracranial pressure. But I don't have to tell you that, you're a doctor. I know you've had one already, but I'd like another scan. I'll call and make arrangements. Is there a particularly convenient time?'

'No. We're at your disposal.' Nico retreated into politeness.

'Thank you. Now let me remind you that the tumour is dangerously large—even for genetic therapy.'

'But you will try to treat it?' Nico interrupted.

I waited a split second before answering, to make sure that he understood that I had given due consideration to his question.

'Yes, if there are no contraindications in the blood test. But none of us should cherish any false illusions.' I paused and then asked, 'Is that understood?'

Nico answered. 'Yes, Doctor. But assuming there are no, uh, problems, how soon could you begin?'

'I could have my nurse take some blood now to get the usual screens out of the way. That would mean, all being well, we can start as soon as we get the results. I would strongly advise you to remain in New York. With a malignant vascular glioma there's always the chance of haemorrhage. And the less moving around the better.'

'There's no question,' he agreed. 'We have an apartment here and a full-time nurse. As it happens, I have to fly to Italy in a few hours, but I'll be back the day after tomorrow at the latest. And I'm always reachable by phone.'

'Fine,' I said. And inwardly questioned how he could be so sublimely overconfident as to leave me alone with Silvia.

After they left, I sat there with my head in my hands, wondering why I was doing this. I was tempted to cancel the rest of my patients. But then, I did not want to be alone with my thoughts. And so, for the next few hours, I lost myself in the mortality of others.

At three o'clock the phone rang. It was Evie.

'How did it go?' she asked.

'All right. She's very sick.'

'I'm sorry. But how did *you* feel?'

'Sad for her,' I answered. Which was part of the truth anyway.

'I can sense there's a lot to talk about. Why don't we meet at the Ginger Man and have a quiet dinner? Debbie's got ballet and Lily has a swimming lesson. By the time I round them up and give them dinner it'll be eight or so. You'll be free by then?'

'Absolutely. I'll call you.'

I hung up and tried to immerse myself in work. Since I had asked not to be disturbed I ignored the phone ringing. After about fifteen minutes, Paula buzzed me to say, 'I know what you said, Matt, but Mrs Rinaldi is very anxious to speak to you.'

'OK, put her through.'

'Hello. Am I disturbing you?'

'That's all right, Silvia. What is it?'

'Can I see you? Can you come to the house?'

I was about to protest the fullness of my schedule when she added, 'I really need to talk to you.'

I glanced at my watch. If I got Morty Shulman to take the afternoon seminar I would have two hours and still could be on time for Evie. I proposed five o'clock and she accepted.

It was an unusually mild February afternoon. I needed to get some air and collect my thoughts, so I walked to their penthouse on Fifth Avenue. All the way I wondered what I was about to hear.

AN ITALIAN MAID in a black and white uniform answered the door, took my coat and accompanied me to the vast terrace overlooking Central Park. Silvia was reclining on a chaise longue, warmly dressed, her knees covered by a blanket. She introduced me to Carla, her nurse, who had been sitting next to her. The woman rose respectfully. I explained that the blood-test results were fine and that I had scheduled the scan for the next morning at ten o'clock. Turning to Carla I enquired, 'How's the patient this evening?'

'The same, Doctor,' she replied, and retreated discreetly.

I looked at Silvia and asked, 'Why did you call me?'

'Nico left and I got very scared.'

'Of what?'

'Of dying.' There was fear in her voice.

'But, Silvia, I promise I'm going to do my best to help you.'

She looked up at me. 'I know that, now that you're beside me,' she answered. And then added tenderly, 'Matthew.' Her look—the way she spoke my name—confirmed that I had not been wrong. Once, at least, however long ago, I'd been the centre of her life. 'Can you stay for a bit?'

I sat down next to her.

'I'm sorry that it had to be for this reason, Matthew. But I'm really happy to see you again.'

I did not reply. I sensed the conversation was leading into areas off limits to a doctor and a patient. But she persisted.

'Do you remember the end of Gluck's opera, when Orpheus loses his beloved and sings that heartbreaking aria "What will I do without Euridice? That's exactly how I felt. And how I feel. There are so many things we have to tell one another. At least I have.'

It would be lying to say that I did not burn to know what had happened back then. That if I did not ask I would go to my grave wondering how she could have loved me one minute and deserted me the next.

'Matthew,' she said passionately, 'there's something you must know. I loved you. I loved you more than anything.'

Though I had fantasised her saying this at least a million times, I never really expected to hear those words again. Now the crucial question once again entered my consciousness. I had to know the truth. I lost control over my better judgment. 'Then why, Silvia? Why did you marry him?'

She looked away and her voice was barely audible.

'It's difficult, so difficult, Matthew.'

'Then let me tell you what I think happened.'

She stared at me, tears welling in her eyes, and listened.

'François didn't have anyone capable of operating on the bullet. You had to get me back to Europe, but the only way to bring me out of Eritrea was in one of Nico's helicopters from the Red Sea rig. You called him.'

She nodded.

'And the price for saving my life was . . .'

She buried her head in her hands and sobbed. 'I loved you much too much to let you die.'

'If only you'd told me.'

'But, Matthew, don't you see—I couldn't. I felt obligated. Especially since the operation was successful.'

I stared at her, scarcely able to believe that what I had imagined was in fact the truth. So, she had loved me after all. I suddenly longed to comfort her physically, but I did not dare.

And in that instant I forgave her everything.

WE SAT TOGETHER without talking, watching the sunset.

Damn it, why did she have to come back into my life?

And then she sighed. 'Now it won't be so bad, Matthew.'

'What?'

'If I die. At least I'll have seen you again.'

'But you won't die, Silvia,' I insisted.

She looked at me. 'Somehow when you say that I believe it. How many have you cured besides the Lipton boy?'

Ah, she had followed my career after all.

'Well, Josh is going to graduate from high school next year. Katie's just had a second baby. Donnie Cohen and Paul Donovan are leading completely normal lives.'

'That's wonderful. Any others?'

I answered her in a professional tone of voice.

'You're a doctor, Silvia. You know there's no such thing as a one hundred per cent success rate.' I hoped she would probe no further and she did not.

I glanced at my watch.

'Must you go now? Don't you have time for a drink?'

I remembered promising to call Evie after eight. I was still OK.

'I've got time, Silvia.'

She had already beckoned to the maid, who now stood awaiting her command. 'Is it still white wine, Matthew?'

'Anything,' I answered.

The servant went off and reappeared quickly with a tray bearing a bottle of Puligny-Montrachet and two glasses.

Perhaps it was the twilight, but there now seemed to be a touch more colour in Silvia's face as we gradually unlocked our memories and began to talk of the past. Around seven o'clock I made another attempt to extricate myself.

'Please,' she implored, 'stay with me for dinner.'

I acquiesced once more.

Half an hour later we were sitting inside a high-ceilinged dining room hung with canvases by Renoir, Cézanne and Pisarro.

'Did you ever see François again?' I asked.

'As a matter of fact, yes,' she said. 'In a way he sold out.'

'What do you mean? He's got two thousand doctors working in thirty-five countries. How can you call that selling out?'

She looked at me and smiled.

'He not only buttons his shirt, he wears a tie and jacket.'

'Oh,' I laughed. 'That really is going bourgeois.'

'We had dinner in Paris last year,' she continued. 'He was trying to charm a contribution out of Nico. By the end of the evening we were three million dollars poorer and he had a field hospital in Gabon.'

'Speaking of hospitals, what did you end up specialising in?'

She frowned. 'I gave up medicine a long time ago.'

'Tell me,' I said. 'I'm curious to know what could possibly have dampened your incredible idealism. I mean, in Eritrea you were so wonderful with children.'

'Well, Matthew, that was Africa. Italy is quite another matter.'

'Meaning?'

'Medicine and marriage don't mix so easily. I don't have to tell you how demanding paediatrics is. Besides, Nico needed me around in the evenings, and the kids of course.'

My pager bleeped. I pulled it out. The display read: CALL YOUR WIFE. I quickly excused myself and dialled the number.

'Are you all right?' Evie asked. 'Where are you?'

'There was an emergency,' I replied evasively. 'I'm on my way.'

'Come home as soon as you can. We've got a lot to talk about. I'll have something ready when you get back.'

'That's OK, I grabbed a bite. I just want to see you.'

'I'll be waiting, Matt.'

I then returned to Silvia.

'I'm afraid I've got to hurry.'

'Of course, I understand. I've kept you too long as it is. Will you play the piano for me tomorrow?'

I felt a sudden chill.

'I'm sorry, Silvia,' I said. 'I've really got to go.'

As we went to the door she took my arm. 'You can't imagine how wonderful this evening was. Thank you for everything.'

I walked slowly home, full of thoughts.

'YOU ARE ARRIVING late,' our elevator man declared.

'Yes, Luigi. An emergency,' I answered, in a tone that I hoped would discourage further dialogue.

Unfortunately I was one of his favourite conversation partners.

'Mrs Hiller is still awake,' he informed me. 'I hear her practising.'

That at least was a valuable piece of intelligence. For when it came to practice, Evie was a day person. The only reason she played at night, unless it was for a concert, was to let off steam.

And who could blame her for being angry? It was nearly eleven o'clock. She was still making music when I entered the apartment.

'I'm home,' I called as I walked in and headed for the studio.

The piano accompaniment to Franck's Sonata in A was booming from the giant speakers. I didn't know if she heard me enter, but she wasn't startled when I kissed her on the back of the neck.

'How was it?' she asked.

'It's been quite a day,' I answered. 'Want something to drink?'

'Yes,' she replied. 'Whatever you're having.'

I returned with a glass of chardonnay for each of us. But she did not leave her instrument. It was as though she wanted the cello as a third-party witness to our conversation. At last she put her bow down and took a sip.

She waited for a moment and then said with studied casualness, 'Was she still beautiful?'

I stared into the middle distance and said, 'Yes.'

She hesitated, then asked, 'Are you still in love with her?'

'No,' I said quickly. Perhaps too quickly.

She picked up the bow and began to play again.

'What did you talk about?'

'The past.'

'Anything in particular?'

'I was right—Nico did force her to marry him.'

'Lucky for me,' she said, not smiling.

She then played a long passage of music. I sensed she was preparing something important to ask me. I was right.

'Is there anything you want to tell me?'

I thought for a moment and then worked up the courage to say, 'Yes. I spent the evening with her.'

She could not disguise the hurt she obviously felt. Why the hell didn't I tell her on the phone?

'I'm tired,' she said. 'I'd like to go to bed.'

Five minutes later she turned off her light and lay back on the pillow. I thought momentarily about putting my arms round her and perhaps initiating something physical. As I hesitated she turned over with her back to me. I murmured, 'I love you, Evie,' but she seemed to have lapsed quickly into slumber.

I closed my eyes but could not sleep. At last I put on my bathrobe and went into the living room to look out at the sleeping city.

And wondered where it all would lead.

TEN

At ten forty-five the next morning, Silvia's driver called to inform us that they were two blocks from the hospital. I dispatched Paula to meet them at the entrance. To hear her tell it later, the limo was as big as a Boeing 747. When she arrived at my department every head turned. Silvia was by far the most glamorous patient I had ever treated. Even though time was of the essence and we were all ready to go, she insisted on making the rounds of the lab to see the futuristic apparatus that we used for restructuring DNA.

I introduced her to my assistant Dr Morty Shulman, lavishly praising his scientific acumen. I wanted her to be completely confident that if I were ever unavailable she would have a clued-in doctor in my place.

Mort and I then accompanied her to radiology on the tenth floor, and stayed with her as she waited for the MRI scan. She was strapped inside what looked like a narrow spaceship that would travel at imperceptibly slow speeds, photographing every centimetre of her head. It would ultimately provide a picture of the inside of her brain so clearly defined that conventional X-rays would seem like daguerreotypes by comparison.

When it was over I asked Morty to take her down for coffee while I hastened backstage to discuss the new photographs with senior radiologist Al Redding. As we walked to the elevator I said to Silvia, 'Mort's a tremendous raconteur. Make sure he tells you all of his legendary elephant jokes.'

By the time I got back, Al and his assistants had the pictures on the viewing box and were studying them closely. Al greeted me sombrely. 'Have a look.'

The damage was visible from halfway across the room, a splotch so large that it first seemed like a defect on the film.

'How can she still walk around with something that big?'

'She won't for long,' Al remarked gravely. 'That woman will be dead in less than a month.'

One of the residents then asked me, 'Dr Hiller, what are the chances of your therapy working with a patient that advanced?'

I was in no mood to share my thoughts and so simply answered, 'I'd like to study it alone for a few minutes. OK, Al?'

'Go ahead,' he agreed. 'The boys and I will grab some lunch.'

They left me in the room with the obscene image of Silvia's brain ravaged by the malign growth that certainly would kill her, barring some unforeseen miracle.

The full reality of it suddenly sank in. My God, I thought to myself. Silvia, my first love. She's still young. She's barely lived out half her life. And now she'll never see her children married or play with her grandchildren.

Or was there still a chance my protocol could save her? I needed an objective view from someone in the field whom I respected.

The timing worked out perfectly. Jimmy Chiu's phone in San Diego started ringing seconds after he had reached his office.

I greeted him laconically and requested that he do me the favour of reading a scan I was sending him by fax that very moment.

Jimmy was a friend. He sensed my urgency and waited for the fax. He was back on the phone to me in minutes.

'What's the difficulty, Matt?' he asked.

'I just want to know what you think, Jim. Could a patient with that tumour still be treated by the retrovirus route?'

'Are you kidding? That glioma's so large if it doesn't kill her it'll cause a haemorrhage that will.'

'Not even worth a try?' I still would not give up. He could sense that I was hoping he might re-evaluate his judgment.

'Come on, Matt, there are limits. We should concentrate on lives that can be saved. By the way, can you tell me who it is?'

'Sorry,' I answered. 'Thanks for your help, Jim.'

I hung up quickly, and with no need to act the stoic professional I buried my head in my sleeve and cried. Then gradually I remembered that Silvia was waiting for me downstairs.

Ironically, I found her laughing. Morty Shulman was regaling her with his best stories. She noticed me approach and brightened further, waving me to join them. 'You two doctors really should be on the stage,' she smiled. 'I mean, Matt could be a concert pianist and Morty have his own television show.'

My younger colleague looked at me with surprise.

'Hey, I didn't know you played.'

'At about the level of your humour,' I volleyed back.

I sat down and looked at Silvia more carefully. Now for the first time I could see a shadow of impending death on her face, and I suspected that she knew it too. Her radiance today was a kind of final blossoming before the flower died.

But either out of denial or sheer wilfulness she kept on talking about her future plans. From the productions that were planned for next season at La Scala to the trips that she would take that summer with her children. All things no longer possible.

Morty and I both saw Silvia to her car.

'Good Lord, Matt. Have you ever seen a bigger limo?' he remarked as they drove off.

'I've never seen a bigger tumour either, Mort. She hasn't a chance.'

'No!' He was genuinely shocked. 'Not that wonderful vibrant woman. I can't believe it—'

'Now, Mort,' I interrupted him. 'I'm going to ask you for a favour. From now on Silvia's your patient. You'll take care of her and see to it that she doesn't suffer for a second. Do you hear me?'

The assignment clearly caused him pain.

'But, Matt, she came all this way to be treated by you—'

'Just do it, Mort,' I ordered. 'Now you and Paula make sure that the infusion for Silvia is prepped as fast as possible.'

Morty must have thought I'd lost control of all my senses.

'Did I hear you right? One minute you tell me it's hopeless and the next you want us to accelerate the whole procedure? I mean, the guys are overstretched already. Can you tell me why?'

'Because,' I answered furiously, 'there still might be a miracle.'

I HAD GIVEN SILVIA strict orders to take a nap when she got home as the morning activities would have taken their toll.

So for the next two hours I sat in my office trying to prepare myself for her inevitable questions about the scan. I'd keep the truth from her, of course, but then I've never been very adept at lying. I only hoped the fact that we were going forward with the treatment would give some credibility to my prevarication.

Eventually I phoned her and she urged me to come over. She explained teasingly, 'I've got a special surprise for you.'

Ten minutes later I was at her front door.

She took my hand as I entered the apartment and led me to the terrace where an elaborate tea had been prepared.

'Sit down, Matthew. You won't believe what fate has brought us.' It was not easy to maintain my equanimity especially since, to the trained eye, her fragility was now much more noticeable.

'You'll never guess what's at the Met tonight.'

'I don't know,' I joked. 'The Three Tenors?'

'No, Matthew, be serious. What was "our" opera? *La Traviata*, of course. And tonight Gheorghiu and Alagna are singing. As you know, they're lovers in real life.'

'I suppose you've got a box there too?'

She laughed. 'By chance, we do. As my doctor, would you allow me to go, and will you join me?'

'Yes, on both counts,' I answered, inwardly rejoicing that there still was something that could bring her such happiness.

'When is Nico coming back?' I asked.

'Tomorrow morning,' she replied without enthusiasm. 'He called just after I got back from the hospital.'

'Sounds like an attentive husband.'

'Yes,' she said vaguely. 'I do believe he loves me very much.'

'How about your children? I know you have two boys. I mean, your lives are so public. Where are they at school?'

'In England, at Eton. They're as different as chalk and cheese. The older one, Gian Battista, is the portrait of his father and there's not a single sport he doesn't excel at. And then there's my little Daniele, so shy and bookish. How many children do you have?'

'My wife has two daughters from her first marriage. I'm very fond of them.'

'I can imagine you would make a lovely father. What's she like, your wife?'

I didn't know where to begin or whether I wanted to. I simply answered, 'She's a cellist.'

'Oh,' said Silvia. 'The two of you must play duets.'

I suddenly felt my privacy invaded and didn't want to answer, and yet I knew the wisest thing was to say yes and change the subject.

She then excused herself to dress for the evening. 'You must have calls to make: your other patients and the lab—'

'Yes.' I reacted with appropriate professionalism. 'I'll check with the lab and see how things are going.' Left alone, I dialled a single number.

'Yes?'

'Hello, Evie.'

'Where have you been? You're not replying to your pager.'

The truth is I had deliberately shut it off along with everything that was not Silvia.

'Sorry, it slipped my mind. Listen, about tonight—'

'Have you forgotten it's Thursday, Matt?' she chided. 'I've got a master class. I won't be home before ten thirty. Anyway, I'm rushing to pick up Debbie. Was there something special?'

'No. I just wanted to hear your voice.'

'Well, you're hearing it say goodbye. See you later.'

Silvia soon reappeared, dressed elegantly.

'It's definitely going to be a repeat of Paris,' I allowed. 'I'm under-dressed again.'

'Don't be silly. Come on, we'll be late.'

We went downstairs. Her car was waiting and we drove off towards Lincoln Center. Only then did I become aware of what a risk I was about to take. The opera house was barely a hundred yards away from Juilliard. If there was any spot in the entire city where the odds of running into Evie were highest, it was there.

And as if by prearrangement, when we stopped for a traffic light on Broadway, I looked out of the window and saw her standing on the corner of 65th Street, carrying her cello. 'Damn,' I muttered under my breath.

Silvia immediately sensed what was happening. 'Don't worry, Matthew, you can't see through these windows from outside.' Then she turned and looked again, remarking, 'The cello's almost as big as she is. Oh, and she's very attractive.'

I said nothing as I stared at Evie's face. I had always thought that the exquisite Silvia outshone my wife, whose true beauty was inward. And yet ironically, this evening Evie looked lovelier than ever. Perhaps it was the aura of sadness in her soft hazel eyes. I felt a strong compulsion to leap out of the car and throw my arms round her.

Oh, Evie, I'm so sorry that I've hurt you.

Lovers playing lovers.

It was perhaps the most memorable performance of *La Traviata* ever given, yet the opera had lost its magic for me. I no longer sympathised with Alfredo's infatuation or believed Violetta's sacrifice. I sat there impassively until Violetta sang her final aria. Now the part that had brought us both to tears in Paris so long ago had acquired a new personal dimension: 'O Lord, to die so young . . . so close to finding happiness.'

I looked at Silvia and noticed she was not crying. On the contrary, her face had a strange look of serenity. She took my hand and whispered, 'I've been close to happiness as well.'

Half an hour later we drew up at the front of her house.

'That was a wonderful evening. Will you come up for a drink?'

'No, Silvia. I can't.'

'Please. Nico's away, it's my nurse's day off. I just can't face being on my own.'

After that appeal I could not leave her.

'All right. Just for a minute.'

Upstairs it became clear that this had not been a sudden whim on her part. An elegant supper for two had been laid out in her dining room. And the maid immediately poured the champagne.

I drank perhaps a little too quickly.

As the meal progressed—I noticed she barely ate anything—she leaned towards me and said with emotion, 'Matthew, there's something I want you to know. Whatever happens, I'm leaving Nico. I've come to realise that life is too precious to waste on idle fantasies. And if you'll have me, I want to be with you.'

At any other moment in my life this would have been the fulfilment of a dream. But not now. Not any more. I tried to extricate myself as gently as I could and said with quiet emphasis, 'No, I'm sorry, Silvia. It's impossible. It's too late for both of us. You can't make eighteen years of marriage just disappear. And I have someone in my life who's very dear to me.'

'Matthew, don't I mean anything to you any more?'

'Silvia, you are and always will be a beautiful memory.' I stood up. 'I really have to go now.'

'No, please don't—' Her eyes filled with tears.

Foolishly I stopped and she drew nearer.

'You can't deny me this.' She threw her arms round my neck and pulled me towards her.

Just then the door opened and Nico entered.

For a moment we were all paralysed.

'Good evening,' he said, clearly restraining his fury. 'I'm sorry my early arrival has disturbed you.' And then pointedly, 'Good night, Doctor.'

'No,' Silvia angrily objected.

Nico turned and overruled her. *'Yes.'*

'I was leaving anyway,' I said. 'Good night.'

Still in shock, I rang for the elevator. A split second later from inside the apartment I heard Silvia shout, 'Nico, you don't understand.'

And then a sudden muffled sound like something falling.

The next moment their front door opened and Nico, ashen-faced, called out to me, 'Doctor, come quickly.'

I raced back inside. Silvia lay on the floor, motionless. I could see instantly what had happened. I bent down to examine her and ordered Nico, 'Call an ambulance!'

As I heard him on the phone frantically summoning medical assistance, I looked at Silvia, and saw for the first time a face that was not only beautiful but finally at peace. I would always remember her like this.

TWENTY MINUTES LATER we arrived at the hospital. Mort Shulman was waiting at the kerb. They immediately rushed Silvia to intensive care. But until the patient is hooked up to the life-support machines the closest relatives—even if they are Nico Rinaldi—are not permitted to go in. I could have, but chose instead to wait outside with him. He looked at me, confused.

'Shouldn't you be in there?'

'She's Dr Shulman's patient now.'

'As of when?'

'This morning. I'm staying here to keep you company.'

If anything, this threw him even more off-balance.

'What the hell's happened?'

'A haemorrhage most likely. It was always a possibility and I'm afraid the tumour had grown considerably since her last scan.'

Suddenly he was silent and a look of immense sorrow had taken over his face. 'No, that can't be true.'

'I'm sorry, Nico. I know this will be hard for you to hear, but it would be merciful if she didn't wake.'

He covered his face with one hand, shook his head and began to moan, 'You're wrong, you're wrong. She has to live.'

He stopped speaking, clearly trying not to let himself break down. I tried to comfort him.

'Nico, if there's any consolation, there was nothing you or anyone could possibly have done to change the outcome.'

'No,' he objected adamantly. 'It's my fault. I should have brought her to you earlier, but I kept her away because . . . It's so difficult to explain. I loved her so much. I've loved her ever since she was a little girl.'

I felt so sorry for him.

Suddenly he looked at me.

'I'm sixteen years older than her, Matthew. I should have been the one to go first. That's nature's way, isn't it?'

He stood rooted to the spot. Just then a nurse appeared to enquire if she could bring us anything. He waved her away. I asked for two cups of coffee.

I took Nico's arm and led him towards a bank of plastic chairs. He had suddenly become docile and even seemed to have grown smaller. I sat him down. He began to weep quietly.

We remained without speaking for a long time. Then out of the blue he turned to me and said without rancour, 'You didn't really know her. Deep down she was a child, a frightened child. How could it be otherwise after what happened to her mother . . .?'

I listened, wondering where this was leading.

'When you were attacked in Africa—when you were shot, she was terrified.'

What was he driving at?

'She begged me to protect her, to marry her right away.'

What was the point of arguing this now? What did it matter? I just let him talk. It was something that he wanted me to know and so I listened.

'I always knew she was a creature of expediency. To her mind, at this moment you were the stronger. You held the possibility of life in your hands. Silvia's first concern was always her own survival. That's what brought her to me eighteen years ago and to you today.'

I looked at him and then said gently, 'Nico, what purpose is there in my knowing this? How does it change anything?'

'Because it's important to me that you understand. She was mine in life and she is mine in death.'

Just then, Mort Shulman appeared. He was clearly ill at ease.

'Mr Rinaldi,' he said barely audibly, 'I'm sorry . . .'

Nico lowered his head and crossed himself. 'May I see her?'

'Yes, of course.'

Mort began to lead him towards the room, then suddenly the grieving husband stopped and turned to me.

'She was extraordinary, wasn't she?' Without waiting for my reply he turned again and walked away.

Yes, Nico. She really was.

EPILOGUE

It began to rain. I turned my collar up and let the shower soak me to the skin. I went down to the East River and began to walk aimlessly. Hardy joggers passed me by in both directions, savouring their masochism. My heart ached.

After a few more minutes it gradually occurred to me: for the first time in nearly twenty years I was free, completely free. The ghosts that haunted me had disappeared.

In the darkness, I suddenly became aware that my pager was bleeping. I reached into my pocket and pulled it out.

The screen displayed a message: YOUR WIFE IS WAITING.

AT LONG LAST, wet and shivering, I put my key in the lock of our front door. I stepped inside and heard the sounds of the Brahms Sonata in F major. It was my wife, embracing her cello, completely engrossed in the music while staring out of the window, her back to me. As usual the piano accompaniment was coming from a loud-speaker. Evie's concentration was so intense that she did not notice my presence. It was only when I shut the hi-fi off that she realised I was there. She looked up. Before she could speak I raised my finger to my lips to silence her.

She watched me wordlessly as I went to the shelf and found the piano copy of the Brahms.

I sat down at the keyboard, put the light on and began to turn the pages till I got to where she'd reached. I then turned to her and said softly, 'Shall we take it from number one nine four?'

She nodded incredulously.

Slowly, tentatively, I began to play to her.

It was not easy but, however awkwardly, I was playing. We joined together and conveyed our feelings to each other in the language of Johannes Brahms.

Miraculously, and yet at the same time in the most natural of acts, we were reunited musically. And as we played I tried to comprehend what had suddenly allowed me to break out from the prison of my muteness. Had let me talk again. Had let me *sing*.

'Evie—' I began.

She cut me off.

'Let's play the second movement.'

She started the slow *pizzicato*, and then continued with long weeping notes, over which my piano part hovered, embracing her melody. For a few moments the only sounds in the entire world were the harmonies of our relationship.

'I've always loved you, Evie,' I said quietly. 'I mean, always. From the very moment that we met at school. I was too shy to put it into words. I tried to tell you sometimes when we played.'

'Yes, I know,' she said, tears streaming down her cheeks. 'If only you had heard me answer you, you never would have let me go.'

'But does it make any difference now?' I asked.

'No, Matt,' she whispered. 'We're together and that's all that matters.'

The next movement was *allegro appassionato*.

'Love is never having to say you're sorry.' Twenty-one years after Erich Segal wrote that famous line in *Love Story*, he has returned to a strongly romantic theme in *Only Love*—a poignant novel with clear echoes of that 1970s tale of young love blighted by tragedy.

Segal's career, straddling the vastly different worlds of popular fiction and academia, is unusual. Born in Brooklyn in 1937, he was educated at a Jewish Theological Seminary with a view to becoming a rabbi, like his father. He eventually decided, however, to study the Classics, and went to Harvard, where he earned a Masters Degree and Doctorate. By 1970, when *Love Story* catapulted him to fame, he was teaching at Yale. Numerous academic prizes followed—and more novels, the most recent of which, *Doctors* (1988), *Acts of Faith* (1992), and *Prizes* (1995), were epic in scale: multi-character stories about doctors, the clergy and scientists respectively, set against panoramic backgrounds. They were in part inspired—like certain scenes in *Love Story*—by the great Classic dramas that Professor Segal deems 'the best stuff ever written'. 'To me,' he says, 'the Classics are very much alive. At many times in my writing career I have drawn upon famous scenes in ancient literature for my inspiration.'

Erich Segal now lives in England, and, although retired from teaching, still writes book reviews and academic papers and is a Fellow of Wolfson College, Oxford. He lives not far from the city, with his wife and two daughters both of whom, he says, are 'inveterate storytellers'. 'Sometimes when I wake up early I can hear the younger one telling herself stories in her room, completely involved in a world of her own creation. It sends a shiver up my spine and I wonder if there isn't something in the genes.'

KILLING

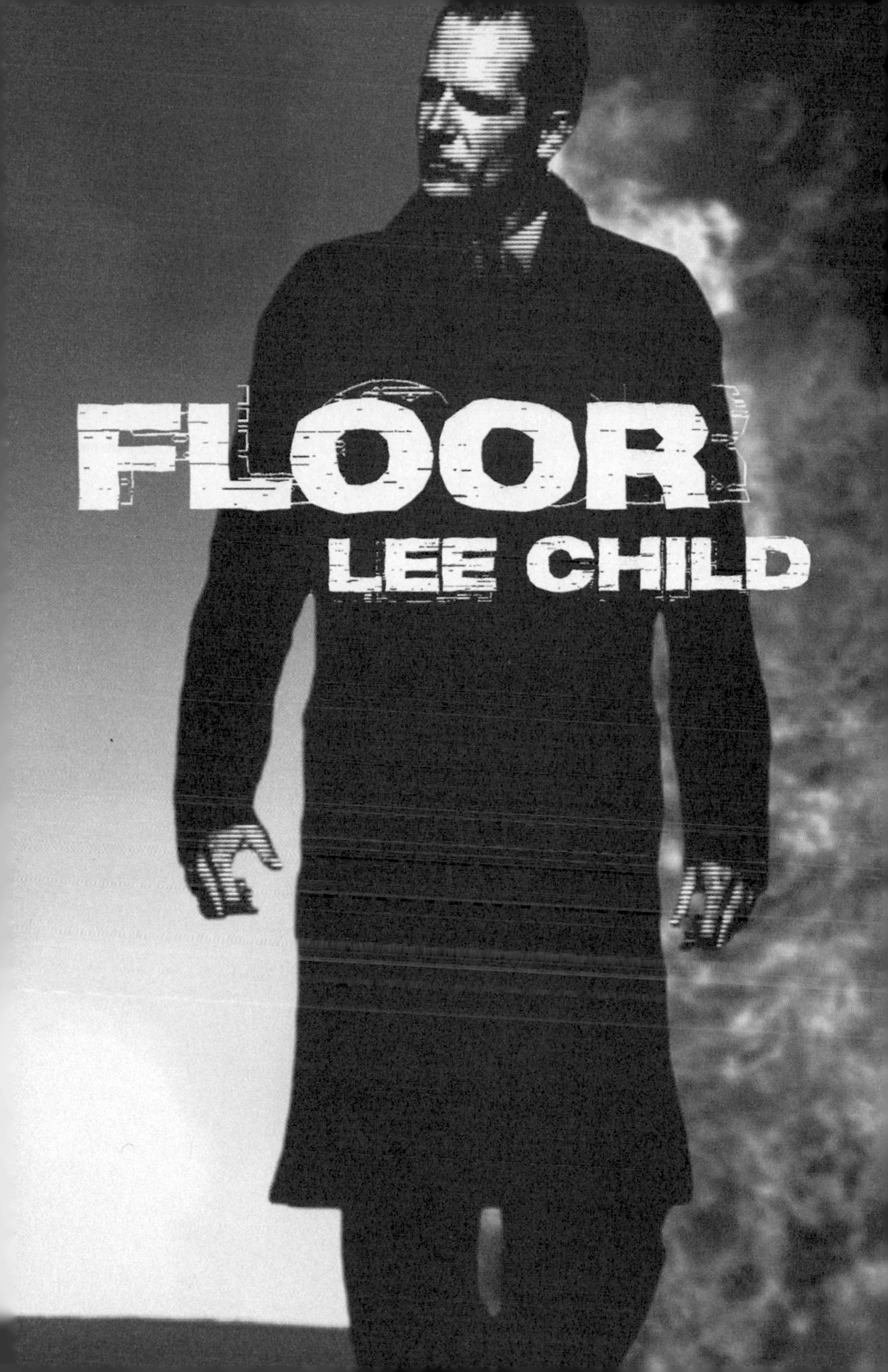
FLOOR
LEE CHILD

There's something strange about Margrave, Georgia. Something that the town's remote location alone cannot explain. The shops are always deserted, the carefully manicured lawns and sidewalks eerily silent in the fierce summer heat.

What dark secrets lie behind the immaculate, apparently respectable façade of this place that hasn't seen a homicide in thirty years? Ex-army investigator Jack Reacher is about to find out.

High-voltage suspense from a talented new British thriller writer.

ONE

I was arrested in Eno's diner. At twelve o'clock. I was eating a late breakfast and I was wet and tired after a long walk in heavy rain. All the way from the highway to the edge of town.

The diner was small, but bright and clean. Brand-new, built to resemble a converted railroad car. Narrow, with a long lunch counter on one side and a kitchen out back. Booths lining the opposite wall. A doorway where the centre booth would be.

I was in a booth, at a window, reading an abandoned newspaper. Outside, the rain had stopped but the glass was still pebbled with bright drops. I saw the police cruisers pull into the gravel lot. Red and blue light bars flashing and popping. Doors burst open, policemen jumped out. Two from each car, weapons ready. Two revolvers, two shotguns. This was heavy stuff. One revolver and one shotgun ran to the back. One of each rushed the door.

I just sat and watched them. I knew who was in the diner. A cook in back. Two waitresses. Two old men. And me. This operation was for me. I had been in town less than a half-hour. The other five had probably been here all their lives. Any problem with any of them and an embarrassed sergeant would have shuffled in and asked them to come down to the station house. I crammed a five-dollar bill under the plate, folded the newspaper and shoved it into my coat pocket.

247

Kept my hands above the table and drained my cup.

The guy with the revolver stayed at the door. He went into a crouch and pointed the weapon two-handed. At my head. The guy with the shotgun approached close. These were fit, lean boys. Textbook moves. The revolver at the door could cover the room with a degree of accuracy. The shotgun up close could splatter me all over the window. I spread my hands on the table.

'Freeze! Police!' the officer with the shotgun screamed as loud as he could. He was blowing off his tension and trying to scare me. Textbook moves. Plenty of sound and fury to soften the target. I raised my hands.

'Out here on the floor!' he yelled.

I slid slowly out of the booth and extended my wrists. I wasn't going to lie on the floor. Not for these country boys.

The guy with the revolver was a sergeant. He was pretty calm. The shotgun covered me as the sergeant moved near, holstered his revolver, unclipped the handcuffs from his belt and clicked them on my wrists. The back-up team came in through the kitchen. Took up position behind me. They patted me down. Very thorough. I saw the sergeant acknowledge the shakes of the heads. No weapon.

The back-up guys each took an elbow. The shotgun still covered me. The sergeant stepped up in front. He was a compact, athletic white man. My age. The acetate nameplate on his shirt said: BAKER.

'You are under arrest for murder,' he said. 'You have the right to remain silent. Anything you say may be used as evidence against you. You have the right to representation by an attorney. Should you be unable to afford an attorney, one will be appointed for you by the State of Georgia free of charge. Do you understand these rights?'

It was a fine rendition of Miranda. He spoke like he knew what it meant and why it was important. I didn't respond.

'Do you understand your rights?' he said again.

Again I didn't respond. Long experience had taught me that absolute silence is the best way. Say something, and it can be misinterpreted. It can get you convicted.

'OK, make a note, he's said nothing,' he grunted. 'Let's go.'

At the door we formed a single file. First Baker. Then the guy with the shotgun, walking backward, still with the big black barrel pointing at me. His nameplate said: STEVENSON. He too was a medium white man in good shape. Behind me were the back-up guys.

Outside in the gravel lot the heat was up. It must have rained all night and most of the morning. Now the sun was blasting away and the ground was steaming. Baker opened the rear door of the first car. My head was pushed down and I was nudged inside.

I was alone in the back of the car behind a thick glass partition. Baker and Stevenson got in the front. Baker drove. Stevenson was twisted around keeping me under observation. Nobody talked. The back-up car followed.

The drive to town was short. The car hissed over the smooth soaked tarmac. I looked out the window. Georgia. Rich land. Heavy, damp red earth. Very long and straight rows of low bushes in the fields. Peanuts, maybe. After a half-mile I saw two neat buildings, both new. The police station and the fire house. They stood together, behind a wide lawn, north edge of town. Three hundred yards south, I could see a blinding white church steeple behind a small huddle of buildings—flagpoles, awnings, crisp paint, green lawns. A prosperous community. Built, I guessed, on prosperous farm incomes and high taxes on the commuters who worked up in Atlanta.

The car slowed to yaw into the semicircular station house driveway. I read on a low masonry sign: MARGRAVE POLICE HEADQUARTERS. I thought: Should I be worried? I was under arrest. In a town where I'd never been before. Apparently for murder. But I knew two things. First, they couldn't prove something had happened if it hadn't happened. And second, I hadn't killed anybody.

Not in their town, and not for a long time, anyway.

We pulled up at the doors of the long, low building. Baker got out of the car and looked up and down along the frontage. The back-up guys stood by. Stevenson walked around the back of our car. Pointed the shotgun at me. This was a good team.

Baker opened my door. 'OK, let's go, let's go,' he said.

I pivoted slowly and twisted out of the car. The handcuffs didn't help. Even hotter now. I stepped forward and waited. Ahead of me was the station house entrance. Baker pulled open one of the plate-glass doors. It sucked against rubber seals. The back-up pushed me through. The door sucked shut behind me.

Inside it was cool again. Everything was white and chrome. Like a bank or an insurance office. A desk sergeant stood behind a long reception counter. He said nothing, just looked at me. Behind him was a huge open-plan space. A dark-haired woman in uniform was sitting at a wide, low desk doing paperwork on a keyboard.

Stevenson was backed up against the reception counter, shotgun pointed at me.

I was pushed into a room to the left. It was an interview facility. No windows. A white table and three chairs. In the top corner of the room, a camera.

I stood there and Baker ferreted into every pocket. My belongings made a small pile on the table. A roll of cash. Some coins. Receipts, tickets, scraps. Baker checked the newspaper and left it in my pocket. Everything else was swept into a large Ziplock bag. A bag made for people with more in their pockets than I carry. It had a white panel printed on it. Stevenson wrote some kind of a number on the panel.

Baker told me to sit down. Then they all left. Stevenson carried the bag with my stuff in it. I heard the lock turning. A heavy, well-greased sound. Sounded like a lock that would keep me in.

I figured they would leave me isolated for a while. Isolation causes an urge to talk. An urge to talk can become an urge to confess. It's a pretty good strategy.

But I figured wrong. A few minutes later Baker unlocked the door and signalled the uniformed woman into the room. The one I'd seen in the open area. The heavy lock clicked behind her. She carried a metal case which she set on the table. She clicked it open and took out a long black number holder. In it were white plastic numbers.

She handed it to me apologetically. I took it in my cuffed hands and held it under my chin. The woman took a camera out of the case and sat opposite me. She rested her elbows on the table to brace the camera. Sitting forward. This was a good-looking woman. Dark hair, great eyes. I stared at her and smiled. The camera clicked and flashed. Before she could ask I turned sideways on the chair for the profile. The camera clicked and flashed again.

Then she took out the fingerprint gear and inked my hands. Her fingers were smooth and cool. No wedding band.

The woman repacked the camera into the metal case. Baker rapped on the door. The lock clicked again. The woman picked up her stuff and left the room. Baker stayed with me. He shut the door and it locked with the same greased click. 'My chief's coming on down,' he said. 'You're going to have to talk to him. We got a situation here. Got to be cleared up.'

I said nothing back to him. Talking to me wasn't going to clear any situation up for anybody. But the guy was acting civilised. Respectful. So I set him a test. Held out my hands toward him. An unspoken request to unlock the cuffs. He stood still for a moment then took out the key and unlocked them. I dropped my arms to my sides. 'OK,' I said. 'Let's go meet your chief.'

It was the first time I'd spoken since ordering breakfast. Baker looked grateful. He rapped twice on the door and it was unlocked from the outside. He opened it up and signalled me through. Stevenson was waiting with his back to the large open area. The shotgun was gone. The back-up crew was gone. Things were calming down. Baker gripped my elbow lightly and we walked to a door at the back of the open area. Stevenson pushed it open and we entered a large office. Lots of rosewood all over it.

A fat guy sat at a big desk. Behind him were a couple of big flags. There was a Stars and Stripes on the left and what I guessed was the Georgia state flag on the right. On the wall between the flags was a big old mahogany clock. I figured it must be the clock from whatever old station house they bulldozed to build this new place. It was showing twelve thirty.

The fat guy at the big desk looked up at me as I was pushed in toward him. I saw him look blank, like he was trying to place me. He looked again, harder. Then he sneered at me and said, 'Get your ass in that chair and keep your filthy mouth shut.'

This guy was a surprise. He looked like a real asshole. Opposite to what I'd seen so far. Baker and his arrest team were professional and efficient. The fingerprint woman had been decent. But this sweating, overweight mess didn't look halfway competent.

'My name is Morrison,' he wheezed. As if I cared. 'I am chief of the police department down here in Margrave. And you are a murdering outsider bastard. You've come down here to my town and you've messed up right there on Mr Kliner's property. So now you're going to make a full confession to my chief of detectives.'

He stopped and looked up at me. Like he was still trying to place me. Then he hauled his bulk out of the chair and looked away. 'I'd deal with this myself,' he said. 'But I'm a busy man.'

He waddled out from behind his desk. I was standing there between his desk and the door. As he crabbed by, he stopped.

'I've seen you before,' he said. 'Where was it?'

He glanced at Baker and then at Stevenson. Like he was expecting them to note what he was saying and when he was saying it.

'I've seen this guy before,' he told them.

He slammed the office door and I was left waiting with the two cops until the chief of detectives swung in. A tall black guy, not old, but greying and balding. Just enough to give him a patrician air. Well dressed, in an old-fashioned tweed suit. Moleskin vest. This guy looked like a chief should look. He signalled Baker and Stevenson out of the office. Closed the door behind them. Sat down at the desk and waved me to the opposite chair.

He rattled open a drawer, pulled out a cassette recorder and inserted a tape. Pressed record. Then he sat right back in his chair and looked hard at me. Did the steepled fingers thing, like tall elegant people can.

'Right,' he said. 'We have a few questions, haven't we?'

The voice was deep. Like a rumble. Not a southern accent. He looked and sounded like a Boston banker, except he was black.

'My name is Finlay,' he said. 'I am chief of detectives here. I understand you have been apprised of your rights. You have not yet confirmed that you understood them. Before we go any further we must pursue that preliminary matter.'

Not a Boston banker. More like a Harvard guy.

'I understand my rights,' I said.

'Good. I'm glad about that. Where's your lawyer?'

'I don't need a lawyer.'

'You're charged with murder,' he said. 'You need a lawyer. We'll provide one, you know. Free of charge.'

'No. I don't need a lawyer,' I said.

The guy called Finlay stared at me for a long moment. 'OK. But you're going to have to sign a release.' He shuffled a form from another drawer and slid it across to me. Then he slid me a pen. I signed and slid the form back. He placed it in a buff folder.

'For the record we'll start with your name, your address and your date of birth.'

There was silence. I looked at him. This was a stubborn guy. Probably forty-five. You don't get to be chief of detectives in a Georgia jurisdiction if you're forty-five and black except if you're a stubborn guy. No percentage in jerking him around. I drew a breath. 'My name is Jack Reacher,' I said. 'No address.'

He wrote it down. Not much to write. I told him my date of birth.

'OK, Mr Reacher,' Finlay said. 'Tell me what happened.'

I had no idea what had happened. No idea at all. Something had happened to somebody, but not to me. I sat there. Didn't answer.

'What is Pluribus?' Finlay asked.

I looked at him and shrugged. 'The United States motto?' I said. '*E Pluribus Unum*? It means one out of many.'

He just grunted at me. I carried on looking straight at him. I figured this was the type of a guy who might answer a question.

'What is this about?' I asked him.

He sat back and steepled his fingers again. 'You know what this is about,' he said finally. 'Homicide. With some very disturbing features. Victim was found this morning up at the Kliner warehouse. North end of the county road, up at the highway cloverleaf. Witness has reported a man seen walking away from that location. Shortly after eight o'clock this morning. Description given was that of a white man, very tall, wearing a long black overcoat, fair hair, no hat, no baggage.'

Silence again. I am a white man. I am very tall. My hair is fair. I was sitting there wearing a long black overcoat. I didn't have a hat. Or a bag. I had been walking on the county road for the best part of four hours this morning. From eight until about eleven forty-five.

'How long is the county road?' I said. 'From the highway all the way down to here?'

Finlay thought about it. 'Fourteen miles, I guess,' he said.

'Right,' I said. 'I walked fourteen miles from the highway into town. People must have seen me. Doesn't mean I did anything to anybody.'

He didn't respond. I was getting curious about this situation.

'Is that your neighbourhood?' I asked him. 'All the way over to the highway?'

'Yes, it is,' he said. 'Jurisdiction issue is clear. No way out for you there, Mr Reacher. The town limit extends right up to the highway and the warehousing out there.' He carried on. 'Kliner built the place, five years ago. You heard of him?'

I shook my head. 'How should I have heard of him?' I said. 'I've never been here before.'

'He's a big deal around here,' Finlay said. 'His operation pays us a lot of taxes, does us a lot of good. So we try to take care of it for him. But now it's a homicide scene, and you've got explaining to do.'

'OK,' I said. 'I'll make a statement describing every little thing I did since I entered your lousy town until I got hauled in here in the middle of my damn breakfast. If you can make anything out of it, I'll give you a medal. Because all I did was to place one foot in front of the other for nearly four hours in the pouring rain.'

That was the longest speech I had made for six months. I watched Finlay struggling with any detective's basic dilemma. His gut told him I might not be his man. But I was sitting there in front of him. So what should he do? I let him ponder.

'No statements,' he said. 'I'll ask the questions and you answer them. You're Jack Reacher. No address. No ID. What are you, a vagrant?'

I sighed. Today was Friday. The big clock showed it was already more than half over. This guy was going to go through all the hoops with this. I was going to spend the weekend in a cell. Probably get out Monday.

'I'm not a vagrant, Finlay,' I said. 'I'm a hobo. Big difference.'

He shook his head slowly. 'Don't get smart with me, Reacher. You're in deep shit. Our witness saw you leaving the scene. You're a stranger with no address, no ID and no story. So don't get smart with me.'

He was just doing his job, but he was still wasting my time.

'I wasn't leaving a homicide scene,' I said. 'I was walking down a damn road. There's a difference, right? People leaving homicide scenes run and hide. They don't walk straight down the road.'

Finlay gazed at me and reviewed his options. Elected to go the patient route. Patient, but stubborn. 'Where are you from?' he asked. 'What was your last address?'

'What exactly do you mean when you say where am I from?'

His lips clamped. But he stayed patient. Laced the patience with an icy sarcasm. 'You don't understand the question, so let me try to make it quite clear. I myself was born in Boston, was educated in Boston and subsequently worked for twenty years in Boston, so I would say that I come from Boston.'

I was right. A Harvard guy. A Harvard guy, running out of patience. 'OK,' I said. 'You've asked the questions. I'll answer them. But let me tell you something. I'm not your guy. So do yourself a favour. Don't stop looking.'

Finlay was fighting a smile. He nodded gravely. 'I appreciate your advice.'

'You're welcome,' I said. 'OK. According to your definition, I don't come from anywhere. I was born on a US Army base in West Berlin. Show me a list of US bases all around the world and that's a list of where I lived. My old man was Marine Corps and my mother was a French civilian he met in Holland. I was a military kid. I did high school in two dozen different countries and I did four years up at West Point.'

'Go on,' Finlay said, making notes.

'I stayed in the army. Military Police. I served and lived in all those bases all over again. Then, Finlay, after thirty-six years of first being an officer's kid and then being an officer myself, suddenly there's no need for a great big army any more because the Soviets have gone belly-up. Which means that now I'm a thirty-six-year-old unemployed ex-military policeman getting called a vagrant by smug civilians. Maybe eventually I'll find something to do, maybe I won't. Maybe I'll settle somewhere, maybe I won't. But right now, I'm just enjoying myself.'

'When did you leave the army?' he asked, making notes.

'Six months ago. April.'

'What rank did you hold?'

'Major,' I said.

A long silence. Finlay drummed a rhythm with his pen.

'So let's talk about the last twenty-four hours,' he said eventually.

'I came up on the Greyhound bus. Got off at the county road. Eight o'clock this morning. Walked down into town, reached that diner, ordered breakfast and I was eating it when your guys came by.'

'Where did you get on the bus?' he asked.

'In Tampa, Florida,' I said. 'Left at midnight last night.'

He rattled open another drawer. Pulled out a Greyhound schedule. Riffled it open and ran a long brown finger down a page. This was a very thorough guy. He looked across at me.

'That's an express bus,' he said. 'Runs straight through north to Atlanta. Doesn't stop here.'

I shook my head. 'I asked the driver to stop. He said he shouldn't, but he did. Stopped specially, let me off.'

'Got family down here?' he asked. 'Or friends?'

'Not down here,' I said.

'You got family anywhere?' he asked.

'A brother up in Washington, DC,' I said. 'Works for the Treasury Department.'

Finlay wrote it all down. Then there was a long silence. I knew for sure what the next question was going to be.

'So why?' he asked. 'Why get off the bus at an unscheduled stop and walk fourteen miles in the rain to a place you had absolutely no reason to go to?'

That was the killer question. Finlay had picked it out right away. So would a prosecutor. And I had no real answer.

'What can I tell you?' I said. 'It was an arbitrary decision. Guy next to me had a map, and I picked this place out. I wanted to get off the main drags. Thought I could loop back down toward the Gulf, further west, maybe. And I thought I'd come and look for Blind Blake.'

'Who the hell is Blind Blake?' he said.

'A guitar player. Died sixty years ago, maybe murdered. My brother bought a record, sleeve note said it happened in Margrave. He wrote me about it. Said he was through here a couple of times in the spring, some kind of business. I thought I'd come down and check the story out.'

Finlay looked blank. It must have sounded pretty thin. He made a note.

'The midnight Greyhound out of Tampa, right?' he said. 'Got your bus ticket?'

'In the property bag, I guess,' I said.

'Would the bus driver remember?' he asked.

'Maybe,' I said. 'It was a special stop. I had to ask him.'

'Why aren't you working?' Finlay asked.

'Because I don't want to work,' I said. 'I worked thirteen years, got me nowhere. I feel like I tried it their way, and to hell with them. Now I'm going to try it my way.'

Finlay sat and gazed at me, evaluating scenarios like a chess player evaluates moves.

'Did you have any trouble in the army?' he said.

'No more than you did in Boston,' I said.

He was surprised. 'What do you mean by that?'

'You did twenty years in Boston,' I said. 'That's what you told me. So why are you in this no-account little place? You should be taking your pension, going fishing. What's your story?'

'That's my business, Reacher,' he said. 'Answer my question.'

I shrugged. 'Ask the army,' I said.

'I will,' he said. 'Did you get an honourable discharge?'

'Yes,' I said. 'Of course.'

He made another note. Thought for a while. 'How did it make you feel, being let go? Were you bitter?'

I thought about it. 'No,' I said.

Being out of the service felt great. Felt like freedom. My only problem was how to make a living without giving up the freedom. But I wasn't about to tell Finlay that. He'd see it as a motive. He'd think I had decided to bankroll my vagrant lifestyle by robbing people. At warehouses. And then killing them.

'Did you specialise?' Finlay asked. 'In the service?'

'General duties, initially,' I said. 'Then the last six years I handled homicide investigation.'

Finlay leaned right back. Gazed at me and exhaled. Sat forward. Pointed a finger at me. 'Right. I'm going to check you out. We'll get your service record. We'll check with the bus company. Find the driver, find the passengers. If what you say is true, it may let you off the hook. Obviously, certain details will determine the matter. Those details are as yet unclear.' He paused. Looked right at me. 'On the face of it, you look bad. A drifter. A vagrant. No address, no history. You may be a fugitive. You may have been murdering people left and right in a dozen states. I can't be expected to give you the benefit of the doubt. You stay locked up until we know for sure, OK?'

It was exactly what I would have said. I nodded.

Finlay clicked off the tape recorder and buzzed the intercom on the big rosewood desk. Asked Baker to come back in. I waited.

When Baker entered, Finlay told him to escort me to the cells. Then he nodded to me. It was a nod that said: *If you turn out not to be the guy, remember I was just doing my job.* I nodded back. Mine was a nod that said: *While you're covering your ass, there's a killer running about outside.*

THE CELL BLOCK was really just a wide alcove off the main open-plan squad room. It was divided into three separate empty cells with vertical titanium bars. The front wall was all bars. A gate section hinged into each cell. No furniture or bed ledge.

'No overnight accommodation here?' I asked Baker.

'No way,' he replied. 'You'll be moved to the state facility later. Bus comes by at six. Bus brings you back Monday.'

He clanged the gate shut and turned his key. I heard bolts socket home all around the rim. Electric. I took off my coat and rolled it up. Lay flat on the floor and crammed the coat under my head. Now I was truly pissed off. I was going to prison for the weekend. Not that I had any other plans.

I tried to finish reading the newspaper I'd picked up in the diner. It was full of the President's campaign to get himself elected for a second term. The old guy was down in Pensacola on the Gulf Coast, aiming to get the budget balanced before his grandchildren's hair turned white. He was cutting things like a guy with a machete blasting his way through the jungle. The Coast Guard had been running an initiative off Florida's coast for the last twelve months, boarding and searching all the marine traffic they didn't like the smell of. They'd seized all kinds of stuff. Drugs, mostly, but guns as well, illegal migrants from Haiti and Cuba. A big success. So it was being abandoned. It was very expensive to run. The Coast Guard's budget was into serious deficit. The President said he'd have to cut it. The economy was in a mess. Nothing else he could do. I stopped reading, because it was just making me angrier.

To calm down, I ran music through my head. The chorus in 'Smokestack Lightning'. The Howling Wolf version puts a wonderful strangled cry on the end of the first line. I lay there with my coat as a pillow and listened to the music in my head. At the end of the third chorus, I fell asleep.

I WOKE UP AGAIN when Baker started kicking the bars. They made a dull ringing sound. Like a funeral bell. Baker stood there with Finlay. They looked down at me.

'Where did you say you were at midnight last night?' Finlay asked.

'Getting on the bus in Tampa.'

'We've got a new witness. He saw you at the warehouse facility. Last night. Hanging around. At midnight.'

'Impossible,' I said. 'Who the hell is this new witness?'

'The witness is Chief Morrison,' Finlay said. 'The chief of police. He was sure he'd seen you before. Now he's remembered where.'

THEY TOOK ME back to the rosewood office in handcuffs. Finlay sat at the big desk, under the old clock. Baker set a chair at the end of the desk. I sat opposite Finlay. He took out the tape machine, pressed the record button.

'The last twenty-four hours, Reacher,' he said. 'In detail.'

The two policemen were crackling with repressed excitement. A weak case had suddenly grown strong. The thrill of winning was beginning to grip them. I recognised the signs.

'I was in Tampa last night,' I said. 'Got on the bus at midnight. Witnesses can confirm that. I got off the bus at eight this morning where the county road meets the highway. If Chief Morrison says he saw me at midnight, he's mistaken. At that time I was about four hundred miles away. Check it out.'

Finlay stared at me. Then he nodded to Baker who opened a file.

'Victim is unidentified,' Baker said. 'No ID. No wallet. No distinguishing marks. White male, maybe forty, very tall, shaved head. Body was found up there at eight this morning, on the ground against the perimeter fence close to the main gate. It was partially covered with cardboard. Negative fingerprint result. No match anywhere in the database.'

Baker waited for some sort of reaction from me. He didn't get one. He riffled through the file and selected another sheet. He glanced up again and continued. 'Victim received two shots to the head. Probably a small-calibre automatic with a silencer. First shot was close range, left temple, second was a contact shot behind the left ear. Obviously soft-nosed slugs, because the exit wounds removed the guy's face. No shell cases were found.'

'Where's the gun, Reacher?' Finlay said.

I looked at him and didn't speak.

'Victim died between eleven thirty and one o'clock last night,' Baker said. 'Body wasn't there at eleven thirty when the evening gateman went off duty. It was found when the day man came in to open the gate. About eight o'clock. He saw you leaving the scene.'

'Why before one o'clock?' I asked.

'The rain began at one o'clock,' he said. 'The pavement underneath the body was bone dry. So, the body was on the ground when the rain started. Medical opinion is he was shot at midnight.'

I nodded. Smiled. The time of death was going to let me out.

'Tell us what happened next,' Finlay said, grimly.

'You tell me,' I said. 'I wasn't there. I was in Tampa at midnight.'

'What happened next is you got weird,' Baker said grimly. 'Your first shot killed him. Then you shot him again, and then you went berserk. There are massive post-mortem injuries. You kicked that corpse all over the damn place. You were in a frenzy. Then you calmed down and tried to hide the body under the cardboard.'

I was quiet for a long moment.

'Post-mortem injuries?' I said.

Baker nodded. 'Just about every bone is smashed.'

'Who was he?' Finlay asked.

I just looked at him. Baker was right. It had got weird.

'What does Pluribus mean?' he asked.

I shrugged. Kept quiet.

'What's your phone number?' he said. Suddenly.

I looked at him like he was crazy. 'Finlay, what the hell are you talking about?' I said. 'I haven't got a phone. Don't you listen? I don't live anywhere.'

'I mean your mobile phone,' he said. He slid a piece of paper toward me. It was a torn-off section of computer paper. On it was printed an underlined heading. It said: Pluribus. Under the heading was a telephone number. 'Is that your number?' Finlay asked.

'I don't have a mobile telephone,' I said. 'I wasn't here last night. You're wasting time, Finlay.'

'It's a mobile phone number,' he said. 'Operated by an Atlanta air-time supplier. But we can't trace the number until Monday. So we're asking you. You should cooperate, Reacher.'

I looked at the scrap of paper again. 'Where was this?'

'In your victim's shoe,' Finlay said. 'Folded up and hidden.'

I sat in silence for a long time. I was worried. I felt like somebody in a kid's book who falls down a hole. Finds himself in a strange world where everything is weird. Like Alice in Wonderland. Did she fall down a hole? Or did she get off a Greyhound in the wrong place?

'Two things,' I said. 'The guy is shot in the head close up with a silenced automatic weapon. First shot drops him. Second shot is insurance. The shell cases are missing. What does that say to you?'

Finlay said nothing. His prime suspect was discussing the case with him like a colleague. As the investigator, he shouldn't allow that. But he wanted to hear me out. 'Go on,' he said eventually.

'That's an execution, Finlay,' I said. 'Not a robbery or a squabble. That's a cold and clinical hit. No evidence left behind. That's a smart guy with a flashlight scrabbling around afterward for shell cases.'

'Go on,' Finlay said again.

'Close-range shot into the left temple,' I said. 'Could be the victim was in a car. Shooter is talking to him through the window and raises his gun. Bang. He leans in and fires the second shot. Then he picks up his shell cases and he leaves.'

'He leaves?' Finlay said. 'What about the rest of the stuff that went down? You're suggesting a second man?'

I shook my head. 'There were three men,' I said. 'Think about it. A guy who uses a silenced small-calibre automatic for a head shot and an insurance shot is not the type of guy who then suddenly goes berserk and kicks the hell out of a corpse, right? And the type of guy who does get in a frenzy like that doesn't then suddenly calm down and hide the body under cardboard. You're looking at three separate things there, Finlay. There were three guys involved.'

Finlay shrugged. 'Two, maybe. Shooter could have tidied up.'

'No way,' I said. 'He wouldn't have waited around. He wouldn't like that kind of frenzy. It would worry him because it adds visibility and danger to the whole thing. You're looking at three guys.'

Finlay thought hard. 'So?' he said.

'So which one am I supposed to be?' I said. 'The shooter, the maniac or the idiot who hid the body?'

Finlay and Baker looked at each other. Didn't answer me.

'So whichever one, what are you saying?' I asked them. 'I drive up there with my two buddies and we hit this guy at midnight, and then my two buddies drive away and I choose to stay there? Why would I do that? It's crap, Finlay. Why the hell would I wait eight hours, in the rain, until daylight, to walk away from a homicide?'

Finlay looked deflated. 'I don't know why,' he said.

His case was crap and he knew it. But he couldn't pursue an alternative when his boss had handed him a suspect on a plate. He could follow up my alibi though. Nobody would criticise him for being thorough. Then he could start again on Monday. So he was miserable because seventy-two hours were going to get wasted. Time to help him out.

'Why don't you just call up the phone number and see who answers?'

'It's a mobile,' he said. 'If I call it up I can't tell whose it is or where it is.'

'Listen, Finlay,' I said. 'I don't care whose it is. All I care is whose it isn't. Understand? It isn't my phone. So you call it up and John Doe answers it. Then you know it isn't mine.'

Finlay drummed his fingers on the desk.

'You know how to do this,' I said. 'Call the number, give some story about a technical fault, get the person to confirm name and address. Do it, Finlay, you're supposed to be a damn detective.'

He leaned forward to where he had left the slip of paper and picked up the phone. Dialled the number. Hit the speakerphone button. The ring tone filled the air. It stopped.

'Paul Hubble,' a voice said. 'How may I help you?'

A southern accent. A confident manner.

'Mr Hubble?' Finlay said. 'Good afternoon. This is the phone company, mobile division. Engineering manager. We've had a fault reported on your number.'

'A fault?' the voice said. 'Seems OK to me. I didn't report a fault.'

'Calling out should be OK,' Finlay said. 'It's reaching you that may have been a problem, sir. I've got our signal-strength meter connected right now, and actually, sir, it's reading a bit low. It would help me to know the exact geographic location of your phone, sir, you know, right now, in relation to our transmitting stations.'

'I'm right here at home,' said the voice.

Finlay picked up his pen. 'Could you just confirm that exact address for me?'

'Don't you have my address?' the voice said. Man-to-man jocular stuff. 'You seem to manage to send me a bill every month.'

Finlay glanced at me. I was smiling at him. He made a face.

'I'm here in engineering right now, sir,' he said. Also jocular. 'Customer details are in a different department. I could access that data, but it would take a minute, you know how it is. You've got to keep talking anyway while this meter is connected, to give me an exact signal-strength reading, you know?'

'OK, here goes, testing, testing,' the voice said. 'This is Paul Hubble, right here at home, that's number twenty-five Beckman Drive, down here in little old Margrave, in the State of Georgia, USA. How am I doing on my signal strength?'

Finlay didn't respond. He was looking very worried.

'Hello?' the voice said. 'Are you still there?'

'Yes, Mr Hubble,' Finlay said. 'I'm right here. Can't find any problem at all, sir. False alarm, I guess. Thanks for your help.'

'You're welcome,' said the guy called Hubble.

The connection broke and dial tone filled the room. Finlay replaced the phone. 'Who the hell is this Paul Hubble?'

'You don't know the guy?' I said.

'I've only been here six months. I don't know everybody.' He turned to Baker.

'Hubble's a banker,' Baker said. 'Some kind of financial guy, a bigshot executive type, works up in Atlanta. I see him around, time to time. Stevenson knows him. Some kind of an in-law.'

Finlay turned back to me. 'I suppose you're going to say you never heard of this guy?'

'Never heard of him,' I said.

He glared at me briefly. Turned back to Baker. 'You better go and bring this Hubble guy in,' he said. 'Go easy on him. He's probably a respectable guy.'

Finlay left the room. Banged the heavy door. Baker walked me back to the cell and removed the handcuffs. Stepped back out and closed the gate. The electric bolts snicked home. He walked away.

'Hey, Baker,' I called.

He turned and walked back. A level gaze. Not friendly.

'I want something to eat,' I said. 'And coffee.'

'You'll eat up at the state facility,' he said. 'Bus comes by at six.'

He headed off to fetch the Hubble guy.

'CAN I GET YOU a cup of coffee?' Standing on the other side of the bars was the fingerprinting officer.

'Sure,' I said. 'Great. No cream, no sugar.'

She went to the machine. Poured me a cup and walked back. She was good-looking, about thirty, dark, not tall. But to call her medium would be unfair to her. She had a kind of vitality. It had come across as a sympathetic briskness in that first interview room. Now she seemed unofficial. Probably was. Probably against the fat chief's rules to bring coffee to the condemned man. It made me like her.

She passed the cup in through the bars. Up close she looked good. Smelled good. I took the cup. I was glad of the coffee. I took a sip. Raised the Styrofoam cup like a toast. 'Thank you,' I said.

'You're welcome.' She smiled. Her eyes were like a welcome blast of sunshine on a rotten afternoon.

'So you think I didn't do it?' I asked her.

'You think I don't bring coffee to the guilty ones?' she said.

'Maybe you don't even talk to the guilty ones,' I said.

'I know you're not guilty of much,' she said.

'Because my eyes aren't too close together?'

'No,' She laughed. 'Because we haven't heard from Washington yet.'

Her laugh was great. I looked at the nameplate over her shirt pocket. Her name was Roscoe.

She glanced around quickly and moved closer to the bars. 'I sent your prints to Washington over the computer link,' she said. 'That was at twelve thirty-six. Big database there, you know, FBI? Millions of records. There's a priority order for checking prints. You get checked first of all against the top-ten wanted list, then the top hundred, then the top thousand. If you'd been near the top, you know, active and unsolved, we'd have heard almost right away. But it's been almost three hours and we haven't heard. So I can tell you're not on record for anything very bad.'

The desk sergeant was looking over. Disapproving. She was going to have to go. I drained the coffee and handed back the cup. 'I'm not on record for anything at all,' I said.

'No.' She smiled. 'I could tell right away. You don't match the deviance profile. You got nice eyes.'

She winked and walked back to her work station. She sat down. All I could see was the back of her head. I leaned up against the hard bars, gazing at the back of Roscoe's head. I liked her.

BAKER HAD BEEN GONE maybe twenty minutes. Outside the big plate-glass doors the sun was falling away into afternoon. Shadows were longer. I saw the patrol car bounce into the driveway. No flashing lights. It came slowly around the semicircle and eased to a stop. Baker got out on the far side and walked around to his passenger's door. He opened it like a chauffeur. Part deferential, because this was an Atlanta banker. Part official, because this was a man whose phone number had been hidden in a corpse's shoe.

Paul Hubble got out of the car and stepped inside the station house. He looked like an advertisement. The sort that uses a grainy photograph of money at play. He was a tall white man in his early thirties. Sandy hair, tousled, receding just enough to show an intelligent brow. Gold-rimmed round eyeglasses. A square jaw. Very white teeth, on show as he smiled at the desk sergeant.

He wore a polo shirt with a small logo, washed chino pants, a thick white sweater draped over his shoulders. The sort of clothes that look old when you buy them for five hundred bucks. I couldn't see his feet because the reception desk was in the way. I was certain he would be wearing tan boat shoes without socks. This was a man who wallowed in the yuppie dream.

He was in a state of some agitation. Uptight. I was a policeman of sorts for thirteen years and I can smell a worried man a mile away. Hubble was a worried man.

I stayed leaning up on the bars, motionless. Baker signalled Hubble to walk with him to the rosewood office at the back of the squad room. As Hubble rounded the end of the reception desk, I saw his feet. Tan boat shoes. No socks. The two men walked out of sight into the office. The door closed. After a moment Baker came back out and headed for his desk.

'Hey, Baker,' I called.

He changed course and walked over to the cells.

'I need to go to the bathroom,' I said. 'Unless I got to wait until I get up to the big house for that, too?'

He cracked a grin. Grudging, but a grin. He shouted something to the desk guy. Probably a code for a procedure. He took out his keys and activated the electric lock. The bolts popped back.

He pushed the heavy gate inward. We walked to the back of the squad room. There was a lobby. Off the lobby were two bathrooms. He reached past me and pushed open the men's room door.

They knew I wasn't their guy. They weren't taking care. Out there in the lobby I could have decked Baker and had his weapon off his belt before he hit the floor. I could have shot my way out of the station house and into a patrol car. They were all parked right out front. Keys in, for sure. No problem at all. But I just went into their bathroom.

'Don't lock it,' Baker said.

I didn't lock it. They were underestimating me in a big way. I had told them I had been a military policeman, and a military policeman deals with military lawbreakers. Those lawbreakers are highly trained in weapons, sabotage, unarmed combat. Rangers, Green Berets, Marines. Trained killers. So the military policeman is trained even better. Better with weapons. Better unarmed. Baker had to be ignorant of all that. Otherwise he would have had a couple of shot-guns aimed at me. If he thought I was their guy.

I came back into the lobby. Baker walked me back to my cell and pulled the heavy gate shut. Operated the electric lock with his key. Walked away into the squad room.

JUST BEFORE FIVE o'clock, I heard a commotion coming out of the big rosewood office. Shouting, yelling, things banging. Somebody getting really stirred up. A buzzer sounded on Baker's desk and the intercom crackled. I heard Finlay's voice. Stressed. Asking Baker to get in there. Baker walked over.

The big plate-glass door at the entrance sucked open and the fat guy came in. Chief Morrison. He headed straight to the rosewood office. Baker came out as Morrison went in. Baker hurried over to the reception desk. Whispered to the desk sergeant.

The intercom on Baker's desk crackled again. Baker headed back to the office. The big front door opened again. Stevenson walked into the station house. It was like the excitement was sucking people in.

Stevenson spoke to the desk sergeant. He became agitated and ran toward the rosewood office. As he got to the office door it opened. Finlay and Chief Morrison came out. And Baker, holding Hubble by the elbow. Stevenson stared at Hubble and then grabbed Finlay by the arm. Pulled him back into the office. Morrison followed them in and the door slammed. Baker walked Hubble over toward me.

Hubble looked like a different guy. He was grey and sweating. He looked like someone had let the air out of him. His eyes behind the gold rims were blank and staring with panic and fear. Baker unlocked the cell next to mine and pushed him inside. Then he pulled the gate shut, locked it and walked back toward the rosewood office.

Hubble just stood staring blankly into space. Then he fell to his knees. Dropped his head. Roscoe stared at him from her desk. The desk sergeant gazed across. They were watching a man fall apart.

I HEARD VOICES raised in argument in the rosewood office. The door opened and Stevenson walked out with Chief Morrison. Stevenson looked mad. He strode down the side of the open area, straight past the reception counter and out through the heavy door into the bright afternoon. Morrison followed him.

Baker came out of the office and walked over to my cell. Didn't speak. Just unlocked the cage and gestured me back into the rosewood office.

Finlay was at the desk. He looked harassed. I sat down in the chair and he waved Baker out of the room.

'We got us a situation here, Mr Reacher,' he said. 'We bring this Hubble guy in, right? You maybe saw him. Banker, from Atlanta, right? Calvin Klein outfit. Very uptight. I ask him if he knows you. Jack Reacher, ex-army. He says no. Never heard of you. I believe him. He starts to relax. Like all this is about some guy called Jack Reacher. He's never heard of any guy called Jack Reacher, so he's here for nothing. He's cool, right?'

'Go on,' I said. I had less than a half-hour before the prison bus came by. I wanted some conclusions pretty soon.

'Then I ask him if he knows a tall guy with a shaved head,' he said. 'Well, my God! It's like I stuck a poker up his ass. He went rigid. Like with shock. Totally rigid. Won't answer. So I tell him we know this tall guy's been shot dead. He starts shaking all over the place. Then I tell him we know about the phone number in the shoe. His phone number printed on a piece of paper, with the word "Pluribus" printed above it.' Finlay stopped again. He was patting his pockets, each one in turn. 'He wouldn't say anything,' he went on. 'Not a word. He was all grey in the face. I thought he was having a heart attack. After a while I realised he was thinking like crazy. Trying to decide what to tell me. He just kept silent, thinking like mad, must have been forty minutes.'

Finlay stopped again. This time for effect. He looked at me. 'Then he confessed. I did it, he said. I shot him, he said. The guy is confessing, right? On the tape. I ask him, do you want a lawyer? He says no, keeps repeating he killed the guy. So I Mirandise him, loud and clear, on the tape. Then I think to myself maybe he's crazy or something, you know? So I ask him, who did you kill? He says the tall guy with the shaved head. I ask him, how? He says, shot him in the head. I ask him, when? He says last night, about midnight. I ask him who kicked the body around? Who was the guy? What does Pluribus mean? He goes rigid with fright all over again. Refuses to say a damn word. I say to him, I'm not sure you did anything at all. He jumps up and grabs me. He's screaming I shot him, I shot him. Then he goes quiet.'

Finlay sat back. Folded his hands behind his head. Looked a question at me. Hubble as the shooter? I didn't believe it. Because of his agitation. Guys who shoot somebody in a fight or in a temper, a messy shot to the chest, they get agitated afterward. Guys who put two bullets in the head, with a silencer, then collect up the shell cases, they just walk away and forget about it. Hubble was not the shooter. Guy like that couldn't shoot pool.

'Got to throw him in the can for now,' Finlay said. 'No option. He's confessed. But it won't hold up.'

I nodded. Sensed there was something more to come.

'He wasn't even there at midnight,' he said. 'He was at some anniversary party. A family thing. He got a ride home at two o'clock in the morning because it was raining. A ride from his sister-in-law's brother-in-law. Officer Stevenson.'

FINLAY LEANED right back in his chair. His long arms were folded behind his head. He was an elegant man. Educated. Civilised. And he was sending me to jail for something I hadn't done.

'I'm sorry, Reacher,' he said to me. He looked unhappy.

'You're sorry?' I said. 'You're sending two guys who couldn't have done it to jail and you're sorry?'

'This is the way Chief Morrison wants it,' he said. 'And he's the boss man, right?'

'You got to be joking,' I said. 'He's an idiot. He's calling Stevenson a liar. His own man.'

'Not exactly.' Finlay shrugged. 'He's saying it's maybe a conspiracy. You know, maybe Hubble recruited you to do it. He reckons the confession is exaggerated because maybe Hubble's afraid of you and is scared to finger you. Morrison figures you were on your way down to Hubble's place to get paid when we hauled you in. Figures that's why you waited the eight hours. Figures that's why Hubble was at home today, waiting to pay you off.'

I was silent. I was worried. Chief Morrison was dangerous. His theory was plausible. Until Finlay did the checking.

'So, Reacher, I'm sorry,' he said. 'You and Hubble stay in the bag until Monday. You'll get through it. Over in Warburton. Bad place, but the holding pens are OK. Meantime, I'll work on it. I'll ask Officer Roscoe to come in Saturday and Sunday. She's the pretty one outside. She's good, the best we got. If what you say is right, you'll be free and clear on Monday. OK?'

I stared at him. I was getting mad.

'No, Finlay, not OK,' I said. 'You know I didn't do a damn thing. You're just scared of that useless fat bastard Morrison. So I'm going to jail because you're just a spineless coward.'

He took it pretty well. His dark face flushed darker. He sat quietly for a long time, glaring at me. 'Two things, Reacher,' he said. 'First, if necessary I'll take care of Chief Morrison on Monday. Second, I am not a coward. You don't know me at all. Nothing about me.'

'I know more than you think,' I said. 'I know you're a Harvard postgrad, you're divorced and you quit smoking in April.'

Finlay looked blank. Baker knocked and entered to say the prison bus had arrived. Finlay got up and walked around the desk. Told Baker he would bring me out himself.

'How do you know that stuff?' Finlay asked me. He was intrigued. He was losing the game.

'You're a smart guy, right? Educated in Boston, you told me. But when you were college age, Harvard wasn't taking too many black guys. You're smart, but you're no rocket scientist, so I figure Boston Uni for the first degree, right?'

'Right,' he conceded.

'And then Harvard for postgrad,' I said. 'You did well at Boston

Uni, life moved on, you got into Harvard. You talk like a Harvard guy. I figured it straight away. Ph.D. in criminology?'

'Right,' he said again. 'Criminology.'

'And then you got this job in April,' I said. 'You told me that. You've got a pension from Boston PD, because you did your twenty. So you've come down here with cash to spare. But you've come down here with no woman, because if you had, she'd have spent some of that cash on new clothes for you. She'd have junked that wintry tweed and put you in a Sunbelt outfit to start your new life on the right foot. But you're still wearing that terrible old suit, so the woman is gone. She either died or divorced you, so it was a fifty-fifty guess. And the smoking thing is easy. You were just stressed up and you were patting your pockets, looking for cigarettes. That means you quit fairly recently. Easy guess is you quit in April, you know, new life, new job, no more cigarettes.'

'Very good, Reacher,' he said grudgingly. 'So if you're so smart, who aced the guy up at the warehouse?'

'I don't care who aced any guy anywhere,' I said. 'That's your problem, not mine. And it's the wrong question, Finlay. First you got to find out who the guy was, right?'

'So you got any way to do that?' he asked me. 'No ID, no face left, nothing from the prints. Hubble won't say diddly.'

'Run the prints again,' I said. 'I'm serious, Finlay. Get Roscoe to do it. There's something wrong there.'

'What something?' he asked me.

'Run them again, OK?' I said. 'Will you do that?'

He just grunted. Didn't say yes or no. I opened the office door and stepped out. Nobody was there except Baker and Hubble over at the cells. I could see the desk sergeant outside through the front doors talking to the prison bus driver.

Finlay came out of the office behind me. Touched my elbow and walked me over to Baker. Baker handcuffed Hubble and me together and then put another set on each of our outside wrists.

'OK, guys, let's hit the road.'

He walked us to the doors. We went out as the driver pushed the bus door inward. Hubble shuffled sideways onto the step. I followed him. The bus was empty. The driver directed Hubble into a seat. He slid over the vinyl to the window. I was pulled alongside. The driver clicked our outer wrists to the chromium hoop that ran across the top of the seat in front, and walked forward to his seat. He started the engine. The gears clashed and ground and the bus moved off.

Beside me, Hubble was slumped in his seat, his left arm inert between us. The life force had just about drained out of him. He was in the grip of a paralysing fear.

WE ROCKED and bounced for the best part of an hour through the huge landscape. Endless rows of bushes flicked past. Endless drills of red earth between. A small stand of trees flashed by on my right. Then way in the far distance, alone in a thousand acres of flat farmland, I saw a complex of buildings. Looked like a chemical factory. Massive concrete bunkers and glittering metal walkways. Tubing running here and there with steam drifting. All surrounded by razor wire punctuated by towers. Searchlights and rifles in the towers.

The bus rattled to a halt at the fifteen-foot-high perimeter fence. Hubble looked up and peered out through his gold rims. He groaned. It was a groan of hopeless dejection.

The gate guard signalled to the driver, waving us through. The bus ground forward into a vehicle cage. We passed a sign at the kerb: WARBURTON CORRECTIONAL FACILITY. Behind us a gate swung closed. We were sealed in. At the far end a gate swung open and the bus ground through. We drove the hundred yards to the next fence. There was another cage. The bus went in, waited, and drove on into the heart of the prison. Stopped opposite a concrete bunker. The reception area. The driver shut down the engine, swung out of his seat. He pulled out his keys and unlocked the cuffs.

'OK, boys, let's go,' he grinned. 'Party time.'

We got out. A door opened opposite and a guard stepped out. Called us over. He was eating a doughnut and spoke with his mouth full. We went through the door, down a corridor and into a small, filthy concrete chamber. Another guard sat on the table reading from a clipboard.

'Sit down,' he said. We sat. His partner with the doughnut locked the outer door and joined him.

'Here's the deal,' said the clipboard guy. 'You guys are not convicted of any crime. In custody pending investigation. That means no uniform, no processing, no big deal, you understand? Nice accommodations on the top floor.'

'Right,' his partner said. 'So what we're saying is this. This damn facility ain't got the manpower to do the job the way it ought to be done. Governor laid off about a half the staff. So we don't want to see you again until we pull you out on Monday. No hassle, right? You, Hubble, you understand?'

Hubble looked up and nodded blankly. Didn't speak.

'Reacher?' the clipboard guy said. 'You understand?'

'Sure,' I said. I understood.

'Good,' he said. 'So the deal is this. The two of us are off duty at seven o'clock. Which is in about one minute's time. So we get you a meal, then you're locked down in here until they got manpower to take you upstairs, maybe ten o'clock, OK? Then the assistant warden will come get you. Spivey's the top boy tonight. You don't like it, you don't tell me, you tell the governor, OK?'

The doughnut eater went out into the corridor and came back with a tray. On it were plates, paper cups and a Thermos. He put the tray on the table and the two of them went out. Locked the door from the outside. It went quiet as a tomb in there.

We ate. Fish and rice. Friday food. Coffee in the Thermos. Hubble didn't speak. His face was full of dejection and fear. I tipped my chair back and put my feet up on the table. Another three hours to waste. A warm evening. September in Georgia.

NOT LONG AFTER TEN the door from the corridor was unlocked and a uniformed man came in. I looked him over. A heavy, fleshy man. Reddened skin, big hard belly, wide neck, small eyes. A tight greasy uniform straining to contain him. Carrying a clipboard in his big red farmer's hands, and a shotgun. Assistant Warden Spivey. Understaffed and harassed. Ushering short-stay guests around by himself.

'Which one of you is Hubble?' he asked in a high-pitched voice.

Hubble raised his hand briefly, like a boy at grade school. Spivey's little eyes flicked over him. Like a snake's eyes. He grunted and signalled with the clipboard. We formed up and moved out.

'Turn left and follow the red line,' Spivey said

He waved left with the shotgun. There was a fine red line painted on the wall at waist height. We followed it through corridors, up stairs and around corners. Hubble first, then me, then Spivey with the shotgun. It was dark. Just dim emergency lighting. Spivey called a halt on a landing. He overrode an electronic lock with his key.

'No talking,' he said. 'Rules here say absolute silence at all times after lights out. Cell at the end on the right.'

We stepped through the door. The foul odour of prison hit me. The night exhalation of countless dispirited men. A nightlight glowed dimly. I sensed rather than saw rows of cells. Spivey walked us to the end of the row. Pointed to an empty cell. We crowded in. Spivey swung the bars shut behind us. He walked away.

The cell was very dark. I could just about see a bunk bed, a steel sink and a steel john. Not much floor space. I took off my coat and lobbed it onto the top bunk.

Hubble sat quietly on the lower bed. I used the john and rinsed my face at the sink. Pulled myself up into bed. Took off my shoes. Big heavy shoes with hard soles. Left them on the foot of the bed. Shoes can get stolen, and these were good shoes.

The bed was too short for me, but most beds are. I lay there in the dark, closed my eyes and thought of Roscoe. I must have fallen asleep because the next thing I knew it was Saturday. I was still in prison. And an even worse day was beginning.

TWO

I was woken up by bright lights coming on. The prison had no windows. Day and night were created by electricity. At seven o'clock the circuit breakers were thrown shut and the building was suddenly flooded with light.

It didn't make the cell look any better. The front wall was bars. Half would open outward on a hinge to form the door. The two stacked beds occupied just about half the width and most of the length. Outside, everything was metal, brick, concrete. Noises were amplified and echoed around. It sounded like hell. Opposite our cell was a blank wall.

I threw off the cover and found my shoes. Put them on and laced them up. Lay down again.

A cleaner moved into view outside our bars. An old black guy with a broom. His orange prison uniform was washed almost white. He must have been eighty. Maybe stole a chicken in the Depression. Still paying his debt to society.

He stabbed the broom randomly over the corridor, caught sight of Hubble and me and stopped. Rested on his broom and shook his head. Gave a kind of appreciative chuckle.

'Well, yes indeed,' he grinned. 'I've been in this joint since God's dog was a puppy, yes sir. But I ain't never seen anybody in that cell wearing clothes like yours, man. Not in all those years.'

'You don't like my clothes?' I said. Surprised.

'I didn't say that, no sir. I like your clothes just fine. It's the fact you're wearing them, man, like not wearing the orange uniform. I never saw that before. Now I seen everything. I really have, yes sir.'

'But guys on the holding floor don't wear the uniform,' I said.

'That sure is true,' the old man said. 'That's a fact.'

'So what's the issue, old man?' I said.

There was a silence. He and I got the message simultaneously.

'You think this is the holding floor?' he asked me. He paused a beat. Lifted his broom and crabbed back out of sight. 'This ain't the holding floor, man,' he whooped. 'Holding floor is the top floor. Floor six. This here is floor three. This is lifers, man. This is the worst. Yes indeed, you boys are in the wrong place. You boys are in trouble. You gonna get visitors. Oh man, I'm out of here.'

EVALUATE. LONG EXPERIENCE had taught me to evaluate and assess. When the unexpected gets dumped on you, don't waste time figuring how or why it happened. Don't figure out whose fault it is. All of that you do later. If you survive. First of all you evaluate. Identify the downside. Assess the upside. Plan accordingly.

We were not in the holding pens on the sixth floor. We were among dangerous lifers on the third. There was no upside. The downside was extensive. We were new boys. We would not survive without status. We had no status. We faced an unpleasant weekend.

Assess. I could call on some heavy training. Not intended for prison life, but it would help. I had gone through a lot of unpleasant education. Not just in the army. Stretching right back into childhood. Between grade school and high school military kids like me get to go to twenty, maybe thirty new schools in some tough places. The first day at each new school I was a new boy. I quickly learned to get status. In many a school yard, my brother and I had slugged it out, back to back. We had got status.

Then in the service itself, that brutality was refined. I was trained by experts. They taught me methods, details, skills. Most of all they taught me attitude. They taught me that inhibitions would kill me. Hit early, hit hard. Get your retaliation in first. Cheat. The gentlemen who behaved decently weren't there to train anybody. They were already dead.

At seven thirty there was a ragged clunk along the row of cells. The timeswitch had unlocked the cages. Our bars sagged open an inch. Hubble sat motionless. Still silent. I had no plan. Best option would be to find a guard. Explain and get transferred. But I didn't expect to find a guard. The prison was understaffed. Unlikely to provide guards on each floor. They would wait in a crew room. Operate as a crash squad responding to emergencies. So the only plan was to wait and see. Survive until Monday.

I could hear the grinding as the other inmates swung back their gates and strolled out to start another pointless day. I waited.

Not long to wait. From my tight angle on the bed, I saw our next-door neighbours stroll out and merge with a small knot of men. They were all dressed the same. Orange prison uniform. Red bandannas tight over shaved heads. Huge black guys. Body builders.

The nearest guy was wearing pale sunglasses. The sort that darken in the sun. He had probably last seen the sun in the seventies. May never see it again. So the shades were redundant, but they looked good. Like the muscles. Like the bandannas. All image.

The guy with the sunglasses spotted us. His look of surprise quickly changed to excitement. He alerted the group's biggest guy by hitting his arm.

The big man looked around. He grinned. 'Look what they sent us,' he said, pulling open our gate. 'Fresh meat.'

'They sure did, man,' the sunglasses guy said.

The big guy looked around his gang and they all grinned back. Exchanged low fives. I waited. The big guy stepped half a pace into our cell. He was enormous. Maybe an inch or two shorter than me but probably twice as heavy.

'Yo, white boy, come here,' he said. To Hubble.

I could sense Hubble's panic. He didn't move.

'Come here, white boy,' the big guy repeated. Quietly.

Hubble stood up. Took half a pace toward the man.

'This is Red Boy territory, man,' the big guy said. Explaining the bandannas. 'What's whitey doing in Red Boy territory?'

Hubble said nothing in reply.

'You got to pay the residency tax, man,' the big guy said. 'Like they got in Florida hotels. Give me the eyeglasses, white boy.'

Hubble flicked a despairing glance up at me. Took off his gold glasses. Held them out. The big man took them and dropped them to the floor. Crunched them under his shoe. They smashed and splintered. The big man scraped his foot, flicking the wreckage into the corridor.

'Good boy,' the big guy said. 'You paid the tax. Now come here.'
Hubble shuffled nearer, trembling.

'On your knees, white boy,' said the big guy.
Hubble knelt.

'Unzip me, whitey.'

Hubble gave a gasp of fear and revulsion and jumped back. He
scuttled backward toward the rear of the cell. Tried to hide behind
the john.

Time to intervene. Not for Hubble, but for myself. Hubble's abject
performance would taint me. We would be seen as a pair. Hubble's
surrender would disqualify us both in the status game.

I swung my feet over the side of the bunk and landed lightly in
front of the big man. 'You're in my house, fat boy,' I said. 'But I'm
going to give you a choice. Either you can walk out of here by yourself, or these other fat boys behind you are going to carry you out in
a bucket.'

'Oh yeah?' he said. Blankly. Surprised.

'I'm going to count to three, so you better choose real quick.'
He glared at me.

'One,' I counted. No response. 'Two.' No response.

Then I cheated. Instead of counting three I headbutted him full in
the face. Came off the back foot with a thrust up the legs and
whipped my head forward and smashed it into his nose. Jarred his
little brain around real good. His legs crumpled and he hit the floor
like a puppet with the strings cut.

I stared around the knot of men. 'Who's next?'

There was no reply. I pointed at the guy in sunglasses.

'Give me the eyeglasses,' I said.

He bent and swept up the twisted gold wreckage. Handed it to me.
I tossed it back at him.

'They're broken,' I said. 'Give me yours.'

There was a long pause. He looked at me. I looked at him. Slowly,
he took off his sunglasses and handed them to me. I put them in my
pocket.

'Now get this carcass out of here,' I said.

The bunch of men in their orange uniforms and their red bandannas dragged the big man away. I crawled back up into my bunk. My
stomach was churning and I was panting. I felt terrible. But not as
bad as I would have felt if I hadn't done it. They'd have finished with
Hubble by then and started in on me.

I DIDN'T EAT any breakfast. No appetite. I just lay on the bunk until I felt better. Hubble sat on his bed, rocking back and forward. After a while I slid to the floor. Washed at the sink. People were strolling up and gazing in. The word had gotten around fast. I was a celebrity.

Hubble stopped his rocking and looked at me. 'I can't take this,' he said.

They were the first words I had heard him say since his assured banter on Finlay's speakerphone. His voice was low, but his statement was definite. Not a whine or a complaint, but a statement of fact. He couldn't take this.

'So why are you here?' I asked him. 'You confessed to something you didn't do. You asked for this.'

'No,' said Hubble. 'I did what I said.'

'Bullshit,' I said. 'You weren't even there. You were at a party. The guy who drove you home is a policeman, for God's sake.'

Hubble looked down at the floor. 'I can't explain it,' he said. 'I can't say anything about it. I just need to know what happens next.'

'You stay here until Monday morning, and then you go back to Margrave. They'll want to know why you confessed, when you didn't do anything. And they'll want to know why the guy had your phone number.'

'I can't tell them,' he said. 'I can't tell anybody anything.'

He looked away and shuddered. Very frightened.

'Why can't you tell anybody?' I asked him.

'Because I can't,' he said. Wouldn't say anything more.

I was suddenly weary. Twenty-four hours ago I had jumped off a Greyhound. Striding out happily down a new road in the warm morning rain. No baggage, no hassle. Freedom. I didn't want it interrupted by Hubble, or by Finlay, or by some tall guy who got himself shot in his shaved head. I didn't want any part of it.

Hubble was thinking hard. I had never seen anybody think so visibly. Weighing things up. I watched him. I saw him make his decision. He turned and looked over at me. 'I need your help,' he said.

I laughed. 'You've had all the help you're going to get,' I said. 'And so far you haven't exactly overwhelmed me with gratitude for that.'

'I'm sorry,' he said. 'I'm very grateful. Believe me, I am. You saved my life. You took care of it. That's why you've got to tell me what to do. I'm being threatened. Not just me. My family. I've got two children. Boy aged nine, girl aged seven. Great wife, great kids. I love them like crazy.'

He meant it. I could see that.

'We've got a nice place,' he said. 'Out on Beckman Drive. A lot of money, but it was worth it. You know Beckman?'

'No,' I said.

He was afraid to get to the point. 'Anyway,' he said eventually, 'it's all falling apart now.' He sat there in his chinos and his polo shirt. Without his glasses he looked older, more vacant. People who wear glasses always look unfocused and vulnerable without them.

I leaned on the cell wall and waited for him to go on.

'They're threatening us,' he said again. 'If I ever tell anybody what's going on, they said they'll break into our house. They said they'll nail me to the wall. Then they'll cut my throat. They said they'll make my wife and children watch and then do things to them after I'm dead that I'll never know about. What should I do?'

He was staring over at me. Waiting for a reply. I stepped to the bars and glanced down the row of cells. Thought for a moment. Came up with the only possible answer.

'Nothing you can do,' I said. 'You've been told to keep your mouth shut, so keep it shut. Don't tell anybody what's going on. Ever.'

He looked down at his feet. Dropped his head into his hands and moaned. Like he was crushed with disappointment.

'Something big is going on,' he said. 'I've got to stop it if I can.'

I shook my head. If something very big was going on around people who used threats like that, then he was never going to stop it. He was on board, and he was going to stay on board. I smiled a bleak smile at him and shook my head again. He nodded like he understood. Like he finally accepted the situation. He went back to rocking and staring at the wall.

I couldn't understand the confession. He should have kept his mouth shut, denied any involvement with the dead guy. Should have said he had no idea why his phone number was in the guy's shoe. Should have said he had no idea what Pluribus was. Then he could have just gone home. I asked him why he confessed. He told me he thought he'd be safe from them if he was arrested and put in prison. But there was a flaw in that logic. Prison was not safe.

'What are you going to do on Monday?' I asked him. 'You'll be back home, walking around Margrave or Atlanta or wherever it is you walk around. If they're after you, won't they get you then?'

'I'm just hoping for the best,' Hubble said. 'I sort of felt they might cool off after a while. I'm very useful to them. I hope they'll think about that. I got scared, because if they'd killed the tall guy they might kill me, too. I can't tell you why. Right now it's a tense situation. But it's going to calm down soon. I might just make it through. If they get me, they get me. It's my family I'm worried about.'

'Hubble,' I said. 'What have you done to them to make you liable to get yourself shot in the head?'

He wouldn't answer. The silence in our cell was terrible. I let it crash around for a while. Couldn't think of anything more to say. My forehead hurt and I wanted to bathe it. 'I'm going to find a bathroom. I need to put a wet towel on my head. It hurts,' I said.

'I'm not surprised,' he said. 'I'll come with you.'

He was anxious not to be left alone. Understandable. I was going to be his minder for the weekend. Not that I had any other plans.

We walked down the cell row to a kind of open area at the end. I saw the fire door Spivey had used the night before. Beyond it was a tiled area clogged with men. I pushed through and Hubble followed.

It was a large square room. A strong disinfectant stink. On the left was a row of open shower stalls. The back wall was a row of toilet cubicles. The right wall was a row of washbasins. Very communal. Not a big deal if you'd been in the army all your life, but Hubble wasn't happy. Not what he was used to at all.

All the fittings were steel. For safety. A smashed-up porcelain washbasin yields some pretty sharp weapons. For the same reason the mirrors over the basins were sheets of polished steel.

I stepped over to a basin and ran cold water. Took a wad of paper towels from the dispenser and soaked them. Held them to my bruised forehead. The water felt good. There was no real injury. No flesh there, just skin over solid bone. Not much to injure.

I checked out the damage in the steel mirror. Not bad. I combed my hair with my fingers. As I leaned against the sink I could feel the sunglasses in my pocket. The Red Boy's shades. The spoils of victory. I took them out and put them on.

As I messed about in front of the steel mirror I saw the start of some kind of a commotion behind me. I turned around. Five white guys were trawling across the room. Biker types. Orange suits, of course, but with black leather additions. Caps, belts, fingerless gloves. Big bears. All five were big, heavy men, with crude tattoos on their arms and their faces. Swastikas. The Aryan Brotherhood. White trash prison gang.

The room's other occupants melted away. Within seconds the big bathroom was empty. Except for the five bikers and Hubble and me. The five big men fanned out in a loose arc around us.

My assumption was they'd come to recruit me, but I was way out. The guy in the middle of the five was looking back and forth between Hubble and me. His eyes stopped on me.

'OK, he's the one,' he said. Looking straight at me.

Two things happened. The end two bikers grabbed Hubble and ran him to the door. And the boss man swung a big fist at my face. I saw it late. Dodged left and it caught me on the shoulder. I was grabbed from behind by the neck. Two huge hands at my throat. Strangling me. The boss man lined up for another shot at my gut. If it landed, I was a dead man. I knew that much. So I leaned back and kicked out. Smashed the boss man between the legs

The strangler was wrenching hard. I was losing it. I reached up and broke his little fingers. He let go.

The third guy waded in, pounding me with short jabs to the arm and chest. He was a solid mountain of lard. I was jammed back between two sinks. Nowhere to hit him. Except his eyes. I jammed my thumb into his eye. He screamed and went down.

The boss man was up on one knee. I kicked hard at his face. He went back down. I spun away from the wall. The guy with the broken fingers ran for the door. The guy with the injured eye was flopping about on the floor. The boss man was nursing his jaw.

I was grabbed from behind again. I twisted away. A Red Boy. Two of them. I was dizzy. I was going to lose it now. But they just grabbed me and ran me to the door. Sirens were going off.

'Get out of here, man,' screamed the Red Boys over the sirens. 'This is ours. We did this. Understand? We'll take the fall, man.'

They hurled me into the crowd outside. I understood. They were going to say they did it. Not because they wanted to protect me. Because they wanted to claim the credit. A race victory.

I saw Hubble in the crowd. I saw guards. I saw Spivey. I grabbed Hubble and we hustled back to the cell. Sirens were blasting. Guards were tumbling out of a door. Shouting and screaming. Inside the cell I splashed water on my face. The sunglasses were gone. Must have fallen off.

I heard screaming at the door. I turned and saw Spivey. He was yelling at us to get out. I grabbed my coat from the bunk and we ran to the emergency door where the guards had rushed out. Spivey shoved us through and ran us upstairs. My lungs were giving out.

There was a door at the top of the last flight painted with a big figure six. We crashed through. He hustled us down a row of cells. Shoved us into an empty cell and flung the iron gate shut. It crashed and locked. He ran off. I collapsed on the bed, eyes tight shut.

When I opened them again Hubble was sitting on a bed looking at me. We were in a big cell. Two beds, one on each side. A sink, a john. A wall of bars. Everything was brighter and cleaner. This was the holding floor. This was where we should have been all the time.

'What the hell happened to you in there?' Hubble asked.

I stared at the ceiling. Thinking hard. Because they had definitely gone through a selection process. They had looked us both over very carefully and chosen me. Then they had tried to strangle me. And Spivey had just happened to be outside the bathroom. He had employed the Aryan Brotherhood to kill me and was waiting ready to burst in and find me dead.

And he had planned it yesterday before ten in the evening. That was clear. That's why he had left us on a convict floor.

But his plan had fouled up. I wasn't killed. The Aryans were beaten off. The Red Boys had piled in and mayhem had broken out. Spivey had panicked and called the crash squad. Rushed us off the floor, up to the sixth, and left us up here. According to all the paperwork, the sixth floor was where we'd been all the time.

A neat fallback. It made me fireproof as far as investigation went. Spivey had a couple of seriously injured convicts on his hands, and he must know I had done it. But he could never say so now. Because according to him, I was never there.

I exhaled gently. Spivey's plan was clear. But what was his angle? What did he have against me? I'd never been anywhere near him or his damn prison before. Why the hell should he operate an elaborate plan to get me dead? I couldn't begin to figure it out.

Hubble slept for a while on the cot across from mine. Then he stirred and woke up. Writhed around. Looked disorientated for a moment, until he remembered where he was. One very miserable guy.

I could understand his fear. But he also looked defeated. Like he'd just rolled the dice and lost. Like he'd been counting on something to happen, and it hadn't happened.

Then I began to understand that, too.

'The guy killed up at the warehouse was trying to help you, wasn't he?' I said.

The question scared him. 'I can't tell you that,' he answered.

'I need to know,' I said. 'Maybe you approached the guy for help. Maybe that's why he got killed.'

Hubble rocked back and forth on his bed. Took a deep breath. Looked straight at me. 'He was an investigator,' he said. 'I brought him down here because I want this whole thing stopped. I don't want to be involved any more. I'm not a criminal. I'm scared to death and I want out. He was going to get me out and take down the scam. But he slipped up somehow. And if they find out it was me brought him down here, they'll kill me. And if they don't kill me, I'll probably go to jail anyway, because right now the whole damn operation is very exposed and very dangerous.'

'Who was the guy?' I asked him.

'He didn't have a name,' Hubble said. 'Just a contact code. I can't believe they got him. He seemed like a capable guy to me. Tell the truth, you remind me of him.'

'What was he doing up there at the warehouse?' I asked him.

'I put him together with another guy, and he was meeting with him up there. But wouldn't they have shot the other guy as well? I don't understand why they only got one of them.'

'Who was the other guy he was meeting with?' I said.

He shook his head. 'I've told you way too much already.'

'Who's on the inside of this thing?'

'Don't you listen?' he said. 'I'm not saying another word.'

'How many people?' I asked.

He thought about it. Counted up in his head. 'Ten,' he said. 'Not counting me.'

I looked at him and shrugged. 'Ten people doesn't sound like a big deal,' I said.

'It's huge,' he said. 'Biggest thing you ever heard of.'

'And right now it's very exposed?'

'Right now it's very risky, getting worse all the time. But it could go either way. If we get through to next Sunday, nobody will ever know anything. But if we don't get through it, it'll be the biggest sensation you ever heard of, believe me.'

'So what's going to happen next Sunday?'

He turned his face away. It was like if he couldn't see me, I wasn't there, asking him questions.

'What does Pluribus mean?' I asked him.

He wouldn't answer. His eyes were screwed shut with terror.

The conversation was over. I gave it up and we lapsed back into silence. That suited me well enough. I didn't want to know anything more. And by next Sunday I planned to be a very long way away from the whole business.

I ROLLED OVER on the narrow cot and tried to float away into some kind of limbo. But Hubble was restless, tossing and turning. He was coming close to irritating me. I turned to face him.

'I'm sorry,' he said. 'I'm very uptight. It was doing me good just to talk to somebody. Can't we talk about something else? What about you? Tell me about yourself. Who are you, Reacher?'

'I'm nobody,' I said. 'Just a guy passing through. I'll be gone on Monday.'

'Nobody's nobody,' he said. 'We've all got a story. Tell me.'

So I talked for a while, lying on my bed, running through the last six months. He lay on his bed, listening, keeping his mind off his problems. I told him about leaving from the Pentagon. Washington, Philadelphia, New York, Boston, Detroit, Chicago. Museums, music, cheap hotels, bars, clubs, roads, buses and trains. Solitude. Travelling through the land of my citizenship like a cheap tourist.

I told Hubble about the crazy decision to bail out from the Greyhound near Margrave. Following a whim. Following some half-remembered note from my brother saying he'd been through some little place where Blind Blake might have died over sixty years ago.

'I did that once,' Hubble said. 'On our honeymoon. We went to Europe. We stopped off in New York and I spent half a day looking for the Dakota Building, you know, where John Lennon was shot. Then we spent three days in England walking around Liverpool, looking for the Cavern Club. Where the Beatles started out. Couldn't find it, I guess they knocked it down.'

He talked on for a while. Mostly about travelling. He'd taken plenty of trips with his wife. They'd enjoyed it. Been all over Europe, Mexico, the Caribbean. Had a great time together.

'Don't you get lonely,' he asked me, 'travelling alone?'

I told him no, I enjoyed it. I told him I appreciated the solitude, the anonymity. Like I was invisible.

'How do you mean, invisible?' he said. He seemed interested.

'I travel by road,' I said. 'Walk a bit, and ride the buses. Sometimes trains. Always pay cash. That way there's never a paper trail. No credit card transactions, no passenger manifests, nothing. If I stay in a hotel, I pay cash and give them a made-up name.'

'Why?' he said. 'Who the hell's after you?'

'Nobody,' I said. 'It's just a bit of fun. I like anonymity. I feel like I'm beating the system.'

He fell back to thinking. We lay on our beds and drifted through the rest of the afternoon. No more talking. We were all talked out.

At seven an orderly came by with dinner. Then we drifted through the empty evening. At ten the power banged off and we were in darkness. Nightfall. I kept my shoes on and slept lightly. Just in case.

AT SEVEN IN THE MORNING the lights came back on. Sunday. I woke up tired, but I forced myself to get up and do a bit of stretching to ease my sore body. Hubble was awake, but silent. Breakfast arrived before eight. The same orderly dragging the meal cart. I ate the breakfast and drank the coffee. As I finished up the flask, the gate lock clunked and a guard stepped into the cell. 'It's your lucky day,' he said. 'You're both getting out. Be ready in five minutes, OK?'

Hubble hauled himself up onto his elbows. He looked more worried than ever. He hadn't eaten his breakfast. 'I'm scared,' he said. 'Once I'm out of here, they can get to me.'

I shook my head. 'It would have been easier for them to get you in here,' I said. 'Believe me, if they were looking to kill you, you'd be dead by now. You're in the clear, Hubble.'

Five minutes later the guard was back. He walked us along a corridor and through two sets of locked gates. Put us in a back elevator. Stepped in and used his key to send it down. Stepped out again as the doors began to close.

'So long,' he said. 'Don't come back.'

The elevator took us down to a lobby and then we stepped outside into a hot concrete yard. There were two cars parked there. One was a big English Bentley, maybe twenty years old but it looked brand-new. There was a blonde woman in it, who I guessed was Hubble's wife, because he was on his way over to her like she was the sweetest sight he ever saw. The other car had Officer Roscoe in it.

She got out and walked straight over to me. Looked wonderful. Out of uniform. Dressed in jeans and a soft cotton shirt. Calm intelligent face. Soft dark hair. Huge eyes.

'Hello, Roscoe,' I said.

'Hello, Reacher,' she said, and smiled.

Her voice was wonderful. Her smile was great.

Ahead of us, the Hubbles drove off in the Bentley, waving. I waved back and wondered how things would turn out for them. Probably I would never know.

Roscoe and I got into her car. Not really hers, she explained, just a department unmarked she was using. A brand-new Chevrolet, smooth and quiet. She'd kept the motor running and the air on and inside it was cool. We wafted out of the concrete yard and shunted through the wire vehicle cages. Outside the last cage Roscoe spun the wheel and we blasted away down the road. I didn't look back. I just sat there, feeling good. Getting out of prison is one of life's good feelings. So is not knowing what tomorrow holds. So is cruising silently down a sunny road with a pretty woman at the wheel.

'So what happened?' I said after a mile. 'Tell me.'

She told me a pretty straightforward story. They'd started work on my alibi late Friday evening. She and Finlay. They'd called Tampa and Atlanta and by midnight they'd gotten hold of the ticket clerk at the Tampa depot. He remembered me. Then they got the bus driver as well. He confirmed he'd stopped at the Margrave cloverleaf to let me out, eight o'clock Friday morning. By midnight my alibi was looking rock solid, just like I'd said it would be.

Saturday morning, a long fax was in from the Pentagon detailing my service record. Then my prints came back from the FBI database. They'd been matched by the computer at two thirty in the morning. US Army, printed on induction, thirteen years ago. My alibi was solid, and my background checked out. Finlay was satisfied.

'What about the dead guy?' I said. 'Did you run his prints again?'

She concentrated on passing a farm truck. Then she nodded. 'Finlay told me you wanted me to,' she said. 'But why?'

'They came back too quickly for a negative result,' I said.

'Too quickly?' she said.

'You told me there was a pyramid system, right?' I said. 'The top ten, then the top hundred, all the way down, right?'

She nodded.

'So what happened with this dead guy?' I said. 'The body was found at eight o'clock, so the prints went in when? Eight thirty, earliest. But Baker was already telling me there was no match on file when they were talking to me at two thirty. I remember the time, because I was looking at the clock. That's only six hours. You just told me my prints were matched at two thirty in the morning. That's fourteen hours after they were sent. If it took fourteen hours to reach nearly to the bottom of the pyramid to find out that I'm in there, how could it take just six to say the dead guy's *not* in there?'

'God,' she said. 'You're right. Baker must have screwed up the scan. If the scan's not clear, the database tries to decipher it, then it comes back as unreadable. Baker must have thought that meant a null result. The codes are similar. Anyway, I sent them again, first thing. We'll know soon enough.'

We drove on and Roscoe told me she'd pushed Finlay to get me out of Warburton right away yesterday afternoon. Finlay had agreed, but there was a problem. They'd had to wait until today, because yesterday afternoon Warburton had been just about shut down. They had told Finlay there had been some trouble and a full-scale riot had started, black and white gangs at war.

I looked over at Roscoe. 'Thank you,' I said. 'I mean it. You worked hard to help me out.'

She waved away my thanks with a blush and a small gesture and just drove on. I was starting to like her a lot.

'I want to take you to lunch,' I said. 'Kind of a thankyou thing.'

She thought about it for a quarter-mile and then smiled across at me. 'OK,' she said, and accelerated south toward Margrave.

THREE

I got her to call in at the station house and bring me out the property bag with my money in it. Then she dropped me in the centre of Margrave and I arranged to meet her up at the station house in a couple of hours. I stood on the sidewalk in the fierce morning heat and waved her off. I felt a whole lot better. I was back in motion. I was going to check out the Blind Blake story, then take Roscoe to lunch, then get the hell out of Georgia and never come back.

So I spent a while wandering around the town. There wasn't really much to the place. The old county road ran straight through, north to south, and for about four blocks, lined with small stores and offices, it was labelled Main Street. There were benches set on the sidewalks, but they were empty. The whole place was deserted. Sunday morning, miles from anywhere.

On the south edge of town I could see a little village green with a bronze statue and a residential street running away to the west. I strolled down there and saw a discreet green sign that read: BECKMAN DRIVE. Hubble's street. I couldn't see any real distance down it because pretty much straight away it looped left and right around a wide grass square with a big white wooden church set on it. The church was ringed by cherry trees and the square was surrounded by cars parked in neat lines. I could just about make out the growl of the organ and the sound of the people singing.

More or less opposite Beckman Drive on the other side of the green was another residential street, running east. And that was it. Not much of a town. Took me less than thirty minutes to look over everything the place had to offer.

But it was the most immaculate town I had ever seen. The roads were smooth as glass, and the sidewalks were flat and clean. No potholes, no cracks, no heave. The little offices and stores looked like they got repainted every week. The lawns and trees were clipped to perfection. Flags flew everywhere, sparkling white and glowing red and blue in the sun. The whole place was so tidy it made you nervous to walk around in case you left a dirty footprint.

The convenience store on the southeastern corner was selling the sort of stuff that gave it a good enough excuse to be open on a Sunday morning. Open, but not busy. I sat up at the little counter and ordered coffee and bought a Sunday newspaper.

The President was still on the front page. Now he was in California. He was explaining to defence contractors why their gravy train was grinding to a halt after fifty glorious years. The aftershock from his Pensacola announcement about the Coast Guard was still rumbling on. Their boats were returning to harbour on Saturday night. They wouldn't go out again without new funding. The paper's editorial guys were all stirred up about it.

I stopped reading and glanced up. A woman came in. Dark hair, very slender, expensively dressed in black. Pale skin. She moved with a kind of nervous tension. I could see some kind of appalling strain in her face.

She didn't stay long. She got through half a coffee, watching the window all the time. Then a brand-new black pick-up truck pulled up outside. I caught a glimpse of the driver as he leaned over to open the door. He was a tough-looking guy. Pretty tall. Broad shoulders and a thick neck. Black hair. Thick knotted arms. Maybe thirty. The pale woman slid off her stool like a ghost and went over to the shop door. As she opened it I heard the burble of a big motor idling. The woman got into the truck.

'Who is that?' I asked the counter guy.

He looked at me like I was from another planet. 'That's Mrs Kliner,' he said. 'You don't know the Kliners?'

'I heard about them. I'm a stranger in town. Kliner owns the warehouses up near the highway, right?'

'Right. And a whole lot more besides. Big deal around here, Mr Kliner. You heard about the Foundation?'

I shook my head.

'Benefits the town in a lot of ways. Came here five years ago, been like Christmas ever since. But Mrs Kliner's a sick woman. She looks like something grown in a closet, right? Could be tuberculosis.'

'Who's the guy in the truck?'

'Stepson. Kliner's kid by his first wife.'

He went away to wipe down some kind of chromium machine at the other end of the counter. I agreed with him the woman looked like something grown in a closet. But not that she looked sick. I thought she was suffering from sheer terror. Terror of what, I didn't know. Not my problem. I stood up and dropped a five-dollar bill on the counter. The pick-up was still there at the kerb. The driver was looking sideways, across his stepmother, staring straight in at me.

There was a mirror opposite me behind the counter. I looked exactly like a guy who'd spent two days in jail. I figured I needed to get cleaned up before I took Roscoe to lunch. The counter guy saw me figuring.

'Try the barbershop,' he said. 'They're always in there. Never exactly closed. Never exactly open, either.'

I pushed out through the door and saw a small crowd of people coming out of the church, chatting on the lawn and getting into their cars. The rest of the town was still deserted, apart from the black pick-up, which was still parked right outside the convenience store. The driver was still staring at me.

I walked north in the sun until I reached the barbershop. Ducked under the striped awning and tried the door. Unlocked. I went in.

Like everything else in Margrave, the barbershop looked wonderful. It gleamed with ancient chairs and fittings lovingly polished, and had the kind of barbershop gear everybody tore out thirty years ago and now wants back. It was run by two old black guys. They indicated they would serve me. Like they were there, and I was there, so why not? And I guess I looked like an urgent case. I asked them for the works.

They mixed up soapy lather in a bowl, stropped a straight razor, rinsed a shaving brush. They shrouded me with towels and got to work. One guy shaved me with the old straight razor. The other stood around not doing much. The busy guy started chatting away, like barbers do. Told me the history of his business. The two of them had been buddies since childhood. Lived here in Margrave since way back. He told me the history of the county from a barber's perspective. Told me about the personalities who'd been in and out of these old chairs.

'You ever heard of Blind Blake?' I asked.

'Yes sir, I heard of him,' the old man said. 'He was here, time to time, way back. Born in Jacksonville, Florida, they say, just over the state line. Used to trek through here, through Atlanta, all the way up north to Chicago, and then trek all the way back again. Very different then, you know. No automobiles, at least not for a poor black man. All walking or riding on the freight cars.'

'You ever hear him play?' I asked him.

He stopped work and looked at me. 'Man, I'm seventy-four years old,' he said. 'This was back when I was just a little boy. You should talk to my partner here. He's a whole lot older than I am. He may have heard him play, only he may not remember because he don't even remember what he ate for breakfast. Am I right?'

The other old guy creaked over and leaned up on the next sink to mine. 'I don't know what I ate for breakfast,' he said. 'Don't even know if I ate any breakfast at all. But listen up. I may be an old guy, but the truth is old guys remember stuff real well. Not recent things, you understand, but old things.'

'Did you ever hear Blind Blake play?'

'No, I never heard him play,' the old guy said. 'But my sister did. Got me a sister more than ninety years old or thereabouts, sang with old Blind Blake many a time.'

'She did?' I said. 'She sang with him?'

'She sang with just about anybody passing through. You got to remember this old town lay right on the road to Atlanta. That old county road out there used to come on down through here straight on south into Florida. Everybody used to stop off here. Workers, crop pickers, fighters, hoboes, truckers, musicians. All kinds of those guys used to stop off and play and my old sister would be right in there singing with them all.'

'What happened to him?' I said. 'Do you know?'

The old guy thought hard. Trawled back through his fading

memories. 'Heard some powerful white folks killed him, right here in Margrave. Killed him 'cos he was blind and 'cos he was black. Some kind of big trouble, got him killed stone dead.'

I sat listening to their old radio for a while. Then I gave them a twenty off my roll of bills and hurried out onto Main Street. Strode out north. It was nearly noon and the sun was baking. Nobody else was out walking. The black road blasted heat at me. Blind Blake had walked this road. Back when those old barbers had been boys this had been the artery reaching north to Atlanta, Chicago, jobs, hope, money. But now the road was just a smooth blacktop byway going nowhere at all.

IT TOOK ME a few minutes in the heat to get up to the station house. I walked across its springy lawn and pulled open the heavy glass entrance door. Stepped into the chill inside. Roscoe was waiting for me, leaning on the reception counter, looking worried.

'We found another body,' she said. 'Up at the warehouse again. The other side of the road this time.'

'Do you know who this one is?' I asked her.

She shook her head. 'Unidentified. Same as the first one.'

'Where's Finlay?' I asked her.

'Gone to get Hubble,' she said. 'He thinks Hubble may know something about it.'

I nodded. Hubble did know something about it. This was the guy he had sent to meet with the tall investigator with the shaved head.

I heard a car in the lot outside and then the big glass door sucked open. Finlay stuck his head in. 'Morgue, Roscoe,' he said. 'You too, Reacher.'

We followed him back outside into the heat. We all got into Roscoe's unmarked sedan. Roscoe drove. I sat in the back. Finlay sat in the front passenger seat, twisted around so he could talk to the both of us at once. Roscoe headed south.

'I can't find Hubble. There's nobody up at his place,' Finlay said, looking at me. 'I need to find out what he knows about all this. What did he tell you about it, Reacher?'

'He didn't tell me diddly,' I said. 'We hardly spoke the whole weekend.'

Finlay glared at me from the front seat. 'Until I get hold of Hubble, I'm going to keep hold of you, Reacher, and sweat your ass for what he told you. And don't make out he kept his mouth shut all weekend, because guys like that never do. I know that and you know that, so don't mess with me, OK?'

I just shrugged at him. If Finlay started blundering around in whatever Hubble was mixed up in, Hubble and his family were going to end up dead. No doubt about that. So I figured I should just stay impartial and then get the hell out of here as fast as possible. Maybe I could get a bus from wherever the morgue was. I'd have to pass on lunch with Roscoe. Pity.

'So what's the story on this one?' I asked him.

'Pretty much the same as the last one,' Finlay said. 'Looks like it happened at the same time. Probably the same weapon.'

'You don't know who it is?' I said.

'All we know is his name is Sherman,' he said. 'Unidentified white male. Same deal as the first one, no ID, no wallet, no distinguishing marks. But this one had a gold wristwatch, engraved on the back: *To Sherman, love Judy*. He was maybe thirty or thirty-five. Hard to tell, because he'd been lying there for three nights and he was well gnawed by the small animals, you know?'

I thought about it. I'd walked right by there at eight o'clock on Friday morning. Right between two bodies.

'Where the hell are we going?' I said.

'Mortuary at the county hospital,' Finlay said. 'Down in Yellow Springs, next-but-one town to the south. Not long now.'

A MEDICAL GUY met us and led us into an office. He sat behind a metal desk and waved Finlay and Roscoe to some stools. I leaned on a counter, between a computer terminal and a fax machine. The guy looked maybe Finlay's age. White coat. He didn't introduce himself. Just took it for granted we all knew who he was.

'What can I tell you folks?' he said.

'Was it the same incident?' Finlay asked in his deep Harvard tones.

'I've only had the second corpse for an hour. But, yes, I would say it's the same incident. It's almost certainly the same weapon. Looks like small-calibre soft-nose bullets in both cases. Probably a twenty-two-calibre weapon. The bullets were slow, looks like the gun had a silencer.'

'OK,' I said. 'Were they killed up there where they were found?'

'No doubt about it,' the medical guy said. 'Take the first guy. He was shot, he fell down dead, he was kicked around in some sort of mad frenzy for a few minutes, then he lay there on the warehouse forecourt for around eight hours. No doubt about it.'

'What do you make of the kicking?' Finlay asked him.

'Some kind of a psychopathic thing, obviously. No way to explain it. It didn't hurt. So it must have gratified the kicker somehow. Unbelievable fury, tremendous strength. The injuries are grievous.'

'What about the second guy?' Finlay asked.

'He ran for it,' the doctor said. 'He was hit close up in the back with the first shot, but it didn't drop him, and he ran. He took two more on the way. One in the neck, and one in the thigh. He made it as far as the raised section of the highway, then lay down and bled to death. If it hadn't rained all night Thursday, I'm sure you'd have seen the trail of blood on the road.'

We all fell quiet. I was thinking about the second guy's desperate sprint across the road while the bullets smashed into his flesh.

'Do we know who the assailants were?' the doctor asked.

'We don't even know who the victims were,' Roscoe said.

'Got any theories?' Finlay asked the doctor.

The doctor nodded and started shuffling his notes. His telephone rang. He answered it and then held it out to Finlay.

'For you,' he said. Finlay took the call. Listened for a moment. 'OK,' he said into the phone. 'Fax it to us here, will you?'

Then he passed the phone back to the doctor and rocked back on his stool. He had the beginnings of a smile on his face. 'That was Stevenson, up at the station house. We finally got a match on the first guy's prints. Seems like we did the right thing to run them again. Stevenson's faxing it to us here.'

The doctor picked up a sheet of paper. 'I haven't got much at all on the first guy. The body was in a hell of a mess. He was tall, he was fit, he had a shaved head. The main thing is the dental work. Looks like the guy got his teeth fixed all over the place. Some of it is American, some of it looks foreign.'

Next to my hip, the fax machine started beeping and whirring.

'So what do we make of that?' Finlay said. 'The guy was foreign?'

The thin sheet of paper fed itself out, covered in writing, and the machine stopped. I picked up the paper and glanced at it. Then I read it through twice. I went cold, gripped by an icy paralysis. I just couldn't believe what I was seeing. I stared at the doctor and spoke. 'He grew up abroad. He had his teeth fixed wherever he was living. He had his tonsils out in the hospital in Seoul.'

The doctor looked up at me.

'They can tell all that from his fingerprints?' he said.

I shook my head.

'The guy was my brother,' I said.

ONCE I SAW a navy film about expeditions in the frozen Arctic. You could be walking over a solid glacier. Suddenly the ice would heave and shatter. A whole new geography would be forced up. Massive escarpments where it had been flat. Huge ravines behind you. The world all changed in a second. That's how I felt.

They walked me through to the cold store to make a formal identification of the body. His face had been blown away, but I recognised the star-shaped scar on his neck. Then they took me back up to the station house in Margrave. Finlay drove. Roscoe sat with me in the back of the car and held my hand all the way.

My brother Joe. Two years older than me. Born on a base in the Far East right at the end of the Eisenhower era. We'd grown up together all over the world inside that tight isolated transience that service families created for themselves. Life was all about moving on at random and unpredictable intervals. A blur of bases. We never owned anything. We were only allowed one bag each on the transport planes. We were together in that blur for sixteen years. Joe was the only constant thing in my life, and I loved him like a brother. Like any pair of brothers two years apart, we irritated the hell out of each other. We fought and bickered and sullenly waited to grow up and get out from under. Most of those sixteen years, we didn't know if we loved each other or hated each other. But we had the thing that army families have. Your family was your unit. The men on the bases were taught total loyalty to their units. The boys copied them. They translated the same intense loyalty onto their families. So from time to time you might hate your brother, but you didn't let anybody mess with him. Joe and I stood back to back in every new school yard and punched our way out of trouble together. I watched out for him, and he watched out for me, like brothers did. And now somebody had killed him. I sat in the back of the police Chevrolet as Finlay drove us back to Margrave and listened to a tiny voice in my head asking me what the hell I was going to do about that.

AT THE STATION HOUSE Finlay led us straight through the empty squad room to the big rosewood office. He sat at the desk. I sat in the same chair I'd used on Friday. Roscoe pulled a chair up and put it next to mine. Finlay switched on the tape recorder.

'I'm very sorry about your brother,' he said. 'I'm going to have to ask you a few questions, I'm afraid.'

I nodded. I understood his position. I'd been in his position plenty of times myself.

'Who would be his next of kin?' he asked.

'I am,' I said. 'Unless he got married without telling me.'

'What was his full name?'

'Joe Reacher,' I said. 'No middle name.'

'OK,' Finlay said. 'Older or younger?'

'Older,' I said. I gave him Joe's date of birth. 'He was thirty-eight.'

'Do you have a current address for him?'

'No,' I said. 'Last I heard, he worked for the Treasury Department in Washington, DC. Doing what, I'm not sure. Before that he was in Military Intelligence.'

'When did you last see him?'

'Seven years ago,' I said. 'Our mother's funeral.'

He paused. 'He wrote you that he had been here, right? You got any idea what brought him down here?'

I shook my head. 'He mentioned the Blind Blake thing. Didn't say why he was here. But it shouldn't be difficult to find out.'

I had no idea why he had come down here. But I knew Hubble did. Joe had been the tall investigator. Hubble had brought him down here and Hubble knew exactly why. First thing to do was to find Hubble and ask him about it. But I didn't particularly want Finlay watching over my shoulder while I was doing it. So exactly how much Hubble knew was going to stay my secret. Just for now.

I left Finlay and Roscoe in the office and strolled through the squad room. Pushed out through the glass doors into the hot afternoon. I needed some air. I wandered through the parking lot, stood on the wide lawn in front, and thought.

The United States is a giant country. Millions of square miles. Best part of three hundred million people. I hadn't seen Joe for seven years and he hadn't seen me, but we'd ended up in exactly the same spot, eight hours apart. I'd walked within fifty yards of where his body had been lying. That was one hell of a big coincidence. It was almost unbelievable. So Finlay was doing me a big favour by treating it like a coincidence. He should be trying to tear my alibi apart. Because a hell of a lot of homicide gets done by relatives. Maybe he was already on the phone to Tampa, checking again.

But he wouldn't find anything, because it *was* a coincidence. No point getting all stirred up about it. The only thing I had to do was to decide what the hell I was going to do about it.

I was about four years old when I figured I was supposed to watch out for Joe the way he was watching out for me. After a while it became second nature, automatic, even when I was grown up.

But now he was dead, and again the tiny voice inside my head was saying: *You're supposed to do something about that.*

I heard the station house door suck open behind me. I squinted through the heat and saw Roscoe step out. She scanned around and saw me. Came over.

'You OK?' she asked.

'I'm fine. I just feel numb, to be honest.'

Maybe it was a weird reaction, but that was how I felt.

'Can I give you a ride somewhere?' Roscoe asked.

Maybe Finlay had sent her out to keep track of me, but I wasn't about to put up a whole lot of objections to that. I realised I liked her more every time I looked at her.

'Want to show me where Hubble lives?' I asked her.

'Shouldn't we leave that to Finlay?'

'I just want to see if he's back home yet. I'm not going to eat him. If he's there, we'll call Finlay right away, OK?'

'OK.' She smiled. 'Let's go.'

We walked back over the lawn and got into her police Chevy. She started it up and pulled out of the lot. Turned left and rolled south through the perfect little town. It was a gorgeous late September day. The whole place was quiet, basking in the Sunday heat.

Roscoe made the turn into Beckman Drive. The street had a rich feel. Cool and shady and prosperous. I couldn't see the houses. They were set far back behind wide grassy shoulders, big trees, high hedges. Occasionally I glimpsed a white portico or a red roof.

Roscoe slowed at a white mailbox and turned left into the drive of number twenty-five, the last house on the road. We nosed slowly up a winding driveway. The house was huge. A palace. Every detail was expensive. Expanses of gravel drive, expanses of velvet lawn, huge exquisite trees, everything shining and dappled in the blazing sun. But there was no sign of the Bentley I'd seen up at the prison. It looked like there was nobody home.

Roscoe pulled up near the front door and we got out. It was silent. I could hear nothing except the heavy buzz of afternoon heat. We rang on the bell and knocked on the door. No response from inside. We were about to leave when the big Bentley appeared around a curve in the drive and eased to a stop at the front of the house. The blonde woman I'd seen driving away from the prison got out. She had two children with her. A boy and a girl. Hubble's family.

The blonde woman seemed to know Roscoe. They greeted each other and Roscoe introduced me to her. She shook my hand and said her name was Charlene, but I could call her Charlie. She was an expensive-looking woman, tall, slim, good bones, carefully dressed, carefully looked after. But she had a seam of spirit, too, enough spirit to make me like her. She held on to my hand and smiled, but it was a smile with a whole lot of strain behind it.

'This hasn't been the best weekend of my life, I'm afraid,' she said. 'But it seems that I owe you a great deal of thanks, Mr Reacher. My husband tells me you saved his life in prison.'

She said it with a lot of ice in her voice. Not aimed at me. Aimed at whatever circumstance it was forcing her to use the words 'husband' and 'prison' in the same sentence.

'No problem,' I said. 'Where is he?'

'Taking care of some business. He'll be back later.'

I nodded. Hubble had said he would spin her some kind of a yarn and then try to settle things down. I wondered if Charlie wanted to talk about it, but knew she wouldn't in front of the children. So I grinned at them. I hoped they would get all shy and run off somewhere, like children usually do with me, but they just grinned back.

'This is Ben,' Charlie said. 'And this is Lucy.'

The girl still had that little-girl chubbiness. Fine sandy hair in pigtails. The boy wasn't much bigger than his little sister. He had a serious face. They were a nice pair of kids. Polite and quiet, standing at their mother's side. I looked at the three of them and I could just about see the terrible cloud hanging over them. If Hubble didn't take care, he could get them all as dead as he'd gotten my brother.

'Will you come in for some iced tea?' Charlie asked us.

'OK,' I said. 'Thanks.'

The kids ran off to play somewhere and Charlie ushered us in through the front door. I didn't really want to drink any iced tea, but I did want to be there when Hubble got back.

It was a fabulous house. Beautifully furnished. Cool creams and sunny yellows. Charlie led us through to the garden room and Roscoe went off with her to help in the kitchen.

A few minutes later the two women came back with the tea. Charlie was carrying a silver tray. She was a handsome woman, but she was nothing next to Roscoe, who had a spark in her eyes so electric it made Charlie just about invisible. Roscoe smiled in my direction and sat down next to me on the cane sofa. As she sat, she pushed my leg to one side. It was a casual thing, but it was very intimate and familiar. A nerve end screamed at me: *She likes you too.* It was the way she touched my leg. All of a sudden I was glad I had jumped off that Greyhound bus. Glad I made that crazy last-minute decision. I suddenly relaxed. Felt better. The tiny voice in my head quieted down. Right now there was nothing for me to do. I'd speak to Hubble when I saw him. Until then I would sit on a sofa with this good-looking dark-haired woman in a soft cotton shirt.

Charlie Hubble sat down opposite us and started pouring iced tea from a pitcher. 'Normally, at this point, I'd ask you how you were enjoying your visit with us here in Margrave,' she said, looking at me, strained, smiling.

I couldn't think of a reply to that. I just shrugged. It was clear Charlie didn't know anything. She thought her husband had been arrested because of some kind of a mistake. Not because he was grabbed up in some kind of trouble that had just gotten two people murdered. Roscoe rescued the conversation and the two of them started passing the time of day. I just sat there, drank the tea and waited for Hubble. He didn't show up. Then the conversation died and we had to get out of there. Charlie was fidgeting like she had things to do. Roscoe put her hand on my arm. Her touch burned me like electricity. 'Let's go,' she said. 'I'll give you a ride back to town.'

I felt bad I wasn't staying to wait for Hubble. It made me feel disloyal to Joe. But I just wanted to be on my own with Roscoe. Maybe some kind of repressed grief was intensifying my feelings. I told myself I had no choice anyway. Nothing else I could do. So we got back in the Chevy together and nosed down the winding driveway.

'Reacher?' Roscoe said. 'You'll be around for a while, right? Until we get this thing about your brother straightened out?'

'I guess I will.'

'Where are you going to stay?'

'I don't know,' I said.

She pulled over to the kerb near the little village green. Nudged the selector into park. She had a tender look on her face. 'I want you to come home with me.'

I felt like I was out of my mind, but I was burning up with it so I pulled her to me and we kissed. That fabulous first kiss. The new and unfamiliar mouth and hair and taste and smell. She kissed hard and long and held on tight. We came up for air a couple of times before she took off again for her place, a quarter-mile down the street that opened up opposite Beckman Drive. I saw a blur of greenery in the sun as she swooped into her driveway. The tyres chirped as she stopped. We more or less tumbled out and ran to the door. She used her key and we went in. The door swung shut and she was back in my arms.

We tore each other's clothes off like they were on fire. She was gorgeous. Firm and strong and a shape like a dream. Skin like silk. She pulled me through to her bedroom and onto her bed. It was frantic. Nothing could have stopped us. We shuddered to a stop and lay gasping. We were bathed in sweat. Totally spent. Held each other and fell into a deep afterglow stupor. Roscoe was snuggled beside me. I was breathing through her hair. Our hands were lazily caressing unfamiliar contours.

We dozed through the afternoon. I called the Hubble place at seven in the evening. He still wasn't back. I left Roscoe's number with Charlie and told her to have Hubble call me as soon as he got in. Then we drifted on through the rest of the evening. Fell fast asleep at midnight. Hubble never called.

MONDAY MORNING I was vaguely aware of Roscoe getting up for work. I heard the shower and I know she kissed me tenderly and then the house was hot and quiet and still. I slept on until after nine. The phone didn't ring. That was OK. I needed some quiet thinking time. I had decisions to make. I stretched out in Roscoe's warm bed and listened to the tiny voice in my head.

What was I going to do about Joe? My answer came very easily. I knew it had been waiting there since I first stood next to Joe's broken body in the morgue. I was going to stand up for him. I was going to finish his business. Whatever it was. Whatever it took.

Hubble was the only link I had, but Hubble was the only link I needed. He would cooperate. He'd depended on Joe to help him out. Now he'd depend on me. What had he said? His masters were vulnerable for a week. A window of exposure wide open until Sunday. I'd use it to tear them apart. I couldn't leave it to Finlay. This was my business. It was between me and Joe. It was duty.

I lay there in Roscoe's bed, filled with restless energy. Got up and
found coffee. There was a note propped against the pot: *Early lunch
at Eno's? Eleven o'clock? Leave Hubble to Finlay, OK?* The note was
signed with lots of kisses. I read it and smiled, but I wasn't going to
leave Hubble to Finlay. No way. Hubble was my business. So I
looked up the number again and called Beckman Drive. There was
nobody home.

I poured a big mug of coffee and wandered through to the living
room. The sun was blinding outside. Another hot day. I walked
through the house. It was a small place. A living room, an eat-in
kitchen, two bedrooms, one and a half bathrooms. Very new, very
clean. Some nice Navajo art, some bold rugs, white walls.

I showered and dressed. Tried Hubble's number again. I let it ring
for a long time. Nobody home. I figured I'd get a ride up there from
Roscoe after lunch. This thing wasn't going to wait for ever.

It was about ten thirty. A mile and a quarter up to Eno's place. A
gentle half-hour stroll in the sun. It was already very hot. Well into
the eighties. Glorious fall weather in the South. I walked the quarter-
mile to Main Street up a gently winding rise.

I turned at the convenience store on the corner and strolled up
Main Street. The sidewalks had been swept. I could see crews of gardeners in the little park areas, setting up sprinklers and carrying stuff
out of smart green trucks marked KLINER FOUNDATION in gold. I
waved in at the two old barbers in their shop. They waved back and I
strolled on.

Eno's came into sight. The polished aluminium siding gleamed in
the sun. Roscoe's Chevrolet was in the lot. I reached the diner and
pushed in through the door. It was more or less empty, just like on
Friday. A couple of old guys and a couple of waitresses. They were
the same women as on Friday. Both blonde, one taller and heavier
than the other. Waitress uniforms.

Roscoe was in a booth, the same one I'd used on Friday. She was
back in uniform and she looked like the sexiest thing on earth. I
stepped over to her and bent to kiss her mouth. She slid over the
vinyl to the window. There were two cups of coffee on the table.

'Is this going to ruin your authority?' I asked her. 'To be seen kissing a vagrant who got arrested in here on Friday?'

'Probably,' she said. 'But who cares?'

So I kissed her again.

'I made a decision,' I said. 'I have to find out what happened with

Joe. So I just want to apologise in advance in case that gets in the way, OK?'

Roscoe smiled tenderly. Looked concerned for me. 'No reason why it should get in the way,' she said.

I sipped my coffee. It tasted good.

'We got an ID on the second body,' she said. 'His prints matched with an arrest for speeding two years ago in Florida. His name was Sherman Stoller. That name mean anything at all to you?'

I shook my head. 'Never heard of him,' I said.

Then her beeper started going. 'Damn,' she said. 'I've got to call in. Sorry. I'll use the phone in the car.'

I slid out of the booth and stepped back to let her by. 'Order me some food, OK?' she said. 'I'll have whatever you have.'

'OK,' I said. 'Which one is our waitress?'

'The one with the glasses.'

She walked out of the diner. I was aware of her leaning into her car, using the phone. Then she was gesturing to me urgently. Miming that she had to get back, that I should stay put. She jumped into the car and took off, south. I waved vaguely after her, not really looking.

I was staring at the two blonde waitresses. I had almost stopped breathing. I needed Hubble. And now I knew Hubble was dead.

One of the waitresses was around three inches taller than the other. Perhaps fifteen pounds heavier. The smaller one was better-looking. Nicer eyes behind the glasses. They were similar in a superficial way. But no way were they hard to distinguish one from the other.

I'd asked Roscoe which was our waitress. And she hadn't said the smaller one, or the prettier one, or the younger one. She'd said the one with glasses. One wore them, the other didn't.

That's what Spivey had seen on Friday night up at the prison. He'd come into the reception bunker with a shotgun and a clip-board in his big red farmer's hands. He had asked which one of us was Hubble. Why the hell should Spivey care which of us was which? He didn't need to know. But he'd asked. Hubble had raised his hand. Spivey had looked him over with his little snake eyes. He had seen that Hubble was shorter, lighter, sandier, balder than me. But what was the major difference he had hung on to? Hubble wore glasses.

But by the next morning I was the one with glasses, not Hubble. Because Hubble's gold rims had been smashed up by the Red Boys outside our cell. I had taken some shades from one of them as a trophy. They looked like ordinary glasses, because they were supposed to react to sunlight. I'd been standing there with them on when the Aryans came trawling into the bathroom. Spivey had just told them: *Find the new boys and kill the one with glasses.* They'd tried hard. They'd tried very hard to kill Paul Hubble.

They had attacked me because the description they'd been given was suddenly the wrong description. Spivey had reported that back long ago. Whoever had set him on Hubble hadn't given up. They'd made a second attempt. And the second attempt had succeeded. Now he was dead. Tortured and butchered. My fault.

I ran over to the counter. Spoke to our waitress. The one with glasses. 'Can you call me a taxi?' I asked her.

She nodded, picked up the phone. 'Just wait out in the parking lot.'

I waited. Five minutes. The taxi drove up. Brand-new and immaculate, like everything else in Margrave.

'Where to, sir?' the driver asked.

I gave him Hubble's address and he headed back to town. We passed the fire house and the police headquarters. The lot was empty. Roscoe's Chevy wasn't there. No cruisers. They were all out. We made the right at the village green and headed up Beckman. In a mile I would see a cluster of vehicles outside number twenty-five.

But the street was empty. I walked into Hubble's driveway. The taxi turned and drove back to town. Then it was silent. No police cars, no ambulances. Just the Bentley, parked up on the gravel. I walked past it on my way to the house. The front door crashed open. Charlie Hubble ran out. She was screaming. She was hysterical. But she was alive. 'Hub's disappeared,' she screamed. 'He's disappeared!'

They'd taken him and dumped him. Someone had found the body and called the police.

'Something's happened, I know it,' Charlie wailed. 'He got back late last night. He was still here this morning. I took Ben and Lucy to school. Now he's gone. He hasn't gone to work. He got a call from his office telling him to stay home, and his briefcase is still here, with his wallet, credit cards, driver's licence. His keys are in the kitchen. The front door was standing wide open. He's just disappeared.'

I stood still. Paralysed. He'd been dragged out of there by force.

Charlie sagged in front of me. Then she started whispering to me. The whispering was worse than the screaming. 'His car is still in the garage. He never walks anywhere. He always takes his Bentley. You've got to find him. Mr Reacher, please. I'm asking you to help us. Hub's in trouble, I know it. He's vanished. He said you might help. You saved his life. He said you knew how to do things.'

She was pleading. But I couldn't help her. She would know that soon enough. Baker or Finlay would come up to the house very soon. They would break the shattering news, drive her down to the morgue to identify the body.

'Will you help us?' Charlie asked me.

I decided to go down to the station house. Find out details like where and when and how. But I'd come back with Finlay. This was my fault, so I should come back. I explained to her where I was going. 'You stay here,' I said. 'You'll have to lend me your car, OK?'

She rooted in her bag and pulled out a big bunch of keys. Handed them to me. I stepped over to the Bentley and slid into the driver's seat. Glided down Beckman in silence. Made the left onto Main Street up toward the station house.

There were cruisers and unmarked units sprawled across the police parking lot. I left Charlie's Bentley at the kerb and stepped inside. Milling around the open area I saw Baker, Stevenson, Finlay, Roscoe, the back-up team from Friday. Morrison wasn't there. Nor was the desk guy. The counter was unattended. Everybody was stunned. Horrified. Distracted. Finally Roscoe came over. She'd been crying.

'It was horrible,' she said. Wouldn't say any more.

I squeezed her shoulder and stepped over toward Finlay. He was sitting on a desk, looking really shaken up. Hubble must have been left in a hell of a mess to be getting a reaction like that from Finlay. He was a twenty-year man from a big city. He must have seen all there is to see.

'Tell me what happened, Finlay,' I said.

He leaned forward. Cupped his mouth and nose with his hands and sighed heavily into them. 'He was naked. They nailed him to the wall. Six or seven big carpentry nails through his hands and up his arms. Then they slit his throat. Ear to ear. Bad people, Reacher. As bad as they come.'

I was numb. Finlay was waiting for a comment. I couldn't think of anything. I was thinking about Charlie. She would ask if I'd found anything out. Finlay should go up there. He should go up there right now and break the news. It was his job, not mine. But I'd go with him. Because it was my fault. No point running away from that. *Believe me, if they were looking to kill you, you'd be dead by now. You're in the clear, Hubble.*

'It sounds pretty bad,' I said.

Finlay leaned his head back and looked around. Blew another sigh up at the ceiling. 'That's not the worst of it,' he said. 'You should have seen what they did to his wife.'

For a moment I couldn't speak. The world was spinning backward. 'His wife? But I just saw her. Twenty minutes ago. She's OK. Nothing happened to her.'

'You saw who?' Finlay said.

'Charlie Hubble,' I said. 'His wife.'

'What's Hubble got to do with this?'

I just stared at him. 'Who are we talking about?' I said.

Finlay looked at me like I was crazy.

'I thought you knew,' he said. 'Chief Morrison. And his wife.'

FOUR

I was watching Finlay carefully, trying to decide how far I should trust him. It was a life or death decision. In the end I figured his answer to one simple question would make up my mind for me.

'Are they going to make you chief now?' I asked him.

He shook his head. 'No,' he said.

'Whose decision is it?' I asked him.

'The mayor's,' Finlay said. 'Town mayor appoints the chief of police. Guy named Teale. Some kind of an old Georgia family. Ancestor was a railroad baron. They've had Teales here ever since. I dare say this one's no worse than the others.'

We walked down to the convenience store. Sat side by side at the empty counter, near the window. We got tall mugs of coffee and a big plate of doughnuts. Looked at each other in the mirror behind the counter.

'Why won't you get the promotion?' I asked him.

He was looking puzzled. He couldn't see the connection. But he'd see it soon enough.

'It's a personal matter,' he said. 'A long story.'

'So tell it to me,' I said. 'I need to know.'

He took a deep breath. 'I finished in Boston in March,' he said. 'Done my twenty years. Unblemished record. Eight commendations. I had retirement on full pension to look forward to. Six months before the end, we were thinking of a cabin somewhere, maybe.

Vacations. Plenty of time together. But my wife started panicking. She didn't want plenty of time together. She didn't want me to retire. She didn't want me at home. She said she woke up to the fact that she didn't like me. Didn't love me. Didn't want me around. I couldn't believe it. It was my dream. Twenty years and then retire at forty-five. But she didn't want it. It got really bitter. We fell apart. I was a total basket case.

'So we got divorced. It was terrible. I was totally out of it. Then in my last month in the department I started reading the union vacancy lists again. Saw this job down here. I called an old buddy in Atlanta FBI and asked him about it. He warned me off. Said the previous guy was a weirdo who hung himself. The department was run by a fat moron. The town was run by some old Georgia type who couldn't remember slavery had been abolished. But I thought I could bury myself down here as a punishment, you know? A kind of penance. Also, I needed the money. They were offering top dollar and I was looking at alimony and lawyer bills. So I applied for it and came down. It was Mayor Teale and Morrison who saw me. I was a basket case, Reacher. I couldn't string two words together. It had to be the worst job application in the history of the world. But they gave me the job. I guess they needed a black guy to look good. I'm the first black cop in Margrave's history.'

I turned on the stool and looked straight at him. 'So you figure you're just a token?' I said. 'That's why Teale won't make you chief?'

'It's obvious, I guess,' he said.

I waved to the counter guy for the check. I was happy with Finlay's story. He wasn't going to be chief. So I trusted him. And I trusted Roscoe. It was going to be the three of us, against whoever.

'You're wrong,' I said. 'That's not the real reason. You're not going to be chief because you're not a criminal.'

I told Finlay I needed to see the Morrison place. Told him I needed all the details. He led me outside. We turned and walked south. Passed by the village green and put the town behind us.

'I was the first one there,' he said. 'About ten this morning. I hadn't seen Morrison since Friday and I needed to update the guy, but I couldn't get him on the phone. So I went up to his house.'

He went quiet. Revisiting in his mind the scene he'd found.

'Front door was open,' he said. 'It had a bad feel. I went in, found them upstairs in the master bedroom. It was like a butcher's shop. Blood everywhere. About twenty-four hours of decomposition.'

'So it happened Sunday morning?'

He nodded. 'Medical examiner says about ten o'clock.'

'Any physical evidence left behind?' I asked him.

He nodded again. Grimly. 'Footprints in the blood. They were wearing rubber overshoes, you know? Like you get for the winter up north? No chance of tracing them.'

They had come prepared. They'd known there was going to be a lot of blood. They'd brought overshoes. They must have brought overalls. Like the nylon body suits they wear in the slaughterhouse. On the killing floor.

'How many people?' I asked, trying to build up a picture.

'The footprints are confused, but I think I can see four,' he said.

Four sounded right. Morrison and his wife would have been fighting for their lives. It would take four of them, at least. Four out of the ten Hubble had mentioned. 'Transport?' I said.

'Can't really tell,' Finlay said. 'I saw some wide ruts in the gravel driveway. Could have been wide tyres. Maybe a big four-wheel drive or a small truck.'

We were a couple of hundred yards south of where Main Street had petered out. We turned up a gravel driveway. At the end of the driveway was Morrison's house, a big formal place, white columns at the front, a lot of police tape strung at waist height between them.

We ducked under the tape and pushed in through Morrison's front door. There was grey metallic fingerprint powder everywhere. I headed for the staircase. Went up and found the master bedroom. Stopped at the door and peered in. There was nothing to see except the ragged outline of the nail holes in the wall and the massive bloodstains. On the parquet in the doorway I could see the footprints from the overshoes, the intricate pattern of the treads. I headed back downstairs and found Finlay leaning on a porch column out front.

'You search the car?' I asked him.

He shook his head. 'That's Morrison's,' he said. 'We just looked for stuff the intruders might have left behind.'

I stepped over to the Lincoln parked outside the house and tried the door. Unlocked. I poked around in the door pockets and under the seats. Found nothing at all. Then I opened the glove box. There was a switchblade in there. It was a handsome thing. Ebony handle with Morrison's name in gold-filled engraving. I popped the blade. Double-edged, seven inches, surgical steel. I closed it up and slipped it into my pocket. I was unarmed and facing big trouble. Morrison's switchblade might make a difference. I slid out of the Lincoln and rejoined Finlay on the gravel.

'Find anything?' he asked.

'No,' I said. 'Let's go.'

We crunched back down the driveway together and turned north on the county road. Headed back to town. I took a deep breath. 'Something I need to check with you,' I said.

Finlay's patience was running thin. He looked at his watch. 'You better not be wasting my time, Reacher.'

'They nailed Morrison to the wall, right?'

Finlay nodded. Looked at me, waiting.

'OK,' I said. 'And his throat was slit?'

Finlay went quiet. Just looked at me. 'Talk, Reacher,' he said.

'First answer another question for me. How many homicides have you had in Margrave?'

He thought about it. 'None,' he said. 'At least, not for maybe thirty years or so.'

'And now you've had four in four days,' I said. 'And pretty soon you'll find the fifth.'

'Fifth? Who's the fifth?'

'Hubble,' I said. 'My brother, this Sherman Stoller guy, the two Morrisons and Hubble makes five. That can't be any kind of coincidence, right?'

'No way. Of course not. They're linked.'

'Right, now I'll tell you some more links. But first you've got to understand I was just passing through here. Until the time those prints came through on my brother, I wasn't paying the slightest bit of attention to anything at all.'

'So?'

'Well, when we were in that cell in Warburton Hubble told me things, but I didn't pay a lot of attention. I wasn't interested, OK?'

'What did he tell you?'

I told him how Hubble had said he was trapped in some kind of a racket, terrorised by a threat against himself and his wife. A threat consisting of the same things that Finlay had just seen for himself that morning.

'You sure about that?' he said. 'Exactly the same?'

'Totally identical,' I said.

'So Morrison was inside the same scam as Hubble?' he said.

'Owned and operated by the same people.'

Then I told him Hubble had been talking to an investigator. And the investigator had been talking to Sherman Stoller. 'Joe was the investigator,' I said. 'Hubble told me the tall guy with the shaved head was an investigator, trying to get him free.'

'What sort of an investigator was your brother?' Finlay asked.

'Don't know,' I said. 'Last I heard he was working for the Treasury Department.'

'Why do you think Hubble's dead?' Finlay asked me after a while.

So I told him how I knew. 'When you pulled him in with the phone number in Joe's shoe, they figured he couldn't be allowed to talk. So they set it up with Spivey. But Spivey's boys blew it, so they tried over again. His wife said he got a call to wait at home today. They were setting him up for a second attempt. Looks like it worked.'

Finlay nodded slowly. 'Shit,' he said. 'He was the only link we had to exactly what the hell is going on here. He gave you no idea what the scam is all about?' he asked.

'No idea,' I said. 'Only that ten people are involved in it. And he did say the scam is vulnerable until something happens on Sunday.'

'What happens on Sunday?' Finlay asked.

'He didn't tell me.'

'Hell, Reacher, you're a big help, you know that?' he said.

'I'm sorry. If I could go back and do it again, I'd do it different.'

'Ten people?' he said again.

'Not counting Hubble himself. But I assume he was counting Chief Morrison. I wonder what the chief did wrong. To get himself dead, I mean.'

'Screwed something up, I guess,' he said.

'Correct, Finlay. He was told to cover up what went down at the warehouse Thursday night. That was his task for the day. He was up there at midnight, you know. He saw Joe.'

'He did?' Finlay said. 'How do you know that?'

'First time he saw me was Friday, at the station house. He was staring at me like he'd seen me before, but he couldn't place where. That was because he'd seen Joe. He noticed a resemblance.'

'So Morrison was there?' Finlay said. 'Was he the shooter?'

'Can't figure it that way,' I said. 'Joe was a smart guy. He wouldn't let a fat idiot like Morrison shoot him. I can't figure Morrison for the maniac, either. That much physical exertion would have dropped him with a heart attack. I think he was the third guy. The clean-up guy. But he didn't search Joe's shoes. And because of that, Hubble

got hauled in. That got somebody mad. It meant they had to waste
Hubble, so Morrison was wasted as a punishment. And as a message
for the next guy in line.'

'You think the next chief will be in the scam?'

'Got to be,' I said. 'They had Morrison inside because they need
the chief on board. So they wouldn't waste Morrison unless they
had a replacement ready. And whoever it is, somebody will have
whispered to him: *See what we did to Morrison? That's what we'll do
to you if you screw up the way he did.*

'So who is it?' Finlay said. 'Who's going to be the new chief?'

'That's what I was asking you,' I said.

We sat quiet on a bench outside the barbershop for a moment.
Enjoyed the sun creeping in under the edge of the striped awning.

'It's you, me and Roscoe,' I said. 'Right now, the only safe thing is
to assume everybody else is involved.'

'Why Roscoe?' he said.

'Lots of reasons,' I said. 'But mainly because she worked hard to
get me out of Warburton. Morrison wanted me in there as a fall guy
for Thursday night, right? So if Roscoe was inside the scam, she'd
have left me in there.'

He looked at me. 'Only three of us? You're a cautious guy, Reacher.'

'You bet your ass I'm a cautious guy, Finlay,' I said. 'People are
getting killed here. One of them was my only brother.'

We stood up from the bench. I noticed the black pick-up across
the street again, the Kliner kid staring out the window at me.

Finlay didn't see him. He was busy rubbing his face with his hands,
like he was washing without water. 'I need to make some calls and
find out from Washington what your brother was doing down here.'

'OK,' I said. I nodded across at the Kliner kid, who had killed his
motor and was walking slowly over. 'I'm going to have a talk with
this guy. He's staring at me.'

Two things happened as the kid came near. First, Finlay left in a
hurry. He just strode off without another word. Second, I heard the
barbershop blinds coming down in the window behind me. I glanced
around. There could have been nobody else on the planet except for
me and the guy in front of me. His eyes told me he probably wasn't
the most rational character I was ever going to meet in my whole life.
He stood in front of me. Just stared.

'You're trespassing,' he said.

'This is your sidewalk?' I said.

'It sure is,' the kid said. 'My daddy's Foundation paid for every inch of it. The Kliner Foundation, that is. But I'm not talking about the sidewalk. I'm talking about Miss Roscoe. She's mine. She's mine, right from when I first saw her. She's waiting for me. Five years, she's been waiting for me, until the time is right.'

I gazed back at him. 'I'm a reasonable guy,' I said. 'First time Miss Roscoe tells me she wants you instead of me, I'm out of here. Until then, you back off. Understand that?'

The Kliner kid was boiling. But then he changed. It was like he was operated by a remote control and somebody had just hit a button and switched the channel. He relaxed and smiled a wide, boyish smile. 'OK,' he said. 'No hard feelings, right?'

He stuck out his hand to shake on it and he nearly fooled me. Right at the last split second I pulled my own hand back a fraction and closed around his knuckles, not his palm. It's an old army trick. They go to shake your hand, but they're aiming to crush it. The way out is to be ready. You pull back a fraction and you squeeze *their* knuckles. If you catch it right, you can't lose.

He started crushing, but he never stood a chance. I crunched his knuckles once, then twice, a little harder, and then I dropped his hand and turned away. I'd gone a good sixty yards before I heard the truck start up and rumble off. Its noise was lost in the buzz of the heat.

BACK AT THE STATION HOUSE there was a big white Cadillac parked right across the entrance. Brand-new.

Inside in the chill everybody was milling around a tall old guy with silver hair. He was in an old-fashioned suit. Bootlace tie with a silver clasp. He must have been about seventy-five years old and he was limping around, leaning on a thick cane with a huge silver knob at the top. I guessed this was Mayor Teale.

Roscoe gestured me over. Wanted me to go with her into the big rosewood office.

'You OK?' I said.

'I've had better days.'

'Finlay give you the spread?'

She nodded. 'He told me everything.'

We ducked into the office. Finlay was sitting at the desk under the old clock. It showed a quarter of four. Roscoe closed the door and I looked back and forth between the two of them. 'So who's getting it?' I said. 'Who's the new chief?'

Finlay looked up at me from where he was sitting. 'Mayor Teale is going to run the department himself.'

'So what do you make of that?' I asked them.

'Everybody else in the department is clean?' Roscoe offered.

'Looks that way,' I said. 'But it proves Teale himself is on board.'

'How do we know he's not the big boss?' Roscoe asked.

'No,' I said. 'The big boss had Morrison carved up as a message. If Teale was the big boss, why would he send a message to himself? No, he's been put in here to run interference.'

'That's for sure,' Finlay agreed. 'Started already. Told us Joe and Stoller are going on the back burner. We're throwing everything at the Morrison thing. Says it's obvious Morrison was killed by some ex-con, just out of prison. Somebody Morrison himself put away a long time ago, out for revenge.'

'It's a hell of a blind alley,' Roscoe said. 'We've got to trawl through twenty years of old files and crosscheck every name in every file against parole records from across the country.'

'Can't you just ignore him?' I said. 'Just do what needs doing?'

Finlay leaned back in his chair. Blew a sigh at the ceiling and shook his head. 'No. Teale's got no reason to think we know anything about any of this. And we've got to keep it that way. We've got to play dumb and act innocent.' He thought for a moment. 'There's a guy I know called Picard. Atlanta FBI. Nice guy, you'll like him. He did a spell in Boston about a million years ago. I'll call him tonight from home. He might be able to help us.'

'Tell him we need it kept very quiet. We don't want his agents down here until we're ready.'

'So what now?' Roscoe asked.

'Maybe I'll go over to Warburton,' I said. 'Spivey was ordered to arrange the attack on Hubble, right? So he must know who gave him the order. I'll go ask him. Might lead somewhere.'

'Take care, Reacher,' Finlay said. 'They see you getting close to what Hubble knew, they'll waste you like they wasted him.'

Charlie and her kids flashed into my mind. They'd figure Charlie was close to what Hubble had known. Maybe even his kids as well.

'Finlay, call your buddy Picard right now,' I said. 'We've got to put Charlie Hubble somewhere safe. And her kids. Right now.'

Finlay nodded gravely. He understood. 'For sure,' he said, picking up the phone. 'Get your ass up to Beckman Drive. I'll organise Picard. You don't leave until he shows up, OK?'

THE END OF THE SCHOOL DAY was the busiest I'd ever seen the town. I passed two people on Main Street and saw another four talking in a knot near the church. I drove the Bentley past them and up Beckman Drive. Turned in at the Hubbles' place.

I parked Charlie's car at her door and rang her bell, not knowing how much I wanted to tell her. She opened up and let me in. I followed her to the kitchen and she switched on the coffee machine. It started with a faint hiss. I sat at a table in a window nook overlooking an acre of velvet lawn. She sat opposite me, looking strained.

'I heard about the Morrisons,' she said. 'Is my husband involved in all this?'

'Yes, Charlie,' I said. 'I'm afraid he was. But he didn't want to be. Some kind of blackmail was going on.'

She took it well. She must have figured it out for herself, but she looked like it had done her good to hear someone else say it. Now it was out in the open. It could be dealt with.

'Is he in danger?' she asked.

'Charlie, I'm afraid I have no idea where he is.'

She got up to pour the coffee. Sat down again. Looked hard at me across the table.

'I panicked this morning,' she said. 'That's not really like me at all. After you left, I calmed down and thought things out. I came to the same conclusion you've just described. Hub's blundered into something and he's got all tangled up in it. So I want to hire you to solve my husband's problem. Would you consider doing that for me?'

'I can't do that, Charlie.'

'Can't or won't?' she said.

I paused for a moment. Tried to figure out how to explain it.

'Your husband felt bad, OK? He got hold of some kind of an investigator, a government guy, and they were trying to fix the situation. But the government guy got killed. And I'm afraid my interest is in the government guy, more than your husband.'

'But why?' she asked. 'You don't work for the government.'

'The government guy was my brother. Just a crazy coincidence, I know, but I'm stuck with it.'

She went quiet. 'I'm very sorry,' she said. 'You're not saying Hub betrayed your brother?'

'No. That's the last thing he would have done. He was depending on him to get him out of trouble. Something went wrong, is all.'

There was a long silence. I sat there at the table, nursing the coffee she'd made for me. 'Would you do it if I didn't pay you?' she said. 'Maybe you could just look around for him while you find out about your brother?'

I couldn't see how I could say no to that.

'OK. I'll do that, Charlie. But don't expect miracles. I think we're looking at something very bad here.'

She went pale and clenched her knuckles. 'I can see you think he's already dead. But I think he's alive. I would know if he wasn't.'

I started worrying about what would happen when his body was found, when she came face to face with reality.

'You'll need expense money,' she said.

I wasn't sure about taking it, but she passed me a thick envelope. I looked in it. There was a thick wad of hundred-dollar bills inside.

'And please keep the car,' she said. 'For as long as you need it.'

I thought about what else I needed to say and forced myself to use the present tense. 'Where does your husband work?'

'Sunrise International,' she said. 'It's a bank.' She reeled off an Atlanta address.

'OK, Charlie,' I said. 'Now you've got to get out of here. An FBI agent is coming to pick you up.'

She stared at me in panic. 'FBI?' she said. 'This is really serious, isn't it?'

'It's deadly serious.'

I sat in Charlie's kitchen with the rest of the coffee for most of an hour while she packed. Then I heard a car horn and the crunch of heavy steps on the gravel. A loud knock on the front door. I put my hand in my pocket and closed it around the handle of Morrison's switchblade. Walked out into the hallway and opened up.

There was a neat blue sedan next to the Bentley and a gigantic black guy standing back from the doorstep. He was as tall as me, maybe even taller, but he must have outweighed me by at least a hundred pounds. He stepped forward with the easy grace of an athlete.

'Reacher?' the giant said. 'Pleased to meet you. I'm Picard, FBI.'

He shook hands with me. He had a casual competence about him that made me glad he was on my side. I suddenly felt a flood of encouragement, and stood aside to let him in.

'OK,' Picard said to me. 'I got all the details from Finlay. Real sorry about your brother. Real sorry. Somewhere we can talk?'

I led him through to the kitchen.

'I could end up with my big ass in a sling for this,' he said. 'But I'll bend the rules for Finlay. We go back quite a ways. But you got to remember, this is all unofficial, OK?'

I nodded. I was very happy with that. Unofficial help suited me fine. It would get the job done without wasting time on procedure. I had five clear days before Sunday.

'Where are you going to put them?' I asked him.

'Safe house up in Atlanta,' Picard said. 'Bureau place, we've had it for years. They'll be secure there, but I'm not going to say exactly where it is. I blow a safe house, I'm in really deep shit.'

'I won't cause you a problem,' I said. 'And I appreciate it.'

Charlie and the kids burst in with their bags. Picard introduced himself. I could see that Charlie's daughter was terrified by the size of the guy. The little boy's eyes grew round as he gazed at Picard's FBI Special Agent's shield. The five of us carried the bags outside and piled them in the blue sedan's trunk. Then they all got in the car and Picard drove them away.

FIVE

I headed over to Warburton a damn sight faster than the prison driver had and I was there in less than fifty minutes. It was a hell of a sight. There was a storm coming in quickly from the west and shafts of low afternoon sun were escaping the clouds and hitting the glittering metal towers and turrets with their orange rays. I stopped the car outside the first vehicle cage. I wasn't going in there. I'd had enough of that. Spivey was going to have to come out to me. I got out of the Bentley and walked over to the guard.

'Tell Spivey Mr Reacher's here,' I said. 'Tell him Chief Morrison sent me.'

The guy went under a Perspex hood and made a call. After a minute he was back out. 'OK, drive on through,' he said. 'Spivey will meet you at reception.'

'Tell him he's got to come out here,' I said. 'Meet me on the road.'

I walked away and stood in the dust on the edge of the blacktop. It was a battle of nerves. I waited. I could smell rain coming out of the west. In an hour, it was going to roll right over us.

Spivey came out. He walked over. Big guy, red face sweating.

'Remember me?' I asked him.

His small snake eyes flicked around. 'You're Reacher. So what?'

'Right,' I said. 'I'm Reacher. From Friday. What was the deal?'

He shifted from foot to foot. He was going to play hard to get. But he'd already showed his hand. He'd come out to meet me. He'd already lost the game, but he wouldn't speak.

I stepped casually to my left, putting Spivey's bulk between me and the gate guard. So the gate guard couldn't see. Morrison's switchblade appeared in my hand. The blade popped out with a loud click. Spivey's small eyes were fixed on it.

'Friday,' I said. 'What was the deal? You tell me the truth, I'll let you go back inside. Want to tell me the truth?'

He didn't reply. His nerves were shot to hell. His little eyes were darting about. They always came back to the blade.

'OK, I'll tell you,' he said. 'Morrison called me Friday. Said he was sending two guys over. I was supposed to get the Hubble guy killed. That's all. Nothing was supposed to happen to you, I swear it. My guys screwed up. But you got out of there, right? No damage done? So why give me a hard time? I just do what I'm told.'

'Who told you what to do?' I asked.

'Morrison,' he said.

'And who told Morrison what to do?'

I held the blade an inch from his cheek. He froze in shock.

'I don't know,' he said. 'I swear it, grave of my mother.'

I stared at him for a long moment. 'Wrong, Spivey. You do know. You're going to tell me.'

Spivey shook his head. His big red face jerked from side to side. 'They'll kill me if I do,' he said.

I flicked the knife at his belly. Slit his greasy shirt. 'I'll kill you if you don't.'

Guy like Spivey, he thinks short-term. If he told me, he'd die tomorrow. If he didn't tell me, he'd die today. That's how he thought. So he set about telling me. His throat started working up and down, like it was too dry to speak. He couldn't get any words out. But he was going to tell me.

Then he wasn't. Over his shoulder, I saw a dust plume. I made out the grey shape of the prison bus rolling in. Spivey looked around at his salvation. As the gate guard wandered out to meet the bus, Spivey backed away and walked over toward him. Then he turned back to look at me, a mean gleam of triumph in his eyes.

The bus roared in and blew dust all over me. I put the switchblade back in my pocket. Jogged over to the Bentley and took off.

THE COMING STORM chased me all the way back to town. I was sick with frustration. I had no back-up, no facilities. I couldn't rely on Roscoe or Finlay—they had troubles of their own at the station house, working under the enemy's nose. And I couldn't expect too much from Picard. He was already way out on a limb. I couldn't count on anybody but myself.

On the other hand, I had no laws to worry about, no inhibitions. I wouldn't have to think about probable cause, constitutional rights. I wouldn't have to think about reasonable doubt or rules of evidence. Was that fair? You bet it was. These were bad people. What had Finlay said? As bad as they come. And they had killed Joe Reacher.

I parked on the road outside Roscoe's house and waited. Her shift finished at six and at twenty after I saw her Chevy winding down the slight hill to her home. Her headlights washed over me as she swung into her driveway. I got out of the Bentley and stepped over to her. We held each other and kissed. Then we went inside.

'You OK?' I asked her.

'I guess,' she said. 'Hell of a day.' She was moving around switching lamps on. Pulling drapes. 'This morning was the worst thing I've ever seen. By far the worst thing.'

'What about the rest of it?' I asked her. 'Teale?'

'I'm not surprised,' she said. 'That whole family has been scumbags for two hundred years. Why should he be any different?'

She went into the kitchen and I followed. She went quiet. She wasn't falling apart, but she wasn't happy. She pulled open the refrigerator door. It was a gesture that said: *The cupboard is bare*. She smiled a tired smile at me. 'You want to buy me dinner?'

'Sure,' I said. 'But not here. In Alabama.'

I wanted to get away from Margrave for the evening. Wanted to get out of Georgia altogether. I figured if we went west for an hour, hour and a half, back past Warburton again, we'd cross the state line into Alabama. That's what I wanted to do. Pull into the first live music bar we came to. Put my troubles on hold until tomorrow. Eat some cheap food, drink some cold beer, hear some music. With Roscoe. My idea of a hell of an evening.

Roscoe liked the plan. She brightened up and went to take a shower, then changed into faded denims and a silky shirt. We turned off the lamps, locked up and headed west.

We were in Alabama before eight thirty. We saw an old roadhouse maybe a mile later. Pulled into the parking lot and got out. The sign at the door said THE POND, LIVE MUSIC SEVEN NIGHTS A WEEK AT NINE. Roscoe and I held hands and walked in.

We were hit by bar noise and a blast of beery air. We pushed through to the back, found an empty booth and slid in. One of the waitresses dived over and we ordered beers, cheeseburgers, fries. Pretty much right away she ran back with our stuff on a tin tray.

Then the band started up. They were called Pond Life. A classic trio. Guitar, bass, drums. Made a good old-fashioned sound.

We were having a great time. We drank a lot of beer, sat tight together in the booth. Then we danced for a while. Couldn't resist it. The room got hot and crowded.

Roscoe looked great. Her silky shirt was damp. She wasn't wearing anything underneath it and the silk stuck to her skin. I was in heaven. I was in a plain old bar with a stunning woman and a decent band. Joe was on hold until tomorrow. I didn't want the evening to end.

The band played on until way past midnight. We were juiced up and sloppy. Couldn't face the drive back. It was raining again, lightly. Didn't want to drive an hour and a half in the rain. Not full of beer. There was a sign to a motel a mile further on. Roscoe said we should go there. I wasn't about to put up objections.

So we stumbled out of the bar and drove down the streaming road. Saw the motel up ahead. I pulled into the lot and roused the night guy at the desk. Gave him the money and arranged an early-morning call. Got the key and went back out to the car. I drove it around to our cabin and we went in. It was a decent place, warm and snug with the rain pattering on the roof. And it had a big bed.

I didn't want Roscoe to catch a chill. She ought to get out of that damp shirt. That's what I told her. She giggled at me. Said she hadn't realised I had medical qualifications. I told her we'd been taught enough for basic emergencies.

'Is this a basic emergency?' she giggled.

'It will be soon,' I laughed. 'If you don't take that shirt off.'

So she did take it off. Then I was all over her. She was so beautiful, so provocative. We ended up in a frenzy on the bedroom floor.

Later we lay in an exhausted tangle and talked. About who we were, about what we'd done. About who we wanted to be and what we wanted to do. I talked to her about Joe. I told her things I'd never told anybody else. All about my feelings for him and why I felt driven to do something about his death. We talked for a long time and fell asleep in each other's arms.

SEEMED LIKE MORE OR LESS straight away the guy was banging on the door with the early-morning call. Tuesday. We got up and staggered around. Within five minutes we were back in the Bentley, rolling through the empty farming country. A floating quilt of morning mist hung over the red earth.

Neither of us spoke. We wanted to preserve the quiet intimate cocoon as long as possible. Arriving back in Margrave was going to burst the bubble soon enough. So in silence I guided the big stately car down the country roads with Roscoe curled up on the big hide seat beside me. She looked very content. I hoped she was.

When we got to Roscoe's place I parked at the kerb and we got out, yawning and stretching. We grinned briefly at each other and walked hand in hand down the driveway.

Her door was open. Not wide open, but an inch or two ajar. It was ajar because the lock was smashed. Roscoe put her hand to her mouth and gave a silent gasp. Her eyes were wide.

I grabbed her elbow and pulled her away. We stood flat against the garage door. Crouched down and circled right around the house. Listened hard at every window and risked ducking our heads up for a quick glance into every room. We arrived back at the smashed front door. Pushed it open and went inside.

We checked everywhere. There was no damage. No disturbance. Nothing was stolen. Roscoe checked her drawers and her bureau. Nothing had been touched. We stood back in the hallway and looked at each other. Then I noticed something that had been left behind.

The low morning sun was coming in through the open door and playing a shallow beam over the floor. I could see a line of footprints on the parquet in the hallway. They had been made by people coming in from the rainy night. At least four people. In and out. I could see the tread patterns they had left behind. They had been wearing rubber overshoes. Like you get for the winter up north.

They had come for us in the night with their knives, their hammer, their bag of nails. They had come to do a job on us, like they'd done on Morrison and his wife.

'So who were they after?' Roscoe said at last. 'Me, you, both of us?'

'Both of us,' I said. 'They figure Hubble talked to me in prison. They figure I've told you all about it. So they think you and I know whatever it was Hubble knew.'

She moved away and leaned against her back door, looking out at her garden. 'Thank God we weren't here last night,' she whispered.

I knew I had to sound confident. Fear wouldn't get her anywhere. Fear would just sap her energy. 'I wish we *had* been here,' I said. 'We could have gotten a few answers.'

She looked at me like I was crazy. 'What would you have done? Killed four men?'

'Only three. The fourth would have given us the answers.'

I said it with total certainty. Like absolutely no other possibility existed. I was willing myself to project all the invincibility, all the implacability, all the protective instinct I felt. I wanted Roscoe to feel safe. I wanted to give her that.

'It's going to take more than four little country boys to get me,' I said. 'Who are they kidding? And I'll tell you what, Roscoe. Someone even thinks about hurting you, they die before they finish thinking.'

It was working. I needed her to be bright, tough, self-confident, and it was working. Her amazing eyes were filling with spirit.

'Promise?' she said.

'You got it, babe.'

She sighed a ragged sigh. Pushed off the door and stepped over.

'Now we get the hell out of here,' I said. 'We can't stay around like sitting targets. So throw what you need into a bag.'

'OK,' she said. 'Are we going to fix my door first?'

'No,' I said. 'If we fix it, it means we've seen it. It also means we know we're under attack. Better if they figure we don't know we're under attack. Because then they'll figure they don't need to be too careful next time. It'll be easier to spot them coming.'

'OK,' she said. She didn't sound convinced. She went off to gather up some stuff. The game was starting. I didn't know exactly who the other players were. But I knew how to play. Opening move was I wanted them to feel like we were always one step behind.

'Should I go to work today?' Roscoe asked.

'Got to,' I said. 'Can't do anything different from normal.'

She nodded. Went to get dressed for work. Within twenty minutes, she came out of the bedroom in her uniform. Patted herself down. Ready for the day.

I hid the Bentley in her garage to maintain the illusion that we hadn't been back to her house. Then we got in her Chevy and decided to start with breakfast up at Eno's. She gunned the car up the hill. Coming down the hill toward us was a van. Smart, dark green, very clean, with fancy gold script on the side. It said: KLINER FOUNDATION. Same as I'd seen the gardeners using.

'What *is* the Kliner Foundation?' I asked Roscoe.

'Big deal around here,' she said. 'The town sold old man Kliner the land for his warehouses and part of the deal was he set up a community programme. Teale runs it out of the mayor's office.'

'Teale runs it?' I said. 'Teale's the enemy.'

'He runs it because he's the mayor,' she said. 'Not because he's Teale. The programme assigns a lot of money, spends it on public things, roads, gardens, the library, local business grants.'

'And what about the Kliner boy? He tried to warn me off you. Made out he had a prior claim.'

She shuddered. 'He's a jerk,' she said. 'I avoid him when I can. You should do the same.'

She drove up Main Street, looking edgy. Her quiet life in the Georgia countryside was over.

We pulled into Eno's gravel lot and went in. The place was empty. We took a booth and ordered coffee, and eggs and bacon with all kinds of extras on the side. A black pick-up was pulling into the lot outside. Same black pick-up as I'd seen before. Different driver. Not the Kliner kid. This was an older guy. Maybe approaching sixty, but bone-hard, tanned and lean. Iron-grey hair shaved close to his scalp. He was dressed like a rancher in denim. Even through Eno's window I could sense his power.

Roscoe nudged me. 'That's Kliner. The old man himself.'

He pushed in through the door and moved up to the lunch counter. Eno came around from the kitchen. The two of them talked quietly. Heads bent together. Then Kliner stood up again and turned toward the door. He stopped, rested his gaze on Roscoe for a second, then moved his eyes onto me. His lips parted in a curious smile. He had amazing teeth. Long canines, yellow, like an old wolf. His lips closed again and he snapped his gaze away. Pulled the door and crunched over the gravel to his truck. Took off with the roar of a big motor and a spray of small stones.

I watched him go and turned to Roscoe. 'So tell me more about Kliner. He looks like an interesting guy.'

'The family made a fortune in cotton processing generations back, over in Mississippi. Invented some kind of a new chemical formula. Chlorine or sodium something, I don't know for sure. Made a huge fortune, but they ran into trouble with the Environment Protection Agency over pollution. There were fish dying all the way down to New Orleans because of dumping into the river. So Kliner moved the whole plant. Set up again in Venezuela. Then he tried to diversify. He turned up here in Georgia five years ago with this warehouse thing, consumer goods or something.'

'So they're not local?' I said.

'Never saw them before five years ago,' she said. 'Don't know much about them. But I never heard anything bad.'

The waitress arrived with the food. We ate in silence. The portions were huge. The eggs were delicious. This guy Eno had a way with eggs. I washed it all down with pints of coffee.

When she'd finished eating, Roscoe said, 'You got no ideas at all why Joe was down here?'

'Money, maybe,' I said. 'That's all I can think of. Joe worked for the Treasury Department. Hubble worked for a bank. Their only thing in common would be money. Maybe we'll find out from Washington. If we don't, we'll have to start from the beginning.'

'OK,' she said. 'You need anything?'

'This is a big deal, right? So I'll need a gun. I can't just go to the store and buy one. No ID, no address, no permit.'

'OK,' she said. 'I'll get you one. One nobody else knows about.'

WE KISSED in the station house lot. Then we got out of the car and went in through the heavy glass door. Saw Finlay in the squad room. He gestured to us to go into the office.

'We need to talk,' he said, closing the door behind us. 'Long call from the Treasury Department. But they wouldn't tell me anything. They want formal authorisation from Teale before they say word one.'

'They confirmed Joe worked there, right?' I said.

'Sure, they went that far,' he said. 'Said he'd been there ten years. He started some new project exactly a year ago, but the whole thing is a total secret. He was some kind of a very big deal up there, Reacher, that's for sure.'

'So that's it? Is that all you got?'

'No,' he said. 'I kept pushing until I got a woman called Molly Beth Gordon. You ever heard that name?'

'No. Should I have?'

'Sounds like she was very close to Joe,' Finlay said. 'She was very upset. Floods of tears. She said she'll step out of line for you, because you're Joe's little brother. You're to call her about one thirty during her lunch break, when her office will be empty.'

'We should start tracing Joe, too,' I said. 'He probably flew down from Washington, into Atlanta, got a hotel room, rented a car, right? We should look for the car. He must have driven it down here Thursday night. It must have been dumped in the area. It might lead us back to Joe's hotel room. Maybe there would be something there. Files, more telephone numbers—like the one you found in his shoe.'

'We can't do it with Teale around. He'll be in soon, no doubt.'

I shrugged. 'We'll have to,' I said. 'You can sell Teale some story. Tell him you figure the escaped con who he says did the Morrison thing must have been in a rental car. Tell him you need to check it out. He can't say no to that, or he's undermining his own cover story, right? Once you find the car, then you twist Picard's arm to trace the hotel through the rental company, OK?'

'I'll try it,' Finlay said. 'Might work, I guess.' He paused. 'I also spoke to the pathologist at Yellow Springs this morning. He has a theory about the second body, Sherman Stoller. Reckons he was a truck driver. Old diesel fuel ingrained in the skin. Too much hydrogen sulphide in the blood gases and the tissues. But because all the traces are old, the doc reckons he was driving a lot for a long period, but then stopped. Maybe nine months, maybe a year ago. That makes him a truck driver, but an unemployed truck driver.'

'I'll get his arrest report from Florida,' Roscoe said. 'And we'll find an address for him somewhere. Got to be a lot of paperwork on a trucker, right? Union, medical, licences. Should be easy enough.'

DURING THE LUNCH BREAK, when the station house was deserted, I dialled Molly Beth Gordon's private line in Washington. She answered on the first ring. I gave her my name. It made her cry.

'You sound so much like Joe,' she said.

I didn't reply. I didn't want to get into a whole lot of reminiscing. Neither should she, not if she was stepping out of line and was in danger of being overheard.

'So what was Joe doing down here?' I asked her.

I heard her sniffing, and then her voice came back clear. 'He was running an investigation. I shouldn't tell you this. Not without clearance. But I will. He ran the Treasury's anticounterfeiting operation. He was head of the department.'

'But why was he down here in Georgia?' I asked her.

'I don't know,' she said. 'I really don't. What I aim to do is find out for you. I can copy his files. I know his computer password.'

There was a pause. Now I knew something about Molly Beth

Gordon. If she knew what Joe's password was, Joe must have told her. He was a professional. He was smart. He wouldn't leave his password on a Post-It note stuck to his monitor. His password would be unbreakable. He had trusted her, been really close to her. So I put some tenderness into my voice.

'That would be great,' I said. 'I really need that information.'

'I know you do. I'll call you again, soon as I can.'

'Is there counterfeiting going on down here?' I asked her. 'Is that what this could be all about?'

'No,' she said. 'It doesn't happen like that any more. Your brother was a genius, Jack. Joe set up procedures years ago for the special paper sales and the inks, so if somebody starts up, they get nailed within days. One hundred per cent foolproof. Counterfeiting just doesn't happen in the States any more. It all happens abroad. Any fakes we get here are shipped in. Why he was in Georgia, I don't know. But I'll find out tomorrow, I promise you that.'

I gave her the station house number and told her to speak to nobody except me or Roscoe or Finlay. Then she hung up in a hurry. I sat for a moment and tried to imagine what the woman who may have been my brother's lover looked like.

TEALE WAS BACK in the station house after lunch. And old man Kliner was inside with him. They were over by the reception counter, heads together. Roscoe and Finlay were by the cells. I walked over, stood between them and talked low.

'Counterfeiting,' I said. 'This is about counterfeit money. Joe was running the Treasury Department's defence for them. You know anything about that sort of a thing down here?'

They both shook their heads. I heard the glass door suck open. Looked up. Kliner was on his way out. Teale was starting toward us.

'I'm out of here,' I said.

I brushed past Teale and headed for the door. Started to walk down to Roscoe's place. Ten minutes at a brisk pace.

I got the Bentley out of the garage. Drove it back up the slope to town. Made the right onto Main Street and cruised along to the barbershop, parked and climbed out onto the kerb. The younger of the two old guys was on his way out the door. He held the door open for me. 'Go right in. My partner will take care of you.'

'Thanks,' I said. 'See you around.'

'Sure hope so, son,' he said.

He strolled off down Main Street and I went inside the shop. The older guy was in there. The gnarled old man whose sister had sung with Blind Blake. 'Good morning, my friend,' he said.

'You remember me?'

'Sure do,' he said. 'You were our last customer. Nobody in between to muddle me up.'

I asked him for a shave and he set about whipping up the lather.

'I was your last customer?' I said. 'That was Sunday. Today is Tuesday. Business always that bad?'

'Been that bad for years,' he said. 'Old Mayor Teale won't come in here, and what the old mayor won't do, nobody else white will do neither. Except old Mr Gray from the station house. Came in here regular as clockwork three, four times a week, until he went and hung himself, God rest his soul. You're the first white face in here since last February, yes sir, that's for sure.'

'But you got enough black customers to make a living?' I said.

He put the towel around my shoulders and started brushing on the lather. 'Man, we don't need customers to make a living.'

'You don't?' I said. 'Why not?'

'We got the community money.'

'You do?' I said. 'What's that?'

'Kliner Foundation,' he whispered. 'The community programme. It's a business grant. Thousand dollars. All the merchants get it. Been getting it five years.'

'That's good. But a thousand bucks a year won't keep you. It's better than a poke in the eye, but you need customers too, right?'

I was just making conversation, like you do with barbers. But it set the old guy off. He was shaking and cackling. Had a whole lot of trouble finishing the shave. 'Man, I shouldn't tell you about it,' he whispered. 'But seeing as you're a friend of my sister's, I'm going to tell you a big secret.'

He was getting confused. I wasn't a friend of his sister's. Didn't even know her. 'It's not a thousand dollars a year,' he whispered. Then he bent close to my ear. 'It's a thousand dollars a week.'

He started chuckling like a demon. He dabbed off the spare lather. Patted my face down with a hot wet cloth. Then he whipped the towel off my shoulders like a conjurer doing a trick.

'That's why we don't need no customers,' he cackled.

I paid him and got out. The guy was crazy.

'Say hello to my sister,' he called after me.

SIX

The trip to Atlanta was the best part of fifty miles. Took nearly an hour. The highway swept me right into the city. I dumped the car and asked a cop for the commercial district.

He gave me a half-mile walk after which I found one bank after another. Sunrise International had its own building, a big glass tower set back behind a piazza with a fountain.

At reception I asked for Paul Hubble's office and the receptionist flipped through a directory. She said she was sorry, but she was new in the job and she didn't recognise me, so would I wait while she got clearance for my visit? She dialled a number and started a low conversation. Then she covered the phone with her hand.

'May I say what it's in connection with?'

'I'm a friend,' I said.

She resumed the phone call and then directed me to an elevator. I had to go to reception on the seventeenth floor.

The seventeenth floor looked like a gentlemen's club. It was carpeted and panelled and full of antiques. As I waded across the thick pile a door opened and a suit stepped out to meet me. Shook my hand and led me into a little anteroom. He introduced himself as some sort of a manager and we sat down.

'So how may I help you?' he asked.

'I'm looking for Paul Hubble,' I said. 'He's an old friend. I remembered him saying he works here, so I thought I'd look him up.'

The guy in the suit dropped his gaze. 'Thing is, you see, Mr Hubble doesn't work here any more. We had to let him go, I'm afraid, about eighteen months ago.'

I just nodded blankly. If I asked him questions straight out, he might go all confidential, like lawyers do. So I waited

'No fault of his own, you understand,' he said. 'Mr Hubble was part of our retail operation. You know, cash, cheques, loans, personal customers. He was our currency manager. He did an excellent job. But the division was too expensive. Big overhead, small margin. We closed it down.'

'So what was Paul's exact role?' I asked him.

The guy got to his feet and gestured for me to join him at the window. He pointed to a figure hurrying along the sidewalk, seventeen floors down.

'Take that gentleman,' he said. 'Probably lives in the suburbs, maybe has a vacation cabin somewhere, two big mortgages, two cars, pension provision, some blue-chip stock, college plans, credit cards, charge cards. Net worth about a half-million, shall we say?'

'OK,' I said.

'But how much cash does he have on him? Probably fifty dollars.'

I looked at him. I wasn't following his drift. The guy changed gear.

'The US economy is huge,' he said. 'Trillions of dollars. But almost none of it is actually represented by cash. That gentleman has a net worth of a half-million dollars, but only fifty of it is in actual cash. All the rest of it is on paper or in computers. The fact is, there's only about a hundred and thirty billion actual cash dollars inside the whole US.'

'Sounds like enough to me,' I said.

'But how many people are there?' he asked me. 'Nearly three hundred million. That's only about four hundred and fifty actual cash dollars per head. Now if everybody chose to make such a withdrawal, the banks would run out of cash in the blink of an eye. So a good currency manager has a constant battle just to keep enough paper dollars on hand in our part of the system. He has to know where to locate them. It's not easy. In the end, it was one of the factors that made the retail operation so expensive for us. We had to close it eventually. We were very sorry to have to let Mr Hubble go.'

'Any idea where he's working now?' I said.

He shook his head. 'I'm afraid not,' he said. 'Professionally, he's dropped out of sight. His institute membership lapsed immediately, and we've never had an enquiry for a recommendation. If he was working anywhere in banking, I'd know it, I assure you. He must be in something else now.'

Hubble's trail was stone cold. I stood up and thanked the guy for his time. Shook his hand and headed for the elevator.

My assumptions had been all wrong. I had seen Hubble as a banker, doing a straight job. Maybe turning a blind eye to some peripheral con, maybe with half a finger in some dirty pie. But he hadn't been a banker. Not for a year and a half. He had been a criminal. Full-time. Right at the centre of the scam.

I DROVE STRAIGHT BACK to the Margrave station house. Parked up and went looking for Roscoe. Teale was stalking around in the open area, but the desk guy winked and nodded me back to a file room.

Roscoe was in there with an armful of old files. She looked weary.

'Hello, Reacher.' She smiled. 'Come to take me away from all this?'

'What's new?' I asked.

She dumped the stack of paper onto a cabinet top. Dusted herself off and flicked her hair back. Glanced at the door.

'Couple of things,' she said. 'Teale's got a Foundation board meeting in ten minutes. I'm getting the fax from Florida about Stoller's speeding offence soon as he's out of here. And Finlay's due a call from the state police about abandoned cars.'

'Where's the gun you've got for me?' I asked her.

'In my desk. We'll have to wait until Teale is gone.'

We stepped out of the file room and walked over toward the rosewood office. The squad room was quiet. The two back-up guys from Friday were paging through computer records. The bogus hunt was on for the chief's killer.

We waited in the rosewood office with Finlay until Teale left for his meeting. Then we went out into the open area. Roscoe turned on the fax machine and picked up the phone to call Florida. I sat down at the desk next to Roscoe's and called Charlie Hubble on the mobile number. It was switched off.

'Damn,' I said to myself. 'Can you believe she's switched it off?'

I needed to know where Hubble had spent his time for the last year and a half. Charlie might have given me some idea.

'Reacher?' Roscoe said. 'I got the stuff on Sherman Stoller.'

She was holding a couple of fax pages. Densely typed.

'Great,' I said. 'Let's take a look.'

Finlay joined us and we all went back into the rosewood office. Spread the stuff out on the desk. It was an arrest report from the police department in Jacksonville, Florida.

Sherman Stoller had been flagged down by a sector car for exceeding the speed limit near Jacksonville Beach at a quarter to midnight on a September night, two years ago. He had been driving a small panel truck eleven miles an hour too fast. He had become extremely agitated and abusive to the sector car crew so they had arrested him. He had been printed and photographed at Jacksonville Central and both he and his vehicle had been searched.

The search of his person produced a negative result. His truck was searched with dogs and produced a negative result. The truck contained nothing but a cargo of twenty new air conditioners boxed for export from Jacksonville Beach. Each box was sealed and marked with the manufacturer's logo and a serial number.

After being Mirandised, Stoller had made one phone call. Within twenty minutes, a lawyer named Perez from the respected Jacksonville firm of Zacarias Perez was in attendance, and within a further ten minutes Stoller had been released.

'Interesting,' Finlay said. 'The guy's three hundred miles from home, it's midnight, and he gets lawyered up within twenty minutes? With a partner from a respected firm? Stoller was some kind of a truck driver, that's for sure.'

'You recognise his address?' I asked Roscoe.

She shook her head. 'Not really,' she said. 'But I could find it.'

The door cracked open and Baker stuck his head in. 'State police on the line,' he said. 'Sounds like they got a car for you.'

'Punch it through here, Baker,' said Finlay.

He picked up the phone and listened. Scribbled some notes and grunted a thankyou. Hung the phone up and got out of his chair. 'OK. Let's go take a look.'

THIS TIME FINLAY DROVE. He was using an unmarked Chevy, identical to Roscoe's issue. He bounced it out of the lot and turned south. Accelerated through the little town, and after a few miles we swung off onto a track that struck out due east. It led out toward the highway and ended up in a kind of maintenance area, right below the roadway. There were piles of asphalt and tar barrels lying around. And a burnt-out car lying on its roof.

'They noticed it Friday morning,' Finlay said. 'Wasn't here Thursday, they're sure about that. It could have been Joe's.'

We looked it over very carefully. Wasn't much left to see. It was totally burnt out. We couldn't even tell what make it had been.

I got Finlay to support the front fender and I crawled under the upside-down hood to look for the number they stamp on the chassis. I called it out to Roscoe and she wrote it down.

'So what do you think?' Finlay asked.

'Could be the one,' I said. 'Say he rented it Thursday evening up at the airport in Atlanta, full tank of gas. Drove it to the warehouses at the Margrave cloverleaf, then somebody drove it on down here afterward. Plenty of fuel left to burn.'

Finlay nodded. 'Makes sense. But they'd have to be local guys. This is a great spot to dump a car, but only a local guy would know about this little maintenance track, right?'

We left the wreck there. Drove back up to the station house. The desk sergeant was waiting for Finlay.

'Teale wants you in the office,' he said.

Finlay headed back there. Roscoe and I went over to her desk. 'Give me the gun,' I whispered. 'Before Teale is through with Finlay.'

She nodded and glanced around the room. Sat down and unclipped the keys from her belt. Unlocked her desk and rolled open a deep drawer. Nodded down to a shallow cardboard box, about two inches deep. I picked it out and tucked it under my arm. Roscoe rolled the drawer shut and locked it again.

'Thanks,' I said. 'Now phone in that number from the car, OK?'

I carried the box out to the Bentley, dumped it on the passenger seat and got in. Pulled the box over onto my lap. It was empty apart from a box of bullets and a gun, a Desert Eagle automatic. A hell of a weapon. I'd used one before. They come from Israel. I picked it up. Very heavy, fourteen-inch barrel. I clicked out the magazine. Takes eight .44-Magnum shells. Not what you would call subtle. It hits the target with more force than anything this side of a train wreck. Not subtle at all.

I checked the weapon over. Brutal, but in fine condition. The grip was engraved with a name. Gray. The dead detective, the guy before Finlay. Hanged himself last February. Must have been a gun collector. This wasn't his service piece. No police department in the world would authorise the use of a cannon like this on the job.

I loaded the dead detective's big handgun with eight of his shells, and put the gun and its box in the Bentley's walnut glove compartment. It was a tight fit. I got out of the Bentley and locked it. Stepped up to the entrance and pulled the door.

ROSCOE WAS AT HER DESK, talking to Finlay. When she saw me she waved me over. Looked excited.

'I called Detroit,' she said. 'It was a Pontiac. Delivered four months ago. Big fleet order for a rental company. DMV is tracing the registration. I told them to get back to Picard up in Atlanta. The rental people might be able to give him the story about where it was rented. We might be getting somewhere.'

'Great,' I said to her. 'Good work, Roscoe.' I turned to Finlay. 'I'm going to borrow the rosewood office so that I can call Molly again. I need some background. There are things I don't understand. Watch your backs, you two, OK?'

When I dialled the Washington number, I got Molly on the second ring. 'Can you talk?' I asked her.

She told me to wait, and I heard her close her office door. 'It's too soon, Jack,' she said. 'I can't get the stuff until tomorrow.'

'I need background,' I said. 'I need to understand what Joe was doing. Why things are happening here, if the action is supposed to be overseas.'

She figured out where to start. 'I guess Joe's assumption was it's maybe controlled from this country. It's a difficult problem to explain, but I'll try. The forging happens abroad, and most of it stays abroad. Only a few of the fake bills ever come back here, which is not a huge deal domestically, though obviously it's something we want to stop. But abroad it presents a completely different type of problem. You know how much cash is inside the US, Jack?'

I thought back to what the bank guy had told me.

'A hundred and thirty billion dollars,' I said.

'Right,' she said. 'But exactly twice that much—two hundred and sixty billion—is held offshore. It's in bank safety deposits in London, Rome, Berlin, Moscow, hidden under floorboards, behind false walls. And that's because the dollar is the world's most trusted currency. People believe in it. They want it. And, naturally, the government is very, very happy about that.'

'Good for the ego, right?' I said.

'It's not an emotional thing,' she said. 'It's business. Think about it, Jack. If there's a hundred-dollar bill in somebody's safe in Bucharest, that means somebody somewhere once exchanged a hundred dollars' worth of foreign assets for it. Our government sold them a piece of paper for a hundred bucks. Good business. And because it's a trusted currency, chances are that hundred-dollar bill will stay in that safe in Bucharest for many years. The US will never have to deliver the foreign assets back again. As long as the dollar stays trusted, we can't lose.'

'So what's the problem?' I asked her.

'It's all about trust and faith,' Molly said. 'If foreign markets are getting flooded with fake dollars and the people in those foreign markets find out, they panic. They lose their faith. They'll get rid of their dollars. In effect, overnight, the government would have to repay a two-hundred-sixty-billion-dollar foreign loan. Overnight. And we couldn't do that, Jack.'

'Big problem,' I said.

'That's the truth,' she said. 'And a remote problem. The fakes are all made abroad, and they're mostly distributed abroad. To foreigners who are happy as long as the stuff looks vaguely like real dollars are supposed to look. That's why not very many are imported. Only the very best fakes come back to the States.'

'And what exactly are we doing about it?' I asked her.

'Two things,' she said. 'First thing is Joe was trying like mad to stop it from happening. Second thing is we're pretending like mad it isn't happening at all. So as to keep the faith.'

I nodded. Started to see some shape behind the big-time secrecy going on up there in Washington. 'OK,' I said. 'So if I were to call the Treasury and ask them about it?'

'We'd deny everything,' she said. 'We'd say, what counterfeiting?'

WHEN I EMERGED from the office, Roscoe was at her desk. She got up and walked over.

'Anything from the car rental people?' I asked her.

She shook her head. 'Tomorrow,' she said. 'Picard's dealing with it. He's doing his best.'

'OK,' I said. 'Let's drive up to Stoller's place.'

We got into Roscoe's Chevy and headed up to Atlanta. Dumped our things in an airport hotel and headed out northwest. Roscoe drove and I tried to direct her from a street map. We battled traffic and ended up roughly in the right place. It was a sprawl of low-rise housing. Small houses on small lots. Old cars up on blocks. Everything bathed in yellow sodium glare.

We found the right house. A tiny one-storey. Small yard, small single-car garage. We rang the bell. An old woman cracked the door against the chain. 'Good evening,' Roscoe said. 'We're looking for Sherman Stoller.'

Roscoe looked at me after she said it. She should have said we were looking for his house. We knew where Sherman Stoller was. In the Yellow Springs morgue, seventy miles away.

'Who are you?' the old woman asked, politely.

'Ma'am, we're police officers,' Roscoe said. Half true.

The old lady eased the door and took the chain off. 'You better come in,' she said. 'He's in the kitchen.'

'Who is?' said Roscoe.

'Sherman,' she said, puzzled. 'That's who you want, isn't it?'

We followed her into the kitchen. There was an old guy eating

329

supper at the table. 'Police officers, Sherman,' the old lady said.

The old guy looked up at us blankly, stopped eating.

'Is there another Sherman Stoller?' I asked him.

The old guy nodded. Looked worried. 'Our son,' he said.

The old lady moved behind him and put her hand on his arm.

'He don't live here,' the old man said. 'Moved out two years ago.'

'Could you give us his address?' Roscoe said.

The old lady gave us the address and told us how to find the place. Very respectful.

'He hasn't lived here for two years,' the old man said again. He was afraid. Trying to distance himself from the trouble his son was in.

We thanked them and backed out. Trooped out through the gate and got back in the car.

'What did you make of those two?' Roscoe asked me.

'They know their boy was up to no good. Probably don't know exactly what it was.'

'That's what I thought,' she said. 'Let's go find this new place.'

After five miles Roscoe swung off the main drag. Nosed along a new road and pulled up by a row of condominiums. Very pleasant. Balconies, garages, ambitious landscaping.

Stoller's building was at the end of the row. I knocked on the door. Waited. Knocked again. The door opened. A woman stood there. Maybe thirty, but she looked older. Short, nervous, tired. Blonde from a bottle. She looked at us.

'We're police officers, ma'am,' Roscoe said. 'We're looking for the Sherman Stoller residence.'

'Well, you found it, I guess,' the woman said. 'You better come in.'

She led us into a living room. A decent-sized space. Expensive furniture and rugs. A big TV. No stereo, no books. It looked like somebody had spent twenty minutes with a catalogue and ten thousand dollars. One of these, one of those, two of that. All delivered one morning and just dumped in there.

'Are you Mrs Stoller?' Roscoe asked the woman gently.

'More or less,' the woman said. 'Not exactly Mrs, but as near as makes no difference.'

'Is your name Judy?' I asked her. The name on the watch, *To Sherman, love Judy*.

She nodded. Kept on nodding for a while. Thinking.

'He's dead, isn't he?' Judy said.

I didn't answer. This was the part I wasn't good at.

'Yes, he is,' Roscoe said. 'I'm very sorry.'

Judy looked pretty blank. She sat down and waved us to sit as well.

'How long did you know Sherman?' Roscoe asked.

'About four years, I guess,' Judy answered. 'He got some kind of a big driving contract up here. So we bought a little place. His folks moved in too. Lived with us for a while. Then we moved out here. Left his folks in the old house. He made good money for three years. Then it stopped, a year ago. He hardly worked at all since.'

'So he was doing well for the first three years?' Roscoe asked her.

Judy gave her a look. 'Doing well?' she said. 'Grow up, for heaven's sakes. He was ripping somebody off.'

'You sure?' I said.

Judy swung her gaze my way. Like an artillery piece traversing. 'It don't need much brains to figure it out,' she said. 'In three years he paid cash for two houses, furniture, cars, God knows what. And he had enough saved so he didn't have to work at all since last September. If he did all that on the level, then I'm the First Lady.'

She was giving us a defiant stare. She'd known about it all along. She'd known what would happen when he was found out. She was challenging us to deny her the right to blame him.

'Who was his big contract with?' Roscoe asked her.

'An outfit called Island Air Conditioning. He spent three years hauling air conditioners down to Florida. Maybe he used to steal them. There's two old boxes in the garage right now. Want to see?'

She didn't wait for a reply. Just jumped up and stalked out. We followed her down some backstairs and through a basement door. Into a garage. It was empty except for a couple of old cartons dumped against a wall, both marked with the logo: ISLAND AIR CONDITIONING, INC. Each box had a long serial number written on by hand, and must have held a single unit. They were both empty. We went back upstairs.

'What happened to Sherman?' Judy asked.

It was a simple question. Deserved a simple answer.

'He was shot in the head,' I lied. 'Died instantly.'

Judy nodded. Like she wasn't surprised. 'When?' she asked.

'On Thursday night,' Roscoe told her. 'At midnight. Did he say where he was going on Thursday night?'

Judy shook her head. 'He never told me much.'

'Did he ever mention meeting an investigator?' Roscoe asked.

Judy shook her head again.

'What about Sunday?' I said. 'This Sunday coming? Did he ever say anything about that?'

'No,' Judy said. 'He never said much about anything.'

She got an album out of a cupboard. 'Want to see his picture?'

I walked around behind her chair and bent to look at a photograph of a sandy, rat-faced man, standing in front of a yellow van. Grinning.

'That's the truck he drove,' Judy said.

But I wasn't looking at the truck. I was looking at a figure in the background of the picture. It was out of focus, but I could make out who it was. It was Paul Hubble.

I waved Roscoe over and saw a wave of surprise pass over her face as she recognised Hubble in the photograph. Then she bent closer. I saw a second wave of surprise. She had recognised something else.

'When was this picture taken?' she asked.

Judy shrugged. 'Summer last year, I guess.'

Roscoe touched the blurred image of Hubble with her fingernail. 'Did Sherman say who this guy was?'

'The new boss,' Judy said. 'He was there six months, then he fired Sherman's ass. Said he didn't need him no more.'

'Is this where Island Air Conditioning is based?' Roscoe asked. 'Where this picture was taken?'

Judy nodded her head tentatively. 'I guess so. Sherman never told me much about it.'

'We need to keep this photograph,' Roscoe told her. 'We'll let you have it back later.'

Judy handed it to her. 'Keep it,' she said. 'I don't want it.'

WE GOT IN THE CHEVY and Roscoe snapped on the dome light. Pulled the photograph out of her pocket. Handed it to me.

'Look at the edge,' she said. 'On the left.'

In the background, on the left of the photo, I could see the edge of a modern metal building. A tall tree beyond. The dark red frame of a door. A big industrial door, rolled up.

'That's Kliner's warehouse,' she said. 'I recognise the tree.'

I looked again. It was a very distinctive tree. Dead on one side. Maybe split by lightning.

Roscoe took back the photograph, clicked her carphone on and dialled DMV in Atlanta. She called in the number from the front of Stoller's truck. Waited a long moment, tapping her finger on the steering wheel. I heard the crackle of the response in the earpiece. Then she clicked the phone off and turned to me.

'The truck is registered to Kliner Industries. And the registered address is Zacarias Perez, Jacksonville, Florida.'

We looked at each other. Sherman Stoller's lawyer buddies. The ones who had got him out of Jacksonville Central so fast, two years ago.

'OK,' she said. 'Put it all together. Hubble, Stoller, Joe's investigation. They're printing counterfeit money down in Kliner's warehouses, right?'

I shook my head. 'There's no printing going on inside the States. It all happens abroad. Molly Beth Gordon told me that. Joe had made it impossible.'

'We need Molly's help,' Roscoe said. 'We need Joe's files.'

She clicked off the dome light. Started the car for the ride back to the airport hotel. I could sense she was getting uptight. She had run out of distractions. Now she had to face the quiet vulnerable hours of the night. The first night after the break-in at her home. 'You bring that gun, Reacher?' she asked.

'It's in the trunk,' I said.

'Bring it inside,' she said. 'Makes me feel better.'

I grinned sleepily in the dark. 'Makes me feel better too.'

We lapsed into silence. Roscoe found the hotel lot. We got out of the car and I opened the trunk. Lifted out the box containing Gray's gun. Went in through the lobby and up in the elevator.

In the room we just crashed out. Roscoe laid her shiny .38 on the carpet on her side of the bed. I checked my giant .44 and laid it on my side. We wedged a chair under the door handle.

I WOKE EARLY and lay in bed thinking about Joe. Wednesday morning. He'd been dead five days. Roscoe was already up. She was standing in the middle of the floor, stretching. Some kind of a yoga thing. She'd taken a shower and was only half dressed. Suddenly I wasn't thinking about Joe any more.

'Roscoe?'

'What?'

'You've got the most wonderful body on the planet.'

She giggled. I jumped on her. Couldn't help it. She drove me crazy. It was the giggle that did it to me. I hauled her back into bed. The building could have fallen down and we wouldn't have noticed it. We finished in an exhausted tangle. Lay there for a while. Then Roscoe got up and showered for the second time that morning. Got dressed again. Fully dressed.

I called room service for breakfast. Removed the chair from under the door handle ready for the little cart. Pulled the heavy drapes. It was a glorious morning. A bright blue sky, no clouds at all, brilliant fall sunshine. The view was spectacular. Right over the airport and to the city beyond. The planes clawed their way into the air and wheeled slowly away like fat, important birds. The buildings downtown grew tall and straight in the sun.

A glorious morning. But it was the sixth straight morning my brother wasn't alive to see.

Roscoe used the phone to call Finlay down in Margrave. She told him about the photograph of Hubble and Stoller on the warehouse forecourt. Then she gave him our room number and told him to call us if Molly got back to us from Washington. Or if Picard got back to us with information from the car rental people about the burnt-out Pontiac. I figured we should wait around in Atlanta in case Picard got a hotel trace on Joe. Chances were he stayed in the city, maybe near the airport.

Breakfast came and we ate it. Pancakes, syrup, bacon. Lots of coffee. Then I started feeling restless. Started feeling like it had been a mistake to wait around. I glared at the telephone. It wasn't ringing. I wandered around the room. Stooped to pick up the Desert Eagle off the floor by the bed. Hefted it in my hand. I was curious about the guy who'd bought the massive automatic.

'What was Gray like?' I asked.

'Gray?' she said. 'He was thorough. You should see his paperwork. There are twenty-five years of his files in the station house. All meticulous, all comprehensive. Gray was a good detective.'

'Why did he hang himself?' I asked her.

'I don't know,' she said. 'I never understood it.'

'Was he depressed?' I said.

'Not really,' she said. 'I mean, he was always very dour. But no worse in February than any other time. It was a total surprise.'

'Why did you have his gun in your desk?'

'He asked if he could keep it in there,' she said. 'He generated a lot of paperwork, so he had no space in his own desk. It was his private weapon. He said he couldn't get it approved by the department because the calibre was too big. He made it feel like some kind of a big secret.'

I put the dead man's secret gun down again and the silence was shattered by the phone ringing.

I answered it and heard Finlay's voice.

'Reacher?' he said. 'Picard traced the car. Rental Pontiac. Booked out to Joe Reacher, Atlanta Airport, Thursday night at eight. The car was delivered right to his hotel.'

He mentioned a place a mile away from the hotel we were using.

'Great, Finlay. We'll get over there now.'

ROSCOE PULLED HER BADGE at the desk where Joe had checked in on Thursday. The clerk did some keyboard work and told us he had been in 621, sixth floor, far end of the corridor.

A manager took us to the room, opened it up with his pass key. We stepped in. It had been cleaned and tidied, ready for new occupants. 'What about his stuff?' I asked. 'Where is it all?'

'We cleared it out Saturday,' the manager said. 'The guy was booked in Thursday night, supposed to vacate by eleven Friday morning. What we do is we give them an extra day, then if they don't show, we clear them out, down to housekeeping.'

'So his stuff is in a closet somewhere?' I asked.

'Basement,' he said. 'Use the stairs from the lobby.'

The manager strolled off. Roscoe and I rode back down in the elevator. We found the service staircase and went down to the basement. Housekeeping was a giant hall stacked with linens and towels. There was a glassed-in office cubicle in the near corner with a woman at a small desk. We walked over and Roscoe held out her badge.

'Room six-two-one,' Roscoe said. 'You cleared out some belongings, Saturday morning. You got them down here?'

I was holding my breath.

'Six two-one?' the woman said. 'He came by for them already. They're gone.'

I breathed out. We were too late. I went numb with disappointment. 'Who came by?'

'The guest,' the woman said. 'This morning, maybe nine, nine thirty. Some kind of a Latino guy. Slender, nice smile.'

'You got a list of the stuff?' I said.

She pulled a small book off a shelf and thumbed it open. She pointed a stubby finger to a small column filled with tight handwriting. It listed a garment bag, eight articles of clothing, a toilet bag, two pairs of shoes. The last item listed was one briefcase.

We just walked away from her and found the stairs back to the lobby. It didn't feel like such a great day any more.

We walked to the car. Leaned side by side on the front fender. 'Roscoe?' I said. 'If you were the guy walking out of here with Joe's stuff, what would you do?'

She stopped with the car door half open, thinking. 'I'd keep the briefcase,' she said. 'The rest of the stuff, I'd get rid of it.'

'That's what I would do as well.'

There was a service road running between the hotel and the next one in line. A row of dumpsters along a twenty-yard stretch of it. I pointed. 'Suppose he drove out that way? Suppose he lobbed the garment bag straight into one of those dumpsters?'

'But he'd have kept the briefcase, right?'

'Maybe we aren't looking for the briefcase,' I said. 'Maybe Joe carried a briefcase but kept his important stuff in the garment bag.'

Roscoe wasn't convinced, but we started walking down the service road. Up close, the dumpsters were huge. I had to lever myself up on the edge of each one and peer in. The first one was empty. The second one was full. Lying right on top of some old cartons was a battered, well-travelled garment bag. I hauled it out. There was a little nameplate fastened to the handle. It said: REACHER.

'OK, Joe,' I said to myself. 'Let's see if you were a smart guy.'

I was looking for the shoes. Two pairs, just like it said on the housekeeper's list. I pulled the inner sole out of each one in turn. Under the third I found a tiny Ziplock bag. With a sheet of computer paper folded up inside it.

'Smart as a whip, Joe,' I said, and laughed.

SEVEN

Roscoe and I danced around the service alley together, then hustled over to the Chevy and raced back to our hotel. The telephone was ringing as we entered our room. It was Finlay, on the line from Margrave again. He sounded as excited as we were.

'Molly Beth Gordon just called,' he said. 'She did it. She's got the files we need. She's flying down here, right now. She told me it was amazing stuff. Sounded high as a kite. Atlanta arrivals, two o'clock. Delta, from Washington, DC. I'll meet you there.'

'See you later, Harvard guy,' I said.

We sat down at a table by the window. Unzipped the little plastic bag and pulled out the sheet of computer paper. The top inch had been torn off the right-hand corner. Half the heading had been left behind. It said: *Operation E Unum*.

'Operation E Unum . . . Pluribus,' Roscoe said.

Underneath was a list of initials with telephone numbers opposite. The first set of initials was P.H.

'Paul Hubble,' she said. 'His number and the other half of the heading was what Finlay found in Joe's shoe.'

I nodded. Then there were four more sets of initials—W.B., K.K., J.S. and M.B.G.—with phone numbers alongside. There was a phone number with a 202 area code against M.B.G. I pointed to it, so Roscoe could see it.

'Molly Beth Gordon,' she said. 'Washington, DC.'

The next item on the list was just two words: *Stollers' Garage*. The last item was three words: *Gray's Kliner File*.

Paul Hubble we knew about. He was dead. Molly Beth Gordon we knew about. She'd be here at two o'clock. We'd seen the garage up at Sherman Stoller's place. It held nothing but two empty cartons. That left the underlined heading, three sets of initials with three phone numbers, and the three words: *Gray's Kliner File*.

'E Unum Pluribus,' I said. 'It's the US motto backward. This more or less means "Out of one comes many". Not "Out of many comes one".'

'Could Joe have written it down wrong?' Roscoe suggested.

I shook my head. 'I don't think Joe would make that kind of a mistake. It must mean something.'

'Not to me,' she said. 'What else?'

'Gray's Kliner File,' I said. 'Did Gray have a file on Kliner?'

'Probably. He had a file on just about everything.'

I stepped back to the bed and picked up the phone. Called Finlay down in Margrave. Baker told me he'd already left. So I dialled the other numbers on Joe's print-out. The W.B. number was in New Jersey. Faculty of modern history, Princeton University. I hung up straight away. The K.K. number was in New York City. Faculty of modern history, Columbia University. I hung up again. The J.S. number had a New Orleans area code. I heard one ring tone and a busy voice said, 'Fifteen Squad, Detectives.'

'You got somebody there with the initials J.S.?' I asked.

'I got three of them,' the voice said. 'Which one do you want?'

'Don't know,' I said. 'Will you ask each J.S. if they know Joe Reacher? Will you do that? It's important. I'll call back later, OK?'

Down in New Orleans, the fifteenth squad desk guy grunted and hung up. I put the phone back on the nightstand.

ATLANTA AIRPORT was vast. We drove for miles before we found the right terminal. The short-term parking lot was packed. I was craning over, looking for spaces. Then out of the corner of my eye I saw a vague black shape slide by in the line on my right.

'Go right, go right,' I said, urgently.

I thought it was the rear end of a black pick-up. Brand-new. Roscoe hauled the wheel over and we swung into the next aisle. Caught a flash of red brake lights in black sheet metal. A pick-up swinging out of sight. Roscoe cornered hard.

The next aisle was empty. Nothing moving. Just ranks of automobiles standing quiet in the sun. No black pick-up. We drove all over the lot. Couldn't find it anywhere.

But we did find Finlay. We parked up in an empty space and started the long walk to the terminal. Finlay had parked in a different quarter and was walking in on a different diagonal. He walked the rest of the way with us.

The terminal was very busy. And it was huge. Flickering screens told us the two o'clock Delta from Washington was in and taxiing. We walked down a long corridor with a pair of moving walkways running through the centre. On the right was an endless row of bright gaudy advertisements. On the left was a glass partition, floor to ceiling, and behind it was a sequence of gates. The passengers came out of the planes and walked along on their side of the glass. Half of them disappeared into the baggage claim areas. The other half, short-haul fliers with no checked baggage, went straight to the doors that led into the main corridor every thirty yards. Each set of doors was mobbed by a knot of meeters and greeters. As we fought through the crowds I felt anxious. The glimpse of the black pick-up in the lot had unsettled me.

We reached the right gate. People were already coming off the plane, spilling out of the jetway and turning to walk up toward the baggage area and the exit doors. On our side of the glass, people were walking down to the gates further on, dragging us down the corridor. We were stepping backward all the time just to stay still.

It seemed like just about any of the women could be Molly. There

338

must have been a couple of dozen candidates. All dressed for business, all carrying efficient luggage. All of them carried along in the swarming crowd.

One of them had a heavy burgundy leather briefcase in one hand and a matching carry-on which she was wheeling with the other. She was small, blonde, excited. As she turned out of the jetway she scanned the crowd through the glass. Her eyes flashed past me. Then they snapped back. She looked straight at me. Stopped. She fought her way over to the glass. I moved in close on my side. She stared at me. Smiled. Greeted her dead lover's brother with her eyes.

'Molly?' I mouthed through the glass at her.

She held up the heavy briefcase like a trophy. Smiled a big wide smile of triumph. She was borne along by the crowd toward the exit. Roscoe and Finlay and I struggled after her.

On Molly's side of the glass, the flow was with her. Our side, it was against us. We were being separated at double speed. Through the glass, Molly was way ahead. I saw her blonde head disappear. I fought sideways and vaulted over onto the moving walkway. It was going the wrong way. I was carried another five yards backward before I made it over the moving handgrip onto the other side.

Now I was going in the right direction, but the walkway was a solid mass of people just standing still. Content with the snail's pace the rubber floor was carrying them. Through the glass, I could see Molly being crowded into the baggage claim. I put my head down and pushed my way through. People were yelling in outrage. I didn't care. I tore through them, vaulted off the walkway and clawed through the crowd at the exit doors.

The baggage claim was a wide low hall, lit with dull yellow lights. I looked everywhere for Molly. Checked every face. But she wasn't in there. I let myself be carried outside on the relentless tide. Roscoe was holding tight to the frame of the exit door, battling the flow.

'She come out?' I said.

'No,' she said. 'Finlay's gone to the end of the corridor. He's waiting there. I'm waiting here.'

We stood there with people pouring past us. Then the crowd coming toward us suddenly thinned. The whole planeload was just about through. I saw something lying in the entrance to the baggage hall. A burgundy leather carry-on, lying on its side, its extending handle still pulled out. From fifteen feet away, I could read the fancy gold monogram on the front. It read: *M.B.G.*

Roscoe grabbed it. Opened it up. It held a change of clothes and a toilet bag. And a photograph of Joe. He looked like me, but a little thinner. A shaved, tanned scalp. A wry, amused smile.

We dived back into the baggage claim. In the few minutes I'd been out of there, the place had just about emptied. The luggage belt was grinding round, empty. Then the rubber curtains covering the hole through to the cargo shed bellied. A briefcase came out. Burgundy leather. The straps slashed through. The case open. Empty.

It wobbled around toward us. We stared at the cut straps. They had been severed with a sharp blade.

I leapt onto the moving carousel. Ran back against the belt's lurching motion and dived like a swimmer headfirst through the rubber slats shrouding the yard-square hole. I landed hard and the belt started to drag me back out. I rolled off and jumped up. I was in a loading bay. Deserted except for tall piles of forlorn cargo and forgotten suitcases.

I ran into one bay and then the next, hopelessly looking for Molly. Glancing around desperately. Nobody there.

I found her left shoe lying at the entrance to a dark bay. I plunged in. She was slumped at the back of the bay, on her back in the gloom, jammed between two towers of crates. Just sprawled there on the rubber floor, a knife in her ribs, blood pouring out of her.

But she was alive. Her lips were flecked with bright bubbles of blood. Her head was still, but her eyes were roving. I ran to her. Cradled her head.

She gazed at me. 'Got to get in before Sunday,' she whispered.

Then she died in my arms.

I STUDIED CHEMISTRY in maybe seven different high schools. Didn't learn much of it, but one thing I remember is how you can throw a little powder into a glass tube and make everything blow up with a bang. It produces a result way bigger than it should.

That was how I felt about Molly. I'd never even met her before. But I felt angry, way out of all proportion.

The other thing I remember from the chemistry lab is stuff about pressure. Pressure does things. It was doing things to me. I was angry and I was short of time. In my mind I was seeing Molly coming out of that jetway. Smiling. Holding up a briefcase of files she shouldn't have copied. Risking a lot. For me. For Joe. That image was building up massive pressure in my mind.

Roscoe and I drove down to Margrave together in her car, stunned and silent. Finlay was in front of us all the way. I had dragged him out of the terminal and marched him to the car, because he had wanted to stay and get involved. But I shouted at him that we didn't have time. That if we got involved it would make the difference between winning and losing.

TEALE WAS WAITING just inside the station house doors. Back against the reception counter. He saw the three of us coming in and limped away into the big open squad room. Sat down at a desk.

We walked past him into the rosewood office. Sat down to wait until he'd gone so that we could look for Gray's file. I pulled Joe's torn print-out from my pocket and passed it across the desk. Finlay scanned it through.

'Not much, is it?' he said. 'What does the heading mean? *E Unum Pluribus*? That's backward, right?'

I nodded. 'Out of one comes many,' I said.

He started reading it through again. There was a loud knock on the office door and Baker came in. 'Teale's on his way out of the building,' he said. 'Talking to Stevenson in the parking lot. You guys need anything?'

Finlay handed him the torn print-out. 'Get me a Xerox of this, will you?'

Baker stepped out to do it and Finlay drummed his fingers on the desk. 'Who are all those initials?' he said.

'We only know the dead ones,' I said. 'Hubble and Molly Beth. Two are college numbers. Princeton and Columbia. Last one is a detective down in New Orleans.'

'What about Stoller's garage?' he said. 'You get a look at that?'

'Nothing. Just a couple of empty air conditioner cartons.'

Finlay grunted and Baker came back in. Handed me Joe's paper with a copy of it. 'Teale's gone,' he said. I kept the original and gave the copy to Finlay.

We hustled out of the office. Caught a glimpse of the white Cadillac easing out of the lot. Pushed open the file room door.

Gray had spent twenty-five years filling that file room with paper. All four walls had floor-to-ceiling cabinets. The K section was on the wall facing the door, left of centre, eye level.

We found a box labelled *Kliner*. I put my finger in the little loop. Pulled the box out. Opened it up. It was full of yellowing paper. But it was the wrong paper. It had nothing to do with Kliner. Nothing at all. It was a three-inch pile of ancient police department memos. Operational stuff. Procedures to be followed if the Soviet Union aimed a missile at Atlanta. I gazed at the three-inch pile and felt the pressure build up.

'Somebody beat us to it,' Roscoe said.

I shook my head. 'Doesn't make any sense. They'd have pulled the whole box and thrown it in the trash. Gray did this himself. He wanted to hide the stuff, but he didn't want to spoil his sequence in the file room. So he took the contents out of the box and put in this old stuff instead. You said he was a meticulous guy, right?'

Roscoe nodded. 'He could have hidden it. He hid his gun in my desk. He didn't mind hiding things.'

I looked at her. Something she had said was ringing a warning bell. 'When did he give you the gun?' I asked her.

'After Christmas,' she said. 'Not long before he died.'

'There's something wrong with that,' I said. 'Why would a senior, respected guy like that feel his choice of off-duty weapon should have to be a secret? That wasn't his problem. The gun must have been a decoy, to make sure you kept the box in a locked drawer.'

'But there isn't anything else in the box,' Roscoe pointed out.

We stood still for a second. Then we ran for the doors. Crashed through and ran over to Roscoe's Chevy in the lot. Pulled Gray's file box out of the trunk. Opened it up. I handed the Desert Eagle to Roscoe. Examined the box of bullets. Nothing there. I tore the box apart. Flattened the cardboard out. Nothing. Then I tore the lid apart. Under the corner flap there was a key. Taped to the inside face. Where it had been carefully hidden by a man who was now dead.

WE DIDN'T KNOW what the key might fit. We discounted anything in the station house. Discounted anything in Gray's home. Felt those places were too obvious for a cautious man to choose. I closed my eyes and built a picture of Gray easing back the corner of that lid and taping his key under it. Handing the box to his friend Roscoe. Watching her lock it in her drawer. I built that picture into a movie and ran it in my head twice before it told me what the key unlocked.

'Something in the barbershop,' I said. 'He used to go in there, three, four times a week. The old guy told me that. He was the only white guy ever went in there. It felt like safe territory. Away from Teale and Klincr and everybody else. He went in there because he liked the old guys. He turned to them. Gave them the stuff to hide.'

I snatched the Desert Eagle back from Roscoe and hustled her and Finlay into the car. Roscoe drove. She jammed the Chevy to a stop outside the barbershop and we ran in. There were no customers in there. Just the two old guys sitting, doing nothing.

I held up the key. 'We've come for Gray's stuff,' I said.

The younger guy glanced at Roscoe. 'OK,' he said. 'Old Mr Gray told us, give it to nobody except his friend Miss Roscoe.' He took the key and stepped back to the sink. Stooped down to unlock a narrow mahogany drawer built in underneath. Pulled out three thick files. He handed one to me, one to Finlay and one to Roscoe. Then he signalled his partner and they walked through to the back. Left us alone. Roscoe sat on the upholstered bench in the window. Finlay and I hitched ourselves into the barber chairs. We started reading.

My file was a thick stack of police reports, a dossier put together by Detective James Spirenza, Fifteenth Squad, New Orleans Police Department, Homicide Bureau. Spirenza had been assigned a homicide, eight years ago. Then he had been assigned seven more. He hadn't cleared any of them. Not one. A total failure.

But he'd tried hard. His investigation had been meticulous. The first victim had been the owner of a textile plant. A specialist, involved in some new chemical process for cotton. The second victim was the first guy's foreman. The next six victims were government people. Environmental Protection Agency employees. The case concerned pollution in the Mississippi Delta. Fish were dying. The cause was traced 250 miles upriver to a textile processing plant that was pumping chemicals into the river: sodium hydroxide and sodium hypochlorite and chlorine, all mixed up to form a deadly cocktail.

All eight victims had died in the same way. Two shots to the head with a silenced automatic pistol. A .22 calibre. Professional hits. Spirenza's approach was to figure out who was benefiting. Didn't take him long to piece it together. The textile processor up in Mississippi State looked like the one. He was under attack from the eight who died. Two of them were attacking him commercially. The other six were threatening to close him down. Spirenza turned him inside out. Pulled in the FBI and the Internal Revenue Service. They'd searched every cent in every account for unexplained cash payments to an elusive hit man.

They'd searched for a year and found nothing. On the way, they turned up a lot of unsavoury stuff. The guy's son was a psychopath.

Worse than his father, in Spirenza's view. The boy had records from a dozen institutions, but the textile processor had protected the boy every step of the way. Covered for him. Paid his way out of trouble.

Nothing would stick. New Orleans FBI had lost interest. Spirenza had closed the case. Forgotten all about it, until an old detective from an obscure Georgia jurisdiction had faxed him, asking for information on the Kliner family.

FINLAY CLOSED HIS FILE. Spun his chair to face mine.

'The Kliner Foundation is bogus,' he said. 'Totally bogus. It's a cover for something else. Gray bust it wide open. The Foundation is spending millions every year, but its audited income is zero.'

He selected a sheet from the file. Passed it over to me. It was a sort of balance sheet, showing the Foundation's expenditures. 'See that?' he said. 'It's incredible. That's what they're spending.'

I looked at it. The sheet contained a huge figure.

'Margrave is a weird place,' I said. 'It's deserted most of the time. There's practically no commercial activity in the whole town. Nobody is earning any money. Look at Eno's, for example. Brand-new place. But he never has any customers. So how is Eno paying the bills? Same goes for this barbershop. I was in here Sunday morning and Tuesday afternoon. The old guy said they'd had no customers in between.'

I stopped talking then. I thought about what else the old guy had said. I suddenly thought about it in a new light.

'The old barber told me something weird. He said they get money from the Kliner Foundation. A thousand bucks. He said all the merchants get it. So I figured he meant some kind of a business grant. But when I said a thousand bucks a year is OK, but it's not going to keep the wolf from the door, you know what he said then? He said it wasn't a thousand dollars a year. He said it was a thousand dollars a week. Made out it was a big secret.'

'A thousand dollars a week?' Finlay said. 'Is that possible?'

'I don't know,' I said. 'At the time, I assumed the old guy was crazy. But now I think he was telling the truth.'

'That's a hell of a lot of money, Reacher.' He was pensive. Thinking it through. 'They've bought the whole town. Very slowly, very quietly. They've bought the whole town.'

'Right,' I said. 'The Kliner Foundation has become the golden goose. Nobody will run the risk of killing it.'

'The Kliners could get away with murder.'

I looked at him. 'They *have* got away with murder.'

'So what do we do about it?' Finlay asked.

'First we figure out exactly what the hell they're doing.'

Roscoe looked over at us from the bench in the window. 'I know exactly what it's all about. Every last little detail.' She held up Gray's file in one hand.

Finlay and I joined her on the bench by the window. Studied the file she'd been reading. It was a surveillance report. Gray had hidden out under the highway cloverleaf and watched the truck traffic in and out of the warehouses. Thirty-two separate days. The results were carefully listed, in three parts. On the first eleven occasions, over a period of a year, he'd seen one truck a day incoming from the south, arriving early in the morning, and he'd seen an average of six outgoing trucks, heading north and west. He'd listed the outgoing trucks by destination, according to their licence plates.

The second section covered a second calendar year. He'd hidden out on nine separate occasions. He'd seen fifty-four outgoing trucks, the same six a day as before, with a similar list of destinations. But the log of incoming trucks was different. In the first half of the year, one truck a day was coming in, like normal. But in the second half of the year, the deliveries had built up to two trucks a day incoming.

The final twelve days of his surveillance were all between last fall and February, when he died. He was still logging about six trucks a day going out to the same wide spread of destinations, but there were no incoming trucks listed at all.

'So?' Finlay asked Roscoe.

She sat back and smiled. She had it all figured out. 'It's obvious. They're bringing counterfeit money into the country. It's printed in Venezuela, at Kliner's chemical place. It comes in by boat and they're hauling it up from Florida to the warehouse in Margrave. Then they're trucking it north and west, up to the big cities—LA, Chicago, Detroit, New York, Boston. It's an international counterfeit money distribution network. The network looks like a candelabra or a menorah. You know what a menorah is?'

'Sure,' Finlay said. 'It's that candlestick Jewish people use.'

'Right,' she said. 'That's how it looks on a map. Florida to Margrave is the stem. Then the individual arms lead out and up to the big cities. It's an import network, Finlay.'

The idea made sense. Almost certainly Margrave itself was the pivot. Almost certainly that warehouse was the actual distribution

345

centre. It was an industrial-scale operation. Huge. It would explain the Kliner Foundation's massive spending. If they ever ran short, they could just print some more. But Finlay wasn't convinced.

'What about the last twelve months?' he said. 'There's been no import flow at all. Look at Gray's list. The incoming deliveries didn't happen. They stopped exactly a year ago. Sherman Stoller got laid off, right? But they're still distributing something. There were still six trucks a day going out. What kind of an import flow is that?'

Roscoe just grinned at him and picked up the newspaper.

'The answer's in here,' she said. 'It's been in the newspapers since Friday. The Coast Guard. Last September, they started their big operation against smuggling, right? Kliner must have known it was coming. So he built up a stockpile ahead of time. See Gray's list? For the six months before last September, he doubled the incoming deliveries. That's why they've been panicking. They've been sitting there on top of a massive stockpile of counterfeit money for a year. Now the Coast Guard is going to abandon its operation, right? So they can start importing again as usual. That's what's going to happen on Sunday. That's what poor Molly meant when she said we have to get in before Sunday. We have to get in the warehouse while the last of the stockpile is still in there.'

Finlay stood up and took Roscoe's hand. Shook it very formally. 'Good work,' he said to her. 'A perfect analysis. I always said you were smart, Roscoe. Right, Reacher? Didn't I tell you she's the best we got?'

I nodded and smiled and Roscoe blushed. Finlay let go of her hand and kept on smiling. But I could see him combing through her theory, looking for loose ends. 'What about Hubble?' he asked. 'Where did he fit in?'

'Hubble used to be a currency manager,' I said. 'He was there to get rid of the fake money, feed it into the system. He knew where it could be slipped in. Like his old job, but in reverse.'

'What about the air conditioners?' Finlay asked. 'Sherman Stoller was hauling them to Florida. What was that all about?'

'Legitimate business, I guess,' I said. 'Like a decoy. It explained the truck movements up and down to Florida. They would have had to run south empty otherwise.'

Finlay nodded. 'Smart move, I guess. No empty run. Makes sense.' He paused. 'We need samples of the money,' he said.

I smiled at him. I had suddenly realised something.

'I've got samples,' I said. I put my hand in my pocket and pulled out my roll. 'Charlie Hubble gave me a wad of hundreds for expense money. She probably got them from Hubble, and I bet he was paid in counterfeit money.'

I pulled a note off the roll and gave it to Finlay. He held the hundred up to the bright light in the window. Roscoe and I crowded him for a look.

'Are you sure?' Roscoe said. 'It looks real to me.'

'If it's a fake, it's damn good,' Finlay said, peering at it, smelling it, feeling it. 'Probably the whole of the Kliner Foundation is funded with fakes. Millions every year.'

He slid the fake bill into his pocket. 'I'm going back to the station house,' he said. 'You two come in tomorrow, about noon. Teale will be gone for lunch. We'll take it from there.'

ROSCOE AND I drove fifty miles south, to Macon. I wanted to keep on the move. It's a basic rule for safety. We chose an anonymous motel on the southeastern fringe of the city.

We showered in cold water and fell into bed. Fell into a restless sleep. The room was warm. We tossed around fitfully most of the night. Gave it up again with the dawn.

Thursday morning. Felt like we hadn't slept at all. We groped around and got dressed in the dark.

'What are we going to do about all this?' Roscoe said.

I didn't answer at first. I was thinking about something else. Then I said, 'What did Gray do about it?'

'He hung himself.'

I thought some more. 'Did he?' I asked her.

There was a silence.

'Oh God. You think they killed him?' she asked.

'I think they lynched him. Made it look like suicide. They killed Joe and Stoller and the Morrisons and Hubble and Molly Beth Gordon. They tried to kill you and me. If somebody is a threat, they kill him.'

Roscoe was thinking about her old colleague. Gray, the dour and patient detective. Twenty-five years of meticulous work. A guy like that was a threat. A guy who took thirty-two patient days to cross-check a suspicion was a threat. Roscoe shuddered.

'I can't believe it,' she said. 'I was at his funeral. Chief Morrison made a speech on the lawn outside the church. So did Mayor Teale. They said he was a fine officer. But they killed him.'

She was silent a while, then said, 'You know what I can't figure?'

'What?'

'There's the two of them, right?' she said. 'Teale and Morrison. Between them, they run everything for Kliner. Their chief of detectives is Gray. An old guy, a wise head, smart and stubborn. Sure enough, one day their smart and stubborn detective sniffs them out, discovers something is going on. So they murder him to keep it all safe. Then what do they do next? They hire in a replacement. Finlay, down from Boston. A guy who is even smarter and even more stubborn than Gray was. Why the hell would they do that?'

'That's easy,' I said. 'They thought Finlay was really dumb.'

I told her the story Finlay had told me about his divorce. About his mental state at the time. What had he said? He was a basket case. An idiot. Couldn't string two words together.

'Chief Morrison and Mayor Teale interviewed him,' I told her. 'He was totally amazed they gave him the job. Now I understand why they did. They really were looking for the worst candidate who applied. And they pick a shell-shocked idiot from Boston. But by the time he turns up to start work, he's turned back into the cool and intelligent guy he always was.'

Roscoe smiled about that for a long time. Then we got ready to return to Margrave.

THE STATION HOUSE was cool and deserted except for Finlay on his way out of the rosewood office. He saw us and hurried over. 'We got a slight problem.'

He hustled us back to the office. 'Picard called,' he said. 'He can't take any more time out. Can't staff the safe house where Charlie and the kids are any longer. And he feels it's not appropriate, you know, Charlie being a woman, and the little girl terrified of him.'

He looked over at Roscoe. She saw where the conversation was going. 'He wants me up there?' she asked.

'Just for twenty-four hours,' Finlay said. 'Will you do it?'

Roscoe smiled. 'Of course I will,' she said. 'As long as you promise to get me back when the fun starts.'

'That's automatic,' Finlay said. 'As soon as we've got the detail, Picard can go official and put his own agents into the safe house. You come back here.'

'OK,' Roscoe said. 'When do I go?'

'Right now,' Finlay said. 'He'll be here any minute.'

She grinned. 'So you already figured I'd agree to it?' she said.

He grinned back. 'Like I said, you're the best we got.'

She and I went back out through the glass door to the lot. Roscoe took her valise out of the Chevy. 'You going to be OK?' I asked her.

'Sure, I'm going to be fine. Can't get much safer than an FBI safe house, right?'

We stood waiting in the sun. Didn't have to wait long. Picard's blue sedan squealed into the lot within a couple of minutes. The big guy folded himself out of the seat and stood up. 'I appreciate this, Roscoe,' he said to her. 'You're really helping me out.'

'No problem,' she said. 'Where is this place I'm going?'

'I can't say where it is,' he told her. 'Not in front of civilians, right?' He nodded toward me. 'And, Reacher, don't you press her about it.'

'OK,' I said. I wouldn't press her. She'd tell me anyway.

Picard said goodbye and threw Roscoe's bag onto his rear seat. Then the two of them got into the blue sedan and headed north. I waved after them. Then the car was lost to sight.

DETAILS. EVIDENCE GATHERING. It's the basis of everything. I was going to have to watch the warehouse operation, long enough and hard enough until I got a feel for exactly how they did it.

I walked back to Roscoe's place and climbed in the Bentley. Headed up north to Atlanta. Took an hour. I wanted the low-rent shopping area and I found it easily enough. I parked in front of a survival shop and went in. The guy at the counter nodded to me.

I found the stuff I needed. I picked up olive fatigue pants and a shirt, a camouflage jacket big enough to fit, a water canteen and some decent field glasses. Humped the whole lot over to the cash desk and piled it up. 'I could use a blackjack,' I told the guy.

He looked at me and looked at my wad of hundreds. Then he ducked down and hoisted a box up. I chose a fat sap about nine inches long. It was a leather tube. Built around a plumber's spring. The thing they put inside pipes before they bend them. It was packed around with lead shot. An efficient weapon. I paid for everything and left.

I moved the Bentley along a hundred yards and parked in front of the first automobile shop I saw advertising window tinting. Leaned on the horn and got out to meet the guy coming out of the door. 'Can you put tints on this for me?' I asked him.

'Sure I can,' he said. 'I can put tints on anything.' He stepped up to the car and ran his finger down the silky coachwork. 'Thing like this, you want a first-rate job,' he said. 'Cost you a couple of hundred.'

'I'll give you two fifty,' I said. 'That's for a better than first-rate job, and you loan me a car while you do it, OK?'

The guy slapped lightly on the Bentley's hood. 'It's a done deal.'

I took the Bentley key off Charlie's ring and exchanged it for an eight-year-old Cadillac the colour of an old avocado pear. It seemed to drive pretty well and it was about as anonymous as you could hope to get.

I CLEARED THE SOUTHERN RIM of the city and stopped at a gas station. Filled the old Cadillac's big tank and bought candy bars and bottles of water. Then I used their toilet cubicle to get changed. I put on the military surplus gear and threw my old stuff into the towel bin. Went back out to the car. Put the Desert Eagle in the long inside pocket of my new jacket. Morrison's switchblade was in the left side pocket and I put the blackjack in the right.

I shared the candy bars around the other pockets. Poured the water into the canteen and went to work. Took me an hour to get back to Margrave. I drove the old Cadillac right around the cloverleaf. Up the on-ramp again, heading north. Backed up about a hundred yards along the shoulder and stopped right in the no-man's-land between the off-ramp and the on-ramp.

I lifted the hood and propped it open. Locked the car and left it like that. Just a broken-down old sedan on the shoulder. A sight so ordinary you don't see it. Then I climbed over the low concrete wall at the edge of the shoulder. Scrambled down the high bank. Ran south and sprinted across the on-ramp. Carried on running for the shelter of the low overpass. I ran under the width of the highway to the other side and holed up behind a broad pillar. Over my head, the trucks coming off the highway rumbled around to the old county road, then branched right for the warehouses.

I settled back and got comfortable behind the pillar. I had a pretty good vantage point. Maybe two hundred yards distant, maybe thirty feet of elevation. The whole place was laid out below me like a diagram. The field glasses I'd bought were clear and powerful. There were actually four separate warehouses. All identical, built in a tight line, running away from me at an oblique angle. The whole area was ringed by a serious fence. Plenty of razor wire at the top. Each of the four compounds had its own inner fence and gate.

The first compound was totally innocent. The big roller door stood open. I could see local farm trucks rattling in and out. People were loading and unloading in plain view. Sturdy burlap sacks bulging with something or other. Maybe produce, maybe seed or fertiliser. Whatever farmers use.

Same went for the second and third. Their gates stood open, their doors were up. All their activity was a cheerful swarm on their forecourts. Nothing secret. Nothing to get excited about.

The fourth warehouse was the one I was looking for. The one at the end of the row. It was screened by the chaos on the first three forecourts. None of the local farmers or merchants would ever need to pass it by. Beyond it, in a field, was the blasted tree. The one Roscoe had picked out of the photograph of Stoller and Hubble and the yellow truck. This was the place, no doubt about it.

The big roller door across the front was closed. The gate was closed. There were two gatemen hanging around on the forecourt. Some kind of a security role. I watched them for a while, but nothing was happening. So I shifted around to watch the road. Waited for a truck bound for the fourth compound.

IT WAS A GOOD LONG WAIT. I sang to myself. I went through every version of 'Rambling on My Mind' that I knew. Everybody has a version. It's a song for people who can't stay around. People like me.

Took me thirty-five minutes to run through every version of that old song. During that time I saw maybe a half-dozen trucks pull into the warehouse approach. All local guys. All little dusty Georgia trucks. Nothing headed for the end building.

It was another hour before anything showed up. A decent-sized panel truck with New York plates rolled in, coming south. It nosed along the tarmac and waited at the fourth gate. The guys in the compound swung open the gate and signalled the truck through, then closed the gate. The driver backed up to the roller door and stopped. Got out of the truck. One of the gatemen climbed into the cab and the other ducked into a side door and cranked the roller open. The truck backed into the dark and the roller came down again. The New York driver was left on the forecourt, stretching in the sun.

I watched and waited. The truck was in there eighteen minutes. Then the roller door winched open again and the gateman drove the truck back out. As soon as it was clear, the roller came down again and the gateman jumped down from the cab. The New York guy hoisted himself back into the seat while the gateman ran ahead to swing the gates. The truck passed through and rattled back onto the county road. It turned north and swung onto the on-ramp headed for the northbound highway.

Pretty much straight away another truck was rumbling down the off-ramp. It was a similar truck. Same make, same size. I squinted through the field glasses. Illinois plates. It went through the same ritual. Paused at the gates. Backed up to the roller door. The driver was replaced by the gateman. The roller came up just long enough to swallow the truck into the gloom inside. Quick and efficient. And secret. The long-haul drivers had to wait outside.

The Illinois truck was quicker. Sixteen minutes. The driver reclaimed his place at the wheel and headed for the highway.

The next hour, nothing happened. Then I saw the third truck of the day come heading in. California plates. Same type of truck, dirty red colour, rumbling in off the highway, heading for the end compound. This time there was no change of driver. The truck just reversed straight in through the roller door. This guy was obviously authorised to see inside the shed. There was a twenty-two-minute wait. Then the roller door winched up and the truck came back out. Drove straight out through the gates and headed for the highway.

I took a fast decision. Time to go. I wanted to see inside one of those trucks. So I grabbed the field glasses and the water canteen. Ran back to the old Cadillac. Slammed the hood shut and got in. Started up and rolled along the shoulder. Waited for a gap and gunned the big motor. Accelerated north.

I figured the red truck might be three or four minutes ahead. After a few miles I spotted it. Eased off the gas pedal and kept a half-dozen vehicles between him and me. I settled back and relaxed. We were going to LA, according to Roscoe's menorah theory.

We cruised slowly north as far as Atlanta, then struck out west, across the country. The theory was looking good.

We rolled on for almost four hundred miles. Eight hours. We drove out of Georgia, right through Alabama, into the northeast corner of Mississippi. It got pitch-dark. It felt like I had been following the guy all my life. Then, approaching midnight, the red truck slowed down. A half-mile ahead, I saw it pull off into a motel and truck stop in the middle of nowhere. Near a place called Myrtle. I followed the truck into the lot. Parked up well away from it.

I saw the driver get out. A tall, thickset type of a guy. Thick neck and wide, powerful shoulders. Dark, in his thirties. Long arms, like an ape. I knew who he was. He was Kliner's son.

The Kliner kid locked up the truck and ambled off toward the buildings. I waited a spell and followed him. I hung around the newsstand and watched him amble into the diner area. He settled at a table and picked up the menu

I headed back out to the parking lot. I wanted to break into the red truck and get a look inside. But there was no chance of doing it out there in the lot. Too many people around. Besides, the whole place was lit up with bright lights.

I strolled back to the Cadillac. Got in and waited. It was a half-hour before the Kliner kid came out again, wiping his mouth with the back of his hand. Looked like he'd had a good dinner. A minute later the red truck rattled by and turned left onto a service road. He was going around to the motel. He was going to stay overnight.

He drove right up to the row of motel cabins and parked against the second cabin from the end. Right in the glow of a big lamp on a pole. He got out and locked up. Took a key from his pocket and opened up the cabin. Went in and shut the door. He must have booked and paid for the room when he was inside for dinner.

It gave me a problem. I needed to see inside the truck. I needed the evidence. And Sunday was only forty-eight hours away. I was going to have to break in, right there in the glare of the light. While the psychopathic Kliner kid was ten feet away in his motel room.

I waited a half-hour. Until the kid was sound asleep. I parked the Cadillac tight up to the red truck, nose in, facing the kid's motel room door. I climbed out across the passenger seat. Stood still and listened. Nothing.

I took Morrison's switchblade from my jacket pocket and stepped up onto the Cadillac's front fender. Stepped onto the hood and up onto the Cadillac's roof. Listened hard. Nothing. I leaned over to the truck and hauled myself upward onto its roof.

A panel truck like that has a translucent glass-fibre roof, a sort of plastic skylight set into the sheet metal. It's there to let a dim light down into the cargo area. Helps with loading and unloading.

My upper body was flat on the glass-fibre panel and my feet were scrabbling for the Cadillac's gutter. I sprang the switchblade. Stabbed it down through the panel, right in the centre of the roof. Used the blade to saw a flap about ten inches deep, eighteen inches wide. Pushed the flap down and peered through.

The truck was empty. Totally empty. Nothing in it at all.

I DROVE JUST OVER four hundred miles back to the Margrave station house as fast as I dared. I needed to see Finlay. Needed to lay out a brand-new theory for him.

I parked the old Cadillac and went inside.

'Finlay here?' I asked the desk guy.

'In the office,' he told me.

I skirted the reception counter and ran through the squad room to the rosewood office. Finlay had bad news for me. I could see it in the slope of his shoulders.

'What's the problem?' I asked him.

'You want the small problem first? Or the big problem?'

'Small first,' I said.

'Picard's keeping Roscoe another day,' he said. 'No option.'

'Hell,' I said. 'I wanted to see her. What's the big problem?'

'Somebody's ahead of us,' he whispered.

'Ahead of us?' I asked him. 'What do you mean?'

'Your brother's list?' he said. 'The initials and the note about Stoller's garage? First thing is there's a telex in from the Atlanta PD this morning. Stoller's house burned down in the night. Totally destroyed, garage and all. Torched.'

'What about Judy?' I asked.

'Neighbour says she bailed out Tuesday night,' he said. 'Right after you spoke to her. Hasn't been back.'

'Smart woman,' I said. 'But that doesn't put them ahead of us. We already saw the inside of the garage.'

'The initials?' he said. 'The colleges? I identified the Princeton guy this morning. W.B. was Walter Bartholomew. Professor. He was killed last night, outside his house. Jersey police are calling it a mugging. But we know better than that, right?'

'Any more good news?' I asked him.

He shook his head.

'Gets worse,' he said. 'Bartholomew knew something. I spoke to some research assistant guy who worked for him. Seems Bartholomew was excited about something, stayed at his office late last night, working. This assistant guy was ferrying him all kinds of old material. Late on, Bartholomew packed up, e-mailed Joe's computer and then went home.'

'What did the e-mail say?' I asked him.

'It just said stand by for a call in the morning,' he told me.

'Shit,' I said. 'What about the New York initials? K.K.?'

'Don't know yet,' he said. 'I'm guessing it's another professor. If they haven't gotten to him yet.'

'OK,' I said. 'I'm going to call him.'

'What about your surveillance?' Finlay asked.

'I followed a truck out the warehouse. The Kliner kid was driving. I got a look inside when he stopped at a motel. It was empty. Nothing in it at all. Just fresh air.'

There was silence in the office for a long moment.

'Damn,' Finlay said. He looked upset. He couldn't believe it. He'd admired Roscoe's distribution theory. 'We've got to be right,' he said. 'It makes so much sense.'

'Yes,' I agreed. 'Except we got one little detail wrong. The direction. We got it back-to-front. Same shape, but it's flowing down here, not out of here.'

He nodded. He saw it.

'So they're not loading up here,' he said. 'They're unloading. Building up a stockpile. But a stockpile of what? You're certain they're not printing money somewhere and bringing it down here?'

I shook my head. 'Molly said that Joe stopped all the printing in the States.'

'So what are they bringing here?' he said.

'We need to figure that out. But we know it adds up to about a ton a week. And we know it fits into air conditioner boxes.'

'We do?' Finlay said.

'That's what changed last year,' I said. 'Before last September, they were smuggling it out of the country. That's what Sherman Stoller was doing. The air conditioner runs weren't a decoy operation. They were the actual operation itself. Stoller was driving the air conditioner cartons down to Florida every day to meet a boat. That's why he got so uptight when he was flagged down for speeding. That's why the fancy lawyer came running over.'

'But the runs stopped a year ago?'

'Correct,' I said. 'They knew the Coast Guard thing was coming, so they got as much out as they could ahead of time. Remember the double runs in Gray's notes? Then they fired Sherman Stoller because they didn't need him any more. They decided just to sit on the stuff and wait for the Coast Guard thing to stop. That's why they're vulnerable right now. That's why they're panicking, Finlay. It's not the last remains of a stockpile they've got in there until Sunday. It's the whole damn thing.'

FINLAY STOOD GUARD at the office door in case Teale came in. I sat at the rosewood desk and called Columbia University in New York. The number reached the modern history department. I asked a helpful woman in their administrative office if they had a professor with the initials K.K. Straight away she identified a guy called Kelvin Kelstein. Sounded like he was a very eminent type of a guy. Then the call got difficult. I asked if he would come to the phone. The woman said no, he was very busy and could not be disturbed again.

'Again?' I said. 'Who's been disturbing him already?'

'Two detectives from Atlanta. They came in here this morning asking for him and they wouldn't take no for an answer.'

'Can you describe these two men to me?' I asked her.

There was a pause as she tried to remember. 'They were Hispanic. I don't recall any details. The one who did the talking was very neat, very polite.'

'Have they met with him yet?' I asked her.

'They made a one o'clock appointment,' she said. 'They're taking him to lunch somewhere, I believe.'

I held the phone tighter. 'This is very important,' I said. 'I want you to go see Professor Kelstein right now. Tell him this is life or death. Tell him those Atlanta detectives are bogus. They were at Princeton last night and they murdered Professor Walter Bartholomew.'

'Are you kidding?' the woman said. Almost a scream.

'This is for real. My name is Jack Reacher. I believe Kelstein had been in touch with my brother, Joe Reacher. Tell him my brother was murdered also. Tell him he must not, repeat, must not meet with the two Hispanic men from Atlanta. Got that?'

The woman swallowed. 'Yes,' she said.

'Good. And he must go right now to the campus security office and wait for me. With a guard right next to him. I'll be there in about three hours. Can you make absolutely sure he does that?'

'Yes,' she said again.

'And give my name to your security desk,' I said. 'I don't want any problem getting in when I arrive.'

I hung up. Shouted across the room to Finlay. 'They've got two guys up in New York. One of them is the same guy who got Joe's briefcase. Neat, polite guy. They've got the list.'

'But how?' he said. 'The list wasn't in the briefcase.'

A clang of fear hit me. I knew how. It was staring me in the face.

'Baker,' I said. 'Baker's inside the scam. You sent him to Xerox

Joe's list. He must have made two copies, given one to Teale. We've got to get out of here, right now. Let's go.'

We ran out of the office. Out through the big plate-glass doors and into Finlay's car.

'Where to?' he said.

'Atlanta,' I told him. 'The airport. I've got to get to New York.'

He headed out north along the county road.

'Baker was in it from the start,' I said. 'It was staring me in the face. That's why he was sloppy and careless with me when I was under arrest. He knew I was innocent. Just a convenient fall guy.'

And then there had been the deliberate attempt to conceal Joe's identity. Baker had deliberately screwed up the prints thing with the computer so that Joe would remain unidentified. He knew Joe was a government investigator. He knew Joe's prints would be in the Washington database. So he'd tried to make sure they didn't get matched. But he had announced the null result far too early. He'd always left the technical work to Roscoe, so he didn't know the system. Since then, he had been poking and prying, a willing helper on the edge of our hidden investigation. And all the time he was running to Teale with the snippets he was getting from us.

Finlay was blasting north fast. 'So what do we do now?' he said.

'Call Princeton back,' I told him. 'Ask that research assistant to try and piece together what Bartholomew figured out last night. Hole up somewhere safe and get busy.'

He laughed. 'Where the hell's safe now?'

I told him to use the Alabama motel we'd used Monday. I told him I'd find him there when I got back. Asked him to collect the Bentley and bring it to the airport and to leave the key and the parking claim at the arrivals information desk. He repeated all the arrangements back to me to confirm them, then he jammed his foot down harder. The big police Chevy eased up over a hundred miles an hour.

EIGHT

I arrived in Manhattan just after four thirty and got the cab to drop me at Columbia University's main entrance. I went in and found my way to the campus security office. Knocked on the glass.

A campus policeman checked a clipboard and led me through to a room at the back. He pointed to Professor Kelvin Kelstein. I saw a very old guy, tiny, sporting a shock of white hair.

'The two Hispanic guys been back?' I asked the college cop.

He shook his head. 'Haven't seen them,' he said. 'The professor's office told them that the lunch date was cancelled. Maybe they went away. What's going on here?'

'Not sure, exactly,' I said. 'I'm hoping Kelstein can tell me.'

The guard walked us back to Kelstein's own office, a small and untidy room crammed full to the ceiling with books. Kelstein sat in an old armchair and gestured me to sit opposite him in another. 'What happened to Bartholomew?' he asked.

'I don't know exactly,' I said. 'Jersey police say he got stabbed during a mugging outside his home.'

'But you remain sceptical?' Kelstein asked.

'My brother made a list of contacts,' I said. 'You're the only one of them still alive.'

'Your brother was Mr Joe Reacher?'

I nodded. 'He was murdered last Thursday. I'm trying to find out why.'

Kelstein inclined his head and peered out of a grimy window. 'Your brother Joe had a keen mind and a precision about the manner in which he expressed himself. It was a pleasure to work with him.'

'Can we start at the beginning?' I said. 'Joe came to you to talk about counterfeit currency, right? Why you?'

Kelstein turned to me and looked amused. 'Because I am the biggest counterfeiter in history,' he said. 'I was going to say I was one of the two biggest in history, but after the events of last night at Princeton, sadly now I alone remain.'

'You and Bartholomew?' I said. 'You were counterfeiters?'

The old guy smiled. 'Not by choice. During the Second World War, young men like Walter and me ended up with strange occupations in intelligence. He and I devised a scheme for shattering the Nazi economy with an assault on the value of its paper currency. Our project manufactured hundreds of billions of counterfeit Reichsmarks. Bombers littered Germany with them. They came down out of the sky like confetti.'

'Did it work?' I asked him.

'Yes and no,' he said. 'Certainly, their economy was shattered. Their currency became worthless very quickly. But, of course, alternative currencies were found. Chocolate, cigarettes, anything. Altogether, it was only a partial success.'

'So Joe was picking your brains?' I asked him.

'Walter and I became experts on counterfeiting history. Some years ago, a Senate subcommittee commissioned a report from us which became the Treasury's anticounterfeiting bible. Your brother was familiar with it, of course. That's why he was talking to us.'

'But what was he talking to you about?' I said.

Kelstein made a couple of precise little motions with his small white hands, like he was moving one scenario aside and introducing another. 'Inside the States your brother had reduced counterfeiting by ninety per cent. He impressed me greatly. But the real problem lay abroad. Did you know there are twice as many dollars outside the USA as inside?'

I nodded. I summarised what Molly had told me about foreign holdings. The trust and the faith. The fear of a sudden collapse in the desirability of the dollar.

'Quite so,' Kelstein said. 'It's more about politics than crime. In the end, a government's primary duty is to defend the value of its currency. We have two hundred and sixty billion dollars abroad. In effect, it's like Washington has raised a massive foreign loan. Raised any other way, that loan would cost us billions of dollars a year in interest payments alone. But this way it costs us nothing at all.'

'So where was the problem?' I said. 'Geographically?'

'Two main places,' Kelstein said. 'First, the Middle East. Joe believed there was a plant in the Bekaa Valley turning out fake hundreds that were practically perfect. But there was very little he could do about it. Have you been there?'

I shook my head.

'Syrian-controlled Lebanon,' he said. 'Joe believed the operation was protected by, or maybe even owned by, the Syrian government. His conclusion was that the only solution was diplomatic.'

'And the second source?' I asked him.

'Venezuela,' he said. 'Outstanding counterfeit hundred-dollar bills are coming out of there. But strictly private enterprise. No suggestion of government involvement.'

'We got that far,' I put in. 'A guy called Kliner, based down in Georgia where Joe was killed.'

'Quite so,' Kelstein said. 'Kliner is running an excellent operation. The very best we've ever seen.'

'The best?' I said.

'Exceptional.' Kelstein shifted his frail weight forward in his chair.

He was about to start a lecture on his favourite subject.

'A good counterfeiter has four problems,' he said. 'The press, the plates, the inks and the paper. The press can be bought, new or used, anywhere in the world. Most countries print money and securities and bonds on them. So the presses are obtainable abroad.'

'What about the plates?' I asked him.

'Plates are a matter of talent,' he said. 'There are people in the world who can forge old master paintings and there are engravers who can produce banknotes. But really good copyists are rare.'

'OK,' I said. 'So Kliner has bought a press, and he's found an engraver. What about the inks?'

'You can't buy any inks vaguely like them in the US,' he said. 'Joe saw to that. But obviously Joe couldn't enforce his systems in every country in the world. So the inks are easy enough to find abroad. It's only a question of colour. They mix them and experiment until they get them right.'

'So we've covered the press, the plates and the inks. What about the paper?'

Kelstein brightened up and clasped his hands like we'd reached the really interesting part. 'Paper is by far the biggest problem. It's the thing Joe and I couldn't understand about Kliner's operation.'

'Why not?' I asked him.

'Because their paper is perfect. One hundred per cent perfect. And that is absolutely unheard of.' He shook his great white head in wonderment. Like he was lost in admiration for Kliner's achievement. 'Don't forget, we're talking about an industrial-scale operation. In a year, they're printing four billion dollars' worth of hundreds. Four billion in hundreds is forty million banknotes. That's a lot of paper.'

'What sort of paper would they need?' I asked.

He eased himself up and took his wallet out of his hip pocket. Pulled out a ten-dollar bill. Crumpled it and pulled it and snapped it.

'It's a blend of fibres,' he said. 'Very clever and entirely unique. About eighty per cent cotton, about twenty per cent linen. No wood pulp in it at all. Currency stock is wonderful paper. Durable, lasts for years, won't come apart in water, hot or cold. Capable of accepting the finest engraving the platemakers can achieve.'

'So the paper would be difficult to copy?' I said.

'Virtually impossible,' he said. 'Even the official government supplier has tremendous difficulty keeping each batch consistent.'

'So the paper supply is really the key to all this?'

Kelstein nodded ruefully. 'That was our conclusion,' he said. 'But we had no idea how they were managing it. That's why I couldn't help Joe, and I can't help you. I'm terribly sorry.'

I looked at him. 'They've got a warehouse full of something. Could that be paper?'

He snorted in derision. 'Currency stock is unobtainable. You couldn't get forty sheets of currency stock, never mind forty million sheets. The whole thing is a total mystery.'

I sat quietly for a spell. Then I stood up. 'I'll figure it out,' I said.

Kelstein put his head on one side and looked at me sharply. 'Do you really think you will? When Joe couldn't?'

I shrugged at the old guy. 'Maybe Joe did. We don't know what he'd figured out before they got him. Anyway, right now I'm going back to Georgia. Carry on the search.'

Kelstein sighed. 'Good luck, Mr Reacher,' he said. 'I hope you finish your brother's business. Perhaps you will.'

I shook his frail hand and left him with the cops in the security office.

I WAS TRYING to figure where Kliner was getting his perfect paper, and I was trying to figure if I could get the six o'clock flight back to Atlanta if I hurried, and I was busy scanning for an empty cab, which was why I didn't notice two Hispanic guys strolling up to me. But what I did notice was the gun the leading guy showed me. It was a small automatic, concealed under a khaki raincoat.

He showed me the weapon and his partner signalled to a car waiting at the kerb twenty yards away. The car lurched forward and the partner stood ready to open a door. I was looking at the gun and looking at the car, making choices.

'Get into the car,' the guy with the gun said. 'Or I'll shoot.'

I was pretty sure he wouldn't fire the gun on a crowded street. It was a small gun, but there was no silencer on it. The other guy's hands were empty. I was unarmed. My jacket with the blackjack and the knife and the Desert Eagle was eight hundred miles away in Atlanta. Choices.

I chose not to get into the car. I just stood there in the street, gambling with my life that the guy wouldn't shoot in public. He stood there, holding the raincoat out toward me. His partner stood on the other side of me. Nobody moved. We were just frozen there like some kind of a display in a store window.

It gave the two guys a big problem. If you say you're going to shoot, you've got to shoot. If you don't, your bluff is called.

They were smart guys. Smart enough not to shoot me on a busy New York street. But not smart enough to walk away.

So I swayed as if I was going to take a step backward. The gun under the raincoat prodded forward at me. I grabbed the guy's wrist with my left hand. Pulled the gun around behind me and hugged the guy close with my right arm around his shoulders. Then I fell forward and crushed him against the car. All the time I was squeezing his wrist as hard as I could, with my nails dug in.

His partner still had his hand on the car door. His other hand was going for his pocket. So I jackknifed my weight back and threw him against the car. And then I ran like hell. In five strides I was lost in the crowd. I dodged and barged my way through the mass of people. Ducked in and out of doorways and ran through shrieking and honking traffic across the streets. The two guys stayed with me for a spell, but the traffic eventually stopped them. They weren't taking the risks I was taking.

I got a cab eight blocks away from where I had started and made the six o'clock nonstop flight. La Guardia to Atlanta. During the descent we flew through storm clouds ten miles thick. Looked like an enormous weather system was rolling in from somewhere. When we got off the plane, the air in the little tunnel was thick and heavy.

I picked up the Bentley key from the information counter in the arrivals hall. It was in an envelope with a parking claim. I walked out to find the car. Felt a warm wind blowing out of the north. The storm was going to be a big one.

I found the Bentley in the short-term lot. The rear windows were all tinted black. The guy hadn't gotten around to the front side glass or the windshield. It made the car look like something royalty might use, with a chauffeur driving them. My jacket was laid out in the trunk. I put it on and felt the reassuring weight of the weaponry in the pockets. I got in the driver's seat and headed south down the highway. It was nine o'clock, Friday evening. Maybe thirty-six hours before they could start shipping the stockpile out on Sunday.

IT WAS TEN O'CLOCK when I got back to Margrave. I had spent the hour's drive thinking about some military philosophy we'd learned back in Staff College. I remembered some theory that said sooner or later you've got to engage the enemy's main force. You don't win the war unless you do that. I knew their main force had started with ten people. Hubble had told me that. Then there were nine, after they ditched Morrison. I knew about the two Kliners, Teale and Baker. That left me five more to find.

I pulled off the county road into Eno's gravel lot. Parked up on the far end of the row and got out. Stretched and yawned in the night air. The storm was holding off, but it was going to break. The air was still thick and heavy. I got into the back of the car. Stretched out on the leather bench and went to sleep. I wanted to get an hour, hour and a half.

Next thing I knew somebody was knocking on the Bentley's windshield. I snapped awake and struggled up. Sergeant Baker was looking at me. The big chrome clock on the dash showed ten thirty. I'd slept a half-hour. That was all I was going to get.

First thing I did was to change my plan. A much better one had fallen right into my lap. Second thing I did was to put my hand in my pocket and snick the safety off the Desert Eagle. Then I got out and looked along the car roof at Baker. He was using his friendly grin. 'How you doing?' he said. 'Sleeping in a public place, around here you could get arrested for vagrancy.'

I grinned a friendly grin right back at him. 'Highway safety,' I said. 'They tell you don't drive if you're tired. Pull off and take a nap, right?'

'Come on in and I'll buy you a cup of coffee,' he said. 'You want to wake up, Eno's coffee should do it for you.'

I locked the car. Kept my hand in my pocket. We crunched over the gravel and into the diner. Slid into the end booth. The woman with the glasses brought us coffee.

'Where's old Finlay tonight?' Baker asked.

'Jacksonville,' I said. 'He had to check something out.'

'What does he need to check out in Jacksonville?'

I sipped my coffee left-handed. My right was wrapped around the Desert Eagle in my pocket. 'Search me,' I said. 'He doesn't tell me anything. I'm just an errand boy. Now he's got me running up to Hubble's place to fetch him something.'

'Hubble's place?' Baker said. 'What you got to fetch from there?'

'Some old papers,' I said. 'Finlay told me to stick them in the mail. Some Washington address. I'm going to sleep up at Hubble's place and mail them in the morning.'

Baker nodded slowly. Then he flashed his friendly grin again. But it was forced. We finished our coffee. Baker dropped a couple of bucks on the table and we slid out and left. He got into his patrol car. Waved at me as he drove off. I strolled over to the Bentley and headed for Beckman Drive.

I HAD TO BE very careful about where I put the Bentley. It had to be left so nobody could get past it. I inched it back and forth until it looked like I'd driven up in a hurry and just slewed to a stop at the top of Hubble's driveway.

I opened the front door with the key from the big bunch Charlie had given me. Walked through and turned on some random lights. Pulled a few drapes so it looked like there might be someone in there.

Then the first stop was the coat closet off the main hallway. I was looking for gloves. Not much call for them in the Sunbelt. But Hubble had some. Dressy things in thin black leather. Banker's gloves.

Next stop was the master bedroom. I found Charlie's vanity table. She had a mass of cosmetics. I found some waterproof mascara and took it into the bathroom. Smeared it all over my face. Then I fastened my jacket, put on the gloves and went back outside. Locked up the front door again.

I could feel the huge storm clouds clamping down overhead. It was very dark. I stood by the front door and checked myself over. Put the pistol in the inside jacket pocket. Spare shells in the outside top right pocket. Switchblade in the left side pocket. Blackjack in the right side pocket. Shoes tightly laced.

I walked down the driveway, past the Bentley. Pushed through the greenery and settled in a spot where I could see up and down the drive. I sat on the cold earth and got ready to wait.

ABOUT MIDNIGHT, the storm broke. Heavy drops the size of quarters spattered the leaves around me. It was like sitting in a shower stall. Awesome thunderclaps crashed about. They ripped and banged and the lightning blazed in sheets. I sat under the lashing rain and waited. Ten minutes. Fifteen.

They came for me at twenty minutes after midnight. The thunder was still crashing and I didn't hear their truck until it was well up the driveway. It was a dark green panel truck. Gold lettering: KLINER FOUNDATION. It crunched past me, about six feet away. Wide tyres on the gravel. That's what Finlay had seen up at the Morrison place. Marks in the gravel made by wide tyres.

The truck stopped a few yards beyond me, just behind the Bentley.

First guy out was the driver. He was wearing a white nylon body suit. It had a hood pulled tight around his face. Over his face was a surgical mask. He was wearing thin rubber gloves and rubber overshoes. He walked around to the rear doors. I knew that walk. I knew that tall, heavy build. The Kliner kid himself had come to kill me.

He opened up the rear door. Four men came out. All dressed the same as the kid. Two were carrying bags. Two had long fat shotguns. A total of five men. I'd expected four. Five was going to be harder.

The Kliner kid was organising them. He reached into the back of the truck and pulled out a crowbar. Pointed to three of his soldiers and walked off with them through the lashing rain to the house. The fifth guy was going to wait in the truck. Because of the rain, he was going to get back in the cab. I pulled out the sap. Forced my way through the bushes.

The guy couldn't hear me. The rain was roaring in his ears. He turned his back and took a step toward the driver's door. I shut my eyes for a second and pictured Joe lying on the slab at the morgue. Pictured Roscoe shaking with horror as she stared at the footprints on her hallway floor. Then I crashed out of the bushes behind the guy. Smashed the back of his skull. He went down like a tree. He lay face down and the rain hammered on his nylon suit. One down.

I dragged the body across the gravel and left it at the back of the truck. Walked around the truck and pulled the keys out of the ignition. Crept up to the house. I put the sap back in my pocket. Popped the switchblade and carried it in my right hand. I stopped inside the front door. The lock was forced and the wood was splintered. I saw the crowbar on the hallway floor.

It was a big house. It was going to take them some time to search it. I could hear them moving through the upper floor. I stepped back outside to wait for one of them to come down into the hallway. Pressed against the wall, sheltered by the overhang of the roof, I waited.

Five minutes later I heard the creak of someone's tread in the hallway. Heard him open the coat closet door. I stepped inside the house. His back was to me. He was one of the shotgun carriers, tall, lighter than me. I fell in behind him. Cut his throat with the switchblade. Two down.

I dragged the body over to the lawn and left him on the grass. Ran back inside. Picked up the shotgun the guy had dropped and grimaced. An Ithaca Mag-10. I'd seen them in the army. There's enough power in them to kill people through the side of a soft-skinned vehicle.

I kept the blade out as my weapon of choice. Silent. But the shot-gun would be better than the Desert Eagle as back-up. A shotgun sprays a wide cone of lead. As long as it's pointed vaguely in the right direction, you're going to score.

I stepped back out through the splintered door and pressed against the wall, out of the deluge. Now my guess was they'd start coming out of the house. They wouldn't find me in there and they'd miss the guy I'd just dropped. Sooner or later, they'd have to come out.

They came out. Two guys together. That made me hesitate a frac-tion. I pulled out the sap again. Swapped it into my right hand. The first guy went down easily enough. I caught him square on the back of his neck. But the second guy reacted and twisted away so that I missed with the next swing. The sap just smashed his collarbone and dropped him to his knees. Took me two more blows to finish him off. Four down.

I dragged the two bodies through the lashing rain to the lawn at the edge of the gravel drive. Piled them with the other guy. Now only the Kliner kid was still on the loose.

I stepped into the house, out of the rain, and listened. Couldn't hear a thing. The roar of the rain on the roof and the gravel out-side was too much. If the kid was alerted and creeping around, I wouldn't hear him. It was going to be a problem.

I crept into the garden room, stood still and listened hard. Heard the kid in the hallway. He was on his way out the front door. If he turned right, he was going to trip over his three dead grunts piled on the lawn. But he turned left. He walked past the garden room win-dows. He was headed across the soaking lawn to the patio area. He looked like a ghost from hell holding a long black shotgun.

I had the garden room key in my pocket, on Charlie's key ring. I unlocked the door and stepped out. The rain hit me like a drenching from a fire hose. I crept around to the patio. The Kliner kid was standing there, looking down toward the big swimming pool. I crouched in the rain, and watched him. Lightning was searing the sky and the thunder was a continuous crashing.

The kid set off down the long sloping lawn to the pool, walking slowly. He was worried. He was on his own. His vision wasn't good. The tight hood around his face was limiting his field of view. He stopped at the edge of the pool. I was a yard behind him, staying out of the edge of his vision as he swung his gaze from side to side.

Perhaps I should have fought him nobly, face to face. I was here to stand up for my brother. And right in front of me was the guy who'd kicked his body around like a bundle of rags. He should have been made aware of why he had to die. But real life wasn't like that. Joe would have laughed at all that noble man-to-man stuff.

I swung the sap with all my strength at his head. Just as he turned to walk back to the house. The sap glanced off the slick nylon and the momentum of the lead-filled tube pulled me off-balance. The kid spun and raised the shotgun. I flung my arm up and knocked the barrel aside. Rolled right under his field of fire. He squeezed the trigger and there was an enormous explosion, louder than the worst of the thunder. The ferocious recoil rocked him back, but as he pumped the second shell I dived at his legs and slammed him backward. The gun fell from his hand as I tripped him into the pool. I jumped in on top of him.

We were in the deep end, thrashing about for the winning hold. The rain was hammering. Chlorine was burning my eyes and nose. I fought on until I got his throat. Tore the nylon hood back and got my hands right on his neck. Locked my arms and thrust the kid's head far under the water. Held him there until he died.

I let his body float off and swam to the side. Clung on until I got my breath. Then I swam back to fetch the body. It was floating a yard down. I towed it back to the side. Hauled myself out. Grabbed a bunch of nylon in each hand and dragged the body out after me. It weighed a ton. I left it there and staggered back up toward the garage.

Walking was not easy. My clothes were soaking wet and cold. It was like walking in chain mail. But I made it to the garage, unlocked the door and hit the light. Just a load of garden gear and the other Bentley in there. Hubble's own car, same vintage as Charlie's. Gorgeous dark green, lovingly polished to a deep gloss. And in the corner I saw what I was looking for, a sort of a wheelbarrow thing with big spoke wheels, and a flashlight left on a workbench.

I wheeled the barrow down to the pool. Scrabbled around and found the two shotguns and the wet sap. Dropped the shotguns in the barrow and put the sap back in my pocket. Heaved the kid's corpse into the barrow. Wheeled it up to the house and down the driveway to the back of the truck. I opened the rear doors and heaved the corpse inside. Then I lifted the first guy's body in and dragged it up next to the Kliner kid. Threw the shotguns in on top of them. Two stowed.

Then I took the barrow up to where the other three bodies were sprawled on the soaking lawn. I wheeled them back to the truck they'd come in. Got all five laid out inside.

The Kliner kid I knew. I pulled back the hoods of the other four and tore away their masks. Played the flashlight beam over their faces. Two of them were the gatemen from the warehouse, I was pretty certain. The other two I knew for sure. No doubt about it. They were police. They were the back-up crew that had come with Baker and Stevenson to the diner to arrest me last Friday. They had been inside the scam. More of Mayor Teale's concealed troops.

I scrambled out of the truck again and took the flashlight and the barrow back to the garage. Now I had to tidy up.

When I was satisfied I went out the front and pulled the splintered door as far shut as it would go. Ran past the Bentley and got into the Kliner Foundation truck. Reversed carefully down the driveway and swung backward out onto Beckman Drive. Rolled down the slope to town. The place was deserted.

I made a right turn and three hundred yards south of the village green I turned into Morrison's driveway. Parked the truck next to his abandoned Lincoln. Locked the door. Ran over to Morrison's boundary fence and hurled the keys far into the field beyond. Started walking back through the rain. Started thinking hard.

The shape of the thing was clear. I had three facts. Fact one, Kliner needed special paper. Fact two, it wasn't obtainable in the States. But fact three, the warehouse was jammed with something.

And something about those air conditioner boxes was bothering me. The serial numbers. The boxes I'd seen had handwritten numbers in printed rectangles. But why? If there were no electrical appliances inside, why write serial numbers on them? That was taking camouflage to absurd lengths. So what the hell had been in those boxes?

FIRST THING I DID back at the Hubble house was root around in Charlie Hubble's expensive kitchen for coffee. Started the machine burbling away. Then I went down to the basement. I fiddled around with the furnace until it kicked in, then I stripped off and shoved all my clothes in Charlie's tumble drier. Set it on low for an hour.

I walked upstairs naked and went into Hubble's bathroom. Took a long hot shower, then wrapped myself up in a towel and went down for the coffee.

I couldn't go up to Atlanta that night. I couldn't get there before maybe three thirty in the morning. That was the wrong time to be sure of talking my way inside. I had no ID to show and no proper status. I would have to leave it until later that day. No choice.

So I thought about sleeping. I wandered through to Hubble's den. Looked around. It was a dark, snug room. Lots of wood panelling and big leather chairs. Next to the television was a stereo. Rows of compact discs. Emphasis on the Beatles. Hubble had said he'd been interested in John Lennon. He'd been to the Dakota Building in New York City and to Liverpool in England. He had all the albums.

Over the desk was a bookshelf. Stacks of professional periodicals and a row of heavy books. Technical banking journals and reports. At the end of the row were some US Treasury Department dispatches and a couple of issues of something calling itself *World of Banking*. A curious collection. I ran my finger along the row of magazines and journals. Some of them were recent issues. Fully a third of them were published after Hubble had left the bank. After he had been let go. Why was he still reading all this complicated stuff?

I pulled out a couple of periodicals, held them in my fingers at the top and bottom of the spines. They fell open at the pages Hubble had consulted. I sat down in Hubble's leather chair, wrapped in his towel, reading what he'd read. I read right through the shelf from left to right. All the periodicals. It took me an hour.

Then I started on the books. I ran my finger along the dusty row. Stopped with a little shock when I spotted a couple of names I knew. Kelstein and Bartholomew. A big old volume. Bound in red leather. Their Senate subcommittee report. I pulled it out and started flicking through. It was an amazing publication. Kelstein had modestly described it as the anticounterfeiter's bible. And it was. It was a totally exhaustive history of every known forging technique. I hefted the heavy volume onto my lap. Read halfway through the night.

It didn't put me to sleep. It had exactly the opposite effect. It gave me a hell of a buzz. It left me shaking with shock and excitement. Because by the time I had finished I knew exactly how they were getting their paper, and where they were getting it from. I knew what had been in those air conditioner boxes last year. I knew. I knew what Kliner was stockpiling at his warehouse. I knew what all those trucks were bringing in every day. I knew everything, with twenty-four hours still to go. The whole thing, from beginning to end. And it was one hell of a clever operation. Old Professor Kelstein had said the paper was unobtainable. But Kliner had proved him wrong.

Kliner had found a way of obtaining it. A very simple way.

I jumped up from the desk and ran down to the basement. Wrenched open the drier door and pulled my clothes out. Dressed, hopping from foot to foot on the concrete floor. Ran back up to the kitchen. Loaded up my jacket with things I was going to need. Ran outside to the Bentley. Started it up and threaded it backward down the drive. Roared off down Beckman and squealed a left onto Main Street. Gunned it through the silent town and headed for Alabama.

'SO WHAT'S GOING ON?' Finlay said to me.

I'd had to bang on the door of his motel room a good long while before he'd come yawning and blinking to the door. Now we were speeding to Atlanta in the Bentley with Finlay behind the wheel.

'Did you call Princeton?' I asked him.

He slapped the steering wheel in frustration. 'I was on the phone for an hour. The guy knew a hell of a lot but in the end nothing at all. He was a history postgrad, working for Bartholomew. Turns out Bartholomew and the other guy, Kelstein, were the big noises in counterfeiting research.'

'That's exactly what Kelstein said. But I've figured it out now.'

'So tell me about it,' he said.

'Wake up and figure it out for yourself, Harvard guy.'

He grunted in irritation. We drove on.

'I'll give you two clues,' I said. 'Think about the heading Joe used on his list. *E Unum Pluribus.*'

He thought about it. '*E Unum Pluribus,*' he said. 'It's a reversal of the US motto. So it means out of one comes many, right?'

'Correct,' I said. 'And what's unique about American banknotes, compared with any other country in the world?'

He thought about it. He was thinking about something so familiar he wasn't spotting it. We drove on. Shot past the prison at Warburton. Up ahead, a faint glimmer of dawn in the east.

He shrugged. 'What?' he asked.

'Dollars are all the same size,' I said. 'Fifties, hundreds, twenties, tens, fives and ones. All the same size. No other country I've seen does that. Anywhere else, the high-value notes are bigger than the small-value notes, right?'

'So?' he asked.

'So where are they getting their paper from?' I asked him.

I waited. He glanced out of his window. Irritated.

'They're scouring the country for one-dollar bills,' I said. 'That was the role Hubble took over a year and a half ago: cash management. He knew how to get hold of cash. So he arranged to obtain one-dollar bills from banks, malls, supermarkets, racetracks, casinos, anywhere he could. They're buying genuine one-dollar bills from all over the US. About a ton a week.'

Finlay stared across at me. He was beginning to understand. 'Go on,' he said.

'The trucks bring them down to Margrave,' I said. 'From wherever Hubble sourced them. They come into the warehouse.'

Finlay was catching on. 'Then they get shipped out again in the air conditioner cartons,' he said.

'Correct,' I said. 'Until a year ago. Until the Coast Guard stopped them. Nice new fresh boxes, sealed with tape. But they used to count them first, before shipping them.'

'How the hell do you count a ton of dollar bills?'

'They weighed them,' I said. 'Every time they filled a box, they stuck it on a scale, weighed it, and calculated the value. Then they wrote the amount on the box. Looked like serial numbers.'

Finlay smiled a rueful smile. 'OK,' he said. 'Then the boxes went to Jacksonville Beach, right?'

I nodded. 'Got put on a boat,' I said. 'To Klincr's chemical works in Venezuela.'

We fell silent. We were approaching the warehouse complex up at the top of the old county road. It loomed up on our left like the centre of our universe. Then we swung up the ramp onto the highway. Headed north for Atlanta.

'Now,' I asked, 'what's that chemical plant down in Venezuela for?'

'Something to do with cotton.'

'Right,' I said. 'Involving sodium hydroxide, sodium hypochlorite, chlorine and water. Bleach, in other words. Bleach for cotton fibre.'

'So?' he demanded.

'What did Bartholomew's guy tell you about currency paper?'

Finlay inhaled sharply. It was practically a gasp. 'Hell,' he said. 'Currency paper is mostly cotton fibre. With a bit of linen. They're bleaching the dollar bills. My God, Reacher, I don't believe it. They're bleaching the ink off the singles and giving themselves millions of sheets of genuine blank paper to play with.'

I grinned at him and he held out his right hand. We smacked a high five and whooped at each other, alone in the speeding car.

'You got it, Harvard guy,' I said. 'That's how they're doing it. They've figured out the chemistry and they're reprinting the blank bills as hundreds. *E Unum Pluribus*. Out of one comes many. Out of one dollar comes a hundred dollars.'

'Hell,' Finlay said again. 'This is something else, Reacher. And you know what it means? Right now, that warehouse is stuffed full to the ceiling with genuine dollar bills. We've caught them with their pants down, right?'

I laughed happily. 'Right,' I said.

'OK. Tell me how you figured it.'

I squirmed around in the big leather seat to face him.

'I wanted to check Joe's list. You recall the second-to-last item? Stollers' garage. Think about the punctuation. If the apostrophe was before the final letter the garage would belong to one person called Stoller. But it wasn't written like that. It was *after* the final letter. It meant the garage belonging to the Stollers, two people called Stoller. Judy and Sherman weren't married. So the only place we'd find two people called Stoller is the little old house where Sherman's parents live. And they've got a garage.'

Finlay drove on in silence. Trawled back to his grade-school grammar. 'You think he stashed a box with his folks?' he said.

'It's logical,' I said. 'The boxes we saw in his own place were empty. But Sherman didn't know he was going to die. He thought he was going to live for years without working. So it's reasonable to assume he had savings stashed away somewhere else. No doubt there are cartons in the old couple's garage stuffed with dollar bills. Anyway, when I went to check Joe's list for the punctuation the list had gotten soaked in chlorinated water. All the writing had bleached off.'

He glanced across. 'You put it together from that?' he said.

I shook my head. 'I got it from a Senate report I found in Hubble's study,' I said. 'There were a couple of little paragraphs. One was about a scam in Bogotá. There was another about an operation in the Lebanon years ago. They were doing the same thing, bleaching real dollar bills so they could reprint the blank paper.'

'So how come Bartholomew or Kelstein didn't get it?'

'I think Bartholomew did get it,' I said. 'I think that's what he finally figured out. That's what the e-mail was about.'

Finlay parked up next to a hydrant in a tow zone near to the FBI headquarters.

We had to tell Picard.

HE MET US in the lobby of his hotel and took us off into a side room. We ran through what we knew. Picard nodded and his eyes gleamed. He was looking at a big case.

'Excellent work, my friends,' he said. 'But who are we dealing with now? I think the Hispanic guys are outsiders, hired help. But locally, we still got five out of the original ten unidentified. We know about Morrison, Teale, Baker and the two Kliners, right? But who are the other five?'

I shook my head. 'We only need to ID one more,' I said. 'I sniffed out four more last night. Only the tenth guy we don't know.'

Picard and Finlay both sat up. 'Who are they?' Picard said.

'The two gatemen from the warehouse,' I said. 'And two more cops. The back-up crew from last Friday.'

'More cops?' Finlay said. 'Hell.'

Picard laid his giant hands on the table. 'OK,' he said. 'You guys head back to Margrave. Try to stay out of trouble, but if you can't, then make the arrests. But be very careful of this tenth guy. Give me twenty minutes to go get Roscoe back, and I'll see you down there.'

We all stood up. Shook hands all round. Picard headed upstairs and Finlay and I headed back out to the Bentley.

'How do you know about the gatemen and the cops?' he asked me.

'Baker,' I said. 'He bumped into me last night. I spun him a yarn about going up to Hubble's place looking for some documentation, then I went up there and waited. Along came the Kliner kid and four of his pals. They came to nail me to the bedroom wall.'

'So what happened?'

'I took them out,' I said. 'Ambushed them. The Kliner kid I drowned in the swimming pool. That's how Joe's list got soaked.'

'Any ideas about this tenth guy?' he said.

'Whoever he is, he's up at the warehouse with Baker, Teale and old man Kline. They're short of staff now. They'll all be on guard duty tonight. Loading duty tomorrow.'

'Unbelievable,' Finlay said. 'How the hell did a place like Margrave start up with a thing like this?'

'It's Mayor Teale's fault,' I said. 'The town sold the land for the warehouses to earn itself some new money, right? Old Teale brokered the deal. But he didn't have the courage to say no when the new money turned out to be bad money.'

'He's a politician,' Finlay said. 'They never say no to money. And it was a hell of a lot of money. Teale rebuilt the whole town with it.'

'He drowned the whole town with it,' I said. 'The place is a cesspool. From the mayor right down to the guy who polishes the cherry trees.'

We drove the rest of the way in silence.

When we arrived at the Margrave station house the place was deserted apart from the desk sergeant. He nodded to us. We walked through to the rosewood office and closed the door.

Finlay looked uneasy. 'I want to know who the tenth guy is,' he said. 'It could be anybody. Could be the desk sergeant. There's been four cops in this already. Could be Stevenson. He was connected to Hubble.'

I shook my head. 'No,' I said. 'Teale pulled Stevenson in off the road when he took over. He wanted him where he could see him. And the desk sergeant never does anything, just sits there all day.'

'So what do we do?' he said.

'We wait for Roscoe and Picard,' I said. 'Take it from there.'

I sat on the edge of the big rosewood desk, swinging my leg, while Finlay paced up and down. Twenty minutes later the door opened. Picard stood there, filling the whole doorway. I saw Finlay staring at him, like there was something wrong with him. I followed his gaze.

There were two things wrong with Picard. First, he didn't have Roscoe with him. Second, he was holding a government-issue .38 in his giant hand, and he was pointing it straight at Finlay.

NINE

'You?' Finlay gasped.

Picard smiled a cold smile at him. 'None other,' he said. 'The pleasure's all mine, believe me. You've been very helpful, both of you. You've kept me in touch every step of the way. You should have spotted it Wednesday. I sent the little guy to Joe's hotel two hours before I told you about it.' He turned the gun on me. 'You disappointed me. Get over there,' he said. 'Next to Finlay.'

'Where's Roscoe?' I asked.

He laughed and gestured with the gun barrel that I should stand up and move over next to Finlay. As I heaved myself off the desk and stepped over, Teale entered the office, his cane in his left hand and a shotgun in his right.

Picard darted his hand up under Finlay's jacket. Took the revolver out of his holster. Slipped it into the pocket of his own jacket. He stepped sideways and patted me down. I was unarmed. My jacket was outside in the Bentley's trunk. Then he stood next to Teale. Finlay stared at Picard like his heart was breaking.

'What's this all about?' Finlay said. 'We go back a long way.'

Picard just shrugged at him. 'I told you to stay away,' he said. 'Back in March, I tried to stop you coming down here. But you wouldn't listen, would you? So you get what you get, my friend.'

I listened to Picard's growl and felt worse for Finlay than I did for myself. But then Kliner stepped in through the door. His bone-hard face was cracked into a grin. His eyes bored into me with hatred. He was carrying another Ithaca Mag-10 shotgun in his left hand. In his right hand, he was carrying a little .22-calibre automatic. Fitted with a silencer. It was pointed straight at me. I stared at it. Nine days ago, the end of that silencer had touched my brother's temple. There was no doubt about that. I could feel it.

Kliner gestured Finlay and me to sit, using his shotgun barrel as a baton. Short jerky movements to move us around. We sat side by side in front of the big rosewood desk.

Teale rattled open a drawer in the desk. Pulled out the cassette recorder. Handed it to Picard, who fiddled a cassette in and clicked the little door shut. Pressed play. The motor whirred and the speaker hissed. Underneath the hiss, I could hear a boomy acoustic. Then we heard Charlie Hubble's voice. She sounded hysterical.

'Hub?' Charlie's voice. 'This is Charlie. I've got the children with me. I'm not at home, you understand what that means? I've got to give you a message. If you don't come back, something will happen to the children. They tell me you know what that something is. It's the same thing they said would happen to you and me. So you have to come back straight away, OK?'

The voice ended on a rising note of panic and then died away in the boomy hiss. Picard stabbed the stop button. Took the tape out and placed it carefully on the edge of the desk. Right in front of me. Then Kliner walked around into my field of vision and said to me, 'You're going to take that with you wherever you've hidden Hubble and you're going to play it to him.'

Finlay and I looked at each other in astonishment. Then I stared back at Kliner. 'You killed Hubble already,' I said.

Kliner hesitated for a second. 'Don't try it on,' he said. 'We were going to, but you got him out of the way. You're hiding him. Charlie

375

told us. We asked her where he was. She promised us you'd be able to find him. She said you'd given him all sorts of advice and guidance. I hope for everybody's sake she wasn't lying. We've got a business to run. So what we're going to do is this. Picard is going to go with you to pick him up. When you get wherever he is, Picard is going to call me. On my mobile. Then you all three come on back here. OK?'

I didn't respond.

'Let me add a couple of factors,' he said. 'We don't know exactly how far away Hubble is. And you're not going to tell us the truth about that. So I'll tell you what we're going to do. We're going to give you a time limit.'

He stopped talking and walked around to where Finlay was sitting. He raised the .22 and put the tip of the silencer in Finlay's ear. Pushed it in hard until Finlay was tilting over in his chair.

'The detective here is going in a cell,' he said. 'He's going to be handcuffed to the bars. If Picard hasn't called me by one hour before dawn tomorrow, I'm going to let my shotgun blow him apart. Then I'm going to give you another hour. If Picard hasn't called me by the time the sun comes up, I'm going to start on the delightful Officer Roscoe. Mayor Teale and I have spent a pleasant hour discussing just exactly what we're going to do to her.'

Kliner was forcing Finlay practically out of his chair with the pressure of the automatic in his ear. Finlay's lips were clamped.

'Understand?' Kliner said to me. 'Call it six o'clock tomorrow morning to save Finlay's life, seven o'clock to save Miss Roscoe's. And don't go messing with Picard. Nobody else knows my phone number. And it isn't written down anywhere.'

I shrugged. Kliner was a smart guy.

'Do you understand?' he repeated.

'I think so,' I said. 'Hubble's run away and you don't know how to find him. You're useless, Kliner. You think you're some kind of a smart guy, but you can't find Hubble.'

I could hear that Finlay wasn't breathing. He thought I was playing with his life. But old man Kliner left him alone. Moved across into my field of vision again. He had gone pale. I was just about getting used to the idea that Hubble was still alive. He'd been dead all week, and now he was alive again. Alive and hiding out somewhere. He'd taken that stay-at-home call on Monday morning and smelled a rat and run for his life. Paul Hubble had given me the tiny edge I was going to need.

'What's Hubble got that you want so much?' I said.

'He's the only loose end left,' Kliner said. 'I've taken care of everything else. And I'm not going out of business just because an asshole like Hubble is running around somewhere shooting his mouth off.'

I leaned forward and stared right into his eyes. 'Can't your son get him for you?' I said quietly.

Nobody spoke. I leaned forward some more. 'Where *is* your son, Kliner? What happened to him?'

His hard face went slack. He knew but he hadn't accepted it. He'd sent his boy after me, and his boy hadn't come back. He wanted to hate me for killing his boy. But he couldn't do that either. Because to do that would be to admit it was true.

'Get him out of here,' Kliner said. 'If you're not out of here in one minute, Reacher, I'll shoot the detective right now.'

I stood up. Looked around the four of them. Nodded to Finlay. Headed out. Picard followed me and closed the door quietly.

PICARD SIGNALLED with the stubby gun barrel that I should get in the Bentley and drive. I didn't argue with the guy. Just got in and drove up to Eno's diner. Reached around to the seat pocket and found the map. Walked over through the bright afternoon sun and pushed in through Eno's door. Slid into an empty booth. Ordered coffee and eggs.

If you've only got one shot, you've got to make it count. You can't afford to miss because you screwed up the planning. Or because you ran out of blood sugar and got sick and dizzy in the small hours of the morning. So I forced the eggs down and drank the coffee. Aware of Picard's huge bulk glowering in the booth behind me. Then I pushed the empty mug and the plate aside and spread the map on the table. Started looking for Hubble.

I spent the best part of an hour with the map. Then I folded it up, picked up the knife and the fork from the egg plate. Palmed them into my trouser pocket. Left one of Charlie's hundreds on the table for the waitress.

Picard pushed me out through the door. It was four o'clock. I hustled over the gravel to the Bentley. Picard followed me with his hand on the gun in his pocket. I eased out of the lot and scooted north up the old county road. When I looked in the mirror I picked up a plain sedan. About a hundred yards behind. Two guys in it. I slowed and glanced left at the warehouses at the top of the county road.

377

Swooped up the ramp and round the cloverleaf. Hit the highway going as fast as I dared. Time was crucial.

The road skirted us around the southeast corner of the Atlanta sprawl. I threaded through the interchanges. Headed due east.

'So where is he?' Picard asked me.

It was the first time he'd spoken since leaving the station house. I glanced across at him and shrugged. 'No idea,' I said. 'Best I can do is go find a friend of his in Augusta.'

'Who's this friend?' he said.

'Guy called Lennon,' I said.

'He's not another damn Treasury spook working for your brother?'

'Friend of Hubble's,' I said. 'Like I told you.'

'Like hell. We checked, he's got no friends in Augusta. Hell, he's got no friends anywhere. He thought Kliner was his damn friend, giving him a job.' Picard chuckled to himself. Then we cruised on in silence. The plain sedan sat steady, a hundred yards back.

'Did old man Kliner shoot my brother?' I asked Picard.

'Sure. That's his weapon, the .22 with the suppressor.'

'And then the kid kicked the body around?'

'The kid was berserk,' he said. 'Wrong in the head.'

'And then Morrison was supposed to clean up?'

'Supposed to. But he couldn't find Stoller's body. So he just left both of them there.'

We drove on in silence for a mile or two.

'We need gas,' I said eventually.

Picard craned over and peered at the needle. It was nudging the red. 'Pull over at the next place,' he said.

I saw a sign for gas near a place called Madison. I pulled off and drove over to the pumps.

'Are you going to do this for me?' I asked Picard.

He looked at me in surprise. 'What the hell do you think I am? A damn pump jockey? Do it yourself.'

That was the answer I wanted to hear. I got out of the car. Picard got out on the other side. The plain sedan pulled up close by and the two guys got out. I looked them over. They were the same two I'd scuffled with in New York. The smaller guy had his khaki raincoat on. I nodded amiably to them. I figured they had less than an hour to live. They strolled over and stood with Picard in a knot of three. I unhooked the nozzle and shoved it in the Bentley's tank.

It was a big tank. Well over twenty gallons. Picard and the two

Hispanics shuffled about in the slight evening chill as they waited.

I slipped Eno's cutlery out of my pocket and pressed the tip of the knife into the tyre tread next to my knee. From where Picard was standing, it looked like I was rubbing my leg. Then I took the fork and bent one of the tines outward. Pressed it into the cut and snapped it off. Left a half-inch sticking into the tyre.

'You paying?' I called to Picard as I replaced the nozzle.

He peeled a bill off his roll and sent one of the guys to pay. Then we got back into the car. I moved out and accelerated gently back onto the highway. The signs started flashing past. Augusta, seventy miles. Augusta, sixty miles. Augusta, forty miles. Still the two guys followed.

The rear tyre went flat about twenty miles from Augusta. It was past seven thirty and it was getting dark.

'Shit,' I said. 'Flat tyre.'

'Pull over,' Picard said.

I slewed to a stop well over on the shoulder. The sedan stopped behind us. We all four got out. The breeze had freshened up to a cold easterly wind. I shivered and opened the trunk. Picked up my jacket and put it on, like I was grateful for the warmth.

'Spare wheel's under the trunk floor,' I said to Picard.

'We'll let the little guys change the wheel,' he said.

He waved the two Hispanics over and told them to do the work. They jacked up the car and took the wheel off. Then they lined up the spare and lifted it into place. Bolted it carefully on. I was standing there next to the car, thrusting my hands deep in my coat pockets and stamping from foot to foot, trying to look like a guy who was getting cold standing around doing nothing.

I waited until Picard stepped around to check the bolts were tight. He put his weight on the lever and when I could hear the metal graunching I dived over the concrete wall at the edge of the shoulder and rolled down the shallow bank. Pulled out the Desert Eagle. Shot at the guy with the raincoat as he came over the wall after me, but I missed my aim and hit his leg. Beyond him I could see Picard fumbling with the jack before dancing over to the wall. I rolled over and aimed up the bank and shot the second Hispanic guy. Caught him through the chest and he came crashing down toward me. The guy with the raincoat was screaming, clutching his leg, trying to free the automatic he'd shown me in New York. I fired a third time and shot him through the head. I could see Picard aiming his .38 down at me.

'Don't shoot me,' I yelled. 'You won't get Hubble if you do.'

He knew that. And he knew he was a dead man if he didn't get Hubble. I ran up the bank and circled the Bentley, forcing him out toward the traffic with the Desert Eagle.

'You don't shoot me, either,' Picard shouted. 'My phone call is the only way you're going to save that woman. That's for sure.'

'I know that, Picard,' I yelled back.

It looked like a stalemate. We circled the car with our fingers on the triggers, telling each other we weren't going to shoot.

I waited until I was next to the Bentley. Then I pulled the trigger. The .44 shell caught him and smashed his huge bulk backward. I didn't wait around for a second shot. I jumped for the driver's seat. Fired the car up and burned rubber, hurtling east.

I was gasping and shaky with adrenaline. I forced my heartbeat down and took big gulps of air. Then I yelled in triumph.

IT WAS DARK when I hit the Augusta suburbs. I stopped at the first motel I saw. Locked the Bentley up and dodged into the office. 'Got a room?' I asked the clerk.

'Thirty-six bucks,' the guy said.

'Got a map of Augusta?' I asked.

He jerked his thumb over to a rack stuffed with maps and brochures. I peeled off thirty-six bucks from the roll and signed the register.

'Room twelve,' the guy said. Slid me the key.

I grabbed a map and hustled out. Ran down the row to room twelve. Let myself in and unfolded the map on the bed. Opened up the Yellow Pages to H for hotels.

There was a huge list. In Augusta, there were hundreds of places where you could pay for a bed for the night. Literally hundreds. So I looked at the map. Concentrated on a wedge a half-mile long and four blocks deep, either side of the main drag in from the west. That was my target area. I put the map and the phone book side by side and made a hit list.

Eighteen hotels. One of them was the place I was in. So I picked up the phone and dialled zero for the desk. The clerk answered. 'You got a guy called Paul Lennon registered?' I asked him.

There was a pause. He was checking the book.

'Lennon?' he said. 'No, sir.'

'OK,' I said. Put the phone down.

I took a deep breath and started at the top of my list. Dialled the first place. 'You got a guy called Paul Lennon registered?' I asked the guy who answered.

There was a pause. 'No, sir.'

I worked down the list. Dialled one place after another. The fifteenth number I dialled got the same question. 'You got a guy called Paul Lennon registered?'

There was a pause. 'Room one twenty,' the fifteenth clerk said.

'Thank you,' I said. Put the phone down.

I lay there. Closed my eyes and breathed out. Put the phone back on the nightstand and checked the map. The fifteenth hotel was three blocks away. North of the main drag. I left the room key on the bed and went back out to the car.

I found the fifteenth hotel and parked at the door. Went into the lobby. It was a dingy sort of place.

'Can I help you?' the desk guy asked.

'No,' I said.

I followed an arrow down a warren of corridors. Found room one twenty. Rapped on the door. I heard the rattle of the chain going on. I stood there. The door cracked open.

'Hello, Hubble,' I said.

HE WAS SPILLING OVER with questions for me, but I just hustled him out to the car. We had to get going.

He looked OK. He'd been running for six days and it had done him good. It had burned off his complacent gloss. Left him looking more tight and rangy. More like my type of a guy. He was dressed up in cheap chain-store clothes and he was wearing socks.

He stopped when he saw the Bentley parked at the door.

'You came in Charlie's car?' he said.

'She was worried about you. She asked me to find you.'

He looked blank. 'What's with the tinted glass?' he said.

I grinned at him and shrugged. 'Don't ask,' I said. 'Long story.'

I started up and eased away from the hotel. He should have asked me right away how Charlie was, but something was bothering him.

'How the hell did you find me?' he asked.

I shrugged at him again. 'Easy,' I said. 'I've had a lot of practice. Spent years picking up deserters for the army.'

I was threading through the busy streets, working my way back to the highway. 'You had no credit cards, no driver's licence, no ID,' I said. 'All you had was cash. So you weren't using planes or rental cars. You were stuck with the bus.'

I found the on-ramp. Concentrated on the lane change and merged with the flow back toward Atlanta.

'That gave me a start,' I said to him. 'Then I put myself in your shoes. You were terrified for your family. So I figured you'd circle around Margrave at a distance. So you'd feel still connected. That's what made it so easy. You were circling Margrave. Counterclockwise. Give people a free choice, they always go counterclockwise. All I had to do was to count the days and study the map. I figured Monday you were in Birmingham, Alabama. Tuesday was Montgomery, Wednesday was Columbus, Thursday was Macon, Friday here in Augusta. My big gamble was you stayed here two nights. I figured you were running out of energy.'

Hubble went quiet. He'd thought he'd been invisible, but he'd been circling Margrave like a beacon flashing away in the night sky. 'But I used a false name,' he said defiantly.

'You used four false names,' I said. 'Five nights, five hotels. But the fifth name was the same as the first name, right?'

He was amazed. 'How the hell did you know that?'

'You're a Beatles guy,' I said. 'You told me about visiting the Dakota Building and going to Liverpool in England. You've got just about every Beatles CD ever made in your den. So the first night, you were at some hotel desk and you signed Paul Lennon, right?'

'Right,' he said.

'Not John Lennon,' I said. 'People usually stick with their own first name. So you were Paul Lennon. Tuesday you were Paul McCartney. Wednesday you were Paul Harrison. Thursday you were Paul Starr. Friday in Augusta, you started over again with Paul Lennon, right?'

'Right,' he said, shaking his head. 'But there's a million hotels in Augusta. How the hell did you know where to look?'

'I thought about it,' I said. 'You got in late morning, coming in from the west. Guy like you walks back the way he's already seen. Feels safer that way. You'd been on the bus four hours, you wanted the air, so you walked a spell, maybe a quarter-mile. Then you got panicky and dived off the main drag a block or two. So I had a pretty small target area. Eighteen places. You were in number fifteen.'

We barrelled on down the road in the dark.

'How are things in Margrave now?' he asked me.

That was the big question.

'We're in deep shit,' I said. 'We've got seven hours to fix it.'

I saved the worst part for last. I told him Charlie and the kids had gone with an FBI agent on Monday. Because of the danger. And then I told him the FBI agent had been Picard.

There was silence in the car. I drove on three, four miles.

'OK,' he said eventually. 'You'll get them back, won't you?'

'I'll get them back,' I said. 'But I'll need your help.'

He nodded. He had crashed through the barrier. He had stopped worrying and was up on that plateau where you did whatever needed doing. I knew that place. I lived there.

'I'm very sorry about your brother,' Hubble said. 'I had no idea. I guess I got him killed, didn't I?'

He was slumped down in the seat, looking out the window. But I wanted to keep him talking. He had to stay on the ball. So I asked him the question I'd been waiting a week to ask.

'How the hell did you get into all this?'

'I lost my job,' he said. A simple statement. 'I was devastated. I felt angry and upset. And scared, Reacher. We'd been living a dream, you know? I was earning a fortune and I was spending a fortune. It was totally fabulous. Then I got canned. And the pay cheques stopped. I was so angry. And I was scared. I had no energy to start again at the bottom of something. I just didn't know what to do.'

'And then Kliner turned up?' I said.

He nodded. 'He had heard about it. I guess Teale told him. Teale knows everything about everybody. Kliner called me within a couple of days. I hadn't even told Charlie at that point. He flew me out to the Bahamas for lunch in his private jet, and we talked.'

'And?' I said.

'He told me to look at it as an opportunity to get out. He was saying I should dump the corporate thing, I should come and do a real job, make some real money, with him. He was clearly a very rich and successful guy. And very, very smart. I was flattered and I was desperate and I said yes. He did a real job on me, flew me up to Jacksonville, sat me with lawyers for a week, signed me up to a huge salary, bonuses, whatever I wanted. After a couple of days he told me exactly what he was doing. But he said now I was involved, I had to stay quiet. I got really unhappy. I told him I wanted out. So he drove me down to some awful place. His son was there with two Hispanic guys. There was this other guy chained up in a back room.

Kliner said this was a guy who had stepped out of line. He told me to watch carefully. His son just kicked the guy to a pulp. Then the Hispanic guys got their knives out . . . It was horrible.'

'Go on,' I said.

'Friday morning, we flew home. We sat together on the little jet and he told me it wouldn't be just me who got cut up. It would be Charlie too. He said they'd nail me to the wall. I was shitting myself. Then we landed and he called Charlie and insisted we go to dinner with him. Charlie was delighted because Kliner is such a big deal in the county. It was a total nightmare because I had to pretend there was nothing wrong. I hadn't even told Charlie I'd lost my job. I had to pretend I was still at the bank. And the whole evening that bastard was asking politely after the children and smiling at me.'

I skirted around the southeast corner of Atlanta, looking for the highway south. 'Then what?' I asked him.

'I started work at the warehouse,' he said. 'Managing the supply and supervising the loading and shipping.'

'Sherman Stoller was the driver?' I asked him.

'Right,' he said. 'He was trusted to do the Florida run. He helped me with the loading, too. We had to work like crazy. A million dollars in singles is a hell of a sight. It was like trying to empty a swimming pool with a shovel.'

'But Sherman was stealing, right?' I said.

He nodded. I could see his face in the dim glow from the old dials on the dash. 'The money got counted properly in Venezuela,' he said. 'I used to get accurate totals back after about a month or so. I used them to crosscheck my weighing formula. Many times we were about a hundred grand down. I figured Sherman was stealing the occasional box. I told him to take care, because Kliner would kill him if he found out. Might get me into trouble as well. I was already worried enough about what I was doing.'

'And what about the last twelve months?' I asked him.

'We had to stop the shipping. The Coast Guard thing made it impossible. Kliner decided to stockpile instead. Now the Coast Guard's finally pulling back, it's caught us by surprise. We're not ready to ship. It's not even boxed yet.'

'When did you contact Joe?' I asked him.

'Was that your brother's name?' he said. 'I knew him as Palo. I called the Treasury a year ago. Couldn't call the police because of Morrison, couldn't call the FBI because of Picard. So I called

Washington and tipped off this guy Palo. I knew his best chance was to strike while they were stockpiling.'

I saw a sign for gas and pulled off. Hubble filled the tank. I found a plastic bottle in a trash can and got him to fill that, too.

'What's that for?' he asked.

'Emergencies?' I said.

He didn't come back on that. We just paid at the window and pulled back onto the highway.

THE BIG CHROME CLOCK on the Bentley's dash said midnight. I needed this whole deal over and done by five in the morning.

'Hubble?' I said. 'I need your help.'

'How?' he asked.

I spent the last ten minutes of the highway cruise going over it, until he was totally solid.

I swung off the highway where it met the county road. Blasted past the warehouses and on down the fourteen miles to town. Slowed as I passed the station house. It was quiet, lights off. The town was silent and deserted. The only light showing in the whole place was in the barbershop.

I made the right onto Beckman and drove up to Hubble's place. Turned in at the familiar white mailbox and pulled up at the door.

'My car keys are in the house,' Hubble said.

'It's open,' I said.

He went to check it out. Pushed at the splintered door gingerly, with one finger, like it might be booby-trapped. I saw him go in. A minute later, he was back out with his keys. It was a hell of a mess in there. His eyes were wide open, but he wasn't seeing me. He was seeing what he'd seen in his nightmares. He didn't speak. Just ducked into the garage. I was left sitting there wondering how the hell I'd ever hated the guy a week ago.

I reloaded the Desert Eagle. Then I saw Hubble drive his old green Bentley around from the garage. He gave me a thumbs-up as he passed and I followed him down the driveway and up Beckman. Two fine old cars, nose to tail through the sleeping town, ready to do battle.

Hubble pulled up forty yards shy of the station house. Killed his lights and waited, motor running. I wafted past him and nosed into the police department lot. Pulled the big automatic out of my pocket. Ran to the station house wall and dropped to the ground.

Watched and listened long enough to be sure.

I stood up and waved a signal to Hubble. I saw his car pull away from the kerb and I ran over to the fire house entrance. Stood to the side of the big red door and waited.

Hubble drove up and slewed his old Bentley in a tight turn. Ended up at a right angle, just about lined up with the fire house entrance, facing away from me. He slammed the shift into reverse. Then he hit the gas and the big old sedan shot backward toward me and smashed into the fire house door. That old Bentley must have weighed two tons and it tore the metal door right off its mountings with a tremendous crash. I was through the gap between the door and the frame before Hubble could drive clear of the wreckage. It was dark in there, but I found what I was looking for clipped to the side of the fire truck. A huge bolt cutter, must have been four feet long. I wrenched it out of its mountings and ran for the door.

Soon as Hubble saw me come out, he pulled a wide circle across the road and lined up with the station house entrance. Paused for a second and floored the gas. Accelerated straight toward the heavy glass doors. This time head on. The Bentley smashed through the doors in a shower of glass and demolished the reception desk. Ploughed on into the squad room and stopped. I ran in right behind it. Finlay was standing in the middle cell. Frozen in shock.

Hubble spun the wheel and reversed. I hauled and shoved the squad room desks out the way to give him a clear run in front. Turned and gave him the signal.

The car shot forward and smashed into the titanium bars at an angle, ripping them open. Came to a stop a yard short of where Finlay was standing and settled in a loud hiss of steam.

I dived through the gap into the cell and clamped the bolt cutter on the link fixing Finlay's wrist to the bars. Leaned on the four-foot levers until the handcuffs sheared through. I gave Finlay the bolt cutter and hauled him through the gap and out of the cell. Hubble climbed out of the Bentley and we all three crunched over the shards of plate glass where the big doors had been to Charlie's Bentley. I started it up and we took off down the road.

I slowed down at the north end of Main Street and rolled gently south through the sleeping town. Hubble was lying in the rear, shaken up. Finlay was beside me in the passenger seat. The clock on the dash showed one in the morning. I wanted to hole up until four and I knew just the place.

I pulled up in the dark behind the barbershop. Killed the motor. Finlay glanced around and shrugged. Going to the barber at one in the morning was no more crazy than driving a hundred-thousand-dollar Bentley into a station house.

'Good job, Reacher,' he said. 'I was wondering how the hell you were going to get me out. What happened to Picard?'

I made a gun with my fingers, like a child's mime. He nodded a sort of partner's nod to me. Then we all got out the car and I rapped softly on the service door at the back of the barbershop. It opened up straight away. The older guy was standing there like he'd been waiting for us. He gestured us down a passage into a storeroom.

'We need your help,' I said. I explained that we needed to hide up for a while.

The old guy held up his palm in a wait gesture. Shuffled through to the front and came back with his partner. The younger old guy. 'Upstairs,' the younger guy said.

We filed up a narrow staircase. Came out in an apartment above the shop. The barber showed us through to the living room, pulled the blinds and switched on a couple of lamps. Waved us to sit. The room was small and threadbare, but clean. It had a cosy feel. The four of us sat down and the barber leaned forward.

'Local trouble?' he asked.

'Big trouble,' Finlay said. 'Big changes coming.'

'Been expecting it,' the old guy said.

'You have?' Finlay said.

The barber nodded and stood up. Stepped over to a large closet. Opened the door and waved us over to take a look. The shelves were stacked with bricks of cash held together with rubber bands. Must have been a couple of hundred thousand dollars in there.

'Kliner Foundation's money,' the old guy said. 'Something wrong with it. I'm seventy-four years old. Seventy years, people are treating me like dirt. Now people are throwing money all over me. Something wrong with that, right?' He closed the door on the cash. 'We don't spend a cent we don't earn. You boys going after the Kliner Foundation?'

'Tomorrow there won't be any Kliner Foundation,' I said.

The old guy just nodded. Closed the door on us and left us alone in the small cosy room.

'Not going to be easy,' Finlay said. 'Three of us and three of them. They hold four hostages. Two of the hostages are children.

We're not even certain where they're holding them.'

'They're at the warehouse,' I said. 'Where else would they be? No manpower available to hold them anyplace else.'

Hubble knew the warehouse well. So we got him to draw plans of its layout, putting in all the doors, the stairs, the distances, the details. We ended up with the sort of drawing an architect would have been proud of.

'I'm worried about guards on the exterior,' Finlay said.

'I'm more worried about the shotguns,' I said. 'It's a big space. And there are two kids in there.'

Finlay looked grim. He knew what I was saying. Shotguns spray a cone of lead over a big wide angle. We went quiet. It was nearly two in the morning. An hour and a half to wait. We would leave at three thirty. Get up there at four. That's when the human body is at its lowest ebb, and so our enemies would be off guard.

WE PILED BACK into Charlie's Bentley. I fired it up, kept the lights off and drove slow. 'I want to get a weapon,' Finlay said.

At the station house, we picked our way through the shattered wreckage of the entrance. Hubble's smashed-up Bentley was sitting in the squad room, inert in the gloom.

Finlay picked his way past the wrecked car to the big office in back. Disappeared inside. I waited with Hubble in the heap of shards that had been the entrance doors. Finlay came back out of the dark with a stainless-steel revolver and a book of matches.

I drove fast the rest of the fourteen miles. Pulled up a quarter-mile short of the target. Turned around in the road and left the car facing toward town. Doors unlocked. Keys in.

I reached under the seat and pulled out the plastic bottle we'd filled with gas. Slipped it into my pocket with the blackjack. It was heavy. Finlay gave me the matches. I put them in the other pocket.

We stood together at the side of the road. Exchanged tight nods. Struck out over the field and headed for the tree near the back of the warehouse. I took the bolt cutter from Hubble and we kept on going until we were opposite the bottom of the fire escape. Finlay and Hubble grabbed the chain-link perimeter fence to put some tension on it and I bit through each strand in turn with the cutter. Went through it like it was liquorice. I cut a big piece out and we stepped through the gap. Walked over to the bottom of the stairs. Waited. I motioned the others to flatten themselves against the metal siding. I still wasn't sure about exterior guards. My gut said there wouldn't be any reinforcements. But just in case, I motioned the others to stay put and crept around to the corner of the massive building. Crouched down and dropped the bolt cutter from a height of about a foot onto the concrete path. It sounded like somebody trying to break into the compound. I flattened myself against the wall and waited with the blackjack in my right hand.

Finlay was right. There was a guard patrolling outside the shed. Sergeant Baker. I heard his tense breathing and his feet on the concrete. He came around the corner of the building and stopped a yard away from me, a .38 in his hand. He looked at the bolt cutter and then swung his gaze along the fence as far as the missing panel.

I swung the sap and hit him. He dropped his revolver and went down. I waited five minutes. Listened hard. Nobody else came.

I went back to where the others were waiting, took a deep breath and stepped onto the fire escape. Eased my way up silently. Finlay and Hubble were behind me.

We stood on the little platform at the top. Hubble pulled out his office keys, clenched in his hand to stop them jingling. He selected the right one, slowly, carefully. Inched it into the lock. We held our breath. He turned the key. The lock clicked back. The door sagged open. No reaction. Quiet. Hubble eased the door back and propped it open with the bottle of gasoline from my pocket.

Light was flooding out of the office, spilling over the fire escape and laying a bright bar down onto the field forty feet below. Arc lamps were lit inside the body of the warehouse and they were flooding in through the big office windows. I could see everything in the office. And I saw I was lucky in a big way.

Because the children were asleep on the office floor. Hubble's kids. Ben and Lucy. Sprawled out on a pile of empty burlap sacks. Fast asleep, wide open and innocent like only sleeping children can be.

I turned to the other two. 'Hubble, take the girl,' I whispered. 'Finlay, take the boy. Put a hand over their mouths. No sound at all. Carry them back to the tree. Hubble, take them on back to the car. Wait there with them. Finlay, come back here.'

I pulled out the Desert Eagle and clicked the safety off. Clamped my wrist against the doorframe and aimed across the office at the inner door. Finlay and Hubble did it right. They clamped their palms over the little mouths. Scooped the children up. Crept back down the fire escape to the ground and vanished into the night.

I lowered the gun. Listened hard. Heard nothing but faint scraping noises from the huge metal shed. I crawled over the floor to the internal windows. Slowly raised my head up and looked down. Saw a sight I would never forget.

There were a hundred arc lights bolted up inside the roof of the vast warehouse. They lit the place up brighter than day. Kliner's black pick-up truck was just inside the roller door. Next to it was Teale's white Cadillac. Both were big automobiles. But they were nothing next to the cash. It was awesome. A gigantic dune of dollar bills piled maybe fifty feet high into the back corner. I was looking at forty million dollars in singles. Higher than a house. Higher than two houses. It was incredible.

Two tiny figures forty feet below me were moving like exhausted troopers at the end of some cruel manoeuvre. Roscoe and Charlie. They were packing armful after armful of dollars from the gigantic stockpile into the boxes. It was a hopeless task. Teale and Kliner sat watching them like overseers, both with shotguns on their knees. Teale was at the far end of the shed, sitting on the lower slope of the mountain, maybe ten feet up. Closer to me, I saw old man Kliner. Sitting higher up on the slope. Sitting on forty tons of money.

I heard the faint clang of Finlay's feet on the fire escape. I crawled back out of the office and met him on the metal platform outside. 'They're back at the car,' he whispered to me. 'How we doing here?'

'Two shotguns out and ready,' I whispered.

It was a hell of a problem. If I walked out to the top of those stairs, Teale would fire, catching the women in the shotgun's murderous spray. But I had an idea. Bent down and picked up the plastic bottle of gasoline. Handed it to Finlay with the matches. Leaned close and told him what to do. He set off slowly back down the metal steps. I crawled through the office and laid the Desert Eagle carefully on the floor by the inner door. Safety off. Crawled back under the window. Eased my head up and waited.

Three minutes went by. I was staring at the roller door. Staring and waiting. Four minutes had gone by. The tiny figures below toiled on. Roscoe and Charlie stuffing boxes, under Teale's careful gaze. Kliner put down his gun and clambered his way over the mountainside to kick a new river of dollars down the slope toward the women. Five minutes had gone by. Six. Seven.

Then I saw the dark wet stain of gasoline seeping under the roller door. It flowed into a semicircular pool at the bottom of the enormous dune of dollars, ten feet below where Teale was sprawled on the lower slopes. Then I saw the flame race in under the door and bloom out over the wide stain like a flower opening. Teale snapped his head around and stared at it, frozen in horror.

I stepped to the door, eased it open and squeezed out. Aimed the gun. Braced my wrist against the balcony railing. Pulled the trigger and blew Teale's head off, a hundred feet away.

Then everything went wrong. I saw it happen in that terrible slow motion you get when your mind is racing faster than you can move. My gun hand was drifting left to track Kliner on his way back to his own weapon. But Kliner dived to the right. In a desperate leap he launched himself down the mountainside to the spot where Teale had dropped his shotgun. He wasn't going back for his own gun. He was going to use Teale's. And Roscoe and Charlie were between him and me, right in his line of fire. Then I heard the crash of the staff door bursting open below and to my amazement I saw Picard stagger onto the warehouse floor.

His jacket was gone and blood was soaking his enormous white shirt. I saw his head turn and his right arm swing upward to point at me. I saw his .38 in his hand. A hundred feet from him I saw Kliner reach Teale's shotgun where it had buried itself in the cash pile. I saw the blue flames bursting upward at the bottom of the huge dune of dollars. I saw Roscoe turn to look up at me. I saw Charlie Hubble turn the other way to look at Teale. I saw her scream.

I swung my gun hand down and fired, and hit Picard's shoulder a tiny fraction before his .38 came to rest on me. I saw him hit the floor as I hauled my aim back over to Kliner.

My mind was detached. Just treating it like a purely mechanical problem. I computed that my bullet would take a hair over seven hundredths of a second to cover the length of the warehouse and that I should aim high up on Kliner's right side to avoid the women.

After that, my brain just shut down. Handed me that information and sat back to mock my attempt to haul my arm up faster than Kliner could haul up the barrel of his gun. His yellow teeth were parting in a wolfish smile. It was a race in agonising slow motion.

My arm got there first. I fired and hit Kliner in the upper chest and the huge .44 slug hurled him off his feet. His shotgun boomed and fired point-blank into the enormous mountain of money. The air was instantly thick with fragments of dollar bills, which swirled like a thick blizzard and burst into flames as they settled into the fire.

I raced down the stairs to the warehouse floor. Flames were ripping through the mountain faster than a man could run. I fought through the smoke and caught Roscoe under one arm and Charlie under the other. Spun them off their feet and dragged them with me toward the staircase.

I ran straight into Picard. He reared up off the floor in front of me and sent me sprawling. He stood there like a wounded giant, his shattered right shoulder pumping blood. As I staggered up off the floor he hit me with his left hand and sent the Desert Eagle clattering over the concrete. The fire was billowing around us, my lungs were burning and I could hear Charlie Hubble screaming hysterically. Picard was swinging his massive left arm back ready for another blow. I threw myself inside the swing and hit him hard in the throat with my elbow. But he just shook himself and stepped nearer. Swung his enormous left fist and knocked me sideways into the fire.

I was breathing pure smoke as I rolled out. Picard stepped nearer, leaned forward and kicked me in the chest. It was like being hit by a truck. Then his body started jerking like somebody was behind him, hitting him with a hammer. I saw Finlay standing there with his revolver. He fired six shots into Picard's back. The agent's legs crumpled and he hit the floor.

Finlay grabbed Charlie and raced away through the flames. I hauled Roscoe off the floor and dragged her up the stairs and out through the office. Out and down the fire escape as the flames boiled out through the door after us. We hurled ourselves through the gap in the fence and ran across the field.

Behind us the superheated air blew the roof off the shed and flames burst a hundred feet into the sky. All around us burning fragments of dollar bills were drifting down. I could feel the heat on my back and Roscoe was beating away the flaming paper that was landing on us. We raced for the tree. Didn't stop. Raced on to the road. Behind me I could hear screeching and tearing as the metal shed distorted and burst. Up ahead Hubble was standing next to the Bentley. He flung open the rear doors and raced for the driver's seat.

The four of us crammed into the back, the children were in the front. Hubble stamped on the gas. The car shot forward and the doors slammed shut. He blasted a mile down the road. Then he jammed to a stop and we untangled ourselves and clambered out of the car. Hugged and kissed and cried, staggering about at the side of the old county road. The four Hubbles clung together. Roscoe and

Finlay and I clung together. Then Finlay was dancing around, yelling and laughing like a madman. Roscoe was huddled in my arms. I was watching the fire spreading to the farmers' sheds next in line. Bags of nitrogen fertiliser and drums of tractor oil were exploding like bombs.

We all turned to watch the inferno and the explosions. Seven of us, in a ragged line on the road. It looked like hell on earth.

'Did we do that?' asked Finlay.

'You did that, Finlay,' I said. 'You dropped the match.'

We laughed and hugged. We slapped each other's backs. Then I lifted Roscoe off her feet and kissed her long and hard.

TEN

It was five o'clock Sunday morning when we stumbled into Roscoe's house. We were both exhausted. But the adrenaline was still boiling through us. We couldn't sleep. Instead, we talked.

Roscoe had been a prisoner the best part of sixty-four hours. In fear of her life, in danger, exhausted and humiliated for three long days. They'd worked her and Charlie Hubble like slaves. The two of them had slept just a few hours a night, lying down on the dune of dollars, handcuffed to the bottom of the office stairs.

Saturday morning, when his son and the two gatemen hadn't come back, Kliner had gone crazy. Now he had no staff at all. So he worked the hostages around the clock. They didn't sleep at all Saturday night. Just ploughed on with the hopeless task of trying to box up the huge pile. Every time an incoming truck spilled a new load out on the warehouse floor, Kliner had become more frantic.

Roscoe and I showered together in her tiny stall, soaping off the stink of the money and the sweat and the fire. And we were still talking. I was telling her about Friday night. The ambush in the storm up at Hubble's place. I told her what I'd done to the five of them. I thought she'd be happy about it.

That was the first faint sign of a problem between us. Not a big deal as we stood there with the hot water beating down on us. But I heard something in her voice. Just a tiny tremor. Not shock or disapproval. Just a hint of a question. That maybe I had gone too far.

I felt somehow I'd done it all for her and Joe. Not because I had wanted to do it. At the same time as feeling I needed no justification at all, I had been justifying it to myself like that.

It didn't feel like a problem at the time. We went to bed. Left the drapes open. It was a glorious day. The sun was up in a bright blue sky. We made love with great tenderness, great energy, great joy. If somebody had told me then that I'd be back on the road the next morning, I'd have thought they were crazy. I fell asleep certain we'd wake up happy and I'd stay there for ever.

WE DID WAKE UP HAPPY. We slept through until late afternoon. Then we spent a gorgeous couple of hours with the afternoon sun streaming in the window, dozing, kissing and laughing. Later, Roscoe took the Bentley up to Eno's for some food.

She came back with news. She'd seen Finlay. She put the food on a tray and we ate it sitting on the bed. 'All four warehouses burned down,' she said. 'There was debris exploding all over the highway. The state police got involved. They had to get fire trucks all the way from Atlanta.' She laughed. 'It sort of snowballed. The Atlanta fire chief called in the bomb squad because of the explosions. The bomb squad can't go anywhere without notifying the FBI, in case it's terrorism. Then the National Guard got involved this morning.'

'The National Guard?' I said. 'Why?'

'This is the best part,' she said. 'When the roof blew off the warehouse last night, the sudden updraught of air blew the money all over the place. There are millions of dollar bills for miles around. In the fields, all over the highway. Most of them are partially burned, of course, but some aren't. Soon as the sun came up, thousands of people swarmed around, picking all the money up. So the National Guard was ordered in to disperse the crowds. And the Treasury Department is sending a team down.'

'What the hell else?' I said.

'Big problems here, of course,' she said. 'Rumours are flying around. Everybody seems to know the Foundation is finished. Finlay says half of them are pretending they never knew what was going on, and the other half are mad as hell their thousand dollars a week is going to stop.'

'Finlay worried?' I said.

'He's OK,' she said. 'Busy, of course. We're down to a four-person police department. Finlay, me, Stevenson and the desk man. But there's nothing anybody can do about rebuilding the station house or hiring new staff without the mayor's approval, and we haven't got a mayor any more, have we?'

I sat there on the bed, eating. The problems started bearing down on me. I hadn't really seen them clearly before. But I was seeing them now. A huge question was forming in my mind. A question I wanted to ask straight away.

'Roscoe?' I said.

She looked up at me. Waited.

'What are you going to do?' I asked her.

She looked at me like it was an odd question. 'Work my butt off, I guess,' she said. 'There's going to be a lot to do. We're going to have to rebuild this whole town. Maybe we can make something better out of it, create something worthwhile. And I can play a big part in it. Maybe I'll get on the town board. Maybe I'll even run for mayor. That would be a hell of a thing, wouldn't it?'

I looked at her. It was a great answer. This was her town. If anybody could fix it, she could. If anybody should stick around, working her butt off, she should. But it was the wrong answer for me. Because I knew then I had to go. The whole thing had got out of hand. Before, it had all been about Joe. It had been private. Now it was public. It was like those half-burnt dollar bills. It was scattered all over the damn place.

Roscoe had mentioned the Treasury Department, the National Guard, the state police, the FBI, Atlanta fire investigators. A half-dozen agencies, all looking at what had gone on in Margrave. All competing like mad to get a result. They'd tear the place apart.

And one or other of them would snarl me up. I was a stranger in the wrong place at the wrong time. It would take about a minute and a half to realise I was the brother of the dead government investigator who had started the whole thing off. Somebody would think: Revenge. I would be hauled in, and they would go to work on me.

I wouldn't be convicted. There was no risk of that. There was no evidence hanging around. I'd been careful every step of the way. And I knew how to stonewall. They could talk to me until I grew a long white beard and they wouldn't get anything from me. But they'd try. They'd try like crazy. They'd keep me two years in Warburton. Two years up there on the holding floor. That was the problem. No way could I stand still for that. I'd only just got my life back. I'd had six months of freedom in thirty-six years. Those six months had been the happiest months I'd ever had.

So I was getting out. Before any of them ever knew I'd been there in the first place. My mind was made up. But it meant my dreams of a future with Roscoe were going to be snuffed out before they were even started.

We talked about it all night. She knew what I was going to do was right for me. I knew what she was going to do was right for her. She asked me to stay. I thought hard, but said no. I asked her to come with me. She thought hard, but said no. Nothing more to say.

AT SEVEN IN THE MORNING I climbed into the back of the Bentley, behind the new black glass. I didn't want anybody to see me. Roscoe drove up the rise from her place and threaded through traffic. The place was swarming. Main Street was parked solid. There were vehicles up on the sidewalks. Television trucks from the networks and CNN. I saw fire chiefs' cars and state police cruisers. I glanced into the barbershop as we crawled past, but the old guys weren't there. I would miss them. I would miss Finlay. I would always wonder how things turned out for him. Good luck, Harvard guy, I thought. Good luck, too, to the Hubbles. This morning was the start of a long road for them. Good luck, too, to Roscoe. I sat there, silently wishing her the best of everything. She deserved it. She really did.

She drove me all the way south to Macon. She found the bus depot. Parked up. Handed me a small envelope. Told me not to open it right away. I put it in my pocket. Kissed her goodbye. Got out of the car. Didn't look back. I heard the sound of the big tyres on the pavement and I knew she was gone.

I strolled into the depot, bought a ticket and got on a bus to California. I had tears in my eyes for more than a hundred miles. Then the old bus rattled over the state line. I looked out at the southeast corner of Alabama. Opened Roscoe's envelope. It was the photograph of Joe. She'd taken it from Molly Beth's valise. On the back she had written her telephone number. But I didn't need that. I had already committed it to memory.

LEE CHILD

Hollywood moguls have recently been battling for exclusive film rights to *Killing Floor*, a block-buster novel penned by an unknown writer from Kirkby Lonsdale in the Lake District.

Asked why he chose an American setting for his first book, the newly famous Lee Child draws an analogy with basketball. 'If I wanted to be a basketball player, I'd always be second best if I stayed in Europe. I would need to go to the NBA in America to find out if I was really any good. It's the same with hard-boiled, tough-guy fiction, which is my favourite kind. You have to find the hardest league in the world, and then get in there and compete.'

Having an American wife of twenty-three years—they met at Sheffield University—has helped: it has meant numerous trips to New York and Chicago to visit relatives which, the author says, 'have added up to a lot of exposure to American culture'. The second thing that worked in his favour was his twenty-year career as a transmission controller for Granada TV. 'Behind the scenes, I dealt with some 40,000 hours of commercial television. It teaches you an absolutely instinctive grasp of the rhythm and pace of popular entertainment. Also, because nearly a fifth of ITV's output is American, you learn it like a second language.'

The catalyst that finally prompted the author to put pen to paper was redundancy, two years ago. 'When you consider I was staring down the barrel of £43.50 a week on the dole, the success of *Killing Floor* is a dream come true. I always felt I could write a successful book, but unless I really needed to do it, I would not have given it one hundred per cent. Redundancy supplied the extra motivation. It was the best thing that ever happened to me.'

THE
SHADOWY
HORSES

SUSANNA KEARSLEY

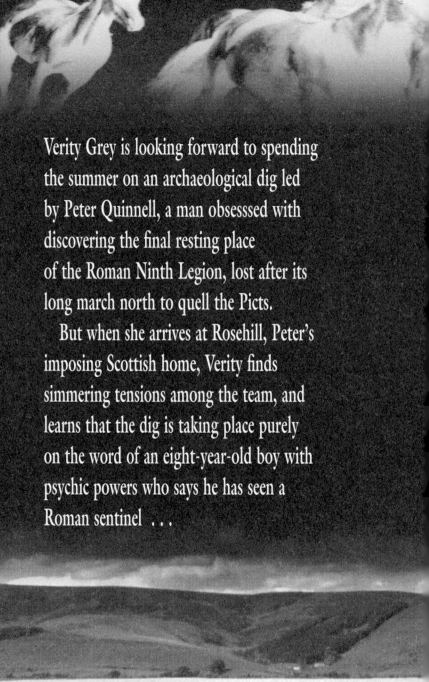

Verity Grey is looking forward to spending
the summer on an archaeological dig led
by Peter Quinnell, a man obsesssed with
discovering the final resting place
of the Roman Ninth Legion, lost after its
long march north to quell the Picts.

But when she arrives at Rosehill, Peter's
imposing Scottish home, Verity finds
simmering tensions among the team, and
learns that the dig is taking place purely
on the word of an eight-year-old boy with
psychic powers who says he has seen a
Roman sentinel . . .

ONE

The bus had no business stopping where it did. We should have gone straight on across the Coldingham Moor, with Dunbar to the back of us and the English border drawing ever nearer, but instead we stopped, and the shaggy-faced cattle that lifted their heads on the far side of the fence appeared to share my surprise when the driver cut the engine to an idle.

A fierce blast of wind rocked the little ten-seater bus on its tyres and drove a splattering of cold spring rain against the driver's windscreen as he shook out a well-thumbed newspaper and settled back. Curious, I shifted in my seat to peer out of my own fogging window.

There seemed, at first glance, nothing to stop for, only the cattle and a few uninterested sheep, picking their way across a ragged landscape that was turning green reluctantly. Beyond the moor, lost somewhere in the impenetrable mist, rose the wild, romantic Lammermuir Hills I'd read about as a child. In the opposite direction, the cold North Sea bit deep into the coastal line of cliffs. I sighed, and watched my breath condense upon the window glass.

Impulsiveness, my mother always said, was one of my worst flaws. After twenty-nine years I'd grown accustomed to her heavy sighs and shaking head, but now, as I squinted out at the bleak, unwelcoming scenery, I grudgingly admitted that she had a point. It had been impulse, after all, that had brought me from my London flat to Scotland in the first place. Impulse, and the slick, persuasive writing style of Adrian Sutton-Clarke. He knew me too well, and he had phrased his summons craftily—with his promise of 'the perfect job' set like a jewel at the centre of a long letter that was so full of hints of grand adventure that I couldn't possibly resist it. And if today was anything to go by, Adrian hadn't been lying about the adventure.

Not that one could really blame British Rail for what had happened. My train had certainly set out from King's Cross speedily enough, and it was only north of Darlington that it had begun to show signs of weariness, creaking and rolling from side to side in a rocking motion that lulled me instantly to sleep. I had stayed sleeping right through Durham, then Newcastle, and finally Berwick-upon-Tweed, where I was meant to get off. When the train lurched to a stop at Dunbar, I'd scrambled down onto the platform where the stationmaster had informed me helpfully, 'There'll not be another train to Berwick now till seven twenty-three.'

Nearly an hour and a half to wait. 'I don't suppose there's a bus?'

'To Berwick? Aye, there is, at six twenty-five. Just round the corner, there, and up the road a ways—that's where it stops.'

And so I'd wrestled my suitcase round the corner and up the road to the small bus shelter, my spirits lifting somewhat as I read the posted timetable telling me the bus to Berwick travelled via Cockburnspath, Coldingham and Eyemouth.

Eyemouth, Adrian had written in his letter, *pronounced as it looks. You'd love it here, a real old-fashioned fishing town with smugglers' ghosts round every corner and the added lure of . . . but no, I shan't give the secret away. You'll just have to come and find out for yourself.*

I'd have been only too happy to oblige, I thought wryly, but for the fact that I was now stuck in the middle of Coldingham Moor. There seemed little point in questioning the stop; apart from a couple of lovestruck kids fondling each other at the rear of the bus, I was the only passenger. Still, my curiosity had almost reached breaking point when the driver finally folded his paper with a decisive rattle and pulled on the lever to open the door.

A man was coming across the moor.

It might have been the wild weather, or the rough and rolling landscape that, like all the Scottish Borderlands, held traces of the harsh and violent past—the echoed din of charging hoofs, of chilling battle cries and clashing broadswords. Whatever it was, it tricked my senses. The man looked enormous, a great dark giant from a bygone age, a fearless border laird who moved over bracken and thorn with an effortless stride.

The illusion only lasted a moment as the stranger jogged the final few steps to the bus door. No Border laird, just a rather ordinary-looking man in his mid-thirties, fit and broad-shouldered and thoroughly modern in jeans and a leather jacket. Well, I amended as he smoothed back his curling black hair and grinned at the bus driver, maybe not *exactly* ordinary-looking . . .

'Heyah,' he greeted the driver, swinging himself up the final step. 'Saw me coming, did you?'

'Aye, well, ye do stick out, lad. Thought I might as well wait for ye, save ye the walk back.' The doors swung shut and the bus sprang forward once again as the new passenger dropped into the seat across from me. He and the driver chatted on like old friends, which I supposed they were, about the weather, and the latest rebellion of the bus driver's daughter, and the health of the younger man's mother. It had been some years since I'd spent time in Scotland, and I'd forgotten just how musical the accent was.

The bus rattled noisily over the moor, dipped into Coldingham town and stopped to let off the teenagers. Shifting round in his seat, the bus driver asked 'You're for Eyemouth, lass, aren't ye?'

'Yes, that's right.'

The man from the moor lifted an eyebrow at my accent and glanced over. I sent him a friendly smile.

The bus driver carried on speaking, over his shoulder. 'Are ye up here on holiday?'

Having received little response from the man opposite, I turned my smile on the driver instead. 'Interviewing for a job, actually.'

'Oh, aye. What kind of job?'

Well, that was just the question, wasn't it? I didn't really know, myself. 'Museum work, of sorts,' I hedged. 'I'm interviewing with a man just outside Eyemouth . . .'

The man from the moor cut me off. 'Not Peter Quinnell, surely?'

'Well, yes, but . . .'

'You don't mean to say you're Adrian's wee friend from London?' He did smile then, and the simple act transformed his rugged face. 'We'd not expected you till tomorrow. David Fortune.' He held out his hand. 'I work with Quinnell as well.'

I shook his hand. 'Verity Grey.'

'Aye, I ken fine who you are. I must say,' he confessed, leaning back again, 'you're not at all as I pictured you.'

Everyone said that. Museum workers were supposed to be little

old ladies in spectacles, not twenty-nine-year-olds in short skirts.
'I'm younger, you mean?'

'No. It's only that, with Adrian recommending you, I'd have
thought to find someone . . . well, someone . . .'

'Tall, blonde and beautiful?'

'Something like that.'

I couldn't help smiling. I was, to my knowledge, the only dark-
haired woman who'd ever received so much as a dinner invitation
from Adrian Sutton-Clarke, and I'd only held his interest until the
next blonde came along. But while our romance had proved temporary, our paths, by virtue of our work, kept crossing and recrossing;
and when one wasn't actually in love with the man, he could be a
quite enjoyable companion. Adrian, at least, understood the restless,
independent streak that had made me chuck my British Museum job
and strike out on my own to freelance. He'd learned I never could
resist a challenge.

I studied the man across from me with interest. I had already
assumed that the job for which I was being interviewed involved
some sort of archaeological dig, since Adrian was one of the best
surveyors in the business. I glanced at David Fortune's hands, and
ventured to test my theory. 'How large is the excavation, then?' I
asked him. 'How many field-crew members are on site?'

'Just the four of us, at the moment.' He looked down, at my single
suitcase. 'You've just come up from London, then?'

'Yes. I'm a day early, I know, but the job did sound intriguing and
I really couldn't see the point in waiting down in London when I
could be waiting here, if you know what I mean . . .'

His eyes held understanding. 'Aye. I wouldn't worry. Quinnell's an
impatient man himself.'

The sea was close beside us now. I could see the choppy froth of
waves beyond the thinning wall of mist, and the jutting silhouettes of
jagged rocks. The rain had stopped. Between the racing clouds a
sudden gleam of sunlight flashed, stretching a searching finger out
to touch the clustered houses curving round the coast ahead of us.

The town of Eyemouth looked like a postcard fishing village, its
buildings tumbling in a tight cascade down to the sea wall while a
gathering of gulls wheeled and dipped above the harbour.

I leaned forward as the bus dived in among the houses. 'Where
would you recommend I stay?' I asked my new acquaintance.

'You'll not be staying in the town?' He raised his eyebrows, clearly shocked. 'Quinnell wouldn't hear of it. He's had a room made up for you at Rosehill, at the house.'

I stared at him. 'Oh, but I couldn't . . .'

He smiled. 'Don't worry. They're all nice people out at Rosehill. They'll make you feel at home, and Quinnell loves company.'

'I'm sure he does. But if he doesn't hire me, it might prove rather awkward.'

'Oh, he'll hire you,' said David Fortune, with a nod of certainty. 'That is, he'll offer you the job. Whether you accept or not, well . . . that's for you to say.'

Something in the offhand way he said that made me tilt my head, suspicious. 'Why wouldn't I accept?'

'Have you eaten yet?' he asked, as if I hadn't spoken. 'You haven't, have you? And it's Thursday night—Jeannie's night off. There'll be no supper on at the house.' He turned to the bus driver, who was following our exchange with interest. 'Danny, do us a favour, will you, and drop us at the harbour road.'

'The Ship Hotel?' The driver glanced at me. 'Aye, no trouble. It wouldnae do for the lass to face old Quinnell on an empty stomach.'

My suspicions growing, I slowly turned to look at David Fortune as the bus came to a halt, but his expression was charmingly innocent. Gathering up my suitcase, I tossed a word of thanks to the driver and clambered down the steps to solid ground.

The wind struck me like a body blow and might have knocked me over if the man at my side hadn't taken the suitcase from me, placing a large hand at my back to guide me up along the harbour's edge. The tide was very high, and the fishing boats creaked at their moorings, masts and rigging swaying with the motion of the water.

David Fortune steered me into the hotel's dining lounge and I felt instantly warmer, out of the wind. Round wooden tables hugged the wainscoting and nestled in padded alcoves that enticed one to sit and relax. My companion plucked a menu from the bar and chose a table for us in a window alcove. 'Order what you like, the bill's on Quinnell,' he told me. 'He'd not want to see you starve.'

The mention of Peter Quinnell's name brought my earlier misgivings sharply into focus. 'Listen,' I began, frowning slightly, 'there isn't anything *wrong* with the job, is there?'

He raised his eyebrows, but before he could respond the barmaid came through from the other side and sent us a welcoming smile. 'Heyah, Davy. What can I get you?'

He looked at me, eyes enquiring.

'Dry white wine, please.'

'And a pint of Deuchars for me, there's a love. Is Adrian about?'

'Upstairs, I think. Do you want me to fetch him?'

'Aye, if you would.'

As the barmaid departed, I gave in to curiosity. 'Adrian's upstairs?'

'Oh, aye. There's just the one spare room at Rosehill, and Quinnell wanted to save that for you, so he's put us both up here instead.'

Our drinks arrived. I watched him down a mouthful of the dark foaming beer, and frowned again. 'Isn't that rather inconvenient?'

He shook his head. 'It's only a mile out to the house. I like the walk.'

I tried to imagine Adrian Sutton-Clarke walking a country mile to work each morning and failed. Adrian, I knew, would use his car.

A door from the corridor opened and a tall, lean-faced man with mahogany hair came, smiling, towards us. 'Verity, my dear, you really must learn some respect for schedules,' he teased me, bending down to brush my cheek with an affectionate kiss. 'Friday, last I checked, comes after Thursday, and you did say Friday.'

'Hello, Adrian.' It always took me a moment to adjust to the sheer impact of his handsome face, even now. I kept hoping, rather foolishly, that he might have chipped one of his teeth, or that his dark, long-lashed eyes would be puffy and bloodshot, but each time he turned up just as perfect as ever, a six-foot-two package of pure sex appeal, and invariably knocked me off-centre. Only for a moment, and then memory reasserted itself and I was fine.

David Fortune had misinterpreted the involuntary change in my expression. He drained his pint and rose politely. 'Look, I'll leave you to it, shall I? I could do with a shower. See you both tomorrow.' Slanting a brief look down at me, he stabbed the menu with a knowing finger. 'Try the lemon sole, it's magic.'

Adrian slid into the now vacant seat opposite. 'Just how,' he asked me, 'did you come to meet Fortune?'

'We were on the same bus. We got talking.'

'Ah.' He nodded. 'The bus from Berwick.'

'Dunbar, actually.'

The waitress came. I closed my menu and ordered the lemon sole.

'I know I'm going to regret asking this,' Adrian said. 'But how did you end up on a Berwickshire bus from Dunbar?'

I explained. It took some time, and I was nearly finished with my meal by the time I'd told him everything.

'So tell me,' I asked, balancing my knife and fork on my empty plate, 'what exactly is this job you've recommended me for?'

'I'm sure Quinnell will be happy to tell you anything you want to know. So let's get you out to Rosehill so you can meet him.'

Ten minutes later, seated in his sleek red Jaguar and speeding inland from the harbour, I tried again. 'The least you can do,' I said evenly, 'is tell me what's wrong with the job.'

He flashed me a quick sideways glance, eyebrows raised. 'Nothing's wrong with the job. It's a great opportunity, wonderful benefits—Quinnell's a wealthy man, so the pay is obscene. And you get room and board with it. It's a marvellous job.'

'You're certain of that?'

'Hell, yes. Why the sudden lack of trust?'

I shrugged. 'Just something your Mr Fortune said, in passing. He was sure that I'd be offered the job, but wasn't so sure I'd accept.'

Adrian digested this thoughtfully. 'I suppose,' he said slowly, 'that he might have been thinking of how you'd react to Quinnell himself. Peter is a fascinating old character—well read, intelligent, one of a kind.' He turned his head so I could see the half-apologetic smile. 'But I'm afraid that he's also quite mad. Anyway, you'll be able to judge for yourself, in a minute. That's Rosehill up ahead.'

I looked, but only saw a tiny cottage set practically at the road's edge, its windows blazing with warmth and light. 'What, *that*?'

'No. That is the groundskeeper's cottage. The drive runs up from there right up the hill to that *big* house, there in the trees . . .'

It didn't look a house at all, to begin with—just a looming block of darkness screened by darker, twisted trees, but then the wind blew and the branches shifted and I saw a twinkling gleam of yellow light. I frowned. 'It looks as if he's gone to bed.'

'At nine o'clock? Not likely. No, I'd be willing to bet that since it's the cook's night off our Fabia's gone out somewhere to have supper, while the old man makes do with egg and chips in his study.'

'Fabia?'

'Quinnell's twenty-year-old granddaughter. Quite fetching. Blonde.'

'Ah.'

He drew up and killed the engine, shifting round to face me. 'Really, Verity, your lack of trust in me is quite appalling. Whatever did I do to deserve this?'

It was my turn to smile. 'You want a list?'

'Ooh,' he inhaled, feigning pain, 'a fatal blow. My ego doesn't stand a chance when you're around, does it? Still,' he conceded, 'I am glad we're going to be working together again.'

'Yes, well,' I said, 'I haven't got the job yet.' I pushed open my door. Without the benefit of light, I couldn't see the house in any detail. I had to rely on Adrian to lead me up a flight of stone steps to the front door. He knocked on it, and after what seemed an age I heard the bolt slide back and watched the door swing heavily inwards. An elegant curse, a sharp click, and the hallway beyond exploded into brilliant light.

It was fitting, I suppose, that in the instant I first saw Peter Quinnell my eyes were dazzled. I tried desperately to focus on the tall black figure in the sudden blinding glare. I heard a smooth poetic voice that made me think of West End theatres.

'What . . . Adrian, my boy,' the voice said, in delighted tones. 'Do come in. Dare I hope that this young woman is who I think she is?'

'Verity Grey,' confirmed Adrian, as we moved from darkness into light and shut the door.

Visible at last, my host reached down to take my hand, and smiled. 'I am so very glad to meet you, my dear. I'm Peter Quinnell.'

My first thought had been that Peter Quinnell wasn't old at all. He fairly towered over me, loose-limbed and lean, not stooping, and the voice and movements were those of a much younger man than I'd expected. Only now, standing in the clearer light of the hallway, could I see the weary lines the world had carved into the long, still-handsome face; the whitened hair; the long languid eyes; the evidence of age upon the beautifully formed hand clasping mine.

I smiled back. 'How do you do?'

'I was about to ask you the same question,' Quinnell said. 'You must be rather tired, if you've come up today from London. We actually weren't expecting you until tomorrow.'

I flushed a little. 'I know. I just . . . well, the truth is I'm not very good at waiting. I thought that I'd be staying at a B&B.'

'What?' His look of horror was quite genuine. 'Oh, my dear girl, that would never do. No, no, we have a room all ready for you. Besides,' he added, 'I was rather hoping to hold you captive here until I'd managed to persuade you to join our motley little team.' The hooded eyes touched mine, with stunning charm, and he smiled again. 'You have your luggage with you?'

'Just one bag. It's in the car.'

'Good.' The smile slid to Adrian. 'Fetch it for her, will you? You can put it in the guest room at the head of the stairs—you know the one? Then come and join us for a drink in the sitting room.'

'Right. Won't be a moment.'

When the front door had opened and closed again, Peter Quinnell drew back a pace to study me with interest. 'I must say, I am surprised. You don't look anything like I expected.'

I smiled. 'That's just what Mr Fortune said. I met him on the bus,' I explained, as Quinnell raised an enquiring eyebrow. 'I gather everyone thought I'd be tall and blonde, and more . . . well, more . . .'

'Quite. Our Mr Sutton-Clarke does have a certain reputation,' he agreed. 'And he did say, my dear, that he knew you rather well . . .'

'Sorry to disappoint.'

'Good heavens, I'm not at all disappointed. And no more, I suspect, was David Fortune. You met him on the bus, you say? Out visiting his mother, was he?'

I admitted I had no idea where he'd been. 'Is he a local man, then?'

'Oh yes. Eyemouth born and bred, is David. He hasn't lived here for some years, mind, but his mother has a cottage on the coast, north of St Abbs.' He turned away to open some French doors behind him, letting the light creep uncertainly into the large front hall beyond. 'Please, do come through. I'll put the light on . . . There.' A switch clicked somewhere and a warm lamp glowed from atop a Spanish chest; glowed again within the mirror hung behind it, and in all the frames of all the prints and sketches grouped around the great square entrance hall. With the weathered Oriental carpet on the floor the overall effect was one of cultured and eclectic taste.

Of the three closed doorways leading off the entrance hall my host chose the nearest on my left. 'The sitting room,' he told me, as he fumbled for the wall switch.

When the light snapped on, I saw deep red walls, set off by more Oriental carpeting and a leather sofa, creased and weathered from years of use, on which two cats were curled round each other, sleeping. A matching armchair sat surrounded in its corner by bookshelves crammed with volumes old and new, and more prints and drawings hung haphazardly about the room.

The front door banged and Adrian went thumping past with my suitcase. His footsteps faded up an unseen flight of stairs.

'Please, do sit down.' Peter Quinnell waited until I had settled myself on the sofa before he folded his own long frame into the armchair, slinging one loose-jointed leg over the other. This was his room, I thought—it had the stamp of him, comfortably masculine. 'Don't mind the cats,' he told me, 'they're quite harmless. Stupid creatures, really, but I'm fond of them. Murphy—that's the big black beast, there—he's been with me seven years now, and his girlfriend Charlie came to us last winter, when we bought this house. Ah,' he continued, as Adrian appeared in the doorway, 'that's done, is it? I don't suppose that you'd be kind enough to fetch us all a drink? No doubt Miss Grey is parched.'

Adrian sent me a winning smile. 'Gin and it for you, darling? And Peter, what will you have? Vodka?'

'Please. And perhaps a cheese biscuit or two?' He waited until Adrian had gone again before he slid his long eyes slowly back to me. 'You met Adrian in Suffolk, did you not? On one of Lazenby's digs?'

'Yes. Though I'm afraid I didn't spend much time at the dig, myself. I'd just started working for Dr Lazenby, then, at the British Museum, and I was rather green when it came to field work.'

'Suffolk,' he said again. 'That was the Roman fort?'

'It was. They built a bypass over it.'

'Ah.' Quinnell didn't take his quiet gaze from my face. 'It was your work with Lazenby, you see, that caught my attention in the first place. He only trains the best. Adrian says you did most of the cataloguing yourself, for the Suffolk dig—and the drawings. Is that right? Impressive,' he said, when I nodded. 'Very impressive. I'd be thrilled if you could do the same for us, here at Rosehill. Of course, we won't have quite the range of artefacts that Lazenby turned up—the Romans weren't here that long—but we're bound to find a few good pieces and a battlefield does have an interest all its own, don't you agree?'

I didn't answer straight away. I was trying to sort out my whirling thoughts. A battlefield? A . . . good God, not a *Roman* battlefield? Right here in Eyemouth? It seemed incredible, and yet . . . My stomach flipped excitedly. I took a breath. 'I hope you don't mind my asking,' I began, 'but what exactly is your team excavating?'

'I am so sorry,' Peter Quinnell said. 'I thought you knew. It's a marching camp, my dear. A Roman marching camp. Early second-century. Though in actual fact I suppose it's more of a burial ground, really.' His eyes captured mine, intense, and for the first time I believed, truly believed, that he might indeed be mad. 'We've found the final resting place of Legio IX Hispana.'

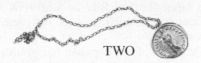

TWO

If he'd told me they had found the Holy Grail, I couldn't have been more astonished. The Ninth Legion—the Hispana—here! It hardly seemed credible, not when so many people had searched for so long, and in vain. I myself had come to believe that the fate of the lost legion would remain one of the great unsolved mysteries of our time.

Historians the world over had hotly debated dozens of theories, but the facts were few. All anyone could say for certain was that, some time in the reign of the Emperor Hadrian, Legio IX Hispana had been ordered north from its fortress at York.

The soldiers of the Ninth, already veterans of the brutal war with Boudicca, were crack troops, rarely called upon to deal with minor skirmishes. It took a true emergency to set a legion on the march. And when several thousand men marched out to do battle, the spectacle would have been stunning. At dawn would come the auxiliary units of archers and cavalry, forming an all-seeing shield for the legion behind. Then the standard-bearer, holding high the sacred golden Eagle of the Empire, symbol of honour and victory. If an enemy touched the eagle he disgraced the legion; if a legion lost the eagle it disgraced Rome. Close round the eagle marched the other standard-bearers, followed by the trumpeters, and then, in ordered ranks, six men abreast, came the legionaries.

They'd been trained to march twenty-four Roman miles in five hours, fully armoured, with weapons and heavy packs, and then at the end of the day's march to build the night's camp—no small task, since a camp needed trenches and ramparts and palisades to protect the leather tents inside. These were hard fighting men, and the legion on the march with all its baggage train and brilliant armour would have been a sight that one remembered.

Which made the disappearance of the Ninth Legion all the more puzzling. Because nobody *had* remembered. At least, there was no record of what became of the Ninth in its northern battle, and the legion had been struck from the military lists. Modern historians offered several explanations—the men of the Hispana might have mutinied, or disgraced themselves by losing the eagle in battle . . . or else, in that barbaric wilderness, they'd met a terrible end. Nearly two thousand years later, the full fate of Legio IX Hispana—all those thousands of men—continued to elude historians like a ghost in the mist of a barren moor.

I looked at Peter Quinnell. 'The Hispana? Are you sure?'

'Quite sure. Adrian can show you the results of his initial radar survey in the southwest corner, can't you, my boy?'

'Certainly,' said Adrian, coming through the door with our drinks. 'It's all on computer. I'll show you tomorrow,' he promised, pressing a glass into my waiting hand.

Relaxing back into the sofa, I took a long sip of cool gin and vermouth and looked across at Peter Quinnell. 'You have a lab set up, then, here on site?'

'Oh, yes. I've converted the old stables, behind the house.'

'Not one but two microscopes,' Adrian enthused, 'and computers— I've never seen anything like it on a field excavation.'

Quinnell's eyes slid sideways to Adrian. He knew, I thought, exactly what made Adrian tick—the clink of coins, the smell of money, the promise of a comfortable position. 'Yes, well,' he said, 'I do like my little gadgets, you know. Sit down, my boy, for heaven's sake—you're making my neck stiff. And mind the cats,' he added, as Adrian narrowly missed sitting on the sleeping tabby.

'You realise, of course,' Adrian informed me, 'that we'll have to shoot you, now, if you don't join our little digging team. Can't risk having our secret leak out.'

They had kept the secret remarkably well, I thought, and told them so. 'I haven't heard so much as a whisper of it in London, and I don't remember reading anything in any of the journals.'

'The journals, my dear, are singularly uninterested in where I choose to dig. No place for instinct, in their books. No place for hunches.' He lifted his glass of vodka. 'I'm considered a rather less successful Schliemann, chasing after fairy tales. Except where Schliemann had his Homer, I have nothing.' He paused and drank, letting his chin droop thoughtfully down to his chest. 'No, that's not exactly true,' he said, at length. 'I do have Robbie.'

Adrian shot me a watchful glance, and Quinnell appeared to rouse himself. 'Anyway, the job is yours, if you'll have it. But I expect you'd like to take a day or so to look around, to think it over. You can give me your answer this weekend, all right?'

I already knew what my answer would be, but I tried to keep my reaction professional. 'All right,' I said, and nodded.

'Good. And now I'm sure you really are quite tired from your travels. I'll show you to your room.'

'I'll take her up,' Adrian offered.

'You most certainly will not.' Quinnell's voice was firm. 'I'd be a thoughtless cad to deliver any woman into your clutches, even one familiar with your Casanova ways. No, you may say good night, and *I* will take her upstairs.'

Adrian was still smiling several minutes later, as he shrugged his coat on in the vestibule. 'So,' he murmured, with a quick glance over my shoulder to where Quinnell stood waiting in the entrance hall, 'what do you think?'

'I think he's rather marvellous.'

'I'm glad. I'll see you in the morning, then.'

I watched him go, then turned and followed Peter Quinnell through the hall and up a winding stone stairway to the first floor. My footsteps dragged a little on the hard steps, and I realised that I actually *was* tired. By the time Quinnell had shown me where the bathroom was and introduced me to the plumbing, I was stifling yawns. When the door to my spacious back bedroom swung open, I saw only the plump twin beds.

Quinnell fussed around, making certain I had everything I needed for the night, and then he left me on my own.

Well, not entirely on my own. One of the cats had come upstairs with us, and when I'd finished in the bathroom I returned to find it perched upon my window ledge, long tail twitching as it stared transfixed at the ink-black pane of glass. It was Murphy, the big black tom. 'You like that window, do you, Murphy? What is it you see?'

I myself could see only my own reflection, and the cat's, until I switched the lamp off. Even then, the view looked ordinary enough. Close by, a large tree shuddered with the wind above a sea of ghostly daffodils that dipped and danced in waves. And beyond that, the fickle moonlight caught a sweep of field that slanted gently up to meet a darkly cresting ridge. 'You see?' I said. 'There's nothing.'

The cat's hair bristled suddenly as it arched itself upon the window ledge, its lips curled sharply back, fangs baring in a vicious hiss.

I jumped. And though the hiss had not been aimed at me, I felt my flesh rising in response, and fought to calm the jerky rhythm of my heart. 'Murphy,' I said sternly, 'stop that.' I snapped the window blind down and nudged the black cat from the ledge with a less than steady hand.

Stupid animal, I thought. There had been nothing out there, nothing at all. Nevertheless, I was glad of the tomcat's company when I crawled beneath my blankets, having chosen the twin bed further from the window. And for the first time since my nursery days, I didn't reach to turn off the bedside lamp.

'Do you always sleep with your light on?' Fabia Quinnell asked me next morning at breakfast.

I hadn't yet made up my mind about Fabia. She was, as Adrian had said, a fetching young woman—quite stunning, in fact. Her pale blonde hair, baby-fine, swung against her soft jaw at an artful angle, leaving the nape of her fragile neck bare. Small-boned and doe-eyed, she looked nothing like her grandfather. Nor did she appear to share his hospitable nature. Her greeting was anything but warm.

In answer to her question I replied, through a mouthful of cold toast, that I normally slept in the dark, like everyone else. 'I just have a foolish imagination sometimes—things that go bump in the night. Especially in strange houses. So I find it helps to leave the light on.'

'Well, you gave me quite a turn last night,' she said. 'I thought it might be Peter, waiting up for me. He drinks and then he wants to talk.' She rolled her eyes with feeling. 'A typical Irishman.'

Taking another sip of coffee, I turned in my chair so I could see out of the narrow kitchen window. From the treeless ridge behind the house a lush green field sloped gently downwards, bounded at its bottom edge by the thick tangle of thorn and briar that hid the road from view. Two men were standing in the centre of the field, eyes fixed upon the ridge. One of the men was Peter Quinnell. The other was larger, broader about the shoulders, with curling jet-black hair. 'They've started early,' I commented.

'Who?' Her uninterested grey eyes flicked towards the window. 'Oh, Peter and Davy, yes. They're always puttering around.'

'What does David Fortune do, exactly?'

'He's an archaeologist, the same as Peter. Lectures at the University of Edinburgh.'

I frowned. 'Wouldn't your grandfather prefer to manage the excavation on his own?'

'I doubt it,' she said, flatly. 'And anyway, he needs Davy's name on his publications, to make the dig legitimate. Peter's name simply doesn't impress people these days,' she explained, her tone offhand. 'Most people think he's past it.' Pushing herself away from the counter, she nodded at my empty plate. 'Are you finished? Come on, then—I've been ordered to give you the grand tour.'

Shrugging on my crumpled anorak, I followed Fabia outside. The morning was crisp for late April, clear and sunny, with a brisk breeze blowing from the southwest.

I turned my back to the breeze for a moment, and took a good long look at Rosehill, pleased to find it looked less ominous by daylight. Pinkish-grey plaster that in places didn't cover all the rose-coloured brick made the plain house seem prettier. A graceful flight of steps curved up sideways to meet the front door, and the narrow white-painted window frames held an abundance of little square panes that reflected the sunlight like glittering faceted gems.

Fabia was looking beyond the house to a corner of the sunlit field just coming into view.

'*Did* anything go bump in the night?' she asked me, slowly.

I glanced at her. 'Only the cats. Why?'

'Just curious.' She shrugged and started up the hill.

The dark wooden stables crouched long and low on the ridge above the house.

It was clear there hadn't been horses there for quite some time, but I forgave Quinnell for their absence the instant my eyes adjusted to the indoor lighting. He had worked wonders.

I was used to doing field work in makeshift labs set up in tents, hauling water back and forth to wash the artefacts and battling for table space. Now, as I looked around, I was made stunningly aware of just what sort of money was involved in the Rosehill dig. To my left, the double row of wooden stalls had been stripped and refin-ished, their clay floors carefully levelled and swept pristinely bare. One stall, ringed round with freestanding metal shelves, held the microscopes Adrian had raved about—not just the ordinary sort, but a dissecting microscope as well, complete with its camera attach-ment. Another stall housed packing materials—boxes of all sizes, self-sealing plastic bags and silica gel for packing metal.

I poked my head round a half-open door leading off the wide stone passageway.

'The finds room,' Fabia identified it. There were brushes of every size and shape, right down to the tiniest toothbrush. Long tables had been set up along the end wall, and beneath them waited stacks of trays and shallow sorting boxes.

'Not that we'll find much,' she continued. 'I'd have had this for my darkroom only Peter thought it better if I had the cellar at the house.'

I felt a spark of interest. 'Your darkroom? Are you the site photographer, then?'

'Peter had to find some use for me, didn't he?' Turning, she led me towards the dark end of the stable building, away from the refinished stalls. 'And this is the student common room,' she told me.

I stared. All the stalls here had been removed, and the walls painted bright creamy white above green pub-style carpeting. In one corner, a large television and video faced two angled sofas. And at the centre of the room stood a massive snooker table.

Fabia folded her arms. 'Showers and loos are out the back. Nothing's too good for the students, you know.' Her mouth quirked. 'Not that we *have* any students. Peter's little fantasy, that. He thinks he can convince the university to support his excavation.'

'But you said David Fortune's from the university.'

'Well, yes. But to hire students for the summer Peter needs the approval of the head of the department, Dr John Connelly. He was once a student of Peter's and I'm told they have a history.'

'Oh, I see. Still, he could always hire regular workers to help with the dig. They don't have to come from the university.'

'Ah, but that,' she said, in a patronising tone, 'would mean he wouldn't get the recognition he deserves.'

She led me back towards the renovated stalls at the other end of the stables, to the last stall but one. 'Your office,' she said.

It put me in mind of a monk's cell, clean and efficiently organised down to the tiniest detail. The grey filing cabinet and metal-topped desk were gleamingly new, as was the state-of-the-art computer in the corner, and the orthopaedic office chair.

'It's lovely.' I delivered my verdict honestly. 'Really lovely.'

'You're right across from Adrian,' she pointed out. 'And Davy's office is in the corner, there, but he's only here a few days a week.'

David Fortune's office looked abandoned, and gave no clue as to the personality of the man who worked there. Adrian's workplace, on the other hand, was easy to identify. He was not the tidiest of men.

I shifted a coffee-stained cup from a stack of his papers and peered with interest at the computer-generated image that topped the pile. It looked like something a child might produce by rubbing a stick of charcoal over a bumpy block of granite. It was, in fact, a plotted section of a ground-penetrating radar survey.

Adrian had already been here a few weeks, I knew. He'd have completed his initial topographic survey of the site, using the measurements to create a detailed contour map of the field where Quinnell wanted to dig. But digging, by its nature, was destructive, and archaeologists didn't do it blindly. There were other ways to see beneath the ground.

Geophysical surveying, Adrian's speciality, could reveal fascinating things. When the results were plotted on a computer, they produced a stratified landscape of black, grey and white, like the one I was looking at now.

The image showed a definite anomaly, a sharp dip spearing down through the black and grey bands. It certainly might be a ditch, I conceded. I picked the paper up and brought it closer for a better look. Funny, I thought, how these things all started to look alike, after a while. This one put me in mind of an image I'd seen only last year. They were very similar. Then I saw the tiny black smudge of a fingerprint to one side of the 'ditch', and I frowned.

Not merely similar, I corrected myself—exactly the same. I'd made that smudge myself; I could remember Adrian ticking me off for doing it. This wasn't an original print-out at all. It was a photocopy, with printing on the top edge changed to read: ROSEHILL, EYEMOUTH, BERWICKSHIRE.

'What the devil is Adrian playing at?' I asked, still frowning. I turned to Fabia. 'Do you know anything about this?'

Her eyes slipped warily away from mine to the paper in my hand. 'Yes, we think that may be some sort of ditch in the southwest corner. Adrian found it last week.'

David Fortune's voice surprised us both.

'It's no use, lass,' he advised Fabia. 'She was in Wales last year as well, with Sutton-Clarke. She'll not be so easily fooled.'

We both turned round to see him standing in the passageway, his arms folded complacently across his broad chest.

Fabia Quinnell shot him an angry look and turned to me, defensive. 'It's not . . . I mean, we didn't . . .'

'I'll do the explaining, if you don't mind,' the archaeologist cut her off. 'Why don't you go and keep your grandfather company?'

Defeated by the determined tone of his voice, she brushed past him, head high. His eyes held firmly to my face.

I looked down, feeling robbed. 'There is no Roman marching camp at Rosehill, is there?'

'I didn't say that.'

'But this,' I challenged him, holding up the incriminating image, 'is a fake. Was it your idea?'

'Fabia's, I think.' He smiled, faintly. 'Adrian shouldered the blame when I caught him, but it's not the sort of thing he'd do on his own. And he has a hard time saying no to Fabia.'

I sighed, and dropped the paper to the desk. 'You knew about this,' I said, slowly, 'and yet you didn't tell Quinnell?'

'I didn't see the point. He'd already seen the image, by the time I learned what Adrian had done. I wasn't pleased about it, ken, but since it didn't do much harm . . .'

'Didn't do much harm?' I echoed, disbelieving. 'How can you say that? Quinnell's digging for something he's not going to find.'

'You don't know Peter Quinnell. He'd dig anyway.'

'Why?'

'Because of Robbie.'

It wasn't the first time I'd heard that name. Quinnell himself had mentioned it, last night. Something about Schliemann having Homer to guide him to the ruins of Troy, while Quinnell had only . . .

'Robbie,' I repeated, shaking my head slowly. 'But who is Robbie? And what does he have to do with this?'

David Fortune took a long time answering. He seemed to be weighing something in his mind. 'Best come and see for yourself,' he said finally, and with that invitation he turned and went out.

It was all I could do to keep up with his long, rolling strides. As we passed the big house, moving onto the drive, I mustered enough breath to speak. 'Where are we going?'

'Rose Cottage,' he replied. 'You'd have passed it last night.'

Even in daylight the cottage looked warm and welcoming as David Fortune stooped to knock at the white-painted back door.

The woman who answered the summons was my own age, with short chestnut hair and a fresh cheerful face warmed by freckles.

'Davy!' she said, in an accent as rich as his own. She pushed the door wider, her gaze sliding past him to me. 'It's Miss Grey, isn't it?' she greeted me, extending a firmly capable hand. 'I heard you'd arrived. I'm Jeannie McMorran. I keep house for Peter. Come inside, the both of you.'

David Fortune ducked his head to squeeze through the narrow

doorway. The kitchen was narrow, too, and though the sunlight couldn't quite break through the small, old-fashioned windows, the lace curtains and gaily painted china plates propped up along the old oak dresser made the room homely and bright.

David sniffed the fragrant air. 'Been baking, have you?'

'Apple tart for Brian's tea. He got back last night. No need to be quiet, though,' she added. 'He'll be sleeping it off for hours yet.'

'Is Robbie about?' asked David.

'Aye,' said Jeannie and she led us along a tiny passageway towards the front of the cottage. 'He'll be fair glad to see you. He's off school today with the smit.' Then, suddenly remembering I wasn't Scottish, she smiled and translated. 'He has a cold. Nothing serious, ken, but I'll not send a son of mine to school when he's ill.'

Her words had only just sunk in when I was ushered through a second low doorway and into the presence of Peter Quinnell's Homer. My first thought was that I'd been brought to the wrong room. The face that looked up from the bed was round and questioning, sprayed with freckles and topped by a shock of unruly black hair. Robbie McMorran could not have been older than eight.

Jeannie laid one cooling hand on the boy's forehead, then rumpled his hair with a smile. 'I'm sure he'll survive a short visit,' she pronounced. 'But just a short one, now. And no Nintendo.' Fixing David Fortune with a stern look, she left us to return to her kitchen.

'No Nintendo!' The Scotsman pulled a face of mock dismay, which he shared with the bedridden boy. 'How's a lad meant to get well?'

Robbie McMorran giggled. 'It's not so bad. The electricity's going off, anyway, some time soon.'

'Is it, now? Did you tell Mr Quinnell?'

'Aye, Mum rang him up, just afore you came.' The frank round eyes looked up at me eagerly. 'Is this Miss Grey?'

'It is Verity Grey,' he introduced me, 'I'd like you to meet Robert Roy McMorran.'

For such a little, gangly thing he had a solemn handshake.

'I think Miss Grey would like to know what part you played in bringing Mr Quinnell here, to Rosehill,' David told him.

'Wasn't me,' the boy replied. 'It was Granny Nan. She wrote to Mr Quinnell, like, to tell him about me seeing the Sentinel.'

I interrupted, with a faint frown. 'The Sentinel?'

'Aye.' Robbie nodded. 'On the hill. My dog Kip found him first. And then Granny Nan showed me this book with pictures in it . . .'

'Granny Nan being my mother,' interjected David, for my benefit. 'She's Granny Nan to everyone round here.'

'. . . she showed me this book, and it had a picture of *him* in it, and she got all excited and wrote to Mr Quinnell. She let me keep the picture.' Rolling onto his stomach, Robbie stretched to reach the lower shelf of his bedside table, and rolled back clasping a colourful sheet with ragged edges. 'I ken you're not supposed to tear a book, but Granny Nan said most of the pages were missing anyway, so it was OK.' He passed the crumpled page into my hands.

Bending my head, I smoothed the picture with careful fingers. 'And this is the man you saw, then, is it? Here at Rosehill?'

'Aye. His name's right there, and all. He walks up on the hill, just there.' The boy pointed in the direction of Rosehill House.

'I see.'

Schliemann had his Homer, I thought, and now at last I understood what Quinnell meant when he said he had Robbie. Understood, too, why David Fortune had told me that Quinnell would dig here anyway, no matter what the surveys showed. If I were a less doubting person, I might dig, too.

My fingers flattened the wrinkled image once again, more slowly, as I read the printed caption:

'The Sentinel At His Post'—A Roman Legionary; Early Second Century, AD.

ADRIAN SNAPPED A BIT of thorn from the low hedge at the roadside and twirled it absently round in his fingers. 'The man *is* six sandwiches short of a picnic, darling. Surely you noticed.'

'Oh, so that's all right then, is it? Lying to someone because he's deluded?'

'Lying,' said Adrian, 'is a relative term. Look, just stop walking, will you? We're far enough from the house, no one will hear.'

I stopped, at a shaded place where the road bridged a shallow stream before beginning its curving downward slope. Here, instead of hedge and fencing, low stone walls edged the road to keep the unwary from toppling into the briskly moving water below.

Adrian turned to settle himself against the stone barricade. 'It wasn't even my idea, to begin with,' he defended himself. 'It was Fabia's. She thought it might be nice to give the old boy some encouragement.'

I sent him an icy look. 'Can you even *spell* the word ethics?'

'I don't know why you're so angry about it.'

'You're supposed to be a professional, for goodness' sake. Professionals don't fake their data.'

'They might if they worked for Quinnell. Saves effort, really. Quinnell doesn't need me, or my surveys, to tell him where to dig. He'll use his little psychic friend for that.'

'I don't believe this.' I rubbed my forehead with a heavy hand. 'I really don't believe you dragged me all the way up here from London for nothing.'

'Who says it was for nothing?'

'Look me in the eye,' I challenged him, 'and tell me you honestly believe there's a Roman camp at Rosehill.'

In a way, it was a trick question. I knew Adrian well enough to know that if he looked me in the eye at all, he was lying.

Instead he surprised me by looking away, squinting thoughtfully. 'I believe,' he said, 'that Quinnell believes it. And for the amount he's paying me, I'm prepared to play along.'

'Of course, I should have known. It all comes down to money, doesn't it?' I studied him. 'Do you know, I'm almost tempted to take the job, if only to protect Peter Quinnell from the lot of you.'

Adrian smiled at my disapproving expression. 'Is that why poor old Fortune wasted no time disappearing when I met you in the drive? Did you tear him off a strip, as well?'

'I don't know the man well enough to tear him off a strip. But he's well aware of what I think.'

David had known, of course, that I'd be disappointed. Known it all along, and still he'd taken me to meet Robbie, had let me hear the whole fantastic tale. And as we'd trudged back up the curving drive, he'd offered no apology. 'So now you ken as much as I do,' he'd told me. 'It's your choice, to stay or to go, but I will tell you one thing: Quinnell's set his heart on your staying.'

He'd said that last bit almost as if it went against his better judgment, and I'd had the curious impression that David Fortune would be happier if I *didn't* stay. But before I'd fully registered the thought, Adrian's red Jaguar had roared up the drive towards us, and with a final, unreadable glance the big dark Scotsman had turned to climb the final hundred yards or so to the stables on the ridge.

'Damn, damn, *damn*.' I spoke the words aloud now with a vehemence that brought Adrian's head round. 'I like Quinnell, Adrian, and I don't want to see him disappointed.'

'So take the job, then, like a good girl.'

'Yes, but if I do that, I'll have to stand by and watch him digging trenches, finding nothing. I don't know which is worse.'

Adrian shrugged. 'One of them pays better.'

'Oh, damn the pay,' I started to say, but my words were drowned by an urgent squeal of tyres on the road, followed by the thud and crunch of metal slamming into metal. In the second of silence that trailed the crash, something began to crack and tear like a tree branch ripped free in a storm, and a softer thud echoed the first.

'That sounded bloody close,' said Adrian.

His reflexes were better than mine. By the time I caught up with him, he'd reached the scene of the accident and was playing referee between a red-faced man with wild eyes and a smaller chap with spectacles who was staring dismayed at the wreckage of his car. I had difficulty making sense of the colourful language spewing from the larger man, but I gathered the other driver had stopped suddenly on the road to get his bearings, with predictable results.

Jeannie McMorran appeared briefly in the doorway of Rose Cottage, took one look, and withdrew with a practical, purposeful air. She's gone to ring the police, I thought, and a few minutes later the wail of a siren proved me right. I moved well back, out of the way, against the cottage wall.

The curtains twitched in a nearby window, and I caught a glimpse of Robbie's small pale face. A road accident, I thought, must surely be a spot of interest in a sick child's boring day. And the boy was, at any rate, getting a language lesson; the large red-faced man had used nearly every curse invented and a few I'd never heard, in explaining his side of things to the beleaguered-looking police officer. 'Will ye just look at what the daftie's done to yon great pole!' he raged. 'The dampt thing's cowpit ower!'

I listened with a frown, intrigued. 'Daftie' was simple enough, I thought, and 'dampt' was clearly 'damned', but 'cowpit ower'? And then I looked where he was pointing. *Fallen over*. The huge wooden pole had split on impact and toppled into the field across the road, crushing a section of hedge in a tangle of thick black power lines.

Power lines . . .

I froze a moment, tried to think. What was it Robbie had said to David Fortune, only an hour ago? I could see his bright-eyed, freck-led face, and hear the confident young voice proclaim: 'The electric-ity's going off, anyway, some time soon . . .'

'IT'S QUITE REMARKABLE,' said Quinnell, 'what the boy knows. If I weren't bothered by ethics I'd take him to Newmarket, make a small fortune.' Smiling at the prospect, he leaned forward to take a chocolate digestive biscuit from the tray between us.

The electricity was on again and he'd made a pot of tea. One steaming sweet sip chased away the lingering chill of the old house and made the red-walled sitting room feel cosy in spite of the west wind that rattled the windowpanes. I would have felt even better, I acknowledged, if Quinnell hadn't used that one word: *ethics*.

'You're not convinced, I take it.'

I hesitated, searching for words that would give no offence. 'I've only just met the boy, really, and we didn't talk much.'

'No, it's quite all right,' he forgave me, crossing one long leg over the other. 'It is the natural response. I think I'd worry about someone who simply accepted the idea, no questions asked. Ghosts and goblins, spooks and psychics—they're so far removed from science, and we are all children of the scientific age.'

I felt a twinge of conscience and I turned my eyes away. 'Mr Quinnell . . .'

'Peter, please.'

'Peter. There's something I must tell you. About the radar survey.'

'Yes?'

My teacup clattered in the saucer with a force I hadn't intended. 'I saw the results today, up at the lab, and I think that there's been a mistake. I don't think the findings are accurate.' There, I thought, I'd said it, and I held my breath, waiting for him to ask me why I didn't trust the survey. When the question didn't come, I raised my head.

The long eyes met mine levelly, with deep approving warmth. 'It is a rare commodity, these days,' he told me. 'Honesty.'

I stared. 'You knew.'

'Suspected. Did he take it from another site, then? One that you and he had worked on?' The answer must have shown in my face, because he nodded, satisfied. 'And you recognised it. Bit of bad luck for Adrian, although it can't have been his idea. I expect he was led astray by Fabia. My granddaughter has rather a knack for leading young men astray. Of course you mustn't tell them that I know.'

'But your excavation . . .'

'Oh, I intended to begin in the southwest corner, regardless. Robbie's very certain that there's something there, and it's as good a place to start as any.'

'I'm sorry to be such a sceptic, but I just don't see what proof you have that the Ninth Legion was ever here.'

'No proof,' he admitted, amiably. 'But I've been chasing the Ninth for fifty years now, and I've developed something of a sixth sense myself, where the Hispana is concerned. You know, of course, most modern historians believe the Ninth was simply sent to Lower Germany, that it wasn't destroyed at all—at least not here on British soil. But I feel it in my bones, my dear. I feel it in my bones.' His mild eyes moved past my shoulder to the window. 'For years, I thought the Hispana must have marched northwest along the Devil's Causeway, the Roman road from York, but now I don't believe that. They came along the east coast,' he said calmly. 'They came here. Even if Robbie hadn't seen his Sentinel, I'd still have found this field. It was the name of the house, you see, that intrigued me.'

'Rosehill?'

'Not after roses,' he explained. 'No, one of the locals told me that this used to be called "Rogue's Hill", until the seventeenth century, when the house was built. The family wanted something more genteel, I suppose. So Rosehill it became.'

'But I don't quite understand,' I said.

'Well, there weren't any rogues, not even so much as a hanging tree. But,' he added, 'it struck me that the word "rogues" could have been derived from *rogus*.'

'*Rogus*,' I repeated slowly. The Latin word for 'funeral pyre'.

It was a possibility. Place names could often give clues about the past, and if the Ninth Legion had perished here, there would of course be bodies, thousands of them—or ashes. Did the Romans still cremate their dead in the reign of Hadrian? I was struggling to remember when Quinnell's quiet voice interrupted my thoughts.

'I must admit, I chose you for your name, as well.'

'I'm sorry?'

'Verity.' He smiled. 'The truth. It's what we're searching for this season, here at Rosehill. It's what I hope to find. And I thought, if you would join us . . . well, I rather viewed you as a good-luck charm.'

Damn the Irish, I thought. They could be so incredibly persuasive. I reminded myself that he'd given me the weekend to decide, and this was only Friday afternoon. Plenty of time to consider things before I gave my answer. Atop the bookshelf by Quinnell's shoulder, the black cat Murphy stirred and stretched and stared at me with placid, knowing eyes. *You're going to say yes, anyway*, he seemed to be saying. *You like the old man, you haven't the heart to refuse him.*

Quinnell leaned forward and reached for the teapot. 'No need to make your mind up yet,' he said. 'Here, have another biscuit.' His eyes, like the cat's, sensed victory, and I knew that when I finally accepted the job, it would come as no surprise to Peter Quinnell.

I sighed, and took a biscuit, and the black cat closed its eyes.

THREE

I woke in the darkness, listening. The sound that wrenched me from my sleep had been strange to my city-bred ears. Trainlike, yet not a train . . . the rhythm was too wild, too random. A horse, I thought. A horse in the next field over, galloping endlessly round and round, galloping, galloping . . . The sound faded and came back again, steadily, bringing others behind it—more hoofbeats, more horses, until it seemed the field must be a sea of heaving flanks and white-rolled eyes and steaming curls of laboured breath. Snorting and galloping, galloping, and then in one thick stream they rushed beneath my window and I knew that I was dreaming, so I closed my eyes more tightly, and I slept.

I woke again in daylight. Reaching over, I flipped the switch on my alarm clock before the buzzer could sound, and heard the minute hand snap forward: eight o'clock. Yawning, I rolled onto my back.

Had it only been a week since I'd accepted Peter Quinnell's job? It seemed longer. I had returned to London to settle my affairs and pack enough clothing to see me through the summer season at Rosehill. Now here I was waking up in this marvellous room, with the morning sunlight edging its way in through the screening chestnut tree.

Tugging a jumper over my standard working uniform of T-shirt and jeans, I quickly washed, wove my long hair into its customary plait and went downstairs, where I found Jeannie McMorran alone in the bright kitchen, mixing a bowlful of biscuit dough.

'Do you never stop baking?' I asked. We'd got on well together last weekend, and I'd decided I liked Jeannie very much. She had a buoyant personality, a deliciously sly wit, and a way of putting Adrian in his place that I found particularly endearing. She turned to face me now and grinned.

'What, with all these men about? They'd never let me.'

'I take it everyone else is up?'

'Aye. Peter and Fabia were on their way out when I got here, half an hour ago. They've gone down to take some photographs, I think, before they start the digging. I've not seen Adrian's car yet, but I know Davy's around. There they go now.'

There were three of them—four if one counted Robbie's dog, Kip. The collie ran energetic circles round David Fortune's legs, jumping up every few paces to bring its head within reach of his hand so he could rumple its ears. Behind them walked an older man I didn't recognise, a short man with a slightly bent back and a dour expression.

'Who's that with them?'

'That's my dad,' Jeannie informed me, in a voice that held affection. 'I forgot, you've not met him yet, have you? He made himself scarce last weekend.'

Scarce, I thought drily, was hardly the word. I hadn't caught so much as a glimpse of the groundskeeper of Rosehill, although Jeannie assured me that was not uncommon. There were, apparently, two things that Wally Tyler hated—living on his own and living within sight of his son-in-law. Inviting his daughter and grandson to fill the empty corners of Rose Cottage after his wife's death meant inviting Brian, too, and so Wally Tyler had reached his own compromise. When Brian McMorran came home, Wally went elsewhere.

Brian, I had learned, skippered his own fishing boat, which meant he must be capable of some responsibility. Yet it was hard to have a good opinion of a man who appared to divide his odd weekend home between the nearest public house and his bed.

'It's not so bad as it sounds,' Jeannie told me, smiling at my expression. 'Brian's away to the fish most of the time. And Dad has friends in town. Right, what will you have for your breakfast? There's porridge made, or I can fix you some eggs—'

'I usually just have toast.'

'You're never thinking to spend a whole day running around after Peter with nothing but toast in your stomach!' She fixed me with a look that made me feel about as old as Robbie, and repeated her offer of porridge or eggs.

Meekly, I opted for the eggs.

Jeannie dropped bread in the toaster and smiled. 'They won't start digging without you,' she promised me. 'Peter and Davy will be busy for a bit yet, organising things. Sausages or bacon?'

One simply couldn't argue with a woman like that, I decided. And the plate of egg and sausages she finally set in front of me did draw a rumble from my stomach. 'This is marvellous,' I admitted, after the third sausage. 'Quinnell is lucky to have found you.'

'He's a good man to work for, is Peter. It's a pity that Fabia's learned nothing from him.'

I smiled, understanding. 'I don't think she likes me much.'

'Aye, well, she wouldn't. You're a woman,' Jeannie said, matter-of-factly. 'Still, I suppose I shouldn't be too unkind. She did lose her father, poor lass, just last summer. It must have been fair hard on Peter as well, to lose his only son like that, but at least he's got Davy to lean on. They're almost like family, those two.'

'Was David a student of Quinnell's, or something?'

'I couldn't tell you,' she admitted. 'But he's kent Peter all his life. Davy's mum was Peter's secretary, like. Afore she married onto Davy's father.'

'Oh. I see.' The relationships were hard to disentangle.

'And Peter was best man at Davy's wedding,' she continued. 'I do mind that, because he had to come all the way over from—'

'David is married?' I couldn't help the interruption, though it worried me that the news had given me such a jolt.

Jeannie replied with a shake of her head. 'He was, aye, but not any more. She left him, stupid lass.'

Stupid lass, indeed, I thought, relieved.

Half an hour later, when I made my way down the gently sloping field to where the men had gathered in the southwest corner and was met by David Fortune's welcoming smile, I decided that stupid was an understatement.

'What kind of time d'ye call this, then?' he asked me.

'It's not my fault. Jeannie made me stop and eat a huge cooked breakfast. Where's Fabia? I thought she was with you.'

Quinnell glanced up. 'What? Oh, she's gone to ring Adrian. He seems to be having a lie-in this morning, and I want to make certain I've positioned this properly.'

By 'this' he meant the long strip of ground at his feet, staked out with string to make a rectangle.

Every excavation took place within an imaginary grid, an unseen plan of lines and squares created by the survey, drawn over the field like a giant invisible graph. Everything we found at Rosehill, no matter how small, would be carefully mapped in relation to that graph. Quinnell had already plotted the location of what would be his trial trench against Adrian's survey markers, and set his own stakes at the four widely spaced corners, but he obviously didn't want to cut the turf until he'd checked his measurements.

Jeannie's father waited patiently to one side, leaning on his spade. In spite of the bent back he had the tough look of a man who'd worked hard his whole life and had no intention of letting up now. He looked at me and raised his eyebrows. 'This isnae the lass frae London?'

Quinnell assured him that I was. 'Verity, this is Wally Tyler. Jeannie's father.'

His eyes, like his daughter's, were alive with canny good humour, and they crinkled kindly at the corners as he took my hand in a firm grip, looking accusingly at Quinnell. 'She's no blonde.'

David smiled broadly. 'Did Jeannie not tell you, Wally?'

'She never let dab. And Robbie only said the lass was a stoater.'

Robbie stopped poking around in the hedgerow and turned, his face colouring. 'Aw, Granddad!'

Quinnell laughed, a warm melodic sound. 'It's all right, Robbie. I don't think our Miss Grey can speak Scots, can you, my dear? She won't know what a stoater is.'

He was quite right, of course—I didn't have a clue, but as no one seemed inclined to enlighten me I acted as though I didn't care.

Instead I looked down at the broad rectangle marked in the grass. The pungent smell of damp earth touched my nostrils like a sweet seductive scent, and I felt that catch of excitement deep in my chest that all explorers must have felt from time immemorial. Because you never knew what worlds were waiting underneath that ground, to be discovered. That was the beauty of it—you never really knew. And on this perfect spring morning, with the sun warming my shoulders, it was easy to forget there was no evidence to support this excavation.

'Adrian's coming,' Robbie announced.

Quinnell relaxed. 'Good, good. Overslept, I imagine.'

Fabia's firm voice corrected him. 'Car trouble.'

She spoke from directly behind me, her sudden arrival startling until I realised that she had not come from the house, but from Rose Cottage, just the other side of the drive. 'Morning,' she greeted me shortly. 'Finally got free of the kitchen I see.'

Quinnell interrupted. 'Car trouble, did you say?'

'Yes. He couldn't get the motor started.'

Robbie, who'd been poking at a hillock with a sturdy bit of stick, looked swiftly upwards and I fancied that his large eyes held a faint reproach. My first thought was: *He's caught her in a lie*; and then I shook myself, remembering that no one could really be psychic.

Still, it wouldn't have surprised me to learn that Fabia was lying. She and Adrian weren't at all eager to see the southwest corner excavated.

Certainly, Adrian's car appeared healthy enough when he finally turned into the drive ten minutes later. He parked by the house and came slowly down to meet us, frowning. 'D'you know,' he said to Quinnell, 'I've been re-examining the results of that ground survey David did for you last week. I can't be absolutely sure, but that anomaly doesn't look quite the right size, you know, for what we're after . . .'

'Ah. Perhaps we ought to double-check.' Quinnell smiled. 'Robbie? Mr Sutton-Clarke's afraid we might be digging in the wrong place for our ditch.'

'The ditch the soldiers dug?'

'That's right.'

Robbie screwed his eyes up while he gave the matter thought. 'No, it's here. It's all filled up, like, but it's here.'

'Good lad.' Quinnell turned back to Adrian like a proud father. 'You see? There's no need to worry. If you'd just be so kind as to verify my measurements . . .'

A few minutes later, as Wally Tyler's spade attacked the toughened sod, my shoulders lifted in a little sigh. Such a pity, I thought, that Quinnell would be disappointed.

'The ditch is here,' repeated Robbie, but he wasn't talking to Quinnell. He'd come round to stand beside me and his blue eyes tilted up to meet my doubting ones, offering reassurance. 'It's OK, he's going to find it.'

'IT MUST BE TEATIME, surely.' Fabia pushed her hair back with an impatient hand, setting down her end of the large wood-framed screen while I reached for the next bucket of soil.

I checked my wristwatch, arching my back in a work-weary stretch. 'Another hour yet, I'm afraid.'

'Well, this is dead boring.' She glared past my shoulder to where the men were sinking ever lower in the trial trench. 'You'd think with four of them digging they'd be able to go a lot faster.'

I halted in mid-stretch, surprised. There were only three of them digging, in actual fact—Adrian, useless with a shovel, had been given the chore of passing the buckets of excavated soil over to us to be sieved. But, even so, the men were making good progress, their shovels scraping steadily, persistently, as they scooped up the soil in thin measured layers, moving deeper by stratified levels. If Fabia thought they could go any faster, she'd never tried digging herself.

And she'd certainly never held a sieve before today. I was beginning to think I could do the work better without her.

Leaving the sieve on the ground for a moment, I tipped over the next bucket, letting the freshly dug soil spill out onto the fine metal mesh. 'I suppose,' I said, 'as Peter Quinnell's granddaughter you've been doing this sort of thing since before you could walk.'

'Hell, no.' She tossed her blonde hair back again and bent to pick up her end of the screen. 'This is a first. I've no interest in dead things. I'm like my father, that way.'

'Ah.' Not wanting to pry, I took a firmer hold on the sieve's wooden frame and we started the shaking motion again, back and forth. The clumps of soil rolled and broke and sifted through the sieve like flour.

'I can't believe, sometimes,' she said, 'that Dad and Peter were related. Dad was so alive, you know? So interested in everything.'

I shot a sideways look at Quinnell, labouring single-mindedly in the trench, and thought I'd never seen a man look more alive. But I kept my opinion to myself.

'Peter isn't interested in anything,' said Fabia, 'except this bloody dig. It's all he cares about.' And then she abruptly switched the subject. 'I can't believe you do this for a living. It would put me to sleep.'

I smiled, hearing the complaint in her voice and knowing she'd imagined archaeology to be more glamorous. Tipping out the remaining pebbles onto the spoil heap, I lowered the sieve and hefted the next bucket, smiling encouragement at Fabia. 'Last one,' I promised.

The heavy tread of footsteps heralded Adrian's approach. 'Last one?' he echoed. 'Then you must have more. That spoil heap's not nearly high enough.' Cheerfully, he swung two full buckets beside the growing mound of sieved soil and rested, hands on hips, waiting for us to call him names.

Fabia, to my surprise, chose not to call him anything. Instead she ran a hand through her hair, in a self-conscious, womanly way, her swift upward glance designed to bewitch the observer. 'Adrian, darling, I desperately need to go to the loo, and I wondered if you might . . .' With a smile, she held up her edge of the sieve.

'Certainly.' Gullible as always, he stepped in to relieve her, watching fondly as she flounced away towards the house. When she'd disappeared from view, he brought his head round to meet my pitying eyes. 'What?'

'Oldest trick in the book.'

'You are a cynic,' Adrian commented.

By the time we'd started into the second bucket his glances up towards the house had grown more frequent. 'She *is* coming back, I hope. I'd forgotten how much I disliked . . . Hang on, what was that?' He peered closely at the sieve.

'What was what?'

'Blast, I shook too hard. I think it's down near you now.'

It took me a moment to find it. Frowning, I held the hard flat lump with careful fingers and gingerly brushed away the clinging dirt. It was a small potsherd with still-sharp edges and the worn remnants of a fine glaze. On any other site I would have been excited by such a find, but now I felt the pricking of irrational anger.

Adrian held out his hand. 'Can I have a look?'

In stony-faced silence I passed him the sherd and watched him weigh it in the palm of his hand. 'It's Samian ware, isn't it?'

'It certainly appears to be.'

'But that's encouraging, surely? I mean, one expects to find Samian ware on a Roman site.'

'Were you planning,' I asked him coldly, 'to fake the whole of this excavation?'

'Verity . . .'

'Mind you, it's not a perfect plant. Samian ware might have been scattered throughout Roman Britain, but I'd think it more common to villas and forts than to marching camps.'

'Verity, I swear.' He raised his right hand in defence. 'This is not my doing. What makes you so sure it's not a genuine find?'

'Oh, don't play the innocent. You know as well as I do that there's nothing here *to* find.'

Quinnell, I thought later, could not have had a better cue. I'd barely finished my sentence when his shout of delight went rolling up the green hill like a thunderclap. I turned towards the sound.

'They've found something,' said Adrian, setting the potsherd back on its bed of dirt.

We put down the sieve and hurried over the grass to investigate. Quinnell looked up from the edge of the trench, beaming. 'We've found the ditch,' he announced. 'Right where we expected it to be.'

Adrian was plainly stunned. 'Right where we expected it . . .'

'Yes.' Quinnell beckoned me closer. 'Just there, do you see? I'm afraid the rampart itself has been levelled at some point, but you can clearly trace its edge against the dark fill of the ditch.'

I looked, enthralled. They'd done an expert job of excavating, and the line where ditch and rampart had once met stood out quite clearly, running crosswise at the bottom of the trench.

The Romans had dug ditches all the way round their marching camps, great ditches nine feet wide and seven feet deep, piling the earth and turf to one side to create a soaring rampart. It must have looked a daunting obstacle to any barbarians trying to attack.

Leaning over cautiously, Robbie watched the work below him. 'Davy . . .'

'Aye, lad?'

'How could *that*'—he pointed at the eroded rampart—'keep anybody out?'

David smiled. 'Well, it used to be much bigger, lad. Like a hill, ken—nearly ten feet tall. And on top the Romans built a wall of wooden poles, to make it taller. And all this,' he added, waving his trowel over the darker area, 'this was a ditch then, like the moats you see round castles.'

'Filled with water?'

'No, just dry. It made it difficult enough to scramble up.'

Robbie pondered this a moment. 'Where'd they get the wooden poles from?'

'The legionaries carried two poles each when they were on the march, along with their armour and their weapons and the things they used for cooking—'

Adrian cut him off abruptly. 'We found a sherd,' he said, as if he'd only just remembered. Not that one could blame him for forgetting: if the sight of the ditch had astounded me, it must have stunned Adrian speechless. It wasn't every day one's lie turned out to be the truth.

Quinnell brought his head round, interested. 'Really? Perhaps, David, you might take a look at it? You're so much better with pottery than I am. And I do want to get this trench photographed, in case it starts to rain. Wally, could you bring the stepladder round, so Fabia can get a shot from higher up? By the way, where is Fabia?'

Adrian informed him she'd gone back up to the house. 'Shall I fetch her?'

'Please. And Verity, would you mind showing this sherd to David?'

Robbie, still crouched beside the trench, looked up hopefully. 'And what can *I* do?'

'You,' David said solemnly, handing over his brush, 'can lend a hand to Mr Quinnell, lad. He likes a bit of help, don't you, Peter?'

The older man glanced round. 'Oh, yes, indeed I do. Come down here, Robbie . . .'

David Fortune smiled. In one easy motion he pulled himself out of the trench and came across to join me. 'Peter does love teaching things,' he confided.

He towered beside me as we walked, our silence broken only by the thump and scuffle of our shoes on the thick green grass. The sieving screen was right where we had left it, balanced on the spoil heap, and David bent to examine the small bit of broken pottery lying nestled on its bed of dirt.

'That was in the last load of soil Adrian brought over,' I told him. 'Careless of us to miss it in the digging.'

I studied the back of his head for a moment. 'You weren't at all surprised to find something, were you?'

He glanced round, his eyes touching mine with level honesty. 'No.'

'But it's . . . I mean, it seems so incredible, when you think about it—Adrian and Fabia going to all that trouble to fake the survey results, and in the end the ditch is exactly where . . .'

'Not so incredible.' His voice held the gentle insistence of a teacher reminding his pupils of a lesson they'd forgotten. 'Robbie said there was something there. When you've known him longer, you'll understand.' He turned the sherd over carefully in his fingers. 'Is this all you found?'

'That, and a few fragments of animal bone—birds and mice, mostly, I think.'

'Right then, let me fetch my notebook, and we'll get this properly recorded. I won't be a minute.'

Left alone, I folded my arms across my chest and frowned harder at the pottery fragment. I ought to have been pleased, I told myself. It was, after all, beginning to look very much as if there really was a marching camp at Rosehill, and Ninth Legion or no, the discovery of a Roman camp was *something*. So why was I feeling uneasy?

I stood there so absorbed in thought that when the footsteps rustled through the grass behind me I didn't turn round. It wasn't until I heard the half-sigh of an indrawn breath close by my shoulder that I realised someone else had come to join me. I fixed a smile of welcome on my face and turned to say hello.

My greeting fell on empty air.

My heart lurched. Over the sudden roaring rush of blood that filled my ears I heard a herring gull cry out its warning high above the twisted trees, and then the whispering footsteps passed me by and faded in the softly blowing grass.

FOUR

'You look as if you'd seen a ghost,' said Adrian, surveying me over the top of his drawing tablet. 'Are you feeling all right?'

'Fine.'

'Because you don't need to stick around for this part, if you're tired. Robbie and Wally have gone home for tea, and as soon as I've done this rough map I'll be taking a break myself.'

'I'm fine,' I repeated stubbornly.

My hands had finally stopped trembling but I kept them clenched deep in the pockets of the windcheater David had insisted on fetching for me when he'd returned to find me shaking from what he'd assumed was the cold.

There are no such things as ghosts, I told myself fiercely.

Below me in the trial trench David sat back on his heels, resting a moment. 'Feeling any warmer now?' he asked.

He had beautiful eyes, I thought vaguely. It really was unfair how nature always gave the longest eyelashes to men. His were black, like his hair, and made his eyes look brilliant blue by contrast. I noticed, also, that his nose, in profile, was not quite straight, as though it had been broken in a fight.

'Much warmer, thanks.'

Adrian sent me an assessing glance. 'Got a headache, have you?'

I sighed. 'No, I'm fine. Honestly.'

Quinnell, at the far side of the trench, raised his head in enquiry. 'Who's got a headache?'

'Verity,' supplied Adrian.

I was on the verge of exploding when the sun abruptly vanished behind a gathering bank of grey cloud. 'Rain,' Quinnell pronounced, in a mournful tone.

'Aye.' David stood. 'I'm done for the moment, at any rate. It's all down to the one level.' He looked at me. 'That's the last of it, for now,' he promised, pointing to the three full buckets to one side of the trench. 'I'll just take them up to the Principia, so they'll not get rained on. You don't want to be sieving mud.'

I smiled at his casual use of the Latin word. 'The Principia? Where's that, the stables?'

'Aye.' He smiled back. 'The nerve centre. Quinnell named it, and the name stuck.'

Most appropriate, I thought. Every Roman fort had its *principia*— the large headquarters building at the centre of the complex, where the legionaries gathered to receive the day's commands.

Our own commander, Quinnell, climbed with great reluctance from the trench. 'Time for a drink, I suppose. There's not much we can do here until the rain passes. We'll meet you back up at the house, David.' Turning, he put a hand on my shoulder to walk me up the hill. 'And I'm sure Jeannie could find some aspirin for you.'

It seemed pointless to protest, and in fact it was heaven to sit in the quiet kitchen at Rosehill and let Jeannie serve me my aspirins with a nice hot cup of tea. 'Is your headache bad?' she asked.

'I don't have a headache, actually. Adrian thought I did and Mr Quinnell suggested the aspirins.'

'Peter,' she corrected me. 'He'll want you to call him Peter. The only one who calls him Mr Quinnell round here is my Robbie.'

She smiled and sat down in the chair opposite. It was, I thought, the first time I had seen her sitting still, not doing something. 'Care for some shortbread? Quietly, though, don't rattle about in the tin, or some man will be in here before you know it.'

'Did I hear you open a tin of shortie?' David Fortune filled the doorway as he walked through it.

'Certainly not.'

'Liar. Verity's eating it now . . . aren't you?'

I went on munching while he helped himself. The unfamiliar Scots terminology reminded me of something I'd meant to ask Jeannie earlier. Chasing down my shortbread with a sip of cooling tea, I casually enquired what a stoater was. 'Someone told me I was one, so I just wondered.'

'Oh, aye?' Her mouth curved in spite of her obvious attempt to keep a straight face. 'And who was it said you were a stoater?'

David smiled. 'Your son,' he said. 'That's who.'

'Cheeky,' she laughed. 'That's his father coming out in him, poor lad. A stoater,' she explained to me, 'is a very good-looking woman.'

'Oh,' I said. Because, after all, there seemed very little else *to* say . . .

David angled his gaze to meet Jeannie's. 'We'll need to be getting her a wee Scots dictionary, so she can understand us. D'ye still sell them at the museum?'

'Aye, I think so.'

I looked from one to the other of them, intrigued. 'There's a museum here in Eyemouth? I didn't know that.'

'A good museum,' David confirmed. 'Not a big one, ken, but the exhibits give you a feel for the past of a fishing town.'

Jeannie nodded. 'I can take you through, if you like. I work there Thursdays, on the desk.' She sent a teasing glance up at the big archaeologist. 'We'd best pick a day when your mum's not there, though, or we're liable to get stuck.'

'Aye.' He leaned across to take more shortbread, and I marvelled at how much more relaxed he was in Jeannie's presence than when we were on our own. 'My mother,' he informed me, 'can be a bit of a blether.'

'She likes to talk,' Jeannie translated. 'Is she still being difficult about having someone to help her?'

'Difficult,' he said, 'is not the word.'

'She'll soon come round,' was Jeannie's optimistic pronouncement. 'It's the funny thing about life, isn't it? If you're not taking care of your kids, you're taking care of your parents.'

'Aye, well, Mum's enough for me, thanks.' Grinning, he glanced at me. 'How's the headache now?'

'I'm fine.' For a moment it occurred to me that I might be wise to have that printed on a T-shirt, for future use.

'Peter'll be glad of that,' he said. 'He sent me in to find out how you were. And unless you want your headache to come back, you'd do well to stay clear of the sitting room. Having to delay work because of the rain does not improve his temper.'

Jeannie studied him with knowing eyes. 'Is that why you're hiding in here, then?'

'I'm not hiding. I'm running errands. I was to see how Verity was feeling, and then go down and check on Fabia's photographs.'

I looked at him, curious. 'Is Fabia a good photographer?'

'Damn good.' His nod held conviction. 'She's been practically raised in a darkroom, that lass. It's what her father did. He could have made quite a name for himself, if he'd bothered to put in the effort.'

'I gather,' Jeannie said, 'that he was something of a . . . well, a . . .'

'Sod,' supplied David, rocking back in his chair. 'Aye, that he was. He and Fabia's mother, they made quite a pair. All their parties and flash cars and Paris weekends. Peter finally had to cut them off— they were spending his money right, left and centre.'

Jeannie frowned. 'She was a fashion model, wasn't she, Fabia's mother? When the money stopped, she left. Fabia was only wee and it's amazing she's turned out as sane as she has, being brought up by Philip. He wasn't all there, if you ken what I mean.'

Giving in to my curiosity, I asked how Quinnell's son had died.

'A bottle of tablets washed down with brandy,' was David's blunt reply. 'Not that it really surprised anyone—we'd all seen it coming a long time ago. And at least Peter got his granddaughter back.'

I frowned. 'I'm sorry . . . what do you mean, he's got her back?'

'Well, Philip wouldn't let him see the lass for years. Never sent so much as a photograph, or a card at Christmas. Not seeing Fabia fair broke Peter's heart.'

'Speaking of which,' said Jeannie, in her motherly tone, 'were you not going downstairs to check on the lass, Davy?'

'Aye, so I was. One more shortie and I'm away.'

He strolled out of the kitchen whistling, and Jeannie rose to salvage what remained of her shortbread. Draining my teacup thoughtfully, I leaned back in my chair.

'He seemed in a good mood,' I remarked. 'Very chatty.'

'Who, Davy? He's always like that.'

THE RAIN FELL STEADILY through the night and when the morning came there was no sun at all, only a dull grey sky and the dreary rhythm of the raindrops beating ceaselessly upon the roof.

There was to be no digging today, not just because of the wet weather but because Quinnell held Sunday to be a day of rest. Which explained why, when I finally extricated myself from my blankets and made my way downstairs in search of coffee, I was surprised to learn that Quinnell had ignored his own decree.

'He's gone up to the Principia,' said Fabia, uninterested. Picking up the Review section of the *Sunday Telegraph*, she shook it out and looked at me over the spread pages. 'He'll have coffee on up there, if you want some. I don't drink the stuff.'

Deciding that Quinnell's company would be more cheering than his granddaughter's, I borrowed a bright yellow mac from a peg in the front entry and made a dash up the hill. I found Quinnell sitting at David's desk, tapping at the keys of the computer with one finger. He raised his head as I came in, and smiled at the picture I made.

'My dear girl, could you have found a larger raincoat?'

'It was the closest thing to hand,' I told him, shaking out the dripping folds as he returned his attention to the computer. 'I thought Sunday was supposed to be a day of rest,' I reminded him.

'What? Oh, yes . . . yes, it is. It's only that this system is giving us some problems. Eating my reports and spewing out all kinds of unintelligible symbols—that sort of thing. Not to worry, though. I'm sure we'll get it sorted out.' Switching off the machine, he stood and smiled warmly. 'If all else fails, I can always hit it with my cricket bat. Would you like a cup of coffee?'

'That would be brilliant, thanks.'

He went through to the common room and came back with two mugs of steaming liquid. 'You look as though you need this,' he said. 'Did the rain keep you awake last night?'

I assured him I'd slept very well. 'I only woke up once, I think, and that was the fault of your neighbour's horses. He really shouldn't be keeping them out in this weather.'

Quinnell's eyebrows drew together. 'Horses?'

'Yes, the ones in the field behind here.'

'There are no horses here, my dear. A few cows, maybe, but . . .'

'I've heard them,' I said firmly. 'Galloping.'

'Ah.' He nodded, smiling faintly. 'Perhaps you've been hearing the shadowy horses.'

'The what?'

'From Yeats's poem *I Hear the Shadowy Horses* . . . *Púcas*, I suppose he meant—evil spirits in the shape of horses, though it's quite the wrong season for *púcas* just now. November's their month.' He tilted his head to one side, thinking. 'Of course, Yeats might have been writing of Manannan's horses. In Ireland, our sea god,

Manannan Mac Lir, is also the god of the otherworld, riding his chariot over the waves in the wake of his magical horses. They carry men off, do those horses—over the water and into the mist, to the land where the living can't go. When I was small,' he said, 'my father would show me the waves rolling in, with their curling white foam, and say: "Look now, boy, look at the horses of Manannan, see their white manes . . . he'll be coming behind in his chariot."'

'And did you ever see him?' I asked.

'Manannan? Oh, no.' The long eyes softened. 'But I shall, my dear, one day. No doubt sooner than I'd like.'

His voice was gentle and resigned, but it bothered me to think of him as old, and I was glad when he changed the subject.

'I've been taking another look at that sherd you found yesterday,' he went on. 'Gave it a bit of a cleaning. It came up rather nicely . . . would you like to see?'

Unlocking the door to the finds room, he switched on the light to show me where the gleaming blood-red fragment, freshly scrubbed, lay drying on a bit of newspaper beside the sink.

'The edges, you see,' he pointed out, 'aren't abraded, they're sharp, so it's possible that fragment was buried soon after it was broken. In fact, I wouldn't be at all surprised if we didn't find a few more sherds nearby—parts of the same shattered pot.' Bending over the three buckets of excavated soil that David had brought indoors yesterday, Quinnell poked about in one experimentally.

'Would you like me to help you look?' I offered.

But before I could lift a finger, a firm feminine voice spoke out from the open doorway of the finds room, telling me that I'd do no such thing. 'It's your day off,' said Jeannie McMorran, turning her reproachful gaze on Quinnell. 'I've something more exciting planned for Verity. Robbie's got his piano lesson in half an hour and I thought she might want to come into town with us. Granny Nan's minding the museum today. We could show Verity the tapestry.'

Quinnell endorsed the plan. 'That's a capital idea. Do go. I shall be quite all right without you . . . don't forget your raincoat.'

And he sent me on my way, the mention of David's mother having clearly settled the matter.

I followed Jeannie to her car, where Robbie sat waiting for us.

It took scarcely any time to drive to Eyemouth. I rubbed the condensation from my window and peered with interest at the maze of narrow one-way streets hemmed in by roughcast square stone houses with bold names painted in the transom windows over their gaily painted doors.

Negotiating a final downhill bend and crossing another road that looked very much like the road I'd first come in on, Jeannie swung the car neatly into a large car park. 'Right,' she said to me, 'I'll just take Robbie in, then you and I can walk along to the museum.'

After waiting a few minutes, I pushed open my door and stepped outside to stretch, pulling my hood tight against the soggy weather. Drawn by the thunder of the waves, I turned and tried to see, through the flat grey mist, if the foam on the crest of the waves really did look like white manes on Manannan's horses, as Peter had said, but I only caught a glimpse of them before Jeannie's footsteps sounded briskly on the pavement behind me.

'This way.' Jeannie steered me along the road past a curving sweep of shops and across the street into a small square edged on two sides by an odd array of buildings. One, with its distinctive symbol set above the wooden door, was obviously the Masonic Lodge, and beside it a white-plastered house in the old style proclaimed itself to be a fish merchant's. The smaller structure, dead ahead, was clearly the museum.

'The Auld Kirk,' said Jeannie, and indeed it could be nothing else with its arching windows and beautiful bell tower.

'Granny Nan will be wanting to show you everything, especially since she kens you're a museum person, too.'

'Has she worked here a long time, then?'

'Aye, since it opened. The doctor tried to make her give up working after her heart attack, but she'd not hear of it. Might as well try to make the sun set in the east.'

As we walked the final few steps, heads bent low into the blowing rain, Jeannie glanced sideways and shot me a mischievous smile. 'You'll want to be taking your raincoat off, though, afore we go in.'

I looked down. 'Is it really so awful?'

'No, but it belongs to Davy,' she informed me. 'And Granny Nan's a noticing sort of woman.'

THE WIND SLAMMED the door at our backs as we came in through the vestibule, and I folded the dripping yellow raincoat tightly over my bent arm. Then my gaze moved past the shelves of books and souvenirs to the reception desk, and I got my first good look at David Fortune's mother.

Having heard her called 'Granny' so often I'd fully expected her to be like my own grandmother, a small saintly woman with withered cheeks and soft white hair pulled back in gentle wings. But Granny Nan, decidedly, was not my Granny Grey.

She put me in mind of those marvellous film stars of the thirties and forties, who'd flouted tradition by dressing in trousers and throwing off witty one-liners. She stood tall for a woman and ramrod-straight, with the same strong, uncompromising angle of chin and jawline that she'd passed on to her son. Her eyes were wider apart than his, and the mouth was different, but her hair, like David's, had once been dark—there were traces of it in the short-cropped steel-grey curls which framed a face that must have been pretty in youth, and in maturity was striking. Her blue eyes held a warm blend of intelligence and humour that I recognised.

Jeannie led me up to the desk and then paused, sniffing the air suspiciously. 'You've not been—'

'Certainly not.'

'Aye, you have so, I can smell it on you.' Jeannie sniffed again, to prove her point, and this time even I caught the faint smell of tobacco smoke, but Granny Nan stood firm.

'You can blame that on your father,' she said. 'He was here not an hour ago, stealing my biscuits and telling me about the ongoings up at Rosehill. He told me a lot about this lass,' she added with a wink. 'I hear our Robbie thinks she's a stoater.'

'Aye, well, I don't think he's the only one.'

'No, even my Davy let dab she had bonny long hair, and he rarely notices a lass unless she's three hundred years dead.'

After which comment it took all my effort to hold back a blush while I stood through our proper introduction. My one relief was learning that she had a real name—Nancy Fortune. I'd have felt dead silly calling her Granny Nan.

'By the way,' Jeannie cut in as we were shaking hands, 'you'll want to sell her one of these.'

I saw the book she was pointing to and, reaching out, took a copy from the shelf. 'Oh, right,' I said. 'My Scottish dictionary.'

'Scots,' Nancy Fortune corrected me. 'Scottish means anything to do with Scotland, ken, but Scots is the name of the language.'

'Oh.' I flipped a page of the pocket-sized paperback, scanning the strange-looking words. *Stoater. Fantoosh. Oose.* Where *did* one come up with a word like that? I wondered.

'Such an uninspired language, English,' David's mother continued. 'Though northern English sounds a bit like Scots; and then there's Ulster Scots as well, in Northern Ireland. Peter always said he had no trouble at all understanding us, when he first came over—it sounded just like home.'

I smiled. 'He's lived in Scotland a long time, I gather.'

'Aye, since the early fifties. He was searching in the west of Scotland then, like all the other Roman experts. When I first went to work for him he'd bought a grand old house near Glasgow, to spend summers in. Ah, those were good days,' she said, eyes softening at the memory. 'We must have walked every inch of Dumfries and Galloway, the two of us, looking for likely battlefields.'

I tried to imagine the two of them young. Peter Quinnell, handsome now, would have been irresistible in his thirties, I thought—tall and lean and full of charm. I found myself wondering what sort of man David's father had been, by comparison. 'Did your husband work for Peter, as well?' I asked.

'Och, no. My Billy was a fisherman, a lad I'd grown up with. Peter had a right canary,' she admitted, 'when I left him to get married onto Billy. But I was thirty-five then, and a woman wants a bairn.'

Jeannie raised an eyebrow. 'He'd have understood that, surely. He was married himself, after all.'

'It's different for men,' David's mother maintained. 'And besides, that was no marriage the two of them had, with Elizabeth a manic depressive and biding in Ireland. She never came out of the Castle.'

Quinnell's life intrigued me. 'The Castle?'

'That's what Peter called his family's home,' said David's mother, fondly, 'in the north of Ireland, near the Giant's Causeway. One of his forefathers made a fair fortune in sugar and slaves in the West Indies, ken, then came back and had someone design him the Castle. Peter never liked it much. Built with blood money, he said. But Elizabeth—Peter's wife—loved a grand mansion. And Philip used to love that house, as well.'

I saw a shadow darken Nancy Fortune's eyes, and commented that it must have been hard on Quinnell, losing his son.

'Aye, well, he's not lost all his family.'

Jeannie's mouth quirked. 'Not yet,' she said. 'I can't say I'm not tempted to stir a few things into Fabia's porridge, some mornings.'

'I hope you've not told Peter that. The problem is,' said Nancy Fortune, her eyes twinkling, 'there's too much of her father in her.'

'So there are three houses, then?' I frowned, still trying to sort out the various properties. 'The one in Northern Ireland, and the one near Glasgow, and . . .'

She shook her head. 'He sold the Glasgow house last autumn, once he'd bought Rosehill. This is where he needs to be.' Her voice was very certain. 'He'll find his Romans here, like Robbie says. He's never wrong, lass. If he sees something in that field, it's there. It's the rest of us who are blind.'

She sent us a purposeful nod. 'Right then, we're away. You can leave the dictionary behind the desk there, and I'm sure you won't want to drag Davy's wet raincoat around with you . . .'

Jeannie's dark eyes caught mine, laughing.

I TENDED TO AVOID museums, when I wasn't working, but this, I reasoned, was a special case. I would be living out at Rosehill for the digging season, so it followed I should do my best to learn the local history. And, to my relief, I found that someone had done a professional job of presenting the town's past in a well-defined sequence of information panels and displays.

David's mother paused before one panel. 'And this, of course, commemorates the day the bard himself came here, to be made a Royal Arch-Mason.'

My eyebrows rose. 'What, Shakespeare came here?'

'Robbie Burns, you heathen,' she corrected me, rolling her eyes good-naturedly. 'Our national poet, no less.'

Jeannie thought it was a wonder Burns had lived to tell the tale. 'Coming to a smuggling town like Eyemouth, and him an exciseman.'

I fancied even smugglers harboured some respect for genius. The poet's image kept proud company with nets and herring barrels and a whopping great cannonball that Jeannie showed off with a smile. 'That came from the fort on the cliffs at the end of the beach. You can see it from where we parked the car.'

'Not a Roman fort, I take it?'

'Tudor,' Nancy Fortune told me.

Conflict, I reflected, was a constant theme along this stretch of coast. Invasion and slaughter and swift retribution, an unending cycle of fire and sword. Small wonder the soil here was red.

I drifted on, attracted by the next display. Instead of relying on pictures alone to give one the feel of a fishing boat, they'd brought the boat itself inside. The front half of a boat, at any rate.

Stepping onto the bridge, I played like a child with the polished wheel and gazed in admiration through the glass window at the ropes and nets and fish boxes piled on 'deck', and the real stuffed herring gull riding the jutting bow into an imaginary wind. I thought the whole thing brilliant, and said so.

'Aye, it's fair impressive,' David's mother said. 'But ye've not yet seen our greatest achievement. That we save for last.'

With great expectations I followed her round the remaining few displays until we arrived back within sight of the lobby.

'There.' She stopped dramatically before the final wall. 'The Eyemouth Tapestry. It took twenty-four ladies two years to make this, for the one hundredth anniversary of the Disaster. One hundred and eighty-nine men were lost at sea in a terrible storm, from all four local harbours—Burnmouth, Cove, St Abbs and Eyemouth. That's what the four maps show, in this third section. And the sea wall, just here, has one stone for each Eyemouth man lost. One hundred and twenty-nine stones'—she gave me the tragic count—'half the men of the town gone in one day. That was the toll of the Eyemouth Disaster . . . October the 14th, 1881.'

I stood a moment, reflecting on the ironies of history. Nearly two thousand years ago, if Quinnell's theories were right, another group of men had faced their own Disaster day in this same place—men who spoke a different language, served a different god, but who had dreams and wives and mothers.

And the shadowy horses had come for them, too, to carry them off to the land of the dead.

FIVE

David Fortune was already hard at it when I went up to the Principia on Wednesday, before breakfast. He swivelled in his chair as I came in, and his face, bathed in the hard blue light of the computer screen, looked beastly tired. 'Morning,' he greeted me, his jaw stiffening as he held back a yawn. He reached for the mug of coffee on the desk before him. 'You're up early.'

'Look who's talking.' I took my own seat in the stall-cubicle opposite and hitched my chair sideways to face him. 'Are you actually doing work at this ungodly hour?'

'I'm just entering my field notes.' The blue eyes flicked me with a friendly challenge. 'So what's your excuse?'

'Couldn't sleep.' I thought of asking him if he had ever heard the horses running in the fields beyond, but decided against it. 'Do you not teach on Wednesdays?'

He shook his dark head. 'We have meetings and such, in the afternoon, but Peter's been wanting to show me the things that he found when he widened the trench.'

'Oh, yes. Potsherds.' I fetched them from the finds room, to show him. 'We found four yesterday. I've not had much of a chance to look at them myself, really. I'd have worked a little longer on them last night, only Peter wouldn't hear of it.'

'Aye, well, he has a thing about us working late. It's like his Sunday holiday, you'll find—meant to be strictly observed by everyone but Peter himself.'

'Yes, I noticed that. He was up here on Sunday morning, but he sent me off with Jeannie. We went down to the museum.'

'So I heard.' He raised his coffee mug to hide the slanting smile. 'I hope my mother behaved herself. You ken she had a heart attack?'

I nodded. 'Jeannie told me. Very recently, was it?'

'Last July. Scared me more than it did her, I think.'

'She seems to have made a full recovery,' I commented. 'I could barely keep up with her; she moves at a fearful pace.'

'Aye, she does that.' The big Scotsman's eyes held affection. 'It'd take being struck by lightning to slow my mother down.' The sound of an engine speeding up the long drive seemed to emphasise his statement. 'That'll be Adrian,' he told me, as I heard a car door closing. 'Either that, or Nigel Mansell's come for breakfast.'

I glanced at my wristwatch, surprised. 'Adrian's normally still half-asleep at this hour.'

'Well, we'll be starting to map out the ramparts today, and Peter was keen on an early start. It's time-consuming, but it shouldn't be too difficult, assuming that we really have a marching camp. We ken the shape a camp would be—we only have to find the corners.'

I nodded. Roman marching camps, and forts and fortresses, tended to follow a playing-card kind of design—square or rectangular, with rounded corners. The Romans, being Romans, had imposed their rigid structure on whatever land they passed through, instead of letting nature dictate what design they ought to use. And so once any section of the rampart had been found, one only had to follow the predicted shape around to plot the whole site's boundaries.

David lifted his coffee mug again and grimaced. 'Yuck, that's awful stuff. I'll make another pot. Did you want a cup as well?'

'Yes, please, if you don't mind.'

'Right.' David rose and stretched to his full height before disappearing in the direction of the common room, and while I waited for him to return I carefully arranged the four new potsherds on my desk and bent over them thoughtfully.

The furtive pad of footsteps broke my concentration.

I felt the hair prickling on the back of my neck and glanced up sharply, seeing nothing. 'Hello?'

No one answered. The silence stretched my nerves to breaking point, and when I felt the brush of cold against my hand I nearly shot straight up into the rafters, until I looked down and saw a pair of liquid brown eyes staring back in mild inquisition, and Kip's long feathered tail gave a tentative wag. Collies, I thought, always looked so damned intelligent, and this one appeared to be weighing the wisdom of making friends with someone this jumpy.

Since I'd always liked the company of dogs, I settled the matter by scratching his ears. 'Hello, Kip. Where's your master, then?'

I saw no sign of either Robbie or Wally, and when I went on stroking him the dog collapsed like a spent balloon on my feet, rolling over slightly to make his tummy more accessible.

'You'll want to watch him,' David warned me, returning along the aisle. 'He'll stay like that for hours if you let him.'

Adrian, coming through the main door, heard the warning and laughed. 'Oh, Verity won't mind. She's a right pushover when it comes to animals.'

And crossing to my desk he set a covered plate in front of me. 'Your breakfast,' he announced, whisking off the cover with a flourish. 'Jeannie said I was to be sure you ate it, seeing as you sneaked off without eating this morning.'

Sighing heavily, I looked down at the great mound of sausages and fried eggs, rimmed with strips of toast and rounds of tomato. 'But I never eat breakfast. A little toast, maybe, but . . .'

'I have my orders,' Adrian said, setting down a knife and fork.

David grinned, and handed me my mug. 'Here's your coffee.'

'I'll give you five pounds if you eat this for me.' I made the offer hopefully, but he refused to play.

'I've had mine, thanks. So, what did you make of the sherds, then?'

I moved the plate out of the way of the four small jagged fragments of blood-red pottery. 'Well, they're definitely Samian ware—a small pot, I'd think, from the degree of curve. Maybe two pots. This one,' I said, touching one piece lightly, 'doesn't seem to match the others.'

'And what date would you estimate?'

I chewed my lip. 'Offhand, I'd say they're earlier than what we're looking for. But then again . . .' Without the support of laboratory analysis, dating pottery could be a rather imperfect science. If the piece wasn't actually stamped by a known maker, one had to rely on comparisons to other bits of pottery dug up at other sites.

Again I touched the suspect sherd. It was a rim fragment, broken from the top edge of a pot or bowl. 'This one strikes me as a later piece. I ought to ask Howard, a friend of mine at the British Museum. He's absolutely mad about Samian ware—knows the name of every potter. He could tell us exactly what they were part of and when it was made. I could send him some sketches, and perhaps, if Fabia would take a few photographs . . .?'

'Good idea, we can tell her on the way,' said David. 'Peter will be thinking we've forgotten all about him. We'll leave you in peace to eat your breakfast. And it's no good trying to give it away to the dog—he can't eat eggs. Bloats up like a balloon, he does.'

His pale eyes were teasing, and I toyed with the idea of pitching a sausage at him, but instead I took a bite of toast, smiling my most amenable smile. 'Right then. Have a good time.'

I waited until I couldn't hear his cheerful whistling any more before I glanced down at the dog sprawled beneath my chair. Kip's tail thumped hopefully against the floor. 'Look, love,' I offered, 'here's the deal. I'll eat the eggs if you'll eat everything else. How does that suit you?'

Evidently it suited the collie fine. The empty plate was positively shining when I set it on the corner of my desk.

Well satisfied, I washed my hands and settled down to start my drawings of the sherds.

I SENT THE DRAWINGS and photographs off by the afternoon post. Howard had always been frightfully efficient and I half expected him to ring me the following day, but it wasn't until Friday morning that I got my call from the British Museum.

'Before I give you my opinion on these sherds,' he said, 'I simply have to ask: What the devil are you *doing* up there? We had to look Eyemouth up on the map, for heaven's sake. Pondered it all through tea break yesterday, but no one could recall an excavation going on in your area.'

I smiled against the receiver, balancing my notepad on the narrow front-hall table. 'Well,' I told him, 'as I'm constantly being reminded by people here, you don't know everything down there in London.'

'So it is an excavation? Led by whom?'

I told him, and waited while he paused for thought. Howard's memory was slow, but encyclopedic.

'Not *the* Peter Quinnell? Don't tell me he's still on the trail of the Ninth Legion?'

'Well . . .'

Howard groaned. 'My dear girl, no one's taken Quinnell seriously since I was in short trousers. And he must be ancient, surely?'

'He's only in his seventies. And I find him rather fascinating.'

'Well, so long as he pays you heaps of money . . .'

'The sherds?' I prompted, patiently.

'Ah. Yes, well, they're Agricolan.'

'All of them?' I felt a twinge of disappointment.

'All pieces of the same bowl, I should think.'

'Oh.' So much, I thought, for my suspicions that the rim sherd didn't match. Howard's knowledge of Samian ware was indisputable.

'So what date are we looking at, exactly?'

'Oh, somewhere between AD 80 and 82, I should think. Not much help to you in finding the Ninth Legion, I'm afraid.'

'You never know. At least it's an earlier date, and not a later one. For all we know the pot might have been forty years old when it was broken,' I reasoned stubbornly. 'And anyway, we've only just begun to map the boundaries of the site. I'm sure we'll find more pottery when we start the proper digging.'

'What you want to find,' he coached me, 'is a sherd that's been hammered down a post hole, so you know for certain that it dates from the time of the . . . what is it, exactly, that you're excavating?'

'A marching camp.'

'Ah,' he said without enthusiasm. 'Not much chance of finding post holes there, unfortunately. Not ones of any real size.'

He was, as always, right. Marching camps, constructed for the one night only, had no permanent structures, and even the stakes used on top of the ramparts were smaller than those used in forts. They often left no trace at all.

'And anyway,' Howard reminded me, 'it's long odds that you'll even find a marching camp. Not if you're working for Peter Quinnell.'

'I'll bet you a fiver that this is a marching camp.'

'Done. Oh, by the way,' he said, remembering, 'you do know Lazenby is looking for you?'

'Dr Lazenby? Whatever for?'

'He's taking a team out to Alexandria in September. Quite a high-profile venture, from what I've been hearing, and he wants you as part of his team. Shall I give him your number?'

I thought of Quinnell, and shook my head. 'No, not just yet. I'll give him a ring in a few days, all right? And Howard?'

'Yes?'

'Thanks. For the expert opinion, I mean.'

'Any time.' The smile in his voice almost made me miss my days at the museum, and I rang off with a small sigh.

And then I cocked my head, listening.

Someone was climbing the cellar stairs. The footsteps were heavy—a man's footsteps—only all the men were down at the far end of the field. I knew that because I'd just left them there, with Fabia as well . . . Even Jeannie, who'd come down to fetch me for my telephone call, had stayed behind to watch the crew in progress. I ought to have been alone in the house.

My mind raced swiftly through the possibilities. A ghost . . . a burglar . . . My brain told my feet to move, but the message took a moment to reach its mark and in that moment the man came up the final stair and into the entrance hall.

He seemed, to his credit, more shocked by my presence than I was by his, then he recovered and came forward, wiping one hand on the back of his denim jeans before holding it out in a friendly greeting. 'Sorry,' he apologised, with a self-deprecating grin, 'I thought you were all down in the field. You must be Miss Grey, am I right? My son's not stopped talking about you.'

So this, I thought, was Brian McMorran. I studied him with interest over the handshake.

He was nothing like I had expected. He was older, for one thing— nearing forty, I judged, with silvered brown hair and rather an appealing sort of face. Not a tall man either, though his body had the hardness of a lifetime of labour and I wouldn't have wanted to take sides against him in a fight. He wore an earring, a small gold hoop that glinted dashingly against his greying hair, and below the rolled sleeves of his flannel work shirt his forearms were a fascinating canvas of dark tattoos. He didn't look a drunkard or a bully, and I found it hard to reconcile the image I had formed with the reality.

'I expect,' he said, 'that I gave you a fright as well. You'd not have known I'd just got in. Is Jeannie anywhere about? I've looked, but—'

'She's down with Quinnell.'

'Is she? If you're heading back there, I'll tag along.'

He didn't talk much while we walked. A brief exchange on the warming of the weather was the closest we came to conversation.

David saw us coming first. 'Heyah, Brian,' he said, coolly. 'When did you get back?'

'About an hour ago. Stealing my wife again, are you?'

'Of course he isn't.' Jeannie moved from David's side to give her husband a kiss in spite of her father's scowl. 'How did it go?'

Brian shrugged. 'Not bad. We netted a fair haul, this trip.'

'Any fish?' Wally asked sourly. I didn't understand the barb behind the comment but it glanced off Brian, who ignored the old man.

'You've been busy,' he noted, looking back at the trail of brightly coloured golf tees that marked our progress along the buried ditch.

From the trial trench in the southwest corner, the western ditch ran roughly parallel to the long drive, travelling up at a slight diagonal for some three hundred yards before it turned a rounded corner, just below the ridge, and started back across the field.

Quinnell followed Brian McMorran's gaze proudly, not appearing to mind the man's presence. 'Yes, we're making good progress.'

'Looks like it. Is that where the walls were, then—where you've stuck all them tees? Bloody big camp, wasn't it?'

'About twenty acres,' Quinnell estimated. 'It's not like a fort, you understand. They only had to house an auxiliary force, but a marching camp was meant to hold the whole legion on campaign. It had to be huge.'

'I see.' Brian's eyes swung back across the field to the southwest corner, where the russet walls of Rose Cottage showed plainly through the frieze of trees edging the drive. 'And what's our Mr Sutton-Clarke up to over there?'

Fabia tossed the short fall of hair from her face. 'Doing a survey, what else?'

Indeed, when I wandered down to join him a few minutes later, I found him preparing the section of field for another pass with the ground-penetrating radar unit, happily laying out neat lines of non-magnetic tape for guidance.

'Guilty conscience?' I asked him.

'What?'

'You've already done this bit of the field, remember? Produced a smashing image.'

'Sarcasm,' he informed me, 'doesn't suit you. And if you must know, Peter asked me to repeat the survey. It seems he's misplaced the initial results, and he wants to have a record for his files.'

'And how did he come to misplace them?' I asked suspiciously.

'I had nothing to do with it.' He raised a hand in Boy Scout fashion, as proof of his sincerity. 'I'm rather pleased the damn thing's gone, mind you, but I had nothing to do with it.'

After scrutinising his face a moment I decided he was telling the truth. More likely, I thought, Peter had pitched the fake survey results on the fire himself. As a solution to a prickly problem it was, I thought, decidedly Peter's style, and endearingly gallant.

Adrian cast a vaguely impatient look at my knees. 'Does that blasted animal have to follow you everywhere?'

I looked down in mild surprise, and Kip looked back at me, one ear flopped softly forward. During the hours when Robbie was at school, the collie had taken to keeping me company, trailing at my heels so quietly that I frequently forgot he was there. Wally had joked that the dog, like its young master, was faintly besotted with me. Personally, I put it down to the sausage.

'It's like you have six legs, these days,' said Adrian. He paused, his eyes flicking past my shoulder. 'Do me a favour, Verity love, and measure how far it is from where I'm standing to that wall over there.'

I measured. At the crumbling stretch of dry-stone wall, I stood up and called back, 'Fifty-six feet, two inches.'

He cupped a hand to his ear. 'What?'

'Oh, for heaven's sake.' With Kip trotting at my heels, I patiently retraced my steps. Across the field, I could see David and Quinnell, heads bent in contemplation of the rough turf at their feet, while Wally stood to one side, frowning, and Brian leaned close over Fabia's shoulder. Jeannie, I noticed, had gone back to the house, as it was now less than an hour till lunchtime. My stomach gave a small anticipatory rumble as I drew level with Adrian.

'Fifty-six feet, two inches,' I repeated.

'Thanks.' He jotted the number down, tossing a quick glance over his shoulder at the others. 'Well, well,' he said slowly. 'I do believe the old man's jealous.'

'What, Peter? Who would he be jealous of?'

Adrian's eyes came back to mine, vaguely pitying. 'Goodness, you are thick, aren't you? No, my love, not Quinnell. The other one. He's looking daggers at me.'

I turned in time to catch the blunt edge of David's scowl before his head angled down again. Staunchly ignoring the tiny, unnamed thrill that coursed through me, I advised Adrian not to be an idiot. 'It's nothing personal. He's been looking daggers at everyone since Jeannie's husband arrived.'

'Ah, yes?' Adrian's tone was dry. 'What did you think of Brian?'

'I thought he seemed rather nice.'

'You always did have rotten taste in men.'

I shot him a sidelong glance. 'Doesn't say much for you, does it?'

'Yes, well, I meant myself excepted. Although,' he mused, 'you did throw me over, didn't you, which only goes to prove my point. Was that a drop of rain, or did I imagine it?'

'I didn't feel anything.'

'Good.' Another pause, while he stretched a length of tape between two surveyed points. 'You've noticed, of course, that our Fabia shares your high opinion of Brian McMorran?'

'Meaning what, exactly?'

'Meaning just what you think I mean.' He jerked his head in the direction of the small group down the hill. 'Look for yourself, if you don't believe me. It doesn't take a rocket scientist.' He broke off, squinting skywards. 'Damn, that *was* a drop of rain. I knew it.'

Beyond his shoulder, Fabia threw back her head and laughed, her artfully tousled mop of hair whipped backwards by the wind to brush against Brian McMorran's jaw. He, too, was laughing, leaning closer, not touching her, but . . .

'She's very pretty,' I commented, slowly.

'Yes, she is. If you like that type.'

'What type would that be?' I teased him. 'The sexy-as-hell blonde type? All legs and eyes and perfect teeth?'

He grinned. 'That would be the one, yes. Mind you, I've gone head over heels on at least one occasion for the dark-haired, smart-talking type as well,' he said lightly.

I knew him far too well to fall for the intimacy of that smile, those dark eyes levelled warmly on my own. I looked away with ease, and held my hand palm upwards to catch the light but unmistakable scattering of raindrops.

'Blast!' Adrian fastened off the final guiding line of tape as the rain began in earnest, a steady soaking shower that made spikes of my eyelashes and tasted sweet on my tongue.

'Come on,' he said, turning to make a dash for it. But I lingered one more minute in the cool and cleansing rain, eyes closed, my face tipped upwards like a child's, wondering why the thought of David Fortune's frowning face made me so damnably happy.

LUNCH AT ROSEHILL was a strictly observed ritual that, while not exactly formal, still carried a faint echo of the grand old days of the country house, when people dressed for dinner and the servants ate below stairs. The impression was made all the stronger by the fact that Jeannie, when she wasn't serving food or clearing plates, kept to her kitchen and left us alone. And the dining room itself seemed to demand a certain degree of gentility.

It was a most impressive room, tucked discreetly away in the rear corner of the ground floor. The walls were panelled in palest oak, the window gleamed wide and uncurtained, a gas fire hissed in the elegant fireplace on the end wall, and beneath the long polished table, which could easily have seated twelve, a thickly cushioned carpet of rich Cambridge blue ran the length of the room.

Because it was Friday, with David not up in Edinburgh giving lectures, we were five, seated in a half-circle around one end of the long table. Peter sat at the head, with his back to the fireplace, and Fabia and I to his left and right, respectively. Adrian had been assigned the seat beside Fabia, which also allowed him to keep an eye on me.

Adrian was an only child; he didn't like to share. If David, at my shoulder, leaned too close or made me smile, Adrian would smoothly intervene, like a child jealously guarding a discarded plaything. As he was past reforming, I ignored him, turning my eyes to the window opposite and its peaceful view of garden, field and sky.

Jeannie had outdone herself, as usual, with plates of ham, and carrots done in mustard sauce, and parsnips and potatoes roasted golden, sweet and crisp. But not even Jeannie's cooking could dispel the curious tension that had settled round the lunch table. Clearly, the change in atmosphere had something to do with Brian

McMorran's coming home, although the man himself was nowhere to be seen. I guessed he would be eating in the kitchen with his wife, and when I next looked out of the dining-room window I knew I'd guessed correctly. Wally Tyler normally lingered long over the kitchen teapot at lunchtime, but today his cap was pacing grumpily back and forth on the far side of the garden wall.

The rain shower had been a brief one, and already the sun was beginning to scatter the clouds. The group of us scattered as well: Peter into town to collect the post; David and Wally back to the ditch, and Adrian, having lured Fabia into assisting with his survey, strolled down to the southwest corner, radar unit in tow.

Since I wasn't really needed anywhere for the moment I chose to spend an hour throwing sticks for Kip, behind the Principia.

Kip was a brilliant fetcher of sticks. He not only brought the stick back, he actually *dropped* it at my feet and waited with a wide grin until I threw it again, then he wheeled like a dancer and bounded off happily to hunt the stick down in the weeds and wild flowers.

He was bringing it back for what seemed the thousandth time when he suddenly stopped and sniffed the warming air. After a second sniff he laid the stick down and looked expectantly towards the drive, his plumed tail waving as he gave a soft, impatient whine. I'd seen him go through this routine a dozen times since I'd been at Rosehill—he did it whenever a car he knew came up the drive, or when one of us came back from an outing. Only this time the drive was empty.

He whined again, and I shook my head. 'False alarm,' I told him.

The collie only wagged his tail harder and raised his head to give a woof of welcome. Picking up his stick again, he bounced past me and began to trot away along the ridge, performing an odd little dance that seemed to demand he turn full circle every several steps, followed by a joyful leap until his head reached a specified level in the empty air. The same level every time, I noticed, hugging myself to ward off the crawling chill of recognition. The same level at which a grown man's hand might hang as he walked beside the dancing dog.

I'd seen him do the same thing when he walked at Wally's side, or David's, or my own. Kip loved to have his head patted. Of course, this time, there was nobody walking beside him. Nobody, I told myself firmly. Certainly not a ghost.

But when the collie turned and started back again, still bouncing and wagging, I turned, too, half in panic, and bolted round the corner of the Principia, to get clear of the Sentinel's path.

'DARLING, WHEN I SAID I'd gone head over heels for you, I didn't mean it quite this literally.' Adrian winced as he picked himself up and brushed grass off his leg. 'Aren't you supposed to yell "fore" or something before you come barrelling round a corner?'

'Sorry.' I dusted the dirt from his sleeve. 'Are you all right?'

'I'll have my lawyers get in touch.'

'Idiot. Have you finished your survey?'

'Mm.' His eyes narrowed thoughtfully as he flexed his right arm, testing the action of his elbow. 'If you promise not to make any sudden movements, I might even let you help me plot the readings on my computer. Or are you busy?'

'No, I'm not busy.' I was glad to have a reason to go indoors, out of sight of whatever was walking the ridge. Relieved, I followed Adrian in through the gaping front doors of the Principia. I wheeled my chair into his cubicle and watched him without really paying attention, content to let the drone of his computer soothe my superstitious fears. In the midst of all this gleaming bright technology, it was difficult to think of things like ghosts.

'I never did ask you,' said Adrian, in a mildly curious tone. 'What did Howard have to say this morning about your sherds?'

'Howard?' I glanced up blankly. My telephone call from the British Museum seemed an age ago. 'Oh, nothing helpful, I'm afraid. He says they're Agricolan. Which only means the pot was made in that time period, really. It doesn't tell us when the thing was used.'

His eyes touched mine with scepticism. 'A forty-year-old pot, in military service? It's a bit of a stretch, don't you think?'

Refusing to concede the point, I changed the subject. 'Howard also said that Dr Lazenby was looking for me.'

Adrian always had been quick at putting two and two together. Swinging round, he raised an eyebrow. 'Not to offer you a place on the Alexandria dig?'

'Apparently, yes . . .'

'Right. That's you gone, then, isn't it?'

'I don't know. I haven't actually spoken to Lazenby yet,' I defended my indecision. 'And there isn't any rush—he doesn't leave until September.'

Adrian smiled briefly before swinging his gaze back to the monitor. 'D'you know, if I'd known you were going to get this attached to Quinnell, I'd have left you down in London.'

'Hindsight,' I reminded him, 'is —'

He cut me off. 'Bloody hell,' he said, staring at the screen of his computer. 'Look at this.' He moved aside to make room as I rolled my chair closer and peered at the jagged black-and-white bands. At first glance, the radar profile bore a striking similarity to the image he and Fabia had faked, the boundary ditch and rampart marked at nearly the same spot by a sharp dip in the lines. But Adrian was pointing to a different, smaller feature. 'There, do you see that?'

'What is it?'

A few clicks on the computer keyboard replaced the single image with six smaller ones, while Adrian explained. 'I made several runs across the area this afternoon, and this is what the chart recorder printed off. You see? There's one blip, there. And that's another.'

I scrutinised the profiles. 'I count three.'

'Right. Now,' he told me, keying in another series of commands, 'let me show you what they'd look like on our site map.'

The image on the screen changed shape again, becoming a topographical map section of the southwest corner, on which the three mysterious blips now showed as small black dots. Then Adrian drew in the known line of ditch and rampart and positioned one more dot on the screen. 'Look,' he advised.

I looked. He was speculating, of course—adding the fourth dot to create a perfect square, set at an angle to the rampart's corner curve. Still, the image *was* suggestive. On any other site, I would have said those dots were post holes, hinting at some buried structure underneath the level turf. And on any other site, I'd have been tempted to identify that structure as a guard tower, only . . . only . . .

Adrian turned his head to lock his eyes with mine. 'This is no marching camp.'

SIX

Quinnell rejected the evidence. 'Your equipment must be off, my boy,' he told Adrian, leaning forward to tap the computer screen with an accusing finger. 'Blips on the landscape, that's all.'

It was obvious to me why Peter didn't want it to be a guard tower.

Roman marching camps didn't have any permanent structures—only forts and fortresses had guard towers. And our site could not have been either.

Roman forts were much too small. Built to defend and supply the spreading imperial forces, they were occupied by auxiliary troops, not legionaries. The famous fort at Housesteads on Hadrian's Wall could have barely held a quarter of a legion, and that only if the men stood cheek by jowl.

At the other end of the scale, a legionary fortress would have been enormous—fifty acres or more. And we knew from our surveys and excavations that our ditch and rampart had enclosed an area of roughly twenty acres. Which left us somewhere in between—too large to be a fort, too small to be a fortress. Marching-camp size, as a matter of fact. But one couldn't deny that the survey had found something in the southwest corner that *did* look like a guard tower.

The three of us frowned at the computer screen until David joined us, took one look, rubbed his jaw and offered another solution.

'Might be a vexillation fortress,' he said.

Which was, I thought, entirely plausible. A *vexillatio* was a detachment of a legion, so a vexillation fortress didn't need to be as large as a full legionary fortress. And since they were only built as temporary campaign bases, they left very little evidence behind, much like a marching camp.

But Quinnell rejected *that* suggestion out of hand. He wanted a site from the early second century, after all, and vexillation fortresses were remnants of the century before—the conquest years.

'No, no,' he said, and tapped the screen again, accusingly. 'A garden shed, or some old fence. That's what we'll find down there.'

But as the days wore on, a careful expansion of the trial trench exposed clear evidence of post moulds, and by the following Saturday Peter's optimism had evaporated. 'A guard tower,' he identified it, sadly. 'It can be nothing else.'

And marching camps did not have guard towers. Which meant that what we'd found could not have been the marching camp that sheltered the Ninth Legion on the eve of its last battle.

Peter sighed and spiked the soil despondently with his trowel. 'This really is the worst thing that could have happened.'

But the *worst* thing turned up half an hour later, on the end of his own trowel.

'THE TERRIBLE PART,' I told Jeannie the next morning, as we sat together in the tiny, homely kitchen of Rose Cottage, 'is that the head of David's department, Dr Connelly, comes to lunch on Tuesday, the day after tomorrow, and Peter seems to have completely given up.'

I'd never seen a man so unutterably depressed, so devoid of any interest in the goings-on around him. Since yesterday at noon I'd hardly seen him, and when I did he looked a shadow of his normal cheerful self, sitting wrapped in morose silence with one or both of the cats to comfort him, a vodka bottle close at hand.

He didn't want company. And so, after breakfast, feeling utterly helpless, I'd come down to Rose Cottage and Jeannie.

'Aye, well, naturally he's disappointed,' she said. 'It was coins that you found, was it?'

I nodded. 'Three Roman *asses*—copper coins—from the reign of the Emperor Domitian. He was Emperor during Agricola's campaigns.'

'And who was Agricola?'

'Oh, sorry. Governor of Britain, for a time. Agricola,' I explained, 'built forts and things all over Scotland, trying to push back the native tribes. Only then Domitian called him back to Rome, and the army withdrew again. Our own fortress, or whatever it is, was probably abandoned within a year or so of AD 86—long before the disappearance of the Ninth.'

'Why AD 86?'

'That's when the coins we found were minted.'

'But the coins could have been old when they were dropped here, couldn't they?'

'No.' I shook my head, positive. 'No, they were all three in splendid condition, unworn. And that kind of coin, once it's in circulation, tends to show wear very quickly. So they had to have been buried just a short time after they were struck. It gives us a very tight *terminus post quem*.'

Jeannie's mouth curved. 'You're worse than Davy, you are, for explaining things.'

'Sorry,' I apologised, again. 'In translation, it would mean the time after which something happened.'

'Like, the Romans left *after* those coins were made?'

'That's right. We use a *terminus post quem* to help set a date range for the site, to say when it was occupied. Here at Rosehill, with the pottery we've found, and now these coins, we're looking at a range of only a few years . . .'

'*Terminus post quem*,' she murmured slowly, testing the sound of the words. 'That's Latin, isn't it? D'ye ken Latin very well?'

'Well enough. It comes in handy in my work.'

'Robbie said you kent it. He was wanting to ask you what a word meant.'

Before I could respond, the peace of the kitchen was shattered by the boisterous return of Robbie and Kip. The collie, muddied from his long walk, greeted me energetically, distracting me while Robbie made a grab for a biscuit.

'Not till you've washed your hands,' Jeannie told him with a firm shake of her head.

I held back a smile as I watched him trudge reluctantly to the kitchen sink, showing the same enthusiasm for soap and water that I'd felt myself at his age. Not that I knew exactly what his age was . . .

'Nearly eight and three-quarters,' he told me, turning as though I'd spoken the words out loud. 'I'll be nine in September.'

I sighed. '*Must* you do that?'

'Do what?'

'Answer my questions before I've even asked them. It puts me at a disadvantage.'

Jeannie smiled. 'Aye, well, we're all at a disadvantage, with this wee laddie around. All of us except his dad, that is,' she corrected herself. 'He can't read Brian very well. Can you?' she asked her son, who simply shook his head.

'Dad's fuzzy.'

'He is that,' Jeannie agreed, her smile widening. 'Och, I'm forgetting now, what was that word that you wanted to ask Miss Grey about? The Latin word?'

'Solway,' came the answer, through a mumbly mouthful of biscuit. 'I looked in Mr Quinnell's dictionary, but I couldn't find it.'

Jeannie frowned. 'Solway?'

The dark curls bobbed affirmatively. 'Aye, that's what he said. I thought he meant the Firth, like, but Granny Nan says it would have had a different name then, and anyways he wouldn't speak English.'

'Who wouldn't?' I asked, thoroughly confused.

'The Sentinel.'

My teacup clattered in its saucer. 'The Sentinel *talks*?'

'Aye. Granny Nan says he's probably talking Latin, like, only I don't ken Latin.'

'He talks.' I repeated the words to myself, surprised that anything still had the power to surprise me. Rosehill had forced me to suspend my natural scepticism. There were no horses in the field behind the house, yet horses ran there in the night. There were no ghosts, yet one had walked right past me. And there could be no psychics, yet I knew whatever Robbie spoke was certain truth.

I cleared my throat. 'Does the Sentinel talk to you often?'

Robbie raised one thin shoulder in a cavalier shrug. 'He just says "solway". And then I don't ken what to say back, so he goes away again. So what does "solway" mean, then?'

'Well, I think he's saying *salve*, Robbie,' I said, and spelled the word out for him. 'The Latin "v" is pronounced rather like our "w". And *salve* means good day, how are you doing, all of that.'

'So he's just saying hello, like.'

'That's right.' It was pointless to tell the boy to say *salve* in return, since he wouldn't understand anything else the Sentinel said to him. Pity I couldn't see the ghost myself, I thought—it would be quite an experience, conversing with a Roman legionary . . .

Jeannie looked down at her watch to check the time. 'Och, it's nearly eleven already. Robbie, finish up now and get ready—you don't want to be late for your piano lesson.'

He pulled a telling face and went scuffing along the back corridor to his bedroom, while I drained my cup of tea. 'I might just beg a lift into Eyemouth, if you don't mind. Just as far as the Ship Hotel, if that's no bother.'

'Oh, aye?'

I nodded, too deep in thought to notice her sudden interest. 'I want to catch David, if I can, before he goes out anywhere. I've got a proposal for him.'

IT WAS DIFFICULT to tell, from his expression, what he thought. He had that damned impassive face that could mask almost anything.

Taking a long drink from his newly poured pint, he settled back and stretched one arm along the top of the padded bench. I shifted in my chair and sent him a smile that felt a little stiff.

'You think it's a silly idea,' I guessed.

'No sillier than some.' His voice was slow and measured. 'No, I'm just surprised you'd think of it, that's all. I thought you didn't put much faith in ghosts.'

'I didn't . . . don't.' I frowned. 'Not all ghosts, anyway. Just this one.'

'Because it's Robbie's?'

'Yes.'

'I see.' He eyed me keenly. 'And so what you're saying is, you think we ought to ask him questions.'

'Well, we know he talks,' I reasoned, 'and we know that Robbie hears him. I assume the ghost hears Robbie, too, though of course since they're speaking different languages there's no real proof of that. But I do think it's worth a try. Peter's already talking about chucking the entire excavation, did you know that?'

'Aye.' He spoke the single word without surprise. 'It'd not be the first time, for him. He's been chasing the Ninth Legion since afore I was born, and he doesn't waste time on a trail that's gone cold.'

'But is it cold?' I challenged him. 'I mean, don't you think we owe it to Peter to examine every possibility?'

His eyes met mine with patience. 'We've got the coins, lass. And the potsherds. Textbook evidence, for dating . . .'

'Yes, I know. But just because the Romans came—and presumably went—in Domitian's day, that doesn't mean they didn't come back later, does it?' Leaning forward, I tried to explain. 'Suppose you're the commander of the Ninth Legion, and you've been ordered to march north to fight the Scottish tribes.'

'I'd have had more sense.'

'Be serious. So anyway, you march your legion north, along the road. If there had been a vexillation fortress here,' I reasoned, 'then there would have been a road. The Devil's Causeway heads up this way from York, and we don't know *really* how far north it went.'

He conceded the point. 'Go on.'

'Well, you have to pitch camp somewhere, don't you? And if you chanced upon an old abandoned fortress . . .'

'A vexillation fortress,' he reminded me, 'was not designed to hold a legion.'

'But suppose the buildings were all gone. The Romans had a habit of destroying their camps when they withdrew. That would leave you a nice level bit of ground, large enough for your legion to pitch its tents on, and protected by a lovely ditch and rampart.'

'We've found no sign of later occupation.'

'We've only been digging a couple of weeks,' I said defiantly. 'It's a big site. And a marching camp won't leave much evidence.'

David settled back a moment, considering my theory. As he drained his pint he studied me above the upraised glass, as though I were a tiny item on his trowel that defied classification.

'You're fair determined, aren't you?'

I set my jaw. 'I just think we ought to make absolutely certain, before Peter packs it in.'

'And we all find ourselves out of a job.'

I bristled. 'It's nothing to do with the job.'

'Aye, in your case, I ken fine that it's not. Adrian, now, he'd miss the money, and I'd miss working where I can keep an eye on my mother, but you . . .' He shook his head. 'I reckon it's the work itself you'd miss. And Peter.'

Actually, I longed to say, *it's you I'd miss.* These past two weeks I'd grown to like the sight of David walking down the field to meet me; the low pleasant roll of his voice; the strong, sure movements of his big square hands. But admitting my attraction wouldn't help. If Adrian had taught me nothing else, he'd taught me that it wasn't wise to get involved with co-workers. Doomed to failure, those affairs were . . . not to mention unprofessional.

Pretending an interest in my barely touched glass of dry white wine, I shrugged. 'Certainly I'd miss Peter. I'm very fond of him. That's why I don't like seeing him like this.'

'He climbs out of his depressions,' David promised me, 'eventually.'

'Yes, well, I'd climb out of my own rather more quickly if I could do something constructive.'

'Like interview the Sentinel?' He smiled faintly. 'Seems to me that you and Robbie can take care of that yourselves. You'd not need me.'

I disagreed. 'I think there ought to be a few of us present, if we do this. So there isn't any question of a hoax.'

'Och, you needn't worry there. I don't imagine Peter would suspect you of twisting the truth.'

'No,' I said, not thinking, 'but you might.'

He arched an eyebrow, as though surprised. But as he began to look at me more closely, I was rescued, rather disappointingly, by a smooth familiar voice that spoke behind me, from the door.

'Now there's a sight one never sees,' said Adrian laconically. 'A Scotsman with an empty glass.'

David took the gibe without offence. 'You'd best buy me another, then.'

Fabia, who'd blown in at Adrian's side, shrugged her coat off carelessly. 'And you can get me a white wine while you're at it.' Sliding onto the bench next to David, she combed her fingers through her bright hair and said to him, half accusingly, 'Does the wind always blow like this? It nearly knocked the Rover off the road.'

David assured her the wind wasn't permanent. 'Sometimes,' he said solemnly, 'it changes and blows from the east, like.'

'Oh, wonderful,' said Adrian. 'Something to look forward to.' He joined our little group at the corner table, his hands wrapped round two dripping pints of beer and a glass of white wine. 'Verity, love, are you all right with that?' He looked at my still-full glass, and I nodded.

David raised his pint philosophically. 'She's been too busy talking to drink it,' he said.

'Ah,' said Adrian, in a knowing tone. He took the seat beside me, stretching an arm along my chair back in an attitude of casual possession. 'So what have the two of you been talking about?'

He voiced the question lightly, but that didn't fool me for a second. *Oh hell*, I thought, *he's jealous.*

'Oh, this and that,' said David, who either hadn't registered the tone of voice or didn't care. He swept a shrewd eye over Fabia. 'How's your Latin, lass?'

She looked up blankly. 'My what?'

Adrian lowered his glass and grinned. 'I didn't do well with Latin myself at school. I'm lost with any language where the words are given genders. Why should *legio* be feminine, for heaven's sake? A legion is made up of men, there's nothing feminine about it. Verity's rather proficient though, aren't you, darling?'

Fabia frowned prettily, still looking at David. 'What difference would it make if I spoke Latin?'

'None. It's only that Verity and I,' he said, glancing at me for consent before continuing, 'are thinking of having a go at Robbie's Sentinel, to see if he'll talk to us.'

Adrian snorted in open disbelief. 'You're joking. Verity doesn't even believe in ghosts.'

'Does she not.' The bland Scottish voice wasn't asking a question, but Adrian answered it anyway.

'No, she doesn't. Practical from head to toe, she is. I ought to know,' he reminded David, in a voice as smooth as polished steel. His smile implied he knew me head to toe in other ways as well, but if he'd hoped to produce an effect he was disappointed.

David merely shrugged. 'Ask her yourself, then.'

Adrian shifted his dark eyes to my face and read my expression. 'My God,' he said, 'you really do believe in our little Roman friend, don't you?'

'Yes.' Lifting my wineglass, I braced myself for the inevitable arguments. Fortunately, Fabia was the first to speak.

'Well, Peter certainly believes in him,' she said. 'Peter thinks that all our troubles with the computer system are somehow the fault of the ghost.'

Adrian rolled his eyes heavenwards. 'I'm surrounded.'

David smiled quietly. 'Since you've no belief in ghosts, then, I assume you'd not be wanting to take part in our wee séance?'

'You assume correctly.'

But the idea clearly intrigued Fabia. 'Do you think you *could* talk to him?'

I nodded. 'He's already tried to talk to Robbie, only Robbie didn't understand the words, you see.'

'So you'd take Robbie with you then, and have him speak to the ghost, is that right?'

I nodded. 'With David and me providing the Latin.'

'And Peter, of course.'

I glanced at David, and he stirred in his seat, adopting the voice of reason. 'I don't think,' he said, 'that we should take Peter with us, lass. Not yet.'

Fabia considered this. 'In case it doesn't work, you mean.'

I bit my lip. 'Or in case the ghost says something Peter wouldn't want to hear. Our Sentinel might be from the wrong legion, after all '

Adrian made a sound between a chuckle and a groan. 'The ghost,' he assured me, 'isn't going to say a bloody thing. You *do* realise this?' He looked across at David. 'Surely you must know how asinine—'

David calmly cut him off. 'We'll not lose anything by trying. Peter will probably scrap the excavation anyway, unless . . .'

'What?' Adrian snapped to attention.

'Unless we turn up evidence of later occupation . . .'

'Well then.' Adrian tossed his beer back as though he needed it. 'I don't suppose that talking to this ghost would do us any harm.'

WE MUST HAVE LOOKED a motley little crew, assembling on the hill behind the stables in the still of the night. Eleven o'clock had been the hour fixed as our gathering time, but it was very nearly half past before we were properly organised. Fabia was the last to arrive.

'That's it, then,' she said, breathless after hurrying up the gentle grassy slope from the darkened house. 'Peter's asleep, I checked. We should be in the clear.'

'Good.' David cast a quick, assessing eye around the group of us.

The end of Wally's cigarette glowed red against the stable wall. 'Best get on with it,' the old man advised, 'and let the laddie hie hisself to bed.'

Robbie, with the legs of his pyjamas tucked deep into his wellies and one of his father's jackets drooping to his knees, cheerfully assured his grandfather there was no need to hurry. 'I don't have to go to school tomorrow.'

'Oh aye?' Wally raised an eyebrow. 'Who's telt ye that?'

'Mum said.'

'He'll be wanting a long lie, the morn,' Jeannie defended her decision, 'and it's only the one day.'

Fabia shifted, impatient. 'Are we ready, then, Davy?'

'Aye.' Davy motioned to Robbie. 'Can you lead us on to where the Sentinel walks?'

Robbie nodded. 'He goes this way.'

It was easy to follow the small bouncing figure in the oversized coat as he headed east along the ridge that marked the boundary of the great deserted field. The moon hanging bright in the midnight sky lit everything plainly, and the wind had died to a whispering kiss.

A large shadow scuttled past and I caught my breath, but it was only Kip.

Beside me, Fabia stopped walking. 'This is far enough, surely,' she said, hunching into her jacket.

Davy agreed that it probably was.

'Perfect night for ghost-spotting,' said Adrian. 'Pass me my flask, will you, Verity love? Or have you drained it already?'

'I only had a taste.' I rummaged for the leather-covered bottle. 'Vile stuff, that.'

'Yes, well, Russian wine is not exactly noted for its subtlety,' he told me, taking a healthy swig.

Jeannie smiled. 'A gift from Brian, was it?'

'Not exactly a gift. I paid him ten pounds for the case, I think.' He offered the flask around, but Fabia was the only one brave enough to accept. She gave a little choking cough and passed it back.

'That is terrible,' she grimaced. Sitting down, she drew her knees up and rested her chin on her hands. 'I was just thinking, we don't really know that this ghost is roaming about at night, do we? I mean, Robbie's only seen him in the daytime.'

'He'll be here,' Wally said. His voice was simple, calmly knowing.

'He walks by night as well as by day. Just ye ask yon dog.'

I looked to where the collie lay sprawled out upon the grass, head up, ears perked, and I remembered it would probably be Wally who took Kip out late at night, when Robbie was in bed. Perhaps Wally had seen what I had seen—the collie dancing at the heels of an invisible companion, begging to be patted, broad tail waving. 'Do you believe in ghosts, Wally?' I asked him.

His shrug was noncommittal. 'Depends.'

'You're all daft.' Adrian pronounced his judgment lazily, leaning back on his elbows. 'A ghost is merely a projection of a less than stable mind.'

David's voice came quietly. 'Is that a fact?'

'It is. I've been working here two months now, and I think I would have noticed anything out of the ordi—'

'*Salve*,' Robbie said.

He was sitting close beside me, and the sudden sound of his small voice made me jump. Just as suddenly, he turned round and showed me a brilliant grin. 'Hey, it works!'

My throat tightened for a moment before the words found their way out. 'That's wonderful, Robbie. Where is he?'

I wouldn't have believed my voice could sound so calm, when I was anything but calm inside. My nerves were thrashing wildly, and my heartbeat pulsed a hard and rapid rhythm in my throat.

'Right there,' said Robbie, pointing to the vacant air.

David slid the few feet down the slope to join us, coming to an abrupt stop directly behind me and steadying himself with a hand on my shoulder. I could feel the warmth of him through the thick folds of my jumper, but I don't believe he even noticed the touch. Above my head, he watched the darkness steadily. 'Say "*salve custos*", Robbie,' he instructed.

'What's *custos*?'

'Sentinel.'

We were all silent now, leaning slightly forward in anticipation as Robbie dutifully repeated the words. I counted my heartbeats . . . one . . . two . . . before the boy turned round a second time, his eyes going over my head, seeking David's. 'He's not saying anything, but he's smiling. He's looking at you, now.'

'Is he?' David frowned a moment at the nothingness, then raising his voice he explained in perfect Latin that we couldn't see or hear our long-dead visitor; he would have to talk through Robbie.

'Now, Robbie,' David murmured, 'if he says anything, if he makes a sound, you repeat it, all right? Like a parrot.'

'All right.'

David nudged my shoulder. 'Go on, then,' he invited me. 'It's your party. You ask the first question.'

I opened my mouth to speak but then the big hand on my shoulder tightened warningly, cutting me off. At the same moment Jeannie breathed an urgent whisper: 'Verity!'

'What?' I brought my head back round, and saw what had alarmed them. The Sentinel had moved.

Robbie, beside me, was watching the air not two feet from my face. I drew a sharp breath and then found that I couldn't breathe out again, so I swallowed instead. 'Robbie,' I said cautiously, 'what's he doing?'

'He's crouched down,' came the reply, 'to see you better, like. Now he's reaching out his hand—I think he wants to touch your hair.'

David swore softly, the word brushing warm down the back of my neck. I might have imagined the ghost's gentle touch and the sweeping thrill of cold—I'd always had a rather wild imagination. But it didn't stop me shivering.

Adrian, unconvinced, raised the wine flask for another drink. 'Go on, then, Verity, my love. Here's your chance to clear up one of history's little mysteries. Ask your friend what legion he belonged to.'

He meant it in jest, of course, but I found my voice and asked the question anyway.

Robbie, if he heard an answer, didn't pass it on. Instead he scrambled to his feet, staring uncertainly into the darkness. Behind him, Kip whined sharply, struggling to break free of Wally's hold, but Robbie didn't seem to hear that, either. Slowly, as though following another's gaze, he turned his head and looked towards the house.

The windows were no longer dark. Lights blazed in both the kitchen and the upstairs hall, and even as I registered the fact, the sound of someone starting up a car came echoing across the field. The motor coughed, and caught, and became a roar, and two clear yellow headlights plunged between the trees that fringed the drive.

'He's going,' said Robbie urgently. 'Davy, he's going. He's . . .'

He didn't finish. His large eyes swung towards us, suddenly anguished, and even as Jeannie leapt forward to catch him he crumpled and fell face-down upon the grass.

'It's all right,' said Jeannie, lifting him gently. 'He's only had a

467

vision, he'll be fine.' But her face, in the cold moonlight, didn't look so self-assured.

Adrian, in his typically selfish fashion, had noticed only one thing. 'That was my car,' he burst out indignantly. 'The bastard took my car!' And then he turned and sprinted for the house, and the rest of us, after an exchange of glances, followed.

On the level sweep of gravel at the top of the drive, we found Brian McMorran brushing off his trousers. 'Crazy idiot,' he said sourly. 'Nearly ran me over.'

Fabia stared at him, disbelieving. 'It wasn't Peter, surely?'

'He took my car,' Adrian repeated bleakly.

Wally eyed his son-in-law suspiciously. 'What d'ye think yer doing, then, coming home at this hour?'

Brian laughed lightly, without humour. 'If I'd known this was the welcome I'd get, I'd have stopped the night in town,' he said, lifting an eyebrow at Jeannie. 'I might ask the same of you, at any rate—the cottage was empty when I got there.'

'We were out in the field,' she answered.

'In the—?' He broke off, seeming for the first time to notice Robbie's condition, and his lips compressed impatiently. 'Aw, bloody hell, you've not been after the ghost? Where's your head, woman? Give him here.' The tattooed arms closed protectively round the little boy. 'You've been putting a strain on him, can't you see?'

'He wanted to help Peter,' Jeannie explained. 'And it wasn't the ghost that made him faint. He saw something else, something . . .'

Robbie stirred at the sound of his mother's voice. 'Granny Nan,' he mumbled weakly. 'Davy, Granny Nan . . . you have to go.'

In the sudden silence, David leaned in closer. 'Go where, lad?'

'Hospital . . .'

'Oh, no. Fabia, get me the keys to the Range Rover.'

Robbie, in his father's arms, slipped back into delirium. Even after David had gone the boy kept calling out to him: 'Davy . . . Davy . . . Granny Nan. Must help, must . . . nona . . .'

'What was that?' Startled, I turned. 'Robbie, what did you—'

'Leave the boy be.' Brian gathered his son closer, staring me down with contempt. 'He didn't say nothing, just leave him alone.'

But I knew what I'd heard.

'Nona'—that's what Robbie had said. It was, I fancied, a belated answer to the question I had asked the Sentinel: *Which is your legion?* And *nona* was the Latin word for 'ninth'.

SEVEN

Somewhere in a shadowed recess of the dining room a mantel clock whirred softly and began to chime the hour: four o'clock. I shifted on my window seat and sighed. The house felt very lonely, with everyone asleep.

Fabia, having sensibly decided there was nothing she could do, had long since said good night and gone to bed. I'd expected Adrian, still worrying about his precious car, to wait up longer with me, but after comforting himself with a well-aged brandy from Peter's drinks cabinet, he had drifted off as well. I'd left him snoring in the sitting room, stretched out full length on the old sofa. Even Wally, who'd displayed no great desire to hurry home with the McMorrans, had eventually taken his leave, and the little cottage slumbered now in darkness at the bottom of the drive.

Which left me on my own, fretful and sleepless, wandering from room to room with only the cats for company.

In the kitchen, I put the kettle on for yet another pot of tea. The two cats exchanged a rather long-suffering glance before beginning to clean themselves. I was disrupting their nightly schedule, and I knew it. Ordinarily at this hour they would be peacefully asleep on my bed, or on Peter's.

But Peter wasn't here, and after what I'd experienced out in the field, I knew that I wouldn't be able to sleep. It wasn't the Sentinel himself that made me jumpy, it was the *idea* of the Sentinel—the knowledge that beyond the window, in the blackness, something walked, and watched, and waited . . .

The kettle boiled. I turned from the window and forced my trembling hands to make the tea. *Don't be such a coward,* I reproved myself. *Fabia's upstairs, and Adrian's only a couple of rooms away, and Peter will be back soon.*

I glanced up at the kitchen clock to check the time again. Four twenty. More than three hours since Peter and David had roared away from Rosehill, and still no word from either of them.

I got to my feet, feeling restless. Peter's sitting room was out, I thought, since Adrian was still asleep in there. But across the hall the drawing room offered warmth and light and a glowing gas fire. I drew an armchair up to the hearth and stretched my legs out. Another half-hour had passed before I saw the gleam of headlights curving up the drive and heard a car door slam. The front door opened and closed. Soft, measured footsteps crossed the entrance hall; paused in the doorway behind me.

'My dear girl,' Peter Quinnell said, his low voice mingling faint surprise and weariness. 'You ought to be in bed.'

I twisted round in my chair. 'I couldn't sleep.' He looked grey, I thought, and frightfully old, and I asked my next question with some hesitation. 'How is she?'

'Resting comfortably, the doctors say, but doctors always say that, don't they?' He crossed to the drinks cabinet. 'Can I get you something? Brandy? It's good medicine for sleepless nights.'

He poured one for himself as well, and lowered his long frame into the chair next to mine, staring at the hearth.

'David found you all right, then, did he?'

'What?' His eyes slid sideways, not really seeing me at first, and then he seemed to pull himself together. 'Oh, yes. He's a good son. He'll stay all night with her, I shouldn't wonder.'

'It must have been a frightful scare for him.' I looked at his face and amended my statement. 'For both of you.'

'Yes, well, it's not the first time.' Quinnell swirled his brandy, turning back to the fire. 'This is her third attack, you know. She never did like listening to doctors. For years now they've been telling her she ought to be more careful, have some help around the house; but she's a bloody-minded woman, Nancy Fortune. She still thinks she can do it all herself. She's always mastered anything she put her mind to.'

I heard the pride in his voice and glanced at him with interest. 'It must have been a great loss, when she left you for David's father.'

'Yes.' He smiled again, a little sadly. 'I'm afraid I was rather ungracious about the whole affair. I never quite forgave her for leaving, but in time I understood. Time,' he told me, 'gives us perspective.'

Of course, I thought, he'd lost much more since then. I tried to think of something suitable to say, but nothing came to mind.

Behind us the floorboards creaked and Adrian said sleepily: 'Ah, here you are. I thought I heard voices.'

He shuffled over to the drinks cabinet, smoothing back his rumpled hair. The gesture didn't help. Barefoot and bare-chested, his shirt slung on loosely, his jeans unbuttoned, he looked like he'd been romping through the sheets with someone.

Quinnell arched an eyebrow in my direction and I hastened to explain. 'He stayed to keep me company, and fell asleep on the sofa.'

Adrian grinned. 'What she means to say,' he told Quinnell, 'is that I've been behaving myself, in spite of appearances. But you did leave me stranded . . .'

The eyebrow lowered again. 'I do apologise, my boy. Couldn't find the keys to the Range Rover, I'm afraid. Fabia puts them in the damnedest places. And when I went to look in the Rover itself, I found your car beside it, with the keys in the ignition, so . . .' He smiled an apology. 'I wasn't thinking very clearly, at the time.'

Adrian sloshed a measure of gin into a glass, and shrugged magnanimously. 'No harm done. Not to me, anyway. Poor Brian McMorran's a bit shaken up, though. You nearly ran him over.'

'Did I?' Quinnell frowned faintly, trying to remember. 'I do seem to recall something leaping into the bushes. That was Brian? Did I do him any damage?'

Adrian shook his head. 'Just rattled him a little.'

'Ah.' The charming voice sounded rather disappointed, to my ears. 'Pour me another brandy, would you, there's a good chap.' He passed his empty glass to Adrian and turned to me expectantly. 'And now, since I have you both here, perhaps you'll be good enough to tell me what you were up to tonight, out in the field. I may be an old man, but I'm not a complete fool. What did the Sentinel say?'

'YE'VE TELT HIM.' Wally Tyler slowly lit a cigarette and nodded. ''Tis well ye did. It'll take his mind off Nancy, some.'

I took a seat beside him on the low stone wall that ran round the small neglected garden at the side of the house, and watched while he threw a stick for Kip.

Already it was early afternoon, and the betraying shadow on the sundial at the centre of the garden shamed me for sleeping away half the day. When sleep had finally found me in the hours after dawn, it had claimed me with a vengeance. I was sorry to have missed what must have been a lovely morning.

Out of the wind, the sun felt exceedingly hot; come Saturday week, it would be June. Which left us three full months still, in the digging season. Time enough to prove our theory. Our theory . . . I smiled faintly, raising a hand to rub my tired eyes. When I'd begun this, I had thought it Peter's theory, and his alone.

'Actually,' I confessed to Wally, 'he wasn't much surprised to learn what we'd been up to. He'd figured most of it out already.'

Brian McMorran sauntered over to join us and settled himself on the garden wall beside me. 'Grand weather,' he remarked. 'I'm surprised you're not out digging, especially after that little panto you staged last night.'

'No work today,' said Wally shortly. 'Peter needs his sleep. He was up all night with Granny Nan.'

Brian shook his head. 'It'd take more than a heart attack to level that woman. She's a tough old bird.'

'How's Robbie?' I asked Brian, then saw from his expression that I'd picked a touchy subject.

'I reckon there's no damage done, no thanks to all of you. He was rabbiting on to Jeannie just now, when I left them. Wanting to go into Berwick to visit Granny Nan in hospital, though I don't imagine she'll be having any visitors today.'

'Was it her heart attack he saw, last night?' I asked. 'Was that what made him faint?'

Brian nodded. 'He didn't get it when it happened, on account of he was already tuned in to your Roman ghost, but once the ghost was gone I guess the signal came in loud and clear. Bit too much for the lad, having all that happen in the one night. His mind's like a fuse box, see. You overload the circuits and the lights go out.'

It was, I thought, an apt analogy.

'Anyhow,' said Brian, 'it won't be happening again.' He looked around. 'Where's Fabia, then? I see the Range Rover's gone.'

'David's got it,' I reminded him.

'Still?' He raised his eyebrows in surprise. 'Inconvenient that. I hope he brings it back by teatime.'

'Why?' Wally speared his son-in-law with a narrowed glance. 'What d'ye want with the Range Rover?'

'Got some boxes to unload off the boat. Our car's too small,' he explained.

Kip, having carried the stick back to Wally, drew back a pace, panting, then suddenly brought his lovely head up and around to stare past our shoulders at the front door of the house. Fabia emerged with a surprisingly cheerful greeting and swung herself over the low garden wall. She looked disgustingly vibrant and full of life. The privilege of youth, I suppose. On top of which she hadn't stayed up all night drinking brandy and discussing whether a child's mumbled '*nona*' was enough to base an excavation on.

'What have you done to Adrian?' she asked me, curious. 'He's dead to the world in there. I had to answer the phone myself.'

I moved to make room for her on the wall, between myself and Brian. 'We were up rather late last night,' I explained, through a yawn. 'Talking to your grandfather.'

'Ah.' Swinging her legs, she looked Brian up and down, assessingly. 'You seem to have recovered from your hit-and-run.'

'Oh, aye.' His golden earring caught the sunlight as he tossed his head back, grinning. 'It'd take more than an old man in a sports car to finish me off. Anyhow, my darling, I promise I'll not sue your granddad for damages, if you'll just do me one small favour.'

Fabia leaned forward expectantly. 'Name it.'

'Let me use the Range Rover.'

'Sure. Davy's finished with it. That was him ringing a moment ago, to say that his mum was all right and he's back at the Ship Hotel. We could walk in now and get it, if you like.'

'Walk, hell,' was Brian's reply. 'We'll take my car. There's two of us, two vehicles. We can each of us drive one back.' He stood up away from the wall. 'Anyone else want to help unload boxes?'

I stood too, and stretched. 'No, thanks. But I think I could do with a bit of a walk.'

I caught the faintest glimmer of amusement in Wally's crinkled grey eyes. 'Away ye go, then, lass.'

Because I didn't want Wally to see where I was going I purposely struck out in the opposite direction, following the road down through the small ravine where the narrow river sang in the green coolness and the trees stretched out protective arms above the primroses and wilting daffodils. Having got safely out of sight of Rosehill I turned back, abandoning the road in favour of a narrow footpath that ran along the river bank.

In time, the footpath led me upwards, and I found myself on the road that led me straight to the centre of Eyemouth.

I didn't see the Range Rover in the car park of the Ship Hotel— Fabia and Brian must already have been and gone. But I did find David, sitting over a mug of coffee in the public bar. He looked rougher than usual, his eyes red-rimmed and dull above the day's dark growth of beard. Seeing him like that, I felt a pang of sharp emotion that I put down to concern.

'You ought to be in bed,' I told him, hoisting myself onto a neighbouring stool and ordering a coffee.

It took him a moment to register my presence, but eventually he turned and slanted me an unreadable look, and meeting his eyes I was forced to admit that concern wasn't all I was feeling.

'How is your mother doing?' I asked him.

'She's over the worst of it; that's what they tell me. They'll be keeping her in for a while yet, though. Not that they want to,' he told me, with an unexpected grin. 'She's not so bad when she's tranquillised, but my mother's aye crabbit in hospital.'

'Aye crabbit?'

'Always in a bad temper,' he translated. 'Have you not got your dictionary with you the day?'

'No, I haven't . . .' Frowning suddenly, I looked down. 'I haven't even brought my handbag, I'm afraid.'

David assured me his means were sufficient to cover the cost of my coffee. But he arched a quizzical eyebrow. 'What were you planning on doing in town without your handbag, may I ask?'

'Just out for a bit of a walk, that's all.'

He watched me for a moment. 'Adrian's not here.'

'No, I know he's not. He spent the night at Rosehill.'

'Oh, aye?' The eyebrow lowered, and I cursed myself.

'On the sitting-room sofa,' I said clearly. 'Peter took his car and he didn't fancy walking back. Adrian's not the walking type.'

David's face relaxed into a smile. 'I had noticed.'

I watched while he took a drink of coffee, curious in my turn. 'You don't like Adrian much, do you?'

'He's all right,' David conceded, with a small dismissive lift of his shoulders. 'But he's sleekit. That means he's sort of all charm on the outside, but inside he's a sly, lying devil.' After a moment's silence he set the coffee mug down again and swung his gaze back to mine. 'So what *are* you doing at the Ship?'

It was a blunt question, and a reasonable one, and it left me with no graceful way of escaping an honest answer. I shifted on my stool and cleared my throat. 'Well, if you must know, I was rather worried about you. We all were.'

The blue eyes softened. 'Were you, now?'

'Yes. And I thought you might need somebody to cheer you up.'

He stroked a thoughtful hand along his unshaven jaw. 'It's not a job for the faint-hearted, cheering me up.'

'No?'

'No.' He looked at me, hard, for another long moment, until I felt certain I'd never be able to breathe again. And then he smiled. 'But we'll see what we can do.'

WHAT WE DID WAS go out onto the quayside in search of fresher air.

I'd never seen the harbour when the fishing fleet was out. It didn't look at all forlorn, as I'd expected. Instead it had the peaceful and serene demeanour of a housewife who, having finished her day's labours, had found an hour of freedom in the absence of her family, and had settled down happily to enjoy herself. Not that the 'family' was entirely absent. A few boats had stayed behind.

'Which boat is Brian's?' I asked David.

'That one,' he pointed out. 'Second up along the middle pier.'

The middle pier, I gathered from the direction of his nod, was the long bit running parallel to us, on the far side of the harbour. Of the three boats moored there Brian's was the biggest—a bright red monster of a fishing boat with *Fleetwing* freshly painted on its prow.

'Want to walk round and take a look?' David suggested. 'I don't ken whether any of the lads are working on the boat, but . . .'

'Brian might be there himself,' I told him. 'He and Fabia were coming down to unload some things from the boat.' I shot him a questioning glance. 'He smuggles, I take it?'

David grinned. 'D'ye work for the Customs and Excise?'

'No.'

'Well then, it's best to keep your head tucked down, lass, in a place like this.' But he yielded to my curiosity, nonetheless. 'He has a friend in one of the Baltic ports. Since the Berlin Wall came down it's not so hard to get things from that corner of the world.'

'Like Peter's vodka,' I suggested.

'Aye. Peter lets him use the cellars at Rosehill for storage, till Brian's mate comes through with his lorry. So Peter gets a bottle or two every month, in return.'

I looked at the little harbour, peaceful in the sunshine with the water lapping smooth and innocent against its walls. 'Is there much smuggling goes on here, now?'

'Only Brian, that I ken about. In the old days, though—and I do mean the old days, back afore my granddad's time—nearly everyone had a hand in the business. That's why they built the old town like they did, all wynds and vennels, twisting lanes. It's fair impossible to chase a smuggler when the streets don't run straight. And that house over there,' he told me, warming to his subject, 'Gunsgreen, that was a smuggler's paradise. It's got tunnels and storage dens built underneath, and every room has two doors—one to the corridor and one leading into the next room along. So you could leave an exciseman standing in the hallway, pounding at the one door, while you took off through the other rooms and made a clean escape.'

We walked a little further on, pausing for a better view of the long fish-market building that hugged the harbour's edge. It was open to the air, most of it, paved like a car park and sheltered by a sturdy roof that rested on squared wooden posts. Outside, a lorry blocked most of the road, and the driver, leaning up against his cab and smoking a cigarette, nodded politely as we passed.

'He's waiting for the fish auction,' David told me when I asked. 'It doesn't start till four o'clock.'

'Oh.' I twisted my wrist to check the time on my watch. 'But it's nearly a quarter past three. And I don't see any fish.'

In truth, the fish market was completely empty; but David refused to tell me how the miracle of the fishes was to be achieved. Instead he led me past the market down to the bottom edge of the harbour, where we started up along the middle pier. To the left of us, the harbour lay serene and almost empty, while on my right a mud-walled channel carried what David assured me was the same river that I'd walked along from Rosehill. I didn't believe him.

'I wouldn't tell you lies,' said David. 'That's the Eye Water. The town takes its name from that wee trickle, ken. Our harbour was built round the mouth of the Eye. Mind the nets,' he added, as we drew level with Brian's boat.

At first glance the *Fleetwing* seemed deserted, but in response to David's call a small, wire-limbed man wearing bright yellow brace-and-bib overalls came out on deck and raised a hand in greeting.

'Heyah, Deid-Banes.' He leaned over the aft end to look at us. 'Heard about yer mither. Bloody shame. She still in Berwick?'

'Aye. And don't you go thinking of burgling the cottage while she's in hospital, neither.'

The other man laughed. 'Ye've no faith. I'm no sae tarry-fingert. And I'd no steal frae yer mither.'

'You'd steal from yours.'

'Aye, but I like yer mither better. Were ye wanting something? The skipper's away the now.'

'Left you in charge, then, did he? Trusting man.'

'Aye, well, he cannae trust Mick, so that only leaves me.'

David tilted his head. 'Do I ken Mick?'

'The new lad, frae Liverpool. Ye dinna wish tae ken that one, Deid-Banes. The lad's been up the jail half his life, and it wasnae fer thieving. I'll no turn my back tae the bastard.' And then, remembering my presence, he shot me a crooked smile. 'Sorry, lass. Ah'm no minding my manners.'

David folded his arms and looked at him. 'Well, now you've switched on the charm, you might offer the lass a wee tour round the *Fleetwing*, show her how a fishing boat works.'

The other man shrugged helplessly. 'I cannae do it, Deid-Banes. I'm painting the day, and the paint's nae dry yet.'

I couldn't see any paint cans on deck, nor smell the faintest whiff of fumes, but David didn't press the point. 'I kent he'd say no,' he smiled, as we turned and walked on, up the pier, 'but I wanted to see what excuse he'd come up with. He's a brilliant liar, is Billy.'

I tipped my chin up, curious. 'What does "Deid-Banes" mean?'

'It's my byname,' he supplied. 'A kind of community nickname, if you like. A lot of folk have bynames, here in Eyemouth.'

'Why?'

'Helps to tell us apart, for one thing. When you've more than one David Fortune running about, things get a bit confusing.'

I was openly intrigued. '*Is* there more than one David Fortune?'

'Oh, aye, there'd be four of us, I think. My Uncle David, and my cousin—and then there was another David Fortune at school with me. If I traced the family history back I'd no doubt find he's a cousin as well. But we're nothing compared to the Dougals,' he added. 'You can't spit in town without hitting a Dougal.'

'So how does one get a nickname, then?'

'Different ways. I was always digging things up as a lad, playing at being an archaeologist, so my granddad called me "Deid-Banes"— dead bones—and it stuck. Some of the bynames are more obscure, ken. There was Deddy; don't know where that came from. And Pamfy and Racker and Duffs. Now Duffs,' he explained, with a broad smile, '*that* came down from a lad who worked as a cook on a fishing boat. All he knew how to make was plum duff, so Duffs he became. His daughter got the byname, too, and I think her son still gets it sometimes.'

I hopped over a coiled fishing net. Encouraged by the growing ease of our companionship, I chanced another question. 'Your dad was a fisherman, wasn't he?'

'Aye, so they tell me. I can't really mind him.'

We'd come to the end of the middle pier, and David leanedt his elbows on the bright red railing at the pier's end, looking across to the harbour's shielded entrance. Every now and then a stiff gust of wind tossed a mist of white spray over the barrier wall, bringing the cleanly biting scent of the cold North Sea.

A white shape glided silently beneath us, where a small metal drawbridge spanned the Eye Water. 'David, look!'

'Oh, aye, the swan. I wondered where he'd got to.'

The bird cocked its head at the sound of voices, turned smoothly and floated back underneath the little red drawbridge, seeking the relative security of the channel.

'He's magnificent,' I said. 'Does he have a mate?'

'Not yet. There was a female here, a few years back, but she only stayed a fortnight. She couldn't seem to settle down to life inside the harbour.' He turned his head and met my gaze unhurriedly. 'And he's well stuck here now, the lad. Too old to change his ways.'

I felt suddenly aware of how near he was, of how little effort it would take to move towards him, feel his warmth. To raise my hand and touch the hard, unshaven contours of his face.

He wasn't warning me off. No, I decided, watching a smile spread slowly from his blue eyes to his mouth, he wasn't giving me a warning. He was issuing a challenge.

And I was already beginning to respond to it when an unexpected shadow fell between us.

'Hello,' said Adrian. 'I thought I'd find you here.'

IT MUST HAVE SHOWN plainly on my face that I wasn't thrilled to see him, but Adrian took no notice. He was doing his dog-in-the-manger again, and his eyes were not on me, but on David. 'You look awful,' he said. 'You ought to be in bed.'

I caught the uncharacteristic gleam of mischief deep in David's eyes as his gaze swung meaningfully to me. He folded his arms across his wide chest and turned to Adrian. 'Plenty of time for that, yet.'

One could almost hear the slap of a gauntlet thrown down upon the pier. Adrian raised his chin a fraction, measuring the challenge.

I frowned at him. 'You don't look very wonderful yourself, you know. Or haven't you seen a mirror recently?'

'My dear girl,' he said smoothly, 'if you will insist on keeping me up until all hours of the night . . .'

Oh no you don't, my lad, I thought, showing him a smile that was dangerously sweet. 'I'm surprised you're up and walking, after all that drink. Peter was rather concerned about you.'

'Was he indeed?' Adrian grinned and let my dart glance off him harmlessly. 'Well, he didn't look at all concerned an hour ago, when he came downstairs and turfed me out. Said he wanted the sitting room all to himself, to write his report for the university . . .'

'Oh, God, Connelly. That's tomorrow, isn't it?' said David, suddenly remembering. 'I clean forgot. Peter'll be needing my notes . . .'

'Peter knows where to find your notes, if he wants them,' I said firmly. 'You'd hardly be a help to him, anyway, the state you're in.'

He raised his eyebrows. 'Would I not?'

'Well, look at you—you're falling asleep on your feet. I'll bet if I gave you a nudge you'd go straight over into the harbour.'

'Come on, then. Give it a try.'

Adrian, always suspicious of bantering that didn't include him, put his oar in. 'I wouldn't dare her, if I were you. It's like waving a red flag in front of a bull. You're liable to find yourself treading water.'

'Och, I'd not be budged so easily,' David promised. 'But if you've a mind to push me in, lass, you'd best do it from the far side of the harbour, or we'll be late for the auction.'

Adrian greened a little. 'The fish auction, do you mean?'

'You don't have to come, you know.'

'No, no,' said Adrian. 'I want to.' His tone had grown intimate again, and as the three of us walked along the middle pier he briefly slung his arm across my shoulders, not in his normal friendly way but with a touch that implied possession.

I stiffened. The male of the species, I thought with a sigh, could be so bloody maddening. As we passed through the shadow of Brian's fishing boat, its nets rolled up alongside the pier, I pretended to lose my footing and ducked neatly out of Adrian's embrace.

We rounded the narrow bottom of the U-shaped harbour and approached the covered fish market. I was just wondering again about the noticeable lack of fish when the first boat came nosing through the narrow channel. It hit the harbour like a bullet, kicking up an arc of spray and bringing behind it a great wheeling halo of gulls that screamed and dived in search of scraps from the deck.

The boat was a small one, just two men on board, both wearing slick yellow overalls. Even with the tide full in, the boat still bobbed a fair distance beneath the quayside, and the man standing on deck had to tip his head a long way up to see us. 'Heyah, Deid-Banes,' he called out, tossing up the mooring rope, 'gie us a hand, will ye?'

David obligingly tied the line off, then stood back as the fisherman scrambled up one of the metal ladders set into the harbour wall.

'How's yer mither the day?'

David dropped into broad Scots as he gave yet another update on his mother's medical condition. Then he introduced us. 'My cousin Danny,' he explained, as the fisherman's ice-cold hand closed firmly around mine.

'The better man o' the family.' The shrewd eyes slid accusingly to David. 'Is this how ye impress a lass, these days? By hanging round the quayside?'

David smiled. 'She's never seen the auction.'

'Aye, well, it's high excitement, that is,' the older man agreed. He turned to me with a wink. 'Ye'll no be getting roses and sweeties wi' this miserable lad, ken.'

Before I could so much as smile in answer, Adrian draped an arm across my shoulders to drag me backwards out of the path of a rattling fork-lift that wheeled to a halt just inches from David's feet. But when the fork-lift driver cut his engine, Adrian didn't let go, even though both David and his cousin had by this time turned their backs to us and were busy lowering chains over the edge of the quay. A moment later they hauled the chains back up again, in practised unison, pulling up a blue plastic box the size of a shallow laundry basket. The box, brimful of steel-coloured fish, was rapidly unhooked and loaded onto the fork-lift, and the chains were lowered once again.

I couldn't see much, thanks to Adrian, but as one boat after another came into the harbour I was able to appreciate the mechanics in greater detail—the speed and rhythm with which the men on the boats slid and sorted and hooked the fish boxes onto the dangling chains, the smooth rattle and pull of the chains sliding over wet concrete, and the final thump and shuffle of the blue and white boxes as they landed on the fork-lifts.

It took David and his cousin less than ten minutes to unload the day's catch. Stacked high, the fork-lift rattled off towards the market.

Behind me, someone called out David's name and all of us looked round to see the barmaid standing in the open doorway of the Ship

Hotel. 'Telephone,' she told him, raising her voice above the rattle and hum of chains and machinery.

My first thought was that it must be someone ringing from the hospital, and from David's face I knew he was thinking the same thing. 'Look,' he said. 'Why don't the two of you go on ahead? I'll meet you down there, at the market.'

He was gone before I could reply, and I had little option but to follow Adrian back down the harbour road.

The fish market fairly bustled now with activity. Young men in wellies and stained jumpers jostled past in purposeful confusion while the lorry drivers hovered close with keen expectant eyes, watching the red-faced auctioneer while he rummaged through the stacks of fish boxes, the bright orange flash of his rubber gloves poking and prodding with knowledgeable speed. 'The lemon sole, first,' the auctioneer decided, then jerked his head up as the Auld Kirk's bell pealed out four times. 'Right, lads, let's go!' he ordered.

The buyers funnelled through into the metal-walled enclosed part of the market. The auction was all very interesting, I thought, and if I hadn't been so worried about David's phone call I would probably have enjoyed myself. As it was, I stood to one side of the crowd, frowning faintly as I tried to concentrate on what was being said and done. Even Adrian, not known for his powers of observation, eventually noticed I wasn't really there.

'Look, if you're bored with this, we needn't hang about. I could do with a pint . . .'

'I'm not bored,' I said, 'and we promised to wait for David.'

'Oh, right.' He put his hands in his pockets and squared his shoulders as he always did when he was about to pick an argument. 'It wouldn't do to disappoint old David, would it? Disappointing *me* is quite another matter. No one seems to care a damn what *I* think.'

Imploring the ceiling to give me strength, I held my tongue.

'At least with Fabia one can understand the appeal. McMorran is a charming devil, and she's little more than a child. But you do surprise me. After all your lectures on professional behaviour, to find you all but bonking our Mr Fortune on the middle pier . . .'

That hit the mark. 'You're a master of hyperbole,' I informed him. 'And bonking in broad daylight on the middle pier, or any pier, is really not my style.'

'Well, you were definitely lusting. Don't bother to deny it.'

'And if I was?'

He looked wounded. 'Well, you might have considered my feelings. We do have a history, you and I.'

'We were only together three months.'

'Three wonderful months.'

My sidelong glance was sceptical. 'Yes, well, I'm sure they were wonderful for you, considering you were also seeing Sally Jackson at the time. And anyway,' I continued, 'that was years ago, Adrian. So back off now.'

'Hey,' he coaxed me, in his best persuasive voice, but even as he raised his arm I turned and froze him where he stood.

'And if you put that arm round me one more time,' I told him, calmly, 'I will not be held responsible.'

'OK, OK.' He pulled back, lifting both hands in a self-defensive gesture. 'I only meant . . .'

The auctioneer's voice cut him off, and looking round I noticed that all eyes had turned in our direction. Adrian paused, lowering his hands with dawning comprehension. 'Damn it, I think I just bought something.' Delighted, I watched him shuffle forward to collect his unexpected purchase.

Close by my ear a deep voice said, 'He'll not do that again.'

Twisting my head round, I looked up at David's face. 'Was it the hospital that rang you?'

'Aye. My mother's just being difficult,' he reported, looking pleased. He watched Adrian poking reluctantly through a fish box packed with ice. 'Gave him a ticking-off, did you?'

I followed his gaze, a little embarrassed. 'Sort of.'

'Well, I reckon he deserved it,' David said approvingly. 'Bonking on the pier, indeed!'

I tipped my head back sharply and my face flamed. 'You heard!'

'Only a few words, like,' he promised me. 'I didn't hear the part about the lusting.'

Growing several shades redder, I hastily lowered my chin again and found myself face to face with Adrian, who'd returned with two great ugly flatfish. He had, if nothing else, recovered his sense of humour. Shifting his burden, he solemnly passed me the keys to the Jaguar.

'And what are these for?'

'I seem to be having a run of bad luck,' he replied. 'In the past hour I've been shat on by a seagull and done *this*.' He held up the two fish. 'And bad luck does tend to come in threes, so you'll have to do the driving, I'm afraid. No point in tempting fate.'

'But you're not superstitious,' I reminded him.

'Better safe than sorry.'

JEANNIE MUST HAVE HEARD the car come up the drive. She met us in the hallway and placed a warning finger across her lips, jerking her head dramatically towards the closed door of Peter's sitting room. 'It's genius at work in there,' she told us, 'and we're not to interrupt him. Come on into the kitchen.'

The four of us moved across the front hall like a band of burglars, wary of every squeaking floorboard, and it wasn't until we were safely ensconced in the warm narrow kitchen that anyone dared to breathe.

'Up to his neck in papers he was, when I took his tea in,' Jeannie continued as she filled the kettle. 'He's wanting to get that report of his finished, before Dr Connelly comes . . .' Her voice stopped as she sniffed the air experimentally. 'What *is* that smell?'

'That would be me,' Adrian informed her. Tossing his newspaper-wrapped parcel onto the table, he sent her a generous smile. 'Don't say I never bring you anything.'

Curious, she unfolded the paper and stared at the fish. 'Lemon sole!' she exclaimed. 'Well, aren't you wonderful? I can do them for lunch tomorrow—they'll be nicer than chops, for our company.' She glanced round at the three of us. 'Been to the fish auction, have you?'

'Aye.' David dropped into a chair. A yawn gripped him, but he tried to get the words out anyway. 'Verity hadn't . . . ever . . . seen . . .'

'Davy,' Jeannie cut him off, shaking her head, 'you'll be making me tired if you don't stop ganting.'

'He hasn't slept,' I explained.

'Has he not?' Jeannie's bright head whipped round. 'Away upstairs,' she instructed him firmly, 'and have an hour's sleep afore supper. You can use the spare bed in Verity's room, she'll not mind—will you, Verity?'

Enjoying the sight of the big Scotsman being firmly ordered about, I solemnly assured Jeannie that I wouldn't mind in the least.

David's dark head rolled in a negative motion. 'I've not got time. My notes . . . there are one or two things that Peter will be wanting.'

'Adrian can take care of all that.' Jeannie waved the excuse aside. 'If you're just wanting to print them off the computer . . .'

'Ah.' Adrian, settled in comfort against the wall, interrupted archly. 'Well, you see, I wouldn't know exactly *what* files to print, would I? There's the problem.'

'So print them all,' Jeannie advised him, with unarguable logic. 'Peter will ken what he wants when he sees it.' Satisfied, she looked from one to the other of them expectantly.

With a sigh of resignation David stood rather creakily. Even Adrian rose to his feet and headed for the hall in David's wake. They looked so exactly like two small boys being sent to their rooms as punishment that I couldn't keep from smiling.

'Now,' said Jeannie, when we'd heard the thud of David's footsteps fading up the stairs, 'I'll make the tea.'

Taking a seat, I watched her in admiration. 'I am impressed. I don't believe I've ever seen Adrian go quite that willingly without being bribed.'

She grinned. 'Well, I've had plenty of practice, living in a house full of men. You know, my dad still can't believe you used to go out with Adrian. He thinks you're far too smart.'

'Well, it's surprising what a handsome face will blind you to.'

Peter poked his head in from the hallway. 'Do I dare hope that you're speaking of me?'

'Well, naturally.' Jeannie's smile held mischief. 'There's not a man so handsome in the house.'

'My dear girl,' Peter said, 'how very kind. Remind me to give you a rise.'

'D'ye fancy some tea?'

He politely declined and turned instead to me. 'I was wondering, Verity, whether you'd seen my red notebook? I've looked everywhere, but I'm afraid the blasted thing's gone missing.'

'Perhaps someone's moved it and forgot to tell you.' Even as I suggested that, I knew it wasn't likely. Quinnell's desk was his domain. No one in the field crew would be fool enough to touch the red notebook containing his field notes.

'Perhaps.' Peter wasn't convinced either. 'It's something of a problem, you see, because without that notebook I can't finish my report for Connelly.'

Forgetting about the tea, I stood. 'I'll go and take a look, if you like. A fresh pair of eyes can work wonders.'

Up at the Principia, having searched Quinnell's desk and come up empty-handed, I shunted Adrian aside to check the floor beneath David's chair. 'Are you sure you haven't seen it?'

'I'm positive.' Patiently he moved his feet to let me finish searching.

I banged my head as I backed out, and massaged my scalp as I straightened. 'Honestly, Adrian, I can't think where that notebook's got to.'

'Maybe your friend took it.'

'Sorry?'

'The Sentinel.' I saw the smirk as he bent to key a command into David's computer, sending the nearby printer into action. 'Come to think of it,' he said, clapping a hand to his cheek in mock horror, 'my coffee cup's gone missing too . . .' And he whistled the theme to The Twilight Zone.

'That's very helpful, thank you.' I looked round with hands on hips before starting on my search again with even greater vigour.

Adrian sighed. 'Right, I'll help you hunt,' he said. 'Just let me get another cup of coffee first.'

Moving over to the tall steel filing cabinet on the end wall, I yanked the top drawer open for a look, even though I knew the odds of Peter's field notes being filed by mistake were slim. I was closing it again when I heard Adrian come back. 'God, that was quick,' I told him. 'Look, I don't suppose you could—'

I didn't manage to finish the sentence. Without warning the cabinet slid a good foot sideways, scraping heavily along the hard clay floor. Startled, I spun round to look at Adrian, and found he wasn't there.

Nobody was.

And yet I knew, as I struggled to move a finger, *anything* . . . I knew that I wasn't alone. I screwed my eyes tight shut and pressed my back to the unyielding bulk of the filing cabinet, drawing reassurance from its cold solidity while phantom footsteps, faint but certain, moved towards me . . . and finally passed me by. Only then did I dare to breathe.

The clink of a spoon in a coffee mug brought my eyes open. 'You'll put your back out doing that,' said Adrian, not noticing anything was wrong.

I licked my lips, to make them move. 'Doing what?'

'Shifting furniture. That's too heavy for you. Still, I see you managed to find it,' he said cheerfully. 'Well done.'

Still rather numb, I peered round at the blank space where the cabinet had been and stared, transfixed, at the large red notebook lying there.

Adrian bent to pick it up, flipping through the dog-eared pages. 'Quinnell must have left this on the cabinet and somehow it got joggled and fell down behind. You see?' Handing me the notebook he hid his superior smile behind the coffee mug. 'Not everything can be the work of ghosts.'

I COULD HAVE TOLD THE TRUTH to Peter—he would have believed me. But when I handed him his notebook he was so delighted I could barely get a word in edgeways, so I let the matter drop.

And if the ghost was on the prowl in the Principia, he didn't seem to interfere with Adrian, who, in an unexpected show of diligence, stayed up there working straight through until dinnertime. He didn't simply print off David's notes, he also took the time to summarise them, creating an impressive report, illustrated at appropriate intervals with sections of his own surveys and my drawings of our Roman-era finds.

Peter, scanning through the pages as we lingered over after-dinner coffee, was ecstatic. 'Brilliant!' he pronounced. 'Marvellous, my boy. I knew those damned computers would be useful. Now, we just have to combine your report with *this*,' he added, waving his own thick sheaf of handwritten jottings, 'and we're all set.'

Adrian's face sagged a little, but I had no doubt he'd manage the revisions. He did his best work when he stood to profit by it, and he had a vested interest in our learned lunch guest's final judgment of our site. If Dr Connelly approved the Rosehill excavation, and agreed to let students from Edinburgh do their vacation work here, then our jobs would be safe for the season. But if Connelly refused . . . well, Peter was a proud man. I didn't know, myself, how he'd react.

Which left us all feeling rather like poor Damocles beneath the hanging sword, expecting any moment that the slender thread might snap. David, freshly showered but still unshaved, sat silently across from me, head lowered, deep in thought. Even Fabia, who'd arrived home in a relatively good mood just as we sat down to eat, showed signs of growing restlessness.

'I'll give Adrian a hand,' she said suddenly. 'I'm much quicker on the computer than he is.'

'Oh, right.' Her grandfather nodded his assent. 'A good idea.'

That opinion was shared, predictably, by Adrian himself, who wasted no time in finishing his coffee. His face, as he guided Fabia from the room, put me in mind of an indolent cat who'd just been handed the keys to the canary cage.

David leaned back in his chair and folded his arms across his chest, awaiting instructions. 'And what can I do?'

'You, my boy,' said Peter, glancing at his watch, 'can drive me into Berwick, if you'd be so kind. I promised your mother I'd look in on her this evening. We can take the Range Rover, if Fabia's left any petrol in it.'

'Aye, all right.' David looked at me. 'You're welcome to come, if you like, but be warned. My mother hates being in hospital, and she's been giving them hell. Unless they've shot her with a tranquilliser dart I'm not sure that she'll be fit for you to meet.'

I smiled. 'That's all right. I should probably stay here, anyway. I want to have a good night's sleep, so as to be alert for Dr Connelly tomorrow.'

When I went up to my room my bed looked different, sheets and coverlet pulled up unevenly, as though someone had turned it down and made it up again. And then I realised that David hadn't used the spare bed, by the window, to take his nap. He'd used mine. Not that he'd have any way of knowing which bed was which, I reasoned— they looked identical. And not that I really minded, come to that.

There was a certain sinful pleasure in knowing he'd been sleeping in my bed; in sliding between sheets that his body had recently warmed, and pressing my face to the pillow that still smelt faintly of him. I tugged the blankets up feeling drowsy and at peace.

The cats, curled at my feet, slept soundly, deeply, silently. And if the horses came that night, I didn't hear them.

EIGHT

'Remarkable.' Dr Connelly excavated a small trench in the middle of his creamed potatoes and pushed in a pat of butter, neatly sealing up the mound again with surgical precision. He was a tidy man, with spectacles, his thinning hair kept closely trimmed to match his still-dark beard. 'It's quite remarkable,' he said again, 'that you've found anything at all. A vexillation fortress, do you say?'

Peter eyed him like a gladiator sizing up a lion. Or was it, I wondered, taking a closer look at Peter's face, the other way round? 'We have come to that conclusion, yes.'

Connelly savoured a mouthful of sole. 'And is it then your theory that the Ninth Hispana came upon this fortress on their northward march, made their camp here, and were then engaged in battle?'

'Yes.'

'Interesting,' Connelly admitted. 'Unorthodox, but interesting.'

Across the table from me, David shifted forward and assumed the role of spokesman. 'We're fairly sure the fortress is Agricolan, and Agricola did bring the Ninth north during his campaigns. It's not so great a leap to suppose that, forty years later, when the Ninth was ordered north again, it chose to camp where it had built before. The land is good here, near a river, and the ramparts and ditch would probably still have been standing.'

Connelly's eyes were sharp behind the spectacles. 'And have you proof that this is what the legion did?'

I looked at Adrian, who looked at Fabia, and for a moment silence hung between us all; a curiously apprehensive silence, as though each of us expected the other to blurt out: 'Well, there's this ghost, you see, who might just be a soldier of the Ninth Hispana . . .' Hardly proof, I thought, for someone as meticulous as Dr Connelly. Any man who cut his carrots into cubes before he ate them was unlikely to put faith in walking ghosts.

Fabia began to point out that we had only been working on site a short time, but Peter cut across her in a ringing voice that sounded not the slightest bit ashamed. 'We have no proof—none whatsoever.'

'I see.'

Adrian's smile had lost some of its certainty. 'We *have* prepared a report,' he said, 'that summarises our initial survey.'

After lunch, we gave Connelly Peter's sitting room, for privacy in which to read the report, while the rest of us waited across the hall. It was, I think, the most unnerving hour I'd spent since my first interview at the British Museum. Fabia paced ceaselessly, while Adrian straightened picture frames and rearranged the objects on the mantelpiece. David, slightly more relaxed, put Chopin's *Études* on the hi-fi and leaned back, eyes closed, to listen. And Peter simply waited patiently, his hand quite still upon the black cat stretched across his knees.

At length the door creaked open and Connelly's head came round it. His expression, I thought, was carefully bland. 'Right,' he said. 'I'd like to see the site now, if I may. Just Miss Grey and myself,' he added, as everyone made to rise, 'if that's all right.'

Surprised, I looked at Peter, and he nodded.

This must be how an Olympic torchbearer feels, I thought uncomfortably, as I led Dr Connelly up the grassy slope to the Principia. I tried hard not to stumble over any of my explanations, but it was difficult to keep my nervousness from showing. Finally we stepped outside again, and after twenty minutes of touring the field I looked at my companion and asked, 'Why did you want me to show you around?'

'Ah.' His mouth curved into a smile that was not unpleasant. 'Because I reasoned you were the only person likely to be truthful.'

'But why?'

'Well, Peter has a rather deep investment here, now doesn't he? His granddaughter, I'd imagine, doesn't want to see him disappointed. That surveyor—Sutton-Clarke—his kind say anything to keep their jobs secure. And young Fortune,' he concluded, 'would swear black was white, if Peter asked him to. Which left only you.'

'Oh.'

'Besides,' he said confidingly, 'I know old Lazenby, and he speaks very highly of the work you did on his Suffolk excavations. I gather that he wants to take you out to Alexandria.'

'So I'm told.' Only I didn't want to think of Alexandria, or the decision I would have to make before the summer's end.

Dr Connelly stopped walking. 'There are people,' he said slowly, 'who'd call Peter Quinnell mad. I have been told he sits out in this field at night and talks to ghosts.'

I looked up sharply, trying to read his inscrutable face. 'Who told you that?'

'Never you mind. Is it true, then?'

'No, it's not. I've never known Peter to come out here after dark,' I answered truthfully. 'You must be misinformed.'

Connelly accepted this with a philosophical nod. 'So tell me, Miss Grey, in your professional opinion, is there anything behind all this Ninth Legion nonsense?' His eyes peered at me like hard, glittering stones. 'Do you believe—honestly believe—that we are standing, right this moment, on something more than a vexillation fortress?'

'I've never been so sure of anything in all my life.'

He studied my face for a long moment, and what he saw there must have satisfied him because at last he gave a fatalistic nod. 'Then I must bow to your conviction,' he said grandly. 'You shall have my students for this digging season. And God help both our reputations if you find there's nothing here.'

THE NEXT THREE WEEKS sped past me like a whirlwind, a blur of motion and emotion and that tingling raw excitement that one feels when starting any voyage.

David's mother came out of hospital and surprised everyone by checking herself into Saltgreens, the local home for the aged. That is, she surprised everyone except Jeannie.

'Have you seen Saltgreens?' Jeannie'd asked me, grinning.

'Is it that modern building beside the museum?'

'Aye, with its front end facing onto the harbour. You'd think it was luxury flats, to look at it. She'll not be suffering in there I expect.'

'Will she sell her cottage, do you think?'

'Oh, I have my doubts. She'll probably stay on at Saltgreens for the summer, like, then go back home and get a wee companion in.'

Robbie, I was sure, already knew what David's mother would decide, but he was much too excited by all the preparations for the arrival of the university students to waste time telling fortunes on demand. This morning he and Kip had been my shadows, dancing up and down between the house and the Principia. Now, as we came into the offices for the third time, with Robbie's constant chatter ringing cheerfully behind me, Adrian looked up from his computer and sighed.

'Robbie, shouldn't you be in school?'

'It's Saturday.'

'Ah.'

'The people come tomorrow.'

'Do they really?'

But all attempts at sarcasm were wasted breath with Robbie. 'Aye,' the boy said, sagely. 'Granddad and Davy are putting up the tents. Will you be living in a tent, Mr Sutton-Clarke?'

'No,' said Adrian.

I smiled, moving past them to my desk. 'Mr Sutton-Clarke would miss his nice room at the Ship Hotel, Robbie.'

'I'd like to live in a tent,' said Robbie. 'Davy's got his own tent, did you see it? It's a big tent, with a window and all.'

'Yes, well, Davy is an idiot,' Adrian replied, rocking back in his soft padded chair. 'Any man who throws over a nice wide bed in a warm room—with private loo, I might add—in favour of a leaky tent on soggy ground, with eighteen students for neighbours, is indisputably an idiot.'

'He just thought one of us should be there, close at hand, in case the students needed anything,' I protested.

'And the location of the camp,' said Adrian slyly, 'is so very convenient. You can see it from your bedroom window, can't you? And vice versa.'

Robbie came to my rescue. Clasping the post that divided two of the box-stall offices, he announced, 'I'm going to be a finds supervisor, when I grow up.'

'Come on, then,' I invited, shifting my chair to make room for Robbie in my cubicle. Taking a few of the less impressive potsherds from the shelf beside me, I set them neatly on my desk and gave the boy a drawing tablet. 'If you're going to do my job, I'd best start training you. Draw me some pictures of those, all right?'

He happily complied. Adrian threw me a grateful glance and in the blissful silence gave his concentration back to the computer.

I spent half an hour sorting the students into threesomes for their tents. As I finished jotting down the tent numbers beside the names, Robbie proudly thrust his drawings in front of me.

'There,' he said.

'Well done.' I studied the papers solemnly. 'And what do you make of our finds, then, Mr McMorran?'

'They're OK.'

'Come now, dear boy,' I said, in a fair imitation of Dr Connelly, 'that's not very scientific.' I chose a sherd and handed it to him, peering closely at him through imaginary spectacles. 'Now, what would your impressions be of this piece, for example?'

Playing along with the game, Robbie frowned in a way that he'd seen David do a hundred times, turned the broken bit of pottery over twice, and frowned still harder. 'It's from a pot, like. And it's red.'

'Anything else?'

'He didn't like it here.'

Across the aisle the steady clacking sound of Adrian's computer keyboard stopped abruptly   silence. 'Come again?' I asked.

'The man who used this pot,' said Robbie, handing back the fragment, 'he didn't like it here. He was always cold, and his tooth hurt.'

'PSYCHOMETRY.'

Peter rolled the word out in his glorious voice, balancing the heavy dictionary in one hand as he ran his finger down the definition. '"The divination of facts about an object from the touching of that object."'

'Well, whatever it's called, Robbie can do it.' I tossed a little ball of paper onto the sitting-room carpet for the cats to chase, and tucked my feet beneath me on the sofa. 'Mind you, he didn't rattle off the chap's name, rank and regiment, and of course we have no way of knowing just how accurate his observations are, but I just thought you'd like to know.'

'Yes.' He closed the dictionary and hefted it back into place on the shelves. 'I'm sure it will be very useful when we're sifting through our finds.'

I knew what he was thinking. Through methods of pure science we could learn an awful lot about an artefact. We could learn when and where it was made, and what culture or group had made it, and identify the tools they'd used to make it with. Quite often, objects spoke to us about their owners: a pair of shoes might tell us that someone had walked with a limp, a shattered helmet might reveal how the man who'd worn it had died. But how the man who'd worn it had *felt* . . . that was a mystery quite beyond the reach of science.

I envied Robbie terribly. I'd spent years holding bits and pieces of the past, poking them and prodding them and willing them to tell me things. And now this little child just touched a potsherd and was instantly connected to the person who had held it several centuries before. How wonderful, I thought wistfully.

Aloud, I said: 'I think I might keep a separate notebook, to record what Robbie says about the things we find. A sort of unofficial record, if you like, to complement the finds register. I know the pundits frown on things like this, but . . .'

'Pundits,' Peter told me, 'frown on everything. I think your notebook is a very sound idea. Would you like another drink?'

'No thanks.' My half-closed eyes drifted guiltily past the empty glass on the coffee table. 'One's quite enough for me.'

Peter smiled to himself as he poured himself another measure of vodka. 'I can't help noticing you've traded in your English gin for good stout Scottish whisky.'

I opted not to respond to that, blaming the good stout Scottish whisky for the growing flame of heat along my cheekbones.

'Rather suggestive, that,' he went on. 'I wonder what—'

His words were interrupted by the rhythmic crunch of footsteps coming up the gravel drive. The front door banged and David materialised in the doorway of the sitting room.

'Heyah,' the deep voice greeted us briskly. 'Getting drunk again, are you?'

Peter smiled archly. 'Would you like one?'

'Wouldn't mind.' Crossing the worn carpet, David helped himself to a whisky and came to sit beside me, sagging into the sofa and stretching out his legs. He turned to Peter. 'Well, the tents are up, if you'd like to have a look. Six, plus mine, plus the big dining tent. We've some fair puzzled cows in the pasture next door.'

'Good, good. When you've finished your whisky, then . . .'

David rolled his eyes. 'I've been up to my ears these past two weeks with exams, ken. Three invigilations and heaps of papers to mark. And today, between the marking, I've been pounding tent pegs. I'm fair jiggered,' he concluded. 'Can you not get Wally to show you?'

Peter looked from David's weary face to mine and back again. 'Of course, my dear boy. You stay here and relax. I'll go and have a good look round myself.'

The room seemed smaller, somehow, with only David and myself and the two cats in it. Or perhaps it was only the sofa that seemed smaller, or David who seemed larger, or . . .

'Just my luck,' he said, in a mild voice. 'I finally get you alone in this house and I'm too damn tired to do anything about it.'

A sharply pleasant thrill coursed down my spine and lodged in the pit of my stomach. Since the day of the fish auction we'd both been so busy I'd barely seen him, and though he hadn't exactly retreated behind a wall of politeness, neither had he given me much cause to hope he shared my own attraction. Until now.

Sinking lower in the sofa, he rolled his head sideways against the leather to look at me. 'Ah well, maybe I'll rally once I get this down me.'

I was truly in bad shape, I thought. Just watching the man my senses went on overload. The clean soap-smell of him that blended with the pungent tang of whisky, the way the fabric of his work shirt strained against the muscles of his arms, the one dark curl that never stayed in place—I noticed all of these. And I felt the most appalling need to touch him. *Deeply unprofessional, my girl*, I reprimanded myself. *Doesn't do to get involved with colleagues.*

Still, when David shifted round to stretch full length upon the sofa, the last shreds of my judgment went completely out of the window. He lay on his back with his head in my lap, quite as if it belonged there, and balanced his glass with both hands on his chest.

'Is this a rally?' I asked, looking down.

His eyes drifted closed. 'I'm afraid not.'

I watched him for a long while, aware of the exact moment when his heartbeat slowed, the lines of strain smoothed gently from his forehead as his breathing shifted subtly to the rhythm of a deep contented sleep.

Then, reaching down, I carefully prised the whisky from his unresisting fingers. 'Damn,' I said, and drained the glass myself.

NINE

The excavation was coming along well. In the beginning, I'd found it strange to have so many bodies working round me in the field, but now that nearly a fortnight had passed I could come round the bend in the road by the thorn hedge and not be surprised by the sight of an army in T-shirts and denims, digging away with true militant vigour.

Two of the students had been assigned to me, as finds assistants, and another two were helping Adrian continue his electromagnetic survey of the site. The remaining fourteen wielded trowels under Peter's watchful eye, like loyal troops that moved according to their general's wishes. And if Peter was a general, I thought, then David was his field officer, always on patrol among the rank and file.

In the Principia my students were hunched over their desks like monks transcribing the Gospels, sorting through the day's finds. I'd always felt a wistful sense of envy of my colleagues who broke open long-sealed tombs, or for film heroes who scraped about in the dirt for twenty seconds before pulling out some rare bejewelled and golden statute perfectly intact. Almost everything I'd ever touched— with the notable exception of one small military dagger—had come to me in pieces, dull with dirt and worn with age.

The Rosehill dig, so far, was no exception. Every new day brought more bits of animal bone, shattered pottery and broken metalwork. And every fragment, no matter how unimpressive it might appear, had to be cleaned, sorted and labelled with an identifying number.

Then, of course, the number had to be written down in the finds register, along with the particulars of the artefact itself—where and when it had been found, in what condition, and what its dimensions were. Before, I'd always kept such notes by hand, but here at Rosehill the 'finds register' was all on computer, in a uniform style.

But that didn't stop me from making odd notes and sketches of the artefacts in my old-fashioned notebook. And every evening, while the students were having their meal in the long tent, I trundled the day's finds down to Rose Cottage, for Robbie to read.

Tonight, I'd chosen to vary our game a little. Taking my seat at the now familiar kitchen table, with the collie sleeping underneath my chair, I watched with special interest while Robbie felt the things I'd brought. His abilities intrigued me. It was already clear to me that certain pieces 'spoke' to him, transmitting some impression of their former shape and usefulness, and of the people they'd belonged to. But did they also speak to him of time?

The fortress we were excavating dated from the late first century, but what we really hoped to find—evidence of the site's occupation by the Ninth Legion—would date from the early second century. A potsherd left behind by the Ninth would be some forty years younger than the ones we'd found so far. Would Robbie, I wondered, be able to tell the difference?

Curious to know the answer, I'd set up a little experiment. Mixed in with the Roman-era sherds was a piece of a Victorian flowerpot that Wally had found broken in the garden. The glaze was red, almost the same colour as Samian ware, and to the untrained eye the pieces looked very much the same, but Robbie picked the impostor out with ease, his fingers closing round it and then opening again abruptly.

'Hey, feel this one—it's hot! You do feel it, don't you, Miss Grey?' Robbie turned his trusting eyes on me, but after dutifully holding the sherd in my hand for a moment, I had to admit that I didn't.

'See, this one's cold,' he said, choosing another sherd. 'That means it's right, like. It belongs to the Roman part. But the hot one belongs to the house.'

I shifted in my chair, wanting to be sure. 'Do you mean it comes from a later time? After the Romans were gone?'

He looked at me in silence, his face perplexed. 'Gone?'

'Yes, after the Roman soldiers left Rosehill . . .'

'But they didn't leave.'

I'd learned, with Robbie, not to alter my expression when he dropped a bombshell in my lap. If I looked at all excited it just seemed to block up all his faculties. I kept my gaze trained now on the grain of the table and asked him very lightly what he meant.

'They didn't leave,' he said once again. 'They're still here. They're everywhere.'

Wally's paper crackled as he set it aside to peer across at his grandson. 'Whit d'ye mean, they're everywhere? Are ye saying yon field's stappit fu wi' deid bodies?'

Robbie was shaking his head. 'Not with bodies.'

'Ye ken whit I mean,' said Wally, who knew as well as I did that Robbie sometimes took things rather literally. 'They'll nae be bodies like ours efter sae lang i' the ground—they'll be banes. Dry banes.'

'No, I don't think there are any bones. Not people bones.'

I cut in, to clarify. 'So the soldiers, the Roman soldiers, they're still here, but their bodies aren't.'

The dark head nodded. 'Aye.'

'What happened to the bodies, Robbie?'

He didn't know the answer to that one, but he had a clear idea who might. 'I could ask the Sentinel for you,' he offered eagerly. 'He'd ken all about it.'

Wally and Jeannie and I exchanged glances. 'I don't think that would be such a good idea,' I said to Robbie. 'It made you ill the last time, remember? We don't want that to happen again.'

'But he wants to talk to you. He tries sometimes, but you can't hear him so he takes himself away again.'

My fingers curved round my teacup. 'He tries to talk to me?'

'He likes you,' was the boy's explanation. 'I think . . . I think you mind him of someone, Miss Grey. He sort of looks at you sometimes and . . . well, he likes to look at you.'

'I see.'

'Follows after you, he does,' Robbie added helpfully. 'So you're always safe.'

Safety, I thought, was a relative term.

Jeannie was watching my face. 'It must be the hair,' she decided. 'Men do have a weakness for bonny long hair.'

I smoothed my plait back with a self-conscious hand and Wally shot me an appraising look, eyes twinkling. 'That's three shadows ye've got noo,' he observed. 'Our Robbie, Kip, and an auld Roman bogle.'

Under the table the collie stirred at the mention of his name, giving a few hopeful thumps of his tail. Wally rose to his feet with a whistle. 'Gaun yersel', then,' he urged the dog, and Kip flipped eagerly onto his feet, padding across to the door while Wally studied me. 'Did ye want tae come wi' us. Back up tae the hoose? I can carry thon thingies for ye,' he added, nodding at my shallow box of potsherds.

It was, I thought, rather gallant of him—not his offer to carry the sherds, which weren't the least bit heavy, but his thinking I might not want to walk home alone this evening. Not in the fading light, with darkness coming on.

'Thanks,' I said. 'That would be a great help.'

'BAD DREAMS LAST NIGHT?' Fabia steadied the camera against her eye and snapped the row of potsherds from a different angle.

I glanced up rather vaguely from my desk. 'No, why?'

'You left the light on.'

'Ah.' She would know, I thought. Fabia was always the last in at night, these days. She had cooled a little towards Brian, and I might have suspected she'd found herself a boyfriend among the students if it hadn't been for David's careful supervision of the camp. He hadn't gone so far as to set an official curfew, but after one or two incidents early on he'd made it clear that anyone who wasn't fit to work would have to answer to him, and now they were usually out of the pubs and tucked into their sleeping-bags well before midnight. If some young man was keeping Fabia out late at night, I could safely say he wasn't one of ours.

At any rate, the late nights didn't seem to be doing her any great harm. She looked lovely this morning, eyes glowing with vigour and youthful good health, her movements quick and fluid. 'Where did Peter want me to go next?' she asked, replacing the cap on her lens.

I tried to recall exactly what Quinnell's instructions had been at breakfast. 'I think he said they were going to start a new trench where the *principia* ought to be, and he wanted you to take a photograph before they stripped away the sod and topsoil.'

Fabia frowned. 'But we're *in* the Principia.'

'No, he means the real one.' When she still looked blank, I stared in open disbelief. 'Don't tell me you're Peter Quinnell's granddaughter and you've never learned the layout of a basic Roman fortress?'

'It's like I said. My father hated all this stuff, and Peter just assumes I know.'

'Then for heaven's sake come here and let me sketch it out for you,' I said, grabbing pencil and paper. 'The average fortress looks like this—a bit rectangular, with rounded corners, like a playing card. A ditch, sometimes a double ditch, outside, and then the ramparts, with a guard tower at each corner. Now . . .' I drew a square, bang in the centre. 'The *principia*, or headquarters building, is here. And running right along in front of it is the *via principalis*, that's the road that links the fortress's two side gates.' I sketched in the gates, too, to keep things absolutely clear. 'From the front gate to the headquarters is another road, the *via praetoria*. And from the headquarters to the back gate there's the *via decumana*. Now, here,' I said, drawing in another square to the left of the *principia*, 'you'd have the granaries and maybe a workshop. And on the other side of the headquarters building would be the *praetorium*.'

'What's that?' Fabia asked, showing a faint spark of interest that made me think she might not yet be past all hope.

'The commander's house. And then the hospital is usually in this spot right here, and most of the rest would be barrack blocks and stables for horses.'

She leaned over to study my drawing. 'So it's really just barracks, and then this row of important buildings, and then more barracks, with a few crisscrossed streets.'

'Pretty much,' I agreed, smiling at her dismissal of the brilliant efficiency of Roman military planning.

'So . . .' Her finger trailed towards the centre of the makeshift map. 'Peter's going to start his new trench up in here somewhere.'

'It shouldn't be too hard to find,' I assured her. 'Just look for a big bunch of people with spades.'

When she'd gone, I put my pencil down and stretched, trying to ease the knot between my shoulders.

My two young assistants were outside, manning the water flotation tank that Peter had installed behind the building. An upright, barrel-shaped device with hoses attached for fresh water and drainage, it sifted excavated soil through screens so fine that we could then recover tiny seeds and insect parts, as well as bits of pottery or bone. Bone, I thought, would have been useful. A nice full skeleton, clad in legionary armour . . .

But Robbie had said that there weren't any bones in our field. That struck me as odd. If the Sentinel was, as he claimed to be, a soldier of the Ninth, and if the Ninth had truly perished here, then there ought to be bones, and plenty of them.

A high-pitched snatch of laughter floated in through the long back wall, from where my two students were working. I sighed and pushed back my chair. As finds supervisor, I reminded myself, I ought to be out there with them.

Outdoors the field was an ant hill of activity beneath a sky of rolling cloud and brilliant bursts of blue. David was down by the road, by the thorn hedge, crouched over a bit of newly exposed earth that a few of the students were clearing with brushes.

Peter, hoping to find evidence of the Ninth's presence in the fortress's *principia*, stood upon a subtle rise of ground near the centre of our carefully staked site, directing Fabia's photography.

Surely any ghost would find activity like that far more interesting than my own boring little scribbles in the finds register. Bolstered by that thought, I took a step away from the stable door.

I stopped. Paused. Listened.

Nothing but the breeze, and that was not the least bit cold or threatening. The laughter drifted out again from the far side of the building and I set my shoulders, walking on more bravely now along the long front wall of our Principia. Just round that corner, I promised myself, hating my sudden nervousness. Just round that corner, and up the deeply shaded side wall, and round another corner, and I'd be with people again. Only when I was satisfied that there was no sound but the distant voices from the dig and the trilling of a bird in the trees . . . only then did I turn the first corner.

I believe I was even smiling as I walked into the strong male hands that waited in the shadows.

WHEN I SAW WHO IT WAS, my terrified posture collapsed into swift indignation. 'You nearly gave me a heart attack,' I accused him. 'When did you get back?'

Ignoring the question, he fixed me with an unimpassioned gaze, making no attempt to be charming. 'You've been using my boy again, haven't you?'

'I'm sorry?' My forehead wrinkled in faint confusion.

'Making him do your work for you. D'you think I'm that bloody stupid I wouldn't find out?'

He'd been drinking. I could smell the lightly mingled scents of beer and sweat that rose from his T-shirt and denims, and could hear the slurred edge to his speech. The dashing pirate with the quick smile was definitely out this morning; the man before me looked a hardened cutthroat, his dark scowl seeking to intimidate.

It had the opposite effect with me. 'Robbie wanted to help me,' I told him curtly. 'I've only let him play with a handful of potsherds and tell me his impressions. It's a game for him, Brian. There's no risk involved.'

Brian McMorran's brown eyes narrowed oddly on mine. 'And how would you know,' he asked coldly, 'just what risks there might be? You're taking advantage.'

'I am not,' I said carefully. 'I'm only letting Robbie do what Robbie wants to do.'

'Is that a fact?' He stared at me hard, but when he spoke again his voice, still slurred, sounded less angry. 'Aye, well, you can keep on with the sherds, then, if he likes it so much, but if I find you've been making him do more than that—and I'll know if you do—'

Oh, great, I thought. *Don't tell me Brian is psychic as well.*

He stopped talking suddenly, still watching me. And, unbelievably, I saw his mouth curve in a knowing smile.

'Did it only just occur to you?' he asked, his smile growing predatory as my instinctive step backwards brought me up against the stable wall. 'Afraid, Miss Grey? Of me?'

'Of course not.'

'Oh, I think you are.' He stopped mere inches from my body, leaning his hands on the wall to either side of my shoulders, effectively pinning me in place. And with a prickling rush of irritation, I realised I was very much afraid. Not afraid of him physically—but knowing that he, like his son, could invade my private thoughts . . . with Brian the very idea seemed a violation.

My mouth tightened. I could have kneed him one, but I'd have had a devil of a time explaining it to Jeannie. And calling for my students was out as well—by the time they'd turned the corner Brian would have backed away and left me looking like a fool. I was trying to decide what to do when I heard someone approaching from the far side of the building, to my right. Someone walking heavily. David, I decided, with a surge of sheer relief.

But even as I formed the thought, David himself proved me wrong as he came whistling round the corner to my *left*. He stopped short, looking at the scene in front of him. 'What the devil's going on?'

Brian shrugged, not bothering to turn his head. 'Just having a bit of fun, Deid-Banes.'

'Aye, well, fun's over. Let her go.'

'Why should I?'

'Because I'll belt you one if you don't.'

I couldn't see David from Brian's shoulder, but although he clearly wasn't pleased he didn't sound particularly violent. So it stunned me when Brian jerked backwards, spun round, and then fell at my feet like a puppet whose strings had been cut.

I stared down in dismay. 'You didn't have to do that, David. I can take care of . . .' But I never did finish the sentence. Because by then I had lifted my head to look at David, and I'd seen that he was standing ten feet from where Brian lay, his face as surprised as my own.

Across the empty shadows his gaze met mine and he arched an inscrutable eyebrow. 'Bloody hell,' he said.

'OH NO, I'M SURE he'll be quite all right,' said Peter, who had come in search of me and stood now looking down at Brian's spread-eagled form with the cheerfully disinterested air of a botanist confronted with a garden weed. 'He's breathing normally. I'm sure there's nothing to worry about.' He smiled at David. 'What did you hit him with?'

'I didn't touch him.'

'No . . . ?' The long eyes shifted, curious, to me. 'Verity my dear, you do amaze me.'

'It wasn't me,' I said, shaking my head. 'I know this is going to sound awfully foolish, Peter, but I think the Sentinel did this.'

'*My* Sentinel? My soldier of the Ninth?'

'Yes.'

'Good man.' Peter looked down at Brian and nodded, highly satisfied. 'Still doing his job, as a good soldier should. Brian making an ass of himself, was he?'

David stepped in diplomatically. 'He'd been drinking.'

'Ah.' Peter nodded again. 'Never mind,' he said happily, turning to me, 'you must come and see what we've been up to. I've a rather good feeling about this new spot where we're starting to dig.'

'But . . . I mean, we can't just leave him here . . .'

'Whyever not? I'm sure he's been laid flat in rougher places.'

'We ought to tell Jeannie, at least.'

Peter lifted his shoulders in a shrug that plainly said I was being unreasonable. 'All right, if you insist, I shall inform Jeannie that her husband is lying up here and let her decide what she wants to have done about it. But then,' he said firmly, 'you really must come and see what we've done.'

David came across to stand beside me as we watched Peter sauntering down to the house. 'Are you sure you're OK?'

'I'm fine. Only . . .' I nodded towards the man at my feet. 'He has second sight as well, did you know that? Like father, like son, I suppose.' The shock had left me feeling a little hysterical, and I could hear it in my voice.

David studied me solemnly for a moment.

'He follows me,' I said.

David frowned. 'Who, Brian?'

'The Sentinel. Robbie says he follows me around sometimes, and tries to talk to me.'

David took my shoulders in his warm hands, reassuring. 'Well, I'd not be worried. He's just taken with your bonny face, that's all—I doubt you'll come to any harm. Poor Brian's proof of that.'

His expression altered slightly as a sudden thought struck him, and before I had time to gauge his intentions the hands on my shoulders tightened and his head dipped swiftly down.

If first kisses were a harbinger of things to come, I told myself, then I was in serious trouble. I couldn't remember a first kiss like this one. There was nothing searching or tentative about it; it was certain and deep and it brought the blood pounding to my ears. Strangely enough, it also seemed to drain all the energy out of my body, so that when he pulled away again I found it took great effort to stand upright. 'David, honestly . . .' I protested shakingly.

'Just experimenting.' His grin was very cocksure.

'Oh, really?'

'Aye. Your Sentinel's protective, but he's not a jealous fool. He's left me standing.'

'So he's a rotten judge of character,' I said, drawing a deep breath to calm my still-racing heartbeat. 'And anyway, for all you know the Sentinel wasn't even paying attention.'

'Give me some credit, lass. I am a scientist.'

I paused, mid-breath. 'And what does that mean?'

'It means that when you're testing a hypothesis, you'd be a fool to trust just one experiment.' As he lowered his head a second time, those laughing blue eyes were suddenly all I could see, and then even those eyes disappeared and for several long minutes I found myself unable to think at all.

'THAT'S THE THIRD TIME you've stopped listening,' Adrian accused me, wheeling his chair round to face me in amused exasperation.

I glanced up, my pencil frozen in mid-doodle. 'I am listening.'

'No you're not.' Settling back in his chair, he stretched his feet out. 'Still, I'll not take it too personally. I expect you're feeling the effects of your morning's adventures.'

I sighed. 'How did you find out about that?'

'I had the whole story from one of your assistants. The redhead, actually.'

'And what, exactly, did she tell you?' I wanted to know.

'Only that you'd knocked our Brian senseless.'

It might have looked like that, I conceded, from a certain angle. I massaged my forehead, closing my eyes. 'And how many people did she mention this to, do you suppose?'

'Does it matter? It can only raise your stock among the students, darling. They'll be in absolute awe.'

'I'm very flattered. But it wasn't me that hit Brian.'

Adrian raised his eyebrows. 'It was never our Mr Fortune?'

'No, of course not, don't be stupid.'

'Who, then?'

'You won't believe me,' I warned him. 'It was Robbie's Sentinel.'

'Oh right.' Adrian rolled his eyes heavenwards. 'Am I the only person on this dig who hasn't gone completely mad?'

Before any higher being could answer him, Peter came striding through the doorway like an actor who'd received his cue.

'Horses!' he announced, in his richly melodious voice.

Adrian looked at me. 'As I was saying . . .'

Coming to a halt beside my desk, Peter reached for one of my hands and pressed into it a flat, round lump of metal, flaking with corrosion. His eyes shone with the exhilaration of discovery as he pointed to the roughened bit of metal and smiled beatifically.

'*There*, my dear,' he told me, 'are your horses.'

TEN

After two months of handling nothing but rough ware and Samian ware and scattered old coins, cleaning that single scrap of Roman horse harness was like polishing Priam's treasure.

I could barely wait for the evening meal to finish so I could make my retreat to the kitchen, spread some old newspapers over the table and set to work again, carefully removing the ugly disfiguring crust of age to reveal the underlying glint of silvered bronze. When Fabia came home several hours later she found me still sitting there.

'You're mad,' she said. 'It's half past one.'

'Is it?' I looked up, blinking like a shortsighted watchmaker. 'Is that what Peter found this afternoon?'

'Mm. A *phalera*,' I said. 'It's sort of a connector for the straps of a horse's harness. You see these little rings, here, on the back? The leather straps went through there.'

'Oh, right.' She peered more closely, pointing. 'What's that little slot thing for?'

'To hang a pendant on. When this was on a harness, there'd have been a pendant hanging from it, a flat metal piece shaped like a wolf's head, or something like that. For decoration.'

'Did the Britons have horses to fight back with?'

'Certainly—and chariots. Didn't they teach you about Boudicca at school?'

'Very probably.'

'Queen of the Iceni,' I elaborated, with a smile. 'A rather fierce woman, who stomped all over our Ninth Legion, as it happens.'

Fabia shrugged. 'The Romans probably deserved it.'

'How do you mean?'

'Well, they were the invaders, weren't they? You can't just go around as you please, making a mess of other people's lives, and not expect some kind of retribution.'

Only a twenty-year-old, I thought, could so neatly dissect history into heroes and villains. I started to explain to Fabia that history could sometimes be more complicated than it first appeared, but she was in no mood to hear my argument.

'Nothing complicated about it,' she contradicted, her tone definite. 'It's only justice, pure and simple. An eye for an eye. Take Robbie's Sentinel, for instance,' she went on. 'He came up here to kill the local tribe, right? So they had every right to kill him back.'

'Well, they didn't make a very thorough job of it,' I commented, 'if he's still wandering about in the field.'

I'd meant it as a joke, but Fabia appeared to be weighing the matter. 'Yes, but then that's the ultimate punishment, isn't it?' she said, finally. 'To take your enemy's life away, to see him lose the people and the things that he most loves, but not to let him die.'

Watching her, I wondered if she was speaking of her own loneliness and devastation, having lost her father and the life that they had shared. Certainly her eyes had grown distant, deeply thoughtful.

I tried to bring her out of it by lightening the mood. 'I see I'll have to keep in your good favour, if that's your idea of the perfect punishment. I don't much fancy being made a ghost.'

She glanced up, shaking off her reverie. 'I wouldn't worry,' she said, smiling. 'Anyway, I'd be afraid to tangle with you, after what you did to Brian.'

THE SUMMER SUN had taken temporary leave and in its place the sky was grey and melancholy, with the hard relentless wind I'd come to think of as a feature of the Borders. Here in the finds room, at least, I was warm and dry and had to contend only with one draught that struck like a pillar of cold near the open door—the fault of the wind, no doubt. At any rate, it was easy enough to avoid.

I was down on my knees cleaning some low shelves when one of my assistants poked her head in. 'Thought you might fancy a cup of tea,' she told me kindly. 'I'll just leave it here, shall I?' She set it down at one end of the long worktable and hovered in the doorway a moment. 'Are you sure you don't want *us* to do that, Miss Grey?'

'Why should you have all the fun?' I asked her, smiling over my shoulder. 'Besides, you're both faster on the computer than I am.'

'Yes, well . . .'

'Aren't you freezing to death in that draught?' I asked, sounding disturbingly like my own mother.

The young woman frowned. 'What draught?'

'The one that you're standing in.'

'I don't feel anything.'

'Well, they do breed you hardier up here.'

As her footsteps retreated, I stood up, turning to walk across to where she'd left my tea.

The pillar of cold had moved.

I walked through it and out the other side before my mind had time to register its presence, before I remembered that, scarcely ten minutes ago, the same spot had been perfectly warm.

Silly, I chided myself. Draughts don't follow a person around . . .

Then the sudden realisation hit me. My heart surged painfully upwards and lodged beneath my collarbone as I wheeled and stretched my hand out searchingly. Into the cold, and back again.

I took a hasty backward step, then stopped and held my ground. Three months ago, if someone had tried to convince me I was facing down a ghost I would have laughed out loud at the very idea; now I had no doubt at all that he was there, directly in front of me, trying to touch me, perhaps; trying to talk to me.

'I can't,' I said aloud, in a raspy voice I hardly recognised as mine. Closing my eyes for a moment, I struggled to concentrate, and stammered out the words again in Latin. 'I can't hear you. I'm sorry. I can't hear you or see you—do you understand?'

Only the silence answered me. I hugged myself to ward off the shivers, my voice dwindling to a whisper. 'I know you want to tell me something, but you will have to find another way . . . this won't work. You will have to find another way . . .'

'Miss Grey?' The voice, close outside the doorway, made me jump. I turned my head. 'Yes?'

'You all right?' My student's head appeared round the corner for the second time, her expression wary. 'We heard you talking, but we weren't sure whether you were saying something to us, or—'

'No,' I told her, 'sorry. I was talking in Latin.'

'Oh, right.' Her look made it clear she considered me strange, but she withdrew again politely, saying nothing.

I drew a deep breath and dived with purpose through the doorway, out of the Principia, crossing the field with swift steps that were just this side of an actual run.

David didn't notice anything amiss when I appeared at the edge of his barracks trench, being happily absorbed in his task. 'Heyah,' he greeted me, his eyes crinkling against the wind. 'Wicked weather.'

I nodded. 'Having any luck?'

'Aye. We've cleared the outline of one of the barracks blocks—I've got the lads putting golf tees in all of the post moulds so that Fabia can take a photograph before it rains.'

'Yes, I see that. So what are you doing down here, with your trowel?'

He grinned. 'Mucking about. I thought this looked interesting, so I'm checking it out. You never ken what you'll find.'

The dark head bent again and for a while I watched him work in silence, drawing comfort from his company, his quiet calming strength. I'm safe here with David, I thought, and the words became a lulling litany: Safe, safe, perfectly safe . . .

The cold passed through me like a knife blade, and I jerked upright. 'David.'

'It's all right,' he said in an excited tone, not looking up. 'I see it.'

I stared down at him. He had tossed his trowel aside and was brushing the dirt away now with his fingers, trying to free something small from the soil. And then he raised his head to whistle sharply across the trench at one of his students. 'Go get Mr Quinnell, lad.'

'David, what is it?' I leaned closer. 'What have you found?'

For an answer he held out his hand, and I saw the small medallion, the shred of a chain and the glitter of gold, and the tiny stamped figure of a woman holding what looked like a ship's rudder.

'It's Fortuna,' David told me.

'Yes, I know.'

I'd come across her image countless times in my career—one of the first things I'd been asked to draw for Dr Lazenby, on the Suffolk dig, had been an altar erected by some unnamed Roman soldier, inscribed 'To Fortune, Who Brings Men Home'. Those few words had moved me, and I'd wished that I could meet the man who'd had them carved in stone.

Be careful what you wish for, my father always said. I ought to have listened to him. Because looking now at the image of Fortuna, goddess of good luck and destiny, steering her ship of fate over the waters, I felt certain I'd already met the man to whom the golden pendant once belonged.

BRIAN WASN'T PLEASED to see me coming down the drive. He'd been making a savage attack on the weeds that grew to either side of the cottage path, his head bent low into the wind, but when he saw me he straightened his back, belligerent.

'I was wondering,' I said, 'if I could talk to Robbie for a minute. We found something this morning, in one of the trenches, and it might be something quite important. I won't stop long.'

He frowned and exhaled sharply. 'All right, you can have ten minutes with the lad. But I'll be there counting them, d'you hear?'

'Thanks.'

It seemed strange to enter the kitchen when Jeannie was absent the cosy little room looked less inviting. Brian kicked off his boots and called to Robbie.

The boy came bouncing in and gave me a buoyant greeting.

'Sit yourself down and look at what Miss Grey's got to show you,' Brian told his son.

Robbie clambered obediently onto his chair. 'Did you find the necklace?'

I stopped in the act of unwrapping the packet, to stare at him. 'The what?'

'The Sentinel's necklace.'

Brian lit a cigarette and smiled faintly, the proud parent, while I peeled away the final layers of tissue and passed the golden scrap of pendant to Robbie. 'Is this it?'

'Aye,' he said, nodding his head. 'He's always got it on. He never takes it off, see, 'cause it belonged to her.'

I opened my notebook, feeling a sudden need to have something to focus my attention on. 'Belonged to who?'

Brian broke in. 'Can you see her name, lad?' To me, he explained: 'He can sometimes pick up names and all.'

Robbie fingered the pendant, screwing up his face as he tried to come up with the answer. 'It starts with a "C", I think . . . C-L-A . . .'

'Claudia?' I guessed.

'Aye, that's it.'

'And the name of the Sentinel, Robbie? D'you know that as well?' Brian asked.

'It's a long name,' said Robbie. 'Hold on.' Closing his eyes, he stayed silent a full minute, thinking. 'Three names. The middle one's the same as *her* name, like . . .'

'What, Claudius?' I asked, and he opened his eyes.

'Aye. And then Maxy . . . Maxy-moose . . .'

'Maximus.' I jotted it down with remarkably steady fingers. 'And the first name?'

'It starts with a "C", too. It's . . . no, I can't get it. It's gone. Sorry.'

'Don't be sorry,' I told him. 'You're doing just fine. This is brilliant.' I looked at the name in my notebook: *C. Claudius Maximus*. No longer a nebulous ghost, but a name. It gave me an odd feeling.

'Claudia and Claudius,' Brian said drily. 'Devoted couple, were they?'

She wouldn't be his wife, I thought. A legionary couldn't marry until he retired from the army. No, it was more likely . . .

I looked across at Robbie. 'Was this Claudia related to the Sentinel?'

'Aye, she was his sister.' Robbie moved his fingers, held the pendant tighter. 'She had long hair,' he told me. 'Long like yours, and the same colour.'

In the brief silence that followed, Brian voiced the question I was too afraid to ask. It must have crossed his own thoughts, after what had happened yesterday. 'Does Miss Grey mind the Sentinel of his sister, then?'

'Aye.' No hesitation there. 'He loves her.'

I kept my attention fixed on Robbie, my pencil resting on the page. 'And she gave him that pend . . . the necklace?'

'Nah, she gave it to the other guy,' said Robbie. 'For luck, like. So he wouldn't be hurt.'

'She gave it to the other . . .?'

'Aye, the Sentinel's friend.' Robbie looked at me as though the details were self-evident. 'The one she was going to marry. He was a soldier, too.'

My ten minutes, I thought, must surely be up, but Brian appeared to be gaining interest, watching while his son rolled the pendant and chain in his small hand.

'He was older, and he kent a lot of things,' Robbie continued. '*He* said the ship would come. He said . . .' He paused, his small face falling. 'Only it didn't. And then the horses came, and the Sentinel had to put him on the fire.'

Enthralled, I leaned forward. 'Why, Robbie? Why did he put him on the fire?'

But the mists through which he viewed these things had swirled again, and Robbie shook his head. 'Sorry,' he said, looking up, and I was shocked to see his eyes were filled with tears. 'He's so sorry. He promised her that he'd protect . . . but he couldn't. He couldn't stop it.'

'Robbie, it's all right, you needn't—'

'Claudia,' he whispered, as if I hadn't spoken. 'So sorry, Claudia.'

'Right,' Brian interrupted. 'That's enough, I think.'

I nodded in agreement. 'That's wonderful, Robbie,' I said, 'you've been a great help. I'll just take this back up to the finds room . . .'

'*No!*' Robbie fixed me with an imploring gaze. 'This can't go in the finds room. It's for protection. You don't understand.'

'Robbie—'

'No.' Wincing, he shut his eyes tightly and shook his head once, as though trying to clear it. 'Must keep my promise . . . must protect . . .'

The boy's head jerked backwards as if a string had pulled it, and his eyes rolled. '*Periculosa*,' he said, in a hollow voice that sounded nothing like his own. '*Via est periculosa.*'

'No, you don't!' Brian surged forward, roaring into the empty air around us. 'D'you hear me, you bastard? You let my son be!'

A sharp gust of wind shook the glass in the windows, and Robbie, the tears forgotten, turned to look up at his father. 'Who are you yelling at, Dad?'

Brian drew in a steadying breath. 'No one, Robbie. Just yelling. Give that back to Miss Grey now, there's a good lad.'

'*VIA EST PERICULOSA?*' Peter rolled his tongue round the words, considering. 'He actually said that, did he?'

'Yes.' I leaned back into the sofa, grateful to be back in the sitting room at Rosehill with its cheerful clutter everywhere and Adrian and Fabia slumped in armchairs on either side of me, drinks in hand. My own dry sherry had been sorely needed.

'How curious,' said Adrian, stretching his legs out. 'He arranges for you to find a medallion of Fortuna, or Fortune, then tells you, "That way's dangerous." Now who could he be warning you *about*, I wonder?'

I rolled my eyes sideways to look at him. 'Must you always be annoying?'

Fabia frowned. 'Davy's not dangerous.' She studied Adrian as she lifted her glass. 'Your eyes are awfully green, aren't they?'

'Frequently.' Their eyes met, and she looked away abruptly.

'*Via est periculosa*,' Peter repeated, thoughtfully. 'Of course, *via* has several meanings, doesn't it? The road, the way, the method.'

'"The road is dangerous"?' Fabia tried the translation. 'That sounds more a warning against your driving, Adrian.'

'Very funny.'

She curled herself into her armchair. 'Where is Davy, anyway?'

Adrian shrugged. 'Still playing scoutmaster, out in the field. He'll be in when he feels like it.'

Out in the field . . . I closed my eyes a moment, seeing the image of a solitary Roman soldier walking back and forth across the waving grass for all eternity, unheard and unseen, with no companions but the silent dead. How lonely that would be, I thought . . . how horribly lonely. I tried to clear my mind, but the soldier would not leave. He walked a little further, looked across the field and thought he saw his sister standing, waiting for him, only it wasn't her . . . not Claudia . . . a young woman with long hair, but not Claudia. Close enough, perhaps, to stir the coals of memory. Did ghosts have memories? I wondered. Did they love?

I opened my eyes, and knew from the dreamy expression on Peter's face that he was wondering the same thing. 'Extraordinary,' was his final pronouncement. 'Quite extraordinary.'

Fabia leaned forward. 'Have you still got the pendant, Verity? I haven't had a chance to really look at it yet.'

I shook my head. 'I gave it to one of my students, to put in the finds room.'

Peter stretched his hand out. 'May I see your notes again, my dear? There's one point in there that makes me rather curious.' He took them from me and flipped the page. 'Yes, here it is. "He said the ship would come" . . . Now, I wonder . . .?' And with that he lapsed into a sort of trance, unspeaking, staring at the carpet.

Archaeologists, I thought, were a breed apart. There was David, still out in the field in a bone-chilling wind with the rain coming on, because he didn't want to stop what he was doing; and here sat Peter, completely oblivious to the world around him while he rebuilt the past in his mind.

Neither one of them sat down to supper.

David stayed out until it grew dark, then came and grabbed a plate of food to take up to his desk in the Principia. He took a plate in to Peter as well, but when I stopped by the sitting room later I found that plate untouched. Peter, lost in his own world, surfaced at the sound of my voice.

'Not off to bed already, are you?'

'Well, it is nearly half past eleven.'

'Oh.' He sounded disappointed, and I hesitated.

'I suppose I *could* stay up a little longer, if you wanted company.'

He beamed at me, delighted. 'Well, if you're absolutely certain. Because I've just been sitting here thinking, you know, about the fate of the Hispana, and I've hit upon a most intriguing theory . . .'

ELEVEN

'So how's Peter?' asked David's mother.

She stepped backwards, hammer in hand, to be sure that the picture she'd just hung was level. We'd been left to ourselves on the mezzanine floor of the Eyemouth Museum, where she was putting together a display that traced the history of Herring Queen Week— *the* big event in Eyemouth's summer calendar.

'He's got a new theory,' I told her. 'He kept me up till dawn, last Saturday, telling me about it.'

Her dancing eyes held sympathy. 'He does like to talk them

through. Used to be me that bore the brunt of it. He'd ring me up at all hours—still did, up until a few years back, but after the first heart attack he stopped all that. Never tells me anything now, for fear it might excite me. And Davy's just as bad.' She hammered in another nail, with a vengeance.

Fondness made me come to Peter's defence. 'It was a good theory, actually. Would you like to hear it?'

'If you think my heart can stand it,' she said.

'Right. Well, you know we found the gold medallion, with the image of Fortuna on it?'

'Aye, Robbie told me.'

'There's a bit more story to the piece than even Robbie knows,' I said, and proceeded to fill her in on all the details. 'Peter thinks that the reason why we haven't yet found any trace of bodies is because the men were cremated. Rosehill used to be "Rogue's Hill", which could come from *rogus* or funeral pyre.'

'That would fit with Robbie saying that the Sentinel put his friend on the fire,' she agreed. 'But still, there were thousands of men.'

'Yes, I know, but . . . maybe I should just run through it all from the beginning. We're assuming that the Ninth came marching north and set up camp at Rosehill, within the ramparts of the old Agricolan vexillation fortress, which presumably had disappeared by then.'

'Aye.'

'And one of the reasons Agricola probably built here in the first place was because of the natural harbour,' I said. 'The Roman navy had to be able to send in ships, to supply the legions on the northward march.' The critical role that the navy had played in the conquest of Britain was all too often overlooked. Absorbed as I was in land-based excavations, I hadn't thought much about the naval connection myself until Peter had leapt on that statement of Robbie's.

'Robbie mentioned a ship that didn't come,' I explained. 'And Peter thinks it might have been a supply ship. Now, if the men depended on that ship . . .'

She nodded. 'Aye, they might have taken ill, or starved.'

'Or even mutinied. At any rate, they probably weren't in any shape to ward off their attackers when the final battle happened.'

'So what became of the survivors?'

'That's a mystery, still. But we do know the Sentinel stayed.'

'Love and honour,' Nancy Fortune told me, 'are a complicated mixture. If he really did promise his sister that he'd keep her man from harm, then he might well have felt he could never go home, that she'd never forgive him for failing.'

'Or he might have been mortally wounded himself,' I suggested. 'Who knows? Still, if we're patient, and stick to our digging, I'm sure we'll find something.'

I felt her eyes on my face. 'You believe Peter's theories, then?'

'Yes, I do. But then it's rather hard *not* to believe Peter, isn't it? I mean, he only has to look at you and give an explanation, and you can't imagine any other way it *could* have happened. You know?'

She smiled. 'Aye, that's what Davy says, too.'

I stayed silent a moment longer, and then said rather tentatively: 'They're very much alike, aren't they Peter and David?'

'Very much,' she agreed.

David's mother watched me, and after a long pause she said, very simply: 'He doesn't ken.'

My head turned. 'I'm sorry?'

'Davy. He doesn't ken who his father is. That's what you're wondering, isn't it?' In the face of my guilty silence she smiled and went on. 'It's no shame for me to tell you, lass. You've more right to the truth than anyone, and if you don't ken why,' she said, cutting me off as I opened my mouth to protest, 'then you're not as clever as I had you pegged.' Her gaze raked me fondly. 'You're very much as I was, Verity Grey. And if you'd gone to work for Peter Quinnell, years ago . . .'

'I should have been in love with him,' I told her, honestly.

'Aye. And so I was. Only, of course, he was married at the time.'

'Not happily.'

'No, not happily. But there it was.'

'Could he not . . .' I paused to clear my throat. 'Surely mental illness, even then, was just cause for divorce.'

'Oh, aye,' she said. 'But there was Philip, too, you see.'

'Well, yes, but—'

'Philip saw us,' she said slowly. 'One day, quite by accident. He had something of his mother's illness, and seeing me with Peter made him crazy. It was an awful thing, for Peter—Philip never did forgive him.' She shook her head. 'Philip had a talent for hating. But Peter loved the lad, and I didn't want him torn in two. I kent, see, that he would divorce Elizabeth if he'd kent I was carrying Davy.'

I blinked at her. 'If he'd . . .?'

'He'd have wanted to marry me,' she said. 'To take care of me. It's his nature. And I'd have hated that.'

'But you loved him.'

Her eyes shifted, and I could see her trying to find the right words to explain. 'Love and marriage, they were two different things to me, then. Marriage meant settling down, giving yourself over to a man . . . losing your independence, like. Much as I loved Peter—and I did love him terribly—I loved my own self more.'

I frowned at it. 'And yet you did get married.'

'Aye, on paper. Billy Fortune was an old friend, and a good man. It was his idea, like—to save my reputation, and to give the bairn a name. We only meant to keep it up two years, and then divorce, but Billy died afore that.' Her voice, I thought, was so amazingly calm. She might have been telling me someone else's story, and not her own. 'Poor Billy,' she said. 'Peter never did fathom why I'd married onto a fisherman.'

I struggled to make sense of it all. 'So Peter doesn't know?'

She shook her head. 'After Billy died he took a hand in Davy's bringing up—he couldn't help himself. But Davy's Billy Fortune's son, so far as Peter kens.'

'And David doesn't know . . . Then why . . .?'

'Why tell you?' The clear blue eyes, so like her son's, touched mine knowingly. 'Because, as you say, my Davy's a lot like his father. And you, lass, like me, are a difficult woman.'

'Well, yes, but . . .'

'I took one road, that's all I'm saying. I went down the one road and, now that I'm old, I can see that it wasn't the best road to take.'

'It's never too late, though, is it?' I ventured. 'I mean, you and Peter, you're both single now, and surely if you wanted to . . .'

She shook her head, and for the first time since I'd met her she looked her full age. 'Life moves on,' she said gently, 'and you can't go back. You've only got one chance to get it right.'

THE INSIDE OF THE TENT was much more comfortable than I'd imagined, lofty and spacious with a camp bed in one corner and a small wooden desk, buried beneath papers.

David, bent over his bootlace, flicked a glance upwards. 'Have I grown an extra head?' he asked me. 'You've been staring at me strange since you came in.' Straightening, he tucked his shirt-tails into the waistband of his khaki shorts and shot me a wicked grin. 'Or is it just that I'm so irresistible?'

He was looking rather irresistible, actually, fresh from his morning

shower with his hair still damp and rumpled like a boy's. I had a
momentary urge to comb my fingers through the curls to tidy them,
but instead I tipped my head back, admiring the canvas overhead.

'I do like your tent,' I said.

'Aye. Pure Abercrombie and Fitch, don't you think? Like being on
safari. I wake up every morning with the feeling that I ought to go
and shoot something. Of course,' he qualified the statement, 'I'd be
bound to feel like that anyway, working with Adrian, tent or no.'

I laughed. 'Adrian's not so bad. He only turns sarcastic when he's
foiled in love.'

'Oh, aye?'

I set him straight. 'And it isn't me he's pining for, whatever you
might think. He's head over heels for Fabia.'

David grinned again, more broadly. 'Is he, poor soul? He and
Brian ought to form a club, then—cry into their beer together. She's
got a new lad in her snares. One of these sub-aqua nutters come
down for the diving.'

'You seem to know an awful lot about it.'

'Oh, I ken everyone's business,' he said cheerfully. 'Especially now
that my mother's sitting up there at Saltgreens looking out on the
harbour all day.'

'Too bad you're not still living at the Ship,' I teased him. 'She
might have kept an eye on you.'

'Just as well I'm here, then.' The light in his eyes was decidedly
sinful. 'There are some things I'd not want to do, in full view of my
mother.'

'Such as?'

He laughed, and took my face in his hands, and showed me.

'Oh,' I said, when I could breathe again. '*Those* things.'

'And others. But I'll have to demonstrate another time. We're running late as it is.'

In the kitchen at Rosehill we found Robbie impatiently swinging
his legs. 'I've been waiting and waiting,' he told us.

David apologised. 'But we'll not be late, I promise you.'

'You're sure it's no bother, now?' Jeannie asked. 'Brian said he'd
meet you down there, when the boats all come back in.'

The fleet had sailed this morning up to St Abbs, near where
David's mother had her cottage, to pick up the young Herring Queen
and give her a royal escort back to Eyemouth as custom dictated.
Their return was timed for high tide, in the middle of the afternoon,

and then there'd be the pomp and circumstance of the crowning ceremony held on Gunsgreen, right beside the harbour. Robbie wasn't keen on seeing the crowning, but he *was* keen on the children's races held beforehand. Jeannie would have taken him, only she'd been battling a headache since breakfast.

'Of course it's no bother,' said David. 'And after the races, we'll take Robbie round to the museum and show him that stunning gown *you* wore as Herring Queen.'

'How do they choose the Herring Queen?' I asked curiously.

'Looks,' Jeannie said, straight-faced, but David didn't let her get away with it.

'Wasn't it school grades, in your day?' he asked her.

'In my day? And what am I, a dinosaur? Which one of us is turning thirty-seven tomorrow?'

Robbie grabbed David's sleeve and hauled him bodily towards the door. 'Come *on*,' he said. 'We'll be missing everything.'

Peter and most of the students had gone into town before us but Fabia was, as usual, running late. As we passed into the front hall she was talking on the telephone.

'. . . in the cellar, yes. Tomorrow? But that's Sunday, are you . . .? Oh right, yes, that's fine,' she said, turning slightly at the sound of our footsteps. 'OK, I will. Thanks very much.'

She rang off with a faintly guilty air, and David grinned.

'You're never ordering more supplies?' he asked.

She opened her mouth, as if to deny the charge, then thought better of it. 'Well, I need them. And anyway, Peter said that I could order anything I liked for my darkroom.' Tossing back her bright hair she gathered up the keys to the Range Rover. 'Are you off to this Herring Queen thing, then?'

'Aye. Any chance of a hurl into town? We were going to walk, but Robbie's in a wee bit of a hurry.'

'Sure, I can give you a lift, if you want.'

She dropped us in front of the museum, where a boisterous group of children appeared to have completely taken over the small paved square, laughing and chasing one another with alarming energy. As I stood watching Robbie run wild with the rest of them, his dark curls tossed anyhow, eyes shining happily, it suddenly struck me that our child would look very much like that—David's and mine. And then the implications of that one stray thought sank home, and I felt my face grow warm.

'If the children's races are run on Gunsgreen,' I asked David, 'then what are we doing here?'

'Waiting for the pipe band.'

My eyes shone. 'What, bagpipes?'

'Like them, do you?' He laughed at my reaction. 'Well, you'll not have long to wait. They come at noon, to gather up the children and pipe them over the water.'

'A pipe band,' I repeated, unable to hide my delight. 'Do we get to follow them, too?'

'Oh, aye. You can run in the races and all, if you're a good wee lassie.' His indulgent smile warmed me as he took hold of my hand, lacing his fingers through mine.

I smiled back, indescribably happy, then turned away as a rising drone of music heralded the arrival of the pipe band. With no ghosts to dog my steps, and the sun shining bright in a perfect blue sky, I felt younger than Robbie as we followed the pipes down to the harbour and onto the level sweep of Gunsgreen lawn.

There were people everywhere. They ebbed and flowed around us like a tidal stream, in colourful confusion. David, still holding my hand, steered me expertly through them and found a spot where we could stand and cheer the races. There was Highland dancing as well, with its bright swirl of tartan and toe-tapping music. I couldn't remember when I'd had so much fun. When the first fishing boats nosed their way into the harbour, I had to check my watch to convince myself it was, in fact, the middle of the afternoon.

David took firm hold of Robbie with his other hand and the three of us shifted with the crowd, to watch the Herring Queen set down upon the small red bridge at the end of the middle pier. She was a lovely girl, fresh-faced and fair, in a beautiful gown.

Robbie fidgeted through the crowning ceremony, bored by the speeches, and finally tugged at David's sleeve. 'Davy, Dad's over there. He's looking for me.' He pointed across the harbour, towards the fish market.

'Right, we'll go and find him.'

Brian McMorran, waiting in the shade of the fish market, didn't appear to be actively looking for his son; but then again, I reasoned, perhaps when both father and son had second sight, finding one another was a simple thing to do.

'Heyah, Dad!' Robbie went bouncing over. 'I saw the Herring Queen. Was mum that bonny when she was Herring Queen?'

'Your mother was the bonniest Herring Queen ever,' said Brian firmly. He propped his shoulder against a post and looked from David to myself. 'Been taking good care of my boy, then, have you?'

'It's no use asking Verity,' David said. 'She's been just as much trouble. I've had to keep the both of them from wandering off.'

Brian smiled and lit a cigarette. 'I'll take Robbie off your hands, at least. I've a few hours yet before my work starts.'

David glanced across the harbour at the *Fleetwing*'s gleaming red-and-white hull. 'Are you taking her out tonight?'

'Planning on it, but I'm a man short at the moment,' Brian answered.

David frowned. 'Who's gone, then?'

'Mick.' The boy from Liverpool that no one liked, as I recalled. Brian's shrug held no regret. 'He took a swing at our cook this morning. It was either me give Mick the shove, or Billy would have killed him.' He pulled at his cigarette, blowing out smoke. 'But I've got a lad lined up to take his place, so we might get a few days' good fishing in before the weather turns.'

'Right, then, we're away. We want to catch the last part of the crowning, ken.' David took my hand again like a teenage lover and led me back onto the middle pier.

In fact the crowning ceremony had ended by the time we made our way back to Gunsgreen, and the Herring Queen was being settled in a horse-drawn carriage while the pipe band started up again, preparing to lead her away on parade.

David's eyes teased me. 'If I'd kent you liked the pipes so much, I'd have taken lessons.'

'It's not the bagpipes, really,' I confessed, 'so much as the kilts.'

'Oh, aye?' David smiled. 'I'll wear mine tonight, to the ceilidh.'

'What does it look like, the Fortune tartan?'

'There isn't one. I wear the Hunting Stewart,' he informed me. 'Sort of an all-purpose tartan, for those whose families never claimed their own.'

But then he wasn't a Fortune anyway, I reminded myself. What did the Anglo-Irish have, I wondered, in place of the Scottish tartan? What was the mark of the Quinnell family?

'You're staring again,' said David.

'Ah.' There was no trace of Peter in his features, I thought. None at all. Except, perhaps, in the sure, unhurried way his eyes slid sideways, angled down to lock with mine.

'Keep looking at me like that,' he promised, putting one arm round my waist, 'and we'll not make it to the ceilidh.'

'Careful,' I warned, as his head began to lower. 'Your mother might be looking out of her window.'

David kissed me anyway.

The voice that spoke behind us wasn't Nancy Fortune's, but it nonetheless brought us apart like a pair of guilty schoolchildren.

'Verity, my dear,' said Peter, in his richly theatrical tone, 'you do have the most appalling taste in men. I'll admit, a Scotsman *is* a marginal improvement on an Englishman, but what you really want now is a nice Irish chap.'

David grinned. 'Away with your Irishmen.'

'Scoff if you will. But if I were some thirty years younger, my boy, I'd leave you at the post. So,' he addressed me 'how are you enjoying your day so far?'

I assured him I was enjoying it very well. 'We've been all over. I'm surprised we haven't bumped into you before now.'

'I've been up to see Nancy. One can see everything from her room, you know, without having to endure the crowds. She's got a lovely big window.'

David winked at me. 'What did I tell you? My mother's a regular spy.'

'Well,' I remarked,' she has to do something with her time, since the two of you insist on keeping her in the dark about the dig. She's longing to know what we're doing. And I must say I think it's dreadful, your shutting her out.'

Peter stared at me. 'But her doctors . . .'

'Are idiots,' I told him bluntly. 'She's not made of glass. I would think the frustration of *not* knowing would do more harm than the ounce of excitement you're liable to give her.'

David lifted his gaze to meet Peter's. 'She may have a point there.'

'Perhaps,' Peter said, 'but she doesn't know your mother, my boy. One might begin by simply telling Nancy things, but it wouldn't end there. She would want to be out in the field, and the minute I turned my back she'd be in there with trowel in hand . . .'

'She could work with me,' I offered. 'Nothing strenuous about what I do.'

Peter turned to David. 'Perhaps we ought to pay your mother a visit, after *this*'—he nodded at the passing parade—'is over. She'll have had enough of my company for one day, but I'm sure she'd be pleased to see the two of you.'

But when we stopped in at Saltgreens half an hour later, Nancy Fortune was not in her room.

One of the nursing staff explained. 'Oh, she took herself off home, for the weekend. Said she wasn't too keen on the crowds, and with the ceilidh tonight there was bound to be noise. The car was coughing a bit, it was, but she reckoned it would run all right once it got going.' The nurse smiled broadly.

'But . . . will she be all right up there, do you think? Alone?' Peter asked worriedly.

'Och, she'll be fine.' The nurse smiled again, confident. 'There's a telephone at her cottage, isn't there? And she's got her medication. It'll do her a world of good, getting away for a wee while.'

THE CEILIDH WAS enormous fun. I had a vague awareness of flushed faces and riotous laughter and wild, reeling music played so loudly that it rumbled in my breast like thunder. I danced until I couldn't breathe, until my head felt light and the room rolled and my legs could no longer support me.

And then it was David's arms supporting me, his shoulders warm beneath my hands, the walls and bright lights spinning past his dark head. I breathed again. The music slowed. People pressed in on all sides, but I saw no one else. Only David.

I might have blamed the kilt. He did look smashing in the blended green hues of the Hunting Stewart tartan, with his white cotton shirt clinging damp to his back. It was as if, by trading in his trousers for a length of tartan, David somehow tapped the pride and wild passion of his ancestors. He seemed to drift in time, not altogether of this century, and his gaze now and then held the glint of a warrior.

Yes, I thought, I might have blamed the kilt; but that wouldn't have been entirely honest. It was the man that held me fascinated.

He stopped revolving, and the blue eyes smiled. Lifting one hand from my waist he brushed back a strand of my hair and I saw his lips moving. 'Too many people.'

'What people?' I asked, and the smile touched his mouth.

'Come on,' he said, 'let's get some air.'

Outside the night was clear and warm, and the wind, for once, was still. The harbour lay like glass beneath a moon that needed one small sliver yet to make it full. High tide had come and gone six hours ago, and the *Fleetwing* had slipped her moorings and gone with it. In her place, a small pale spectre floated on the water. It might have been a mere reflection of the moon until it turned and stretched a searching neck along the blackness. The swan.

'David.' I stopped walking, grabbed his arm. 'Look at that.' A second ghost had glided from the shadows, neck arched smoothly, wings at rest. It met the first and touched it and the two moved on together. 'Oh David, look—he's finally found a mate.'

David looked and said nothing. After a long moment he smiled faintly and started walking again, his arm across my shoulders.

I didn't really notice which direction we were walking. After several long minutes the pavement ended and the ground became rougher. I sensed that the sea was below us now, the waves kicking spray on the rocks and the beach.

Clearing my mind with an effort, I took a proper look around. 'Where are we?'

'Up on Eyemouth Fort.'

Of course, I thought. That massive spear of land that jutted out into the sea, the red cliffs topped with long green grass. In the shelter of a ridge David sat and pulled me down beside him, our backs fitted to the angle of the grass-covered slope. I tipped my head back and watched the stars glittering into infinity.

David stayed silent, hands linked behind his head. And then he said simply: 'What are you going to do about Lazenby's job offer?'

I rolled my head sideways to look at him. 'How do you know about that?'

'Adrian told me.'

Reminding myself to smack Adrian next time I saw him, I pointed out that I hadn't actually been offered *any* job, as yet. 'Lazenby hasn't been in touch, he hasn't asked me —'

'When he does,' said David calmly, 'what will you tell him?'

For a moment, in silence, I studied his profile. Then I said, 'If he'd asked me two months ago, I think I would have said yes.'

'And now?'

'Now I'm not sure.' I pulled a clump of grass with idle fingers.

'And why is that?'

I tossed the grass away and sighed. 'Look, I'm never very brilliant at this sort of thing . . .'

He smiled faintly at my choice of words. 'Happens a lot, does it?'

'No, it doesn't. In fact, it's never . . . well,' I stumbled, as he slowly turned his head to look at me, 'that is to say, I've never felt . . .' But that sentence faltered as well.

He held my gaze a long while, silently, his eyes turned silver by the moonlight. And then he stood and held a hand out. 'Time we were getting back,' he said.

'David . . .'

'I'm no saint. I can't stay here like this and not touch you,' he told me, his tone carefully even. 'And fond as I am of the fort, I would rather our first time took place in a bed, if it's all the same to you.'

I thought of his camp bed, and of my twin-bedded room at Rosehill, and of the other people who were constantly around us. 'But David . . .'

'Some things,' he said, 'are worth waiting for.'

The fort path led out past the caravan park, and a snatch of music gave way, as we walked, to the muted sound of a couple quarrelling. David kept possession of my hand, whistling softly under his breath as though he were well pleased. As we passed the last row of caravans he slowed his step and the whistling ceased. 'There you are,' he said quietly. 'What did I tell you?'

Two figures were standing locked in an embrace alongside the furthest caravan. The man I couldn't see too well, but he was clearly kissing Fabia. One couldn't mistake her, even at this distance.

'Hard luck on poor Adrian.'

'Aye.' David smiled.

He didn't take the road towards the harbour, but led me uphill instead, along a curve of darkened houses and out again onto the road that would take us back to Rosehill. It seemed no time before we were turning up the long drive, in companionable silence.

David didn't kiss me good night at the door. He followed me into the entrance hall and up the curve of smooth stone stairs, and when I turned in the middle of my bedroom he was still there behind me, putting the cat out.

'David,' I asked him, 'what are you doing?'

He glanced over his shoulder, as though it were plainly self-evident. 'I'm locking the door.'

I heard the key catch. And then he was coming towards me and I found myself suddenly at a loss for words, nervous in a way I hadn't been in years. I was trembling—actually trembling—when he touched my hair, his fingers working to undo the plait, arranging the long strands over my shoulders. 'Do you mind?' he asked me gently.

I found a smile then, to show him. 'What happened to "some things are worth waiting for"?'

'My God, woman. I've waited half an hour as it is.'

I caught the flash of his grin in the near darkness. And then he took my face in his hands and kissed me, and it was a very long while before I noticed anything else.

TWELVE

The horses woke me in the dark hour before dawn. Snorting and stamping, they thundered past beneath my window and were swallowed by the lonely field and the wind that swept through the chestnut tree like a wandering lament.

I shivered into wakefulness and forced my leaden eyelids open, momentarily confused by the heavy weight of something warm across my waist. And then I remembered.

'David. Did you hear that?'

But it was obvious he hadn't. Still half-asleep, he tightened his arm round my waist to gather me closer against him, his powerful body shielding me from harm. 'Whatever it is,' he murmured soothingly, 'it'll have to come through me first. Go to sleep.'

And closing my eyes I turned my face against his shoulder and felt all my fears flow from me while his strong and steady heartbeat drowned the shrieking of the wind.

It might have been a minute or a lifetime later when I heard Jeannie's voice calling my name. She sounded close, I thought drowsily. A good thing David locked the door, or else . . .

'Come on, Verity— waken up, now.' Jeannie's hand jostled my arm and my eyes flew open with a guilty start to focus on her face. 'Jings! You do sleep like the dead.'

The warm weight across my stomach shifted, and looking down I saw that it was Murphy, rolling over on his side to test his claws against the blankets. He had not quite recovered from the indignity of being chucked out of my room last night, and his level stare was icily aloof. Beside me, the mattress was empty and cold.

'It's nine o'clock,' said Jeannie briskly. 'Peter said to knock you up at nine.'

Closing my eyes again, I let my head drop back against the pillows. 'On a Sunday?'

'He didn't want you missing all the excitement. There's a big storm on the way.'

I opened my eyes as the realisation struck and levered myself onto my elbows. 'The excavations . . . we'll have to cover—'

'It's already done,' she informed me. 'Davy and Peter and Dad did all that, afore breakfast. And they're moving the students up into the stables, in case those wee tents don't stand up to the storm.'

'Will it be bad, do you think?'

Jeannie nodded. 'Brian brought the boat back in at half past two this morning, and there's not much makes my Brian cautious. Oh,' she said, as an afterthought, turning at the door, 'you do mind that it's Davy's birthday, don't you?'

As if I needed reminding. Hopeful that Jeannie wouldn't see the tiny flush that touched my cheeks, I nodded, feigning nonchalance. 'He's thirty-seven, isn't he?'

'Aye. Not that you'd ken that from looking at him. He's been bouncing about like a lad Robbie's age all the morning.'

Where he had found the energy to bounce, I didn't know. I felt deliciously lazy, myself. Simply dressing and brushing my teeth took me all of twenty minutes, and my fingers were so clumsy with my plait that in the end I gave up the effort. The wind caught the loose strands as I stepped outside, blowing them across my eyes.

I nearly walked straight into Adrian's red Jaguar, parked at a crazy angle just a few steps from the house, the keys still dangling in the ignition. Adrian had been quite cautious with his keys since the night we'd sat up in the field, and this was hardly his usual parking technique, but when I caught up with him in the Principia a few minutes later I saw the reason for his carelessness. He put me in mind of a stylish corpse—deathly white draped artistically across his desk.

'Late night?' I asked him.

'You have no idea.' Raising his head, he propped it up with a hand and half opened one eye. 'Blasted Herring Queen, herds of people milling about underneath my window. It was impossible to sleep.'

I filled my coffee cup and took my chair. 'Where is everybody?'

Adrian shrugged. 'I haven't the faintest idea, but I'm sure they'll be back. They've been in and out all morning . . . every time I start to nod off.'

'Very thoughtless of them,' I agreed.

Hearing the smile in my voice, Adrian opened his eye wider, to stare at me suspiciously. 'You're looking rather ragged yourself, my love. Almost as ragged as our Mr Fortune. He's—'

'Adrian,' I interrupted, not listening, 'how long have you been sitting here?'

He consulted his watch. 'About an hour and a half. Why?'

Frowning down into the drawer of my desk, I pushed aside a pen to get a better look at the tiny gold medallion gleaming in my pen tray. The Fortuna pendant. 'You didn't see who put this in here, I suppose?'

He squinted as I held it up. 'No, I didn't. But that doesn't mean anything. Even I have difficulty seeing with my eyes shut.'

It must have been one of my students, I told myself. They both had keys to the finds room. But still . . .

'Here's the watchdog,' Adrian announced. 'Ask him.'

Kip came dancing through the arched door with energy to spare, half running down the aisle between the desks, then bounding back to watch Wally and Peter manoeuvre a bundle of sleeping-bags into the room.

'Dear oh dear,' Peter said, when he caught sight of me. 'You ought to be in bed, Verity.'

'Well, I'm up now. So there.' Smiling to soften the comment, I held up the golden pendant. 'You didn't put this in my desk drawer, by any chance?'

'No, I'd imagine David did that. He found it on *his* desk, as I recall, but as none of us had our keys to the finds room handy he must have thought your desk was the safest option. Now,' he said, turning his attention to the common room, 'I'm wondering if we shouldn't bring the camp beds up as well?'

David was struggling through the doorway with another load of sleeping-bags. 'No,' he said, with feeling. 'They're students, Peter—they *like* sleeping on the floor.' He dumped his armful of sleeping-bags and turned to me, his smile warming the air between us. 'Morning.'

'Good morning.'

Adrian, aware that he was missing something, was glowering across at me when I was suddenly saved by Fabia. Waltzing through the stable door, her blonde hair fetchingly ruffled by the fierce rising wind, she provided a welcome distraction. Adrian's eyes left my face like a compass needle swinging to magnetic north.

But she didn't appear to notice. She'd come looking for David. 'Your mother just rang,' she said. 'She says she's having trouble with the car, and can you please go up and get her.'

'What, now? Right this minute?'

Fabia nodded. 'She didn't sound too keen on being stuck up there alone, with this storm coming.'

'Nonsense,' Peter said. 'Nancy's rather fond of storms, as I recall.'

David smiled. 'All the same, I'd best not keep my mother waiting, not when I've been summoned.'

'You can take the Range Rover, if you like,' said Fabia.

'Aye, all right.' Turning, he held out his hand. 'Give us the keys, then, and I'm away.'

Brian came through the doorway as David went out, and shuddered as a sudden gust of wind shook the building. 'It's worse up here than it is at the harbour.'

Peter arched a solicitous eyebrow. 'How's the boat?'

'Oh, the boat's fine,' said Brian. 'But we had the bloody Customs and Excise officer around this morning. Scared poor Billy half to death. Good job we'd only been out a few hours—the boat was clean. And the last shipment's safely up here, where nobody would think to . . .' He suddenly stopped, and his head came up.

I'd seen that expression before, I thought—that strange, fixed expression. I'd seen it on Robbie.

Fabia, beneath his stare, swallowed apprehensively. 'What?'

'You stupid cow,' he told her slowly. 'You bloody stupid cow.'

Adrian stood up, protectively. 'Brian . . .'

'I'd figured it was Mick who grassed,' said Brian, heedless of the interruption, seeing only Fabia. 'But it was you put the officer onto the *Fleetwing*.' His tone was certain, and I remembered what I'd heard of Fabia's telephone conversation yesterday, in the front hall. *Tomorrow morning*, she'd said. Had she been ringing the Customs and Excise then, telling them to inspect Brian's boat? But why?

Brian had his own theory. 'What, angry with me, were you, for giving your boyfriend the shove?'

'Her boyfriend . . .' Adrian frowned.

'Oh, aye. She and young Mick have been having it off for a month or more, now. You and I,' he told Adrian, 'outlived our usefulness.'

The storm was drawing closer. I could feel the pricking heat of it, the dark oppressive heaviness that dulled the dead air around me. Peter, standing by the wall, shook his head slightly. 'Brian, my dear boy, this hardly seems . . .'

'I didn't make that call because of Mick,' said Fabia, rising to

Brian's bait. 'And I never wanted them to search your stupid boat. I wanted them to come *here*.' Her eyes freezing over, she turned to face Peter. 'They will come, you know—they'll be on their way now. And they'll find what you're keeping down in the cellar. And what will Connelly say, do you think, when he finds you've been using the dig as a cover for smuggling?' The tone of her voice was pure venom.

Peter's eyes held a terrible sadness. 'Fabia, why?'

'Because,' she said, 'I want to see you suffer.'

Adrian, shocked, burst out: 'Fabia!' and she wheeled on him in a temper.

'You don't know anything about it!' she accused him. 'He killed my father, understand? He made my father's life a living hell.'

Peter seemed to age before my eyes, his features collapsing with the weight of painful memory. 'Fabia,' he tried to explain, 'your father was ill . . . he was ill but I loved him.'

'Liar!' She hissed the word. 'You never loved Daddy as much as you loved your precious work, your precious reputation. He told me.' Her eyes, filled with hate, found her grandfather's stricken ones. 'He told me everything.'

The lights flickered briefly and I suddenly realised how dark it had grown outside—the shadows closed around us and vanished again as the warm glow hummed to life. And then the sky exploded, and the storm came down like vengeance.

Jeannie, blown into the big room on a wet and swirling wind, seemed scarcely to notice the tension. She was too busy looking at Brian. 'Where's Robbie?'

Forgetting the drama in progress, he turned. 'Is he not with you?'

She shook her head. 'I thought you had him down the harbour.'

'Right, I'll go and have a look. Did you ring round his friends?'

'I couldn't,' she said. 'It's the wind, see. Our phone line's been out of order since breakfast.'

'It can't be out,' said Adrian. 'Fortune's mother rang not long ago, from her cottage.'

But Jeannie disputed the fact. 'She couldn't have. I've been check-ing the line myself, every ten minutes, like.'

'But Fabia said . . .'

In the space of an instant my own mind sifted through a hundred things that Fabia had said, and fitted the statements together like the pieces of a jigsaw puzzle. I didn't like the picture that was forming.

Above all, I remembered her saying that the perfect revenge on one's enemy would be to take from him everything and everyone he loved, yet make him go on living. Everything Peter loved . . . that would be his work, his reputation. And as for the 'everyone' . . . My mind baulked, not wanting to follow that thought, but I forced it.

If Fabia knew what her father had known—if he had, as she said, told her everything—then she knew about Peter and Nancy. Was she trying to harm Nancy, somehow? And had she needed to get David out of the way first by inventing that telephone call; by sending David out alone on the road to St Abbs?

The storm rose and wailed like a living thing, beating its fists on the shuddering walls, and I clenched my own fist convulsively. *The road. The road is dangerous.*

'Oh, God,' I breathed. My head jerked round, to stare at the tiny gold medallion sitting atop my disordered papers. The Fortuna pendant. It had been on David's desk this morning—that's what Peter had told me. *David's desk.*

Oh, how could I have been so stupid? Stupid, stupid—thinking that the warning was for me. It was David that the Sentinel had tried to warn, David who had found the pendant in the first place. What had Robbie said? *It's for protection. You don't understand.*

And now, too late, I understood.

I understood why Fabia had chosen Mick to be her boyfriend. She needed a violent, unprincipled man to help her destroy what her grandfather loved. She needed a man who could murder. And now that same man, I felt sure, was somewhere near St Abbs, where Nancy Fortune—an old woman with a weak heart—sat waiting out the storm in her cottage, alone and unprotected. And where David, unaware of the danger, would shortly walk into an ambush.

I was not aware of moving, but I heard my own voice saying 'No' quite loudly, and somebody reached to take my arm, but I pushed them away and was through the great arched doorway before anyone could stop me. Kip howled after me, and I thought I heard Adrian shouting my name, but the sound of the wind swallowed both of them and I was running, running, the rain in my eyes and the bitter wind tearing the breath from my throat.

The Jaguar roared to life at the first twist of the dangling key. I hauled at the wheel, spinning gravel, and took the drive at twice the prudent speed. The bonnet kissed the big stone gatepost with an ugly grating sound, but I barely noticed.

I was too busy praying. 'Please,' I whispered to the furies that were beating on the windscreen. 'Please let me be wrong.'

The rain was so thick I could scarcely see and the windows steamed, but I kept my foot to the floor through the village of Coldingham, taking the turnings blindly, letting the tyres shriek their protest through a stunning arc of spray. I tightened my grip on the steering wheel. 'Please let me be wrong.'

But as I came out onto the Coldingham Moor, the wiper blades swept cleanly through the pounding flood of water and I saw what I'd been fearing.

He had lost control of the Range Rover, and it had rolled, coming to rest on its battered roof. One metal door, bizarrely twisted, lay drowning in the river that had been the road. What remained of the windscreen was pure white with splinters, like smashed river ice. There was no sign of life.

The Jaguar spun out as I hit the brakes. The car came to rest against a rail fence at the far edge of the road, directly across from the battered Range Rover. Fumbling with my door latch, I stumbled out, uncaring of the storm.

'David!' I screamed in panic, raising my hands in a futile defence against the lashing wind. He wasn't in the Range Rover. My hands scraped raw against the battered metal as I pulled the vehicle apart in search of him, but he wasn't there. Sobbing now, my body trembling with shock and pain, I turned away and staggered through the tangle of gorse and thorn at the side of the road. 'David,' I called again, but the storm stole my cry and I sank to the ground, defeated.

The wind passed through me like a frozen blade and a deep voice called me, indistinct. I raised an anguished face. But it wasn't David.

It wasn't anybody. A jagged spear of lightning showed the empty moor, the blowing thorn. But as the thunder rolled and died I heard the voice again, strangely hollow, as though straining to reach me across a great distance. 'Claudia.'

Struggling to resolve itself, the faint transparent outline of a man took form and faded in the slashing silver rain. And as I blinked against the stinging wetness, he made a supreme effort and his shadow reappeared. Dark eyes, not wholly human, met mine.

He raised what might have been an arm, a hand, as if he meant to touch me, and I saw the effort this time, saw him fight to frame the words. '*Non lacrimas, Claudia.*'

Don't cry.

I felt a gentle trail of ice across my cheek, as if he sought to brush the tears away, and then I half believed the shadow smiled. '*Non lacrimas*,' he said again, and melted in the rain.

Afraid to move, I went on staring at the place where he had been. Then the lightning split the clouds again, and flashed across the roughened ground, and all at once I felt the breath tear from me in a sob of pure relief.

A man was coming across the moor.

He looked enormous to my eyes, a great dark giant moving over bracken and thorn with an effortless stride. It was as if the hourglass had tipped and the sands were spilling back and I was sitting on the bus again, and watching for the first time while he came to me across the wild moor.

He was carrying something, wrapped up in a bright yellow mac. I saw him stop, and standing square against the storm he stared at the Jaguar, its bright red bonnet buried at a crazy angle in the rail fence. Then his chin jerked upwards and I knew he'd seen me, crouched amid the wreckage of the Range Rover, and even as I raised my voice to call him he began to run.

I COULDN'T SEEM TO let him go. We were safe inside the Jaguar, but my hands had fastened to his wet shirt and I couldn't let him go.

David, one-handed, had made use of Adrian's cellphone to check that his mother was safe, and now he rolled me sideways so he could replace the handset in its cradle. We were both of us wedged in the passenger seat, and he settled me against his chest, one arm wrapped warm around my shoulders.

The bundle he'd brought with him sat propped on the driver's seat, small head lolled sideways, and I reached my hand to smooth one darkly dripping curl away from Robbie's pallid face. He was unhurt, breathing normally, and tucked within the folds of David's raincoat he slept soundly, deeply, unaware.

Which was just as well, I thought. The things I'd said to David as we'd clung to each other outside in the rain . . . such things were not intended to be overheard by anyone. Least of all an eight-year-old.

'You're sure he's all right?'

'Aye. Though how a wee laddie like that got himself all the way out here . . .' David put his hand out to pull the folds of the raincoat tighter round Robbie's shoulders.

'He's so pale.'

'I'm the one that should be pale. I nearly ran him over. The lad bolted clear across the road in front of me—fair scared me to death. I barely had time to see that it was Robbie afore I rolled the Rover, and after I got myself clear of that mess, I had to go chasing after him. I couldn't leave him out on the moor in this storm,' he explained. His voice trailed away and his chin shifted a fraction further, so he could look to where the moor stretched out towards St Abbs, beyond the fogging window.

I had explained, as best I could, what had happened, but my words had tumbled out incoherently, a confusing narrative that leapt from Fabia to the Fortuna pendant, with yawning gaps between. I'd have to do a better job, I told myself, and sort things out more clearly, so that he could understand them.

But not now. Not now. There would be time enough for talking when we all got back to Rosehill.

'David? I think I've lost the car keys.'

He laughed. 'Not to worry. They'd not be much use, from what I can see. We're stuck in this fence.'

I moved my head, to look out in dismay at the crumpled bonnet of the Jaguar, but David's hand drew me back again, holding me close while the gusting wind set the car rocking. 'It's all right,' he assured me. 'If I ken my mother, we'll not have to wait long for the cavalry.'

He barely got the sentence out before the blue lights flashed behind us and the storm itself was drowned beneath the stronger wail of sirens.

THE STORM HAD PASSED by teatime but the sullen sky, flat grey and dreary, pressed heavily upon the dripping walls of Rosehill.

'For goodness' sake,' Peter said, 'do put a light on, somebody.' Stretching himself in his cracked leather armchair he stroked Murphy's black back. 'I've had enough of shadows for one day.'

I reached to switch the lamp on, and the red walls warmed. The grey cat, Charlie, on my lap, stirred and blinked in the sudden light, then burrowed her small face against my leg with a tiny sigh. She and I, I thought, were the odd ones out in this room—two females being suffered by a gathering of men. But then it was, essentially, a man's room. Wally, with his feet up in one corner, eyes half closed against the drifting haze of his cigarette, looked perfectly at home here, as did David, slouched beside me on the old worn leather sofa, one arm slung lazily along my shoulders while the other cradled Robbie close against his other side.

Robbie, wide-awake now, showed no ill effects from his morning's adventure. He couldn't remember leaving Rosehill, or walking cross-country to Coldingham Moor—a trip that must surely have taken him two and a half hours. Nor could he even clearly tell us why he'd done it. 'The Sentinel needed me,' was the only explanation he gave.

I suspected that the Sentinel, lacking human hands, had needed Robbie to fetch the Fortuna medallion from the finds room, as well, and leave it on David's desk. But Robbie couldn't recall being in the Principia, either. His memory of the day's events was blurred at best. 'Was I really in Mr Sutton-Clarke's car?'

'Indeed you were.' Adrian was lounging in a corner chair. 'I've got the water stains on the seats to prove it.'

Adrian, I thought, was bearing up remarkably well. I'd expected histrionics when we'd arrived at Rosehill with the Jaguar in tow, but Adrian had merely looked in mournful silence at the dents and scratches, then he'd sighed and turned to David. 'Well, at least *you're* in one piece. That's something, anyway.' With which surprising speech he'd left us and gone back inside the house.

David had raised his eyebrows. 'What was that, d'ye think?'

'A beginning,' I'd told him, linking my arm through his.

Adrian, I knew, had meant it as a peacemaking of sorts; a gesture of conciliation and acceptance. Not that he and David were ever likely to become firm friends, I admitted, but still . . . I had seen stranger things today, and could no longer call anything impossible.

The comforting thing about the past, to me, had always been that it repeated itself in predictable patterns. But today the past had come loose like a runaway cart and the present ran on in confusion, a horse still in harness with nothing behind it and no one controlling the reins. And so Adrian, who had always read me the riot act if I so much as slammed his car door, was now sitting across from me, holding his tongue. And Wally, who had always hated Brian, had spent the past hour praising what his son-in-law had done.

And what Brian had done, I decided, was in itself a fine example of how the patterns of the past had been disrupted. Brian, selfish and conceited, who lived by his own whims for pleasure and gain, had today risked his own neck to save Peter's. Once word had reached him that Robbie was safe, he had set about clearing the cellar of anything incriminating. At the height of the storm and in three separate carloads, he'd shuttled the crates of vodka and cigarettes from Rosehill to their new hiding place, in the town. 'And efter a' that,'

Wally'd told us, complaining, 'the excisemen didnae even come.'
But at least, if they did come, the house would be clean. There'd be
no scandalous headlines, no ruinous charges. The only news would
be that Peter Quinnell's granddaughter, still suffering from nerves
after her father's suicide, had been admitted to an undisclosed private hospital, where she'd be receiving counselling and treatment.

'So it was Fabia,' said David, 'who did all that messing about with
the computers.'

'And mislaid Peter's notebook,' I added. 'And told Connelly about
our ghost hunt in the field that night, saying it was all Peter's idea.
She would have done anything to be sure our dig didn't succeed.'

Peter gently reminded me that he, and not the dig, had been the
target of Fabia's sabotage. 'At the end of the day,' he said, 'it all
comes down to her wanting to discredit me, to see me suffer.'

Had she been able to see him now, I thought, she would have felt
quite satisfied. The lines of suffering were still etched plainly in his
handsome face, for all of us to see. Still, Peter, I reflected, had
remained consistent in his actions. Saddened but unbowed, he'd
spent the afternoon dispensing drinks and comfort, telephoning
lawyers, taking care of everything. It was, as Nancy Fortune said, his
nature—taking care of things.

'Good heavens,' I said to David, suddenly remembering. 'Your
mother. She'll still be waiting for us to come and fetch her at the cottage, won't she?'

'Aye, well,' David shrugged, 'I can't do much of anything until
Jeannie and Brian come back—I've no car.'

Peter eyed him thoughtfully. 'I really think, my boy, it might be
best to let someone else collect your mother. You've had bad luck
with borrowed cars today.'

Robbie twisted to look up at David's face. 'You didn't take the
necklace,' he said, as if that explained everything. 'You were supposed to wear it, like.'

'Aye, well,' David smiled, 'next time we're talking to your Sentinel,
Robbie, you mind me to tell him why no self-respecting archaeologist
wears artefacts.'

'Why?' Robbie asked.

Peter explained. 'Because we'd damage them. We shouldn't dig
things up at all unless we can take care of them.' He was silent a
moment, mulling something over. 'Can he really hear us, when we
speak? The Sentinel, I mean.'

Robbie nodded. 'He can see you and all. Only you've got to speak Latin, or he doesn't ken what you're saying. I can say "hello",' he announced proudly.

'Well done,' said Peter vaguely, deep in thought. The crunch of tyres on the gravel roused him and he raised his head expectantly. 'Ah, here are Jeannie and Brian now.'

Jeannie looked relieved to have the whole thing over with. 'It wasn't so bad,' she said. 'It was just an identification, like.'

'It did take us a while, though,' Brian admitted. 'Just to be sure, with the bandages and all. What the devil did your mother hit him with, anyway?'

'Teapot,' said David. 'Her famous tin teapot.'

Brian winced. 'Bloody hell!'

'Will they have enough,' asked Adrian, 'to make the charges stick?'

'Oh, aye,' Brian nodded.

'What makes you so certain?'

'Well, for one thing,' said Brian, leaning back with a thoughtful expression, 'the police are going to find Mick's caravan is filled near to bursting with black-market vodka and fags.'

David looked at him. 'Brian, you didn't.'

'I did. He's a right bastard, and he needs to get more than your mother's blinking teapot in his eye.'

Peter glanced at Jeannie, suddenly remembering. 'I do hate to ask you this, my dear, because I know you've just got back, but would you mind very much driving over to fetch Nancy?'

'Of course not.' Picking up the car keys, she held out her free hand. 'Come on, Robbie, let's go get Granny Nan.'

'And don't take her to Saltgreens. You're to bring her back here,' Peter said. 'For dinner. It's high time she had a look at what we've been up to.'

Jeannie stared at him for a long moment, and her slowly spreading smile was beautiful. 'Aye,' she said, 'I think you're right.'

'Any chance of a lift into town?' Adrian asked, rising with a self-indulgent stretch. 'I have a dinner date myself, as I recall, with a rather smashing redhead.'

I sent him a mildly suspicious glance. 'One of my finds assistants is a redhead. Just see that she's not late for work in the morning.'

'My dear girl,' he asked me, 'do I look the sort of person who'd corrupt an innocent student?'

None of us answered him, but his words set Peter off on a new train of thought. 'The students,' he mused. 'I must go and check on them. I don't believe we'll have the tents set up again before tomorrow, but—'

'Aye, well,' said David, stretching himself, 'maybe Wally and I can go down now and take a look round at the damage.'

Brian went with them. Which left only me, sitting there with the cats, in no hurry to do much of anything.

It was the telephone, jangling in the front hall, that finally got me off the sofa. With a sigh, I lifted the receiver, wishing the thing could have stayed out of order till dinnertime, at least.

'Verity?' A voice I knew. 'It's Howard. Remember those photographs you sent me a while back—the Samian sherds?'

'Yes.'

He coughed. 'The thing is, I was clearing my desk up last Friday . . . you know how my desk gets . . . and anyway, I found the envelope you'd sent the photos in, and I was just about to tear it up when I realised there was a photograph still stuck inside it. Got wedged in the bottom somehow, and I simply hadn't noticed . . .'

'Howard. What are you trying to tell me?'

'I told you those sherds were Agricolan. But this last one . . . the one in the photograph I *didn't* see, it's entirely different.'

Remembering the one sherd that I'd thought was younger than the others, I gripped the handset tighter, hoping. 'In what way?'

'The rim pattern is quite distinctive, you know, and . . . well, I'd have to see the actual sherd, naturally, before I could give it a positive date, but it certainly couldn't have been made before AD 115.'

My heart gave a tiny, joyful leap. 'You're sure?'

'It is my job,' he reminded me drily.

'Not before 115? Oh Howard, that's wonderful.'

'Helpful, is it?'

'You have no idea.'

'You still owe me five pounds,' he said. 'As I recall, the bet was that you'd find a marching camp, and the word down here is you've found a good deal more.'

He meant our digging team, of course, but the statement struck me personally. 'Yes,' I told him. 'Yes, I have.'

'Well, well,' said Howard. 'Look, just send that sherd to me tomorrow, will you?'

'Right,' I promised. 'And Howard?'

'Yes?'

'If you're talking to Dr Lazenby . . .'

'Yes?'

'Would you tell him I'm not interested in Alexandria?'

A pause. 'Are you ill?'

'No, I'm perfectly healthy. And perfectly happy, right here.'

I did feel almost ridiculously happy as I rang off. Odd, I thought, how good and bad things always seemed to come at once, as if some unseen force were seeking balance. Peter, for all his brave exterior, had suffered today as no man deserved to suffer. And now he was about to learn that Rosehill had been twice occupied—not only during the Agricolan campaigns, but later, after AD 115, around the time the Ninth Hispana had started its fateful march northwards.

It wasn't proof, not concrete proof, but it was enough to make the archaeological establishment show some respect for Peter Quinnell. Even those who mocked his theories could no longer call him mad.

Not that he was *entirely* sane, I thought fondly, when I went outside to find him. He was standing in the field, alone, a rather tragic figure with his white hair blowing in the wind, his jaw set high and proud. He looked round as I approached, and smiled wistfully.

'And they say the gods don't hear us.'

'Sorry?'

'I've been pondering the truth, my dear,' he said. 'And here you are. In Latin, truth is feminine, is it not? *Veritas.* Verity.' My name flowed out in his melodic voice like a phrase from a very old song, and he turned his gaze away again. 'The truth is buried in this field, somewhere. But if I fail to prove it, can it still be called the truth?'

I considered the question. 'Well . . . I can't see the Sentinel, and I've no scientific proof he exists, but I do know that he's there.'

'Ah, but you did see him, didn't you? Whereas I . . .'

'Whereas you have a potsherd that dates from the end of Trajan's reign,' I said, and smiled as he turned again to stare at me.

'I beg your pardon? I have what?'

I repeated the statement, and told him about Howard's telephone call. 'He said he'd be happy to give us a firm date if we could send him the sherd.'

'Good heavens.' He stared at me a moment longer, and then crushed me with a hug. 'That's marvellous, my dear. That's absolutely—'

The slam of a car door interrupted us, and Robbie came running over the blowing grass with Kip bounding close at his heels. 'Heyah,' said Robbie. 'We got Granny Nan. She's going to change her shoes, she says, and then come out.'

'Wonderful,' Peter said.

The collie brushed past us, tail wagging, and Robbie nodded at the field. 'You found him, did you?'

I looked where he was looking, and saw nothing. 'Who do you mean, Robbie? The Sentinel? Where is he?'

'Just there, where Kip is.'

Not ten feet in front of us. 'Poor chap,' Peter said. 'I would have thought he'd find some peace, after what he did today. I would have thought that he could rest.'

Robbie wrinkled his freckled nose, looking up. 'He doesn't want to rest,' he said. 'He wants to take care of us.'

'Does he, indeed?' Peter smiled. 'Well, I can understand that.'

I thought I understood, as well. And where I'd once been frightened by the thought of being watched, I now took comfort in the presence of the Sentinel. I felt a satisfaction, too, in knowing that today he had been able to keep his promise, saving the life of the man that his 'Claudia' loved. And he would go on protecting us, here at Rosehill. The shadowy horses could run all they wanted; they'd never come near while the Sentinel walked.

Kip suddenly sat and whined an eager little whine, eyes trained upwards, waiting. And then, as though someone had given him a signal, he broke away and bounded off to meet the older woman coming round the house behind us. Robbie turned and said: 'Granny Nan's coming.' And I was turning myself, to wave hello, so I might have imagined what Peter said next. His words were quiet, very low, and I wasn't meant to hear them.

He was speaking to the Sentinel. 'Thank you,' he said simply, in his lovely, cultured Latin. 'Thank you for saving my son.'

He dropped his gaze, but not before I saw his wise and weary eyes, and knew for certain that he knew. And then his eyes lifted again, and in place of the sadness there was only a smile as he held out his hands to greet David's mother.

DAVID WAS SITTING on the bank of the Eye Water, watching the swans. The harbour must have been too rough for them during the storm, so they'd swum further upriver in search of calmer waters. They drifted now under the trees, snow-white and regal.

I spread my anorak over the wet grass and sat down beside him. 'Your mother's here. Peter's giving her the grand tour.'

'We'll be waiting for our dinner, then.'

I nodded, hugging my knees. I ought to have told him about Howard's discovery, only I knew that if I did we'd end up talking about the dig, and I didn't want to talk about the dig right now. Instead I watched the pale swans drifting in the shallows. 'They're beautiful, aren't they?'

'Aye.'

'I'm glad there are two. The one looked so lonely, by himself.'

David smiled, not looking at me. 'He'll not be lonely again. They mate for life, swans do. She's stuck with him now.'

And I was stuck with David Fortune, I thought fondly, studying his now familiar face—the deep lines of laughter that crinkled his eyes, the thick slanting fall of black eyelashes touching his cheekbones, the firm, unyielding angle of his jaw, and the nose that, in profile, was not quite straight, as though it had been broken in a fight. One day, I promised myself, one day, when we were sitting in the red-walled room at Rosehill, watching Peter and Nancy dandle their grandchild, I would ask my husband how he'd broken his nose.

But till then I could wait—I was in no great hurry. Like the swans, I had mated for life.

David, whose thoughts had obviously been drifting along the same lines, turned his head, and his warm blue eyes caught mine. 'D'ye ken that in Eyemouth, when a woman marries onto a man, she takes his byname as well? Verity Deid-Banes—' He tried the combination on his tongue, and grinned. 'It's a fair mouthful, that.'

'David . . .'

'Of course, you could always be just Davy's Verity.'

So much for independence, I thought. Still, I took a final stab at it. 'I am not,' I said, setting him straight, 'Davy's Verity.'

But my protest had no real effect. He only laughed, and rolling to his side he reached for me, his big hand tangling in my hair as he drew me down towards him. 'The hell you're not,' he said.

And proved it.

SUSANNA KEARSLEY

It is no surprise to learn that Canadian-born author Susanna Kearsley is passionate about Roman history and archaeology. 'What I love more than anything,' she says, 'is a historical mystery—anything that can't be easily explained—and the disappearance of the Ninth Legion intrigues me for that reason. When I was a child I was present at a dig and it made a huge impression on me. Later on, I was a museum curator for many years and regularly came into contact with archaeologists. While writing *The Shadowy Horses*, I was able to call upon the expertise of a Canadian field archaeologist and on the University of Edinburgh's Archaeology Department.

'For my fictional solution to the fate of the Ninth Legion, I chose the setting of Eyemouth. It is in an area of the country that fascinates me because my mother's father's family originally came from there—the western Borders region near Kirkcudbright. I'm very grateful to the people of Eyemouth who were wonderfully helpful when I told them I was writing about their village. I spent several weeks there, and everyone, from the owners of the B&B where I stayed, to local fishermen, gave me a hand.'

And does she believe in psychic powers such as those that eight-year-old Robbie displays in *The Shadowy Horses*? She maintains a neutral position, but says that part of the inspiration for Robbie's role came from a real-life experiment involving psychics in an archaeological exploration of the city of Alexandria.

Susanna Kearsley has had two previous novels published, one of which, *Mariana*, won the 1993 Catherine Cookson Prize. After spending last autumn and winter in Wales, researching a new book, she moved to Whitby on Lake Ontario, where she now plans to turn her energies to full-time writing.